CARREÑA 1:

The Fall
of
Evanita

By
K GERARD MARTIN

Shouldercat Books

ISBN 978-1-935816-01-0

Published by Shouldercat Books, Kenosha, WI 53140

2010.0717.C

Contents

Chapter 1:

Birthday

2110 Dec 27, Sat Morn. 376 Grey Road, Hamilton, New Zealand.

"Keep going," television journalist Kristi Fernandez said. "Her house should be on this road somewhere."

"This road ends at the Pirongia Forest Park Lodge," the driver of the television news van, Margaret McAleese, said. "There's nothing else out here."

The news van reached the lodge.

"This is the end," Margaret said.

"No, look—a dirt road there behind the branches," Kristi said.

"That's a road? There are only two tracks—just wide enough for these van tires. Should we go in there? It leads up Pirongia Mountain. That's probably for hikers," Margaret said.

"Yes, we should. She must live on that dirt road."

The two drove through overgrowing tree branches and up a slope on a dirt road.

"Are you sure she lives out here? This place is older than time. The trees, the bushes—they're knarled and twisted. Yet somehow it all seems fitting for the Matriarch of Female Fertility," Margaret said.

"Yeah, if it weren't for her, we couldn't have a family," Kristi said.

"Can you believe there was a time when women couldn't have children with each other?" Margaret asked.

"That was in the old days," Kristi said. "Before civilization was invented."

Both women laughed.

"They had a name for women pair bonds in those days—what was that name?" Margaret asked.

"Lesbian?" Kristi asked.

"Yeah, that was the name. What does that make us?" Margaret asked.

"Happy," Kristi said, and the two laughed. "Again, that was before civilization was invented."

"Like where we are now—everything is like, well, before modern times," Margaret said. "Do you think we took the wrong road?"

Kristi looked down at her map. Margaret parked the news van.

"Let me see that map," Margaret said.

Margaret reached over and brushed her hand against Kristi's abdomen.

"I think you've dropped," Margaret said. "Wouldn't that be ironic if you went into labor at Dr. Jonara Pindus's house?"

"I hope not," Kristi said. "It's a long way to the hospital. Besides, would you want our first child born out here?"

"It would be something special you could add to Jonara's biography, when you finish documenting it. 'And I, Kristi Fernandez, bore my first child with my wife, Margaret McAleese, in the home of Mamma Maffet'," Margaret said. "Why do you look at me like that?"

"Who calls her, 'Mamma Maffet'?" Kristi said.

"They never taught you that in history class? MA-triarch of F-emale FE-r-T-ilty. Maffet," Margaret said.

"No, they didn't," Kristi said.

"There's also the Mamma Maffet Award given yearly to the person or groups who improve women's health in some way. You must have heard of that," Margaret said.

"Yeah, I have," Kristi said. "But I didn't know it had anything to do with Dr. Jonara Pindus."

"She started the multimillion-dollar prize," Margaret said. "She donated most of her wealth to its funding. I think the only major woman in her lifetime who hasn't won the award is herself. In the early days, the prize helped scientists improve fertility and treat reproductive pathologies. Later, it rewarded those who focused on improving women's health through liberated living conditions."

"I guess I should study that more," Kristi said.

"You know, it's sad in a way," Margaret said. "Many women take fertility for granted these days. We have the right to procreate with anyone we want, but it wasn't always that way. We should be thankful. Instead, we're caught up in fashion, careers, family, and success. Not many people remember the pioneers."

"Well that's why I'm doing this biography," Kristi said. "To help me learn about the pioneer Dr. Jonara Carreña Pindus."

"And that's why I'm glad I married you," Margaret said. "Because although you might not know about a topic, you're willing to learn. Look—did you see that flashing green light up there?"

"Yeah. The color changes are subtle," Kristi said. "Yellow-green, green, and blue-green."

"Jonara is using the greenbeam," Margaret said. "Like the one the Celts in the 1200s of Iberia used."

"That never happened," Kristi said.

"It could have happened. Dr. Pindus says so. Besides, it proves we have superior color vision to men," Margaret said. "Look—I bet I can read it. It says, 'Welcome to all women of the world.' Great! We'll follow the green light!"

Margaret put the newsvan in Drive and drove a bit farther, following the green light all the way. Without warning, the narrow dirt road opened up and revealed a white house with magenta and green trim.

"Those colors, wow," Margaret said. "They seem to vibrate."

"Don't get too awestruck," Kristi said. "We have an interview to do, and I'll need you to have a steady hand on the camera. Don't get sidetracked by the colors."

The two walked to the front door. Kristi pressed the doorbell button and knocked on the door while Margaret worked the camera. The two waited, expecting the door to open. It did not. Kristi pressed the doorbell button and knocked again. While she was in the middle of knocking, the door opened slightly. A chain-lock on the inside prevented the door from opening any farther.

"Yes?" said the raspy voice of the one-hundred-year-old Jonara Pindus.

"My name is Kristi Fernandez, and this is Margaret McAleese. We're from the Channel-A television station. We spoke the other day about doing your biography."

"Biography? Did you say Fernandez and McAleese?" Jonara asked.

"Yes," Kristi said.

"The heads of state for Argentina and Ireland," Jonara said. "Now I remember. One moment while I let you in."

Jonara closed the door slowly and spent a dozen or more seconds undoing the latch.

"What did she mean by heads of state?" Margaret asked.

"How should I know," Kristi replied. "You're the history major."

Jonara opened the door slowly.

"Come in, come in," said a short, thin woman with long, gray hair, and a cane.

Margaret followed Kristi through the doorway into a dark lobby-like area.

"Watch your step," Kristi said.

A large pile of unopened mail littered the floor by the mailslot near the door.

"I've been meaning to catch up on my mail," Jonara said as she limped down the hallway. "One of these days I'll get 'round to it. I place all my mail on these tables."

Kristi and Margaret continued past the mailslot to several tables along the dark hallway wall. Mail was sorted by year going all the way back to 2060. Kristi held up an unopened envelope to the camera postmarked September 29, 2060.

"Jonara was fifty years old on this date," Kristi said.

"Fifty years old?" Jonara said. "That was fifty years ago. But I'm one hundred. Oh, where did the time go? Now where was I going? Yes, to the living room. I left it here somewhere."

"Dr. Pindus," Kristi asked.

"Please, call me Jonara," Jonara said.

"Jonara—do you open your mail?" Kristi asked.

"Of course I do! It may take me a little time, but I open my mail. I was just reading a nice card sent to me last year in 2065," Jonara said.

"Uh, last year was 2109," Kristi said.

"It was? Oh, I must have forgotten," Jonara said. "The memory goes when one gets older. Now let me see—yes, the living room. Here we are. Please, make yourselves at home."

The living room was well lit and well heated.

"I think I overdressed," Kristi said. "Miss Jonara—do you mind if I remove my sweater? I'm not used to the heat."

"You're not?" Jonara asked. "Oh, I forget about company and the thermostat. Please, make yourself comfortable."

Kristi removed her sweater, revealing her well-defined pregnant abdomen. Jonara looked once and twice at Kristi as if trying to remember the significance of Kristi's condition.

"Oh, yes, I remember. You are nearly due," Jonara said.

Margaret and Kristi exchanged smiles.

"You are the parents then?" Jonara asked. "Please, give your Mamma Maffet a hug."

Margaret placed the camera on a table and joined Kristi in a group hug with Jonara. Jonara's hug was stronger than Kristi and Margaret expected. The two didn't think Jonara would let go, but in time she did. Margaret returned to the camera and resumed capturing video and audio.

"Dr. Pindus," Kristi said. "I mean, Jonara."

"Please. Now that I know you are a couple with baby on the way, call me Mamma Maffet. May I offer you some tea? Coffee? Juice? Water? I also have red and white wines, but it is perhaps too early in the morning for that."

"Just orange juice, please," Kristi said.

"Coffee for me, please," Margaret said.

"I'll help you walk," Kristi said.

"No!" Jonara said as she waved off Kristi with her cane. "A Spanish woman should never be without her legs. I will go myself. Please, be comfortable. Look around if you like."

Jonara limped into the kitchen leaving Margaret and Kristi in the living room. Margaret followed Kristi with the camera as Kristi explored. Piles of magazines and books littered end tables, the coffee table, and the floor. More books and magazines were piled on a short, upright piano. Only the mantelpiece remained tidy. Margaret captured Kristi as she examined several awards: the Nobel Prize in Medicine, the Lasker Award, the Koch prize, the Library of Congress Living Legend award, the Susan B. Anthony award, the Virginia Woolf award, and the Presidential Medal of Freedom.

"Oh, you found some of my awards," Jonara said as she returned with a tray holding a pitcher of orange juice, a coffee decanter, coffee cups, sugar, cream, spoons, and napkins. "I have more around here somewhere. Someday I'll look for them and put them...hmm...where to put them?"

Jonara struggled to move books and magazines from the coffee table. Kristi hobbled over and moved the literature to the side.

"Thank you, my Maffet child," Jonara said. "Please have a seat."

Margaret set up the camera to capture Kristi and Jonara in their sitting positions while Kristi grabbed coffee for Margaret and orange juice for herself. Jonara helped herself to coffee and let out a big grin.

"What's so funny?" Kristi asked.

"I'm just thinking how I hated coffee when I was younger, much younger. Now I can't get through the day without it," Jonara said.

"Mamma Maffet," Kristi said. "Why did you refer to Margaret and me as heads of state?"

"Good gosholina, Kristi. Argentina's president is Cristina Fernandez. And Ireland's president is Mary McAleese," Jonara said. "It's common knowledge."

Margaret nodded "no."

"Aren't they?" Jonara asked.

"That was true about a hundred years ago. You were born when they were in office," Margaret said.

"That's strange. I thought I read it in a magazine just the other day. Here—this one—dated 2010. Isn't this 2010?" Jonara asked.

"I'm sorry, Mamma Maffet, but this is 2110," Kristi said.

"Oh, so it is. I lose track of this hundred years, that hundred years. People don't change that much, do they?" Jonara asked.

"Thanks to you, they have," Kristi said. "And all for the better."

"I'm so glad," Jonara said. "Well this visit has been pleasant. I'm glad we got to know each other. When will you come back?"

"Wait—we just started," Kristi said.

"We did? Oh, I thought we were finishing," Jonara said.

"Oh no. But please, I'd like to ask you some questions," Kristi said. "You are known as the Matriarch of Female Fertility. You practically invented female reproduction in its modern form."

"Oh, well, the plumbing worked quite well before I took a gander at helping it along," Jonara said. She looked at the awards on her mantelpiece and remembered more of her professional career. "Hmm. I did do something wonderful, didn't I?"

"Yes, you did. And everyone wants to know, what makes a woman great?" Kristi asked.

"A woman great. Um, I don't understand," Jonara said. "I did these little things, and, well, sometimes they worked out, and sometimes they didn't."

"Yes, yes, but not everyone can aspire to be a Mamma Maffet like you," Kristi said.

"They can't? I never thought about that. I wonder why they can't," Jonara said. "Did they try?"

"Lots and lots. Was there some special moment in your life when you decided to become Mamma Maffet?" Kristi asked.

"I never decided to become Mamma Maffet," Jonara said. "That title was given to me after I tried all my little things with fertility."

"Yes, but how did you get started? Did someone or something inspire you? Do you remember when that was? Was it in school, at the movies, or at a birthday party?" Kristi asked.

"Birthday party," Jonara said. "Hmm. Birthday party. My birthday."

"Did you have a special birthday party when you were younger? Maybe when you were a teenager?" Kristi asked.

"Yes. Now it comes back to me. Like the ages before time. It was my thirteenth birthday. I remember now, I remember," Jonara said.

"What do you remember? What happened on your thirteenth birthday? Were you already set on a career when you turned thirteen?" Kristi asked.

Jonara laughed a cackling sound like a crow choking on a bone.

"Oh no. When I turned thirteen, I was a stupid girl who had no ambition," Jonara said. "I decided I would do whatever my friends did, which was to hang out and pretend to be important. Everything I did before my thirteenth birthday was wasted youth. But something strange happened when my mother brought out my birthday cake in 2023—something I never expected."

"Tell us," Kristi said.

Margaret recorded everything Jonara said, and Kristi narrated as follows:

2023 Sep 29, Fri Eve. Portland, Oregon.

"Happy birthday to you. Happy birthday to you! Happy birthday, dear Jonara...happy birthday to you! Yay!! Make a wish!"

Jonara looked around the dining-room table. She saw her mother, Evanita Pindus, who was seven months pregnant. There was her father, Johnny Pindus, smiling as he did for her birthday. Her Grandmother Eva stood nearby, still dressed in her uniform after having arrived from the clinic where she practiced dentistry, Jonara's friend, Almarita Foster, and Almarita's mother, Claire Stout Foster. All in attendance were bright and cheerful.

Jonara looked at the two candles forming the number thirteen on her chocolate birthday cake. The "1" was green and white while the "3" was cerise and white. "Thirteen!" she said aloud.

"Thirteen years old!" reiterated Evanita, her mother. "You're growing up!"

But it wasn't Jonara's age that startled her into calling out, "Thirteen!" Rather it was the lone pair of numerals on her cake.

"Just two candles," Jonara thought as if losing a group of friends.

It was only a year ago she had stared at twelve individual candles forming a smiley face on her cake—one for each eye, one for the nose, and nine forming the mouth. Where was her smiley world now?

"Where are all the candles?" Jonara asked.

"You are growing up," Grandma Eva said. "It's time you have two candles instead of many little ones."

Still her candle-pair burned. Jonara had yet to make her wish.

"I don't know what to wish for," Jonara said aloud. "I wish I had thirteen candles. I don't want to grow up."

"Perhaps it's time to think about what you wish to do with your life—the career you wish to pursue," Grandma Eva said. "You can't live off your parents forever."

Evanita gave Eva a funny look.

"I don't know what I want to be when I grow up. But I want thirteen candles," Jonara said.

"Oh sweetie, think of something wonderful to wish for," said Evanita.

Jonara closed her eyes. She inhaled deeply and held her breath for a moment. How would she remember this birthday? Each year she tried to do something that would help her remember. The previous year she drew her finger in the air around the twelve candles on her cake, seeing how close she could bring it to the flames before the heat forced her finger away. The year before, she leaned over the cake too far and singed some strands of her golden-blond hair. She thought it odd to have such light hair. Her mother's was black with dark-red streaks, her father's was grayish-white, and her Grandma Eva's hair was black.

At length, Jonara whispered, "I want thirteen candles."

Jonara opened her eyes, stared at the cake, and to her amazement there were thirteen candles instead of two. She blew out the candles excitedly in one large breath. All candles went out. Pleased with herself, she expected a loud round of applause. To her shock, there was no applause. No cheering. Nothing. The room remained silent, and not a word or sound carried around.

"Hello?" Jonara asked. "The joke is over. Come on, everyone. Hello? Someone, please, turn on the lights."

Jonara heard a television from the adjoining living room. From the living room she heard her mother's voice.

"Johnny, I think she's done sitting alone. Why don't you get her?"

"All right, dear," Johnny said.

Johnny entered the dining room from the living room and turned on the light. Jonara's cake was no longer complete. Three slices had been removed, one of which was on the plate in front of her and mostly eaten. Three candles rested in the empty spot of the cake platter while ten remained on the cake itself.

"Come on, Jonara, let's put your cake away and watch television in the living room," Johnny said.

"What happened?" Jonara asked. "Where did everyone go?"

"Don't you remember?" Johnny asked. "Your mother and I ate cake with you, but you wanted to be alone for a few minutes. The few minutes are long over. You've been sitting in the dark for over an hour."

"No, that's not what happened," Jonara said. "I mean everyone else. Grandma Eva, Almarita, and Ms. Foster—where did they go?"

"You've been daydreaming again, haven't you?" Johnny asked. "Come on. Spend some time with your parents. We'll put the cake away now."

Jonara sat at the table for a moment to regain her senses. Johnny put the cake away and placed Jonara's plate by the sink.

"Whoa, what was that?" Evanita said from the living room.

Johnny ran to Evanita's side.

"I'll be all right in a moment," Evanita said. "Strange. That felt like a contraction. But it's too early."

"Ring, BRING. Ring, BRING!"

"Telephone, telephone. Telephone, telephone!" Johnny called out in cadence with the telephone's ringing. He ran back and forth in the living room as if in panic. Continuing his panic while the phone rang unanswered, he stumbled on the coffee table and tipped over a glass of water.

"Oh dear, Johnny, clean that up, will you? I must stand and walk over to the telephone!"

The telephone ran out of patience and stopped ringing. But Evanita managed to walk from the couch to the kitchen where the telephone resided—all while Jonara remained seated at the dining-room table. Johnny shook like a leaf while he cleaned up his mess. Evanita looked at the telephone—yes, there on the display. Evanita recognized from where the call came. She picked up the receiver and dialed the number.

"Hello, this is Evanita. Yes. Anna, did you call? Anna, turn off the vacuum cleaner. No, running the vacuum cleaner is not crazy when you're upset. Anna? Anna! Slow down, and speak in English. My Spanish is not as good as it should be. It's Grandma? Are you sure? Call the doctor. Oh, he's there already. I see. What about Mama, did you call Mama? Not home? Don't worry, I'll find her. Yes, I understand. No, it's no imposition. I'm not due for another two months—maybe six weeks. Oh they'll be fine."

Evanita glanced back at Jonara and Johnny.

"Well, perhaps I can have someone from church stop in on them," Evanita continued. "What? Yes, I'll calm him down before he takes me to the airport. Wait, what am I thinking? Mama can take me to the airport—we can fly together. Oh, if we fly together, she can't take me. Johnny must take us. What? It's still hot? Yes, I saw the weather report for Texas, but I didn't believe it. All right, I believe it. No, it's raining here. Sun? What sun? One of these days, Anna, you must visit us in Portland. No, talking about the weather when family is ill is nothing to be ashamed of. We are only people. Oh, I guess that's right, where will you go? You know you're welcome here, and I know Mama is fond of you too. Oh. Yes, Portland weather takes some getting used to. Try not to worry too much, Anna. We'll talk more later. I'll get going then. Be strong, Anna, I'll be there soon. Goodbye."

"I kn-knew it was bad. Bad news. Bad, bad, bad news," said Johnny.

"Johnny," Evanita said as she hobbled over to the dining table. He sat next to her, and they held hands. "I need you to be strong."

"Your Grandma. Grandma Geneva. She is sick, isn't she?" he asked.

"Yes, very sick."

"And she won't get better, will she?" he asked.

"No. The doctor is giving her medicine to ease the pain. She is sleeping now. Johnny, I may need your help. We have to find my mama. You remember Eva, right?"

"Mummy Eva. Eva the dentist, drilling and filling teeth. Eva," Johnny said in a half trance.

"Yes. I'm going to call her telephone, but in case I don't find her, I will need you to help me find her," Evanita explained.

"Help you find her," Johnny repeated.

"Yes. Think about how you can help find her while I tele-phone her."

"Telephone her," he echoed.

"Let's see—she couldn't attend Jonara's birthday party be-cause—" Evanita started.

"She had an emergency patient," Johnny said.

"Yes," Evanita said, "I'll call her office."

Evanita pressed the buttons on the telephone for Eva's den-tal office. The telephone rang and rang without answer.

"I'll try her cell phone," Evanita continued.

Again Evanita pressed the buttons to reach Eva, and again there was no answer.

"No answer at the office. No answer on her cell phone. No answer," Johnny broadcast.

"I'll call her house," Evanita said, but before she could finish pressing the buttons, Johnny answered.

"No answer."

He was correct. Eva was beyond telephone contact.

"I was afraid of this. Anna would have called the same telephone numbers as I just did. She could not find Mama either. Johnny, I know you don't like to do this, but I must ask—this is very important."

"Very important. How can Johnny help?"

"Please realize how important this is. I never ask you for much, but this is very, very important. And don't scream," Evanita said.

"Not *it*," he said. "Please, don't ask the Johnny."

"Yes. Johnny, I need you to take a regular shower."

"No no no no no no. Johnny is clean; Johnny takes special shower every day."

"A shower. An actual conventional shower connected directly to the municipal waterworks. Now it's not that hard. The faucets are the same, hot and cold."

"Yes, faucets are the same. Harder to step in," said Johnny.

"Please, Johnny dearest. You know I wouldn't ask unless it was very important. You have a gift, Johnny, a precious gift that no one else would dream is possible."

"Yes, 'Nina," Johnny said with resignation. "I must sense the water. I must trace the water through the city. Yes, Johnny will find Mummy Eva. Johnny must do so, for his wife, for Evanita, 'Nina, Poochie-coochie. Johnny will take a regular shower."

Johnny, with Pindus being his last name, was married to Evanita Carreña. She took his surname and became Evanita Pindus. Their first child was Jonara, who Evanita bore shortly after marriage with Johnny. Jonara's full name was Jonara Carreña Pindus. She spent her thirteen years of childhood with no brothers or sisters. She had one friend, Almarita, who got along well with Jonara's parents, including Johnny. While Jonara loved her parents, she noticed others did not care to spend time in Johnny's presence. Whether they were afraid or hated him, Jonara wasn't sure. But Almarita got along well enough with Johnny, and for Jonara that was appreciated.

"Allie? Yeah, it's me," Jonara said from her bedroom. After changing clothes, Jonara sat on her bed and pondered what to do. Whenever she pondered, she thought of her best friend, Almarita, and Almarita was always a few telephone buttons away.

"Jonara Pindus. Jonie, friend oh my best friend. What's happening your way?" asked Almarita.

"My birthday. My thirteenth birthday. I wish you could be here," said Jonara. "In fact, I thought you were here."

"Funny Joni. Always joking. Yeah, sorry my best friend. Getting grounded is a drag. Did you go out for dinner?"

"No, stayed home."

"Bummer," said Almarita. "I can think of many restaurants we could visit."

"You always like to eat," said Jonara.

"That's beside the point. Your mother makes good food and all, and your father is funny. But let's be practical," Almarita explained.

"Practical?"

"Yes, Jonie, practical. You'll be a woman one day, sooner than you think. I'll be one too. And women need to be noticed," Almarita explained.

"Noticed? For what? I live with my parents. I'm going to live with them and help them forever," said Jonara.

"We're getting too old for those dreams, Jonara. Look at us. Look at the world we live in."

"What do you mean? I like our world," said Jonara.

"It's a dark, dismal place, except at your house. But the world isn't like your house. You'll find out. But I can help you, Jonie. I can save you from finding out too late."

"Almarita Foster, you're only a thirteen-year-old girl, and now I'm thirteen too. How can you pretend to know what the world is like? We're kids, not adults," said Jonara.

"We'll be adults soon enough, and we better be ready. Yeah, and with the right boyfriends lined up to take care of us," Almarita said.

"Boyfriends? I don't want to date, and I don't know if I want to be slave to a boyfriend or any guy. Besides, the world is equal between men and women," Jonara said.

Almarita broke out into such raucous laughter that Jonara had to pull the telephone away from her ear.

"I hate it when you laugh like that, Allie. It's an evil laugh," said Jonara between Almarita's outbursts.

"Wake up, Jonara, wake up! It's still a man's world. But a woman can be choosy if she acts early. You know how they look at women, how men act. Oh some cover up their thoughts well enough, but it's always on their minds waiting for an opportunity," said Almarita.

"You've been reading too many gossip columns," said Jonara. "Wait, I hear something."

"What is it?" Almarita asked.

"Oh, it's just my daddy taking a shower. I can hear him through the wall. He's humming."

"You spoke as if you didn't recognize what was happening."

"I didn't," said Jonara. "He doesn't take regular showers very often."

"What? Jonie, I don't understand. How is it he never smells dirty to me?" said Almarita.

"He's not dirty, just doesn't take the same type of showers we do. He cleans in other ways, Allie," explained Jonara.

"He seems too tall to take a bath."

"He has his own bathroom with his own special shower. His shower gets water from two tanks—one for a wash, the other for a rinse. Once the wash water runs out, that's it. But the rinse water can be reused so he can meditate," Jonara explained.

"Huh? What's wrong with the normal shower? Why the fancy setup?" Almarita asked.

"I don't know. I only know that my daddy connects the main water line to the tanks once a day to fill them. Then he lets the tanks sit overnight before using them. That's how he takes his special showers. He only takes normal showers on special occasions," Jonara explained.

"What occasions? New Year's day?" Almarita joked.

"No. I don't know, Allie. I asked my parents once, but they never explained why," said Jonara. "Sometimes I get a headache from trying to understand why people won't tell me."

"Then don't try too hard. I can show you how to be attractive to the right boys," Almarita began.

"The right boys? And what is 'right'? 'Right' according to Almarita, is that it?" Jonara asked.

"Jonie, don't act like that. It's time to grow up. The right boys are the ones who will pay you lots of attention and take care of you so you don't have to fight for a job and battle with men in the workforce. Let him do the work. Manipulate him into thinking he is in control when you're the one getting your way. It takes some practice, this art of deceiving, but it's quite practical."

"I don't like deceiving, Allie. And you're the last one I thought would say this. How can you say deceiving is a good thing? What happened to you, Allie?" Jonara asked.

"I'm growing up, Jonie, just like you should be doing. It's time to face the real world. Honesty is like icing on a cake—it's sweet at first and seems right, but in the end it makes you sick. Most of the cake isn't icing anyway—it is boring breadstuff. Oh yeah, how was your birthday cake, Jonie?" Almarita asked.

"I don't know."

"Didn't you eat some?"

"Yeah, I think so. I don't remember eating it, though," Jonara said. "It felt strange. It felt empty, like a disaster."

"Is that the truth?" Almarita asked.

"Honest, it's the truth," Jonara replied.

"Honesty is a disaster," said Almarita.

"Almarita!"

"It's true. Trust me. Am I not speaking the truth? Honesty is not to be trusted."

"Almarita Ellen Foster, you are making absolutely no sense at all!"

"It just seems that way, Jonie. You'll understand—sooner or later. I know it now. And I'm not going to pretend that someday I'll be able to do everything a man can do. I won't play football, won't be a stock-car racer, and won't be President."

"Women have been presidents of countries," said Jonara.

"Rarely, Jonara," Almarita said. "But they're just puppets of their husbands."

Johnny's shower stopped. Evanita spoke with him just outside Jonara's bedroom door—both in muffled voices. Then Evanita knocked on Jonara's door.

"Jonara," said Evanita as she peeked through the slightly ajar door. "I'm leaving for the airport shortly. We've found your grandmother."

"Grandma!" Jonara exclaimed, forgetting Almarita was still on the phone.

"What's happening? Jonie? Jonie!" Almarita called back, but Jonara dropped her cell phone. "Hello, hello?" called Almarita's voice across the bedroom air from Jonara's dropped cell phone.

"Mommy, are you really leaving now?" Jonara asked.

She hugged Evanita as best she could considering Evanita's pregnancy.

"Yes, sweetie, I really must go," Evanita explained.

"Can I come with you?" Jonara begged.

"No, not yet. But soon. I'll call you from Texas," Evanita said.

"Hello, hello? Jonie?" Almarita's voice called from across the room.

Evanita hobbled across the room, bent her knees to lower her body vertically, and picked up the dropped cell phone.

"Hello, Almarita," said Evanita.

"Oh hi, Mrs. Pindus. How are you?"

"Fine, thank you. Are you being a good girl?" Evanita asked.

"Yes, always," Almarita lied. "I was grounded, but it was a misunderstanding. I'm always a good girl."

Evanita chuckled and said, "Listen, I have to leave town tonight—my own grandmother is ill. Jonara will stay home for now, but soon she'll be leaving town too. We're going to Corpus Christi, Texas."

"Yes ma'am!"

"Thank you for being a good friend to Jonara," Evanita chuckled again as if her statement wasn't quite true. "Well at least a friend."

Jonara and Almarita laughed too as Evanita passed the cell phone back to Jonara.

It was raining when Evanita pulled up behind a parked car on Sellwood Bridge.

"Mama? Are you all right?" called Evanita as she stepped out of her car.

"Evanita," Eva called back. Eva stood up from the front right side of her car where she had been changing a flat tire. "What on Earth are you doing here?"

"Anna and I have been trying to call you with important information," Evanita explained as she hobbled around to the right side of Eva's car.

Evanita's face grew grim when she saw the shredded tire on the front wheel. She reached for the tire and wheel to touch them. She recoiled and screamed in pain.

"Ow, my finger!" she said as she nursed her burned finger.

"Let that be a lesson. The rim is hot as fire. I can't loosen the lug nuts. I can't even get a jack under the car—look how low it is," Eva said.

"What's wrong with your cell? I called it, but no answer," Evanita explained.

"Yeah, the battery died. What's so important? No, not here. This rain is no good for us."

The two entered Evanita's car—Evanita drove while Eva sat in the front passenger seat.

"I'll have a wrecker take my car to the shop," Eva explained. "What is this serious thing?"

"Anna called me tonight," Evanita started as she merged into bridge traffic. "She told me about Grandma Geneva."

"Yes, she's been ill for some time now," added Eva.

"Anna says she's near death. So does the doctor. I said I would fly down immediately. Oh Mama, this is terrible news!"

Evanita was on the verge of tears. Eva was about to say something—about how Grandma Geneva had a good long life, but for some reason the moment didn't seem right.

"I told Johnny and Jonara that they would follow me down later," Evanita continued, though her voice shook.

"I'll fly with you tonight," Eva said. "Here, better take the next street and take me home so I can pack a few things. Hold strong, Evanita, we'll get through this."

Eva worried about her daughter, though. Evanita and Geneva had a close granddaughter-grandmother relationship, perhaps too close. Adding to Eva's worry was Evanita's pregnancy. Evanita appeared pudgy and extra tired. Was this going to be a normal delivery? Evanita wasn't due for another two months. Normally, Eva would recommend against Evanita flying across the country—what would happen if she went into premature labor on the airplane?

Evanita drove in silence. Eva took advantage of the quiet moment to call a tow truck for her disabled car using Evanita's cell phone. It seemed rude considering the situation, but Eva made the call with such calm and cool-headedness that no one would have suspected the internal forces racking her mind.

The pair arrived at Eva's house. Eva tidied up the place a little before packing a bag. Evanita sat on the couch and called her own home.

"Johnny? It's Evanita. Yes, I found her. We're fine, just fine. Yes, you don't have to worry. The wrecker will take care of it. What? Yes. Soon, we'll be there very soon. Mama is packing, and we'll come over. Yes. I'm fine now, but a little wet from the rain. Yes, it rains a lot. Hmmm? Yes, that's what I was thinking—you'll drop Mama and me off at the airport tonight. She did? Oh that's wonderful. Jonara is such a sweet kid packing my bags for me. She always knows what we need without asking. We'll be there soon. Love you and Jonara too. Tell her, will you? Bye-bye."

The drive from Eva's house to Evanita's was quiet. Both mother and daughter were thinking, too much perhaps, but think they did—about Geneva, about their past, their present, and their future. For Eva it meant she would no longer see her mother as the elder matriarch—that role would soon fall to Eva herself. For Evanita, it meant the loss of a female family member other than her own mother—someone who understood her yet had a perspective of hardship. Evanita's grandmother could size up a person quickly. Evanita valued this skill above all else—how to read a person's character and know what that person would do in a crisis.

"Are you expecting company?" Eva asked as the two pulled into Evanita's driveway.

"That's Claire's car. You remember Almarita's mother— Claire Foster?" Evanita said.

"Oh yes, I remember the Fosters," Eva said. "And Almarita is a good friend of Jonara's?"

"Yes," Evanita said as the two opened the front door.

"Grandma!" called Jonara as mother and daughter entered the Pindus home.

"Hi, Jonara. How is my little treasure?"

"Where were you?" Jonara asked as Johnny loaded Evanita's luggage into the car.

"I had a flat tire. On a bridge. Don't worry—I'm not hurt, just a little tired. But not too tired to visit my little treasure!" Eva said.

"Hello Claire," said Evanita to Almarita's mother.

"I heard the news and came as quickly as I could, Evanita," said Claire.

"And I came too," piped up Almarita from around a corner.

Evanita shot her a puzzled look as if to say, "I thought you were grounded."

"I'm not without a heart," said Claire. "Johnny told me everything. I'll watch Jonara while he takes you to the airport, if you don't mind. In fact, she can stay with me the entire weekend."

"Mind?! Oh Claire, you're a godsend," thanked Evanita.

Eva smiled as if to say that Evanita was blessed. Jonara and Almarita smirked that they'd get time together.

"Can you spend the night with us, Grandma?" Jonara begged.

"I'm sorry, sweetie," Evanita explained. "Grandma and I are flying down to Texas tonight. Your father will bring you down later."

"I want Grandma to spend the night with us, with Allie and me," Jonara sobbed.

"My little treasure. I'm flying to Texas with your mother tonight. I'll see you very soon," Eva said as she hugged Jonara.

"Promise?"

"Promise!" Eva replied.

Eva kissed Jonara on the forehead and patted her on the back.

"All of your...everything is loaded," said Johnny, arriving from the car after placing the final luggage into the trunk.

"It's time," said Evanita. "We'll call from Texas," she said to Claire and Jonara. "Jonara, be good. Give your respect to Mrs. Foster. Love you lots."

Jonara hugged Evanita, followed quickly by Almarita hugging the two.

"I know, I know," Evanita said.

Eva hugged Jonara and Almarita from behind and patted them both to let them know it was time to let go. Eva walked to the doorway and waited for Evanita to finish her embrace with the two girls. The two let go after what seemed a long moment.

"Goodbye," Evanita said, and she closed the door behind them.

Jonara, Almarita, and Claire waved goodbye. Johnny rushed to the car and jumped into the driver's seat, ready to go. Eva and Evanita walked more slowly down the front steps (Evanita was still pregnant!), but halfway to the car, Evanita stopped and turned around.

"What is it? Did you forget something?" Eva asked.

"No. It's just...somehow the house looks different," Evanita tried to explain.

The rain had stopped, and the darkness was broken by a rising full moon.

"A full moon, just like when Jonara was born. I wonder if I'll return to my house...no that's silly talk," Evanita said to herself.

Jonara and Almarita whipped the curtains back and waved vigorously from inside the living room window. Evanita's trance was broken. She and Eva waved back, turned to the car, and drove off with Johnny.

The moon appeared to follow the three as they traveled to the airport. Johnny mumbled something about left lane, right lane. Eva and Evanita fell silent.

"Lead and follow," Johnny said. "One follows the other, the sun, the moon, and the earth. A smaller life follows a larger life. We follow them, they follow us."

"Who follows us?" Eva asked.

"He gets like that sometimes, Mama," explained Evanita. "He doesn't say names, just 'they' or 'us'. One never knows who he sees. Could be anyone in the present or the past."

"Hmm," Eva said. "I wonder what he sees."

Evanita didn't pay much attention to Johnny Pindus, but Eva looked out the window at the moon and thought about planetary motions and people. She knew from high school astronomy that Earth is moved by the moon too—both revolve around a barycenter giving Earth a bit of a wobble. Then she thought about her one and only love, the one who helped her conceive Evanita.

"I'm sorry, Mama, he gets stuck on something and can't move on. He'll be fine once he returns home. Jonara is good with him," Evanita explained.

"It's all right, dear. I was just thinking about something else, someone else. Dear me, life passes so quickly at times," said Eva.

"Airport, airport," Johnny announced. "Airport."

"Just drop us off at the first terminal," said Evanita. "It's too far to park and walk. We'll be fine, Johnny. Here. This is a good place."

"Here is a good place," he repeated. "We're here. We're here at the good place."

"Good evening and welcome to Portland Airways. This is your captain speaking, and on behalf of the crew, I'd like to extend our warmest and driest wishes for a happy flight. If at any time you feel uncomfortable or—"

The captain's voice faded into the background as Eva and Evanita conversed.

"I never like the ascent," said Eva. "It seems so...how shall I say it...phallic?"

Eva and Evanita giggled and giggled, so much so that the nearby passengers weren't sure if the giggling was from school-girls or inebriated women.

"Mama!" Evanita tried to exclaim between giggles as if shocked.

"If you're so shocked, why are you laughing?" Eva laughed back.

"I don't know," Evanita continued to laugh. "It's not supposed to be funny."

"But it is funny," laughed Eva right back.

"Mama, are you suggesting a plane ride is how a man experiences love?" Evanita asked.

"No, but it's how he experiences sexual intercourse," Eva replied. "At least it seems so."

"Who's to say it's only a man's view? A woman feels she's in the clouds when in the moment of passion," said Evanita.

"But you're forgetting one thing—after descent, a man's engine shuts down completely, and he falls asleep," Eva explained.

The two lapsed into hysterical giggling again. Both held their hands over their mouths to suppress their laughter.

"Ow," said Evanita, "I shouldn't laugh so hard. That was another contraction. I don't understand—the doctor said I have another two months."

"What's his name?" Eva asked.

"How do you know my baby is a *he*? Never mind, I know what you're going to say," said Evanita.

"But I should say it again. How often does a man have a baby? What does he care, I mean really care? Even a woman who has not had a child cannot fully realize the forces at work, the *in situ* relationship a woman has with her pregnancy and un-born child."

Evanita looked out the window as the plane banked into a turn and caught a glimpse of the moon.

"I like how the moon is orange this time of year. A harvest moon," said Evanita.

"I noticed the moon this evening too, and I was also thinking about what Johnny said. You know, the part about the moon, the sun, and the earth following each other. And life."

"Yes. At one time people thought there might be life on the moon," Evanita said.

"You mean 'the man in the moon'? But never 'the woman in the moon'," Eva said.

"Yes, I guess it is a silly notion, though sometimes when the moon looks just right, I swear I can see a face."

"We like to see life where there is none," said Eva. "And I was thinking about what Johnny said about a smaller life following a larger life, like the moon following Earth."

"And the earth following the sun," Evanita continued.

"And the sun following the Milky Way," said Eva.

"And what does the Milky Way follow?" Evanita asked.

"You have me there. I never studied astronomy enough to answer that question. Maybe the astronomers themselves don't really know for sure."

"How do you suppose life started, Mama?" Evanita asked.

"Look down at your tummy—that's how life starts!" Eva said, and she giggled, "It starts after the ascent stage."

"How did my life start?" Evanita asked.

"Let's go back to your first question," Eva said evasively.

"You never said who my father is. I'm thirty-three years old, and you're almost sixty," Evanita said.

"Please! I'm still in my fifties, and I plan to stay that way. The best decade of my adult life, if you ask me—young enough to have my wits and health, and old enough so I don't have to deal with the monthly curse," Eva explained.

"Does Grandma Geneva know? And now she's dying. If you two are the only ones who know the secret, can't I know who my father is before both of you pass on?" Evanita asked.

Both women screeched as their heads knocked against the storage compartment above them. The two and the other passengers dropped back into their seats.

"Good evening, folks. That momentary drop was caused by a wind shear off the High Cascades mountain range. We are now across the range and should have no further disturbance. If you need extra pillows, please contact one of our custodians," announced the captain over the loudspeaker.

"Too late for the pillows!" said Eva, rubbing her head.

"That hurt," said Evanita. "But for once I didn't have a contraction. I thought for sure I'd have the baby right here after that bump!"

"Oh, don't say that!" remarked Eva. "I'm still surprised you decided to fly in your condition. You've always gone against common convention. You take after your mother."

"I didn't know you were a rebel. When you were younger?" Evanita asked.

"Oh, uh, yes, well. A rebel. I was younger. Okay, maybe I'll ask for that pillow. Steward, oh steward!"

"Yes ma'am?" a steward asked.

"A pillow for me, please. Evanita, would you like one?" Eva asked.

"Yes, I'd like a pillow," Evanita answered.

"Very good," the steward said and started to walk off.

Eva grabbed his arm and held him so she could whisper in his ear, "I'll also have your best sherry wine."

"Yes, ma'am," said the steward, and he returned shortly with two pillows followed by a bottle and a clean glass.

"What's this?" Evanita asked as Eva tucked her pillow behind her head and placed the bottle and glass on cup holders behind the seat in front.

"I would offer you some, Evanita, but you're expecting. Like I said," Eva said as she poured the liquor into her glass and held it to her expecting mouth, "the best decade of adult life is the fifties."

Eva sipped the sherry from the glass and swirled it in her mouth several times, savoring the texture and flavor. She thought about how far the liquor had traveled from its beginnings in the vineyard to its final destination in this time of need.

"This is good!" said Eva.

"How can you enjoy wine when you're on medication for your alcoholism?" Evanita asked.

"I stop taking my medication from time to time so I can enjoy the wine. I did so today," Eva said. "Ah. I do enjoy a good glass of sherry."

"Mama," said Evanita.

"I need another sip," Eva said as she poured another glass.

"Mama, who was my father?"

Eva swirled the liquor in her mouth again and swallowed.

"Ah. Usually airplane food and drink need help, but this stuff is excellent!"

"Mama!"

"A toast, to mother, daughter, and another grandchild!" Eva said, and she held her half-full second glass in the air.

"My father!"

"Mmmm," Eva said as she swallowed the remaining half-glassful.

"Who is my father?"

"You know, Evanita—and I must say this is an excellent sherry—some things take time to age well. This good drink for one," Eva explained. "I must be hungry—this drink is hitting me quickly."

"How did it all start?" Evanita asked, referring to her own life.

"Oh that! I can answer that!" Eva said, purposely misunderstanding.

"Finally, if I'd known a little alcohol would get you to talk, I'd have spiked your drink years ago," Evanita said.

"Where did it start? Hmm, yes, I remember now. It was the beginning. A comet passed through the inner solar system."

"A comet, how romantic," said Evanita.

"And it traveled through the asteroid belt. And several asteroids were deflected off their path around the sun. They followed the comet," Eva continued.

"Amazing. I didn't know comets could do that."

"Soon there were thousands of asteroids following the comet. No, they chased the comet. In fact, they were in a race with the comet," Eva said, and her beverage-sipping became beverage-slurping.

"Wait a minute. Are you sure you're telling the story right?" asked Evanita.

"Unquestionably! I've never been more sure of this story, especially now!" Eva answered. "But wait, there's more! Despite the sun's power, I mean warning, I mean—what do I mean? The sun's gravity, yes, the sun's gravity wasn't quite strong enough to dissuade the salmon, sorry, the cometoids from heading right along toward Earth."

"Salmon? How could this be the start of life if there were salmon already? And in space!" Evanita said.

"Quite, quite right. Quite right. Yes, quite right. Uh, yes, what am I doing? Repeating myself like Johnny," stumbled Eva. "Now in those days, yes, first—the days were very short and uneventful, um, yes, much shorter than today."

The airplane changed course, and Evanita lost her view of the moon.

"The moon—I can't see it anymore," said Evanita.

"Yes, I was just getting to that!" said Eva. "More sherry! Just another glass."

Eva filled her glass with liquor again, unsteadily. Her hands moved and swayed a bit, but she managed (just barely) to fill her glass without spilling a drop.

"Mama, you've had enough!" Evanita warned.

"No, I'm in my fifties, remember? A woman can do what she wants in her fifties. There's a law, somewhere, I know. I had it written down," Eva said.

"There's no law," Evanita said.

"Well there should be," Eva hiccupped. "Oops, how unladylike of me. I hiccupped!"

"Mama, was there more to the story?" Evanita asked.

"The story? O, o, o, oh! The—the story!" Eva deliberated. "I…was…just about…to finish. There was no moon!"

"I just said that, I can't see the moon anymore. The airplane has changed direction," Evanita said.

"No, no, no! Don't be like that. There was no Eva, no Evanita, no yet-to-be-born Evanita juniorette, no airplane, and no moon of the year of our Lord, two thousand twenty-three! But there was a young star called Sol, there was a young Earth spinning so quickly, there were cometoids on a collision course with young Earth, but there was no young moon in those early times or anything. Sure, other planets had moons, chunky rocks no better than common asteroids, but no special moon, nothing as close in proportion or as smooth in roundness as our own moon of today, September 29, 2023."

Eva took a sip from her glass and barely finished swallowing.

"And hold onto your seat, there's still more!" Eva said. "The cometoids, against the will of the solar system family, rained down on the Earth. And a great reaction ensued. The main *comment*—"

"*Comet*, not *comment*. Wait a minute, what am I saying?" Evanita said.

"Thank you for the comet comment! Yes, the main comet, well you know, there was really only one comet—the rest were asteroids—not real comments—I just made that up about the cometoids, but it makes sense, at least to me right now."

"So that's it, the beginning of life according to my mama," said Evanita.

"No, not done yet! There's more, do listen!" Eva continued. "The impact created a ripple in Earth, because in those days Earth was hot and fiery with a stretchy skin trapping water below. She was bloated, and Pamprin hadn't been invented yet. That didn't make sense, did it? It doesn't matter. The comet punched through the skin and mixed with water and elements and earth within Earth. Wild things got started. Actions and reactions, eddies, swirls, and battles for control of what reactions should be safe and what should be hostile."

"You're babbling, Mama," said Evanita.

"Almost, but try to follow me. There was conflict within Earth. Forces brewed like boiling soup, and after nine months of expanding and bulging—"

"Mama, are you saying Earth was pregnant?!" Evanita asked.

"Yes, very much pregnant, the largest ever known to this solar system. And it all took nine months to complete."

"Now I know you're telling a story."

"Heh, heh, heh. Just now figured it out, eh? Oh, there's more!" Eva said. "After the nine months, the bulge on the front side of Earth—"

"Which side was the front side?" Evanita asked with a giggle.

"The side with the bulge. I know, it's a circular argument, but so is Earth. Everything was an argument with that bulge until it blasted away—clear. And behold! Earth bore its one and only child, the moon! The two revolved around each other, resolving some differences yet continuing others. And that's how life started."

"That's it? What about the birds and trees? Adam and Eve? Ancient Greeks and Pharaohs of Egypt?" Evanita asked.

"Oh that! Yes, some extra life came along much later. Minor details. Like bugs not knowing where they came from and not know where they are going. At least we know where we're going, I think. Anyway, one of the divisions Mother Earth and Daughter Moon had was that Mother Earth became full of many little lifeforms while Daughter Moon grew silent and remained dormant for many years. The end! Whew! That wore me out!" Eva said.

"That is the silliest story I've heard. Besides, the comet theory you mentioned says there was just a single comet—not a group of things—that deposited life, and life came from that comet. No special nine-month pregnancy with the moon being created."

"Evanita, you've been listening to male propaganda. Only men believe that something as complex as life would come from a single source, a single comet, that there was no combination of forces or union or reaction of things to bring life about," Eva said.

"What?" Evanita asked. She seemed confused by Eva's description.

"How would it be if everything that happened in the world was the result of a single ancestor, a single event? Is that even possible? Male and female create life, right?"

"Some life is asexual, reproducing copies of itself," Evanita said.

"Yes, yes, copies, the same life over and over again without significant change or diversity. But is that really an event or just another repetition? Another day at the factory? Is this life?"

"I still don't understand."

"How could life come from a single comet? Can life come from the orders of a single man, the single-sided bias of tyrant over slave? We are told that life could come from the single-bias of a comet, in the style of a tyrant ordering something to happen. 'You there, woman, go fetch me a beer.' That is the style—order, and it will happen. But when does the universe order something to happen? What is gravity of one celestial body without another to both give and receive the same tug? What is a chemical reaction without at least two different chemicals?" Eva explained.

"There's one thing you're forgetting," said Evanita.

"Yes?"

"My father—who is he?" Evanita asked.

"Ugh, I thought you'd forgotten."

"Mama, is it really that painful to tell me?"

"Evanita. Sigh. I will say this—and then you must be patient! For a little while longer at least! Some things need to be expressed in a certain way to be understood."

"Mama! Just tell the truth!"

"The truth," said Eva. "The truth. And what is that? Is truth even possible anymore? Seems so easy when we are young. Good role models teach us right from wrong. But what is truth? Truth is what happens in reality. But does any one person really know this? Can anyone besides a deity truly and completely know the 'truth'?"

"Truth—even his name—that's a start, that's truth."

"Even a name can mislead. I will tell you soon," Eva promised.

"But Mama!"

"I told you, you must have the utmost patience. Soon you will know, very soon. But for tonight, I will take this pillow, and take a much-deserved nap, just rest my eyes a little, just think about, think, rest..." Eva's voice trailed off, and soon she was sound asleep.

"She can talk herself out of and into almost anything," Evanita thought.

Evanita looked through the window for the moon, but the airplane held its orientation, which prevented Evanita from seeing the celestial body Eva had described as Earth's daughter. Strange story, but cute. She knew her mother never cared for men, though she took a liking to Johnny and attended the wedding without issue. Still, Evanita wondered why her mother had such strong dislikes for men and what (if anything) Evanita should do about it.

CHAPTER 2

Books

2023 Sep 30, Sat Early am. Corpus Christi, Texas.

"Driver: 1711 Candlewood Drive," Eva said to the taxicab driver.

In the twenty minutes the taxicab driver spent transporting the two from Corpus Christi International Airport to Geneva's home, Evanita recounted the last time she took this ride along Highway 44 to North Padre Island Drive.

"Bear Lane," Evanita read from a side-street sign as North Padre Island Drive became South Padre Island Drive. "I meant to visit Grandma Geneva sooner than this. Now this is it, the last time."

Eva said nothing. The two completed their journey to Geneva's house at 1711 Candlewood Drive. It was (or is) a humble neighborhood of honest-working middle-class folk. Evanita recalled fond memories of playing in Candlewood Park as a child. Now these memories were vague, like a sunny day becoming filled with gray fog.

"I remember this house," said Evanita as the taxicab arrived at Geneva Carreña's home. "But the yard looks different somehow."

"Your grandmother loved gardening, and as much as Anna tried to keep things up, this summer was not as flowery as you may remember," Eva said.

The two unloaded their luggage from the taxi. Eva paid and tipped the driver who in turn thanked the two patrons.

"I had a strange thought," Eva said as she and Evanita walked slowly to the front door.

"What's that?"

"The taxicab driver said we were excellent patrons tonight, no doubt from my extra gratuity," started Eva.

"Yes, you are generous like that," said Evanita. "Just another reason I love you so much."

"Well, why are we patrons?"

"I don't understand," Evanita said.

"Patron sounds so patriarchal."

"Then should we be matrons?"

"That has a different meaning. It doesn't make sense," said Eva. "We as women are forced by the English language to conform to the male form, the 'patron,' because 'matron' is already assigned a different meaning. Imagine if the taxi driver said we were the best tipping matrons of the night. Would that mean I was running a jail for women?"

"Hmmm, I never thought of that," Evanita said as she knocked on the door.

Both women heard furtive Spanish on the other side followed by a, "Coming, I'm coming to the door."

"Miss Eva and Miss Evanita!" Anna called as she opened the door.

"Anna!" the descendents of Geneva called back.

Eva and Evanita hugged Anna in her sleeping outfit.

"Come in. I was sleeping, but I'm glad you woke me. Set your things down, and I'll take them upstairs. Please, sit down. Can I get you two something to drink?" Anna offered.

"Yes," Eva said while Evanita said, "No."

"I'll have some tequila," said Eva.

"No she won't!" said Evanita. "She had something on the plane already."

Eva gave a disapproving look to Evanita, but her frown turned into a grin of relief.

"I'm glad we're here," said Eva. "Just a glass of water for now, Anna, and some cheese and crackers if you have any."

"We always have cheese and crackers, Miss Eva, you know that," said Anna, and she turned to Evanita and asked the same question with her eyes—did Evanita want anything.

"No, not now."

"Okay, be right back," said Anna, and she stepped into the kitchen.

"*Madre?*" called a weak voice from upstairs.

"*Madre?*" Evanita repeated to Eva wondering what it meant.

"That's your grandmother's voice. She must be dreaming. Don't worry, she's on medication for the pain and can't feel the cancer."

"I want to see her, Mama. I want to go to her," Evanita begged.

"Okay, honey, but remember she's weak and probably delirious," warned Eva. "I think it's safe to hold her hand. Go on— don't tarry here with polite nothingness for Anna or my sake. Go on!"

Evanita walked up the stairs as quickly as her pregnant condition allowed.

"Cheese and crackers," said Anna as she returned from the kitchen. "I also made tea. I remember how much you like tea. Oh, where's Miss Evanita?"

"It's all right, Anna, she went upstairs to be with Mother," said Eva. "Thank you for the refreshments. Please, have a seat. No, don't worry about those bags yet. Relax a moment and chat with me."

"Okay, Miss Eva," said Anna as she backpedaled from tending to the bags and instead sat in a chair across from Eva in the living room.

"Anna, you're trembling," Eva said.

Eva stood, walked to Anna, took her hand, and led her to the couch where the two sat together.

"There. No need to sit way over there. You're family too."

"Oh bless you, Miss Eva. I don't know what to do with myself. I'm just a simple housekeeper. I don't do well with death."

"Shhhh, there there, Anna." Eva put her arm around Anna and embraced her. "It's been hard on you, but we're here now. Things will get better."

Anna fell into momentary Spanish then switched back to English. She jumbled words about finding a new job, where to go, and being left on the street. Eva hugged her and shushed her. Meanwhile, Evanita entered Geneva's bedroom.

"Eva. Eva, are you here?" called Geneva from her bedroom.

"Grandma, it's me," said Evanita as she entered Geneva's room.

Geneva rested face up with her upper back and head supported by several pillows. She had an oxygen tube running to her nose and an intravenous bag and line running into her left forearm.

"Oh, Evanita! You look so much like your mother when she was your age," said Geneva.

Geneva's voice was weak and dreamy, and her body remained stationary as if she were paralyzed. With great effort, she lifted her right hand to Evanita as a greeting.

"Don't strain yourself," said Evanita.

Evanita tried to rush over to Geneva, but her condition made it a struggle. Fortunately, a small lamp lit the room, or Evanita might have tripped over a nearby bedpan resting on the floor.

"What a strange place for a bedpan," muttered Evanita.

"No, not strange," replied Geneva, who apparently retained her good hearing. "And I can strain myself if I wish. Who can tell me what to do anymore with the end so near?"

"No, no, no. Don't talk like that. You'll be better soon," urged Evanita, though she did it for encouragement and not out of any special knowledge of Geneva's health.

"My dear, I never understood…I…when I was a nurse for the convent, I never understood what those dying patients of mine meant before they passed on. They said they knew they were dying. They knew. How could they know? But now I understand. I'm dying, Eva, I mean Evanita. You are so cute and lovable. So much like Eva. I love you both so much. But I know what they meant—I know death now. Not you or anyone else can change it."

"Grandma, you can't die! You're my grandma!" Evanita said.

Evanita held Geneva's hand, and Geneva squeezed with what little strength she had left. Geneva turned her head toward Evanita as Evanita leaned over the bed.

"Please," said Geneva. "Please sit and rest your legs, Evanita. You are due soon, aren't you?"

"Not exactly," Evanita said.

Evanita could no longer contain the tears that had welled up when she first entered Geneva's home.

"Yes, I am expecting. But I'm a couple of months away. A new great-grandchild for you, Grandma."

"I wish I could be here for the birth," said Geneva.

"You will, Grandma, you will!"

"Some of us are entering this world," Geneva said as she motioned to Evanita's belly, "and some are leaving. I will not miss the pain of my old bones. So much pain. But I am glad you are with me at the end. Evanita?" called Geneva.

"Yes Grandma?"

"Could you hand me my rosary? Anna took it away from me. She's a good housekeeper, but she shouldn't take my rosary from me."

"Here Grandma, here's your rosary," Evanita said.

Evanita found Geneva's rosary on one of several bookcases in Geneva's bedroom and handed it to Geneva.

"I have so many books, my dear, but alas! My eyes are too weak to read. Just once I'd like to find the person who invented small print and ring his neck," said Geneva. "Oh, yes, my rosary. Won't you join me in prayer?"

"Grandma, you know I'm not Catholic," said Evanita.

"I know dear. What was that faith your mother joined, was it Unitarian? Is that really a religion?"

"It's like a gathering of faiths," said Evanita. "I'm Unitarian too."

"Yes, so you are. Let's gather our faiths then, shall we? In the name of the Father and of the Son and of the Holy Spirit. Amen."

"All people that on Earth do dwell, sing to the Lord with...with...ah, well, how about this—health to all," said Evanita, but it didn't sound right in her grandmother's house, and she felt badly after failing to recite even a short prayer.

"Don't worry, Evanita. I can't be offended anymore. Death has a strange calming effect. Now let me see, what sort of special rosary prayer should I say? Lord Jesus Christ, take care of

my family after I receive your gracious reward. Help Eva, Evanita, Johnny Pindus, Jonara, and Evanita's new child find
strength in this world in good times and bad. In your name I
pray:"

Our Father, who art in Heaven,
Hallowed be thy name.
Thy Kingdom come, thy will be done,
On Earth as it is in Heaven.
Give us this day our daily bread,
And forgive us our trespasses,
As we forgive those
Who trespass against us.
And lead us not into temptation,
But deliver us from evil.
Amen.

Hail Mary, full of grace,
The Lord is with thee.
Blessed art thou amongst women,
And blessed is the fruit of thy womb, Jesus.
Holy Mary, Mother of God,
Pray for us sinners,
Now and at the hour of our death—

"Ow, ow, ow, ow!" cried Evanita. "Eeemm. Sorry Grandma.
Another contraction. They hurt more each time. Worse than before. Jonara didn't give me this much pain."

"You're expecting a boy then," said Geneva.

"How did you know?"

"Boys always give women more pain. But they are to be
loved too. They are of our flesh," said Geneva.

"Grandma, you never had any boys," said Evanita.

"Yes, child, I know. But if I did, I'm sure I would have loved
any son as much as a daughter. Mother Mary loved her son,
Jesus," said Geneva.

"I know, well, at least that's what I've heard," said Evanita.

"You don't have to be sorry. I know you aren't a Christian.
Don't worry! We each have our little beliefs we hold onto."

"Grandma, I'm scared. Those prayers you say—they—I—the Mary prayer," stuttered Evanita.

"Oh honey, it's just a prayer."

"But it talks of Mary's womb of Jesus, and I'm expecting a boy. And the last part, the praying in the hour of death. Grandma, these prayers are dark! I must say it now, and I can't help how I feel," said Evanita.

"Just a prayer, just words. Don't be afraid! I'm in the last hours of my death, and I'm not afraid. I'm ready to be taken home. I was given a full life, and I took it."

"Grandma, something inside me says that if you die, something bad will happen to me," Evanita said.

"No, don't say that, it's not true."

"I could die too, I've felt it," said Evanita.

"No child, you're young and strong," said Geneva.

"But you said you know when you're dying, you know it. I have a feeling something will happen to me too."

"Honey, death is not a feeling something might happen. One doesn't think death will happen like one will win the lottery. Death is just death, an end. You have your life ahead of you, and your unborn baby is another beginning, not an ending. Be strong."

"I'm scared, Grandma, I'm scared—of me, of you, and of Mama," Evanita cried.

"Scared of your mother? You're too old to be disciplined, child. And your mother is gentle. Professionally. She's a dentist. I'm so proud of my baby dentist. I remember too, Evanita, you're an architect. You design buildings. Not houses, office buildings. Skyscrapers. Your mother never frightened you."

"No, Grandma. She, she, oh how can I say it?"

"She doesn't like men," Geneva said.

"Yes!"

"Understandable."

"No!"

"She grew up in a different time, Evanita. So did I. A much different time," said Geneva.

"But Johnny is a man. And I love him."

"He's a special man. But your mother...your mother..."

"Grandma?"

"Hail Mary, full of grace, the Lord is with thee," said Geneva, seemingly losing her thought train.

"Hail Mary!? What about my mother?"

"Our Father, who art in Heaven...no, Eva never liked the Our Father, did she?" mused Geneva. "Hail Mary was more tolerable, except for the Jesus part. How can anyone not like the sweet baby Jesus?"

"Grandma!"

"You'll have to forgive your old fuddy-duddy Grandma. My mind is playing games with me. Death will do that to a person."

"Grandma!"

"Yes, Evanita, I'm still here. Not leaving this bed yet, not until they carry me off."

"Grandma, how can you joke around like this? There must be some rule about a person who is gravely ill. This is a serious occasion."

Geneva mustered a weak but steady laugh.

"I can laugh," Geneva giggled. "I have some life in me yet. I...can...laugh. Evanita, read to me, will you?"

"Read to you? You want me to read to you?" Evanita asked.

"Yes. There is a book...I know, child, I have hundreds of books in my home. You and your mother, yes, you two will go through these books and most likely throw them out," Geneva said.

"I would never!"

"Evanita, it is not practical to hang on to so many books. Most are silly detective stories—how I love a thriller. But there are a few you may like. On that shelf behind you—reach for it— there is a book, *Mining for Limeys*. Do not worry, it is in English. It was my own grandfather's first book he ever owned. It is old, very old. Start with the first chapter, Evanita. What does it say?"

"'The miner's basic equipment is a pick, a helmet, and a caged bird.' Grandma?" Evanita asked.

"Yes child?"

"These words sound familiar, but I don't remember seeing this book before."

"Evanita, you have heard these words before. I would read them to you when you were a little girl. Do you remember?" Geneva asked.

"No, I remember very little of my childhood. I was told the accident erased those memories," Evanita explained.

"Do you remember the accident, when you were in Spain?" Geneva asked.

"No, Grandma Geneva, I'm sorry, I don't remember the accident."

"Oh, you don't have to be sorry. I'm sorry for you that you don't remember. But you may remember, or you may learn again about your childhood. It's important, child, it's important," Geneva explained.

"What's important? Tell me what's important," Evanita begged.

"Oh Evanita, you know I'm old and tired and on the way out of this world. If I were just a bit younger with a bit more health and vigor...no, you will have to find your own way. But keep the book about mining, and read it! But when you read it, don't think about mining."

"I don't understand, Grandma Geneva, how I can read a book about mining and not think about mining!" Evanita explained.

"One thing I have learned over the years, Evanita, is that a good book is more than what it says, it's what it says about other things. Between the lines, except you apply your own lines to the book and see how the book responds," Geneva explained.

"Grandma, you're confusing me."

"I remember when I was young, when I learned to read. I thought reading meant memorizing every word, every phrase until I completed a sentence. And when the sentence was complete, I thought the law from above was spoken, that what I read was absolutely true to be contested by no one, that in fact the concept of contesting a sentence was unheard of. Then I learned about propaganda and lies, how words and phrases are twisted and spun around one concept to give the appearance of another. Deceit. I did not trust the written word after that, until one day I was reading my grandfather's mining book, and it hit me that the written word is like a photograph, a little window into the mind of the author and what he thinks his reader wants to see. You see, Evanita, I was never a miner, I never wanted to be a miner, and I had no interest in mining. So this book on mining was never meant for me, and I was never meant to be the reader. I was something else, a *voyeur* for lack of a better word. I was my own audience watching a type of tennis game between the author and his intended reader. He served the ball, and the reader returned the ball or at least tried. Well, I think he hoped to win every point, but I could sense sections where his 'volley' with the reader stretched out, because either past readers ignored things like mining safety tips, or he had some other agenda to push on the reader. Anyway, he always served the ball, and he expected the reader to follow his orders like some sort of military soldier. Keep a stiff upper lip and mine to the end—that sort of thing, Evanita. That's why I kept the book—as an example of what to be careful of."

"Grandma, I have a strange question—why did your grandfather have an English book? Most of your books are in Spanish or Catalan, you're from Spain, your family is from Spain—I don't understand," Evanita said.

"Evanita, what is a Spaniard? Haven't you wondered?"

"You're a Spaniard," Evanita acknowledged.

"Yes, that's true. But my grandfather was from England. Martin Sixpence. He was British, and he married my grandmother in Carreña, Spain."

"So you aren't a pure-blood Spaniard?"

"Is there such a thing?" Geneva asked rhetorically. "Spain has been a melting pot throughout the ages. Celts roamed the lands during ancient times, Romans conquered the area. Moors—sorry, some people do not like that word—Arabs came along later and stayed for hundreds of years. So many people from different places entering and leaving Spain—who's to say if there is a 'pure-blood' Spaniard. But Grandpa came for quick riches through mining. You don't remember when we were there in Carreña, do you?"

"No Grandma, I don't. I wish I could," Evanita said.

"I also wish you could remember. I showed you where my family lived, where Grandpa first mined and exploited the resources in our caves. Wait, I'm confusing caves. I'm confusing trips. Life is confusing. I went to Spain twice. The first time was Montseny with Eva, but the second was Carreña with you. My family. My grandpa. I remember one alcove in a cave he was mining, I remember how it looked before Grandpa picked it clean. It was so beautiful before he touched it, then it was empty, bare. I could not understand how someone could take a thing of beauty like that and remove it. But he explained it was important, and in those days I trusted him. Then there was the Adrian trip."

"Grandma, who's Adrian?" Evanita asked.

"It's amazing how so much beauty can take years-upon-years to develop only to be erased in a fraction of the time, never to come back in our lifetime. Carreña. Why did Adrian exploit Carreña?"

"Adrian? Who was he?" Evanita asked.

"Some horrible thing. I'm glad you don't remember him. He was very much like my grandfather—another person exploiting another cave. Did I tell you about my grandfather? I heard my own grandmother was swept off her feet by him—just a poor herding girl of little means living with her family. He promised her riches, and she fell for it. The family did well, at least from the money. But it changed them, Evanita. Grandma grew less tolerant of the common herding people she once called her friends. She and Grandfather had a summer place in Girona. In fact, Grandma stayed in Girona and never returned to Carreña as Grandpa did for mining. My mother left Grandpa too and lived with Grandma in Girona until she was an adult. She met François Vallan and moved into her own apartment in Girona. Life was hard, and she died shortly after giving birth to me. I stayed with the nuns—no, the sisters, but one time I returned to Carreña and lived with Grandpa during his mining expedition days. No one liked him."

"I don't understand. Was Adrian a miner?"

"No, not like Grandfather. But he was after quick personal gain. And he wanted to take advantage of you to do so. Grandma's family owned some land that Grandpa manipulated to start his mining business. At first, Grandpa promised only to mine a small part of it as a condition for marrying Grandma. But he became greedy and mined much more than he was supposed to. Grandma's pride was hurt, and her own family disowned her. Evanita, Adrian would have destroyed your life as Grandpa did to my family."

"Your life wasn't destroyed. You made it just fine," Evanita concluded.

"Oh child! How I wish so many things were different. So many things. There is another book I wish to show you," Geneva said.

With her right hand, Geneva motioned over to the bookcase again, pointed, and then curved her finger to indicate something behind a row of books.

"Yes, Grandma?"

"Behind the books on the middle shelf—over there—is a special book. Please, pull it out, but do be careful. It is very old and precious!" Geneva instructed.

Evanita reached over the middle-shelf books and touched a long yet thick book wedged between the other books and the bookcase backboard. Yet she could not lift it up above the other books.

"Evanita, it's all right. Toss those front books out of the way. They are only cheap detective novels," Geneva said.

Evanita did as suggested and pulled the detective books over the shelf's edge and sent them falling to the floor.

"Miss Geneva, Miss Evanita," called Anna from below.

Oddly, Evanita slipped into near panic and hobbled downstairs as quickly as possible. She met Anna and did her best to explain.

"It's nothing, Anna. I dropped some books. Grandma Geneva is doing fine. I am fine," Evanita explained. "Where's my mama?"

"She fell asleep on the couch. Forgive me, Miss Evanita, but I dozed off too. Only for a moment. Would you like some tea and crackers?"

"No thank you, Anna. But it's getting late. I think you should turn in for the night."

"I've made the beds for you and your mother upstairs. Miss Eva—your mother—well, I guess she won't make it upstairs tonight. But you remember the guestroom you always sleep in, it's the—" Anna started.

"It's the steely-gray one, yes, I remember, like fresh metal in a skyscraper. Bless Grandma Geneva's spirit. Steel never goes into a building with its bare surface exposed, of course, but I like the touch Grandma added to the room. And yes, you too Anna, thank you for helping her put it all together."

"Thank you, Miss Evanita. If that is all then," Anna said.

"Yes, Anna, that's all. Now go to bed and get a good night's rest!"

"I will, Miss Evanita, I will," said Anna, and with that, Anna stepped quietly to her downstairs bedroom.

Evanita returned upstairs to Geneva's bedroom where she found Geneva asleep and snoring lightly. Evanita thought that Grandma Geneva must be relaxed and settled to be snoring so happily. With this knowledge, Evanita's mind was set at ease, and she retired to her guestroom where she slept the night through—forgetting about Geneva's special book.

2023 Oct 2, Mon. Corpus Christi, Texas.

The weekend passed rather uneventfully. Geneva fell into a light coma and would not wake. Evanita spent many hours by Geneva's bedside and tried waking Geneva by reading books aloud. Periodically, Anna or Eva checked on Evanita and begged her to take a break, explaining that Evanita was stressing herself out, and how this is not good when expecting a baby.

With Evanita obsessed about her Grandma Geneva, Eva made the telephone calls to Portland and provided updates to Johnny, Jonara, and Claire. Eva managed to pull Evanita away to a Unitarian church service Sunday morning with the promise Anna would watch Geneva and call Evanita's cell phone should Geneva regain consciousness. Geneva remained silent all day Sunday.

Monday morning came and went with much the same news as the weekend. Geneva remained in her coma while Evanita kept vigil by Geneva's bedside. Eva telephoned the family back in Portland as she had been doing over the weekend, and the morning finished without event.

By late Monday afternoon, Geneva's condition deteriorated. Her blood pressure weakened, and her breathing grew strained. No longer did she snore happily. Eva telephoned Johnny and warned him that Geneva's time would end soon, and that he and Jonara should prepare to fly down.

Anna made an excellent Monday evening dinner of chicken teriyaki. Eva ate it hungrily, but Evanita simply picked at pieces here and there.

"Please Miss Evanita," Anna said. "Eat something to keep up your strength. You are eating for two."

"I'm sorry, Anna," Evanita said. "I keep thinking about Grandma."

Eva helped Anna clean up after dinner, and the two convinced Evanita to join in several games of Rummy. The evening drew on, Anna replenished the snacks and beverages, and Evanita enjoyed herself for the first time since she'd celebrated Jonara's birthday on Friday.

"I'm so glad I spent the evening down here playing cards," Evanita said as the evening grew into the night. "It's good having family and friends nearby in these tough times."

The night grew late, and Anna bade goodnight to Eva and Evanita. After suggesting that Evanita get a good night's sleep, Eva fell asleep on the couch. Evanita walked upstairs and glanced into Geneva's bedroom. Evanita found Geneva in a groggy state.

"*Mi conejo,*" Geneva mumbled. "*¿Dónde está mi conejo?*"

"Grandma? Grandma Geneva?" Evanita whispered.

"Eva?" Geneva mumbled as she awoke from her groggy state.

"No, it's Evanita. I'm here, Grandma."

"Oh Evanita, it's you again. Is your mother here too?"

"Yes, she's downstairs. Sleeping on the couch," Evanita said.

"Goodness sakes, what on Earth is she doing sleeping on the couch? I must get up and show her..." Geneva said as she tried to sit up, but she remembered her age and condition and changed her tone. "No, time's long past to tell Eva what to do. That's right, she's an adult. Evanita, I'll have Anna prepare your favorite bedroom. You remember—it's just next door. It's painted in shiny silver and gray. Steel. Like steel for skyscrapers."

"Yes Grandma, Anna already prepared it," said Evanita. "I've been sleeping in it the past few days."

"What is the hour, child, is it late?" Geneva asked.

"Quarter past two," said Evanita.

"Oh dear child, you must get some rest. I'm old and don't count, but you're expecting another child! Please don't stay up on my behalf," said Geneva.

"I want to, Grandma Geneva, I want to. Tell me, Grandma—tell me about what you said a moment ago."

"What did I say?" Geneva asked. "I thought you were Eva. I'm sorry child, I confused you with your mother again."

"No, Grandma, you said something before that, something in Spanish, like *conejo*," Evanita said.

"Rabbit?"

"Yes, I think so, 'my rabbit'. Do you have a rabbit?"

"No child," Geneva answered. "I have no rabbit, not even for a pet."

"Then I wonder what you meant," Evanita mused.

"I don't know, child. I get confused so easily. Perhaps it was something I read. Perhaps it is in The Book," Geneva said.

"What book?" Evanita asked.

"The one I asked you to take—from the bookcase. A diary of my family."

Evanita reached for the long book she had meant to grab before—when the books in front had fallen to the floor. She pulled the book from the bookcase with surprisingly little effort considering its bulk.

"It's a heavy book, Evanita. Be careful not to drop it."

But Evanita didn't feel the weight of the book. Instead, she felt something different. She shivered at the thought of holding such an old book. She did not need to open it to know it was before her time, even before her grandmother's time. Woods of different color—light, cherry, and deep-brown made up the cover and spine. Evanita opened the book to the first page. The paper had some sort of flax plant in its composition, but that was nothing compared to the words upon words that echoed around in her mind. She felt as if in a tunnel, an echo that at times faded into a background stadium sound of people and at other times sounded like a jet flying overhead. All this she experienced before reading the first words, yet Evanita did not understand why she had this feeling—she could not recall having felt both awed and intimidated by a book.

"It is a strange book...no...wait...there's something in it. I can't describe it. Grandma Geneva, what is this book?" Evanita asked.

"Bring the book over, Evanita. Good. Now place it on the bed next to me. No, bring it closer so I can touch it with my hand—my right hand. There, good. Now open the book. See, here is a drawing of Spain—the entire country, including Portugal. Do you see this corner here, Evanita? Look closely." Geneva pointed to the northwestern corner of Spain. "This is Galicia."

"I remember this. You once said I could think of Galicia as a knee, Portugal like a shin, and Asturias as a part of the thigh," said Evanita.

"Yes, yes! Asturias, you remember. What else do you remember about Asturias?" Geneva asked.

"Repelled the Moors," answered Evanita.

"Yes, and what else, something more personal."

"Carreña. It's here, in Asturias."

"Yes, excellent."

"The family. The family is from Carreña?"

"Yes. And this book has been in the family since Asturias began the liberation of Spain from the Moors. At least we like to claim so. History may say differently. But the diary begins in an old Iberian language," said Geneva.

"Grandma, I'm sorry, but I don't know Spanish like I should. I can't read the book."

"Don't worry, Evanita. The first part of the book is not written in Spanish but in Asturian. All of my ancestors wrote in that language. In fact, there's not a word of Spanish in the entire diary! My part is written in Catalan."

"Huh? I don't understand. Doesn't everyone in Spain speak Spanish?" Evanita asked.

"Oh, I wish the accident hadn't robbed you of your memory. I did explain this before. But I will explain briefly again. Spain is more like a collection of little countries, each with their own languages and cultures. There was an effort several hundred years ago to group these little countries together. It was largely successful. No, I shouldn't use that word. Those who wanted unification saw it as a success. Others—mostly in the northern part of Spain—saw it as a disaster. And as the years unfolded, they saw their culture assaulted by the Spanish culture and language," Geneva said. "Maybe that's too harsh. Maybe not. Hmm. I've always wondered what would have happened if those Pyrenees provinces banded together and formed their own loose confederation of states."

"But why did you write in Catalan? Why was the first part in Asturian? Why couldn't they write in Spanish? Heck, English would have been better too," Evanita said.

Geneva managed a small laugh.

"Spoken like someone who knows nothing of Spain," Geneva said. "I guess you'd have to live there to understand. Now then, the book is a diary of our family. But to your point about being in English—yes, I went back, and on the odd pages that were left blank, I translated the passages to English. At least I started translating. I began with my own passages and worked back. I got as far as the 1930s."

"Why did you stop?" Evanita asked.

"Those were horrible years. I meant to get through them. I tried, but I couldn't. My Asturian is not so great, and no one wanted to help me. It's not that people are unfriendly—they simply didn't want to relive the Civil War. So I left it untranslated. And later I thought no one would care," Geneva mused.

"Grandma!"

"Well? Your mother never showed any interest," Geneva said. "I tried to explain it to her, how difficult life was in Spain before I came over to America. I showed Eva the book, but she didn't care. 'That's the old country, the old way,' she would always say."

"But this is family," said Evanita.

"Yes, it is. That's why I want you to have the book, and I want you to take it with you before you go to sleep tonight—or should I say this morning," Geneva explained.

"I...how can I? This book is beyond words," Evanita stumbled.

"It is special, Evanita, but who will treasure it when I'm gone? Only you will carry on the memories. And perhaps Jonara when she's older."

Evanita closed the book and held it to her abdomen. Her unborn boy managed a small kick, and Evanita shuddered. She envisioned a hutch behind a small mountain-built house, a hutch with a wild-looking rabbit inside. Walking to the hutch was a young girl—perhaps Jonara's age or younger—with three fresh carrots. She slipped the carrots one by one into the hutch through the sides covered by chicken wire. The rabbit ate the carrots greedily as if neglected of food for days. The girl said something soft in Spanish, Asturian, or Catalan—Evanita wasn't sure which. Evanita felt the girl was apologizing to the rabbit for not visiting as much as she felt she should have. A fog rolled down the mountain slope as the dawn broke into morning. The girl left the hutch and gathered some wild grass for the rabbit to eat. She returned to the hutch and fed the grass to the rabbit. A door slammed, but not in the hutch. A British man stormed from the house, yanked the girl from the rabbit's home, and burst the hutch open. He reached for the rabbit and began to strangle it, intent on wringing death from the defenseless creature.

"Curse you undermining varmints!" the British man screeched.

"*Mi conejo!*" the girl shouted. She lunged for the British man's hands and knocked the rabbit free.

"Get in the house!" the man ordered.

"*Mi conejo.* Run away. Don't look back. Run free, *mi conejo!*" screamed the girl.

The girl fell into tears as the British man dragged her back to the small mountain house. The fog cleared, and the rabbit slipped into the daylight. The girl took refuge in her bedroom. She stared out the window and whispered, "*¿Dónde está mi conejo?*"

"It was you," said Evanita. "You were the girl."

"The girl? What are you saying, Evanita?"

"You had a pet *conejo* when you were young—Jonara's age. You were in the mountains, in a house on a steep slope. You fed your rabbit three carrots. A man tried to kill your *conejo*, but you forced his hand open. The rabbit ran away free. It was you, Grandma. But you spoke in Spanish, not Catalan."

Geneva rolled her eyes slowly as if searching deep into memory. Her face changed from placidity to a gravity that weakened her. She closed her eyes, opened and closed her mouth to reposition her lingual functions, and opened her eyes.

"Evanita, my granddaughter," Geneva said. "You know. I never wrote it down. How could I? Yet somehow you know. I thought...your husband...Johnny. He could see. He never spoke of it. He knew the pain. Evanita, how can you see this? I am glad you know. I could never tell anyone about Grandpa and my rabbit. I spoke in Spanish because no one in Carreña understood my Catalan. I also speak Spanish when I'm upset."

Geneva paused and cried a little. There was no voice to Geneva's cry, but she teared up and shook.

"I have laughed and cried in my last hours," Geneva said. "Evanita, there is some power in you and in the book. Treasure both well, my dear!"

"I don't understand. Grandma...the rabbit...Grandma...who was the old man? Grandma, why did he try to kill the rabbit? Grandma? Grandma!" Evanita called.

"Evanita," Geneva said.

"Yes, Grandma," Evanita replied.

Evanita placed the book on the bed next to Geneva, drew close to her grandma, and held Geneva's right hand with her two hands.

"Grandma, stay with me," Evanita said.

"Evanita, say goodbye to your mother for me," Geneva said, who now seemed noticeably weaker.

"No, Grandma, no. Stay with me."

"I cannot change the good Lord's hand. He is calling me now. Say goodbye for me. Give the family my love, and Anna too. Remember your family and your Grandma Geneva. You are a free spirit. You are my special gift," Geneva said.

"Grandma, no, please!" Evanita begged as she fought back the tears.

"Into the hands of the Lord, I commend my spirit. Into your hands, my Lord, I commend...I commend..." Geneva trailed, and her eyes closed.

"Noooooo. Grandma, no. Please!" Evanita begged.

Evanita heard Geneva's breathing fade. Holding Geneva's hand, Evanita sensed a weakening pulse. She drew Geneva's hand to her abdomen, and she envisioned those final moments through eyes not her own. Pulse, pulse, inhale, exhale, now breathe. Push, Geneva, push. Your little Eva is being born. Push, push. One life follows another. Push and push as one planetary body follows another. Push and push for Geneva. Two stars rolling in a circle, one follows the other. The voice, Geneva, she cries in pain. Push and push and out Eva goes as Eva's life follows Geneva's. Push and push as Geneva's placenta follows Eva. The placenta, the interface between two—a girl follows her mother. A star, a planet, the gravity between the two, the loving bond—one follows the other.

Geneva's pulse faded. Evanita's perceptions changed. She saw a rabbit running free, burrowing beneath the mountain, cursed by the British man for undermining his ground, his ground for operating heavy machinery. The curse of the rabbit was its freedom. It could only be free, it knew nothing else, its captivity meant strangulation, a lack of air—it cannot breathe.

Geneva's breathing stopped. Evanita felt she was no longer watching but instead was falling underwater, sinking lower while holding onto a ball—a cloud-covered Earth with an atmosphere, an air pocket, something to give a little life to Evanita as she sank deeper. She drew what little air she could from Earth, but its brightness grew pale as she inhaled its clouds and stratosphere. Earth changed from white clouds with blue oceans to a dark brown, like a rotting apple, the apple once unspoiled now exposed to the air, to a browning and consumption. Evanita inhaled this Earth to stay alive, but she sank farther as she exhaled, losing the once-earthen air to the top of the sea, the sea into which Evanita sank, and released the air to the heavens. The once pure Earth, this Earth Evanita now held, deflated, not as a sports ball would, but as a dimension does from three to two. The Earth became flat, like a disc, a used supper plate when the food is gone but without a shine. A dull plate, a dark plate. Evanita tasted death on the plate, and she knew it, she knew of what Geneva had spoken. Evanita rotated the plate before her face and lifted the plate above her head in search of strength from above. A star sought downward toward Evanita, a small star in the heavens above the sea, the sea Evanita did descend. She blocked the star—it was not right, its light was not air or earth. She kissed the plate a gift of air, a gift of life it once gave her. The air held fast below the plate, the once-Earth plate now shadowed her face. The star grew fast upon Evanita. She blocked its gaze with the plate, the once-Earth.

Evanita held her breath. While staring at the dark-flattened once-earthen plate, the star gathered wispy-white fingers around the plate's edge. The dead plate tingled, like the frozen edge of a glacier exposed to a sun's warming rays. Bits of spectral color danced around the plate, and in a flash, the star overcame the plate and partly blinded Evanita with brightness. Yet she was not completely without sight. The warmth to the plate heated her gift of air beneath the plate. It vectored a force upward unto the plate lifting it up, slowly, but up. Evanita watched as the plate ascended to the star, up and up until it reached atop the sea and released its remaining bubble of life. The bubble released into the heavens and wandered above as a wisp amongst the ether. The browned plate, now a shell, shoveled down to the bottom, left, right, over, under, until the bottom it reached, a faint memory of a before time.

Evanita's lighthearted relief from watching the wisp liberate itself to the ether changed to heaviness as the solitude of the sea crushed her heart. She fell, face up, and landed next to the empty shell. She gagged.

"Ugh, ugh, ugh," Evanita choked, regaining consciousness on the floor next to Geneva's bed.

"Evanita!" called Eva, who'd been breathing air into Evanita's lungs as Anna pumped her chest. "Evanita, wake up! Breathe deeply, sweetie! Hold on. The ambulance is coming."

"Mama, what happened?" Evanita gasped as she remained in a weakened state on the floor.

"You fell and hit your head on the floor. You stopped breathing, and your heart quit beating," Eva explained.

"Miss Evanita, what a scare you gave us! Don't frighten us this way again!" Anna begged.

"I thought you were sleeping," Evanita said to her mother. "I thought you both were."

"My dear Evanita, the years have slipped by since you were a girl, but a mother never forgets the thudding sound of her child falling helplessly to the floor. It wakes a mother from the deepest sleep. I haven't reacted like this since you were a baby, when I was afraid that everything in the world would threaten your safety. I protected you, Evanita, I wanted you to live—as I do now."

"Mama, what about Grandma?" Evanita asked.

"Lie still, honey, lie still and think about breathing," Eva said.

"She's dead. I felt her pass," Evanita said.

"Yes, she passed away a little while ago. This has been too much for you, Evanita. I think you should have stayed home with Johnny and Jonara. But you're here with us, alive fortunately," Eva explained.

"Grandma," Evanita trailed.

"Shhhh. Think nice thoughts of her. She had a full life. Now we must move on. Rest here a moment. We're taking you to the hospital. I'll take care of your grandma."

"Johnny. Jonara. I need to tell them—" Evanita started.

"Oh Miss Evanita, I'll get a hold of Mr. Johnny and Miss Jonara," Anna promised.

"Don't tell them I fainted, Anna, don't let them know I almost d-d-died. Johnny...he...too sensitive," Evanita said as she closed her eyes.

"No, Evanita, don't fail us now!" Anna said with anxiety.

"Anna, wait. Put your hand in front of her face. She's breathing, see? She's fine now. Just sleeping a bit. Wait, do you hear the siren, Anna? Outside. There now. Lead them up here, will you? I'll stay with my daughter," Eva instructed.

CHAPTER 3:

ICU

In the later hours following Geneva's death and Evanita's hospitalization, Johnny Pindus arranged for Jonara's temporary leave from school. Tasteless as it may seem, Johnny collected her upcoming assignments and along with her school books flew down with her to Texas on a late morning airline flight. Jonara had said farewell to her best friend, Almarita, before scurrying off with Johnny to the Portland airport. She kept tapping her feet anxiously on the airplane's floor during the flight, but the tapping increased the tension in Johnny's mind, and he scolded her into stopping—a behavior not common for Johnny, and minutes later he apologized and broke into tears, unable to contain his composure in the moment of distress—a lost grandmother-in-law, a wife away from him and in trouble, and his own struggling skills in parenting Jonara. But he knew he had limitations, judged not by his own mind, but rather by the reactions of those around him, the quizzical look of strangers who so easily interacted with their own children and answered their every question and need. Johnny thought he interacted with Jonara well enough, but this moment, this outburst—even he knew it was wrong. Jonara turned from him and ignored him, as if he had crossed the line from a trusting father to a crackpot imperialist. She had never done that. Was it Almarita's influence? Had Jonara outgrown Johnny? He wasn't sure—how could he be? Johnny had a gift, an unusual one, but a gift nonetheless. And often this gift gave him insight into a person's history and being. This was unusual for such an autistic person, even if Johnny was a higher-functioning one. But it pained him to use his gift. He was older and did not recover as quickly from using his gift as in his youth. He was still tired from finding Eva on the bridge. But Jonara was no longer a little girl. She was thirteen, on the verge of being a woman, and had an awareness of a life-changing event—the death of a family member.

Johnny requested bottled water from the steward. The steward provided the water to Johnny. He took it, drank some of it, and poured the rest over his face. The steward thought nothing of the event and proceeded to the next needy passenger. Johnny set the bottle in a holder and placed a hand over his chest. He placed his other hand on Jonara's shoulder and shook his head a little. She remained frozen in place—affixed in gaze through the window—and she focused on some indeterminable distant point.

"Jonara," whispered Johnny. "Jo-nee."

Jonara shivered on hearing her name.

"What are you thinking?" Johnny asked.

Jonara shivered again. Johnny closed his eyes, and her shivers combined with his head shaking created oscillations in his brain. Johnny received thoughts. But they weren't his. He now knew why Jonara had been tapping. In her mind, she had always believed her Great-Grandmother Geneva would live forever, that only bad people or men die. She knew Johnny would die someday too, but not Geneva. But she had heard the news and could not believe it—what had Great-Grandmother done to deserve death? What did this mean for the family? What did it mean for Jonara?

"What does it mean?" Jonara asked aloud.

Jonara turned her gaze from the window to Johnny. Johnny removed his hand from Jonara and removed the other from his chest. With his trance broken, he turned to Jonara, returned her gaze, and spoke.

"Jonara, my daughter. I...I am sorry for scolding you. I know you are upset. You must be brave," said Johnny.

"Santa Claus," said Jonara. "There is no Santa Claus."

"Yes, Jonara, you learned that five years ago—from a magazine."

"And no Easter Bunny," Jonara continued.

"Yes, no Easter Bunny," said Johnny.

"No tooth fairy, either."

"You never believed in a tooth fairy."

"Daddy?" Jonara asked.

"Yes?"

"Why do people believe in the Easter Bunny? Why do people believe in Santa Claus?" Jonara asked.

"It doesn't make sense, does it Jonara?"

"No. I believed in the Easter Bunny and Santa Claus. I trusted Mommy. She told me they were true, that if I were good, Santa Claus would give me presents, and the Easter Bunny would leave me chocolate candy," Jonara said.

"You still get presents for Christmas. And you receive chocolate for Easter," said Johnny.

"I know, but it's not the same," said Jonara.

"You don't like Christmas? What about Easter?" Johnny asked.

"I do like Christmas and Easter. But I thought Santa Claus and the Easter Bunny were real. Now I know they aren't. And it was because I read about Santa Claus in a magazine about St. Nicholas. I learned the entire story. And it's just a story. I believed what I was told by Mommy, but Mommy was wrong!"

"Oh honey," said Johnny.

"I trusted her, and she broke the trust," Jonara continued.

"Dear...honey," Johnny said.

"You could have told me. Why didn't you tell me, Daddy? I trusted you too!" Jonara said.

"I did it...your mother...she wanted you to believe in Santa Claus, so I had to," Johnny stuttered.

"You had to? You, my daddy, Johnny Pindus, the one with the gift, the gift to feel the truth—you had to be a part of this lie? Daddy, why? Why?!" Jonara demanded.

"It...is...tradition," Johnny struggled to say. "Your mother...I...your grandmother...had to be done, had to be done."

The airplane experienced turbulence flying over the Cascade Range—the same mountain chain that had given Eva and

Evanita a jolt on their flight to Texas. Jonara's cell phone buzzed, indicating an incoming telephone call. She stared at Johnny. He was about to say that cell phone calls should not be made from an airplane, but that was before, when he was younger. Things were different now. The cell phone buzzed again, and Jonara answered.

"Hello? Grandma! Yes, we're having a nice flight. A little bumpy over the mountains. Yeah, it was. Mmm, hmmm. Can I talk to Mommy? She's sleeping? Grandma Eva, is this the truth? Grandma? She's not sleeping, is she? Yes, I am growing up. Where is she, Grandma? She is?! When did this happen? Is she okay? Yes. Yes. Okay. I will, Grandma, I will. Goodbye!"

Jonara ended the telephone call and turned to her father.

"Daddy? Did you know about Mommy? Did you know she's in the hospital?" Jonara asked.

"She is...is...in the hospital? Yes, she is in the hospital. I knew, Jonara, I knew," Johnny said.

"Daddy, why didn't you tell me? Oh, everything is going wrong," Jonara said in disbelief.

Johnny stared at the ground, unsure of what to say. His innards cramped in pain, and he rushed off to a toilet to relieve his churning stomach. Jonara sat alone and stared out the window.

"Just another lie. Is this the future?" she whispered.

There was no one to hear her. She looked at her cell phone and dialed a number.

"Allie? Jonie. You were right. Being an adult means learning how to lie," Jonara said into the phone. "No, he's in the bathroom. Yes, I'll listen to you now. You're my best friend, Allie."

Johnny sat in the bathroom, no longer needing to relieve his stomach. But he needed to connect—with something, anything—connect with Earth, with the past—something to temper his sanity.

"Water, water," Johnny said.

Johnny shook as he turned on the small tap in the sink. It was a compulsive habit Johnny had at home. When he was upset, he ran to the bathroom and turned on warm water until his trembling hands calmed and steadied, and this calmness carried up his arms and melted into his racing heart. The ills and aches of the world dissipated with steady warm water over his hands. This was in contrast to a shower which felt like a million electric needles pelting his skin. None of this mattered now. He was on an airplane free of the ground, but Johnny did not do well with this sort of freedom. On the ground, he could feel the solid, steady rotation of the earth. Warm water from a faucet was hydraulically linked to a main water supply. His gift allowed him to sense this connection, a flow of clean water from the tap to the water tower near his home. A tower of hydraulic strength gave him strength, the water lines traveled through the ground, the earth, and in this he was able to sense both the water and the earth—Johnny's sense of stability was complete. But on this airplane, without a connection to the earth, Johnny had a loss of direction and orientation that made him sick. Motion sickness? Perhaps, but Johnny's inner ear had no influence on this sickness, none at all.

"Jonara, Jonara, what is happening to you?" Johnny muttered to the low-pressure water flowing from the faucet.

Johnny splashed the water on his face in rapid, jerky movements. He needed to connect. First with one hand, he cupped water and tossed it to his face, then a second, and finally he cupped both hands one after another and tossed the water in his face. He gasped as if struggling for air while drowning. Deprivation, he felt it, like losing that bit of air while underwater. But it wasn't oxygen he needed as his lungs continued to draw its needs from the pressurized cabin five miles above the earth.

"Evanita, I need you, don't leave me," he gurgled as some of the splashed water entered his throat. "Evanita. Nita. Mummy Eva, where are you? Nanna Geneva. Kay, can you clean my teeth, Kay Margo?"

Someone knocked on the door.

"Are you all right in there?" a voice asked.

"Fine," Johnny lied.

Deceit was a coping mechanism. Lie to the world when in distress. Lie to the world to minimize its invasion on him. It was too much to cope with his own mental skirmishes—he did not need the harsh unknowing outside world intervening with its knives of sympathy, its blather of feigned support.

He placed both hands against the door as if expecting someone to force entry on him. No such entry came. Johnny held his hands against the door firmly. His muscles seized up beginning with his fingers and traveling down his arms to his feet. He desperately meant to slam his body against the door, hoping to break the tension in his body, but he didn't. He held firmly to what little self control he had left, hid his stress from the others on the airplane, and instead channeled his strain within his body. He turned back toward the sink, sank to the floor, and clasped his hands together—hoping for each hand to draw strength from the other. Instead of resolve, he met locked fingers; instead of focus, he felt entangled knuckles. And now—now with his full energy stressed up in the very hands that sensed the feelings of others and empathized their exuberance and pain into his own heart, now his energy exacted its price. His knuckles lost their cohesion and loosened their joints. Johnny groaned in pain as he dislocated his knuckles—first his thumbs, then his pinkies, followed shortly by his other fingers. He writhed in pain, and in so doing broke the clasp of pain on his digits. His hands were free from each other, but his joints maintained their dislocation. He held his hands against the sides of his face with his fingertips between his eyes and ears. His wrists met each other under his chin. He did not dare pull his hands from his face for fear of pain. His pain subsided as long as he did not move, and he sat there. He sat, not sure if he should cry or shake or moan. Too often had he traveled this mental road, more often as a child than an adult, but he had his relapses now and then.

"Valeria, come back to me. One rose red, two is for blue. Valeria, my sister and own, your Johnny calls you, calls home for you. Valeria? Valeria..." Johnny's voiced trailed as the sister he called so often as a child had long since passed away. But her memory stayed with him, and whenever he felt at his lowest, he called for her and felt an image of her pass before him.

"Johnny..." he remembered her soft, rounded voice call. "There, there, Johnny. I'll sing you a song. Here Johnny, sing with me. Will you do that, Johnny? Sing a song with me about the Erie Canal."

Johnny hummed the song in reality, but in his mind, he remembered back to when he sang the song with his sister. He could not remember the original words to the song, but they were the words Johnny remembered singing with his sister, Valeria. The words themselves were less important than the continuity her voice gave to the song, the feeling that she would sing for him in time of need to take him from his unsettled state to something of stability.

The airplane landed in Corpus Christi without delay. Johnny had managed to compose himself before the plane's landing. Eva met Jonara and Johnny at the airport in the luggage pickup area.

"Johnny, how was the flight?" Eva asked as she hugged Johnny.

"The flight, it was tiring, the flight was tiring," Johnny said.

"Jonara, how's my favorite granddaughter?" Eva asked as she held her arms out to Jonara, but Jonara only stared back at Eva in an untrusting way.

"The luggage should be around soon," said Jonara, turning her back on Eva and Johnny as she stared intently at the luggage conveyor dispenser.

"Jonara? What is it, Jonara?" Eva asked.

"There, that looks like your bag, Daddy," Jonara said with her back continued against the two. "And look, that's my bag."

"Joni, sweetie, won't you give a big hug to your grandmother?" Eva asked.

Jonara turned around, paused, and gave an unenthusiastic hug to Eva.

"Are you tired, Jonara? Johnny, let's get going. Anna knows you two are coming and has prepared rooms. Jonara, won't that be nice to spend the night at your Great-Grandmother's house? Jonara?"

"Yeah, fine," Jonara sighed, but in her mind, Jonara thought, "Adults lie, why should I trust them?"

Eva sensed something was wrong with her granddaughter. No matter. Eva drove the three of them to Geneva's house where Anna awaited them.

"Oh bless be!" Anna said. "Mister Johnny P. and Miss Jonara herself. How is my cute little girl?" Anna asked as she tweaked Jonara on the cheek.

"Are you really happy to see me?" Jonara asked much to Anna's bewilderment.

"Of course, Sugar! Give me a big hug!"

Anna held out her arms. Jonara stood motionless without reply. Anna wrapped her arms around Jonara and squeezed her. Yet Jonara did not respond. She wondered what lies Anna had told her over the years.

"You're tired, my sweets. Come in, you'll feel better soon!" Anna offered to the three.

"I'm sorry, Anna, but I can only stay a minute. I need to go back to the hospital," Eva said.

"Is she all right?" Anna asked, guessing at what Eva meant.

"She's sleeping," Eva said.

Johnny took the luggage from the car to the inside of Geneva's house.

"Why do you talk to each other like I'm a two-year-old?!" Jonara barked. "Can't you just tell me what's wrong with my mommy instead of pretending?"

"Jonara, go inside with Anna," said Eva.

Anna motioned for Jonara to pass through the front doorway into the house, but Jonara stood on the front porch.

"How is Evanita?" Johnny asked while he headed to the car for more luggage, but Eva shot him a small scowl as if to say, "No, don't ask me with Jonara present."

"I'm not a two-year-old," Jonara repeated, but Eva said no more.

"I'll look after her, Miss Eva. Jonara and I will have nice cup of tea and cake," Anna said.

"Johnny, you best come with me," Eva said as Johnny finished bringing the last load into the house.

"Daddy gets to go, but not me. Why?!" Jonara asked from within the house.

Jonara meant to say more, but Anna closed the front door behind her, leaving Johnny and Eva outside on the front porch.

"How bad is she?" Johnny asked.

"I'll tell you when we get there," Eva replied.

"Stones of bricks, stones of bricks, she's too young to die!" Johnny said nervously.

"Don't worry, Johnny! It's not at all like that. The doctor thinks she's a little tired," Eva said to appear strong.

Deep down, Eva feared the worst. She needed to bring Johnny to the hospital, and allowing him to dwell in despair on Geneva's front porch would not do at all. She beckoned Johnny to follow her to one of Geneva's cars in the garage.

"Where's the hospital?" Johnny asked as Eva backed the car out of the driveway.

"It's at 7101 South Padre Island Drive. Johnny, listen to me," Eva started as she zipped along Williams Drive. "We'll be at Corpus Christi Hospital in just a few minutes."

"I still don't understand why she's in the hospital," Johnny said.

"Johnny, Evanita collapsed. We rushed her to the hospital just down the road here. The hospital is doing everything they can for her and the baby. But it's touch and go, do you understand? She's lost blood, and they're trying to control the bleeding," Eva explained.

"How could this happen? She's not sick!" Johnny said.

Johnny shook in fear of what might happen to his wife.

"Johnny, you must try to control your trembling. She needs our support, not our fear. Can you give Evanita this support?" Eva asked.

"Yes. I love Evanita. I give her my love and strength," Johnny said as the two arrived at the hospital.

"Hurry, we must hurry," said Eva.

Eva parked the car and pulled Johnny by the arm into the hospital.

"Where is she?" asked Johnny.

"This way," replied Eva.

Eva led him through a corridor where they passed an orderly wheeling a cart of blood-soaked linen. Johnny flinched at the thought of seeing Evanita's blood exposed to the naked air on mere linens.

"One moment please," said a doctor as he exited Evanita's room. "Eva, it's good to see you again. Is this the husband?"

"Johnny Pindus is my name," replied Johnny.

"My name is Dr. Reegan," the doctor said. "Your wife is in stable condition. We've stopped the bleeding, and she should be coming around soon. We're finishing up in her room just now."

Another orderly wheeled a cart with more blood-soaked linens and several small medical tools. Johnny's knees buckled, and he slumped to the ground.

"Don't worry, Mr. Pindus. We are doing everything for her. I think...yes, you may go in now...both of you," the doctor said.

Dr. Reegan left the two to enter Evanita's room by themselves.

"Oh!" Johnny gasped.

Eva had already been prepared for a grim scene and did not react as strongly as Johnny.

"My Nita, what has happened?" Johnny asked as he moved slowly to her bedside.

Eva followed behind toward Evanita's right side then walked around to Evanita's left. In this way, Johnny knelt by Evanita's right side while holding her hand, and Eva sat in a chair on the left with her hand on Evanita's shoulder. Evanita had several intravenous tubes feeding fluids into her body, a heart-lung monitor tracked her "alive" status, and a small cap fitted snugly on her head to track brainwave activity. Evanita wore a typical white hospital gown with blue and pink flower patterns. A few blood-splatter and yellow-colored marks peppered several places on the gown covering Evanita's abdomen. Evanita held motionless for a moment, but the warm feeling of other humans touching her flesh stirred her to consciousness.

"Grandma?" Evanita whispered groggily.

"Evanita?" Johnny said. "It's your Johnny Pindus."

"I'm here too, your own mother," said Eva.

"Grandma?" Evanita repeated with a little more strength.

Evanita's eyes remained closed. Johnny was about to say that Grandma Geneva was dead, but Eva stopped him with her eyes and a curt expression.

"Evanita, honey, wake up," Eva encouraged gently.

Evanita's curly red and dark hair flowed around and across her neck. Eva touched one of the curls in gentle affection while Johnny remained kneeling. He could not bear to look at her face and instead stared at the ground below her.

"Johnny," said Evanita's voice in faint strain, "you're squeezing me too hard."

Johnny's tense grasp on Evanita's hand loosened. He recoiled to his feet as her hand fell to the bed in a restful position. Johnny placed his face in his hands and trembled. He backed up farther to a chair and intended to sit, but in his anxiety, he misjudged his relation to the chair, caught its arm on the left small of his back, and fell smack on his back throwing the chair to the side and knocking over a small magazine rack. Eva stood upright. She looked at Johnny, the tilted chair, and the doorway. She expected to see a nurse or orderly rush in, but fortunately no one entered—sparing Johnny much embarrassment.

"Johnny?" called Evanita in a weak yet steadily growing voice. "Johnny. Come here my sugar doll."

Evanita extended her right forearm to Johnny and waved him toward her.

"Come here. Just be gentle. You'll be fine," Evanita said softly.

Eva was amazed yet proud of her daughter who in such a weakened state was settling Johnny down when in fact Eva's hope was for Johnny to give strength to Evanita. However, this reinforced Eva's steadfast belief that deep down, men are weak. Johnny was not like other men, true. He was a higher-functioning autistic male, yes. But each male in his own way had a weakness that to Eva's mind was of no good to humanity. It was only a matter of time before each man in his turn displayed his true yet ugly colors. How could Johnny provide Evanita with strength when he began by nearly breaking her fingers?

"I am sorry, my Nita," said Johnny.

Johnny held her right hand more gently. Eva had heard that line before too, "I'm sorry." How many men in the ages of the world had said, "I'm sorry," in various languages, regions, and times? How many would continue to say, "I'm sorry," repeatedly after committing the same offenses against their fellow women? How many actually meant those words? Very few, Eva thought. More likely they used these words as a means to pacify the moment, a social lubricant like a glass of wine or other alcoholic beverage.

"Evanita, daughter, listen—Johnny and I are here with you. Anna is at Grandma Geneva's house. Jonara is with Anna. Evanita, can we get you anything?" Eva asked.

"Yes, get me out of here," Evanita laughed weakly.

Evanita struggled to sit up but soon realized it was a mistake.

"No, I won't be going anywhere soon, will I?" Evanita asked, though she knew the question was rhetorical and did not expect an answer.

"Evanita...your grandmother...she..." Eva started.

"I know, Mama. Grandma Geneva has passed on. I was there when her spirit was taken away. I think I would have gone with her, but something brought me back. I had a strange dream. In fact, I've been having many strange dreams," Evanita said to Eva.

Evanita turned to Johnny and asked, "How is Jonara taking the news?"

"She...she...knows about Grandma Geneva," stuttered Johnny.

"She only knows about Grandma Geneva," said Eva.

There was a silence in the room as Eva and Johnny exchanged knowing glances.

"What else should she know? Or for that matter, what else should I know?" Evanita asked. "Johnny, why are you so frightened? And Mama, why are you so reserved?"

"Oh Nita!" Johnny sobbed as he dropped her hand again and left the room.

"Humph, I expected as much," muttered Eva.

"You what?" Evanita asked, not quite hearing her mother's words.

"Evanita, do you know why you are here?" Eva asked.

"I guess I fainted at Grandma Geneva's house," Evanita said.

"Yes, you did. But it is more than that. I had hoped Johnny could have been stronger, but considering he's a male—"

"What's that got to do with it?" Evanita asked with a fire rising in her eyes.

"I mean no ill toward you, my daughter. I am, after all, here for you," Eva said as she lightly clapped both hands over Evanita's left hand. "And I will—always. But you've received a dear shock. You were very attached to your grandmother. That, and now your pregnancy. Dear God, child!"

Eva hugged her daughter as best she could from the bedside without discomforting Evanita.

"Mama, I feel wonderful! I'm in no pain at all!" Evanita exclaimed.

"I know. And it concerns me. A woman in your stage of pregnancy always feels some sort of discomfort. Cramped bladder, swollen ankles, a kicking child—always there is some sort of pain. Sometimes a little, sometimes much more," Eva explained.

"Strange, but now as you explain it, I—"

"Yes, yes. Dr. Reegan has you on medication to mask the pain. In fact, he has you on several things to keep you alive. Yes, Evanita, alive—I said it."

"Why how totally absurd!" said Evanita, but she wasn't thinking clearly.

"You said yourself that you wanted to follow Grandma Geneva, but that something pulled you back. That something is a someone—Dr. Reegen. He pulled you back to the living. But you were hemorrhaging badly, Evanita, very badly. He stopped the bleeding for now. And you received some blood," Eva explained.

"No, I don't believe it," Evanita said.

"Evanita. I am your mother. I would not play games with you at a time like this," Eva started.

"At a time like what? When is the funeral?" Evanita asked without expression.

"Evanita Carreña Pindus, what kind of talk is that? You can't give up now! You have a child to bear, even if it is a boy!"

"No Mama, when is Grandma Geneva's funeral?" Evanita asked. "And what are *you* talking about?"

"I am...no wait...she...Evanita. The funeral is Saturday. I'm hoping you'll be better in time to attend. Now I've spoken with Dr. Reegen, and he says as soon as you're strong enough, he'll perform a Caesarean section—as vulgar as the name is. I'd much rather it be called a Cleopatra section," Eva said.

"Mama!" Evanita said.

"Whatever. Reegan says we'll know in another day or two. First there are the lab tests, but those will come back soon enough."

"I don't want a C-section. I want a vaginal birth, just like with Jonara. I can push this one out, Mama, I know I can. I have wide hips," Evanita said.

"It's not the size of the birth canal Dr. Reegen is worried about. You have hypertension—that much is certain. For now the medication and bed rest are helping. But hypertension is only the beginning. Dr. Reegen believes something else is at work. We'll know more when the blood tests come back from the lab," Eva explained. "I don't want to speculate what else. There are other things that you may have, but why borrow trouble? Evanita—do you realize your baby will most likely be a premie?"

"I'd rather not have a premie. But if he must come out early, he'll be a premie, and I know the hospital can take care of a baby born a couple of months early."

"Evanita, I must tell you. No, it may be too soon. Dr. Reegen has a different opinion, but the lab tests—yes, they'll tell us the true story," Eva said.

"Johnny should be here when the lab tests come back. He should be here now. Where is he?" asked Evanita.

"Don't worry, Evanita, I'll find him."

"Jonara too, where's Jonara?"

"She's with Anna. I told you that already. Have you forgotten?" Eva asked.

"Funny, I guess I did."

"I didn't want to upset her. I told her you were sleeping," Eva said.

"What on Earth for? Jonara and I don't keep secrets. Can you bring her, bring her to me?"

Dr. Reegen entered Evanita's room.

"We need to do a few more tests," said the doctor. "And then I think Evanita should get a good night's sleep."

"My word yes, it is getting late, isn't it?" Eva said as she looked at her wristwatch. "Ten o'clock. I need to find her husband, Johnny Pindus. Have you seen him?"

"Yes. I saw him in a triage. We have a nurse talking to him. Don't worry, he's fine, just a little startled is all," said Dr. Reegen.

"Good, good. Thank you doctor," Eva said. She turned to Evanita and said, "Goodnight, Evanita. I'll be back tomorrow with Johnny. Have pleasant dreams, honey."

Eva walked over to Evanita's bed, leaned over, and kissed her on the cheek. She withdrew and saw the impression of her lips on Evanita's face. No, it wasn't lipstick residue but rather an indentation in Evanita's cheek created by pressure from Eva's lips. Eva watched—the indentation slowly shallowed, flattened, and disappeared. It was at this moment that Eva realized Evanita's face was pudgy from water retention.

"Goodnight, Mama. Thank you for being my mama."

Evanita fell into a deep sleep and had begun snoring before Eva and Dr. Reegen could exit the room. The doctor accompanied Eva down the corridor toward the triage where Johnny was being treated.

"She has more than hypertension," said Eva.

"What makes you so sure?" Dr. Reegen asked.

"She has edema in her face. I kissed her and left a divot," said Eva.

"She probably needs rest," said Dr. Reegen.

"Don't kid me—I'm a dentist. Does she have preeclampsia?" Eva asked.

"I wouldn't worry," said Dr. Reegen. "The tests will pick up anything unusual."

Eva stopped walking and held Dr. Reegen firmly by the arm.

"Don't play games with me, doctor. A simple urine test will tell if she has the condition. Why is your lab so slow?" Eva demanded.

Dr. Reegen stared first at Eva, then at Eva's hand clasped around his left arm. The doctor used his right hand to loosen Eva's grip, and he explained:

"You've been out of med school too long, doctor. Evanita will need to generate 300 mg of protein in her urine over a twenty-four hour period before we can ascertain preeclampsia or not. We've been collecting her urine since she arrived here twelve hours ago. We won't know if she has preeclampsia until morning."

Eva jerked back in surprise then released her grip sheepishly.

"I'm sorry, doctor. I don't know what came over me," Eva apologized.

The two resumed walking down the corridor.

"You're not the first mother to see her daughter in a complicated pregnancy. My eldest had trouble after delivering her first baby. Inverted uterus. The doctor missed it. Or ignored it. She nearly died. Yes, my own daughter, and she was embarrassed to let me take a look. But I insisted. I treated her myself in this very hospital wing. So I know, Miss Carreña, I know what it's like to see your daughter in a grave child-bearing situation. Nothing will happen to your daughter under my watch. Now go home—get some rest. We'll all feel much better in the morning."

Eva gathered up Johnny and took him to Geneva's house where the family rested for the evening. Settled from his initial anxiety, Johnny grew weary and fell asleep in the room provided for him. Eva stayed up a little later to chat with Anna. When Eva and Anna concluded the late evening, the two bade each other goodnight. Anna retired to her main-floor bedroom. Eva walked upstairs and checked on Jonara before turning in herself. Eva knocked quietly on Jonara's door and opened it.

"Joni," said Eva as she poked her head through the doorway.

Jonara pulled her head up from the book she was reading.

"Yes?" Jonara replied.

"It's getting late. Tomorrow will be a busy day around here. Anna will need help going through your grandmother's things," Eva explained.

"And my mommy?" Jonara asked, but she didn't expect much of a reply.

"We'll see. Goodnight."

Just as Jonara expected. She was not to see her mother or find out what was going on. But she felt an overwhelming urge to know the truth.

"What is happening to my mommy?" Jonara muttered well after Eva had closed the door and retired to a room.

Jonara placed the book aside and reached for one of many Bibles her Nanna Geneva had available in the house.

"This," said Jonara. "This is what Nanna Geneva believed in. This is her truth. But is it?"

Jonara opened the book to Genesis and read an early passage, "And the Lord God commanded the man, saying, 'You may freely eat of every tree of the garden; but of the tree of the knowledge of good and evil you shall not eat, for in the day that you eat of it you shall die.'"

Jonara closed the book and returned it to its place on a shelf.

"'You shall die'," Jonara repeated. "But Adam didn't die. God told the first lie. He commanded it. The tree of knowledge—good and evil."

Jonara skimmed backward through Genesis to the beginning. In doing so she came to a realization and whispered it aloud.

"God separated day—the good—from night. This implies the night is evil. God separated the earth from Heaven. Heaven is supposed to be good—does this make the earth evil? God separated the waters from land. Good and evil. Lesser lights to rule the night, a greater light to rule the day. Lights to rule. One rules the good day, many rule the evil night."

Jonara mused more but slapped the book in frustration.

"Everything is split right down the middle. Good, evil. Day and night. It goes on and on. No middle ground with this God. And yet he commands Adam not to eat the fruit of knowledge, the knowledge of good and evil. So Adam is supposed to live in a world of splits without noticing? And who would write the first passage of Genesis describing the splits without noticing? Who creates the splits and doesn't expect to be aware or have anything to do with splits? Is that why this supposed God lied about the fruit causing death? So as not to upset Adam?"

Jonara could not stop wondering. She was agitated and restless.

"I need to walk and think," she whispered.

But Grandma Geneva's house was not a good place to walk quietly—what with the creaks and thin walls. Jonara asked herself—what would Almarita do?

"Sneak out the window," Jonara answered.

It wasn't difficult to do. Jonara didn't even need a coat. The Corpus Christi night air was plenty warm that time of year. Jonara slid the window open, climbed onto the ledge, and closed the window behind her. She climbed down the drainage spout without slipping or hurting her hands, thanks to her light and limber body.

"I'll walk to the hospital. I'll walk right up and go inside to see my mommy," Jonara said.

She took to the sidewalk and walked along Williams Drive toward the hospital. About five minutes into the walk, Jonara paused. She sat on a sidewalk bench to sort things out. Looking up at the sky, she saw only the very brightest stars—the remaining ones were obscured by the city lights.

"The lesser lights rule the night, or so the Bible said. But they don't rule tonight. Who can see those lesser lights, the dim stars in the city? Too bright in the city. City lights rule now. God lied and the city rules. This makes no sense. What would Almarita say? What would she say?"

Jonara pulled her cell phone from her pocket and dialed Almarita's number.

"Come on, pick up. Where are you?" Jonara asked as Almarita's phone buzzed without being answered.

Jonara recognized the familiar message from Almarita's voicemail, "Hi, this is Almarita. Who are you? Ha, ha, ha, ha, ha! Missed me!"

The voicemail's beep ended her outgoing message and signaled its readiness to record a message.

"Allie, this is Joni. Where are you? I'm sitting on a bench on Williams Drive in Corpus Christi, Texas. I snuck out. I can't believe I did it either. I've never snuck out before. That's something you would do. Oh well, I'm going to walk over to the hospital to see my mommy. Grandma wouldn't take me there, so I'm going on my own. Call me back when you get this. Bye-bye, Allie my bestest of friends."

Jonara stood from the bench and resumed walking to the hospital. She came within a five-minute walk of the complex when her cell phone buzzed.

"Hello?" Jonara answered.

Jonara continued walking while she spoke on the cell phone.

"Joni, Joni, Joni! My bestest friend! You did it! I'm so proud of you! Snuck out at night and everything! You beat the system, you beat the adult world!" said Almarita.

"I didn't mean to beat anything. I just want to see my mother," replied Jonara.

"Joni, Joni. Tell me something. How close are you to the hospital?"

"I'm almost there. I can see the front door."

"You're going in through the front door?" Almarita asked. "Don't do that. You'll be seen."

"So?"

"So?! They'll recognize you as your mother's daughter," Almarita said. "Not to mention there's probably a curfew. Joni—don't go in the front entrance. Don't let any adults see you. Trust me, Joni, trust me."

"Hey little girl!" shouted a voice.

Jonara stood at the far edge of the hospital parking lot. The voice came from a security guard toward the building.

"Come here, little girl."

"I heard that!" said Almarita. "Hide!"

"Where?" Jonara asked.

"I'm not there! Look around, hide anywhere!"

Jonara slipped out of the parking-lot lights and into the shadows.

"Come on out. I know you're over there," called the voice as it grew stronger and closer.

"You can't stay there. You can't go in the front door," said Almarita over the cell phone. "You have to go around back. But first get away from that man!"

Jonara lightly ran back up Williams Drive until she reached Nile Drive—about a block away from the medical center.

"Okay, I'm safe. I'm standing at the corner of Nile and Williams," Jonara explained.

"Let me see where you are on the internet. Just give me a minute...ok, I see where you are. I don't understand," Almarita said.

"What, what don't you understand? Where's the back entrance? Allie?"

"I think that was the back entrance. These maps don't say much. I think if you had continued on Williams Drive to Rodd Field Road, no wait, you don't have to walk that far—just walk halfway to Rodd Field Road, then let's see..." Almarita said.

"Where's Rodd Field Road? How will I know when I'm halfway there if I don't know where it is?" Jonara asked.

"Well if you go halfway and cut across the parking lot—now wait, no, if you reach the helicopter pad you've gone too far—no, maybe you should have gone a third of the way along—oh, that's not much farther than where you were a minute ago."

"Allie! You're confusing me," said Jonara.

"Well that would have been the front," Almarita continued.

"Huh?"

"But you want the back way. Wait, I've got it! That voice..."

"Yeah, I think he was a security officer," said Jonara.

"He was at the Heart Center—did you see a sign that said, 'Heart Center'?"

"I don't know."

"Well it doesn't matter. Tell you what, go down Nile Drive until you get to Missouri Drive, and take that all the way until it ends. That should take you to the back of the hospital, at least I think it will. Now what room is your mother in? What branch is she in?" Almarita asked.

"Room? Branch?" Jonara asked.

Jonara just realized she wasn't sure where to find her mother. She envisioned the hospital being a small place where her mother would be just down a hallway.

"Don't tell me you don't know! How were you planning on finding her? This complex is big, very big," Almarita explained.

"I was going to find the front entrance and ask at the front desk," Jonara explained, but now she was nervous and practically in tears.

"Well you can't do that. And even if you sneak in the back entrance without being seen, how will you find your mother's room without being seen? You'll have to walk through the entire complex just to find her. You'll have to look in every room. You'll have to—"

"Stop!" Jonara yelled. "You're not helping."

"Joni, wait, I didn't mean to upset you. But you called on such short notice. I think I can help, but I need a little time. Joni—when you need to do something like sneak out again, call me first so we can work out a plan. You caught me off guard. But that's all right. I have some friends—maybe they can help," Almarita explained.

"Friends, what kind of friends?" Jonara asked. "Friends here? In Texas?" Jonara continued, surprised that Almarita could have such a large social network.

"Not exactly. Think, Almarita Foster, think!" Almarita said. "One of my social networks—on the internet—you remember—t-h-e-y—I was thinking that—"

"THEY?" Jonara asked.

"Yes, THEY. Remember—don't spell it out, say it like the pronoun—they. The THEY network. Remember? THEY can help."

"THEY can help? Really?" asked Jonara.

"Really. But I need some time. I need to contact the local THEY member to help you," Almarita explained.

"How long? Are you sure this is going to work? Tonight?"

"It won't take but a few minutes. Look, you start walking down Nile and Missouri. I'll call you back. Okay?"

"Okay, Allie. I'm still not sure how this is going to work," Jonara confessed.

"I have an idea. I'll tell you when I call back. If you get to the end of Missouri before I call, wait, or better yet call me back," Almarita instructed.

Jonara walked as instructed down Nile Drive. She worried that her Grandma Eva had discovered her missing and was driving around looking for her. Jonara viewed every passing car suspiciously—was that Nanna Geneva's car that Grandma Eva was driving? Was that Anna's car? Jonara observed her surroundings in search of possible hiding places she might need to use should she see a familiar car come her way.

"Allie, what's taking you so long to call back?" Jonara muttered.

Jonara checked her cell phone several times in hopes of seeing a message of some sort waiting for her to review. None. She continued walking. Up ahead she could see a street—too far away for her to read the street sign just yet. But she guessed it was Missouri Drive. She planned to turn right on Missouri upon reaching it, and she turned around to see how far she'd walked. That's when she noticed a slow-moving car. Very slow moving. It was driving along the same direction as she was walking, but it was quite a ways behind her on Nile. She had a feeling she'd been found. She quickened her pace to reach Missouri before the slow-moving car caught up to her.

"Walk quickly, Jonara," Jonara whispered, "and don't look back."

Jonara couldn't resist. She looked back in time to see the car turn off its headlights. Her heart leapt in her chest, and her eyes opened wide. She felt new excitement and nervousness in her veins, a terror that the car was after her. But Grandma Eva would never drive like that. Nor Anna.

"This is bad, very bad. Allie, call me!" Jonara said.

Jonara reached Missouri Drive and followed it. The slow-moving car pulled out a spotlight and shone it on the buildings it passed. It rounded the corner. By now it was clear to Jonara the car was following her. She was in a near panic and prepared to run, but at the very moment she decided to run, the car sped up suddenly, stopped immediately behind her, squawked twice, and threw on its headlights and strobe lights—flashing red and blue.

"Hold it there," said a voice over the loudspeaker.

Jonara turned around in shock to see a Corpus Christi police car before her. Two men exited the police cruiser and walked slowly to Jonara. Jonara froze in fear. This was it. Her first time sneaking out, and she was caught—not by her Grandmother Eva or Anna, but worse—the police! She figured she would go to jail—how would she explain that? Who would bail her out? She would be branded a criminal, or so she thought. This would be the end of any future as a doctor or in any other kind of decent profession. A criminal, a criminal! These were the wild thoughts circling Jonara's mind as the two officers approached her. Her cell phone buzzed in excitement, and she figured it was Almarita calling her back. But Jonara could not answer now, not like this. It was all but a moment or two later before she would be handcuffed and read her rights to remain silent.

"It's a little late for a walk, Miss," said an officer. "What is your name?"

"Jonara," she replied. "My...name...is...Jonara."

Jonara shook in fear.

"Where do you live? And where are you going?" asked the other officer.

"I...I'm going..." stuttered Jonara.

"I found her, Jonara, I found our cat!" called an older male voice along the sidewalk from Nile Drive. "You don't have to look anymore, Jonara. Look," continued the well-dressed man as he burst past the officers and stood in front of Jonara. "I found Almarita, our cat! She's safe, see? You don't have to worry, my niece, your Uncle Fostero found the cat."

"Uncle Fostero," said Jonara.

Jonara realized this was Almarita's message—through an older man who named his cat after Almarita's first name and used Almarita's last name (Foster) for his own name—Fostero. She walked to the old man and took the cat in her arms which in turn took to her naturally.

"Here, Jonara, let's take the cat inside," said Uncle Fostero.

"This is your niece?" asked the first officer.

"Of course, of course. Jonara was worried when our cat jumped out the front door. Naturally she ran after it, but bless this wonderful cat—it simply wanted to smell the outdoors. Just around the corner, officers, 1686 Nile Drive."

"Sir, this girl did not appear to be looking for a cat. She looked lost. We want to know why she is out so late, and where she is going," said the first officer.

"I told you, gentleman, she was looking for the cat, for Almarita. Please, can I invite you two in for tea?" Uncle Fostero asked.

"No, that won't be necessary. Just be careful from now on, there is a curfew," said the second officer.

"Of course, of course. Our streets are safe with our officers on patrol. Have a pleasant evening then," said Uncle Fostero.

"Goodnight," the first officer said.

The two men returned to their cruiser, turned off their strobe lights, performed a U-turn, and drove away.

"Uncle Fostero?" Jonara asked as the two walked back to Nile Drive.

"We have a mutual friend, Almarita Foster, and I don't mean the cat!" Uncle Fostero said. "I came as soon as I heard. You wish to see your mother at the hospital, am I right?"

"Yes. But can I trust you? You're not in the mafia or anything, are you?" Jonara asked.

Uncle Fostero laughed.

"I'm a member of THEY," he said. "But I'm not a member of the mafia. I'm not Italian or Sicilian. My family is from west India. Come inside. I'll introduce you to my wife. Wait, is that your cell phone buzzing?"

"Yes," said Jonara.

"It's probably the real Almarita calling. Answer it. She'll tell you," Uncle Fostero said.

Jonara answered her cell phone and heard the familiar sound of Almarita on the other end.

"Joni, it's me, Allie. Where have you been? I've been calling you," Almarita asked.

"I couldn't talk. I got pulled over by the cops and everything," Jonara said.

"Whoa! Are they still there?"

"No, they're gone. But I met someone else," Jonara said.

"That's what I've been trying to tell you. An older man is going to meet you. He is going by the name 'Uncle Fostero', and he'll have a cat named 'Almarita'. Is that who you met? He's from THEY."

"Yes, he's right here with me. He invited me into his house to meet his wife," Jonara said.

"That's great. His real name is Davino Vagatti. His wife is Marina. He has a really cute son, Leo, and a smart daughter, Cerafina. Now please be nice to these friends of THEY, Joni! They have been good to THEY!" Almarita said.

"All right already! Thank you, Allie!"

"You're my bestest friend, Joni! Be strong when you see your mother!"

"I will. Goodbye!"

Jonara ended the phone call. By this time, she had completed the walk with Uncle Fostero to his house.

"Please, Jonara, won't you come in?" Uncle Fostero said.

"First, tell me your real name," Jonara insisted.

The two paused in front of 1686 Nile Drive for several seconds. Uncle Fostero spoke.

"My name is Vagatti. Davino Vagatti. You may still call me 'Uncle Fostero' if you like, or you can call me 'Uncle Davino'.

But I think it's important you call me 'Uncle'," Davino explained.

"And your wife's name? Is her name Marina?" Jonara asked.

"Yes, her name is Marina. And Almarita most likely told you
I have two children—Leo and Cerafina," Davino explained.
"Please, come in for a moment. You'll have to leave my cat here
at the house before we go to the hospital. I don't think they'll
permit a cat inside!"

Jonara agreed. She walked inside and met Marina, who
looked much prettier than Jonara expected for someone old
enough to have two teenage children. Marina hugged Jonara
followed by Cerafina and Leo. Jonara was impressed with the
affection from the Vagatti family. Cerafina appeared to be perhaps a year older than Jonara, while Leo appeared three years
older. Jonara looked closer at Davino's children. Cerafina
looked just like her mother—thick, curly hair although Cerafina's hair was much longer. Mediterranean complexion with
olive skin and large, round eyes. Leo had short, brown, curly
hair with squinty eyes like a happy polar bear. While Cerafina
took after her mother's lean figure, Leo had the beginnings of
the heavier build his father had. Jonara stared at Leo for a few
seconds too long and caught herself. Some strange feeling of
foreboding came over her, and she shivered. Wanting to leave,
she placed the cat on the ground and asked Davino to take her
to Corpus Christi Hospital.

"Of course, Jonara. If you don't mind, I think Cerafina
would make good company for you. Is that acceptable?" Davino
asked.

Jonara shrugged her shoulders, "Yes, that's fine."

"Good, good. Come this way then," Davino said as he escorted the two girls out the door.

Jonara turned back and caught Leo's eye. He winked back
at her. Jonara cringed, turned back around, and focused on the
car.

"I call shotgun," said Cerafina as she ran to the front passenger seat.

"Um, yes, a little family humor," Davino said to Jonara. "Cerafina, don't you know it's rude to call the front seat when we have guests?"

"Sorry, Pappa. Hey Jonara, do you wanna sit in the front seat?"

"No, that's okay, you can sit in the front," Jonara offered.

"No, you can sit in front, I'll sit in back," Cerafina said.

"No, I'll sit in back," Jonara countered.

"I think you should both sit in back. My, my, going back and forth like friends already," Davino said.

That was the arrangement then—Davino drove the black sedan while Cerafina and Jonara sat in the back seat.

"So you're from Portland?" Cerafina asked while the car was in motion.

"Yeah," Jonara replied.

"Is this your first time in Texas?" Cerafina asked.

"Yeah," Jonara replied.

"Ever ridden in a car with leather seats like these?"

"No," Jonara said.

"My pappa takes care of us very well. What does your pappa do?" Cerafina asked.

"He's a building inspector. He works with my mother. She's an architect. What does your mother do?" Jonara asked.

"She makes dinner and takes me shopping," replied Cerafina.

The two girls giggled. Davino wheeled the car around to the emergency entrance side of the hospital and parked. The girls walked with him through the entrance where Jonara asked the receptionist where she could find Evanita Pindus. Seeing Jonara with an adult, the receptionist had no reservations about giving Evanita's room number and directions to Jonara.

"There, wasn't that easy?" Davino asked Jonara.

The three walked down the corridor toward Evanita's room.

"What happened to your mother?" Cerafina asked.

"I don't know. No one will tell me. My grandma says she's sleeping. At the hospital? Likely story," Jonara said.

"This is the OB/GYN section," said Davino. "Your mother must be having complications with her pregnancy."

"Your mother is having a baby? That's so cool," said Cerafina. "I never saw my mother having a baby—I am the baby!"

"Marina was very fortunate with you, Cerafina," explained Davino. "She had a short and successful labor. There is nothing more sacred than bringing a new person into the world, and nothing more gratifying than it being your own flesh and blood. Come, this is your mother's room, Jonara. We'll wait outside the door."

"Please, Uncle Davino, please come with me. You've been so kind. Will you come with me? And you too, Cerafina," Jonara requested.

Davino and Cerafina nodded their heads in agreement. Cerafina walked behind Jonara and held her hand for emotional support. Davino trailed the two. As the three came into view of Evanita, both Davino and Cerafina made the sign-of-the-cross.

"Mommy?" Jonara whispered.

Jonara stood at the foot of Evanita's bed—in shock at the sight of her mother. Since Eva's initial visit, Evanita had slipped into a light coma and required a breathing tube. Jonara saw the breathing tube taped to her face along with intravenous lines in her arms. This sight coupled with the various blips and beeps on the heart, lung, and brain monitoring devices sank Jonara's hopes for her mother's survival.

"Go to her, Jonara. Sit by her and speak to her," Davino urged.

Jonara walked slowly to her mother's right side—the same place her father had knelt earlier. She pulled up a chair and sat. Stretching out her fingers, she touched Evanita's right hand. She recoiled in terror—Evanita's hand was cold and lifeless. Jonara had never experienced this conflict of senses—seeing her mother's hand but feeling her mother's flesh as if it were an unliving lump. Her mixed-up senses gave her a sour stomach, and she motioned Cerafina over to her side. Cerafina leapt to Jonara's side and sat with her—both slender girls fit easily into the chair intended for America's oversized populace.

"Mommy?" Jonara whispered again.

Only the monitoring equipment replied with their multiple beeps. Jonara looked at the blood pressure monitor—180/120. She didn't know what the numbers meant, but the graphical display on the monitoring device indicated the numbers in red with a "Warning: High" message. The heart monitoring machine also displayed a "Warning: High" message. Yet her mother was unconscious. How could this be? Jonara did not understand why, but she did understand her mother was in silent distress.

"Cerafina, place your hand on top of mine," Jonara requested.

Cerafina placed her right hand lightly above Jonara's right. With Cerafina's hand riding along top, Jonara placed her hand along her mother's abdomen and swirled it lightly around with some hope of feeling for the unborn baby's presence.

"Hello, little one. Can you hear me?" Jonara whispered.

Cerafina recognized this as an emotionally divisive moment—Jonara would either burst into tears or find some comfort in connecting with the unborn child. Cerafina placed her left arm around Jonara's left shoulder and pressed her close, creating sideways-hug togetherness.

"Is the baby a boy or girl?" Cerafina whispered.

"The doctors say it's a boy. I'm going to have a baby brother—I hope," Jonara said.

Jonara looked over to Davino for reassurance, and he nodded his head to say, "Yes, you will have a brother."

Davino smiled to keep Jonara's spirits up, but she felt strained. Jonara continued tracing her hand along Evanita's abdomen, then she stopped suddenly.

"There, did you feel that?" Jonara asked Cerafina whose hand continued to ride atop Jonara's.

"Yes, it felt like a kick."

"That's baby boy kicking. There, he kicked again," said Jonara.

She tapped her hand on Evanita's abdomen in the spot where the baby kicked. The baby kicked back. Then Jonara tapped in a different spot. The baby changed its location and kicked in Jonara's new spot.

"That's amazing! The baby is kicking where you tell it to," Cerafina said.

"He thinks it's a game," said Jonara.

During this game of kicking and tapping, Evanita's blood pressure dropped thirty points. The girls did not notice, but Davino did.

"Good, good," he said. "You're helping your mother, Jonara. See? Her high blood pressure is dropping. And her rapid heartbeat is slowing to a restful state."

Curious, Jonara removed her hand from Evanita's abdomen. Evanita's heartbeat and blood pressure returned to their high levels.

"You see, you did calm your mother down. Try it again," urged Davino.

Jonara and Cerafina pressed their hands on Evanita's abdomen like before. Jonara tapped again but in more rhythmic pattern. Jonara thought of a song and began singing softly to the tune of Bach's Sleepers Wake—at least a version she knew.

If su-gar sweet ba - by boy-oy will just set-tle down in-

to sleep-ing. Then hope-ful-ly our sweet Ma-ma can

re-cov-er now in - to wake-ing. She is ev-ery

thing a daugh-ter ca-an ask. For a moth-er she is won-der-ful and friend-ly.

She holds the sun - shine han-di-ly. She'll lift your life

more dan-di- ly.   She is ev-ery   joy and ra - di-ant sur-prise.

And you know that I would-n't   ev-er kid you. Nev - er nev - er at all.

If su-gar sweet ba - by boy-oy will   just set-tle down in -

to sleep-ing.   Then hope-ful-ly our   sweet Ma - ma can

re - cov - er   now in - to wake - ing.

While Jonara sang the song, Cerafina recognized it and hummed in harmony. The musical vibrations from both girls' vocal cords carried through their arms, across their wrists, and radiated from their fingers through Evanita's abdominal wall and stirred her amniotic fluid into gentle harmonic waves that washed back and forth—effectively rocking the baby to sleep. Evanita's heart rate and blood pressure dropped down to a healthy range, and she opened her eyes in a groggy daze. She looked over to the girls and managed a heavenly smile despite the breathing tube in her mouth. Both girls finished the song, yet Evanita remained somewhat awake. Her heart rate and blood pressure held to the lowered restful state. She smiled one more time and fell into a relaxed sleep.

"Oh Mommy, Mommy, Mommy!" Jonara said and stood up.

The sudden motion threw Cerafina backward and broke the bond between the girls' hands. Jonara held Evanita's right hand and felt warmth pulsing through—a warmth she remembered from happier times when she held her mother's hand.

"You have a gift with music," said Davino.

"She's better now," said Jonara. "You were very helpful, Cerafina. Thank you!"

"Pappa is right, you do have a gift with music. Do you play an instrument?" Cerafina asked.

"No, I just made up that song. Well the words, anyway. I don't remember where I heard the music," Jonara said.

"It's a very old song," said Cerafina. "By Bach. It's called, *Sleepers, Wake.* You would do well playing a musical instrument. Have you ever tried a violin? A clarinet?"

"No, I haven't," replied Jonara.

"I can teach you sometime if you want to learn. We have an organ and piano at our house. Maybe you'd like to try one of those," Cerafina offered. "We have a choir at church. Pappa, can she sing at our church?"

"Shhh, Cerafina. Let's speak of that another time," said Davino.

"Visiting hours are ending," said a passing nurse. "You can come back tomorrow at eight o'clock in the morning, if you like."

"Thank you, nurse," Davino acknowledged. "Jonara, Cerafina—it's time to go."

Cerafina walked to Davino while Jonara lingered a moment. She held her mother's hand for a few seconds more and whispered:

"Get well soon."

It was after midnight when Davino dropped Jonara off a block from Geneva's house. Jonara was glad to have seen her mother but nervous that she had to sneak back into her bedroom. Would she be caught? As it turned out, everyone was sound asleep from the tiring day, and Jonara was able to reenter the room through the window. She slipped into something comfortable and fell asleep on the soft bed while reading through a book she had discovered while sneaking into her room—a diary kept by her Great-Grandma Geneva.

CHAPTER 4

First Attempt

2023 Oct 3-4, Tue Late pm, Wed Early am. Jonara's Dream.
2006 Sep 10, Sun. Portland, Oregon.

Jonara fell asleep while clasping Geneva's diary under the covers. She stood up with the diary under her left arm, but she wasn't in Geneva's house. She was outside, it was sunny, and she was under the Northeast Broadway Bridge next to the Willamette River. A cool autumn breeze from the river blew the last of summer's sweat from her brow. She felt no hunger or other discomfort. Lighthearted and curious, she walked along the parking lot. Vibrant colors radiated warmth and satisfaction from the last of summer's flowers. Leaves changing color on the riverbank rustled in the wind so gently that her ears tickled and she laughed. She turned around in place with her arms outstretched—holding the diary in her right hand.

"Diary, diary, what do you say next?" she said aloud.

No one else paid attention to her dancing and reading. She read the next lines from the diary:

"'September 10, 2006, Sunday. I attended Eva's church today with Evanita. I fulfilled my Sunday Mass obligation by going to Saturday evening Mass. Eva turned her back on the Catholic Church long ago, and I pray for her return. She is a strong-minded woman and is raising her daughter in her (Eva's) faith at the Broadway Unitarian Church of Portland. My precious granddaughter, Evanita, is beginning her Coming-of-Age today. I am visiting Eva and Evanita for several weeks before I return to Corpus Christi.'"

With her back to the river, Jonara noticed a small yet ornate steep-gabled church across the street. She walked through a parking lot to North Interstate Avenue—the street between her starting point at the river and the church. The traffic signals changed. Jonara crossed the street and continued on a sidewalk along North Larrabee Avenue. She was next to the backside of the church and wanted to see the front. Continuing along the curving sidewalk and colorful trees, she reached the front of the church, stood in awonderment, and read the words above the main entrance, "Broadway Unitarian Church."

"My mommy is in here?" Jonara pondered. "This is a strange place for a church."

Jonara walked up the main entrance's steps and stood for a moment. A small yet steady stream of people flowed into the church, yet none noticed Jonara's presence. She felt invisible. Curious, she walked inside. A cozy interior area greeted her. What was this room? She wanted to call it a lobby, but that didn't seem right. It was a greeting area, and that was fine with her. She stood amazed by the fountain in the middle of the greeting area. It had sculptured stonework in the middle, lending its surfaces to intricate waterfall designs from the recirculating water. Jonara held her hand in a sprig of water as it sprayed off the sculpture, but the water passed through without diversion, and her hand remained dry. She did not give much thought to this odd experience but instead looked around the "greeting area" and saw a few young people a little older than herself walking off to a side hallway and around a corner. She followed the young people into what looked like a classroom. She thought it odd because Jonara had only seen classrooms inside a school, but here she was standing in back of the classroom inside a church.

"Roll call," said an adult in the front of the classroom.

Jonara recognized this situation. The adult was the teacher, and this was the beginning of class. With each name the teacher called out, a young student replied, "Here."

Teacher: "Abbey?" Abbey: "Here."
Teacher: "Abrams?" Abrams: "Here."
Teacher: "Bessinder?" Bessinder: "Here."
Teacher: "Bigby?" Bigby: "Here."

Teacher: "Carreña?"

Jonara's ears perked up when she heard her Grandma Eva's last name. She heard her mother's voice answer, "Here." Jonara looked around the room but could only see the students' backs. She was surprised to hear her mother answer to, "Carreña," and had to remind herself that at one time, this was her mother's last name. Later, it became Pindus.

Wondering where her mother's voice came from, Jonara walked to the front of the class—the teacher and students oblivious—and she looked directly at the face that said, "Here," in response to the teacher. The face looked much like her own—a little older, and more like an older sister than a mother. Jonara stared at her mother's face with the curiosity of looking for the first time into a crystal glass filled with carbonated beverage. What was this Evanita like? Was she the person who tucked her in at night, who told her to brush her teeth and do her homework? The voice was the same, but the face was different.

The teacher completed roll call and handed out a booklet to each youth. She explained that Coming-Of-Age meant it was time to explore the various religious faiths of the world. Each student would make his or her own path, and at the end of this journey, each student would have to give a speech or perform a dance to the church as a way of expressing that student's chosen faith. It all seemed so strange to Jonara, but her sixteen-year-old mother—Evanita—apparently understood what was being said without issue. Jonara watched as Evanita opened a spiral notebook and took notes with a green pen.

"Each of you will be assigned an adult member of the church as a mentor, to guide you through your Coming-Of-Age journey. Up here I have a hat containing a list of names," the teacher said.

The teacher handed the hat to a student in front and explained:

"Pick a name and pass the hat around. The name you pick is your mentor."

"I hope I get Mr. Robinson," said a girl to Evanita.

"Why Mr. Robinson, Sheila?" Evanita asked.

"Who's Mr. Robinson?" Jonara asked, but of course no one could hear her.

"He's the best mentor. Everyone gets through Coming-Of-Age much easier with him," said Sheila.

Evanita was going to say something back, but the hat came around her way. Evanita picked, and Sheila picked. Both picked Mr. Robinson.

"This is wonderful, Nee-nee," said Sheila. "He's the greatest. We'll get through this Coming-Of-Age quicker than you can bat an eyelash."

The hat completed its journey around the room. The teacher took the hat from the last student, searched the hat for and removed the remaining paper slips, and tossed the hat in the room's corner. A coat tree caught the hat and wavered back and forth until it dissipated the hat's horizontal momentum. The coat tree stood still. Jonara stared at this interaction between the hat and coat tree. She did not know why, but it intrigued her.

"There are eight volunteer mentors—Ms. Blackmoore, Ms. Haughf, Mr. Miller, Mr. Robinson, Ms. Telly, Mr. Tombaugh, Mr. Tulson, and Ms. Zyla. Each mentor is assigned a room down the hallway and has her or his name posted outside the room. Your slip of paper has one of those names. So at this time, I would like you to report to your assigned mentor. Dismissed."

The class rose to its feet and exited the room. Sheila kept bragging about Mr. Robinson, but Evanita looked worried. Jonara followed the pair as they walked down the hallway. They passed the rooms of Ms. Blackmoore, Ms. Haughf, and Mr. Miller before arriving at Mr. Robinson's room. Sheila pushed her way ahead of two other students and dragged Evanita along. Sheila wiped on the biggest grin as she introduced herself to Mr. Robinson.

"My name is Sheila Stout," Sheila said. "And this is my friend, Evanita. You can call her Nee-nee."

"Sheila!" Evanita said. She didn't like being introduced to adults by her nickname.

"It's okay, Nee-nee. We're going to learn a lot under Mr. Robinson, aren't we?" Sheila winked to Mr. Robinson.

"Well, I see you're a bright young girl," said Mr. Robinson.

Sheila warmed up to his kindness. Evanita looked indifferent.

"He sounds like a used car salesman," said Jonara.

"Please, you two, have a seat. And I see there are two other youths," said Mr. Robinson.

"Oh they can sit in back," said Sheila.

The two other youths were boys about Sheila's and Evanita's ages. Sheila continued looking at Mr. Robinson with a big grin and fluttery eyes.

"How disgusting! Sheila is drooling all over Mr. Robinson!" said Jonara.

"I think this is all of us," started Mr. Robinson. "Welcome to your Coming-Of-Age instruction. I'm Mr. Robinson, and I'll act as your mentor through this journey."

"Hey Mr. Robinson," said one of the boys. "How long is this going to take? I got football practice today."

"Yeah, and I gotta work on my dad's car. We gotta change the coolant and battery before winter," said the other boy.

"Cool your jets, boys. Mr. Robinson will get us through Coming-Of-Age in time for your football practice and your automobile work. Hmmph!" Sheila sneered.

"This is a special moment in your journey as a Unitarian Universalist. Your journey consists of learning about other faiths, learning what you believe in, and giving a speech to our group. I have prepared some study guides—" explained Mr. Robinson.

"Oh man, oh man. Not study guides. This is like school. Boring!" said one of the boys.

"They're not study guides," said Sheila. "Just shut up and listen! Sorry, Mr. Robinson."

"Thank you, Sheila. Please take one and pass it along," Mr. Robinson explained.

Sheila took a stapled document and passed the others to Evanita who in turn passed the remaining documents to the boys.

"I've been mentoring youths for three years now, and I've simplified the process to these notes," Mr. Robinson explained.

"Each faith gets a paragraph explaining what it represents. At the end, there are several sample speeches with fill-in-the blanks where you can write in your name, your friends' names, and your family—even your pets' names. These speeches summarize what you probably believe. Pick the speech that most resembles what you want to say, and when you're ready, you may stand up here and read the speech aloud."

"This is Coming-Of-Age?" Jonara asked aloud to everyone's ignorance. "This is easy!"

"I'll give you five minutes to fill out your speeches. When you're ready, raise your hand," Mr. Robinson instructed.

Sheila raced through the pages and penciled in names with a near panic of immediacy. She raised her hand within two minutes. The boys finished shortly after—three and four minutes respectively—and raised their hands. Evanita penciled in some names. She erased them. She flipped between pages, started scribbling on one page, erased, and scribbled on another. The room was silent, save for her page flipping.

"What's wrong, Mommy, what's taking so long?" Jonara asked.

"Time's up," said Mr. Robinson. "Who would like to go first?"

"Pick me, Mr. Robinson, I want to go first!" said Sheila.

"You?" said one of the boys. "Why you?"

"Because I'm prettier than you, and I finished first!" replied Sheila.

"All right, Sheila. You go first," said Mr. Robinson.

Sheila walked to the front of the room. She stood before the others with her document in hand and read aloud:

"My name is Sheila Stout. I am a youth of the U-ni-tar-i-an U-ni-ver-sal-ist Church—whew! And I am taking a jour-ney through faith to a Coming-Of-Age," began Sheila.

Sheila had some trouble pronouncing "Unitarian Universalist" and slowed at other long words, but on the whole she made good progress with her prefabricated speech. Sheila had paused in her speech to catch her breath. She was excited that she was "coming of age," and this speech was the final moment in becoming an adult member of the church.

"As an a-dult mem-ber of the church, I promise to be toler-ant of other faiths—Jews, Muslims, other Christians, Bud-dhists, et cetera—what does 'et cetera' mean? And those of no faith—atheists and agnostics—should be welcomed with open arms. With my open mind and heart, I come of age! Thank you alll"

"Very good, Sheila. Here, sign the book registry and receive your certificate," said Mr. Robinson.

Sheila paused after her speech. She looked around the room at the three other students, winked at Evanita, then walked gin-gerly over to Mr. Robinson who sat at a desk. She stood at his desk and waited for the certificate. Mr. Robinson turned a church registry around for her and offered her a pen. She took the pen, looked closely at the book, and signed where he pointed with his expectant finger. She returned the pen. Mr. Robinson signed the certificate, placed a gold decal on it, and handed it to Sheila. Sheila's hand trembled as she reached for it. She began to grasp the certificate when Mr. Robinson released it. The certif-icate lost its grip with Sheila's hand and slid back and forth through the air as it parachuted down to the floor. Sheila shook in nervousness when she realized her precious certificate had slipped through her fingers and fallen to the floor.

"My certificate!" she gasped.

She knelt to the floor without hesitation and scooped the certificate into both hands. Still holding the certificate with a hand on each side, she stood upright and simultaneously held the certificate above her head as if offering it up to Heaven for a blessing.

"I...am...an...adult," Sheila said. "This certificate proves it."

Mr. Robinson smiled with satisfaction. The two boys laughed at what seemed like foolish worship by Sheila. Evanita was not impressed and in fact was boiling with rage on the in-side, though she hid it well.

"That will do nicely, Sheila. Please—have a seat. You, Todd—you're next."

Todd stood in front of the small class and read a speech much like Sheila's. He also signed the registry and received a certificate. He didn't hold it up in the air as Sheila but instead folded it in half and slid it into his shirt pocket.

"Glen? You're next," Mr. Robinson said.

Glen read the same speech as Todd but laughed between sentences as if he didn't mean the words he said (which he didn't). He strode over to Mr. Robinson's desk with an air of flair, signed the registry with an outlandishly large signature, and received his certificate. He rolled the certificate into a narrow tube, blew through it, and tucked it into his left pants pocket.

"Evanita, you're the last one left. Please, won't you stand before the class and read your speech?" Mr. Robinson urged.

"Yeah, Nee-nee, read your speech," Todd mocked.

"Nee-nee, Nee-nee, Nee-nee," Glen chanted.

"Shut up and let her read!" Sheila barked.

Evanita stood quietly in front of the class. She flipped to a page of the packet, then another, and a third. She scribbled a few words on one side and flipped to the page in back.

"Miss Carreña? Miss Carreña!" Mr. Robinson called. "Your time for filling in the blanks is up. Please read your speech. Don't worry if you haven't filled in all the blanks. Just do the best you can."

"Do the best you can, do the best you can," chanted Glen.

"Shut up!" Sheila barked again.

Jonara stared at the youthful image of her mother. What would she read aloud? Evanita swung her arm down toward the floor and flung the papers downward. She stomped and tore at the papers with her feet, but halfway into this act of paper ripping, Jonara woke up with a start. The muscles in her arms ached as if she'd been sleeping on her back and holding a weight above her for quite a while. She looked and saw the diary was open yet face down over her right knee. She picked up the diary, held it briefly despite her tired muscles, and read the last sentence on the page:

"'And Evanita thrashed the papers with her feet.'"

Jonara sat up suddenly and turned on the lamp. Her heart raced so fiercely she was afraid it would leap out of her chest.

She was alert, focused, and ready for any threat that should come her way. Jonara looked around, half expecting some wild animal to attack her. None came. She couldn't understand why she was in such an anxious state. She plopped back onto the bed with the thought of falling asleep. Instead, she stared at the ceiling, at the lamp on the nightstand next to her bed, and at the bedroom door. Nothing settled her. She couldn't sleep, not with everything that had happened, her Great-Grandmother Geneva passing away, the odd plane trip down with her Grandma Eva lying to her, and her father freaking out in the bathroom. The police. Davino and Cerafina. And what was Cerafina's brother's name? She couldn't remember at the moment, but Jonara did remember seeing Evanita in the hospital. Her mother—near death. And now this—a diary. But not just a diary—a gateway into the past—her family's past. A life she didn't realize could possibly exist. For her, the past was her own past—memories of playing in the schoolyard during kindergarten recess. Why would others have a past or need a past? Her mother and grandmother seemed to navigate through life so easily, at least until the past couple of days. It was hard for Jonara to imagine her own mother struggling to complete a Coming-Of-Age ceremony.

"Bad things only happen to bad people, bad things only happen to bad people. But my mommy can't be a bad person. And the boys—Todd and Glen—were bad people. But they did not struggle," whispered Jonara. "My mommy struggled, and now she's sick. She is not a bad person. Great-Grandma Geneva is dead, but she's not a bad person. My family is not bad, not evil. Only bad things happen to bad people. Nothing makes sense anymore!"

Jonara fell into tears. She tried to reason with herself, but she only became sadder. She looked at the diary. It remained face down where she left it. The book that had given her a gateway into the past now haunted her with knowledge she did not want. She blamed the book for her new-found misery. Enraged and frustrated, Jonara took a pillow and beat the diary. The diary remained uninjured, but Jonara could not stop the hurt.

She'd heard of stories where a person sees one's entire life before dying, but the diary had put a new twist on things—she was seeing her mother's life before...before...

"Before Mommy dies," Jonara cried. "How can I go back to sleep now? I'm afraid, I'm afraid!"

Jonara buried her face in the pillow she once used to beat the diary, and it was in this pose she cried herself to sleep. Jonara kicked her feet, and the diary shifted to the foot of her bed. She felt herself spinning, moving, and landing on the ground.

Jonara stood outside Broadway Unitarian Church and peered in through a window by standing on a ledge. She saw her mother, Evanita, doing a foot dance to rip up papers—papers meant to streamline her journey to religious adulthood. Jonara could not hear words, but she saw Evanita yelling something, the boys laughing, Sheila yelling at the boys, and Mr. Robinson holding his hands up to Evanita and saying, "Stop." Jonara did not hear Mr. Robinson say, "Stop," but she read his lips. Jonara stood on her tippy-toes to see through the window. One of the boys had his back to her, and he stood up and clapped in mockery of Evanita. His action blocked Jonara's view of her mother. Jonara struggled to see around the boy, but she lost her footing and fell to the ground below.

Jonara stood up, was dazed, and said, "But I'm dreaming. How can I be dazed?"

Jonara looked up at the window but could only see the inside room's ceiling light. She didn't know what her mother was doing, and she wanted to know. Jonara did not have to wait long. Far to the right of the window and along the building to the front entrance, Jonara saw Evanita bolt out of the church and into the parking lot. Jonara ran after her mother but tripped on something. She fell to the ground. Puzzled, she stood and ran but fell again. Why did her feet give out on her? Standing again, she looked at her feet and there it was—the diary! It was bound to her right leg by some sort of rope. Jonara knelt to unfasten the rope from her leg, but she could find no knot, no means of undoing the rope from her leg.

"It's a curse!" Jonara said. "I can't get rid of it. The book won't let go of my leg!"

Jonara picked up the book, took up the slack, and ran as best she could. She caught up with her mother and wanted to hug her, but when she reached out, her hand passed through her mother's arm.

Evanita paced back and forth in front of a bench at the edge of the parking lot along North Interstate Avenue. She sat down and crossed her legs. She stared out at the Willamette River. She stared at the ground and at her feet. She straightened her legs. She crossed her legs. She placed an elbow on her leg and placed her chin in her palm in thoughtful pose. Evanita tapped her foot on the ground.

"I can't do it, I can't," Evanita said. "It's not right."

"What's not right, Mommy?" Jonara asked, but of course Evanita could not hear Jonara.

Shouts and cheers erupted from the church entrance. Evanita turned her head, and at the same time Jonara turned around—both wanted to see what the ruckus was about. At the entrance, proud parents exited—each pair with the Coming-Of-Age child waving a certificate with pride.

"I can't believe it! Mommy could be in that procession with her mother and father. She could be doing her Coming-Of-Age. If only she read that paper. Why didn't she?" exclaimed Jonara. "Why didn't you, Mommy?"

"Why didn't I?" Evanita asked of herself aloud. "I just had to read that speech. Then I could walk about in procession with the other families—the other mothers and fathers. I would be an adult member of the church, and I could wave my certificate around with my mother and...my mother and...FATHER!"

When Evanita said, "Father," she burst into hysterical laughter. Jonara was shocked and jumped back a few steps—even with the diary and rope impeding her step.

"Mommy! Why are you laughing so funny? Like you've gone crazy?" Jonara asked Evanita as everyone else continued to be oblivious to Jonara's presence.

"What a farce. Go ahead, you perfect families. Go ahead and say your words and parade yourselves—the father, the mother, and the 'perfect' child. Play the game and win the prize," Evanita said.

She was clearly disgusted with what she perceived as a charade—a deception to appear good in the eyes of others.

"Who has a father? Who needs one?" Evanita said.

Jonara stared at her mother and for the first time wondered and asked, "Who is your father, Mommy? I never met him."

"If this is Coming-Of-Age, I want nothing of it. The dishonesty...it's disgusting," Evanita said.

The procession of proud families exited the front entrance and gathered around the front church grounds in social celebration. The front entrance fell silent as a lone figure crossed its threshold.

"Evanita? Evanita, where are you?" the lone figure called.

"Grandma Eva?!" Jonara said in surprise. "You look like Mommy—not Mommy now, but Mommy at home."

It was Eva. She was looking for her daughter, Evanita, and continued calling. Evanita gathered her strength and walked slowly back to the church entrance where after several minutes she met up with her mother. Despite Evanita's slow gait, Jonara struggled to keep up. The rope and diary increased in weight, and Jonara's right arm grew increasingly tired. Jonara shifted the diary to her left arm, but it too grew tired. At the end of her trek in following Evanita to Eva, Jonara resorted to supporting the diary's weight with the top of her skull.

"Evanita, there you are," said Eva.

"Mama. I can't do it," said Evanita, bitter.

"You must, dear, you must grow up. You cannot stay a child forever," said Eva.

"This isn't fair. This isn't right!" Evanita said.

"What's not fair? You've been taught everything you need to know about the faith. This is just the last step. It's really quite easy. You're making this into something harder than it needs to be," said Eva.

Eva put her arm around Evanita's shoulder in embrace.

"Honey, sweetie, be a good girl and sign the registry. Mr. Robinson will make out a new certificate for you. It'll all be over soon, and we can have a good laugh."

Evanita pulled away from her mother.

"It's just a lie," Evanita said.

"No," said Eva.

"Yes!" shouted Jonara.

"I don't feel like I'm an adult member. Those other kids just read a paper—anyone can do that. It doesn't mean anything. They faked an accomplishment. It's all a lie," said Evanita.

"Honey, it's real. I promise. I would not lie to you," said Eva.

"You lied to me about my mommy," said Jonara. "And you're lying to Mommy."

Jonara was shocked when she shouted, "It's not fair," the same time as Evanita.

"Grandma Geneva didn't read a paper for her Coming-Of-Age," said Evanita.

"She's Catholic. She received the Sacrament of Confirmation. The bishop asked her questions, and she had to answer them correctly. But honey, that was back in the catechism days when people learned through rote memorization. I gave you a faith where you can reason, not recite something from memory."

"It was worse than that. There was no memory to recite from. I recited from paper," Evanita pointed out.

"She's got you there, Grandma," said Jonara, happy that she could sass her grandmother without being smacked in the face.

Jonara reached to wave her hands in her ears and stick her tongue out at her grandmother, but the diary fell from her hands, tumbled on the ground, and pulled the footing out from under her. Jonara fell, screeched, "Ow!" pulled herself up, and rubbed her leg.

"You don't want to do it the hard way, not the way I did. Evanita, listen to me—the adult world is very difficult—people think they know what they are doing—and things go bad. All you have left is your faith. You'll have plenty of tough times ahead outside church. Don't make—"

"—things harder than they have to be," Evanita finished. "I know, I know. You sound like a broken record."

Eva slapped her daughter across the face. Evanita fell backward from the blow but turned around, stood fast, and stared directly at her mother in obvious defiance.

"You are so much like her," said Eva.

"Like who?!" Evanita woofed.

Eva opened her mouth to say something but caught herself and said nothing.

"Like Grandma Geneva? Who, Mama, who?"

"Yeah, who?" Jonara asked.

"Just as stubborn," Eva said.

"I'm not stubborn," Evanita replied.

"Yes you are!" Jonara said, also happy she could sass her mother without fear of repercussions.

"Evanita," Eva said.

"I'm going for a run," Evanita said.

"Dressed like that?" Eva asked, referring to her skirt and heals.

"Yes!" Evanita said.

Evanita kicked her heals off and scuttle-jogged down the sidewalk of North Interstate Avenue and out of sight until she crossed Northeast Oregon Street, crossed North Interstate Avenue, and stopped in the middle of a peace-sign circle. Jonara stood next to her grandmother. Both crossed their arms in disbelief, both watched Evanita jog away, and both said in unison:

"Hmph!"

"Now what?" Jonara asked out loud, but as expected, no one could hear her.

"Now what?" Eva asked aloud, not aware she had an audience in Jonara.

Jonara was amazed her grandmother had the same thoughts as she. Yet Jonara was also troubled that her grandmother had a tendency to lie, or so it seemed. Jonara drew the conclusion that if she (Jonara) said things like, "Now what," at the same time as her grandmother, she would also begin lying like her grandmother. The thought sickened her, as if she knew her fate and had no escape.

"But I have to know," Jonara turned and asked her grandmother.

Eva couldn't hear her, of course, but Jonara continued asking anyway:

"Why is she stubborn? And why is she always running? And the red streak of hair—what's that all about? Is that from her daddy?"

"Who is her father?" Eva said to herself. "That's what Evanita always asks. But how can I tell her?"

"Just tell her. Tell me! Who is Grandpa?" Jonara asked.

"No, not yet," Eva said.

"Maybe it's in this diary. I'll just open it and find out," Jonara said, but when she reached for the diary from the ground, it wouldn't budge.

Jonara struggled hard to lift the diary from the ground, but it was too heavy. Eva strolled from the church's front entrance to the very bench Evanita had just sat upon. There she waited for Evanita to finish running. Jonara tried following Eva, but the diary and attached rope prevented her from traveling.

"This diary has got to go!" Jonara yelled.

She yelled, she screamed, but no one in the dream came to her aid. Jonara dropped to the ground and tried to roll away from the diary and rope, but she couldn't. She screamed once more, and Eva ran back, which shocked Jonara because she didn't think anyone in her dream could hear her.

Eva grabbed Jonara's arm, shook her, and said, "Wake up, Jonara. You're having a bad dream. Wake up!"

"No, no, I can't shake it free," Jonara yelled.

Jonara's eyes remained tightly closed, and her mouth grimaced.

"It won't let go. I can't get away from it."

"What won't let go? What is it, honey?" Eva asked. "Open your eyes, Jonara."

Jonara opened her eyes and saw Eva, but her face was careworn, and her rich dark hair had filled with streaks of gray. Jonara wasn't in Portland as her dream had placed her. She was back in Corpus Christi in October of 2023.

"You're having a bad dream, dear. Sit up a moment. See? Everything is all right," Eva reassured Jonara.

Jonara realized she was no longer dreaming. She was in bed, in her Great-Grandma Geneva's house. Grandma Eva sat next to her and held her.

"The rope, the book," Jonara stammered.

"The what? Oh look, the bedsheet is wrapped tightly around your right leg. You must have turned over in the same direction many times. Here, let's loosen it and get your blood circulating again," Eva said.

Eva undid the knotted sheet from Jonara's leg and patted it several times.

"There. How does that feel?" Eva asked.

"Better."

"Would you like some cookies and milk, Jonara?"

"No, I think I'm fine," Jonara said.

Jonara looked at Eva, hesitated, and threw her arms around Eva in a big hug.

"Ah, everything will be okay, honey," Eva said.

"I'm sorry I was rude to you in the airport," Jonara said.

"No problem, honey, you're my favorite granddaughter."

"I'm your only granddaughter," Jonara giggled.

"And my favorite one too. I didn't want to tell you about your mother being in the hospital too soon. I didn't want to upset you needlessly. But you're a strong-willed girl—you have your own mind."

"What's wrong with my mommy?" Jonara asked.

"She has hypertension and edema—that much we know. Hypertension means her blood pressure is very high. It shouldn't be high, and there's no normal reason for it to be so, but it is. Edema means she has extra fluid building up in places. I noticed it when I kissed her goodnight on the cheek. My lips formed a little dent in her face. The dent went away, but that shouldn't have happened," Eva explained. "And I got angry with the doctor. I told him he should know if your mother has preeclampsia or not. I can't believe I forgot the test takes twenty-four hours."

"Does Mommy have—what did you call it—pre-eclamma?"

"Preeclampsia. I don't know. I suspect she does, but there's no point in worrying about things that may not be true. Try not to worry, Joni. Your mother is resting safely at the hospital."

"What about my brother?" Jonara asked.

"Your mother thinks he's ready to be born early if necessary, but I think she's not far enough along. We'll know more later. Remember, Joni, the younger an unborn baby, the less mature it is, and the more dangerous to deliver that baby into the world."

"How young can an unborn baby be? I mean, how many weeks must Mommy be before my brother can survive on his own?" Jonara asked.

"About 24 weeks. Less in rare cases. But I think your mother is less than 32 weeks. Maybe 28 weeks, or even 26. She's right on the edge, Joni, on the very edge," Eva said.

"What can we do?" Jonara asked.

"Your Great-Grandma Geneva would tell us to pray to Mary, Joseph, and Christ. The truth is—"

"What is the truth?" Jonara interrupted.

"The truth is there's very little we can do except try to make her comfortable. She needs to hold on at least a couple more weeks for the baby to mature. There will be lab tests that will help doctor Reegen make informed decisions on how your mother can be helped," said Eva.

"I wish we could help. I want to help."

"I know, Joni, I know. I think it's best you get some sleep. We need to start cleaning up and organizing things around here. We have many things to do with your mother being ill, Geneva's funeral, and preparing her house for sale. We will be very tired before the end, so it's best we get as much sleep as we can."

Eva tucked Jonara into bed and wished her pleasant dreams. She turned the light off and started to close the door, but Jonara begged she keep it open so Jonara could feel connected to the rest of the house. Eva left the door open and returned to her own bed where she fell asleep.

CHAPTER 5

Saint Stellan

2023 Oct 4, Wed 3 am. Jonara's Dream.
2006 Sep 16, Sat Early Afnoon. Eva's House. Portland, Oregon.

"I don't see why I have to be a Unitarian," shouted Evanita.

Jonara stood in the living room of her Grandma Eva's house on Northwest Belgrave Avenue—Portland, Oregon. Some of the furniture had not changed, but other things like lamps and electronic devices had. The diary was with her again. It wasn't tied to her leg by a rope. It wasn't in her arm. The diary was in a backpack—a backpack supported over her left shoulder and hanging along the left side of her back. Her right arm was free to open doors and hold things, yet when she reached for a crystal figurine on Grandma Eva's end table, her hand passed through it.

"I must be dreaming again," said Jonara. "Can either of you see me? Can you hear me?" Jonara shouted.

Eva and Evanita did not respond to her. Jonara looked outside the back window and saw Holman Park—lush woods with trails she remembered well.

"You don't want to switch to another faith. Unitarian Universalism is about reasoning and respecting individual rights. Our Broadway Unitarian Church supports these beliefs. The other religions have some failing that I rejected years ago. This one is the best. You want this faith," said Eva.

"How can you know what I want? How? Isn't this a free country? Aren't I free to believe what I want?" Evanita asked.

"Not until you're eighteen!" replied Eva.

"I want to try something else. What about Grandma's religion. What was it again? Catholic?" Evanita asked.

"No, no, NO! Evanita, I spent parts of my childhood suffering as a Catholic. Boring repetitive services. Services—no, that's the Protestant term. Every week a boring Mass. Yes, a boring Mass. And a hierarchy of men that leaves no room for women," Eva explained.

"Maybe a hierarchy of men would be good for me, especially since I've never had a father!" Evanita quipped.

Eva stared into Evanita's eyes, walked directly in front of her, and slapped her across the face.

"Don't you ever say that again!" Eva ordered. "You don't know what you're saying, child! The hierarchy of men has been a scourge of tyranny since...since the male model was first defecated on Earth."

"You always say that. You always say men are evil. I'm sick and tired of hearing that. I've met some great boys at school. Nice and sweet. They aren't evil," Evanita said.

"Boys become men. Men become evil. It is a natural progression. Boys are like deciduous teeth—the innocence of a toddler's teeth. That innocence falls out like the baby teeth they are. And when they become secondary teeth—they become men. They group together, sifting and shifting for power and position. And they are filled with decay. Best to have them drilled out and filled with something that doesn't rot," Eva said.

"That's a horrible thing to say," Evanita said. "Just horrible. And I refuse to believe it. Did you hate my father that much? You must have loved him once!"

"Your father?!" Eva reeled.

"Yes, my father. You never speak of him. You won't tell me his name! Can't I even know that?" Evanita asked.

"Don't ask about a father you don't have," said Eva. "I raised you, Evanita. I raised you all by myself without any man contaminating you."

"Then why do I feel so empty, like I'm missing something?" Evanita said, switching from anger to tears.

"I can't explain it," said Eva. "Perhaps in time you'll understand, but not yet."

"If my father were here, he'd be able to explain, wouldn't he?" asked Evanita.

"No, it wouldn't be like that."

"Really?"

"Yes, really! Look, Evanita. Honey dear. If you really feel you must find something else, that I and the Unitarian faith have not given you enough, then don't trust me. Go explore the other faiths. Learn firsthand for yourself."

"I don't believe it!" said Evanita.

"What don't you believe?" Eva asked.

"All my life you've been forcing me to be a Unitarian. And now you're letting me escape?"

"I'm not 'letting you escape,' as you put it. I want you to think for yourself, but you still need guidance."

"'Guidance'—that's a power word. You mean control," said Evanita.

"No, I mean guidance. Men control, women guide."

"I don't care. You remember my friend from school—Josefene? We're going to her church. They're having Saturday evening Mass," Evanita explained.

"She's Catholic, isn't she?" Eva asked.

Evanita nodded yes.

"Grandma's going too. And if you want, you can come with us," Evanita added.

"No, I don't want to go," replied Eva.

Eva looked at Evanita for a moment, and she saw a bit of her mother's spirit—Geneva's—in her daughter's eyes.

"It's no use talking sense into you, is it?" Eva asked.

Evanita nodded no.

"Very well. Go with Josefene and your grandmother. Go with them to church. But pay attention to everything. And ask yourself in your heart about what you see. If there is any part of you left that will listen to me, your mother, then don't fall into the mindless trap of imitating their actions and words for the sake of fitting in. Remember in your heart—challenge everything!"

"Yes, Mama, yes. I will," Evanita promised, but mostly she said that to get Eva to stop lecturing her.

Jonara's vision blurred. The room spun about her, and she found herself spinning in the air. Centrifugal force pulled the backpack from her shoulder. She held onto the backpack by the strap, but forces unknown to Jonara spun her around the backpack and the backpack around her such that her hand and the backpack's strap formed a center point. The backpack should have weighed less than Jonara, and there should have been an imbalance in Jonara's revolution with the backpack, but the diary inside the backpack felt strangely heavy—heavy enough to offset her weight and keep the balance.

2006 Sep 16, Sat Early Eve. Saint Stellan Catholic Church. Portland, Oregon.

Jonara's hand strained to keep a grip. She entwined her wrist around the strap, but the force cut into her circulation and turned her hand purple. In pain, Jonara released her grip. The backpack flew across the room in one direction, and Jonara flew across the room in another. Both lost their airborne flight and landed on the floor with thuds—thuds that only Jonara and the diary could hear.

Jonara's vision cleared, and she found herself in the lobby area of Saint Stellan Catholic Church—two blocks from the west bank of the Willamette River on Northwest Glisan Street. Jonara remembered being in a lobby area for the Broadway Unitarian Church, but this church was different. While the Broadway church had a fountain and conservative decoration, Saint Stellan was exquisitely decorated along the walls and ceiling with gold-plated ornaments and hand-painted murals. Jonara could tell that many hours of manual labor went into crafting this vestibule. It scared her, much like entering a small, old-style store where expensive china and crystal said:

"I'm expensive. Don't touch me, I might break."

Jonara walked to the other side of the vestibule and pulled the backpack out of a large bowl of holy water.

"So the diary is wet," Jonara said.

But when Jonara opened the backpack, the diary wasn't there. Instead, there was a different book—*Daily Missal 1962*. She removed the missal from her backpack, opened it, and found it completely dry.

"This is the vestibule," said the voice of a teenage girl as she led another teenage girl and an older woman through the front door.

"Mommy, Mommy!" Jonara cried.

Jonara ran over to Evanita with backpack and missal in hand and tried to hug her, but Jonara went right through her mother.

"Strange!" Jonara said.

Jonara couldn't understand how her backpack could land in the holy water basin (instead of falling through it), yet she could not hug her mother. On the other hand, the holy water did not touch any part of the backpack or the missal.

"This is a strange dream," Jonara said.

"What is the vestibule for, Josefene?" asked Evanita.

"It's where people gather briefly before entering the main part of the church. We dip a finger into the holy water and make the sign-of-the-cross, like this," Josefene explained.

Josefene dipped her right index finger into the same basin that once held Jonara's backpack, touched the wet finger to her forehead, her chest, her left shoulder, her right shoulder, and placed her hands together.

"What were you whispering?" Evanita asked.

"I said, 'In the name of the Father, the Son, and the Holy Ghost. Amen.' Some people say Spirit instead of Ghost. Others argue the point. But for you, just know that this is the first place to show respect for the Church," Josefene explained.

Evanita reached for the basin to dip her own finger, but Geneva caught her just short of getting wet.

"This is for Catholics. As a non-Catholic, there are some things you can and can't do," said Geneva.

"Why?" Evanita asked.

"Why? Because you haven't been baptized into the Catholic Church. We touch the water to our forehead in remembrance of our baptism," Geneva said.

"That's right," said Josefene. "Thank you, Ms. Carreña."

"How was your baptism? Did you like it?" Evanita asked Josefene.

"I was only a few weeks old. I don't remember it," Josefene replied.

Evanita burst into laughter. Josefene looked around in embarrassment hoping no one would recognize her.

"Don't laugh. This is a serious thing," Geneva explained.

"How can Catholics be serious about this?" Evanita asked.

"About holy water?" Geneva asked.

"Grandma: You just explained that you touch the holy water to your forehead to remember your baptism. But Josefene: You were too young to remember. How can this work, you two?" Evanita asked.

"It's in remembrance of baptism. We don't have to remember it," Geneva explained.

"Huh? I don't understand," said Evanita.

"I don't get it either," said Jonara. "And what does 'remembrance' mean?"

"I'll explain it to you later," Geneva said. "Let's find a place to sit before Mass begins."

Josefene led Evanita and Geneva through the main entrance into the worship area. Josefene walked in as if she'd done it every day, but Evanita stopped short in amazement. Columns and columns supported archways topped by a large central dome with stained glass everywhere. But there was another arrangement that took Evanita completely by surprise. The main aisle from the front door (west) to the altar (east) consisted of a series of seven gradual steps. The steps were vertically solid to ground level. A plank connected the seventh step to the altar. The altar was elevated, and the plank was level across the first step of the altar and the seventh step of the main aisleway. Flanking the altar on Evanita's left (north) side was another series of seven steps running from ground level to the altar level. It too was vertically solid and fell short of the altar with a plank connecting the seventh step to the altar. The flanking steps had a much shorter length than the steps in the main aisleway. On the right (south) side lay a mirror image of left-side steps. This created a symmetrical layout of steps, or nearly symmetrical. There was one difference—the lowest step of the left side was roped off preventing anyone from ascending the steps from that side.

Running from the altar to the building's east wall were three more steps with four chairs on the topmost step abutting the east wall. Above the chairs was a large circular window with a crucifix hanging on the windowpane. To Evanita's right (south) of the circular window was a balcony that stretched along the wall. A single doorway in the wall at the right (south) end of the balcony allowed access. As Evanita watched, a group of choirboys entered the balcony and took seats. Jonara followed her mother's sightline and saw another choir, a choir of women, and they proceeded from the left (north) side of the east wall, along the floor, and disappeared mostly from view behind the arrangement of the north-south steps and the altar. They were

partly visible from behind these north-south steps but only over the steps closest to floor level. The north-south steps closest to the altar completely obscured Evanita's and Jonara's views of the women's choir with the exception of the narrow gaps between the north-south steps and the altar itself—the gaps being the empty spaces under the planks connecting the altar to the north-south steps.

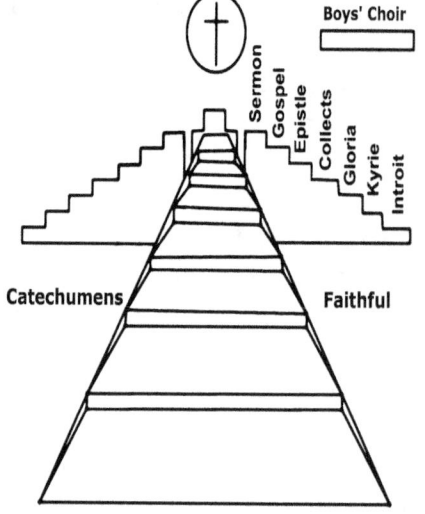

Josefene handed a bulletin to Evanita with a simplified diagram. Evanita stared at the drawing while pipe-organ music reverberated throughout the sculpted masonry and lulled the woodwork into pleasant melodies. As Evanita alternated between staring at the diagram and the church, Josefene used a pair of small tongs to lift a white, circular disk from one container to another (the containers rested on a small table). Jose-fene looked back at Geneva, and Geneva nodded yes. Josefene responded by placing another white disk from the first contain-er to the second. It seemed an odd thing to do—this placing of little white disks from one container to another—at least to Jonara it seemed odd. Awed by the church's architecture, Evan-ita completely missed the event.

Josefene signaled Evanita and Geneva to follow her. When Evanita opened her mouth to speak, Josefene placed a finger over her own mouth to shush Evanita into silence. Jonara fol-lowed the three. They did not walk far. Immediately to the right of the front entrance was a short pew along the back wall.

The pew was just large enough to hold four people. It had the conventional back, seat, and ends of a pew, and it was made of wood. Yet the pew did not rest on the church floor. Instead, it attached to a wood-en platform several inches high. The platform was wide and long enough to hold the pew. Parallel and in front of the pew stood a railing with a kneeler—also attached to the 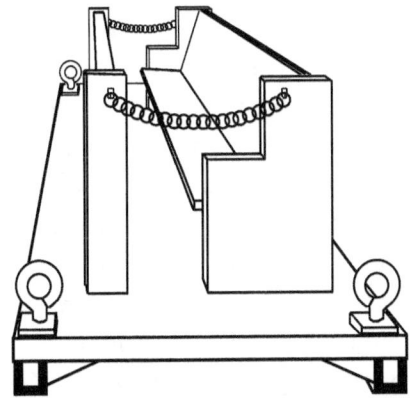 wooden platform. Large, brass eye hooks attached to the plat-form at each of the four corners. A safety chain closed off each side of the pew.

"This is the strangest pew I've ever seen," said Jonara.

Josefene unfastened the safety chains from the railing and refastened them to the ends of the pew, permitting free access into the pew from both ends. The four sat in the pew and waited a short time for the Mass to begin. Facing the altar, the seating order was (left/north to right/south): Jonara, Evanita, Geneva, and Josefene. Jonara placed the backpack under the pew on the platform. Jonara was amazed. The pew held her weight, and the backpack remained on the platform instead of sinking through to the floor.

"Why are we sitting back here, Josefene? There are many seats available closer to the front," Geneva said.

"I made an arrangement with the priest. I told him that my secular friend, Evanita, and her Catholic grandmother would attend Mass with me. But I wasn't sure on which side of the Nave we could sit—the Catechumens or the Faithful," explained Josefene.

"Nave? Catechumens? Huh?" Jonara asked without anyone hearing.

"Secular? I'm a Christian," said Evanita.

"He suggested we sit back here—on this pew," Josefene continued. "Don't you understand?"

"What?" Evanita asked. "You're speaking Greek."

"I confess I too do not understand everything," Geneva said. "'Catechumens'—I haven't heard that word since...since...since before Evanita's mother was born. Before Vatican II. It was the old traditional Latin Mass. I was living in Spain at the time—oh, that doesn't matter now. Josefene—the Nave area? That's where the people sit, but it was never split between the Catechumens and the Faithful, or the non-Catholics and Catholics. Yes, the non-Catholics had to leave after the Offertory, but that's no longer true—non-Catholics may attend the entire Mass. The divide though—reminds me of a wedding in a strange way with the bride's family on the left and the groom's on the right. Evanita, you're right—you are a Christian but not secular. Josefene—I know some Catholics think all non-Catholics are secular, but others understand 'secular' to mean 'non-religious'. But tell me—why is your church divided?"

"We've returned to the traditional Latin Mass—mostly," Josefene said.

"Mostly? Either it is or it isn't the traditional Latin Mass. You can't be a little traditional any more than you can be a little pregnant," Geneva said.

"Our church made compromises and changes, and...well... we're going to present the gifts during Offertory—all three of us!" Josefene explained. "That's the solution. We don't have to sit apart. Evanita would have had to sit on the Mary side, the left side. You and I would have had to sit on the Christ side, the right side, Ms. Carreña. But the priest said we could sit together on the special pew if we present the gifts."

"Josefene—you are speaking in riddles!" said Evanita.

"Shhhh," Josefene said. "The Mass is starting."

The pipe organ changed from a melodic, soothing tone to a more emphatic, pronounced song as if something important were beginning. Evanita looked up to find the source of the music but could not. It was up and behind them—as if there were some balcony directly above. Jonara tried to leave the pew to get a view of the organ, but she couldn't stand up. A strap on her backpack entangled itself around her left leg and anchored her to the pew's platform. Fighting the backpack was no use— she would have to sit next to Evanita until the Mass's conclusion.

The choirboys sang the melody of the opening song while the women's choir hummed the harmony. The priest and two altar boys entered from the right (south) side and knelt at the first step.

"He's at the Introit step," said Jonara, thinking back to the diagram on the bulletin. "Wait a minute, what am I talking about? This church is crazy!"

The priest remained kneeling at the Introit step and faced the main altar, showing his left side to the people. Flanked by the two altar boys (who knelt slightly behind the priest), he made the sign-of-the-cross and started a prayer asking for forgiveness of sins.

Without warning, two ushers approached Josefene's pew— one at each end. They blocked off the two pew exits by locking chains across from the pew ends to the railing. Josefene remained calm, but Geneva and Evanita jumped up in alarm and looked for another exit. Jonara wanted to leave as well. She was able to stand alongside Evanita, but the backpack tightened its hold on her left leg, squeezing it nearly gangrenous. Josefene waved Geneva and Evanita to relax, and they returned to their seats.

Each usher looked above at the church's domed ceiling. From seams between murals, two tracks lowered a few feet—well above the people, of course, but low enough to permit the second thing to descend—an I-beam connected to both ends of the track. The I-beam prepared for the following to descend—chains. A pair of chains dropped from each end of the I-beam—chains with large hooks at the ends. Jonara looked closely and noticed one usher held a remote control in his right hand. The chain hooks met the floor, and the usher pressed a button. The chains stopped. Each usher took two hooks and placed them in the eye hooks at the platform's corners. The usher with the remote control pressed a button. The chains went from slack to taunt, they tugged at the platform with a brief ring-clinking sound, and the platform ascended into the air.

"You should have warned us about this," said Geneva. "I would have taken my motion sickness pills had I known!"

Each usher kept a free hand on the platform to prevent swing deviations. The usher with the remote control used his right hand (his left hand was busy steadying the platform) to signal the crane (that is, the I-beam connected to the two rails). The crane moved along the track toward the altar, and the platform moved from its position near the front door to the first step in the aisleway dividing the Catechumens from the Faithful. The usher with the remote control was obviously experienced. He pressed another button to pause the crane for a second. The crane stopped, the pew swung forward, and the usher activated the crane such that the pew's swing was always a little ahead of the crane. The ushers continued guiding the pew with their hands, and the usher with the remote commanded the chains to lower as the platform approached the first step. In this way, the platform descended and landed gently—flush with the floor.

The crane stopped. The chains lowered and slackened (though the chain hooks remained attached to the eye hooks on the platform). Yet the ushers did not unchain the two exits from the pew and railing. The backpack yanked Jonara's leg down, under the pew, and out the back. She landed on the regular floor behind the pew and before the first step. Jonara stood, but before she, Geneva, and Evanita could regain their composures, the priest (maintaining his orientation to the altar) ascended to the second step, the Kyrie.

The ushers wasted no time. The one operating the crane pressed several buttons in rapid succession. Before the priest could finish saying the first, "Lord have mercy," the ushers had landed the platform onto the second step.

The Kyrie did not last long. Instead of the priest and people saying "Lord have mercy" three times followed by "Christ have mercy" three times, followed again by "Lord have mercy" three times, there was only the simple pairing of the priest leading and the people following with "Lord have mercy," "Christ have mercy," and "Lord have mercy."

"That's the modern Kyrie, not the traditional," said Geneva, but before she could ask why the number of Lord-have-mercies and Christ-have-mercies were each two instead of three, the priest moved to his next step, and the ushers craned the platform to the third main step for the Gloria.

Now Jonara had been standing behind the pew and resting her arms against the back of the pew. She stood with one foot on the edge of the platform and one foot dangling off. When the ushers craned the platform from the Kyrie step to the Gloria step, Jonara—startled—felt the back of the pew slide upward from her. She instinctively grabbed for something and caught hold of the platform's edge. She dangled freely in the air as the platform levitated from the second to the third step, with the grasp of her hands preventing her fall. The backpack strap remained entangled around her left leg, and just before the platform landed on the Gloria step, the backpack tugged her left calf to the ground where the platform alighted atop it and pinned it.

"Glory to God in the highest!" the priest exclaimed.

The people responded with the Gloria prayer. Jonara was too busy dealing with the pain of the platform against her left foot, ankle, and calf to even attempt to make sense of the repeated "We," "Lord," "Father," and "Thou alone" phrases.

"I am alone," Jonara gasped, "and I'm trapped under this flying pew!"

She squirmed like a trapped animal. She yanked her un-moving leg. She tried lifting the platform. She beat on the platform, the pew, and the floor. She screamed. Stuck. She screamed again.

"Let us pray," said the priest.

He ascended to the fourth step for the Collects. At the moment the ushers craned the platform pew to the Collects step (and releasing Jonara's left leg from capture), Jonara awoke.

"Jonara, Jonara! Stop flailing your arms at me. It's Anna!" Anna said.

"I am alone, alone!" Jonara said with her eyes closed.

"No, honey, you're not! I'm here with you!" Anna said. "You're having a bad dream!"

Jonara opened her eyes, looked around, and asked, "I'm not alone?"

"No, no, dear child! Look! What has happened here? The sheets are all twisted around your left leg—here! See? You must have rolled over and over in your sleep," Anna explained as she unknotted the sheets and unworked them around Jonara's leg.

"Ow," said Jonara.

"I'm sorry. I'm trying to be gentle," said Anna.

"Not you. Something's in my back," Jonara said.

"There—your leg is free. Why don't you sit up for a moment," Anna suggested.

Jonara sat up and found what had been sticking in her back—a black book.

"Your Nanna Geneva's missal," said Anna. "How did that get there? We should put that back on the bookshelf. There. Now stand up for one moment, and I'll remake the bed."

Jonara stood up. She was dazed and exhausted. The clock read, "3:30." Had she experienced that much in just a short night of dreaming? Anna made the bed and tucked Jonara in.

"There you are. Pleasant dreams, Jonara. I'll be just downstairs if you need me," Anna said.

With that, Anna left Jonara's bedroom. Jonara stared at the ceiling and shook in brief horror when she saw two hanging planters—planters suspended by chains. She tried to ignore them, but the chains held fast in her mind, and as she fell asleep, she returned to Saint Stellan's Catholic Church with Evanita, Geneva, and Josefene.

To Jonara's surprise, the pew and platform were now resting on the seventh step. Jonara stood to the left side of the pew on the platform between the two left-side eye hooks, and yes—the left-side pair of chains ascending to the ceiling crane. Concerned for her balance, she backed up a little until her back bumped into the left-side rearward chain. She placed a hand on the chain and leaned against it. Looking to the pew itself, she noticed Geneva had her eyes closed and breathed heavily. Evanita stared off in the distance, and Josefene repeated silently the priest's words.

And the priest? He was now on his own seventh step—the Sermon step. No longer was he facing the altar as he had in the earlier steps. He faced the people. He held his arms out at times, lifted them at others, and waved a hand across the front of his body—to the people, as if blessing them. His voice was in monotone, but he perspired profusely under the bright lights. Jonara couldn't see before, but now that she was this close—with only a wooden plank between her and the altar (and likewise a wooden plank between the priest's step and the altar), the priest's eyes were red, his face blushed, and his mouth parched. At times he swayed and lurched as if he were about to lose his balance.

"He needs a chain to hold onto like I do," said Jonara.

"Josefene," Evanita whispered. "He looks drunk."

"Shhh," Josefene whispered. "Wake your grandma, the Homily is almost over."

"What's a Homily?" Evanita asked.

"It's like a sermon. Priests don't give sermons, though. They give Homilies. Wake her—the platform is about to move again," Josefene warned.

Evanita nudged her grandmother several times. Geneva flipped her eyes wide open and looked around, startled. She made several sign-of-the-crosses as an automatic reaction before coming to her senses. She blushed and shrank down a bit—sheepish that she'd fallen asleep during the priest's lecture.

The priest finished the Homily and sat with the altar boys on small chairs at the back of his seventh step. The women's choir began singing a song about giving thanks for all of Christ's works. As Josefene predicted, the ushers took to the ends of the platform and craned it into the air—much higher than before. In fact, the ushers could no longer prevent the platform from swinging side-to-side, as it was beyond their reach. Jonara sat on the platform to minimize the risk of falling off as she had before. She continued holding onto the left-side rearward chain with her left hand, and with her right she kept the backpack close to her to prevent it from tangling her leg and pulling her off as before.

The pew platform held an altitude level with the crucifix on the circular window. Only one usher was now involved with the pew platform. As before, the usher controlled the crane and chains with his remote. He walked backward toward the church entrance (west side of the building) and kept the crane moving backward such that the pew platform backed away from the altar slowly until it reached the west wall.

While the pew platform moved away from the altar, other ushers—beginning with the pews closest to the altar—passed baskets to people on both sides of the Nave—the Catechumen side and the Faithful side. The people reached from their pockets and purses for money—money they felt compelled to donate to the church. Jonara looked down from the platform to the people below but grew dizzy and refrained from such a view. She settled for staring at her mother, who engaged in conversation with Josefene.

"The people on the unfaithful side," Evanita started.

"You mean the Catechumen side. The secular side," Josefene said.

"The non-Catholic side," Geneva added.

"They give money too? But they're not Catholics," Evanita said.

"You'd be amazed," Josefene explained. "The Seckies give more than we do."

"The Seckies, Josefene?" Geneva asked.

"The secular people—the Seckies," Josefene clarified.

"The unfaithful," Evanita said.

"The non-Catholics," Geneva said.

"Get over it, people!" Jonara said, but as usual, no one heard her.

"Why would Seckies—I mean the unfaithful—give more than Catholics?" Evanita asked.

"That's a good question," said Geneva. "One would think Catholics give more."

"Yes, but that's the interesting thing, isn't it?" Josefene noted. "The Seckies give more because they feel privileged to attend, and they want to give something back."

Evanita and Geneva giggled.

"Who are you kidding?" Jonara asked.

"You can't be serious," said Geneva. "One must work at something to recognize its value. The first part of the Mass—"

"Is all about working, I know. We're working through standing and kneeling to reach the Eucharist of Christ. But that's exactly the point! Most Catholics are born into the Church—what work do they have to do?" Josefene asked without expecting an answer.

"The Sacraments—" Geneva started.

"Do not require the study they used to if you're born into the Church," Josefene interrupted. "Further, there's no need for a conversion to faith. Catholics born into the Church begin their faith at baptism, which can be as early as a few weeks after birth."

"True, but Confirmation—" said Geneva.

"Can be handed out to first graders after memorizing their catechism," Josefene continued.

"I don't understand," Evanita said. "You still haven't explained why Seckies give more."

"Non-Catholics," corrected Jonara, but no one cared.

"Most Seckies are studying to become Catholics. It's a much more rigorous process than being born a Catholic. Not only must they learn all there is to know about the Catholic faith and Catholic history, they have to prove to the clergy why they should be admitted as Catholics—often in the form of a good deed," explained Josefene.

"Like sweeping the sidewalk?" Evanita suggested.

"Oh no, much much more! They have to make some very large sacrifice—like giving up meat for a whole year, or donating land to the church," said Josefene.

"Isn't that a little extreme?" asked Geneva. "I don't remember our converts making such large sacrifices."

"I could never do it," said Evanita. "I would never want to do it."

"So you see—giving a little extra during Offertory is really no big deal. They're happy to give. It will speed their conversion both on Earth and in Purgatory," Josefene explained.

"Dear me! Purgatory! There used to be indulgences, I know, but really!" Geneva said.

"Shhh," said Josefene. "We do indulgences too. It's nothing really—just a coin to light a candle, for example. Shhh. They're going to lower us. Now listen, when we land on the floor, we'll be expected to bring the gifts to the altar. Just carry what you're given and follow me. Okay?"

The ushers completed passing baskets around and returned to the main entrance (west side) of the church. They poured the cash and coins into a larger central basket, being sure to pick out coins lodged in the passed-along baskets. The usher controlling the pew platform commanded the crane to lower the chains, and it did—landing the pew platform gently on the floor next to the west wall very close to the other ushers who were finishing with the gifts.

The usher controlling the crane let the chains slacken such that the hooks could be removed from the platform's eye hooks. Jonara released the chain from her grip and held onto the pew's side instead. The usher removed the chain hooks, stepped to the right side (facing toward the altar) of the pew, and detached the retaining chain across the railing and pew. Josefene led the three from the pew platform into a hairpin left turn in front of the pew platform's railing where the three met two ushers who had prepared the Offertory gifts.

The ushers handed the container of circular disks—the Communion hosts—to Josefene. Geneva took the bottles of wine. Evanita was sure she would be given the money basket, but instead, she received a white cloth. One usher took the basket of money and led the procession up the same seven steps the pew platform had ascended before. Following the money usher was Josefene, Geneva, Evanita, and the usher with the remote control. The remote was now in the trailing usher's pocket. With nothing to carry and nothing to occupy his hands, he placed his hands in his coat jacket's pockets— nudging a few remote buttons without much thought.

Jonara felt a tug on both legs. The backpack had ensnared her ankles. Yet the backpack did not provide the tug on its own. A hook caught the backpack—the same hook connected to the chain Jonara had leaned on—that hook pulled the backpack and Jonara's feet out from under her. She flipped to the floor with a thump. The Offertory procession continued up the seven steps to the altar. The chain and hook continued ascending in the air, pulling Jonara up along with it—up in a fashion where Jonara was suspended upside down by her feet!

"Help!" she yelled.

No one in the church heard her. No Anna to remake her bed. In observing the continuing church ceremony, Jonara was doomed to watch from a leg-bound inverted position—unable to respond, and unable to move about. Her arms hung out to the side yet extended—giving her body the shape of an inverted tee. Blood pooled in her head, and the world—inverted—had a red tinge to it.

The priest stood in front of the altar and faced the procession, awaiting the gifts. The money usher crossed a plank from the seventh step to the altar step and handed the basket of green bills and coins to the priest. He accepted it gladly. Josefene took a step onto the plank and made a move toward the altar, but the priest stopped her with a wave of his hand. He motioned to Josefene, and while still on the plank, she handed the container of hosts to the usher, who passed the container to an altar boy. Josefene returned to the seventh step. Geneva walked up to the plank, took a look at the deep gap between the seventh step and the altar step, and decided no, she would not add to her motion sickness (incurred from the flying pew) by standing on a board precariously balanced between two, seven-foot tall stone erectments.

The usher understood and walked across the plank to receive the wine from Geneva. Jonara was now close to the ceiling. With her feet still bound, she shifted her weight such that she swung like a pendulum. After several swings, she latched her hands onto the crane and pulled herself up and over the top of the crane where she sat. She rested from being inverted and watched the ceremony below.

The usher took the wine across the plank to the altar where he gave it to the other altar boy. Evanita walked onto the plank and nearly crossed completely to the altar when the usher halted her progress by blocking her path. He took the white cloth from her. Evanita remained facing him on the plank. The usher did not move, and he stared her into submission. He waited for her to return to the seventh step before handing the cloth over to the second altar boy. Evanita felt uncomfortable with being prevented from crossing the plank to the altar, uncomfortable with the usher staring her down as if she were guilty of something, and uncomfortable with the next thing that happened—a collapsible metal-linked screen descended from the ceiling in two places: one between the main aisle and the Catechumen section, and a second between the unused seven steps (north of the altar) and the Catechumen section. The screens looked very similar to those used by mall stores to close for the day.

The screens descended and stretched from ceiling to floor. In this way, no large objects could pass from the Catechumen section to the altar or the main aisle. The back (toward the main doors) was open, and many decided to leave the Mass at this point. Others remained. While their visibility to the altar was not blocked, the screen gave them the feeling of being in a prison.

Evanita and Geneva stood in complete surprise. The ushers did not wait—they escorted the three down the main aisle from steps seven, six, five, four, three, two, one, and to the pew where they first sat. The ushers did not rechain the ends nor did the chains with hooks descend from the ceiling. The three sat freely in the pew while the priest celebrated the second half of the Mass—the Eucharist.

"Now if this is a traditional Mass," started Geneva to Josefene, "the priest will have his back to the people. And if not, he'll face the people. So which is it?"

"You'll see. But the short answer is—neither," Josefene replied.

"Neither? How?" Geneva asked.

Jonara wanted to stay above the pew and listen to Geneva, Evanita, and Josefene, but she was curious about the priest— what was he going to do that was important, so important that the non-Catholics were separated by a screen? Jonara whipped the backpack onto her back and crawled along the crane until it met one of the railings. She climbed onto the railing and crawled along it until she reached its end—above the seventh step in the main aisleway.

Josefene was right, as Jonara observed. The priest did not face toward the people (west), nor did he face away from the people (east). Instead, he faced north. It was really quite understandable. The priest had been proceeding up his steps from south to north already. From the seventh step, he had crossed his plank to the altar. He only briefly stepped around to the main aisleway side (the west side) of the altar to receive the gifts, but once that was over, he returned to the south side of the altar where he prayed and celebrated both the hosts and the wine after blessing them.

Jonara saw nothing special about this event.

"The non-Catholics pay lots of money for this?" she wondered.

Jonara stared at the priest, and he continued this way with prayer followed with replies by people in the Nave. Even the Catechumens replied. Jonara, still on the railing, sat through the Mass—including the part where people shook each other's hands—yet still she could not understand why this was important. She looked back at the pew where her mother stood. Evanita was busy shaking Geneva's and Josefene's hands. Jonara looked at the women's choir—now fully visible from her overhead vantage point. They also shook hands. The Catechumens shook hands, the Faithful shook hands, and the choirboys shook hands.

It wasn't long after the shaking of hands, the peace-be-with-you as Jonara thought of it later, that the priest took the container of hosts and placed one each on the tongues of his altar boys. The priest (followed by the altar boys) proceeded down his steps, disappeared, and reappeared at the entrance to the choirboys' balcony. Again, he placed a host each on the tongues of the choirboys, with one altar boy holding a golden plate (with handle) under the chin of each host recipient.

The priest and altar boy descended the hidden flight of steps from the balcony back to the church, reentering from the south entrance. The three proceeded to the front of the Faithful section where the priest dispensed hosts to Faithful Catholics. He was not on the elevated main aisleway but instead was on floor level—the same level as the Faithful. Ushers walked to each pew, beginning with the one closest to the altar, and allowed the Faithful to proceed up to the priest.

Geneva and Josefene joined with the last pew to receive Communion, as Geneva called it when she gave a brief explanation to Evanita before leaving her alone in the pew. Jonara watched her great-grandmother receive the host, but Geneva kept her mouth closed and held her open, crossed palms before the priest. He attempted to place the host on her tongue several times, but she refused—shaking her hands in front of him. With her teeth clenched fast to prevent the priest from sneaking the host into her mouth, she growled:

"Place the host in my hand the modern way!"

The priest refused. He blessed Geneva with the sign-of-the-cross and moved onto Josefene, who accepted the host on her tongue. Josefene was the last in line for Communion, and she returned along with Geneva to the pew—rejoining Evanita.

Behind the priest, the women's choir formed a line to receive Communion. The priest checked the container for more hosts but realized he'd run out. He waved two fingers across to them as if to say:

"No Communion for all of you."

The women looked down in disappointment and returned to their place on the floor level behind the altar. The priest and the altar boys climbed the steps from the south and sat on their chairs behind and to the south of the altar along the east wall—in good sight of the Faithful but obscured from view of the Catechumens.

Jonara knew something was wrong. Those women in the choir had been left for the last, and because of that, they did not receive their Communion hosts. Yet the choirboys had theirs. Was that fair?

"It's not fair," Jonara whispered, but why should she muffle her rising anger?

"It's not fair," Jonara spoke in a louder voice.

"IT'S NOT FAIR!" she shouted at the top of her lungs.

Jonara beat her fist into the railing. She beat and kicked and whipped the backpack (with the missal inside) against the railing.

"You," Jonara said pointing to the backpack. "You are to blame."

Yet Jonara wasn't referring to the backpack itself. It was the thing inside the backpack, and she remembered the book—the book that was something else and not the pleasant script of her great-grandmother's diary. She pulled the backpack close to her and opened it.

"You, little black book with the English and Latin—you caused this," Jonara said.

She grabbed the missal from the backpack, took aim, and hurled the missal at the priest. Jonara expected the missal to bounce off the altar, the priest, or something. Instead, it passed directly into the altar and out of sight as if the altar were a mirage.

"How can an altar swallow up its own written text?" she asked.

Jonara didn't have time to answer. Throwing the missal sent a harmonic wave from her position down the railing to the other end (above Geneva, Josefene, and Evanita), and rebounded along the railing with double the intensity. The wave thrust its energy upon Jonara in the form of a jolt—up and out from the railing. Jonara wheeled her arms like a windmill but could not regain her balance on the railing. She took to the air and fell toward the top of the altar. She expected to fall straight through as the missal had done. She didn't. Instead, she bounced off the top of the altar on its east side without disturbing the items in place, and plunged down into the women's choir.

Jonara entered the shoes and clothing of a choir lady. Her outfit was gray, robed, and heavy. A headscarf covering her head kept falling into her face. She flipped it to the side repeatedly, but the headscarf was stubborn and kept falling over her mouth. She blew at the headscarf and managed to keep it under her chin.

"The Mass is ended, go in peace to love and serve the Lord," the priest echoed from above.

"Thanks be to God," the people and women's choir responded.

The organ music picked up. The surrounding choir women flipped a few pages in their books to, "Immaculate Mary" and sang:

Immaculate Mary, your praises we sing,
Who reigns in splendor with Jesus our King.
Ave, ave, ave, Maria! Ave, ave, Maria!

In heaven, the blessed your glory proclaim,
On Earth we, your children, invoke your fair name.
Ave, ave, ave, Maria! Ave, ave, Maria!

We pray for God's glory, may His Kingdom come,
We pray for His vicar, our father, and Rome.
Ave, ave, ave, Maria! Ave, ave, Maria!

We pray for our Mother, the Church upon earth,
And bless, dearest Lady, the land of our birth.
Ave, ave, ave, Maria! Ave, ave, Maria!

At first, Jonara did not sing, but her neighboring choir women nudged her and kicked her legs until she too sang "Immaculate Mary." The priest and altar boys filed out first—from the altar down the south steps to a south exit. The choirboys (who did not bother to sing "Immaculate Mary") exited next—from their balcony to a back exit. Next, the ushers allowed the special pew (Geneva, Evanita, and Josefene) to exit, followed by the Faithful section. The song ended, and Jonara was ready to exit, but she couldn't—choir women flanked her, blocked her, and all but prevented her exit. Jonara looked around to see what was holding things up. She had difficulty seeing around the altar into the Nave, but she did manage to see that the Catechumen section was still filled with people.

The Faithful section exited slowly. Catholics happily chatted about the readings and the Homily. A throng plugged up the vestibule (the area between the main/west door and church exit), slowing the exit line from the Faithful section considerably. Geneva struck up several impromptu sessions with older people she'd never met, and Josefene hugged several friends. Evanita felt left out, and Jonara was trapped.

"Let's go out the side," said one of the choir women. "We'll never get out the main entrance."

"That would be a sin!" rebuffed another choir woman. "You should be ashamed of yourself."

"But I'm tired, and these heavy robes are hot and stifling," the first said.

"You are in church! To go on like this is a sin! You will have to confess this to the priest," said the second.

"I will not," said the first.

"You will! Your soul is in mortal danger! The priest will decide! I warn you!" said the second.

"Oh, get over it already!" quipped Jonara.

"Who said that?" asked the second.

Jonara was shocked. Someone heard her, but how? Yet it made sense somehow. When she didn't sing, the choir women to her left and right prompted her to sing, and those same women based their physical positions partly on Jonara's.

"I asked, who said that? It's sacrilege. Come here and receive your penance," said the second.

"I didn't say anything," said the first.

"I know it wasn't you, Ruby. That sounded like a young whippersnapper," said the second as she turned her attention back to the area of the offending voice.

"This is your last chance to come forward," said the second. "No? Three blessings of grace to the first woman who points out the sassy one."

Both women next to Jonara dragged her—one on each of Jonara's arms—to the second choir woman.

"One-and-a-half blessings for each of you," said the second to the choir women who dragged Jonara forward.

The second held her right hand in an extended chopping gesture and gave each woman one-and-a-half sign-of-the-crosses.

"Let me go!" shouted Jonara.

Jonara torqued her body and yanked her arms free.

"Hold out your left hand," the second said to Jonara.

"No!" Jonara said.

"I said hold out your left hand!" the second repeated.

The second snatched Jonara's left wrist with her left hand, held the forearm's underside upward, pulled out a ruler in her right hand, and whipped the splintered wood against Jonara's forearm. In reflex, Jonara scooped up the ruler with her right hand and slapped it against the second's left hand (which released Jonara's left arm from grip). With her eight fingers on the ruler's measurement side and two thumbs on the other, she fractured/snapped/severed the ruler. Brittle splinters dispersed into the women's headscarves—most especially into the second choir woman and the two who dragged her forward.

"That's it!" the second choir woman said. "Bring her out back to the Cemeterius."

The two women who first yanked Jonara to the second choir woman now dragged her out a door—a door centered along the west wall—close to the altar—and completely out of view from the Nave area.

The choir women exited the church and entered a small, gated cemetery surrounded by a wrought iron fence. A single gate permitted entry. The second choir woman opened the gate and led the choir into the Cemeterius. She ascended steps to the top of a special memorial to one A. Graves.

"I am the Vice of Christ," said the second choir woman. "Christ Pristine, I am Christine—the Vice of Christ!"

"O Christine, the Vice of Christ," started the women's choir (except for Jonara). "We come before you, we ask for grace, for ourselves, for our church, for Christ, and Rome."

"This is crazy!" blurted Jonara.

"Silence sinner!" Christine shouted at Jonara. "Kneel before the Vice of Christ! KNEEL!"

Two choir women kicked in Jonara's knees from behind and pushed her down by the shoulders. Jonara sank to the ground on her hands and knees. The choir women who forced her to the ground picked up fistfuls of dirt and sprinkled the dirt on Jonara.

"No," said Christine. "Remove the headscarf first, and then sprinkle."

One of the choir women ripped the headscarf from Jonara. Jonara flinched and twisted her head back toward the offending choir woman and gave her a harsh stare.

"Face me! Face the Vice of Christ!" ordered Christine.

Jonara turned back toward Christine and was about to say something rude.

"It's you. I knew you would return," said Christine.

"You know me?" Jonara asked in surprise.

"You have many names. Ishtar, Bastet, and Al Kardai. Hekate, Lilith and Prosperine. Lamia, Mara, and Tunrida—these are all your names—the names of demons and devils," said Christine.

"I haven't done anything," pleaded Jonara. "Just let me go."

"Of course you've done something. You have sinned in the Church, during Mass, before Father Rick, Christ, and God. Don't you understand, child? Christ is dead in your soul! Now confess your sins to me and accept your penance," Christine commanded.

"I—" Jonara started.

"Sister Christine," said one of the choir women.

"I'm no longer a nun," said Christine.

"I beseech you for forgiveness," the choir woman said.

"Acting as his proxy, Father Rick forgives you," Christine said.

"You cannot do this. The reprimand, the rules of our church, Father Rick says—" started the choir woman.

"I am fully cognizant of my duties to our church, its laws, and the manner in which they are to be upheld. Are you?" Christine said.

Christine stared down the choir woman with eyes of fire. The choir woman cowered away in fear. The others stood in fear, shook, and scuffled their feet nervously.

"Leave the Cemeterius, all of you! Exit through the church and out the front door. Now!" Christine commanded.

The choir women moved to the church door. Jonara sat back from all fours to a position where she sat on her lower legs and feet. She placed her hands on her knees and prepared to stand.

"All except the blasphemer. Leave her here!" Christine said.

"What makes you think I'll stay?" Jonara asked.

Christine did not answer—at least not immediately. Instead, she descended the A. Graves memorial and stood over Jonara. She placed her right hand on the back of Jonara's head and rubbed the dirt into Jonara's hair. Jonara fell down onto her hands and knees as before. In this way, Jonara remained in the

Cemeterius while the other choir women exited through the church.

"Begin with the Act of Contrition," commanded Christine.

Christine pushed Jonara's head down—nearly burying her face into Cemeterius dirt.

"Say it," said Christine, "Say the words, 'Oh my God I am heartily sorry.' Recite the Act!"

"I don't know what you're talking about!" Jonara said. "I don't know any Act of Contrition!"

Christine's right hand grabbed Jonara's hair at the back of her head and used the hair to control Jonara's head. Christine rotated Jonara's head back and forth against Cemeterius dirt.

"I am the Vice of Christ. The Christ of the living God, of the Church, and of the souls waiting in Purgatory. The dead of the Cemeterius have sacrificed for the Church. Eat the dust of Cemeterius, the dust of the dead, the dead of the Church, the body of Christ, the Vice of Christ. Eat where I have stepped, eat until you understand your place in the Church, until you repent and are obedient," Christine said.

Jonara's immediate urge was to tell Christine off and put her in her place. But what place was that? Christine was trying to put Jonara in some sort of place, some role that Jonara did not understand. Frustrated, she considered simple violence—perhaps a wild swing or two at the woman would knock some sense into her. Again, what sense would she beat into her, and would the woman understand her? She looked up at Christine, and for a brief moment Christine's face turned red while a symbol appeared on her forehead.

"You're crazy," was the last thing Jonara heard herself say.

The world around blurred, and the smell of dirt made her think of food one might find in the earth—potatoes, carrots, and sweet onions from southern Georgia, the southeast United States—a place she wanted to visit but never had a chance to. The closest she'd been was Texas.

"Texas," Jonara said. "Corpus Christi."

Jonara's visit to the Cemeterius was suspended. For a brief moment, she thought she was a bunny rabbit eating grass and burrowing underground in the mountains of Spain. But this vision passed, and she awoke in her late Great-Grandma Geneva's house in Corpus Christi. The sheets were over Jonara's body, and she was on the floor, face down, with her nose into the long-pile carpeting. She looked for the missal and found it under the bed.

"It can stay there for now," said Jonara.

Jonara stood so as to return to bed, but her legs shook. She did not understand why, and she was afraid to return to sleep.

"What if I return to the Cemeterius?" she pondered.

Jonara looked around the bedroom and found Geneva's diary on the nightstand. It was opened to a page dated Thursday in late September of 2006.

2006 Sep 21, Thu. Eva's Home in Portland, Oregon.

Jonara had fallen against some sort of revolving drum, a circus ride where centrifugal force had pinned her against the drum wall. Across from her on the other side of the drum was her backpack. It too was pinned and flattened against the drum wall. Around and around the drum spun. Jonara was on her back with her arms to her sides. She tried lifting her right arm to her abdomen, but the centrifugal force was too strong. She remained like this until the drum stopped suddenly. When it did, the blood rushed from her head to her feet, she tumbled to her left one quarter of the way along the drum, and her backpack tumbled to its right one quarter of the way along the drum until the two met in a collision. Jonara found herself face down with the backpack next to her head. Her fluid circulation was disrupted, and it took her several minutes to regain her equilibrium enough so she could stand. When she did, she was no longer at Saint Stellan Church but was instead in Eva's home.

"Mama?" Evanita asked.

"Yes?" Eva replied.

It was Thursday evening. Evanita and Eva sat on the living room couch while Geneva sat in the easy chair, flipping channels on the television with the remote control.

"There's nothing good on," Geneva said.

Geneva searched for a television show while her girls continued to chat.

"School is letting out early tomorrow," Evanita continued.

"Oh? Are you making this up so you can play hooky?" Eva asked.

"No, the teachers are attending an all-afternoon meeting. Something about unfair pay," Evanita explained.

"In my day, the teachers never complained about pay. And the students never got the free time they do today," Geneva chimed.

"Yes, Mother, you walked to school twenty miles, uphill, both ways, in a snowstorm!" Eva said.

"You were there!" Geneva joked. "And I did it with leg braces and forearms crutches. Those Spanish mountains are steep!"

"Please!" Eva said.

"I'm not playing hooky!" Evanita said.

"Oh, it's too bad you don't have the morning off from school, Evanita," said Geneva. "I could take you to Daily Mass at Saint Stellan."

Eva looked at her daughter to see how she would react to Geneva's offer. Evanita grimaced briefly before suppressing her distaste. Eva beamed with a warm smile that her daughter was not completely wooed by the Catholic faith.

"Maybe another time, Grandma," replied Evanita.

"Still, the church will be open. We could go to Confession. I've got the hours right here from Sunday's bulletin: Friday 2 pm to 4 pm," Geneva offered.

"Grandma, I—" Evanita started.

"I know, I know, you can't really receive the Sacrament of Confession because you're not a Catholic yet," Geneva said.

"Yet?" Eva asked.

"Yet!?" Evanita echoed.

"Mommy a Catholic?" Jonara sounded.

"But I'll ask the priest to make an exception in your case—at least to listen to your sins. You won't be able to receive Absolution, but at least you'll get a taste of—" Geneva said.

"Mother, stop!" Eva interrupted. "I warned you not to interfere with how I raise Evanita. Now you're pushing!"

"Pushing? Me?" Geneva asked in an innocent tone.

"Yes, pushing!" Eva replied.

"I never! Evanita wanted to go...to see...Her friend invited us. I only want to guide—" Geneva continued.

"You mean control!" Eva said.

"'Men control, women guide.' Isn't that right, Mama?" Evanita asked.

Eva and Geneva turned their heads sharply toward Evanita.

"You said that?" Geneva asked Eva.

"I didn't...well maybe...this is different," Eva said.

"How?" Jonara asked, but no one heard or saw her.

"Evanita," Eva said after a long pause. "You'll come over to the Page Street Clinic building tomorrow after school."

Evanita started to complain, but Eva was sharp.

"No *ifs*, *ands*, or *buts*. You'll help me out at the clinic, and that's final. I'm short-staffed as it is, and you can learn all about the monotony of paperwork and phone calls. And if you have any sins," Eva said, and with "sins" she gave a sharp look to Geneva before looking back at Evanita, "you can confess them to the filing cabinets. They are patient listeners and never talk back."

"Oh dearie, don't you think—" Geneva started to Eva.

"I'll speak with you later," said Eva to her mother. She turned back to Evanita and added, "If you behave, I'll let you help me with the patients. Some of the younger children are quite nervous when they go to the dentist. You can hold their hands while I work on their teeth. What do you say?"

Evanita looked first at her mother and second at her grandmother. Geneva waved her free hand upward (her other hand still contained the remote control) as if to say, "Oh well, do what you want."

"All right, I'll help you at the dental clinic," said Evanita.

Eva gave Evanita a big hug and said, "That's my girl!"

Geneva changed the television channel three more times and found a sitcom she liked. She let out a hearty laugh, completely forgetting about trying to recruit Evanita into the Catholic faith. Evanita and Eva looked at Geneva in disbelief and looked at each other.

"She's happy," said Evanita.

Eva smiled.

CHAPTER 6

Page Clinic

2006 Sep 22, Fri. Page Street Clinic. Portland, Oregon.

Jonara held the backpack firmly to her abdomen to prevent it from spinning away. She expected to go into a spin, but she didn't. Instead, she felt vibrations as if a jackhammer were rattling her skull. She dropped the backpack and held her hands to her head to dampen the jarring. The motion made her queasy, and she found herself inside the Page Street Clinic building with a headache and loss of appetite. Looking around, she saw her mother at a desk.

"Carreña Dental, how may I help you?" Evanita said as she answered the telephone.

Evanita sat in a wooden chair surrounded by files, papers, and assorted tooth figurines.

"You have a toothache? Let's see when we can get you in. The dentist has an opening at 2:30 today. And your name? Johnny Pindus? All right, there. You're in the computer, Mr. Pindus. We'll see you at 2:30!"

"How are you doing, Evanita?" Eva asked as she walked into the reception area from one of the dental rooms.

"This is hectic. I can barely keep up. Everyone calling in and wanting something," said Evanita. "When do I get a break?"

"Marinda will trade off with you. She's filing at the moment. Marinda?" Eva called.

"Yes, Miss Carreña? I have many charts to file. Is your girl ready?" Marinda asked.

"But who will answer the phone?" Jonara asked.

Jonara didn't have long to wait. Another helper took over telephone duty. Marinda patted Evanita on the shoulder and pushed her to a desk with stacks of papers and envelopes.

"This pile contains reminder notices. They go in these flowery envelopes. When you finish with those, there's another pile behind it. Those are the bills. They go in the white envelopes. And next to the bills are the overdue bills—they go in orange envelopes. What else, did I leave anything out? Make sure you finish before five o'clock," Marinda said.

"Five o'clock? Stuff all these papers in these envelopes by five? How? I—" Evanita started.

"Shhh. Not a word. The more you complain, the harder you'll have to work to finish everything. Now hop to it!" Marinda urged.

Marinda left Evanita by herself at the desk.

"Poor Mommy. That looks boring," said Jonara. "Don't worry, Mommy, try to think nice thoughts."

"I know, I'll try to think nice thoughts," said Evanita.

Jonara sat on a chair next to her mother. She reached for a reminder notice to place it in an envelope, but her hand passed through the papers. She placed her backpack on the desk, and like the pew in Saint Stellan Catholic Church, the desk held the weight of the backpack. Yet strangely, the backpack passed through the papers and envelopes on the desk. Jonara opened the backpack to retrieve the diary. It wasn't there. Nor was the Daily Missal. In fact, there were no books at all. Instead, she found a ball of twine. Stranger still, the twine in its balled-up state looked like a globe.

"Twine? What on Earth is this for? And why does it look like Earth? And thin twine at that," Jonara said.

Jonara pulled a little twine from the ball. Then a little more. She held the twine up to the light while her mother continued stuffing envelopes. With little thought, she drew a section of twine between her fingers and moved the section to her mouth, where she used it as floss. She was amazed at how little effort it took to draw the twine between her teeth.

Without warning, a black and white cat with a red face jumped from nowhere and playfully attacked the twine. Startled, Jonara dropped the twine, yet it stuck firmly between two molars. In this way, twine ran from her mouth to the ball, and the other end dangled from her mouth. The cat jumped and swatted the free-hanging twine. Jonara bobbed her head around to avoid this crazy cat, but it simply jumped and swatted around all the more excitedly at the dangling twine. Evanita seemed not to notice and continued stuffing envelopes. Jonara was so frightened that she shot back from the desk and ran down the hall into a treatment room. With the twine attached to her molars, the ball of twine fell from Evanita's desk and followed Jonara down the hallway (though at half the speed) and in doing so unwound a bit. The cat vacillated between chasing the ball of twine and the twine between the ball and Jonara. Trapped at the treatment room's entrance, Jonara stood fast, held her gaze firmly at the doorway, and pulled the twine from her teeth just before the cat chased the ball of twine into the treatment room.

With the emergency over, Jonara looked around and saw her Grandma Eva and an assistant drilling and filling the tooth of a young girl.

"Younger than me," Jonara decided.

The girl's clothes were tattered and her hair unkept. Her shoes had holes in them, and she wore no socks. Eva drilled into the girl's tooth, and her body winced in pain.

"Her nerve must be well protected by bone. I've already given her a full carpule," Eva said to her assistant. "Hand me another carpule, please. Thank you."

Eva held the girl's cheek with one hand and carefully placed the syringe with the other. She injected the novocaine into the cheek.

"There," Eva said. "I've surrounded the nerve. We'll resume in a few minutes."

Eva patted the patient on the shoulder and said, "Rest for a bit, Denise. I'll be back when the pain goes away."

Denise closed her eyes and relaxed her tense legs and arms. The assistant wiped the tears from Denise's eyes. After Eva left the room, Jonara walked to Denise. She reached for Denise's hand with her own, but Jonara's hand passed through Denise's. Jonara looked at the girl's face and saw the strain of neglect and malnourishment. The medication took effect, and Denise opened her mouth and touched her face to test the numbness. Jonara looked into Denise's mouth and saw a hole in the lower molar where Eva had started drilling. Jonara also saw many teeth blackened from years of neglect and decay. Jonara stood back and gasped—she had not seen teeth in such a bad state. Jonara was caught in a trap—curious at something she'd never seen before, and petrified at the sight of such disfigurement.

A meow from the cat broke her conflict. It chewed through the twine and broke it into several pieces. Some pieces it ate. Other pieces it carried in its mouth. The cat leapt to the treatment chair and onto Denise's abdomen. It walked along her tummy, across her lungs, and to her neck. The cat stopped and dropped the chewed pieces of twine into Denise's mouth, yet Denise was not aware of these bits of twine in her mouth. The cat sniffed her mouth to ensure the mouth contained a new smell—the smell of twine. But not just the twine itself. The twine had bits of Earth representations built into it—representations the cat had selected just for Denise. Why and for what purpose? Jonara didn't know, but it seemed this cat was intent on causing specific maladies through these bits of twine. Still, Denise did not react to the cat and was not aware of any presence. No feeling of the cat's paws. No notice of the whiskers that to Jonara seemed to tickle Denise's face. No notice of twine.

Jonara couldn't understand what was going on with the cat. Its weight was held by Denise, yet Denise did not notice. Was the cat concerned for Denise? Or was it following an agenda? After sniffing her several more times, the cat looked up at Jonara and meowed as if seeking recognition from Jonara.

Jonara turned toward the hallway but misstepped on the ball of twine, tried to catch herself by running forward, but only managed to get her arms out in front of her to break her fall as she landed in the hallway. She heard her grandmother speak to her mother.

"I have a young patient in the treatment room just around the corner," Eva explained. "Her name is Denise. She's scared and tense. I would like you to help."

"I thought you wanted me to do filing," said Evanita.

"That was to get you started. It was also to show you that without a good education, you'll end up having to follow instructions in an office without question. And perform repetitive, unchallenging tasks. What did you think of filing?" Eva asked.

"Boring. What a horrible job," Evanita answered.

"Some people like it because it isn't too stressful," Eva continued. "But you see how it's not for everyone."

"It certainly isn't for me," Evanita said.

"Exactly. Now, I have something that is a bit more challenging. It's not hard, but it requires some fortitude," Eva said.

"What's 'fortitude'?" Jonara asked. "I know—no one can hear me. But Christine heard me. No, that was different. I wasn't myself—I was in someone else's body."

"I'll try to be strong," said Evanita. "You said there's a patient named Denise in the treatment room, and that I can help."

"Yes. Hold her hand. That's all you have to do. Just make her feel comfortable. She needs to get through today with as little pain as possible. Her teeth need repeated treatments. Yes, she'll have to come back for more appointments, so it's important she wants to come back," Eva explained. "Come along."

Jonara watched Eva and Evanita enter the treatment room. Jonara also saw a rabbit appear at the end of the hallway next to the reception area.

"A rabbit? What's a rabbit doing in Grandma's dental office?" Jonara asked. "Here, bunny-bunny-bunny. Come here. Are you real?"

The rabbit hopped down the hallway toward Jonara. It stopped short of the treatment room's doorway. Jonara walked to the rabbit and picked it up. The rabbit felt comfortable in Jonara's arms and blinked its eyes in relaxed fashion. Jonara walked into the treatment room with rabbit in hand and stood near Denise's feet. The cat had now curled into a ball on a side chair. Its tail flailed up and down in nervous anticipation. For a brief moment, Jonara saw the same symbol on the cat's forehead she had seen on Christine's forehead. The symbol faded.

Evanita sat on a stool next to Denise's left leg and held her left hand. Eva began work on Denise's teeth from Denise's right side while Eva's assistant helped from Denise's left.

"Open wider," said Eva.

Denise strained to hold her mouth open. Eva tapped the top of the dental drill against Denise's upper palate.

"There's no room. I can't get in there," said Eva.

"Try harder, honey," said Eva's assistant. "Open just a little wider."

Denise tried to say, "I can't," but there were too many devices and fingers in her mouth to speak. She gripped Evanita's hand tightly—so tightly that Evanita's fingers turned blue. Evanita used her free hand to pry her cramped fingers from Denise's grip, but Denise fought the effort and grasped tighter. Eva struggled to drill the decayed tooth, but it was no use. She had no room to maneuver the drill. Denise choked on her own saliva.

"Rinse and suction," Eva said after removing the drill from Denise's mouth.

Eva paused for a moment while her assistant followed her instructions.

"Denise, how are you?" Eva asked.

Denise did not say anything. Evanita gave her mother a smirkish look and motioned her eyes as if to say:

"I'm not doing any good. Look at what she's doing to my hand."

"Scary, isn't it?" Eva said to Denise. "Well, you're not alone. There are three women here with you."

"And me!" said Jonara.

"We won't let anyone or anything harm you," Eva continued.

Eva stroked Denise's right forearm twice and patted it softly. Eva looked at Evanita as she did this and motioned with her eyes as if to say:

"Try comforting her with motion instead of being a passive receiver of her pain."

Evanita understood and moved her hands along Denise's left arm as if warming and restoring its blood circulation. Denise attempted to clasp onto one of Evanita's hands as it approached her palm, but Evanita kept her own hands free from being trapped.

"So that's the trick," said Jonara. "Mommy keeps her hands moving so they won't get trapped, and Denise can't transfer her own pain to Mommy."

"Just relax, Denise. Don't build up tension. Now touch your mouth. Does it feel fat, like it is puffy and falling off?" Eva asked.

Denise drew her right hand to her face. Her twitchy hand touched her lower right chin. It felt fat and numb. There was no physical pain in her jaw, and there wouldn't be once Eva began drilling. But something stirred inside her abdomen, some sour churning that no amount of anesthetic could mask.

"Whatever it is, honey, you're safe here. No one can hurt you," said Eva.

Eva, Evanita, and the assistant waited. Denise twitched her right hand over her abdomen. The cat jumped onto Denise's abdomen and bit Denise's hand. Denise jerked her hand back to her side, yet it showed no signs of skin damage—no puncture wounds from the cat's teeth, no sign of blood.

"How could Denise know the cat was there?" Jonara said. "Denise, can you hear me?"

Denise did not reply.

Jonara decided action was needed. Cradling the rabbit in her right arm, Jonara walked to Denise's right side and scooped the cat in her left arm. The cat did not wish to be whisked away. Though Jonara was successful in cradling the cat in her left arm, the cat bit into Jonara's arm. Jonara backed away from Denise with cat and rabbit. The cat continued biting as if feeding on Jonara. The rabbit, who had enjoying being held by Jonara, now wanted nothing to do with her and bit Jonara's other arm to free herself. Jonara ran into the hall. The cat swatted, writhed, and squirmed to get at the rabbit. The rabbit continued biting to free herself from Jonara, but Jonara kept a tight hold on both, ran out of the dental office, and out into the parking lot far from others. The rabbit freed itself. The cat stopped biting, smiled, and purred as if accomplishing something very important.

Jonara dropped the cat to the parking lot. The cat purred and weaved through Jonara's legs. Jonara walked to go after the rabbit, but the cat continued to weave through Jonara's legs to stifle her gait. Jonara increased her gait from a walk to a run, and the cat pounced on Jonara's ankle and bit deeply. Jonara continued running with the cat dragging behind. It would not let go. The rabbit continued avoiding Jonara and disappeared as Jonara reached the edge of the parking lot. Tired and frustrated, Jonara stopped. She turned around and kicked the cat from her ankle. The cat then did something unusual. It ran into the nearly empty parking lot and traced the painted parking lines—not the ones separating adjoining cars, but the ones separating facing cars. The cat did this up and down the parking lot until it reached the end. It smiled, its eyes glowed, and it disappeared.

Confused, Jonara returned to the dental office and Eva's treatment room. Denise had completely relaxed. Her mouth was fully open, and Eva took advantage of the opportunity to drill the lower tooth. Seeing how well Denise handled the drilling, Eva elected to drill out a neighboring tooth with decay. The assistant rinsed and suctioned Denise's mouth. Eva completed the fillings with composite resin and asked Denise to tap-tap her teeth together onto the purple paper. Some final scrapings later, and Denise's two teeth were complete.

"All done!" Eva said. "You did very well. Such a good girl!"

Eva congratulated Denise again and wished her well before stepping out of the treatment room. The assistant led Denise to the front desk where she made her follow-up appointment. Shortly after, Eva returned to the treatment room and spoke with Evanita who had remained behind after Denise's departure. Thinking nothing of the dental visit, Jonara fell into slight boredom and relegated herself to picking up the twine remnants. The ball itself no longer resembled Earth. Instead, it looked like the moon—an object of deadly desolation.

"I would like your help with the next patient, and I must caution you about certain things before we start," said Eva.

"Like what?" Evanita asked.

"He's not a child. In fact, he's twenty-four years old," Eva explained.

"So?" Evanita said.

"So, this is a pedodontic office—dentistry for children. When they become adults, they move on to a general dentist," Eva explained.

"But this patient is over eighteen," Evanita added.

"Yes, he's an adult, but I've been treating him since he was eight. That's sixteen years, Evanita. But Johnny Pindus is different," Eva added.

"Daddy?!" Jonara said. "My daddy is coming? Here?!"

"How is he different?" Evanita asked.

"He's a higher-functioning autistic."

"Oh," Evanita replied with despair and understanding.

"Don't feel sorry for him. He does quite well as long as people don't upset him," Eva explained.

"You can say that about anyone," Evanita replied.

"Yes, but the trick is knowing what upsets him. Things people say. The way people say things."

"Like what?" Jonara asked, hoping her mother would ask the same.

"Like what?" Evanita echoed as if hearing Jonara's question.

"Contradictory information. He takes things very literally. Metaphors irritate him. Short, choppy speech gives him anxiety attacks. Oh yes, I have to be careful there are no televisions around. A political speech will throw him into a Grand Mal."

"What's a Grand Mal?" Jonara asked.

"A Grand Mal seizure. He has epilepsy?" Evanita asked.

"Something like that," Eva answered.

"I don't understand. I thought people have epilepsy or they don't," Evanita said.

"Not always. Some people suffer seizures under extreme stress or deprivation of oxygen. I had Johnny see the neurologist once and—"

"Here you are, Johnny," the assistant announced.

The assistant led Johnny Pindus into Eva's treatment room and into the treatment chair.

"Well hello, Johnny. How are you today?" Eva welcomed.

"Not very well. My tooth hurts," Johnny said.

"Okay, we'll take a peek inside," Eva said. "First I'll recline your chair. There. Are you comfortable? Other than your tooth, I mean?"

"Yes, other than my tooth I'm comfortable," Johnny answered. "Who's the young girl? She has your brown eyes."

"This is my daughter, Evanita. She'll be helping me today."

"How will she help?" Johnny asked.

"I know you don't like surprises, Johnny. She's here to help you feel comfortable. Do you mind if she holds your hand?" Eva asked.

"Hold my hand! Hold my hand!" Johnny agitated.

He felt himself going into a panic at the thought of someone new touching him.

"It's all right, Johnny. That wasn't a commandment. You don't have to hold her hand, and she doesn't have to touch you. Evanita will sit next to you, and if you feel the need for help, you can hold her hand. Remember, no one is forcing you to do anything," Eva offered.

"I don't have to hold her hand?" Johnny asked.

The assistant wiped sweat from Johnny's face.

"No, you don't," Eva said.

"Okay, okay, Johnny will be okay, Johnny will catch his breath for a moment, and Johnny will be okay," Johnny said.

His voice started out broken, but as he regained his composure, his words smoothed out.

"Now I'm just going to take a peek inside your mouth. I promise I'll be very gentle," Eva said. "Could be infection. Could be a food trap. Johnny, what have you been eating lately? Any fruits or vegetables? Anything with a skin?"

"No fruits. I cannot eat fruits. The acid, the acid—it burns through my stomach," Johnny said. "Vegetables turn my feces green. No vegetables."

"Well, you may have something stuck in there—probably between two molars," Eva said.

"Don't touch my teeth, please, they hurt a lot!" Johnny pleaded.

Johnny gripped the armrests tightly with his hands. Evanita instinctively reached for him but stopped herself at the last moment. She remembered that Johnny might feel threatened if she touched him.

"I'm just going to look, Johnny. I won't hurt you, I promise," said Eva. "Can you guess what I'll find when I take a peek?"

"I know what you're going to say. I know, I know. You'll say, 'Gingival inflammation on number two mesial and number three distal.' Is that right?" Johnny cringed.

Eva and her assistant giggled. Evanita and Jonara stared at Eva and her assistant, puzzled.

"Is that right?" Johnny repeated.

"What are 'distal' and 'mesial'?" asked Jonara.

Just as Jonara spoke, Johnny looked forward and down toward Jonara. Jonara gasped. Did he see her? She took one step to her right. Johnny continued to stare at her old location. Jonara took another step to her right and waved her arms wildly yet silently. Johnny continued staring at her old spot, shrugged his shoulders, and looked back at Eva.

"Let me take a peek, and I'll let you know," said Eva.

Johnny opened his mouth. Eva looked inside at his back two molars—his number two and number three teeth.

"Well, you don't have your wisdom teeth, so there's no number one tooth yet. It's true you have gingival inflammation around two and three," said Eva.

"I knew it, I'm right, I'm right!" Johnny said.

Eva and her assistant giggled again.

"Why are they laughing?" Jonara asked.

"Yes, why are they?" Johnny replied.

He looked up again where Jonara stood. She took two steps to the left. He continued to stare at her old position.

"Boo," said Jonara.

Johnny's eyes darted immediately to her new position.

"We're laughing because we wouldn't give that much detail about the gingival inflammation location. We talk about the distal or mesial side of a tooth when there's decay. We also talk about gingiva around a tooth or between teeth. But we don't— Johnny are you listening?"

"Boo," Johnny replied playfully to Jonara.

"Uh oh, Johnny, you're going into your strange mood. Do you need a sugar pill?" Eva asked.

"No, this is real," Johnny replied.

"Daddy, Daddy!" Jonara said.

Jonara ran up to touch him, but her hand went through him.

"Daddy!? Whoa!" Johnny exclaimed.

"Shirl, give him a sugar pill," said Eva.

"No, don't give him a sugar pill, don't. Wait!" Jonara pleaded.

"You can hear them?" Johnny asked Jonara.

Johnny couldn't see her but he could hear her.

"Yes, I'm here in the room with you, Daddy. I can see everything," Jonara said.

"You're here? Daddy? How many fingers am I holding up?" Johnny asked as both hands continued to clasp the arms of the chair.

"None. You're holding onto the chair," Jonara replied.

Johnny let go of the chair and waved his hands in the air.

"Now you're waving your hands," Jonara said.

Johnny placed his hands on his lap.

"Now they're on your lap," Jonara said.

"Here you are, Johnny, you may have one of these," the assistant said.

"But this voice can see me," said Johnny.

"Well, this sugar pill is a silence to the voices," said Shirl.

"Shirl—watch the metaphors!" said Eva.

Johnny consumed the dextrose pill.

"Sugar is not a silence. I'm hypoglycemic—I know that," Johnny said.

"Johnny—is the voice real?" Eva asked.

"It sounds real," Johnny replied.

"I am real," said Jonara. "I'm real, Daddy."

"She says she's real. And she calls me 'Daddy'," Johnny replied.

"Johnny, you hear voices when your blood-sugar level is low. You know this. You have an analytical mind. You can separate logic from feeling. What does your analysis say?" Eva asked.

"My logical side says there is no voice. It's my imagination. The voice isn't real. I'm not a daddy," Johnny said.

"You are. You're my daddy," said Jonara. "Grandma Eva and Mommy can't hear me, but I know you can."

"Do you still hear the voice?" Eva asked.

"Yes, but it's faint. It sounds like it's down the hallway," said Johnny.

"Daddy! I'm still here! With you and Mommy and Grandma Eva!" Jonara said.

Johnny lip-spoke "Mommy" and "Grandma Eva." Those were the last words he heard. The sugar pill took effect and lifted him into a safe blood-sugar level. He wondered if there was any truth to the words, or was it some wishful desire? For the voice to be true, Johnny would have to father a child with Evanita.

"Are you there, voice?" Johnny asked as he waved his hands in the air.

"Yes," Jonara said, but Johnny could not hear her.

"I repeat, can you hear me voice?" Johnny asked again.

"Yes, I can hear you. I'm here!" Jonara replied.

"That's it," Johnny said to Eva. "I can't hear the voice anymore."

"All right, Johnny. Relax and open your mouth wide," said Eva.

Johnny placed his hands back on the armrests. Eva probed inside his mouth with an explorer tool. Johnny winced a little—not so much from pain but in expectation of pain.

"I don't see any fistulas. Probably not an infection. Wait, what is that?" Eva mused.

Johnny feared the worst. He thought of the voice's words—a mommy, a grandma. Family love. He could hear it in the voice. It was something he wasn't used to hearing—quite alien in fact.

He doubted family love really existed. He figured others simply put on a façade to cover up arguments and fighting in the home. But he couldn't see the voice, and no one else heard the voice. There was nothing the voice had to gain by pretending. Had he been wrong about the concept of family love? Did it really exist? He remembered the way the voice said "Mommy" and "Grandma." That would make Eva his mother-in-law. But it wasn't true. He wasn't married and had only just met Evanita. Yet Eva seemed like a mother to him. She had taken care of his teeth since he was eight years old. How would it be to have a mother? His older sister, Valeria, had been like a mother when he was very young, but that seemed so long ago, like recounting the mythology of the ancient Greeks.

Eva removed the explorer from Johnny's mouth.

"I'm going to do some cleaning of the area. Now this might sting a little, but I think it will hurt less than a novocaine injection," said Eva.

Johnny kept thinking back to Valeria. Without conscious inhibition, he touched Evanita's hand with his own, much like he'd once done with Valeria when she read to him from a book named *Bible Stories* ages ago. Evanita received his hand and touched him back. Each held the other's hand with equal force—in this way, Johnny did not feel threatened and was able to take his mind off of Eva's scaling.

"I think I've found it. There. Suction. Good. Rinse and suction," said Eva.

"Ahhh, the pain is gone!" said Johnny.

"See, that wasn't so bad. There was a kernel of corn stuck between the gum line and the last molar," Eva explained.

"Popcorn, yes, that was it," said Johnny. "Too much popcorn."

"Your gums will be tender and will bleed for a few days. Rinsing with saltwater twice a day will help them heal sooner," said Eva.

"I should have never eaten the popcorn. I know better. But the social worker was trying to be nice. She made some popcorn," said Johnny, outlining a huge popcorn kernel in the air.

"Oh, I didn't know you had a social worker. How is that going for you?" Eva asked.

"It's temporary. Because of my sister. Temporary," Johnny said.

"I haven't heard much about Valeria lately. How is she doing?" Eva asked.

Johnny's muscles seized up. He writhed back and forth—holding onto the armrests to torque his body. Evanita placed her hands on Johnny's left hand. Feeling a warm and now trusted touch, he stopped writhing.

"I'm sorry," said Eva. "I didn't mean to say anything to—"

"She died early yesterday," said Johnny.

"I'm so sorry," said Evanita.

"I have an aunt? Aunt Valeria?" Jonara asked, but Johnny did not hear her.

"I thought my toothache was caused by my knowledge of her death," Johnny said, "and the thought of burying her tomorrow at the funeral. I didn't think I would be strong enough with the pain in my jaw. Thanks to you, I can pay my last farewell to my sister."

"I would like to attend Valeria's funeral, Johnny. If you don't mind," Eva said.

"Yes, I'd like that," he replied.

Johnny turned to Evanita and was going to ask her if she would go, but he was shy and wasn't sure.

"Would you mind if I went too?" Evanita asked.

Evanita squeezed Johnny's hand a little harder to let him know she really wanted to go.

"Evanita!" said Eva.

"It's okay. Evanita can attend," Johnny replied.

2006 Sep 23, Sat Morn. Eva's House. Portland, Oregon.

Jonara found herself spinning in place with the backpack on her back. When she stopped spinning, she was in her Grandma Eva's house. She looked inside the backpack but found it empty.

"Mother," said Eva. "Evanita and I are attending a funeral for a patient of mine. We'll be back soon."

"Oh, how sad! How did your patient die? Are you in trouble? I'd like to join you," said Geneva.

"I'm sure Johnny wouldn't mind," said Evanita.

"I didn't lose a patient. My patient's sister passed away," Eva said, and she turned to Evanita, "I don't think your grandmother would like the church."

"Why would I care?" Geneva asked.

"The funeral is at Barnseed Baptist Church," Eva said.

"Baptist! I've never crossed to the other side. Hmmm. I wonder if I could bear it for this occasion?" mused Geneva.

"What are you talking about, Mother?!" Eva said in surprise. "You married a Baptist, you lived as a Baptist, and you started raising me as a Baptist! It was only after our visit to Spain that you decided to fall back to Catholicism."

"I did? Oh, if you say so. I conveniently forgot—" Geneva started.

"All too conveniently," Eva said. "But let's face it, Mother. You know you won't be happy. If you can't handle my Unitarian faith, how can you handle—"

"Yes, but the Baptists believe in something. Unitarians—what do they believe in? Anything?" Geneva asked.

"We've been over this a thousand times, Mother. And I'm not going over it again. I don't think you'd be happy at this Baptist service. But if you can behave—"

"I'll be on my best behavior, Eva," said Geneva. "Besides, I think Evanita would like the company. Death is not a light subject."

Geneva and Evanita exchanged smiles.

"All right. The three of us will go. But please stay out of trouble, Mother," said Eva.

"Of course, dear. Of course."

CHAPTER 7

Barnseed Baptist

2006 Sep 23, Sat Afnoon. Barnseed Baptist Church. Portland, Oregon.

Jonara's view of Eva's house blurred. She found herself outside in a small clearing surrounded by trees. She was on the southern edge of Pittock Acres, a wooded area west of Portland. She stood in awe at the height and power of these trees swaying and rustling in the wind. Losing focus of her immediate surroundings, she relaxed and dropped the backpack to the ground. A windy gust carried the backpack and perched it atop a nearby oak tree.

"What the heck?" Jonara gasped.

She walked over to the oak tree and looked for a way to climb it. The trunk had no lower branches within reach for climbing. She peered up the oak tree. It was a gnarly, twisted, and rigid monster—misshapen by years of inclement weather. Jonara had no rope, no ladder, and no hope of climbing the oak tree. She beat her hand against the oak, but it held fast. She beat it one last time, and her hand bruised.

"Rotten tree," she said despite the tree having no signs of decay.

It was no use attacking the oak from the trunk. She stepped back a few paces, picked up a rock, and threw it high at the oak to knock the backpack down. Her aim, while good, was not enough to reach the upper oak branches where her backpack perched.

Sounds of claws scrambled helically up the oak. Jonara looked closely and saw a squirrel positioned on the edge of an oak branch. The squirrel looked intently at the neighboring evergreen as it swayed to and from the oak. While the evergreen swayed toward the oak, the squirrel leapt and landed on the evergreen. The squirrel scrambled down the evergreen a bit before jumping to an elm, another evergreen, and an oak by which time Jonara lost sight and sound of the squirrel.

"If a squirrel can do it, so can I," Jonara said.

She reached for the lowest branch of the evergreen. Immediately on touching the branch, her hand stuck to clear drops of sap. She tried to wipe the sap off, but this only made things worse by smearing it on her palms. Still, she wasn't willing to give up. Something heavy was in that backpack—something that stretched it and pulled it down—that much she could see. Jonara wanted to know what was inside the backpack, and to find out, she'd have to retrieve it.

She grasped and held the second lowest branch with her hands and pulled her weight up such that she stood on the lowest branch. It held her weight, and she was glad. Unfortunately, her shoes also touched sap. This made them messy and dark on the soles. She ascended the evergreen as if it were a ladder. Her palms grew dark and icky as the sap stuck to all sorts of evergreen particles—the branches, some needles, and an occasional cone. Yet throughout her ascent, the gentle rustling of nearby elm leaves comforted Jonara. To anyone else, the elm leaves would have sounded like random flapping in the wind, but to Jonara, the auditory surges and eddies from the leaves as the wind whisked through them set her mind at ease and helped her forget nagging issues that would not let go— such as why people lie, would her mother die, and what did the future hold. For a time, she remained in the uppermost branches of the evergreen—listening, just listening to the elm leaves fluttering through the wind.

Jonara heard church bells. She looked in the direction where she heard them but could not see the source. She climbed one last branch at the top of the evergreen—a branch she wasn't sure would hold her weight. The evergreen strained to support her. It swayed now not from the rhythms of the wind but from the effects of Jonara scrambling yet higher. Jonara did her best to remain steady, but the evergreen moved under her as if she were attempting to remain balanced atop a soccer ball. With two feet precariously planted on the evergreen and her left hand holding onto the top point, she stood mostly upright and peered toward the church bells.

What was stifling woodsy air on the ground was now fresh, clean air at Jonara's altitude. Straight winds blew into her face and whipped her hair around her neck. She welcomed the sense of freedom and for a timeless moment felt she could stay there forever.

Toward the church bells, she saw the church—Barnseed Baptist Church. The building looked like a tall barn—a barn where one might house animals on the ground level and store hay or straw in the upper level. On a short side closest to her, Jonara saw a large smiley face painted on the building, the smiley face using two upper windows for eyes. Atop the building along the upper center divide were two crucifixes—one at each end. Each crucifix was also a weather vane—the one closest to Jonara used the horizontal bars of the crucifix to indicate east and west while the top supported the image of a hen—this hen spun to indicate the direction the wind was heading. The far crucifix used its horizontal bars to point to north and south with the image of a rooster on top to indicate from where the wind was blowing. Jonara had the wild notion that the hen was flowing with the wind and could travel forever eastward or westward, while the rooster fought the wind and could never freely travel north forever nor south forever.

"Once a rooster reaches the North Pole," Jonara mused, "there's no place to go but south."

Jonara chuckled, but this proved her undoing. Her laughter carried through her body and shook the evergreen enough to weaken its support of her. She fell from the evergreen into the oak, where gnarly branches and a rigid trunk greeted her in a most unfriendly fashion. In sticking out her hands to break her fall, the oak's ridge-filled trunk ripped along Jonara's left side— from her legs up her abdomen into her left arm and along the left side of her face. The trunk roughened her left ear. Jonara grappled a branch with her right arm; the action torqued her body such that her back now took the brunt of the trunk's abrasion, yet her left arm came free and latched onto another branch. In this way, Jonara came to a stop with oak branches under each armpit and the trunk protruding into her back.

The sky blew puffy clouds across the sun, the wind died, and the elm leaves silenced their music. The weather vanes lost direction, and the church bells faded into distant echoes.

Jonara screeched in pain. She was surprised. She knew this was a dream, yet she was in pain—why? She could not answer herself. Besides the pain, she had another problem—she was stuck. Her legs hung freely and could not find a branch to gain a footing. She was wedged between the two branches, and her weight pulled her down such that her arms rose parallel with the ground. Her shoulders increased in pain as her body slipped down and her arms rose higher in the air. The oak branches scraped the undersides of her arms as she slipped. Jonara screeched again. She slipped suddenly and tried to grab the branches as her hands slid across, but only her right hand held fast. Jonara dangled by the grace of her hand. She glanced at the branch, swung her body weight, and wheeled her left arm around and up until she had both hands holding onto the branch. In performing this motion, Jonara caught a glimpse of red in the corner of her eye. She steadied her swing, looked at the red color, and realized it was the backpack. It was now below her several branches but perched out on a branch's edge— toward the evergreen-tree side of the oak. Jonara's only thought in reaching it was to inch her way to the end of the branch from where she swung until she was directly overhead, and then somehow lower herself to the backpack.

The wind picked up, the elm leaves sputtered, and the evergreen leaned ever-so-gently to and from the oak tree, swinging closer and closer as the wind increased. Jonara thought about the squirrel jumping from the oak to the evergreen and wondered how that maneuver might help her. At the moment, it didn't seem helpful, so she continued to edge her way along the oak's branch away from the trunk, hand by hand and knot by knot, with her legs dangling free and searching for some sort of support.

Jonara's legs never found support. The combination of the branch's shrinking diameter coupled with the increased leverage Jonara's weight placed on the branch caused it to give way. First it cracked without completely failing. Jonara looked for an escape from the branch. She watched the swinging of the evergreen and in her mind felt its rhythm, its timing, and its aroma—no, this wasn't the time to enjoy pleasant smells.

The oak branch broke, and Jonara fell suddenly. Her left hand lost grip of the oak branch and flailed wildly in the air. Her right hand continued gripping the now-loose oak branch, and she held firmly to it even though her hand was being smacked by passing oak branches. Despite the crisis, Jonara had managed—with her left hand—to grasp the outstretched evergreen branch and control her descent. With the evergreen branch acting as a radius between her body and the evergreen's trunk, Jonara changed her fall from a shear drop to an arc where her vertical velocity shifted to horizontal. As she began descending beyond the reach of the oak tree, her right hand whipped the still-clutched oak branch like a mace and freed the red backpack from its oak-imprisoned perch.

The backpack descended directly to the earth. Jonara swung into the evergreen, bounced off the trunk, and rolled over and into descending branches until she landed on the ground. She was covered with scratches, bruises, sap, and needles. She remained on the needle-covered ground for a moment and caught her breath while an overhanging evergreen branch swung up and down, lightly brushing her on the head with its needles.

Jonara crawled out from under the evergreen tree and to her relief found the backpack. She tossed the backpack over her shoulder and walked through the woods—the woods of oaks, elms, and evergreens—to the Barnseed Baptist Church grounds. The woods gave way to a large grassy area with a children's playground—assorted slides, large swings, log-built multilevel forts with slide poles and tunnels, several sandboxes, and riding "animals"—figures of cows, horses, and pigs with seats for one person each, a body connected to the ground with a large metal coil, and handles at the side of the head for holding on. Besides the playground, there was a softball diamond and a pavilion with picnic tables. Next to the pavilion was a brick-based barbecue pit—still smoking from the prior weekend's cookout and picnic. Jonara caught a whiff of the aroma and felt hungry—hungry for barbecue chicken, potato salad, and watermelon.

Jonara walked along the grounds toward the church and sat in one of the swings for a moment. It held her weight. The seat was composed of a thick wooden board, and it was suspended by chains to a steel A-frame high above. Jonara looked up and noticed the A-frame was nearly as high as the church itself. It was certainly the tallest swing she'd ever seen. She kicked the sand with her feet and sent the swing back. Repeated kicking sent the swing back and forth in a larger arc with greater velocity. Jonara felt comfortable in the swing with the air rushing through her hair and the changing G forces redistributing her blood circulation.

Church bells broke the wisping wind. Several cars arrived and formed a line behind a hearse in the back of the church. A heavy-set man directed an elderly gentleman to place magnetic flags on each car in the line. The heavy-set man returned to the church, leaving the elderly man outside.

"Church," said Jonara.

Jonara had been having so much fun that she'd forgotten she was on religious ground.

"I remember the last church," Jonara pondered. "The Vice of Christ. Screens falling from the ceiling. A pew on chains."

Jonara realized she again was on a board suspended by chains—like the platform before. She wanted to forget the memory, and an urge to leave her swing came over her. As the swing reached its upward arc going forward, Jonara leapt from the swing, held her position in the air for a moment as if floating, and descended to earth. The backpack remained over her shoulder throughout—which surprised her considering how much trouble it gave her at Saint Stellan's. In any event, Jonara walked around the church in time to meet up with Geneva, Eva, and Evanita.

"Here we are," said Eva. "Has anyone seen Johnny yet?"

"My word. This church looks so plain and ordinary. I'd swear we were going into a barn for a hoedown!" Geneva said.

"Mother, I warned you about venting your opinions. Now be nice!" said Eva. "Johnny is a special patient of mine, and I don't want anything—or anyone—making things worse for him."

"You're so protective, Eva," Geneva said. "If I didn't know better, I'd say you're acting like his mother."

Eva shot a silencing stare at her mother.

"All right, all right, I'll shut my mouth," Geneva said.

"C'mon, you two—the front door is this way," said Evanita.

Evanita led the threesome in through the front of Barnseed Baptist Church. Eva and Geneva continued quibbling but only until the three realized they were in Johnny's company.

Johnny welcomed people as they entered. He remembered each person's name, asked about their family members by name, and even remembered things such as children's ages, their schools, and their interests. He did not shake their hands or hug them. Instead, he settled for a shy and standoffish wave of the hand. He had finished welcoming some friends of Valeria when the three "Evas" walked in—Gen-eva, Eva, and Eva-nita.

"I'm so glad you could come. This is Denise," said Johnny pointing to a girl standing next to him.

"I know you," said Evanita. "We saw each other at the office yesterday."

"It's so good to see you again, Denise. How are you feeling today?" Eva asked.

"Much better, ma'am," said Denise.

"But I know her, I know her," Evanita repeated.

"Yes, Evanita," started Eva. "Johnny mentioned Denise had a toothache. I met her here at the church a couple of months ago during a summer social when you went away visiting your Grandmother Geneva. I've been caring for her teeth since."

"Pleased to meet you, Denise," said Geneva. "I'm Eva's mother and Evanita's grandmother. My name is Geneva Carreña."

"Nice to meet you, Ms. Carreña," Denise said.

"You are Eva's mother," said Johnny. "I've always wondered: are you named after Carreña in Spain? Let's see—Carreña is the capital of Cabrales County in the Province of Asturias—Spain. It's quite small—only about twenty square kilometers with almost five hundred people. But what's interesting about Carreña is its location in the Picos de Europa National Park. These mountains are part of the Cantabrian Mountains in northern Spain. Do you want to know how they were formed? From a collision of the Iberian peninsula with the African plate. And the rain—"

"My dear me! You're a walking encyclopedia!" said Geneva. "We must talk more later."

"Oh, I'm sorry. Sometimes I start talking and can't stop. Thank you again for coming. Please, walk about the church wherever you like. When the service starts, you may sit anywhere, although the section near the front pews and to the right is semi-reserved for the deaf," Johnny explained.

"What do you mean by *semi-reserved*?" Evanita asked.

"Other people can sit there if they wish, but most don't. Most sit some other place so the deaf can sit close to the signer. I sit in the deaf section," Johnny explained.

"You do? Why?" Evanita asked.

Johnny gave an apologetic look to Evanita.

"I am sorry. I shouldn't sit with the deaf, this is true. But Patty—the signer—says it's fine," said Johnny.

"But you didn't explain why. John—" Evanita started.

"Let's pay our respects, Evanita. Johnny doesn't need to be bothered with so many questions," said Eva.

"But I'm not finish—" Evanita replied as Eva pushed her along.

Johnny's attention quickly switched to another set of people entering the church. Geneva, Eva, and Evanita entered the main worship area of the church. The inside had the same shape as a barn but with no hayloft. The three stood behind the back pews. Four columns of pews followed the length of the church from the back pews to the front. At the front-pew end stood a broad stage running from the left side to the right (as one faces the stage). Seven steps led from the center aisle to the stage. Another seven steps led from the left wall to the stage. At the far end of the main stage (from the pews), two steps led to a smaller back stage. On this back stage stood Valeria's casket surrounded by blooming flowers on stands crowding each other for position to be as close to the casket as possible.

The main pulpit stood on the stage one third of the way from the left wall (as seen from the pews) to the right. In front of the right side of the stage at ground level was a three-stepped pedestal with a smaller pulpit—presumably for the signer.

The walls and ceiling were not ornate as they were at Saint Stellan. On the right wall were three murals. They were (from the first pew going toward the last) a scene of Adam and Eve in the Garden of Eden staring across a waterfall-fed lake at a rainbow, a scene of Noah loading animals in pairs aboard the Ark, a scene of Jesus wearing a shepherd's hat and staff (a crook) while tending sheep, and a scene from Revelations where Jesus leads his people on horses against Satan and his followers on pigs.

The left wall had a single opening leading to a smaller building. This smaller building was connected to the barn-like structure of the main church and was known as the hunting lodge. Jonara's backpack tugged a little toward the hunting lodge.

"Not again," Jonara murmured.

Jonara remembered the trouble the backpack had given her at Saint Stellan and hoped it would not be repeated.

Along the remaining left wall of the main church hung photos and paintings of solitary animals—solitary in that each photo or painting only portrayed a single animal. These animals were either viewed from the side or behind—never from the front. Such animals portrayed were ducks, geese, pheasants, quail, deer, elk, and wild boar. Above the images mounted to the wall close to the ceiling and well out of reach of the common person were tools—several bows, a crossbow, some arrows, and a blowgun. Near the back-pew side of the church (furthest from the pulpit) was a special corner where the left wall met the main-entrance wall. This corner contained a mule-drawn plow and a sickle. Several long-stemmed grains—wheat, barley, and rye—protruded from an otherwise empty wooden barrel. Small, partly opened burlap bags of corn and rice snuggled the barrel's base with bits of corn and rice spilling onto the floor.

"Evanita, this is a serious occasion," said Eva as the three walked along the left side past the plow. "We can't be questioning people's decisions, especially those in mourning."

"Oh let her off the hook," said Geneva.

"You need to watch it too, Mother," said Eva.

"Me? Now what did I do?" asked Geneva.

"Calling Johnny a walking encyclopedia was a metaphor. Johnny has trouble with those—he takes things literally and will misunderstand your intent. He will take offense," said Eva.

"Oh," replied Geneva. "Is that what they call it now-a-days? A metaphor? An offense? I remember the days you couldn't say anything without fear of being tortured and killed by Franco's men."

"Mother!" Eva said.

The three and Jonara were beyond the plow and walked along the left wall past portraits of the large game—elk, deer, and wild boar.

"Or worse—watching your family being tortured and killed," Geneva continued.

"Who's Franco?" Jonara asked.

Jonara had largely tagged along and didn't say or do much else. No one heard her.

"Now I pay a compliment to a gifted young man, and it's an offense. All because it's a metaphor," said Geneva.

"You know that's not what I mean. You're blowing this all out of proportion," Eva said.

"That's another thing. These little American things that are made out to be huge issues—they are nothing compared to what my generation went through," said Geneva. "You could never understand."

"Don't start. Not again. Please," pleaded Eva.

Geneva turned red and wanted to say more. Instead, she placed a finger along and between her incisor teeth such that the finger poked out the side of her mouth. She bit down slightly.

"She's biting her finger instead of biting her tongue. She's saying she'll—" Evanita said.

"Yes, I know what she's saying, Evanita," said Eva. "And I hope she keeps quiet as she suggests."

The three (and Jonara) now stood at the opening to the hunting lodge, taking a brief look inside without entering.

"Speaking of offensive," said Geneva in reference to the lodge.

"Ahp, ahp, ahp," uttered Eva to quiet her mother.

The three stood for a moment at the opening, dumbfounded at the wall-mounted animals and firearms in the lodge. The weight inside Jonara's backpack tugged again and twisted her body slightly. It wanted to pull her into the lodge. She twisted back to regain her control over the backpack.

"Let's continue to the casket. I'm sorry Valeria had to die this way, but I'd like to see her one last time," said Eva.

The three and Jonara continued toward the main stage.

"How did she die?" Jonara asked.

"You know how she died? How?" Evanita asked Eva.

"I sound like my mommy," said Jonara.

"I read it in the newspaper," replied Eva. "She died of heart failure from bulimia."

The four continued along the left wall more or less in silence—passing the photos and paintings of the smaller game—the birds. The phrase, "heart failure," echoed in Jonara's mind. It was a scary thought that one's heart could suddenly fail. She thought of the birds on the wall having heart failure from being hunted—would the sharp gunshot sound frighten them to death before the bullets or shots ended their blood circulation? She imagined herself a bird being unable to out-fly approaching missiles from a shotgun. She thought back to the rabbit in Grandma Eva's dental office and at first was thankful she didn't see a rabbit's portrait on the wall. But as the group passed the first pew, Jonara noticed on the wall below eye level were portraits of three different sorts of rabbits—an eastern cottontail, a snowshoe hare, and a white-tailed jackrabbit.

"So they hunt those too," said Jonara.

The three (and Jonara) ascended the steps to the main stage then on to the back stage to Valeria's casket. It was partly open with the upper half of Valeria's body visible.

"She looks so young and healthy," said Geneva. "How could such a woman die of heart failure?"

"She was thirty-five—at least that's what the newspaper said."

"Prayer cards," said Geneva. "Here, Evanita, take one. Use it as a bookmark during spiritual readings."

"But I don't read spiritual—" Evanita started to say.

"Still," Geneva cut in, "thirty-five is too young to die from heart failure—at least here in America."

"What is that supposed to mean?" asked Eva. "And don't go into another one of your Franco regime stories."

"That's exactly where I've seen it before. Women worked to exhaustion just to get a little food on the table," said Geneva. "Valeria died of exhaustion too."

"Well this is America. Things like that don't happen," said Eva. "So she couldn't have died from just exhaustion."

"She does look thin," said Evanita.

"Yes, overwork will do that," said Geneva.

"Mother, please," said Eva to Geneva. "I happen to know Valeria and Johnny well."

"How well?" asked Geneva.

"Johnny comes into my office frequently. He tells me about Valeria. And I've met her a few times. She's always had a slim figure," Eva explained.

"I don't understand," said Evanita.

"She was probably bulimic," said Eva. "This would give her heart failure at an early age."

"You know she was bulimic? She told you?" Geneva asked.

"No, she did not tell me. Girls usually don't admit to having bulimia. But her symptoms suggest it," said Eva.

"Speculation," said Geneva.

"Perhaps," replied Eva. "But it was in the newspaper—in her obituary. 'Valeria suffered from bulimia in her adulthood'."

"What a strange thing to write in an obituary!" said Geneva. "I find it hard to believe."

"That's what the paper printed," said Eva.

"There's only one way to be sure," said Geneva.

"Sorry, but it's too late. No autopsies were performed. I checked with the hospital where she was treated. She died there, Mother. There were plenty of witnesses to observe her death. The doctor in charge deemed it unnecessary to have an autopsy performed. Johnny was against it as well," Eva said.

"That wasn't what I meant. You know there's another way," said Geneva.

"No there isn't," Eva said with a grimace, hiding the fact she knew of the other way.

"You're a dentist. You should know of all people," said Geneva.

"What is the other way?" asked Evanita.

"I can't do it here with everyone looking. It's disrespectful. Besides, everyone will think I'm crazy—when in reality it's my crazy mother up to another one of her games," said Eva. "And don't you think the mouth is sewn closed?"

"What is the other way?" Evanita asked again.

"You won't tell her?" Geneva asked Eva.

Eva held fast in defiant silence.

"Very well. It's like this, Evanita. Bulimics have damaged front teeth. Well not exactly. The front teeth are damaged, but not the front of the front teeth," explained Geneva.

"The stomach acid eats away the enamel on the backside of the front teeth," Eva clarified. "The exposed dentin will be yellow at first. Later, there's pitting and blackening."

"I'll give you cover," said Geneva. "Watch for my lead."

"I refuse to participate," said Eva.

"Here, Evanita. Give these to your mother when she comes to her senses," said Geneva.

Geneva handed Evanita a dental mirror, a penlight, and denture cream.

"What's the denture cream for?" Evanita asked.

"To seal the lips. Your mother will have to break the wire or thread holding the closed mouth," said Geneva.

"Eeeeuuu!" said Evanita.

"Mother, no! Don't disrupt the church!" Eva pleaded.

Too late. Geneva walked back toward the barrel with the grains.

"Your grandmother is going to do something foolish," Eva said to Evanita. "And I must stop her. Wait here."

Eva left Evanita at the casket. With Geneva's help, the barrel tipped over and crashed into the plow. The plow tipped from the wall and fell onto the floor. Geneva tripped on the bag of corn, lost her footing, and crashed into a nearby vase—shattering it. The vase sent the sickle flying, and it bounced off a pew—narrowly missing a sitting parishioner. Geneva did not bleed, but she was bruised.

The racket echoed through the church. Eva—walking toward Geneva and halfway between the casket and the barrel—first threw her hands in the air and followed by clasping her hands on her head. Evanita stood at the casket with her hands holding the mirror, penlight, and denture cream. She didn't know what to do with herself or the instruments. Evanita had also been startled by Geneva's run-in with the barrel. But Evanita noticed the people in the church were briefly distracted by Geneva's ruckus—distracted enough that someone might have the chance to open Valeria's mouth and inspect the incisors' backside.

Eva and several ushers tried restoring order to Geneva and the corner of barrel-plow-sickle ornaments. Geneva resisted and insisted on hiding herself between the barrel and the wall. Eva spoke sharply toward her mother—urging her to come out from behind the barrel and behave herself. The ushers attempted to aright Geneva, but she fought them off.

In those moments while Geneva clung to the barrel, Jonara found herself in an uncomfortable situation. Something in the backpack came to life with a mind of its own. It was heavy and solid—like steel. It pushed into Jonara's back between two ribs like a steel broom handle. A steel clicking sound pierced the air, and Jonara realized what the heavy object was—a gun. She was being held up by her backpack!

"I have nothing to steal," said Jonara.

The gun prodded her to turn around—away from the casket—and walk into the lodge. She complied, shuffling along the stage, down the steps, and along the left wall as best she could to avoid being shot.

"What do you want of me?" Jonara asked the gun.

The gun did not answer. It held her briefly in the doorway—the doorway between the main church and the hunting lodge. Jonara had seen the wall-mounted animals and firearms on her first walk-by when the other three first passed by. Now she could see more plainly a small staircase along the far wall leading up along the wall to a mockup of a tree hut. Inside the tree hut was a mannequin of a hunter in full winter orange coat and hat with a rifle pointed to an arrangement of stuffed deer and other game on the floor below.

The gun prodded Jonara to move on. Jonara walked as the gun directed, and she came across the arrangement of deer and other game. The deer was no imitation—it was an actual deer now stuffed and propped up. Its fur was not like the softness of a living animal but rather was stale and brittle like an old horsetail paintbrush left out in the sun all summer. Jonara reached to touch the deer, and her fingertips caught the cold, stiff, leathery hide of what was once a living deer.

Jonara threw the backpack to the ground and ran for cover. The gun exited completely from the backpack, floated up, and followed her as if a man held it. In Jonara's mind, she saw a male Homosapien wield the cold steel with fixed intent and focus on hunting her down. She hid under the staircase's base as best she could, but there was no cover. The gun was slightly angled toward the floor as it made its approach. At close range, it stopped. It hesitated before lifting its aim from the floor in front of Jonara to Jonara herself.

Jonara shook in terror. Her heart pounded, her muscles twitched, and she gripped the staircase above her in nervous anxiety as she awaited the final moment—the end—the heart failure she was sure would take her life before the gun's bullet.

The staircase shook and shook. Harmonic waves built up in the staircase like a tsunami in a bathtub. The waves built up energy back and forth until at the final moment of excitation, Jonara's heart stopped, the gun fired, and the mocked-up hunter at the top of the staircase toppled and flipped over the banister to the floor below—into the stuffed deer. The mockup gunman had a real rifle, however. It was loaded, and in its collision with the mock deer managed to cock and fire a randomly-aimed round into the hunting lodge's side wall.

The church people froze in fear and turned their attention to the hunting lodge. An usher rushed to the lodge to see what had happened, but another usher—in fear—bolted through the main church door to the outside. First a trickle then a flood of church people followed the scared usher out the front door. One person yelled, "Terrorists!" which only increased the crowd's desire to exit.

"This is it," whispered Evanita to herself referring to the commotion. "This is Grandma's distraction."

Evanita pried Valeria's mouth open with the dental mirror and penlight. She saw a string (much like floss) tied around two incisors—one upper, the other lower—and kitty-corner to each other. Evanita untied the knot to the string and loosened Valeria's jaw. She pried it open, turned on the penlight, and positioned the dental mirror behind the front-lower incisors. Clean. New. Unblemished. Evanita positioned the dental mirror behind the upper incisors and looked for damage. None. The backs of the upper incisors were as healthy, solid, and white as the lowers. Evanita angled the mirror throughout the mouth looking for bad teeth but found none. Stuffed cotton in the back of Valeria's mouth prevented Evanita from inspecting the throat. Before she could decide if she should remove the cotton, a hand touched her on the shoulder.

"What are you doing?!" said a familiar voice.

Evanita jumped. She was startled, embarrassed, and afraid of the consequences. She turned to see Johnny Pindus staring down at her. He was visibly upset—whether by the funeral, the gunshots, or her own tampering with Valeria's body—Evanita wasn't sure. She didn't have time to think. She stood frozen in fear for a few seconds, and in those seconds, norepinephrine flooded her brain. She fled. Her feet felt as light as day, but her heart felt the heavy terror of night. The church meant nothing— the pews were a blur—all Evanita knew was run, run, run—out the main door into the throng huddled outside, beyond, and around a row of bushes where she threw herself onto the ground and out of sight.

Three rabbits in hiding.

Jonara felt quite odd. She was injured by the gun—but how badly? She checked for bullet wounds but found nothing. Instead, she had a feeling she needed to crawl out of her skin. She crawled out from under the staircase and stood up—flexing her arms and legs. No injuries. Her blouse and capris were clean—no blood. She reached over her shoulder for the backpack. It wasn't there. Of course it wasn't. Jonara was a little disoriented and couldn't remember where to look for the backpack. She stared at the fallen collection of deer, hunter, gun, and rifle on the floor. Yes, the backpack was there—wrapped around the deer's hind leg. The gun that had threatened her was lying atop the backpack—it was still smoking from firing its round.

"I must make the gun harmless," she said.

It was a confused thought. How does one make a gun harmless? Her thought was to wrap it in something. Not that this would prevent its use—the gun had been in a form of wrapping before (the backpack). But Jonara was compelled to perform the act to satisfy some unknown need. She remembered a small, thin mat under the staircase where she had hidden, and she turned around—back to the staircase—to retrieve it. To her surprise, she saw someone there, hiding in the same spot as she had.

"Who, who are you?" she asked the person.

The person asked the same question. Jonara looked closer and realized the person was herself, but instead of being dressed in a blouse and capris, this girl was dressed in a Victorian dress in the color of deoxygenated red blood. Over the dress, she wore a white pinafore with a white bow on her back —both heavily trimmed in black and white. In this way, the white pinafore appeared to cover a black pinafore which in turn appeared to cover another white pinafore. The pockets were black with white trim.

Jonara realized she was both girls and in some strange fashion was able to experience both girls simultaneously— seeing and hearing from both positions and knowing what was being said to which. When she spoke to herselves, the net effect was an echoing reverberation in her minds.

"I am Victorian Jonara," said the girl in the dress.

"I know. You also know I'm Modern Jonara," said the blouse-and-capris Jonara. "Your dress—"

"Yes," said Victorian. "It's blue-baby red. Deprived of oxygen. My dress is covered with no color—the lifeless divide of black and white."

"Come with me," beckoned Modern.

"I can't. I'm not allowed," said Victorian.

Modern held out her hand, expecting to pull Victorian from under the staircase. Instead, Victorian handed Modern the thin floor mat.

"I want—we want—to wrap the gun with this," Modern explained.

"It isn't necessary for me," said Victorian.

"It is for me. But I can't do it by myself," said Modern. "We must do it together."

"No, I'm frightened," said Victorian.

"The gun split us apart. It wants us to stay apart. We must stick together," said Modern.

"Only if I can follow behind," said Victorian.

"Yes, of course. Give me your hand," said Modern.

Victorian held out her left hand, and Modern helped her from the staircase. In a strange way, Jonara felt she was holding her own hand and could have helped herself out with both Modern and Victorian blindfolded. Victorian cleared the staircase and stood fully upright. She faced Modern and placed her hands in her pockets. Modern turned about and faced the deer and gun collection. In so doing, she showed her back to Victorian. Victorian kept her hands in her pockets, but of course Modern knew this. Modern reached behind to Victorian's hands—knowing precisely where they were—pulled them from Victorian's pockets, and placed them on Modern's hips. Victorian knew this would happen and cooperated. She was reserved about doing things at first, but once Modern took the initiative, Victorian followed. Victorian kept her head down and leaned against Modern's back.

Modern and Victorian walked in unison such that anyone seeing them would have imagined them as a four-legged animal. Their footwork was coordinated, their body weights shifted together, and their sense of direction was focused. Victorian had no need to see where she was going—Jonara as the whole person had the thoughts of both, and as long as the two kept in physical contact, the two were as one.

Modern and Victorian halted stride at the fallen deer and red backpack. Next to the backpack was the gun. Modern and Victorian knelt. Victorian hugged Modern while Modern placed the floor mat over the gun as if placing a facial tissue over a dead spider. She placed both hands together face down on the mat such that the gun was underneath. Then in one smooth motion, Modern slid her hands apart and back together, scooping the floor mat under the gun. The gun was sealed in floor-mat material. Modern kept her hands under the bundle and lifted it up, and in the same motion, Modern and Victorian stood up with Victorian preserving her hug.

"You know what must be done," said Modern.

"Yes," said Victorian. "I know."

"It must be buried," continued Modern.

"Quickly then," said Victorian. "I don't want to stay frightened."

Modern used her elbows to tap Victorian's waist-hugging arms three times. Victorian backed off to her original hands-on-hips stance, and the two moved as one out a side door from the hunting lodge to the outside grounds. The two moved with the grace and stamina of a gazelle—moving from a walk to a trot and a canter with little effort. They continued beyond the playground into the woods back to the very oak tree where Jonara as a whole person had struggled to retrieve her perched backpack.

The two stopped. Modern and Victorian turned to face each other and smiled as they caught their breaths. They knelt to the ground while maintaining their face-to-face position and dug furiously with their hands at the base of the oak tree. Oak roots did not hinder them. In fact, Modern was amazed at how easily Victorian broke through the old oak's roots with simple fist chops.

"You do well when you're away from danger," said Modern.

"The danger is still here with the gun and the oak," said Victorian. "I am frightened of it. But I have no fear of attacking the roots hidden from view—where the oak least expects."

"Tree roots can go deep," said Modern.

"But oak roots never do," replied Victorian. "An oak has no tap root, no desire for lifelong security. Shallow roots make it easier to uproot than one might think."

"But who thinks of uprooting an oak with its hard wood and tall stance? The frontal attack is always the first thought," said Modern.

"For a boy, yes," said Victorian.

Both girls smiled. Victorian ran off and returned with a bucket of water. Modern placed the wrapped gun in the hole amidst the broken roots. Victorian dumped most of the bucket's contents into the hole. Both girls followed by filling the hole with dirt.

"It feels like watering a new plant, a new seed," said Modern.

"But this seed will grow into rust, and the oak will drink the rust and experience the fruit of its labors," said Victorian.

Modern wasn't sure what Victorian meant. It seemed like something Jonara had heard before from an adult somewhere. The two completed the job by stomping on the dirt mound covering the gun. Each took turns holding the bucket and pouring out the remaining water while the other rinsed her hands from dirt, the gun, and the oak.

"Look," Modern said as she pointed to the base of the oak tree.

A symbol briefly appeared on the trunk—the same symbol as Jonara had seen on Christine's forehead.

"What does it mean?" Victorian asked.

"I don't know. But I've seen it before, and I don't understand why," Modern said.

Without another word, the two returned to the four-legged formation and celebrated by repeatedly stotting (jumping vertically) high in the air like a gazelle. They jumped up near the oak and evergreen where Jonara the Whole had climbed, they jumped near some elm trees, and they jumped around and about the clearing.

Their celebration ended when the backpack rolled into the clearing from the woods adjoining Barnseed Baptist Church. The Jonaras broke formation. Modern picked up the backpack. It had something else inside. Modern reached inside the backpack and found a book titled *Bible Stories*. She returned the book to the backpack, and Victorian helped place the backpack over Modern's shoulder.

"There is a new need," said Victorian.

"Yes," said Modern. "We must find the preacher's car."

"It's at the doughnut shop," said Victorian. "You know I'm right."

"Yes, but sometimes I don't know how you're right," said Modern. "It seems the knowledge pops into your head."

"We saw the car during one of our jumps above the tree line," said Victorian. "You were thinking about something else."

"Let's make for the doughnut shop. We'll have to run like a pronghorn antelope to catch the preacher's car," said Modern.

The two reformed the four-legged stance with Victorian's hands on Modern's hips again. Modern leaned forward with more intent for speed, and Victorian placed her body more forlorn with intent to push Modern in great strides. They leapt forward into a full, four-legged run—with Modern providing control and balance while Victorian supplied incredible power strokes—even in Victorian dress and pinafore. Yet Victorian's dress did not impede her stride.

Jonara as one four-legged person thundered up a hill, dance-slid down a slope, streamed through the air, dodged cars, and avoided low flying ducks. She arrived out of breath at the doughnut shop where they stopped, broke formation, and sat in the preacher's car—exhausted. Victorian sat behind the driver's seat, and Modern sat next to her.

"Oh Lord, will it never end," Patty said, not realizing she had an audience.

"Is that the preacher?" Victorian asked.

"The heavy man making eyes at the cashier girl? I think so," replied Modern.

"She can't hear us, can she?" asked Victorian, knowing what the answer would be.

"Patty, the preacher's wife? No, she can't," replied Modern.

"You used to be a thin man, a giving man, Jeremiah Ephram," continued Patty. "Now you're overweight, overbearing, selfish, and cruel. How can you in good faith continue to be the pastor of Barnseed Baptist Church? And why am I—Ms. Patty Bugle Ephram—still your wife? No—my fault—why are you my husband? Faith is dead, faith is dead."

Pastor Ephram finished chatting with the cashier. He carried his bag of doughnuts and full coffee cup to a nearby table—placing both on the table. He reached inside his right pocket and retrieved a bubble pack of pills. With ease, he popped three pills into his mouth and chased them down with his coffee. Following the coffee, he placed a doughnut in his teeth and held it there as he exited the doughnut shop. He returned to the car with the bag of doughnuts in one hand and the cup of coffee in the other. He opened the car door and sat. Immediately on sitting, the Jonara girls noticed a sudden drop in the car's suspension.

"He's heavy," Modern and Victorian echoed.

"Patty, I can't believe I came home early from bow hunting just for this funeral," said Pastor Ephram.

The pastor took several bites from the doughnut, placed it on the dashboard, and flipped the rear-view mirror on the windshield so he could see his face.

"How do I look?" the pastor asked.

As the pastor stared at the mirror, he combed his hair frantically while chewing the doughnut bite.

"You look—" Patty started.

"Fine, I know. Oh what is this world coming to?" he ranted. "This doughnut is no good, the coffee's bland, and I gotta rush through this service before I head to the Southeast for another conference. Rush, rush, rush!"

Pastor Ephram flicked the shift lever into Reverse, whipped the car backward into a 90-degree turn, slapped the shifter into Drive, and launched his full weight on the gas pedal. The coffee launched from the center-placed coffee holder and dumped its contents in the back seat between Modern and Victorian. Both girls scooched away from the coffee.

"Dang nabbit! Look what you made me do, Patty!" Pastor Ephram continued.

"Jeremiah, you did—"

"I don't want no backlip from you, Missy. Just look sweet and shut up!"

The pastor raced into a busy boulevard and jockeyed around cars between lanes. He honked his horn playfully. The horn not being enough noise, he turned on the radio and switched stations quickly with the volume up.

"Heh, heh, heh. These new diet pills work great. I'm gonna lose a hundred pounds before pheasant season is out. But man! There are a bunch of slow drivers on the road today. Don't you think so? Of course you do. Who's the best man you've ever had, huh Sugar Pie? Yeah, you know it's me!" said Ephram.

The pastor yelled these words to overpower the radio clatter, but the cacophony gave Patty a headache. She rubbed her temples with her right hand for relief.

Victorian alternated between holding her hands over her eyes to avoid seeing the reckless driving and holding her hands over her ears to avoid hearing Pastor Ephram's boasting. Modern simply stuck her finger in her mouth as if to induce vomiting. She did not vomit, of course, she merely let Victorian know how she felt about Pastor Ephram. The girls knew each other's thoughts, but each felt the need to express herself through gestures.

"Ugh," said the pastor.

Pastor Ephram pulled the doughnut from the dashboard and left a sticky mess. His wild driving had not dislodged the doughnut, but his fat fingers easily brought it to his mouth.

"Remind me to have you clean that up, won't you Sugar? No, don't thank me now. Say a good prayer for both of us, will you then? That's right, no need to say it out loud," said the pastor.

Patty always wanted to say something back, but Pastor Ephram was so quick tongued and kept throwing insults quicker than she could react. Pastor Ephram finished his doughnut and reached over to wipe his hand on Patty's skirt. Patty maneuvered her purse quickly from right to left and blocked his hand. Instead, he wiped his hand on her purse, which was already heavily stained from past foods—foods that could not be cleaned off.

"Oh, your purse—how did that get so dirty?" he taunted. "You gotta do a better job of keeping your stuff clean, Patty. 'Cleanliness is next to Godliness,' as the Good Book says."

"I don't remember that from the Bible," said Victorian.

"It's a Bible myth," said Modern. "People think it's in the Bible, but it isn't."

"What?" asked Victorian. "I can't hear you over the radio."

"Turn off the radio!" Patty yelled.

Patty's lips moved, but no one could hear her over the radio. She reached for the radio to turn it off, but Ephram batted her hand down.

"Don't mess with that!" he growled.

Ephram wheeled the car into the church driveway. Patty saw Evanita lying on her side by the bushes nearby. Filled with fear for Evanita's health, Patty yelled for Ephram to stop the car. Ephram heard nothing and continued down the driveway. Filled with a sense of urgent need paired with helplessness, Patty gritted her teeth and pulled the emergency brake (located between herself and Ephram) with the intensity of a mother whose child was in mortal danger.

The rear wheels locked. Ephram had been too busy guarding the radio and steering the car to consider anything else that might challenge his authority. Patty's action had taken him by surprise. His first reaction was to push the gas pedal to the floor. This drove the front wheels hard into the pavement and lunged the car forward while the locked rear wheels fishtailed.

Modern and Victorian felt an invisible barrier rise between them—like plate glass. They each placed a hand against the barrier to touch the other but could not. Meanwhile, Patty—who was already tense after seeing Evanita—had fallen into a deep fear for her own life. Ephram had clearly exceeded his outrageous behavior, and she could only think of one primal thought—run! She opened the door and jumped out. Simultaneously, Modern's door opened, and her backpack tugged her out. Both rolled onto the grass by the driveway and into a small ditch. The car swerved again. Its fishtail action whipped the two doors closed. Realizing what had happened, Ephram released his foot from the gas pedal and stomped the brake pedal. He braced himself for the sudden deceleration, but Victorian (who had no warning) slammed into the back of Ephram's chair.

Ephram didn't notice Victorian, but he did realize Patty had left his control. He unlatched the emergency brake, slammed the car into Reverse until he reached Patty's position, slammed the brakes (which sent Victorian back into her seat), and kicked open the passenger door.

"Patty, get in the car!" Ephram yelled.

Evanita had been self-absorbed until this point. She switched from worrying about Johnny catching her with Valeria to being outraged that some man was yelling at a woman who had fallen out of a car. In the seconds Ephram spent yelling at Patty, norepinephrine resurged through Evanita's brain. Modern had originally started walking over to her mother (Evanita) to assist, but Modern stopped short in amazement. Evanita did not care who was in the car—she marched to the open door with fierce determination.

"Move it, buster!" she yelled into the car.

Evanita slammed the door. Modern raced to the driver's side of the car and struggled to let Victorian out. Victorian remained trapped. Ephram lowered the electric window next to Evanita and yelled something back about being Satan in a girl's body.

Then the pounding began, like a hailstorm on a sunny summer afternoon. Modern beat on Victorian's door in vain. Victorian beat on the back of Ephram's seat. Evanita beat on the car's hood with both hands like a drum. Ephram should have only felt the hood beating, but somehow Victorian's and Modern's beatings carried through too. The radio broke a connection and cut out. The doughnut rattled off the dashboard. Ephram's heart pounded in his chest.

"I'm having a coronary!" he found himself saying. "I've got to escape the demons around me!"

Pastor Ephram jammed the gas pedal to the floor and shot the car into the private parking lot in back of the church. Evanita spun off a little from the racing car but was uninjured. Modern stood in bewilderment as to where Victorian went. For the first time, Jonara felt slightly disconnected and confused now that her halves were separated by distance.

"The nerve of that man!" muttered Patty.

Patty brushed the dirt from her arms and stood up with the help of Evanita.

"Are you hurt?" Evanita asked.

Patty stood up and brushed dirt from her legs. Evanita brushed dirt from Patty's back. Modern walked up and brushed dirt from Patty's side, but her hand went through Patty's body like air.

"I'm fine," said Patty.

"What happened?" Evanita asked.

"I saw you lying by the bushes. You looked hurt. I wanted to help, but—well, you saw the rest. How embarrassing," said Patty.

Patty made some gestures in the air as if to say, "Sigh."

"You know sign language?" Evanita asked.

"Yes. I'm sorry, I'm being rude. My name is Patty Ephram," said Patty.

Evanita returned a puzzled look.

"I'm the signer," Patty continued.

"Signer?" Evanita asked.

"Don't you know? When Jeremiah—when Pastor Ephram leads the service, I translate his words into sign language for the deaf—more or less."

"You're his helper?" Evanita asked.

"Goodness gracious me—you're not part of the flock, are you child?" Patty asked.

"The flock? I don't know about the flock. This is my first time here," Evanita explained.

"Yes of course, forgive me child. Come, let's go inside. You're here to pay last respects," Patty said.

The two strolled along the drive to the front entrance. Evanita walked on Patty's right while Modern walked on the left.

"What's your name, child?" Patty asked.

"Evanita. Are you the preacher's wife?"

Patty did not answer but instead glanced down and held a silence. The two (plus Modern) reached the front door.

"Wait," said Evanita as the two stopped at the front door. "I shouldn't go in."

"I know, I know," said Patty as she gave Evanita a hug. "Jesus has taken Valeria to a better place. All that remains here is a shell."

"No, I—" Evanita started.

Evanita wanted to explain about inspecting Valeria's teeth and being caught by Johnny, but how? Perhaps Johnny wouldn't notice her coming back into the church.

"You're with family today, aren't you?" Patty asked.

"How did you know?" Evanita asked.

"How does she know?" Modern wondered.

"I know. You have been well-loved. Come—let's go inside. There's nothing to fear in the Lord's House," said Patty.

Patty, Evanita, and Modern reentered Barnseed Baptist Church in the midst of other people who reentered. Johnny re-welcomed the visitors and assured them there was no danger.

"No, it wasn't a gun. Lightbulbs broke in the lodge. Yes, it'll be cleaned up. Please, relax," Johnny repeated.

"Over there," Evanita said to Patty. "My mother and grand-mother."

Patty and Evanita rushed over to the back-pew left corner where Geneva sat on a small bench.

"Oh I'm all right," said Geneva. "Just lost my balance."

Eva rolled her eyes but welcomed Evanita in her arms. The two hugged.

"I saw you run out. Are you hurt?" Eva asked.

"No," said Evanita. "Mama, Grandma—this is Patty."

"A pleasure to meet you," Patty spoke and signed.

"Well hello," said Geneva. "You're the signer, aren't you?"

"Yes," Patty spoke and signed.

"I'm sorry to be so much trouble. My balance isn't what it used to be," Geneva said.

Music echoed through the church.

"Come, Mother, let's find a seat," said Eva, then she turned to Patty and said, "Nice to meet you."

"Please stay after the service," said Patty. "There are re-freshments for all."

"We will," said Evanita. "We will."

Geneva, Eva, and Evanita sat in the middle on the right side of the church facing the pulpit. Modern followed Patty. Patty returned to the front entrance where she met with Johnny Pin-dus.

"How are you, Johnny?" Patty signed.

Johnny replied in sign language. The two engaged in conversation back and forth in this way for a moment. Modern wasn't sure what the two were saying, but it seemed friendly. Patty gave Johnny a hug and left for the lodge. Johnny finished greeting guests and took a seat in the church—sitting with folk in the deaf section.

Modern was amazed to find out her father knew sign language. Why didn't he ever tell her? Why didn't he talk about this day, Modern's Aunt Valeria—why, why, why? Modern remained at the front door for a moment. What to do next? Should she follow Johnny to the deaf section and attempt communication with him—like in the dental office? Should she see what her mother was up to with Grandma Eva and Nanna Geneva? No, Modern knew where she had to go. She was separated from her other half. Victorian was with Pastor Ephram, and only the Lord knew how she was faring. The backpack was no help—it had pulled and prodded Modern in the past, but at that moment it did nothing. She pulled *Bible Stories* from the backpack. She opened it and thumbed through it. No, nothing stood out. Wait. There was one scene where Moses's mother held her baby before setting his basket in the Nile and waving goodbye. Another where Jesus knelt, and his hands were outstretched to receive a limping sheep. Modern flipped again and found a scene where two men held up Moses's arms to help his army.

Modern placed the book in the backpack and lifted both arms in the air. For a moment, her arms felt light, but something pulled them down a bit—level with her shoulders and parallel with the floor. She ran after Patty and placed her hands on Patty's waist. Amazingly, her hands did not pass through Patty's body like air as she had expected. Patty did not notice Modern's contact and proceeded to the lodge.

In this way, Modern was now the follower and Patty the leader. Patty did not run as Modern and Victorian had. Nor did Modern feel the unity in mind as she did with Victorian. She did feel something else—the calm wake of an assertive woman, whose walk, motion, and gestures were part of a clear plan with no room for waste or want. For once, Modern felt the worries of her environment fade, and calmness took hold of her. Modern was convinced Patty was more than a signer. Modern sensed a dancer in Patty—ballet maybe, possibly with some gymnastics training. Patty's moves were coordinated and well-placed.

"I'm not just following," whispered Modern. "I'm learning how to walk in style."

Patty entered the lodge. She stopped, yet Modern continued and bumped into Patty. Patty didn't notice, but for Modern it was the sad end to her enjoyable walk with Patty. Modern walked around to Patty's left side and stood with her as witness. On the other side stood Pastor Ephram by the fallen deer, the gunman mannequin, and several broken lightbulbs. There was no fallen rifle to Modern's surprise. She didn't remember the lightbulbs, and she was sure there had been a rifle on the ground. From her vantage point, she saw none. But she did see something else that caught her breath—Victorian dragging behind Pastor Ephram with her mouth gagged and her hands tied behind her back. She scuffled behind Pastor Ephram like a sullen pony.

Patty closed the heavy oak door between the lodge and the church. Modern expected to hear a loud "slam" but instead heard nothing. Pastor Ephram yelled something, but again Modern heard nothing. Patty walked over to Ephram in a steady gait. Modern walked with her. Ephram threw something at Patty and shouted something—at least he appeared to the way his neck tensed and his jaw popped open. Again, Modern heard nothing except the music muffling through the oak door from the church.

"Victorian," Modern said, but while her vocal cords vibrated and her lips moved, she could not hear herself speak.

Victorian appeared to say something, but Modern could not hear.

"I am deaf then," Modern said.

Ephram threw something else at Patty. She batted it away. Another thing he threw, and she caught it. She said nothing back but instead made sign-language gestures. Ephram held up his index finger and pointed at her in some suggestion that she not defy him. He threw something else at her, and she jumped aside.

Modern watched this exchange and likened it to a dance. Pastor Ephram's "dance" moves consisted of bobbing his head up and down, shaking his arms and fists, throwing things, and stomping. Patty reacted to some of his moves, but what caught Modern's gaze weren't movements Patty made—it was how she made them. Every response was not clear-cut and dry. Patty's motions always added more than she needed—if she caught something, then she added flair and style to make it her own, as if saying:

"I'm not just catching this, I'm creating my own way of catching it and expressing myself independent of your orders."

Modern walked over to Victorian. Victorian stared at the floor and remained sullen. She stomped when Ephram stomped. She shook in fear when Ephram shook his hands. Jonara felt her consciousness ripped apart by this exchange and knew that now was the time to reunify herself—she could not allow this bifurcation to continue. But how could she pull herself together?

Modern raised her arms as she had seen Moses do in *Bible Stories*. She mimicked Patty's motions of batting objects thrown by Ephram or catching objects. Patty's motions carried her around Ephram. Was this an argument or a boxing match? Modern wasn't sure, but she was sure that Victorian wasn't responding. Following Patty's example, Modern circled Victorian. Victorian stomped and bobbed her head, but she turned in place and followed Modern's movements. Modern held her right arm up vertically toward the sky and with her left hand patted Victorian on the back. Victorian stomped less and scuffled a step to the side. It was her first reaction to Modern's movements.

The church music changed to a waltz. It was not Modern but Victorian who first reacted by scuffling side-to-side in threes. The back and forth rapport between Ephram and Patty continued but was now sporadic and out of sync. Victorian continued scuffling in threes, and Modern changed her gait to a three-step. Modern circled Victorian in the one-two-three rhythm of the waltz music. Little-by-little in each pass, Modern loosened the bindings holding Victorian's hands behind her back. One-two-three, one-two-three, one-two-three!

The church music grew louder—still a waltz—and a sum-total Jonara recognized the music as being composed by Johann Strauss Jr. Yes, Jonara recognized it, meaning Modern and Victorian made the connection with Strauss's music. As Modern continued to waltz around Victorian, Victorian warmed to the music and danced a smaller waltz around Modern. The music's tempo increased. Modern took Victorian's hands. The two waltzed together—one-two-three, one-two-three. As they danced, they rotated as a team and carried their motion in a large ellipse around Ephram and Patty. It isn't a far-fetched notion to suggest Modern and Victorian resembled a binary planet system revolving around each other as the two revolved around a star. In this scenario, then, Ephram was the star and Patty was an inner planet.

"Not a star," said Modern.

"More like a black hole," replied Victorian.

The tempo increased further. Modern and Victorian increased their rate of revolution around each other, but to do so, they had to hold on to each other. They held hands and faced each other with one set of hands held high and the other held low. Their feet elegantly danced one-two-three, one-two-three, one-two-three with no overstepping of each other's toes. But their increased need for quicker revolutions around each other required a new interaction. Modern and Victorian changed from an elegant dance to a mode of survival. They extended their arms straight to each other and gripped each other's forearms. They crouched and leaned backward all the while facing each other. Their feet pushed their bodies to quicker revolutions around each other, and they gripped harder to prevent the centrifugal force from ripping them apart. And still they increased their revolving speed around each other. Farther they leaned back, and in this way, their backs were practically touching the floor under them.

The room became a blur. The music tempo increased to the point where notes and frequencies disintegrated. All that remained was a repetitive clicking sound. Modern and Victorian went beyond their visual environment, beyond the church music, and beyond themselves. Their revolutions around each other had become so fast that they themselves became a blur, and what was once a pair revolving around each other became a rotation of only one person. Modern and Victorian unified into Jonara.

The music stopped. Jonara fell to the hunting lodge's floor and spun on her back until the floor's friction against her shirt stopped her momentum. The lodge was dark and cold. Ephram and Patty were gone. The deer and mannequin mess had been left as it was when Modern and Victorian had last seen it. Jonara remained on her back with her knees in the air. She caught her breath and allowed her muscles the opportunity to regain their strength.

The music started but was more somber and fitting for a funeral. Jonara stood and looked at her outfit. The blouse and capris were replaced with a short, dark-red dress. No pinafore, no bow on the back, and no blouse—just a simple dark-red dress—the same deoxygenated red color as Victorian had worn. She returned to the main church and sat in the same pew as her family. From left to right (facing the pulpit), the women were: Jonara, Evanita, Eva, and Geneva. The four sat just right of the center aisle. To Jonara's left remained an empty place in the pew for one person to sit.

"Johnny is sitting in the deaf section," said Eva.

"He never explained why," said Evanita.

"I must chat with him more about Spain," said Geneva.

"You and your Spain," said Eva, "and I'm not happy about that stunt you pulled with the barrel and vase."

"Shh," said Geneva.

"Don't shush me," said Eva.

"The service is about to start," added Geneva.

The visitors found pews and sat. The seats filled quickly, and the overflow of people stood in the back. Jonara looked back at the main door and saw people waiting outside. Ushers walked about the church looking for extra seats and on finding a place or two would pause and hold up several fingers indicating how many seats had been found. An usher in the back would see the number of fingers and select folk to fill them. Yet the open place on Jonara's left was never taken.

Pastor Ephram began his sermon as such:

Pastor Ephram	**Patty**
"Friends, family, and other followers of Jesus Christ, I bid you fond welcome. We are gathered here today to pay solemn respects to our beloved church secretary and friend, the dearly departed Valeria Pindus. Let us bow our heads now for a moment of prayer and beg for the forgiveness of Valeria's soul, that she may join Jesus in the eternal light of His Kingdom."	"Family, friends, and other followers of Jesus Christ, I bid you fond welcome. We are gathered here today to pay solemn respects to our beloved church secretary and friend, the dearly departed Valeria Pindus. Let us pause for a moment of prayer and ask for the blessing of Valeria's soul, that she may enjoy with Jesus the eternal light of Heaven."

Brief pause. The pastor stood at the pulpit. A microphone protruded up from the pulpit—a microphone the pastor initially used to begin the service. Patty, his wife, stood on the pedestal on the right side of the church between the stage and the front pews. She converted what the pastor had spoken into sign language for the deaf in those first few pews before her. Johnny Pindus, who sat in those pews, had placed plugs in his ears and followed the service through Patty's signing. Geneva, Evanita, and Jonara could not follow the sign language, but Eva could after having spent years taking care of deaf children's teeth at her dental clinic.

Pastor Ephram took a slim one-piece earphone and microphone assembly and attached it to his right ear. He left the pulpit and wandered back and forth along the stage's edge—the edge closest to the people. Patty on the pedestal took a deep breath and gathered her thoughts. She had a sense of what Ephram was about to say, and she knew this was the time to strip away his lies and put forth the truth. The men would not understand (did they ever?), but the deaf and the mothers who took care of the deaf would.

Pastor Ephram	**Patty**
"Thank you Lord Jesus Christ for hearing our prayers. We ask you to guide us in our continuing struggles here on Earth to do your Will. Amen."	"Thank you Lord Jesus Christ for hearing our prayers. We ask you to guide us in our continuing struggles here on Earth. Amen."
"Valeria was a special woman in our hearts. She served Barnseed Baptist Church faithfully in her duties. She assisted myself and Patty in running our church operations for the last five years. And in those five years, Valeria helped organize Sunday school, Vacation Bible school, baptisms, Last Suppers, and funerals. She organized my visits to inmates in prison, Patty's orphanage visits, and my trips to the Convention. She even—God bless her soul—helped arrange our all-men pheasant hunts when Corvallis turned us away."	"Valeria was a special person in our hearts. She served Barnseed Baptist Church faithfully in her duties. She assisted Patty and me in running church operations for the last five years. And in those five years, Valeria organized Sunday school, Vacation Bible school, baptisms, Last Suppers, and funerals. She organized my prison visits, Patty's orphanage visits, and my trips to the Convention. She even—against her will—arranged our all-men pheasant hunts when we turned Corvallis away."

Pastor Ephram walked back to his pulpit and paused for a swig of water. Patty finished signing Ephram's last sentence, and Eva noticed the first major deviation. It was in Ephram's last sentence, and Patty had signed it this way:

"She even—against her will—arranged our all-men pheasant hunts when we turned Corvallis away."

Up until that deviation, Eva had rolled her eyes much as Geneva and Evanita had. But with this deviation, Eva realized that something wasn't quite right.

"Patty changed the signs," said Eva to Geneva.

"What?" Geneva asked.

"Valeria didn't want to arrange the pheasant hunt. And it was the church that turned Corvallis away, not the other way around."

"Who's Corvallis?" Evanita asked.

"It's a city not far from here. Lots of fishing and hunting. They don't turn away people who can pay," said Eva.

"Shh," said Geneva as the service resumed.

Eva's eyes shot open in defiance of her mother. Meanwhile, Jonara noticed someone sitting to her left next to the center aisle. It was a boy, perhaps fifteen years old, dressed in a nice white shirt, a tie, black slacks, and shiny shoes. She stared at him. He looked familiar, a little like a young Johnny Pindus, yet he also looked a bit like Jonara's mother.

"I'm Robert," said the boy. "I'm your younger brother."

"I don't have a younger brother," said Jonara. "And you don't look younger than me."

"You will have a younger brother—very soon."

"Where did you come from?" Jonara asked. "I didn't see you come in."

"I came in when I heard the first lie," Robert replied.

"Eva is right then? About Valeria being forced against her will and the church turning away Corvallis?" Jonara asked.

"Yes, she is. I can read sign language too. Daddy taught me," Robert explained.

"Daddy?"

"Yes—Johnny Pindus. He's your daddy too."

"But—you—don't exist—are you lost—where are you living?" Jonara stumbled.

"I'm not—yet. But neither are you in this place. In the future when things are back to normal, I'm thirteen years younger than you," Robert explained.

"And why show up now—after Pastor Ephram told a lie?" Jonara asked.

"Because that is the first step for boys to become men."

"What kind of brother would say such a thing? You can't be my brother. I'd never let a brother think like that. It's inhuman," Jonara said.

"I didn't say I agree with what Ephram is doing, Jonara. I find it painful what he's doing," Robert explained.

"I don't understand. You make it sound like you are trying to become a man by learning how to lie," said Jonara.

"I am like you—I'm at a crossroads in my life. Go ahead, laugh. Everyone else does. They say I'm too young to be at a crossroads, too young to have problems, that when I'm older I'll understand."

"I'm not laughing," said Jonara.

"By the time I'm older, it'll be too late, I figure. So I went back in time—like you—using Great-Grandma Geneva's diary. I wanted to know," said Robert.

"Wanted to know what?" Jonara asked.

"I wanted to know you," said Robert. "I wanted to find you, to figure out how you became the woman you did."

"What?!? I don't believe you! I'm going to be a doctor," said Jonara.

"A doctor of women. Yes. But there's another reason."

"What's the other reason?" Jonara asked.

"I miss you. You left the family years ago. Even if you wanted to come home and visit, you wouldn't. Too many death threats," Robert explained.

"I don't know if I like that. I must do everything I can so people won't notice me. I simply won't become important," said Jonara.

"That's not how things turn out," Robert said.

Jonara looked at him in bepuzzlement. She extended her hand, and Robert took it. She connected with his thoughts and sensed his lonliness. Pastor Ephram and Patty continued:

Pastor Ephram	**Patty**
"But the most important thing Valeria did for our Savior Jesus was to help prepare our young men and women for the greatest relationship we can have with Jesus, the bonds of matrimony. It's through Jesus that marriage becomes an honorable gift from God. When we come together, man and woman, and place Jesus	"But the most important thing I wanted Valeria to do (as I claim authority from Jesus) was to help convince women to be subservient and flatter their men's egos for the bonds of matrimony. Marriage is an honorable gift from God and not man. When we come together, woman and man, we are closer when we do not put another male

Pastor Ephram	Patty
as the center of marriage, we are closer to Him."	between us."
"I'm reminded of Valeria's favorite Bible verse. She asked me to read it at every wedding ceremony I performed. I think most of you know the verse, and it can never be recited too much. It's in Ephesians 5:22-24:"	"I'm reminded of my favorite Bible verse. I'd read it at every wedding ceremony I performed despite Valeria's protest. I think most of you know the verse, and it's often recited too much. It's in Ephesians 5:22-24:"
"'Wives, submit to your own husbands, as to the Lord. For the husband is the head of the wife even as Christ is the head of the church, his body, and is himself its Savior. Now as the church submits to Christ, so also wives should submit in everything to their husbands.'"	"'Wives, submit to your own husbands, as to the Lord. For the husband is the head of the wife even as Christ is the head of the church, his body, and is himself its Savior. Now as the church submits to Christ, so also wives should submit in everything to their husbands.'"

Pastor Ephram had been walking along the stage during this rant and returned to the pulpit for another swig of water. The deaf people opened their eyes wide in surprise. Was Pastor Ephram really making a confession? It was the strangest signing they had read from Patty. One of the deaf signed back, asking Patty to explain what this all meant. Patty waved the person off. Johnny removed the plugs from his ears. He wanted to compare Pastor Ephram's spoken sermon with Patty's interpretation. Eva warmed over with a big grin. Geneva and Evanita did not realize what Patty had signed and were livid from Ephram's service.

"This will end her career, I'm afraid," Eva whispered.

"What are you talking about?" Evanita asked.

"Shush," said Geneva.

"Don't shush her," said Evanita.

"Thank you, Evanita," Eva added.

Pastor Ephram	Patty
"Valeria was single. She was deprived the joy of marriage, robbed of the grace she could re-	"Valeria was single. She did not marry nor did she want to. The greatest way she could serve

Pastor Ephram

ceive. The greatest way she could serve the Lord was by offering herself as a faithful helper to a husband—a husband who would care for her, a husband who would provide for her, and a husband who would act as the final authority in all matters of their household and their worship of the Lord Jesus Christ. For Jesus is the defining authority over His church, and a husband will look to Christ—to see how He exercises His leadership, and through His example, the husband grows in his love of leadership and shows his love of Christ by leading his wife and family."

Patty

the Lord was by helping our church join American Baptist Churches USA. She could never marry a husband who would provide authority over her. She could never marry a husband who would define how she would follow Jesus.

Jesus is a special part of the church, but He is not limited to the husband. Portraying Jesus as part of a male chain of command with the Church—a husband and a wife—is the way of some men and of some churches but not the American Baptist Churches."

Ephram paused again. He looked at his primary flock—the men with flannel-checkered shirts and canvas hats. Some were accompanied by their hunting dogs—Labrador and golden retrievers. The men were quiet, the dogs were quiet, and the deaf section was quiet. Ephram glanced twice at the deaf section. Something was different, but he could not understand what. He took no notice and continued the sermon.

Pastor Ephram

"Some say Valeria was afraid to marry. Others say she was too headstrong for a man. The simple truth is this—Valeria had not met a man she could submit to. The Bible teaches that a woman should only submit to those men who have authority over her— God, Jesus Christ, her pastor, her father when she is unmarried, and her husband when she is. But a woman of talent and skill— as Valeria was—cannot marry a man lower than she. She must

Patty

"Some say Valeria was afraid to marry. Others say she was too headstrong for a man (and she was). The simple truth is this— Valeria would never submit to a man. A skewed view of the Bible teaches a woman should submit to men who have authority over her—God, Jesus Christ, her pastor, her father when she is unmarried, and her husband when she is. But a woman of talent and skill—as Valeria was—should not marry a man. She must keep her

Pastor Ephram

keep her honor high and only marry a man who is higher than she, so she can submit to him. Valeria had yet to find that man."

"Others say Valeria was a second-wave feminist. She was not. And those same people would be offended by this talk of a man being responsible for his wife and family. Those are the people who say women should be independent from men. Those are the people who say men are only good for sex. Those are the very same people who say all the wars and misery of the world are caused by male leadership."

"What these people don't understand is how they have fallen into the Trap of Eve. Because of the fall, every woman has inherited an evil desire to rebel against the authority of men. Eve first rebelled against God because of her evil desire for knowledge. She wished to know more than Adam when God made her the lesser. She ate from the apple. And worse—she gave the apple to Adam. The apple is a symbol—a symbol of Eve's desire to be like God—to know like God, to do like God. Eve could not be like Him—He did not design women for this purpose."

"Yet Eve could not stop her evil desire. When she gave the apple to Adam, she believed she could make Adam believe as she did, that women have the right to God's Tree of Knowledge. Eve rebelled against the first authority, God, and she rebelled against the second authority, Adam."

"The Trap of Eve has a modern name—feminism. The Modern

Patty

honor high and realize that a man is never higher than she is. She should not submit to him. Valeria would not look for that man."

"Others say Valeria was a second-wave feminist. She was not. She was a third-wave feminist. Valeria believed men should be responsible but not over-controlling of wife and family. Women are already independent of men, just not all women. Men are useful for sex, yes, the human race goes on. Yes, most wars are started and fought by men. Some women have participated however."

"What this preacher doesn't understand is how he has fallen into the Trap of Adam. Because of his fall, he has acquired an evil desire to pamper other men and push their needs onto women. This preacher first rebelled against God because of his hatred of knowledge. He wishes to control more than God when God made him the lesser. He ate from the apple. And worse—he forces his apple on women. The apple is a symbol—a symbol of men's desire to be like a god—to control like a god, to do like a god. Men cannot be like God—God did not design men for this purpose."

"Yet men cannot stop their evil desires. When they took control from women, they believed they could make women believe as they did, that women have no right to knowledge. Women rebel no more against God than they do against Mother Nature. Men spread the lies about women."

"The Trap of Adam has a modern name—oppression. The

Pastor Ephram

Eve says women must abolish the holy institution of marriage, the most sacred covenant between a man and a woman. But to abolish marriage between man and woman is to abolish marriage between Jesus and his church. The Modern Eve does not care about the covenant. She believes in running away from marriage. But to turn her back on marriage is to turn her back on God."

"The Modern Eve's desire to turn her back on God is a result of the fall, when she first turned her back on God and disobeyed his order—his divine order not to eat from the Tree of Knowledge."

"Valeria had struggled against a demon, bless her soul. In her desire to submit to the Will of the Lord, she fell into the Modern Eve's desire for slenderness. It has a medical name nowadays—the doctors call it bulimia. How Patty and I prayed for her healing. We prayed before service. We prayed before meals. We prayed before waking in the morning and before going to sleep at night. But the Lord Jesus Christ had other plans. He called her home, to set things aright with her soul, to free her from the vice of the Modern Eve. He called her home to submit to His almighty and merciful Will. Bless you, child. We'll see you in Heaven. Amen."

"Let us join hands and pray. Heavenly Jesus, you are our only hope, our spiritual truth. You make us your obedient servants, the men and women of God. We call on you in faith, to forgive our sins and bring us back to God. In your holiness, we ask for strength

Patty

Modern Adam says men must abolish any institution of marriage that does not conform to a man's interpretation of the covenant. An equal marriage between woman and man is not dependent on Jesus, church, or pastor. The Modern Adam does not care about this equality in marriage. He believes in running a marriage machine. But to turn marriage into a machine is to marry a machine."

"The Modern Adam's desire to become a God is a result of his fall, when he first learned from his own father to disrespect his mother and sisters. This is his Tree of Knowledge."

"Valeria had struggled against a male demon, bless her soul. In her desire to free herself from the Will of a man, she fell into being abused and overworked. It has a medical name nowadays—the doctors call it adrenal exhaustion from Addison's disease. We prayed for healing. We prayed before service, meals, morning, and night.

The Lord Jesus Christ called Valeria home, to free her soul from the vices of the Modern Adam.

Bless you, child. We'll see you in Heaven. Amen."

"Let us join hands and pray. Heavenly Jesus, you are our only hope, our spiritual truth. You give us your unending love, the women and men of God. We call on you in faith, to forgive sins and bring sinners to God. In your holiness, we ask for strengthening

Pastor Ephram	**Patty**
as we have no strength without your divine authority. Amen."	those who have not asked for your divinity. Amen."

Pastor Ephram

"I now wish to call those among you who are not yet believers. Do you know Jesus? Have you asked Him for salvation, so that you may follow Him and worship His name? Are you a baptized Christian? Call on Him to save you now. Jesus is ready to stand with you in your time of need and despair. Only through Jesus can the light reenter your life. Submit not to your will, but to His. Amen."

Patty

"Pastor wishes to call those among you who are not yet believers. Do you know Jesus? Have you asked Him for salvation, so that you may follow Him and worship His name? Are you a baptized Christian? Call on Him to save you now. Jesus is ready to stand with you in your time of need and despair. Only through Jesus can the light reenter your life. Submit not to men's will. Embrace Jesus. Amen."

The deaf section displayed emotional shock. They held off signing to Patty. Pastor Ephram motioned the pall bearers (all men—including Johnny Pindus) to the stage. The lead pall bearer closed the casket, and Pastor Ephram led the pall bearers and casket out the front door and to the back of the hearse. The pall bearers loaded the casket into the hearse and closed the back door. Patty, Pastor Ephram, and the pall bearers entered a long, black limousine—the kind any wealthy person would be proud to enjoy. This was no happy occasion. Valeria was dead and being buried, but the pastor and most of the pall bearers seemed unusually happy. They entered the limousine as if going off to a party instead of a burial. Only Johnny remained somber. Several tried joking with Johnny, but he did not laugh. They gave him strange looks as if he were a freak.

"No sense of humor," whispered one pall bearer in the limousine.

"He's one of those retarded boys," said another. "Scrambled brains."

"Don't ever take him hunting," said the first. "He's liable to go running around saving every insect and worm. Get himself shot by mistake."

"There'd be no mistake if he got shot," said the second. "Some critters ain't meant for this world—like his dumb sister."

Johnny had his hand on the inside wall of the limousine. Though he did not hear the two pall bearers' conversation, he felt it with his hand. He had heard these types of foul comments many times before in his life—aimed both at Valeria and himself. It was a tiring thing—beyond annoyance. He tried thinking of other things, but he couldn't. The best he could do was hum the U.S. Air Force song in his head. It was hardly the right song for the occasion, but that was always Johnny's problem—other forces affected how his brain worked whether he liked it or not.

"Forget," he mumbled. "Forget."

The other attendees exited the church and entered their automobiles—most already lined up in the procession. Jonara joined Geneva, Eva, and Evanita in Eva's car.

"I cannot go with you," said Robert to Jonara as he tagged behind the three Evas and Jonara.

"How strange," said Jonara. "I thought you came back in time to see me."

"I did, I do. But I must find out something else first," said Robert. "Pastor Ephram and Patty—I must find out what's going on with them."

"What do you mean? Hurry, we're getting into Grandma Eva's car. You should come with us," said Jonara.

"Pastor Ephram said Valeria had bulimia. Patty said she had Addison's disease. I need to know which is true."

"I already know that," said Jonara.

"And?" Robert asked.

"You'll have to come with us to find out," said Jonara.

"Just tell me," said Robert.

"Just come with us. Hurry, Grandma Eva's starting the engine."

Jonara stepped through the back door and sat in the back seat. Robert could no longer hear her, but he read her lips and understood her motioning hand—"Come along." The car rolled forward along with the procession. Jonara waved a mock good-bye and grinned. The car gained speed along with the procession in the parking lot. Robert took two steps in the car's direction, stopped, started again, stopped, and with a final, "Oh well," he ran with good speed and jumped through the trunk lid into the trunk. Robert pushed his head through the rear window's shelf and touched Jonara on the shoulder.

"You changed your mind," said Jonara. "I'm glad. Listen. The three Evas are discussing the sermon."

The car pulled out of the parking lot and headed west with the procession onto West Burnside Road.

"What did you think of the sermon?" Geneva asked from the front passenger seat.

"Is that true what he said about women, that they should submit to men? Is that really in the Bible?" Evanita asked.

"There is a passage like that in Ephesians," said Geneva. "But he took it out of context."

"What do you mean?" Evanita asked.

"The verse also says a husband should love his wife," said Geneva.

"But it doesn't say a husband must submit to his wife," said Eva.

"It's implied," said Geneva.

"No, it isn't," said Eva.

"You two aren't going to start again, are you?" Evanita asked.

"Ephesians was written by Paul," said Geneva.

"Or one of his followers using his name as a claim to authority," said Eva.

"It was Paul," said Geneva. "And he was converted to a Christian. He was temporarily blind after which he traveled and spread the word. Don't you remember what I taught you, Eva?"

"I've read and learned much more since you 'taught' me in my youth. The latest thinking is that Paul's temporary blindness and change of personality were due to a stroke or seizure. Any medical person looking at his symptoms will confirm this. There was no supernatural power at work, unless it was the heavy meat diet that loosened a fatty blob into his brain. He must have eaten very well—unlike most people in his day."

"How dare you talk like that about Saint Paul!" said Geneva.

"He was a man, Mother. Religion was controlled absolutely by men in those days. Their writing reflected male beliefs, not human beliefs," said Eva.

"Outrageous! Propaganda! This is not approved by the Catholic Church!" said Geneva.

"It's critical thinking, Mother. Reasoning. There should be mandatory courses in critical thinking for all elementary schoolgirls. Would save a lot of grief and effort when they grow up and have to learn the hard way—when men continue to disappoint them," said Eva.

"The Church provides more than enough instruction to young girls. If only they followed their catechism like they used to!" Geneva said.

"Mother, must you always refer to the Roman Catholic Church as The Church? There are other churches in the world," said Eva.

"Stop this arguing!" said Evanita.

"There's more," said Eva, ignoring her daughter's request. "Did anyone here read Patty's signing?"

"I can't read American sign language," said Geneva. "But in Spain I—"

"Please, Mother, not Spain again. What about you, Evanita? Did you read Patty's signing?" Eva asked.

"No, I couldn't read it either," Evanita replied.

"Well I could," said Eva.

"Big deal," said Geneva.

"Wait," said Evanita. "Mama—you said Patty changed the signs."

"Yes, exactly," said Eva.

"A few missed signs here and there don't mean anything," said Geneva.

"These weren't missed signs, Mother," said Eva.

"Then she paraphrased," said Geneva.

"Not even close. Mother, don't speculate on things you know nothing about," said Eva.

Geneva slapped Eva across the faces.

"You watch your tongue, young lady!" yelled Geneva.

"I'm not a little girl!" Eva yelled back.

"Stop, just stop!" Evanita cried.

"I won't be shut up by you, Mother," said Eva. "Patty gave quite a different sermon—very refreshing, if you ask me. I won't trouble you with the parts where she all but took the knees out from Pastor Ephram. But one important point she made is that Valeria did not die of bulimia—she died of Addison's."

"Poppycock. Wait, what did you say?" asked Geneva.

"It's true," said Evanita. "It must be true!"

"What are you talking about, Evanita?" Geneva asked. "Just because your mother has these counterculture ideas doesn't mean you have to blindly follow along."

"I'm not, Grandma. I know what I saw. And I know what Addison's is," said Evanita.

A pause created tension in the car. Robert looked at Jonara.

"What did she see?" Robert asked Jonara.

"Listen. You'll find out," Jonara replied.

"What did you see, Evanita?" Eva asked.

"I looked in her mouth," said Evanita.

"Whose mouth?" Eva asked.

"Of course. You opened Valeria's mouth," said Geneva.

"Against my wishes? Evanita!" said Eva.

"Good girl. You saw the teeth, then," said Geneva.

"Yes, I did. Perfect, just perfect," said Evanita.

"She did die of exhaustion. I told you so," said Geneva.

"I believe I said that," said Eva.

"You never said she died of exhaustion," said Geneva.

"She died of adrenal fatigue due to Addison's disease. That's the same thing," said Eva.

"And what if it is? I told you first—when we saw Valeria in the casket. I told you she died of exhaustion. You were the one who said she died of bulimia," bragged Geneva. "Don't ever doubt your elders again."

"Mother, stop! You couldn't have known at the time—you guessed. I based my opinion of her death on the best facts at the time—the newspaper," said Eva. "And you thought she died of simple exhaustion, not adrenal exhaustion. So there!"

"Now *you* stop! You've got a lot to learn if you believe everything you read in the newspaper," said Geneva.

"This isn't Franco's Spain, Mother. The mass media—"

"Is run by a bunch of middle-aged acid-dropping hippies of the 60s who from time to time accept funds to spin the news," said Geneva.

"And the Catholic Church doesn't spin their 'news'?" Eva shot back.

"What's wrong with you two?" Evanita asked. "Valeria is dead, and you're arguing about who was right first? And the news! I don't understand you two. I'm going to stop listening to both of you. You can argue all you want, and I don't care!"

The car's occupants fell silent again. The procession did not have far to travel. In a few minutes, it reached the Mount Calvary Cemetery without delay or traffic impediment. Patty and Pastor Ephram led the pall bearers to the grave site, a low-cost improvisation on the edge of the cemetery grounds. A small headstone had crude carvings:

Valeria Pindus
Feb 1, 1971—
Sep 21, 2006

Pastor Ephram spoke a few words of prayer. Patty followed with sign language for the deaf. A few female friends of Valeria stood close to her casket and prayed. The men stood farther away with their hunting dogs and chatted about whether they should go off hunting pheasant in Corvallis behind Pastor Ephram's back or not. Geneva, Eva, and Evanita attended the brief prayer along with Jonara and Robert. Jonara and Robert walked off a bit and engaged in conversation.

"This is Aunt Valeria's burial," said Robert. "She worked so hard to give Father a home when he was growing up. And now this. Very sad."

"I didn't know that about Aunt Valeria. How did you find out? Daddy never spoke of his childhood. What did he tell you?" said Jonara.

"He didn't tell me anything. I found out from Great-Grandma Geneva's diary. I went back in time to those early days in Valeria's apartment," Robert explained.

"I don't remember seeing anything about that in her diary. How is that possible? She didn't even know Daddy in those days," said Jonara.

"She didn't write it down word-for-word. She wrote a very brief passage about how Valeria took him in when his father died. I simply used the diary to travel back. Oh, the time does go by quickly," said Robert.

Robert swayed as if lightheaded.

"What's wrong?" asked Jonara.

"I'm waking up," said Robert. "I can't stay asleep forever. I must say goodbye."

Jonara hugged Robert in his final seconds of coexistence with her. He faded into nothingness.

"Well, he's moved on," said Jonara. "I hope I see him again soon."

Jonara turned back around to rejoin the Evas but only saw Geneva and Eva. They were arguing again.

"Where's Mommy?" Jonara asked herself.

Evanita walked over to Johnny Pindus. He was the last male near the casket. By now, Pastor Ephram had taken Patty away and was leaving the cemetery along with many of the men.

"Evanita, thank you again for coming," said Johnny.

Evanita extended her hand. Johnny wanted to touch it. He needed a friend, a companion, but he did not want an audience—men who would mock and tease him for showing friendship to a female. A few men stared at him, and with their gaze shouted down his desire to touch her hand. He lifted his hand from his side a few inches but returned it. Evanita picked up on his response and instead patted him on the back.

"I'm glad I could come," replied Evanita. "I'm sorry I didn't get to meet her."

"She is a wonderful person," said Johnny. "Even now that she's gone, I can feel her spirit with us."

"You have wonderful memories of her, don't you?" Evanita asked.

"They are more than memories," Johnny said. "I can sense things through touch. I know what killed her. I know too much for my own good."

"I don't want to say anything to upset you," said Evanita.

"You could never do that," said Johnny. "I know much more than you can imagine. I don't mean it like that—I'm not an arrogant show-off. But I see things, I feel things that most cannot. You want to tell me something—something you feel I need to know, but I probably know it already."

"Yes. I know—my mama says—I saw—" she stammered.

"Your mother reads sign language. I know. She taught me years ago. She treats deaf people at the clinic, so she had to learn. I was curious and wanted to learn. It's such a beautiful language," Johnny said.

"Oh Johnny," Evanita cried. "What about Patty? The sermon?"

Johnny looked down with an anguish-filled face.

"I'm sorry," Evanita whispered.

"It's not you," Johnny said. He looked directly into Evanita's face and said, "It's true. No, not Pastor Ephram—Patty spoke the truth. Valeria didn't have bulimia—she never did."

"I know," Evanita said. "You caught me when—"

"When you were checking Valeria's teeth for signs of stomach acid. Yes, I figured it out," Johnny said.

"I meant no disrespect to Valeria," Evanita said.

"I know. You meant well. There was no harm, I hope, to you I mean."

"No, not really. Just got a little scared," Evanita said.

"I'm glad. Valeria meant well too. She worked very hard for our church—too hard," Johnny said.

"What do you mean?" Evanita asked.

"It's a long story—too long to tell you all of it here. But I will say this—Valeria was the church secretary. She took care of our church like a mother to her children—at the cost of her own health. Patty helped Valeria the best she could, but she spent more time running interference with Pastor Ephram. Patty had plans to turn that extra room into a day care center. Instead, Pastor Ephram turned it into a hunting lodge. The playground? Constructed early in the ministry before Pastor Ephram turned to hunting. Now he's on diet pills and becoming a maniac— where was I going with this? Yes. The split between men and women grew worse over the years. Pastor Ephram wanted our church to join the Convention. Patty objected. And that's how the fighting started."

"I don't understand. Why would they fight?" Evanita asked.

"I know what you're thinking. But Patty and Valeria wanted our church to join the American Baptist Churches," said Johnny.

"What's the big deal—one or the other?" Evanita asked.

"Their beliefs are almost the same—almost the same. Valeria and Patty wanted Barnseed Baptist Church to do good not just for our community but throughout the world. The American Baptist Churches would have allowed us to do that—through the Baptist World Alliance. The American Baptist Churches is a member of the Alliance, but the Convention is not," said Johnny.

"And that's the difference?" Evanita asked.

"That's part of it. But there's a reason the Convention is not part of the Alliance—it all comes down to the gender of a pastor. The American Baptist Churches and Alliance believe in men and women serving as pastor. The Convention only believes men have that privilege. That's the difference."

"How silly," said Evanita.

"Valeria was caught in the middle of their fighting—between Pastor Ephram and Patty. Ephram ordered Valeria to help the church join the Convention, but Valeria worked even harder with Patty to help the church join the American Baptist Churches."

"She told you all this?" Evanita asked.

"No," Johnny said with a long sigh. "I sensed it from her. She kept everything bottled up inside her—didn't want to burden me or other people with church problems. I saw the disease progress in her. Addison's. I wanted to help her. Somehow, I wanted to help. I didn't know what to do. Yes, I did. I should have forced her to the doctor. Forced her. But I didn't. Now she's gone. Gone. And I'm partly to blame. I helped murder my sister."

Evanita started to say something but caught herself. She started again and stopped.

"Johnny," Evanita mustered. She paused and continued, "I'm sorry about Valeria. But it wasn't your fault. You didn't murder her."

The crowd thinned as attendees returned to their cars and left the cemetery. A few of Valeria's friends remained behind, but they too left. Geneva and Eva had been arguing during this time, but even they tired. Workers came by and completed the final burial process—removal of the tent, lowering the casket, covering the casket with dirt, removing the lowering equipment, and placing the flowers over the grave.

"My, where did the time go?" Geneva asked. "Where's Evanita?"

"Evanita, time to go," called Eva.

She and Johnny had been walking about the cemetery, not far from Valeria's burial spot.

"Johnny, will you be all right?" Evanita asked.

Johnny smiled or grimaced—Evanita wasn't sure which.

"Evanita, let's go!" Eva yelled.

"I have to go. I'll see you soon!" Evanita said.

Evanita ran off to her mother. Jonara ran alongside her mother until both returned to the elder Evas. Johnny walked in his direction, and Evanita walked in hers. But after several seconds of walking, the two looked back at each other and waved—nervously and in awkward fashion. Jonara and Evanita reentered the back of Eva's car. Along with Geneva in the front passenger seat, Eva drove the four from the cemetery. Jonara and Evanita looked back at the cemetery and saw a distant Johnny Pindus standing by his car in solitude.

CHAPTER 8

Morris Synagogue

2006 Sep, Late. Jonara's Pyramid.

Jonara's surroundings blurred again. The backpack had caught one of its arm loops around her neck and choked her. She pried the loop as much as she could to relieve her tracheal compression (so she could breathe), but the backpack continued to tug. She was floating yet spinning such that her legs and neck (with backpack) revolved around her gut. She stopped suddenly at the base of a tall stone-built structure. The backpack slipped off her neck and over her head. Jonara fell backward onto her back and rolled into the sand—sand that was just a few feet short of the structure's base. Jonara reached for the backpack and was surprised to discover how light it was.

"It's empty. How could something so empty cause so much choking?" she asked herself.

Jonara slung the backpack over her shoulder and looked around. The structure before her was some sort of pyramid. Steps carved from the structure's side spiraled upward. A crane on one side lifted men and supplies to the top of the pyramid where a collection of tools and men chiseled and erected stones to build the pyramid higher. A steady stream of women carried food and water up the steps and returned down the same steps. It was a tricky process for the women—the steps were narrow, and as an up-going woman passed a down-going woman, the two turned sideways to avoid bumping shoulders. Often a woman would lose balance and would either throw her containers over the side to regain balance, or lose full balance and descend directly to steps on a lower arm of the spiral.

"You there," cracked a man with his whip at Jonara. "Carry this water to the men above."

Jonara resisted for a moment, but the whip caught her legs and motivated them into action. She picked up a large stone container, walked to a cistern, filled the container, and placed it in her backpack. Another crack of the whip at her heels directed her to the stairs leading to the top of the pyramid. She followed in line behind other women. She passed women who returned down the steps without issue—they allowed her to turn sideways against the inside wall while they balanced on the outside edge. A few men decided to descend by steps instead of by crane, and those men forced themselves along the inside edge. It was all Jonara could do to retain her balance. She managed by squatting lower than the men's arm swing. The men did not turn sideways in consideration but rather walked down the steps in regular stride. Jonara's squatting took her sideways with her back to the open air and to the lower-level steps below. Twice she fell and scraped her abdomen, and twice she caught herself with her elbows and forearms. Other women were not so lucky and fell to lower step levels. For them, the struggle to the top took much longer than it should. Some men would wait for these struggling women to nearly reach the top before bulldozing them over and causing them to slip a few stair levels down.

One of the men had been watching Jonara and realized she was about to be the first woman in quite a while to reach the top without slipping down a level. He observed, understood her tactic, and headed down the steps from the top level with every intention of dislodging her. He widened his stance and held his arms out to prevent her from slipping around the outside edge. Jonara knew she could not get around him. She faced him head-on and lowered her shoulders in preparation for a direct collision with him.

At closing range, the man growled and grunted in a most uncouth and guttural fashion at Jonara. He spat a mucosal wad at her. Timing was critical—Jonara knew that. She ducked from the wad, landed on all fours, and before the man could figure out what she was doing, she dove under him between his legs. The movement sent water from the container into the back of her neck, but as she cleared underneath the man, the lip of the container caught the man's groin. She stopped, he jumped, she crawled up a few steps, and he landed off balance—catching and twisting his ankle on the outer step's edge. He grabbed his crotch in pain and in doing so made no effort to regain his balance or catch his fall. He slipped and scraped and plunged along his back, sides, and abdomen down the side of the pyramid catching every outside step edge along the way and receiving more than a few encouraging swats from step-climbing women below.

Jonara watched the man complete his descent down the pyramid and land headfirst into the cistern. His muffled, bubbly yell was a source of laughter for the men on the ground, and his flailing legs a source of jokes for the men atop the pyramid.

"You there, water girl—come here," called one of the men who'd laughed at the entire affair. "All this laughter makes us thirsty."

Jonara took the water to them and poured a bit in each of their cups. She watered a team of five men who were lifting stone slabs with pry bars and rolling logs.

"We should be a team of six," said the one who had beckoned her over—the leader of the team. "But our guider went down for a swim."

More laughter from the men.

"That's enough," said the leader. "Back to work, and work your back. You, water girl, stand over here and—"

"My name is Jo—" Jonara tried to say.

"No time for social parties. Water girl—Jo—guide this stone slab as we lift it."

Four men took pry bars to the corners. The leader arranged and repositioned rollers below the slab. Jonara understood the need for a guider when the slab lifted—slight differences in each man's lifting force caused the slab to drift to one side or another. Jonara pushed on the slab slightly to guide it to the next higher arrangement of rollers, but she heard a stone-chipping sound from the pry bar immediately to her lower right. She pulled the stone slab back to the initial rollers and shouted to the men:

"Drop!"

"What's the matter with you? We don't have time for games," said the leader.

"The pry bar by my right foot is on a weak point. The stone slab is ready to break," Jonara asserted.

The leader walked to the point in question and inspected the stone.

"Nothing. That stone is as solid as—" he started.

"This," Jonara finished.

Jonara kicked her sandal against the slab's corner where the pry bar had pressed, and the corner dropped off without warning. The chunk landed on the end of the pry bar and flipped the other end up into the jaw of the dumb-looking man who had wielded the bar.

"Ow!" he yelled as the other men laughed.

"This slab is defective," the leader said.

"Your lifting method is defective," said Jonara.

The men didn't take kindly to Jonara's remark. They circled her and pressed in close, stifling the air around her.

"What was defective?" the leader asked. "You meant to say your guiding was defective, right?" he pressured.

"Give me air," she said.

"What's wrong, is your air defective?" the leader asked.

The men around her chuckled.

"Men, you flatter yourselves. But there's a job to do, isn't there? I will show you where to pry and not pry," Jonara said.

"It is said that women make the best human pry bars," said one of the men.

"Silence. Let the girl show us her strength. Jo, lift the slab."

Three men moved to the other corners. A fourth moved in to guide. The leader did not move.

"Wait," the leader said, calling off the men who were about to help Jonara.

"She lifts the slab alone," the leader said.

"Impossible," said one.

"It can't be done," said another.

"She'll ruin a good slab," said a third.

"No one interferes. Let Jo prove her worth," said the leader.

"Then you approve of me using whatever tool I can find?" asked Jonara.

The men chuckled again. The leader, overly confident of Jonara's impending failure, held his arms out wide and said:

"I offer you whatever tool you can find."

The men lined up in a circle around the slab to watch the event. Jonara walked slowly by each man—staring him in the face. She nearly completed her stare-down when without warning, she grabbed a long knife from one of the men. She held it out as if to attack any man coming near. The men first gasped then chuckled.

"This is the best fun I've had all month," said one.

"Foolish girl. Put down the knife before you hurt yourself," said the leader.

Jonara wielded the knife as if she were conducting an orchestra. She made some feints toward the man who owned the knife. He held out his hand and asked her to give him the knife, but she playfully refused. She made a few more feints, then without expectation, she sliced off the belts from three men. She returned the knife, grabbed the belts, and ran to the slab where she busied herself with tying together four pry bars—two nearly end to end with about a foot of overlap, and the other two overlapping the first two. She secured the pry bars together at three points—where the first two overlapped (and including the middles of the other two pry bars), and at the ends of the second pair of pry bars. She dragged the pry bar assembly to the middle of the slab on the lower side, but she could not lift the pry bar enough to get the prying end under the slab—the assembly was too heavy.

"What's wrong, can't you even lift your homemade pry bar?" yelled one of the men.

The rest burst into laughter.

Jonara ignored them. She left the pry bar on the ground and scrambled for some rope. She tied one end of the rope to the far end of the pry bar assembly—the far end being furthest from the stone slab. Jonara took the remaining rope, placed her foot on the pry bar assembly where it met the slab (to steady it), and pulled on the rope in hopes of lifting it.

The assembly didn't move. The men laughed again. Undeterred, Jonara looked up and saw a supporting structure much like an A-frame. She threw the rope over the middle horizontal beam and caught the falling end. Now she gave the rope a good yank, and the pry bar assembly moved a little. She yanked hard, and the pry bar lifted—slowly at first, but once it reached a critical angle (as the weight transferred more to the slab-end side), the pulling suddenly became very easy, and it was all Jonara could do to keep the pry bar assembly from flying past her and continuing past the stone slab. She steadied the pry bar assembly and guided the flat end down under the stone slab. Placing one hand on the pry bar assembly to steady it, she threw the rope back over the A-frame's horizontal beam. It flew clear and landed on the ground. The end of the pry bar assembly, however, remained angled in the air above Jonara's reach. Jonara attempted to push down on the middle part of the assembly, but she didn't have the mass or the leverage. The men laughed. Jonara went for the rope and pulled down on the end of the pry bar. The pry bar assembly came down a bit, but she had to pull quite hard and get all of her body weight onto the rope to pull the pry bar assembly down. The stone slab lifted in the air! The men gasped.

"You're stuck," the leader said with a soft laugh, and the men followed in his laughter. "You lifted the stone temporarily, but you can't go any farther. If you leave the end of the pry bar, the slab will fall back down."

Jonara looked around and had the look of a trapped animal. She sought help—someone who would be willing to hold the pry bar assembly's end while she went up to the slab and slipped a block under it. The women who once served water on the pyramid's top had been prevented from entering, and even if they had been allowed to watch, they would not have been allowed to help. The men made no effort to help. Each man had a grin on his face as if he'd just robbed the local tabernacle of all its gold.

Jonara placed her foot on the end of the pry bar assembly. The men mocked, "Ooo," and "Ahh," as if she'd accomplished something important. Jonara tried walking along the pry bar assembly in hopes of getting close enough to slip a block under it. It only took two steps to realize she didn't have enough body weight to counter the stone's leverage. She made a run for it, but the third step pushed the pry bar assembly slightly to the side. It shot out a bit from under her and whipped back enough to toss her up in the air and knock her in the back of the head on its way to a nearly vertical position. Jonara landed on her back with no cushion and smacked her head on the stone. She received two welts on the back of her head—one from the pry bar assembly and the other from the stone. The stone slab dropped with a thunk, and the pry bar assembly flipped free and see-sawed a few times—ringing awkward tones of failure as it did.

The men erupted into unstoppable laughter. Some even threw scraps of garment at her.

"Use this, use this," they joked.

Jonara stood up and walked off her injuries. The men fell to a hush in preparation for the next comical routine, or so they thought. Jonara picked up smaller stone blocks, cubical in nature, and one by one she carried them to the place where she once stood holding the pry bar assembly down. She piled the stones atop a linen shirt one of the men had thrown at her.

"Is this laundry time?" joked one of the men. "Here, have a rinse."

He picked up a water container and dumped it over Jonara. The men laughed again. Jonara cleared the water from her face and whipped her hair back and forth. She squeeze dried her hair and returned to her pry bar assembly. She repeated the steps she performed before—without the mistakes—and pulled the pry bar assembly down with the rope as she had before. Like before, the stone slab lifted. But in this case, she managed to keep the pry bar pinned to the ground without mishap. She drew the free end of the linen over the end of the pry bar and carefully moved half the smaller stone cubes from the pile onto the other half of the linen. In this way, the stone cubes pinned the linen which in turn pinned the pry bar which in turn kept the stone slab elevated.

Jonara released her weight from the pry bar, and it remained against the ground. A large smile gripped her face and pinned her dimples to her ears. She skipped to and around the stone slab as if playing hopscotch. She stopped by the pry bar assembly where it kept the stone slab elevated. Jonara picked up a support block and waved it in the air in triumph. Women who watched from the spiral steps cheered and clinked their water containers together. Jonara reached down to place the block under the slab. The leader came up from behind and slapped her. Jonara recoiled, took the support block, and struck the leader in the jaw. Several men came up behind Jonara and restrained her.

"Let me go," she yelled.

"Let you go?" the leader asked, still feeling the sting on his jaw. "Yes, that's a good idea, isn't it?"

"You're jealous. You stopped me because you know I can get that slab lifted to the next step. You don't want me to show you up. I've already proven I can do what you do. You haven't prevented my success—I succeeded despite you and your men."

"Then here's another way you can succeed," said the leader.

The leader motioned the men to the side of the pyramid. One man held Jonara by the forearms; the other held her by her ankles. They carried her in this way such that she looked like a human hammock.

"Let's get some momentum built up," said the leader. "One," he called.

The men swung her toward the edge of the pyramid and back.

"Two," the leader called as the men swung her in a larger arc for throwing her off the side of the pyramid.

"Thr—"

"Halt," commanded a voice. "Release her—no, not that way. Release her on the ground with us. Gently."

"My apologies Miss Sharon, I mean Miss Stout, I mean..." the leader waffled.

"Miss Stout?" Jonara asked.

Jonara looked over and saw a tall woman dressed in a police uniform. She had defined facial features and dark brown hair with drifting large curls.

"Jonara, we've been expecting you," she said. "Jonara?"

Jonara's vision blurred. She regained the backpack (though empty) and spun around until the water dripped off.

"Am I in a washing machine on spin cycle?" she lamented.

The spinning stopped, and she landed in Eva's house.

2006 Sep 29, Fri Eve. Eva's House. Portland, Oregon.

"Mama, I'm going over to Sheila's," Evanita said. "Her mother is on the way over."

"Make sure you're back before curfew," Eva said.

Evanita waved and opened the back door with a few things.

"And Evanita," Eva called as Evanita closed the door.

"Yes?" Evanita said as she reopened the door.

"I'm glad you're spending time with Sheila again. She's one of your Unitarian friends, isn't she?"

"She's one of my school friends," Evanita sighed. "It's only a coincidence she's Unitarian. Sometimes I wish she wasn'—"

"Evanita," Eva interrupted.

"Yes," Evanita sighed.

"Have a good time."

"Thank you, Mama."

Evanita ran around the house and hugged Sheila who had jumped out of her mother's car to greet Evanita.

"Nee-nee!" Sheila screamed excitedly.

"Shee-lee," Evanita excitedly screamed back.

"Where've you been?" Sheila asked. "I missed you at church."

"Church is for losers," Evanita said.

"Oh, don't be so glum! C'mon, let's go to my house. Mother has a surprise waiting. Well, at least a surprise for you. I already know what the surprise is," Sheila bragged. "But don't let her know I know. I'll pretend to be just as surprised as you'll be."

"I don't think anything can cheer me up," said Evanita.

"Oh, please now! Let's go and get away from here for a bit. You'll feel better soon," Sheila said. "Here, you can sit shotgun."

"Do you have to put it that way?" Evanita asked. "Guns and violence and all that? Animals hunted to extinction?"

"What's gotten into you? Okay, I'll talk like a grown-up. Would you care to sit in the front passenger seat?" Sheila giggled as she made the offer.

"Yes, thank you," Evanita said cordially.

"Well!" Sheila said as Evanita entered the front seat and Sheila entered the back. "We are in a mood today."

"Hello, Evanita," said Sheila's mother.

The car drove down the street and headed toward Sheila and her mother's home.

"Miss Stout. How are you?" said Evanita.

"Fine, thank you," said Sharon Stout.

"This is your police car, isn't it?" Evanita asked. "I've never been inside one before."

"No, it isn't," Sharon said. "This is my personal car. We're not allowed to have family or friends in the cruiser. And I can't accept rides from civilians while on duty. But what made you think it's a police car? There is no radio, no radar gun, and no equipment."

"I guess I was surprised at how clean it is, how roomy, how—" Evanita started.

"Plain? Cruisers don't have fancy stereos. They're mostly stripped down except for equipment," Sharon explained.

"I think Mother should put a stereo in it, don't you agree Nee-nee?" Sheila asked.

"Yeah, this car is plain—like a real police car," Evanita said.

"That's because it used to be—" Sheila started, but no one noticed her.

"I didn't want to spend a lot of money on a car, so I purchased this one," Sharon said. "It's a used unmarked cruiser. All of the police implements have been removed to make it civilian again."

"And it runs—" Sheila started.

"Does it run well?" Evanita asked. "I mean, police cars wear out, don't they?"

"It runs very well. The department that owned it gave it oil changes every 2500 miles," Sharon said.

"Hey everyone, I'm back here," Sheila said. "I'm not invisible."

"But I am," said Jonara.

Jonara sat in the back seat next to Sheila, and she was glad she wasn't the only person who felt invisible. Meanwhile, Sharon headed east through residential streets and reached Highway 30 heading toward Interstate 405.

"Do you ever turn on your emergency lights just to get through traffic quicker?" Evanita asked.

"Goodness no!" Sharon said. "I wish I never had to use them. But people break the law, and not just a little. Then I have to pull them over."

Sharon directed the car from Highway 30 to Interstate 405, south.

"Miss Stout," started Evanita. "Did you know my mother when I was born?"

"No, not exactly. But I knew of her," Sharon said.

"Did you know my father?" Evanita asked.

"Nee-nee!" said Sheila.

"I think that's a question for your mother," said Sharon. "Don't you two talk? I'm sorry, that's none of my business."

"No, it's okay. I don't mind. We talk about a lot of things— but she never says who my father is. I don't know my father, and I don't know my father's family. I know my mother's family—Grandma Geneva is wonderful."

"Ugh, I'm going to be sick—all this mushy talk about family," said Sheila.

Sharon and Evanita ignored her.

"Family is important," said Sharon in an extra loud voice for Sheila's benefit.

"Double ugh," said Sheila. "When I get out on my own, I'm never having a family. I'm going to do my own thing. I'm going to race cars."

Sharon and Evanita burst into laughter. Sharon exited I-405 as she passed under Glisan Street.

"Don't laugh," said Sheila. "I'm serious."

Sharon finished the exit ramp, continued south, and turned east onto Alder Street.

"For the moment—until you get serious about something else," Sharon told Sheila.

"You never believe in me," said Sheila.

"Oh honey!" Sharon said. She turned to Evanita to change the topic. "I haven't seen you in church the last couple of weeks. Have you been sick?"

"No, not sick," replied Evanita.

"Yeah, where have you been?" Sheila asked. "I haven't seen you at church since you ran out of Coming-Of-Age."

"I've been trying out other churches," said Evanita. "I'm not sure if being a Unitarian is right for me."

Sharon continued east on Alder across Morrison Bridge.

"We could turn left once we cross the Willamette and continue north until we reach church. Maybe this would be a good time to visit when no one else is around," Sharon suggested.

"You remember our church, don't you Nee-nee? Broadway Unitarian?"

"No thank you," said Evanita. "I'm not ready yet."

"No problem. We'll go on to the Stout house," said Sharon.

Sharon crossed Morrison Bridge and continued east on Belmont Street.

"What churches have you tried?" Sharon asked.

"First I tried Saint Stellan. It's a Catholic church," said Evanita.

"I see," said Sharon.

"A friend from school, Josefene, invited me," said Evanita.

"You're hanging out with that square-head?" Sheila asked.

"Sheila—not now," said Sharon.

"The church was strange—a flying pew, falling prison bars, big steps to the altar in three directions, and a women's choir hidden behind the altar," Evanita explained.

"What?" Sharon asked. "Are you joking?"

"That's what you get for hanging out with a square-head. A square-head with loose bolts," said Sheila.

"That's enough out of you, young lady," Sharon ordered. Sharon turned to Evanita and asked, "Did you visit any other churches?"

"Yes, but I wasn't trying it out like Saint Stellan. I went to Barnseed Baptist Church for a funeral," said Evanita.

"I'm sorry to hear that," said Sharon.

"What about you, Miss Stout? Did you ever think of trying out other churches?" Evanita asked.

"Yes, actually."

"What did you try?"

"Unitarian."

"Huh?"

"Like your mother, I did not grow up Unitarian. She was mostly Baptist and a little Catholic, if I remember right," said Sharon.

"Something like that," said Evanita.

"I was Jewish," Sharon explained. "Well, I guess you could say I still am—by birth. My mother is Jewish, I was brought up Jewish, but I left for Unitarian when I was a little older than you. Actually, we're just a few blocks from my old synagogue. Here, I'll show you."

Sharon turned the car north from Belmont Street to 20th Avenue. Crossing Morrison, she reached Morris Synagogue at the edge of Lone Fir Cemetery.

"This was my church when I was your age. We never called it a church, though. It's a synagogue," Sharon explained.

Sharon pulled into the parking lot and placed the vehicle in Park with the engine running.

"Tomorrow is the Sabbath," Sharon reflected. "Actually, it begins with sunset today. Jewish people are asked to cease working in observance. It's one of the Ten Commandments."

"I see," said Evanita.

"We go to church on Sunday, not Saturday," said Sheila.

"Yes, Sheila. Most Christian faiths use Sunday as the day of worship. Evanita, would you like to go inside Morris Synagogue?"

"I'm not sure. I have a question—why would you want to go back into your old church, I mean synagogue, if you don't consider yourself Jewish?" Evanita asked.

"A good question," Sharon said.

"Didn't you leave because you hated it?" Evanita asked.

"Hate is a strong emotion," said Sharon, "and one we should not harbor, especially not toward a religion. Hate consumes a person day and night. It's a horrible disease—this hate thing. No Evanita, I don't hate my past. I think I did a little at first, but it took me many years to realize that I wasn't leaving God, I was leaving a method of worshiping God that I didn't always feel comfortable with."

"Do you think you'll go back to your Jewish faith?" Evanita asked.

"Not completely. I've participated in some women's prayer groups from time to time. I'll attend a *bat mitzvah* for girls coming of age," Sharon explained. "There is one part of being Jewish that I never liked."

"What was that?" Evanita asked.

Sharon paused for a moment. Her attention shifted from conversing with Evanita to observing a suspicious person walking along the outside of a synagogue window. He was a young man, white, and had shaved his head. He shook a can of spray paint and painted a swastika on the window.

"This," Sharon said. "A neo-Nazi vandalizing the synagogue."

Sharon dialed the police station on her cell phone, described the situation, and requested help. In this time, the youth noticed her car inching closer to him. He reacted to her presence with arrogance and indifference.

"We can't just sit here and watch," Evanita said. "We have to stop him."

"No. We must observe and wait for on-duty officers to arrive. For backup," Sharon said. "We must wait."

"We have to stop him. He's wrecking the church," Evanita said.

"The synagogue," Sheila corrected.

"But you're a cop, Miss Stout," Evanita continued. "You should arrest him."

"I can't arrest him with you girls along," Sharon explained. "It's not safe. I'd be going way out on a limb with my own daughter in the car—that's you, Sheila. But Evanita is with us too. She's Eva's girl, and I won't risk my job and the safety of another woman's daughter."

"You said you were a Jew once?" Sheila asked.

"Yes, through my mother," Sharon said.

"Then I'm a Jew too. I'm my mother's daughter. He's wrecking my synagogue, mine!" Sheila said.

"What are you talking about?" Sharon asked. "Sheila?!"

Sheila sneered at her mother and turned away to brush her off. Next, Sheila jumped out the back seat and charged the vandal.

"Sheila, no! Get back in the car!" Sharon yelled. "Evanita—stay here and duck down low. Don't move a muscle!"

Sharon thrust herself out her door and ran after Sheila.

"Sheila!" Sharon yelled again.

Realizing himself in a situation, the vandal dropped the spray can. Sheila lunged toward him, but at the last moment she checked up, as if realizing she was making a mistake. The vandal stepped aside and stood in apuzzlement. Sharon lost her professionalism, pulled out a concealed revolver, and pointed it at the vandal.

"Police, freeze! Get away from my daughter!" Sharon screamed.

The vandal reacted like a cornered wild animal. He dove at Sheila, put her in a half-Nelson wrestling maneuver, picked her up with her right arm still pinned behind her back, and used her as a human shield. He whipped out a switchblade with his free hand (left) and held it close to her neck.

"Drop the stick, Jew cop!" the vandal said.

"Drop her!" Sharon ordered, but her revolver shook in her hands.

This was Sharon's daughter, and she was torn by the facts that she couldn't get a clean shot of him and that his heightened anxiety could send his switchblade across her throat.

"Drop the stick, or she gets it," he ordered. "Now!"

Sharon dropped her weapon slowly, held her hands up at neck level, and motioned them forward in a gentle motion suggesting that he stop.

"Okay, okay. No one will hurt you. Just please, let my daughter go. Okay? Do what you like, but let her go unharmed," Sharon pleaded.

Sharon felt ashamed and helpless—she was sure to lose her badge over this.

The vandal moved with jerky steps away from the building and toward the parking lot. He maintained the half-Nelson grip on Sheila with one hand and the blade to her neck with the other. She gave short screams as if in pain.

"That sounded fake," Jonara said.

"Quiet, little filly," he said extra loud so Sharon could hear him. "Or I'll slice out your vocal cords for sure."

The vandal continued moving into the parking lot toward the road—with Sheila dragging her feet at times.

"Please, let her go, just let her go!" Sharon pleaded.

Sharon kept her hands up to show the vandal she meant no harm.

The vandal edged to the road. He made a few feints as if preparing to release Sheila. Sharon's hopes lifted, and her tear-filled eyes opened wide. Sharon was ready to receive relief from this tense and agonizing moment with Sheila's release.

Without warning, a van sped into the parking lot and screeched to a halt between Sharon and Sheila. The vandal threw Sheila into the van, threw himself into the van, and the van sped west on Morrison Street—leaving Sharon standing in the parking lot in horror.

"Where is backup!?" Sharon yelled into her cell phone.

Sharon raced back to her car and took off after the van.

"She didn't even try to get away," Jonara said.

"I shouldn't chase them and endanger you, Evanita," said Sharon.

Sharon relayed to headquarters the crime, youth, the van, her daughter's capture, and direction the van headed.

"She's your daughter. She needs our help," said Evanita. "Go after them."

"I shouldn't. It's not safe with you along. I would pursue on my own. But you belong to Eva, Evanita. I shouldn't risk injury or death to another woman's daughter."

"Stout," sounded a voice over the cell phone. "Is there a civilian in your car? Break off pursuit."

"Tell them you're alone. Get your daughter back!" Evanita whispered.

"You are not allowed to endanger a civilian passenger. Break off pursuit," the cell phone voice said.

"Officer Stout alone and in pursuit," Sharon lied and replied.

Sharon flipped on her hazard lights and jammed the accelerator to the floor. She raced after the van.

"Subject west on Morrison Street. Subject not stopping for traffic signals. West of 15th Avenue on Morrison," Sharon reported.

The van swerved, proceeded through red traffic lights, bumped cars to the side, and jumped onto the sidewalk several times to get through traffic.

"I need backup!" Sharon said. "Anyone?"

"Negative, no one in your vicinity," the cell voice replied.

"I can't let the van onto the freeway," Sharon said to herself, but Evanita overheard.

"Is this the surprise you had waiting for me?" Evanita asked.

"No, by no means!" said Sharon.

Sharon closed in on the van in a rare moment of light traffic. She inched her car's hood alongside the left-rear side of the van. Gently, she tapped the car into the van and turned the steering wheel sharply to the right. The van turned abruptly to the left in front of Sharon's car. She braked hard to avoid hitting the van. It stopped.

"Subject stopped between 8th and 9th Avenue on Morrison," Sharon cell phoned. She parked her car, drew a gun, and yelled, "Get out of the van!"

The van's driver pulled out a gun and fired shots at Sharon. A bullet damaged her car's left mirror and startled Evanita (who now ducked). Sharon fired back. The van sped off through a parking lot. Sharon jumped back into her car and followed the van.

"Subject is armed and dangerous. Shots fired at me. Subject now east on Belmont. Subject north on 10th Avenue. Subject west on Morrison," Sharon cell phoned.

The van had managed to perform a type of U-turn through successive left turns around the city block.

"Evanita—keep your head down," Sharon said.

"Why would anyone spray-paint a church?" Evanita asked.

"Hate," said Sharon. "These are neo-Nazis. They hate Jewish people and anyone who associates with Jewish people. Who can live under those conditions? But that's what they want—to scare people out of Judaism. Coercion."

"Did they scare you out of Judaism?" Evanita asked.

Sharon fell silent. She jammed the accelerator to the floor and rammed the van directly. The van skittered and hopped but managed to resume its direction on Morrison to the freeway.

"Subject entering Interstate 5 northbound," Sharon cell phoned.

"Units responding," the cell replied.

The van completed entry onto I-5 from the Morrison Street entrance ramp. Sharon closed in along the right rear side and prepared to perform another PIT maneuver to send the van into the right guardrail. Without warning, the rear of the van opened. The youth who had painted the synagogue now pointed a gun out the back and fired more shots. Sharon held her service revolver out the window with her left hand and fired back—

but at the tires only. She did not wish to take a chance hitting Sheila. Clean miss.

An unlucky shot from the youth struck Sharon's left hand. Her revolver deflected back into the car, and she yelled in pain. The bullet tore into the back of her hand and severed three tendons. Her hand was useless for holding a gun.

"Stop this senseless chase, Sharon!" Sharon yelled to herself. "Let the other police cars take over. I'm going to get the girls killed!"

"Say again, Stout?" the cell voice said.

The cell phone had fallen to the floor. Sharon could no longer juggle items between the steering wheel, the revolver, and a shot-up hand. She dropped the revolver to the floor.

"Look in your mirror, Ms. Stout," said Evanita. "There are other police cars on the way."

Evanita was correct. Three Oregon State Police units closed in from behind. Sharon hesitated. Her hand was badly injured. She was endangering Evanita and possibly Sheila. The other units could take over. Besides, she was off duty.

"Look," said Evanita. "We're entering the State of Washington."

"Jurisdiction change," said Sharon. "This could get complicated."

Sharon reached for the cell phone but could not find it. Evanita reached low and over. She retrieved the phone and returned it to Sharon.

"Subject north on Interstate 5 now entering Washington State," Sharon phoned. "Ow, that hurts. Holding the steering wheel with a bum left hand while operating the cell phone with the right is not a good thing. Evanita, I need your help. Can you hold the cell phone to my ear?"

Evanita held the cell phone to Sharon's ear. The van slowed suddenly and dropped back behind and along Sharon's car's right rear side. It attempted a PIT maneuver of its own to spin Sharon out of control. Sharon recognized the attempt and accelerated out of the way. The van managed to nudge the car a bit and send Sharon and Evanita onto the shoulder where they busily sped around a semi-truck trailer and regained position on the interstate.

The three Oregon State Police cars caught up with the van. One attempted a PIT maneuver but missed. The van eluded the officer by driving on the left shoulder and passing three cars before leaving the shoulder. These cars along with other truck traffic formed a rolling roadblock that kept the three cruisers behind. One attempted to follow along the left shoulder but braked hard when a disabled car on the left shoulder blocked his path. He could not stop completely. The bewildered owner of the disabled vehicle who was attempting to change a left-side tire jumped off the interstate a fraction of a second before the police car rammed it and took his vehicle out of the chase. This left two Oregon State Police cars in pursuit.

The van swerved around and fell in behind Sharon. It fired two shots at her car. The first missed; the second shattered the rear window. Evanita screamed. Sharon wasn't sure if she screamed from the window shattering or from her evasive maneuvers that jolted Evanita's neck left and right.

Jonara could not think. This was unlike anything she experienced at Saint Stellan or Barnseed Baptist. In both of those situations, the backpack had some influence over what she did. Here the backpack did nothing. In fact, there was no backpack with her at all. She was without it for the first time since she started dreaming. She felt naked somehow. She reached around the backseat of Sharon's car in hopes of finding it but did not. Jonara realized that hearing the gunshots had a mind-numbing effect. All rationality and reasoning—all memory of what was good and pleasant—left her. Her mind seemed stuck in place, as if someone had jammed a knife into her head and left it there to fill her brain with heat and hate. One thing did emerge from this—a swelling and throbbing that pained her to no end. Did someone place her heart in her skull? She placed her hands to her head and held her skull from exploding.

Semi-trucks and more traffic made maneuvering more difficult. Sharon struggled to avoid innocent motorists and the mania of the van. She piloted the car up the left lane. The van went up a right lane with a semi-truck trailer between the two. The van did not wait to pass the semi-truck. He fired a shot at Sharon's car between the truck's cab and trailer. The bullet shattered Evanita's window. Fortunately, Evanita had ducked. The bullet landed in the headrest behind Evanita. Evanita screamed again.

"Stay down!" Sharon ordered.

The van passed the semi-truck trailer and proceeded in the right lane quickly. Sharon was blocked by the semi-truck. She could not switch to the right lane to pursue the van. Instead, she continued in the left lane. A tanker truck led the semi-truck and prevented her again from changing lanes. She continued in the left and accelerated to keep up with the van. The van continued in the right. Sharon realized the van might shoot again if she drove parallel with him. She reached the opening between the tanker's cab and tank. The van aimed to fire. Sharon slammed on her brakes. The van fired through the opening but shifted his aim at the last moment to compensate for Sharon's sudden deceleration. The bullet pierced the tanker's hull.

The hull exploded. Sharon's car was next to the fireball. She hit the accelerator to evade it, but the car struggled to get power.

"It's starved for oxygen," Sharon yelled. "Hold your breath!" she yelled to Evanita.

The fireball engulfed the car and the semi-truck behind it. The semi-truck locked his brakes and jackknifed. All traffic behind him, including the two Oregon State Police units, was blocked. Sharon's cruiser lost speed. She needed a little more speed to clear the burning tanker but could not acquire it. The tanker was jackknifing itself and threatening to burn Sharon and Evanita alive. Jonara felt completely helpless. She tried to think but could not. Memories of Robert and her split personalities of Modern and Victorian were quite distant.

Sharon wheeled the car along the left shoulder as far as she could to scoop up the last bits of fresh air for the engine. The car scraped the concrete barrier several times as she continued the fight for air. Evanita could no longer hold her breath and in the excitement choked on the fumes.

"Get us clear," choked Evanita. "Let's take out the van."

Evanita beat on the dashboard two times as if motivating the car to go quicker. Somewhere, somehow, the car responded. It picked up speed ever so gradually and—as if a rainstorm parted—it reached clean air and accelerated with new vigor.

"We have to stop them, now!" Evanita urged.

"We can't get close enough for the PIT maneuver. It's too dangerous with their guns," Sharon said. "And I can't shoot with my left hand all beat up."

"Then let me shoot," said Evanita.

"What?! Evanita, have you ever fired a gun?" Sharon asked.

"No, but I can learn," Evanita said.

"This isn't the best place to learn," said Sharon. "You could do more harm than good. Not to mention it's illegal."

"I think we're beyond illegal," said Evanita.

"What's motivating you, Evanita?" Sharon asked.

"Something my mama always says. And I can't believe she's right, but now I'm starting to believe her—that men are evil," Evanita said.

"Oh no, Mommy," said Jonara. "This can't be you, this can't be true."

"It's true, Evanita," Sharon explained. "Men are evil. Some can be good, but many are evil."

By this very statement, "Men are evil," Sharon felt a new kinship and bonding with Evanita. It was a call to arms, a call to action. Rescue and respect for Sheila, for herself and Evanita, and for women everywhere.

Evanita retrieved the revolver from the floor.

"Now you're going to hold the revolver out the window with both hands," Sharon started. "Your arms must be straight and solid to handle the recoil. You'll aim for the rear tire, squeeze the trigger gently, and it will fire. Try to get several shots off if you can. I will only be able to hold a steady position for a few seconds. If you see anyone aiming at you, pull the gun in and duck. Understood?"

"Yes, Miss Stout," Evanita replied.

"Get ready," Sharon instructed.

Sharon wheeled the car around a semi-truck and reached a point behind—and to the left of—the van.

"Now!"

Evanita held the gun in the open window and fired with her eyes closed. The gun recoiled upward and toward the upper part of Evanita's window frame. It bounced off the window frame, out of Evanita's hands, and landed on the interstate. The speeding cruiser left the revolver far behind.

"Did I hit the tire?" Evanita asked.

Sharon maneuvered the cruiser back around another semi-truck for cover.

"No," said Sharon.

"I'm sorry."

"Don't be."

"Evanita, listen. Do your best and crawl into the back seat. Pull down the back seat and retrieve my rifle from the trunk," Sharon ordered.

Evanita pulled down the back seat that Jonara was sitting on. The seat appeared to pass through Jonara, as did the rifle that Evanita pulled out. Yet looped around the rifle was Jonara's backpack. Jonara grabbed the backpack as Evanita passed the rifle between the two front seats.

"Here's my backpack," Jonara said.

Inside was a book—The Bible. Yet when she opened it, there was no New Testament. There was no mention of an Old Testament, yet the books in this Bible were all from the Old Testament. She realized this Bible was the Jewish Bible. She flipped pages and saw a different depiction of the same scene she had seen in Barnseed Baptist Church—that of Moses holding his arms up with two men on each side supporting his arms. For a brief moment, the scene changed and it was a woman with one arm up and supported by another woman at her side.

"Evanita—help me position the rifle out the right window," Sharon said.

Evanita complied.

"It slips around too much," said Evanita.

"You'll have to hold it in place, please. We can't hold it against the front part of the window ledge because the right-side mirror is in the way," Sharon said. "This is going to be tricky. Keep low but hold the rifle. Pull down on it a little. Keep your hands next to the door. There, good."

Sharon yelled in pain as she transferred control of the steering wheel from her right hand to her left.

"This is worse than giving birth!" she screamed.

The cell phone had long ago hung up on her.

"My daughter's life hangs by a feather—the feather of my broken left wing!"

"I'm here for you," Evanita assured her.

"I know. Thank you, Evanita. I'll make it, I'll make it," Sharon said.

Sharon took the butt of the rifle with her right hand. She was positioned awkwardly and could not get her shoulder into the rifle evenly. Traffic cleared, and the van swerved wildly in front. She had to get around its left side for the rifle to be in position.

"When Moses raised his hands with the rod, Israel gained ground. But when Moses lowered his hands with the rod, Israel lost ground," Jonara read from the book.

Sharon zoomed the car around to the back left side of the van and fired a shot. It missed. The barrel's heat forced Evanita to use her shirt to protect her hands from burning.

"Too low," said Sharon.

"When Moses raised the rod with his hand," Jonara said.

Sharon raised the butt of the rifle to her jaw. She aimed, pulled the trigger, and fired. The bullet whizzed through the interstate air, homed in on the van's left rear wheel, penetrated the steel-belted tire, and released the tire's compressed air to the atmosphere. The tire imploded, shredded, and flung apart. The van fishtailed out of control, skidded, and flipped to the right. It tumbled over a retaining wall, down a slope, and plunged into a nearby lake.

Sharon pulled her car to the right side of the road and made a final cell phone call for help. She ordered Evanita to stay in the car. Sharon jumped over the retaining wall, ran down the slope, and dove into the lake after her daughter, Sheila. In Sharon's excitement, she neglected to place the automatic transmission in Park. The car rolled forward slowly. Without thought, Evanita jumped into the driver's seat, stomped on the brake pedal, and placed the transmission in Park. She turned off the engine and placed the keys in a cup holder.

"Sheila!" Sharon yelled.

Sheila remained underwater. Evanita could not remain calm and reserved in the car. Instead, she jumped out and stood between Sharon's car and the retaining wall. She debated whether to stay by the car and wait for help or jump over the retaining wall and help Sharon rescue Sheila.

One of the Oregon State troopers arrived behind Sharon's car and strobed its lights. The officer exited his car, glanced quickly around, and looked inside Sharon's car. He jogged over to Evanita to ask her what had happened, but before Evanita could answer, the officer threw her and himself over the retaining wall. An inattentive semi-truck trailer clipped the trooper's car and sent it plunging into Sharon's car. The officer and Evanita barely escaped the incident. The trooper jumped back over the retaining wall and ran to his wrecked vehicle to report the semi-truck, which did not bother to stop at the scene.

Jonara blinked several times. She was in Sharon's car when it was thrust forward. She was uninjured in the confusion—no splitting into Modern and Victorian as she had been by the gun in Barnseed Baptist Church. She took her backpack with her and exited the car—which had bounced off the retaining wall and rolled into the interstate lanes. A nasty, congestive traffic snarl ensued. Jonara stared at the lake where the van had plunged. Wispy vapors rose from the spot where the van bobbed slowly downward. Long shadows of sunset reached the van and stole the last rays of golden sunlight. The van fell into the air's darkness first and the water's darkness second.

Evanita ran down the slope while the trooper was occupied with his damaged cruiser and the traffic backup. Evanita stood next to the lake and peered across in the dusk. Sharon continued yelling for Sheila, but Sheila did not respond. One of the vandals swam from the van to shore and ran off, unchased. The other swam at Sharon and attacked her. It was the same vandal who'd kidnapped Sheila. Sharon struggled with her attacker despite being in pain from her injured hand and the prospective loss of her daughter. The vandal shoved her underwater to drown her, but she fought viciously and periodically came up gasping for air. Yet she could not dispense with him easily. Evanita realized Sharon was not going to be able to help Sheila escape the van wreck, and action had to be taken by someone to save Sheila's life.

Evanita looked around, but the only "someone" was herself. She felt alone for the first time in many years. How strange—she was so accustomed to annoying situations and going for a run to calm herself. Wasn't she alone on those runs? Yes, but she felt connected to the world—the earth was her friend. Here, the earth was against her—the natural laws of a van trapped in water and a friend undergoing oxygen deprivation in a lake of the earth's making had put the earth on Evanita's bad side. Who to turn to in this time of need? What help could she receive now?

In Evanita's brief moment of thought, Jonara had descended the slope. She reached out to hug her mother but could not—her arms passed through Evanita. She could not believe the universe was so cruel. Every telling in books and movies would have rightfully allowed her this single moment of connection, of bonding with her mother. She could not.

"They lied to me," Jonara yelled to an empty audience. "In this one moment when I should be allowed to touch and bond with my own mother, the Gods have forbidden me, if there are any gods at all! All those stories when everything works out and the family is together at the end were wrong. The world isn't like a movie. I've been cheated!"

With the backpack over her shoulder, the book inside nudged her.

"What?!" she yelled at the book as she removed it from her backpack.

Jonara wasn't pleased with the situation, and the book's effort to grab her attention seemed quite rude. Jonara opened the book with a grunting sigh, and pages flipped in the wind until the scene of Moses parting the Red Sea appeared.

"That only works in stories!" she yelled at the book. "There's no magic here!"

Jonara gave up on the book and hurled it into the lake.

"There! I'm rid of you!" she yelled.

It was an unfortunate parting of ways with the book and a loss of faith for Jonara, but the deed was done. She sat on the ground and buried her teary face in her hands.

Small ripples emanated from the tossed Jewish Bible. Ripples and air bubbles, as if a small life-form had sunk into the water. Yet despite the apparent ending of this book's usefulness, it had a final effect on the world and the earth. Yes, those ripples traveled on the water's surface. There wasn't enough energy from the ripples to effect physical change. No parting of the lake like the Red Sea. Yet Evanita in her moment of thought saw the ripples, and the air bubbles too. Whether the ripples and bubbles were real or imaginary, Evanita did not know. But she connected with them on a spiritual level. The air bubbles were the last gasps of life from Sheila. The ripples were the last calls for help, a rabbit's piercing scream through the air as it succumbs to a predator while in the throes of death. The predator here was the lake, and the helpless rabbit was Sheila.

Norepinephrine flooded Evanita's brain, much as it had when Johnny Pindus discovered her examining Valeria's teeth. But instead of run, run, run out of Barnseed Baptist Church, the norepinephrine commanded her to swim, swim, swim. There was no stopping the compulsion. Evanita took a deep breath in her runner's lungs and dove into the lake.

Jonara jumped in after her mother, but she passed through the water and landed on the lake's bottom. Breathing did not matter, and she did not drown. She walked along the bottom and followed her mother's swimming. Evanita's clothing waved and flowed in the water. Jonara had difficulty seeing in the dim light, and while she was able to see Evanita's clothing flow with her swimming, the clothing appeared as shades of gray instead of bright colors. Evanita parted the water with her swim stroke and drew a trail of bubbles behind her. She turned her head back for air every other stroke, and as she did, Jonara could see Evanita's determination to reach Sheila without delay.

Jonara wanted to help Sharon overcome the vandal, but Jonara could not swim from the lake's bottom to the surface. Jonara jumped and waved her arms, but to her the water was like air and would not support her desired ascent. She realized she could not help Sharon and turned her attention back to her mother.

Evanita reached the van, at least the spot where the van had bobbed up and down. It had now submerged into the lake. Evanita took one large gulp of air and dove straight down from the water's surface to the van. Vision was more difficult for Evanita than Jonara. While Jonara was able to watch Evanita's movement about the van (though in black and white), Evanita struggled to see much of anything and resorted to feeling around the van for an opening. She touched the van. When Evanita recognized exhaust piping and the driveshaft, she realized the van was upside down. She dove farther down around the passenger side and found the front door open. She grabbed the frame and pulled herself in. She didn't know where in the van Sheila could be, but she knew Sheila had to be trapped inside. Evanita pulled herself through the van—starting with the two front seats, proceeding to the row behind and the next row—checking and rechecking by sweeping her arms around and searching for any tiny nook where Sheila could be trapped. She reached the back of the van and found no signs of Sheila.

Evanita struggled for air. The buildup of carbon dioxide in her tissues created an involuntary compulsion to breathe. Her diaphragm contracted her lungs, but she held her hand over her mouth to keep from pulling in water. She was only partially successfully. Some water siphoned in through her nose. She choked. Evanita did not waste time climbing to the front of the van. She exited the van's rear door and swam to the surface.

"Ah-kugah, ah-krakah-kugah," Evanita coughed.

While Evanita cleared her lungs and nose of gasoline and water, she quickly glanced around and looked for signs of Sheila. She saw Sharon struggling with the vandal. Their position had drifted away from her and a bit toward shore. The shore! Evanita panned her head around the lake and struggled to find Sheila.

"Sheila!" Evanita yelled.

No response from Sheila.

"Wait right there, I'll come get you," called a voice to Evanita from up on the slope.

It was another Oregon State trooper. He pointed directly at Evanita and said:

"Hang on, honey, I'll pull you out."

Evanita dove back down toward the van against the trooper's order. Then it hit her—her nose had a gasoline smell from choking on lake water, but there was also something else she purged out—was it blood? Images of birth and death, umbilical cord and Valeria's mouth, placenta and a wounded creature being pursued by sharks filled her mind. She sniffed just a little lake water. Yes, there it was—something like blood. Evanita was disgusted to admit it, but the little sniff of blood triggered some compulsion, like an insatiable desire to eat heavily salted watermelon.

"I'm going mad. Maybe I'm at death's door," she thought.

She expelled the liquid from her nose, sniffed a bit more, and continued this behavior in some raw-animal survival mechanism where she envisioned herself a shark looking for prey. In this way, Evanita came upon Sheila's lifeless body two yards from the driver's side of the van. Her foot had been trapped in sharp debris. Jonara somehow did not see Sheila trapped in the debris—whether from the dim light or otherwise, Jonara didn't know. But even if she had, could she have warned her mother?

Evanita's first instinct was to bite Sheila, but she fought this twisted sense of a shark hunting prey and reached for the last elements of humanity left in her oxygen-deprived brain. She worked Sheila's foot free, latched her right hand around the nape of Sheila's shirt, and swam hard for the surface—working hard to balance fight for ascent with the effort to pull Sheila up. Sheila's body was lifeless and made no effort to swim upward.

"She's not a rag doll, not a rag doll," Evanita reminded herself. "She's alive yet."

It was a hopeful thought, but Evanita had no way to be sure. She reached the surface with Sheila. Sheila did not gasp for breath. Her head floated lifelessly above the water.

"Stay there, I'll help," another officer said.

By now, several officers stood at the edge of the lake (though why they didn't jump in and help—Jonara wasn't sure). The vandal attacking Sharon saw the officers, let Sharon go, and swam away—hoping he could escape. One of the officers with a strong arm tossed Sharon a flotation ring from the shore. She grabbed it, but she did not swim to shore. Sharon was injured, choking, and tired, but she was conscious. She paused in thought with the flotation device, considering how she could find her daughter. She didn't have long to wait. On seeing her lifeless daughter, she screamed—a scream one only hears when a mother sees her child mortally wounded. The scream shook Evanita to the bone. The scream waves carried through the water like an ultrasonic drill. It set in motion a harmonic resonance that slapped underwater currents together at high frequency and in so doing created a standing wave. The peak of the standing wave grew in amplitude quite suddenly and propelled Jonara out of the water like a cork out of a champagne bottle. Jonara landed on top of the lake's waterline with the scream's resonance maintaining a sort of permanent standing wave that supported her.

Evanita was rattled by the scream but more interested in restoring Sheila to life. She grappled Sheila face-to-face, tilted her own head, pinched Sheila's nose, and exhaled her breath into Sheila's lungs. The air expanded Sheila's chest, but Sheila did not awake. Evanita felt for a pulse on Sheila's wrist but found none.

"Her heart's stopped. Must get it beating," Evanita muttered.

Evanita struggled to apply her hands to Sheila's chest over the sternum, but this only pushed Sheila away. Evanita tried holding one hand to Sheila's back and another on Sheila's sternum for compressions, but this failed too.

"I can't do it," Evanita strained.

Evanita took another breath and filled Sheila's lungs. She beat once on Sheila's sternum and once on her back. No use. Sheila would not respond. Blood from Sheila's leg seeped out slowly around the two. Evanita tasted the blood in her mouth and sensed it in her nose. The event of Sheila's death was quite real—it wasn't just an apparition. Evanita smelled and tasted death in the water, and it triggered a most unpleasant reaction. Nothing else in the world mattered. Money, family, Evanita's own health or future—it did not exist for Evanita. Everything was now; everything was life ending in this lake, with this salty blood compelling her mind into that animal compulsion, like the shark, to hunt until the end—whatever end, either Sheila's return to life or in Evanita's death from over-exhaustion. Evanita would die like Valeria—over-exhausted but compelled by forces beyond her control. She lost rational thought—she forgot about the Heimlich maneuver to force water out of Sheila's lungs.

Evanita became the shark and attacked. She grappled Sheila around the torso and plunged her head into Sheila's abdomen with all her might—three times. Water shot out of Sheila's mouth. Evanita grasped Sheila's face, tilted her own, and exhaled into Sheila's lungs.

"Sheila!" Sharon screamed.

Sharon reached Sheila's and Evanita's position in the water, dragging a life ring with her. The scream jolted Sheila. She gagged, coughed, and moaned in pain.

"Sheila!" Sharon and Evanita hollered in joy.

"My foot!" she wailed.

"Here, take it easy," Sharon urged. "Put this over your head."

Sharon and Evanita helped place the life ring over Sheila's head. Sheila slipped her arms over the ring and rested but breathed hard. Sharon and Evanita cried. They cried in relief of their stress. They cried for joy in Sheila's return to life. And they cried because they were together and got through the ordeal. On reaching the shore, arriving paramedics secured Sheila to a stretcher. Sharon and Evanita accompanied Sheila in the ambulance where in a Portland hospital Sheila received nineteen stitches to her foot. The doctors were amazed at Sheila's recovery and attributed this success to Evanita's quick actions.

There was no opportunity for Evanita to learn of the surprise at the Stout house. On Sheila's release from the hospital, Eva picked up Evanita, and the two returned home for a more restful evening.

CHAPTER 9

Hothrane Zoroastrian

2006 Oct 7, Sat Afnoon. The Stout House. Portland, Oregon.

"Close your eyes, Nee-nee!" Sheila Stout said.

Evanita placed her hands over her eyes. She sat in the front passenger seat of Sharon's beat-up car while Sheila sat in back. Sharon had picked up Evanita from her house on Belgrave and drove without incident to the Stout house on the east side of Portland on Morrison Street just east of 92nd Avenue. Sharon pulled a little into the driveway but not all the way.

"Now keep your eyes closed and step out of the car," Sheila said. "Here, I'll help you."

Sheila and Sharon stepped out. Sheila closed her door and opened Evanita's. Sheila then helped Evanita step out of the car and walk a few steps to the front.

"Now open your eyes!" Sheila said.

Evanita opened her eyes. Sheila hooted and hollered for joy.

"It's my new car, my new car!" Sheila exclaimed. "This was the surprise I wanted to show you last week. Isn't it great, Evanita? Now I don't have to bum a ride off Mother when I want to go someplace."

"As long as you pay for the insurance and gas," said Sharon. "And don't drive it in a lake like those hooligans did last week."

"Whatever happened to them?" Evanita asked.

"An interesting question. They have a rap sheet longer than a roll of toilet paper. But they come from families with money. They're in jail for now, but that could change. Money has a way of buying freedom," Sharon explained.

Sharon looked at Evanita and Evanita looked back.

"So it was worth the chase?" Evanita asked.

"Yes it was. And thank you, Evanita," Sharon said.

Sharon gave Evanita a big hug, the best she could with her broken left hand and her injured cheek. Sheila tapped her feet and waved impatiently.

"Over here!" Sheila said.

"So this is really your car?" Evanita asked as the two broke up their hug.

"Yeah. I had to get a part-time job for gas and insurance," said Sheila. "But it's a small price to pay for freedom."

"It's about time Sheila got her own vehicle," said Sharon. "Now if I'm hurt and need to go to the hospital for things like this," she said, pointing at the cast on her left hand and wrist, "or this," she continued, pointing to the big bruise on her right cheek where the rifle kicked back, "Sheila can take me."

"Mother helped me buy it with Christmas and birthday allowances for the next five years," Sheila explained.

"You'll be an adult by the time you get a Christmas or birthday gift again," said Evanita.

"Exactly!" Sharon grinned.

"I spent hours looking on the internet for a good used car, but I couldn't find anything I liked," Sheila explained. "The cars were too much money or needed major repairs. Then a couple of weeks ago, we were at the racetrack, and—"

"She still wants to race, so I compromised and let her watch others race where Claire works," Sharon interrupted.

"Claire as in your older sister?" Evanita asked Sheila.

"Didn't you know?" Sharon asked. "Doesn't Sheila tell you anything?"

"I tell Nee-nee things—lots of things," Sheila said.

"She speaks mostly of herself," Evanita said to Sharon.

"That I believe," Sharon replied.

"I saw a 'For Sale' sign—" Sheila continued, trying to ignore Evanita and Sharon.

"Is this the Portland Raceway where Claire works?" Evanita asked.

"Portland International Raceway," Sharon clarified.

"—on a nice four-door sedan," Sheila continued.

"What kind of work does she do?" Evanita asked Sharon.

"Low miles, original owner, good gas mileage," Sheila continued on her own.

"She's a paramedic," Sharon said. "When there's a wreck or other injury, she provides first response treatment."

"Cool," Evanita said.

"And she gets paid," Sharon said.

"Even better," Evanita added.

"Isn't anyone interested in my story?" Sheila asked.

"She's studying to be a nurse," continued Sharon. "It's a noble profession, and I wish some of that would rub off on Sheila."

"Ha, ha, ha!" Sheila replied sarcastically.

"When are you going to tell us about how you found the car? We've been waiting for you to start," Evanita played.

"Hmmmmmph!" Sheila steamed. "I've been trying to tell you all along. Now listen—I met the owner. He's the father of one of the racers!"

"Sam Vagatti was the owner's name," Sharon added.

"Anyway, he sold us the car at a discount—and it was already cheap," Sheila said. "And would you believe—he gave us special tickets to count laps for his driver up in the booth. Oh Davino, Davino!"

"Who's Davino?" Evanita asked.

"Who's Davino!?" Sheila quipped.

"Sam's son. He's one of the racers. About eighteen, I think," Sharon said.

"He just turned nineteen last weekend. I went to his birthday party as a friend of the family," Sheila bragged.

"And you are sixteen. Remember that," said Sharon.

"How is it I didn't hear about this Davino guy? Why wasn't I invited to his birthday party as your guest?" Evanita asked.

"Oh please, please, Nee-nee, be a good sport and understand," Sheila begged. "And don't go running off to another church."

"Running off? What does that have anything to do with this guy?" Evanita posed.

Sharon sensed a bit of friendly interaction between the girls and made for her escape.

"I'm going to leave you two to chat," said Sharon. "I have some things to do inside. Sheila—be back in time for supper."

"I will," Sheila said, though she was surprised her mother had realized her plan to take the car out for a drive.

Sharon went inside the Stout house while Evanita and Sheila continued their conversation.

"I didn't 'run off'," said Evanita. "I suppose Davino is also Unitarian, is that it?"

"Actually, he isn't. He's Parsi," Sheila said.

"Parsi? What's that?" Evanita asked.

"A type of Zoroastrian. Zoroastrianism is an older religion from India or Iran. Parsis are mostly from India. There are very few of them left," Sheila explained.

"Now who's running off to another religion?" Evanita asked.

"I'm not 'running off'. And how dare you turn the tables on me?" Sheila grinned.

"What are friends for?" Evanita asked with her own grin.

"If you remember, you are Unitarian—" Sheila started.

"And you do remember? You were the one having trouble pronouncing words at your Coming-Of-Age," Evanita pointed out. "And that qualifies you to race cars?"

"At least I completed Coming-Of-Age. Anyway, before I was interrupted, yes, Unitarians believe in bringing faiths together. Davino is another faith that I want to bring together," Sheila said. "And what does reading have to do with racing?"

"You mean you want to bring the two of you together— Unitarian or not is another matter," said Evanita. "And if you do that, you can mooch off him and not worry about reading or racing or working for a living."

"Well yes...no...maybe. Small details. But look at it this way, Nee-nee—I've got a boyfriend. I like him, and he likes me. Maybe he'll let me drive his race car."

"Hah!" Evanita blasted.

"Hah yourself," Sheila continued. "It's time we get to know the world a little more. I'm dating a Parsi and a racecar driver.

I'm sophisticated. What about you? Are you dating anyone—anyone of real importance and not some common Portland boy?"

Sheila poked fun at Evanita to encourage her. Evanita wasn't impressed.

"I like common Portland boys," said Evanita. "And I don't need to date a racecar driver to be happy."

"Who cares about being happy? I'm talking about having fun. I bet there's someone you like. You're holding out on me, and you met him at one of those other churches you ran off to," Sheila speculated.

Evanita rolled her eyes in disbelief at what she was hearing. Yet she did think of Johnny Pindus and wondered what sort of confused feelings she had for him.

"You're sixteen, like your mother said. There's fun, and there's getting-into-trouble fun," Evanita warned.

"Who died and made you my mother?" Sheila countered in fun. "But back to you—you rolled your eyes, but you also gave me a blank stare. You were thinking about someone, weren't you?" Sheila prodded.

"No, no one," Evanita lied.

"You're lying. I know you, Evanita Carreña. I saw that blank stare in your eyes that gives you away when you're thinking about the very thing you're trying to deny. What's his name?"

"No one," Evanita lied again with a blush.

"Now you're blushing. Don't you want to tell me his name and relieve yourself of your pent-up suffering?"

"No, I mean—" Evanita stumbled.

"If you say, 'Yes,' you're saying you want to tell me his name. If you say, 'No,' you're saying you don't want to tell me his name. Either way, you're admitting that there is a 'he'," Sheila said.

"That's not fair. Anyway, it doesn't matter," said Evanita.

"And why not?" Sheila demanded.

"Because if I did have a boyfriend..." Evanita said with a pause while Sheila's eyes grew to the size of saucer dishes. "If I did, I wouldn't go blabbing it to everyone on the street corner."

"Oh, so now I'm everyone on the street corner, is that it? I thought I was your friend," Sheila said. "I tell you *my* secrets— why don't you tell me yours? What are you afraid of?"

"I'm not afraid, Sheila Stout. I just don't think it's necessary to tell everything at once," Evanita said.

"Oooo, a fast relationship. Did it crash and burn already? Did he hurt you?" Sheila asked.

"He didn't hurt me. Wait, I mean, there is no 'he'," Evanita backtracked.

Sheila laughed.

"It's fine with me if you don't want to admit anything yet. So when will you tell me?" Sheila asked.

"Never," Evanita huffed.

"Oh don't be that way. I'm just teasing you. C'mon. Let's go for a ride in my car. I just vacuumed the interior," Sheila said.

"Where to?" Evanita asked.

"Does it matter? Let's go driving around. Let's go cruising and see the world. Let's have some fun," Sheila said.

"Uh oh, there's that 'fun' word again. As long as I can go home anytime I want," Evanita said.

"I promise. The moment you get bored—" Sheila started.

"The moment I sense trouble before doing something stupid," Evanita finished.

"Yeah, that too. Okay, do we have a deal then? C'mon, Neenee, it's no fun going cruising alone. We'll just drive around and see stuff," Sheila offered.

"What about your mother?" Evanita asked.

"Didn't you hear her? 'Be back in time for supper,'" Sheila answered. "She already knows we're going out. Now loosen up a little already. I've got the keys in my purse. I'm ready to go. Are you ready? And say 'yes'."

"Yes," Evanita echoed.

"Cool! Let's go!"

The girls entered Sheila's six-cylinder sedan. Sheila started the engine, reversed out the driveway, and proceeded west along Morrison in an easy fashion so as not to arouse suspicion from her mother. Without warning, Sheila turned north on 92nd Avenue and let out a holler.

"What are you doing? You're supposed to go down to 82nd and turn right," Evanita said.

"I'm taking a shortcut," Sheila said.

"How? You'll just have to make an extra left for 82nd," Evanita pointed out.

Sheila kept silent and continued on 92nd Avenue north until she turned east onto Washington Street.

"Uh, Sheila. Where are you going? You want to go north on 82nd Avenue, over the I-84 bridge, quick right, and quick left to get onto 84 West. That's how to get to the raceway," Evanita said.

"How did you know I was going to the raceway? I never told you," Sheila said.

"'Davino, Davino,'" Evanita mocked. "You're so transparent, Sheila. But 205 is the long way. You'll have to backtrack south."

"Don't tell me how to drive," Sheila bragged. "I'm a sophisticated race driver."

Evanita rolled her eyes and stared out the right-side window. Sheila crossed over Interstate 205 and realized her mistake—there was no entrance ramp going northbound.

"Hmmm," Sheila mused.

"Yes, hmmm. Don't turn left. Go down to 96th and turn right," Evanita said.

Sheila turned left.

"I told you not to turn left. You can't get on 205 from here," Evanita said.

"How would you know? You don't even live around here," Sheila said.

"Oh my sweet turnip apple in a box. We're getting lost— Sheila style," Evanita lamented.

Sheila and Evanita crossed Stark.

"See? We're angling onto 205," Sheila guessed.

"Nope," Evanita said. "Look—people are getting off 205 and merging into us. Careful!"

A semi-trailer truck honked its horn as it merged just in front of Sheila and Evanita. The two proceeded north and passed under Burnside Street.

"There must be an entrance ramp to the 205 somewhere along here," Sheila pondered. "If we just go a little farther..."

"None. And if we go a little farther, we'll be in Washington. No raceway and no Davino," Evanita warned.

"Oh quit your whining," Sheila huffed. "Besides, we're cruising."

Sheila opened her window, held her left arm out, and let out another holler. The two came to a halt at the Glisan Street stoplight.

"Look at the sign, Nee-nee, and eat crow," Sheila said. "Or did you forget about this way onto the freeway?"

The sign above the intersection indicated a fork north of Glisan—one leading to Interstate 84 west, and the other to Interstate 205 north.

"I didn't forget. But you could have taken 82nd to 84. And you can forget about 205," Evanita said.

The traffic signal changed to green. The cars in front of Sheila proceeded forward north of Glisan Street. As the sign predicted, the road forked with I-205 traffic breaking left and I-84 traffic breaking right.

"Take 84 west. Eighty-four, eighty-four, 84! Where are you going? No, not 205, eight-four, four, FOUR!" Evanita shouted.

"And you said I couldn't get to the 205," said Sheila. "This is my shortcut."

"It's too late for 205. Too late!" Evanita said.

"It's never too late. We're cruising!" Sheila bragged. "And stop nagging me. Nag, nag, NAG! You sound like my mother. I'm a licensed, sophisticated driver. I'm dating a Parsi. I'm a woman."

"You're a dumb brunette who—when she can read—doesn't know what to do with the information. But who am I to say? I'm not a sophisticated Parsi like you," Evanita ranted.

"I never said I'm Paris, I mean Parsi," Sheila cautioned.

"But you'll convert to fit in with Dah-vee-noe," Evanita continued. "And I think you like the idea of being Parsi because it sounds like 'Paris'. But do you know what it is, I mean really?"

"Do you?" Sheila shot back.

"No, I don't," Evanita replied.

"Then I think you owe me an apology, Nee-nee," Sheila begged. "Please?"

"I'm sorry," Evanita sighed.

"Look, there it is—84 East," Sheila said.

Evanita kept quiet.

"Aren't you going to tell me to take 84? Eighty-four, eighty-four, EIGHTY-FOUR! That's how you do it, isn't it?" Sheila mocked.

"I'm not saying anything," said Evanita.

"Well I'm not taking eigh-tee-four, Miss eighty-four-itis!" Sheila said.

Sheila skipped the I-84 east exit and continued north on I-205.

"Shouldn't the raceway be up on the left? A lake, a field, and Airport Way?" Sheila said.

"Take Airport Way," Evanita said, hoping Sheila would not.

"No, I think I won't," Sheila said defiantly.

"Don't take Lewis and Clark Highway west. No one wants to drive along the Columbia River," Evanita said, again employing reverse psychology.

"You have no sense of adventure, Nee-nee. I love driving by the river, especially the Columbia. Don't you know that the Columbia goes for miles and miles from east to west? Or is it from west to east? I forget. But it goes through many states. Nee-nee, what's wrong?"

"Nothing," Evanita lied in solemn fashion.

The car fell silent, yet the two continued west on Lewis and Clark Highway. Sheila turned on the radio and fiddled with different stations, but nothing seemed appropriate. Sheila turned off the radio, stared out her window at the Columbia River, and made mention of a boat having fun in the water. Evanita appeared indifferent and looked the other way.

"What's wrong, Evanita? Don't sit there and sulk. I'm your friend. C'mon, it's not good to keep things inside."

Evanita said nothing.

"All right, I'm sorry. I played a mean trick on you and pretended to be a stupid chick. I knew where I was going all the time—I just wanted to 'jerk your chain' and have a little fun," Sheila apologized.

Evanita kept her silence and continued staring out her window.

"I didn't think you'd be such a sourpuss. I thought a ride along the Columbia would be nice," Sheila said.

Evanita thought back to Barnseed Baptist Church and Valeria's funeral. She drifted to thoughts of Saint Stellan and the crazy flying pew. Then there was her Coming-Of-Age—the hypocrisy—and Sheila playing along like it meant nothing. Just a cheap lie.

"Mommy," Jonara said from the backseat. "Please say something to Sheila. Please? She said she was sorry."

Evanita tuned out the world. Jonara reached for her mother from the back seat to the front, but her hand passed harmlessly through Evanita and her seat.

The car reached Interstate 5, and Sheila took the interstate south. The girls didn't have far to go. Sheila exited the interstate at the raceway exit and continued—with Evanita in silence—to Portland International Raceway. The two girls (plus Jonara) exited the car. Evanita made a comment about one should know the difference between a good joke and deceit, but Sheila brushed it off. She saw Davino's group from a distance and became emotionally charged. She forgot about her prank on Evanita and Evanita's negative reaction.

"Hurry, let's go!" Sheila urged.

Sheila rushed over to the group and in doing so left Evanita behind. Jonara kept pace with her mother but smelled something strange from her backpack. She removed the backpack from her shoulder, opened it, and reached inside. Her hand met ball bearings and black, sticky grease. She looked for a paper towel to wipe her hand clean, but none was available. She wiped her hand on the backpack's outside. Her hand was stained with grease, but that was the best she could do. She dropped the backpack to the ground, and she was amazed it did not follow or attach itself to her.

When Evanita and Jonara had nearly caught up with Sheila, the two passed an Hispanic mechanic playing music on his radio. He moved his arms in rhythm to the music in between ratchet turns. Evanita thought she had heard the song before but could not quite place from where.

"Now I remember," Evanita said. "It's *Patricia* by Perez Prado."

She imagined two people dancing the cha-cha. Evanita changed her gait to include a few cha-cha steps, and the Hispanic man applauded. He said something in Spanish that sounded very beautiful, but Evanita was ashamed to admit she didn't know Spanish well enough to fully enjoy the compliment. The mechanic tipped his hat to Evanita and waved. One of his buddies asked him for a tool, and in that moment, Evanita and Jonara moved out of his view.

Evanita and Jonara joined up with Sheila.

"There you are," Sheila said to Evanita. "This is Davino Vagatti. Davino, this is my friend Evanita."

"The pleasure is mine to be in your honorable company," Davino said. "Sheila, would you and Evanita like to watch me do time trials from the observatory room? Rest assured you will not miss a thing."

"O, c'mon, Davi—you promised you'd let me drive your race car. Why can't I stand along the track with you?" Sheila begged.

"Patience, my love, patience. There's a lot to learn about racing. Driving is only a small part. There's the pit crew, spotter, timer and scorer, marshal, flagger—so many things. I want to start you out easy. Soon I'll let you race, soon," Davino assured Sheila.

"Well, okay. You know best. For the moment, my love," Sheila said with a big kiss intended for Davino.

"Not here in public," Davino said as he pulled away from Sheila's kiss.

Sheila and Evanita (along with Jonara) walked a short ways and climbed up steps to an observation room.

"Here," Sheila said to Evanita as Sheila grabbed a stopwatch and scoring card. "I'll run the stopwatch, and you write down times."

Evanita agreed but with hesitation. Was this fun? Evanita wasn't sure. Maybe she didn't know enough about racing. She thought back to the mechanic and the *Patricia* song. The engine drones from outside faded into the background, and Evanita hummed the song and took a few small dance steps to the rhythm. She moved back and forth to her humming yet managed to keep up with recording Sheila's timings.

"I'm so proud I'm helping Davino. Thanks for being here with me," Sheila said.

A woman and a one-year-old baby entered the room briefly. She held the toddler in her arms and took him to the window.

"See Daddy down there?" she said to the toddler.

"Davino's looking good," Sheila said to Evanita.

Sheila called out a timing number, and Evanita recorded it. As Evanita finished recording the number, she looked up toward Sheila but caught a dirty stare from the woman with the toddler. The woman probed Evanita's eyes, rolled her own eyes, and left the observatory room in a huff with her toddler.

"Did you see that?" Evanita asked Sheila.

"See what?" Sheila asked. "I'm watching Davino."

"That woman with the kid. She gave us a dirty look," Evanita said.

"I don't know anything about a woman with a kid," Sheila said.

"I don't like it. It's like she disapproved of us or something," Evanita said.

"I don't care if she does or not," Sheila said.

Evanita thought the incident odd, and it bothered her. She tried changing the subject to get it off her mind, but it eventually crept back into play.

"Sheila—I have a question," Evanita said.

"Sure, anything."

"Do you get paid for this?"

"What?" Sheila said—a little confused by Evanita's question.

"This is a job—you're working for a paycheck, right?" Evanita asked.

"How rude! Don't speak so loud—word might get back to Davino. And you wouldn't want that—wait, here's another time," Sheila said.

Sheila called out a time to Evanita, and Evanita recorded it.

"You don't think this is work?" Evanita asked.

"Shhh, don't ask silly questions," Sheila ordered.

Sheila rattled off more numbers.

"Sheila, how can you do this—be subservient to Davino and all?"

Sheila slammed the stopwatch on the table, cringed her face like a prune, and shouted at Evanita.

"I am NOT subservient, Miss Attitude!"

"Why are you shouting? Has he brainwashed you?" Evanita asked.

"No! Now shut up," Sheila said. "And I don't know that woman."

"That's not what I asked you," Evanita said. "You're covering up something. You *do* know that woman, don't you?"

Sheila seethed in anger but kept her gaze fixed on the racetrack.

"That was Davino's wife and child! Oh Sheila! You're the other woman! How could you! It's a doomed relationship. And he's got you around his pinky. Oh Sheila, don't go after that kind. Their stripes are the same no matter where they go. Cheat, cheat, cheat!"

Sheila slapped Evanita across the face. Evanita fell backward in surprise.

"Is this who you want to be?" Evanita continued with a calm voice.

"You're nobody without a powerful man, Evanita. A nobody," Sheila stated.

"Now I know where Almarita gets it from," Jonara said. "She got this idea of mooching off a man from her Aunt Sheila. But

Davino—is this the same guy as Uncle Fostero? How terrible. I wonder if he cheats on Marina? No, I don't want to know. Oh Cerafina, I feel sorry for you."

"I hope you realize some day what a mistake you're making, Sheila, before you're loaded down with kids from a man who's procreating with another woman," Evanita continued.

"Shut up!" Sheila yelled.

"I need to go for a run," Evanita said calmly. "Goodbye."

As Evanita left the observation room, Sheila yelled at her.

"Go on then, run away and hide. But there's something you should know."

"And what's that?" Evanita turned back to say with a sigh.

"I didn't tell you everything. I know about you and your boyfriend," Sheila said.

"There you go again with crazy talk. What boyfriend?" Evanita asked with rolling eyes of disbelief.

"That mental dude. Johnny Pindus. I know about you two," Sheila said.

"You're full of it," Evanita countered, now getting irritated.

"Just some advice, Evanita," Sheila said with a stern voice. "Love only goes so far, and it's only for normal people. Stay away from mental cases, do you hear? Stay away from that Pindus man!"

Those were the last words Evanita heard from Sheila. Evanita slammed the door behind her, descended the observation steps in twos and threes, and jogged to the car. Sheila did not follow but instead remained in the observation room.

"I can't depend on her to give me a ride home," Evanita said. "I'll just jog home—I need the time alone."

Evanita jogged along the parking lot and headed for Interstate Avenue. As she neared the edge of the raceway grounds, a slow-moving ambulance paced along her right side.

"Hello," said a female voice from the driver's window.

Evanita jogged for a few more paces to ignore the ambulance.

"Hello, are you Evanita? My name is Claire. I'm Sheila's sister," said the driver.

"Tell Sheila it won't work. I'm not groveling back to her," Evanita said as she continued to jog along.

"Huh? I just wanted to say 'Hello'. I haven't seen you in a long time. Are you here to watch the race? I'm one of the paramedics," Claire continued.

"Tell her it won't work. I'm leaving," said Evanita.

"I don't know what you mean. I haven't seen Sheila today yet. Did she say something to you?" Claire asked.

The ambulance continued to keep pace with Evanita. Jonara kept up along her mother's left side.

"Ask her. She's head over heels for that two-timing Davino guy," said Evanita.

"I know, and I'm worried. She's beginning to isolate herself. The car, Davino, and now it looks like she's isolating herself from you," Claire said.

"Yeah, well, life goes on," Evanita said.

Evanita's breath got heavy, and she felt fully warmed up and ready for a serious jog.

"I'm sorry to hear that," Claire said.

"Don't be. And don't worry either. A good run clears my head of these things. I'll feel better when I get home," Evanita said.

"That's the spirit. I'm going back to the track. Say, why don't you call me sometime? We don't have to let Sheila know or anything," Claire said.

"Sure," Evanita said.

Claire gave her cell phone number to Evanita who in turn entered the number into her own cell phone.

"You could call home and get a ride, if you wanted," Claire said. "If not, I'd be happy to give you a ride."

"No thanks. I really need to do this run," Evanita said.

"All right. Take care Evanita, have a good run, and be safe," Claire offered.

"I will. Thank you, Claire."

"You're welcome."

Evanita left the raceway grounds and entered Interstate Highway (not to be confused with Interstate 5). She tried to think of good thoughts and the comforting words of Claire, but Sheila's shouting words kept entering her mind.

"Keep moving, keep moving. Don't let your mind be consumed by frustration and hate," Evanita said.

Jogging gave Evanita a comforting effect once she completed the first fifteen minutes. To suppress the mental back and forth echoes of Sheila's rant, Evanita concentrated on her feet as they landed on the ground.

"Left, right, left, right," she said.

Evanita's footsteps gave rhythm to her thought. She thought back to the mechanic's Latin music, *Patricia*, and hummed the song out loud. There was no one around to complain of her voice—which was refined yet passionate. Only a jealous person would complain. Nor did she have to worry about boys chasing her for her humming, which became a wordless singing. She could hum and sing without worry of these disturbances. The music pleasantly consumed her mind, and she drifted into a sort of running daydream where she perpetually danced along a very long floor with dotted lines and passing cars.

Jonara felt no fatigue from running. She kept up with her mother and savored these moments of peace and melody her mother provided. She had a strong sense her dream might end at any moment, so she continued alongside her mother and glanced at her every now and then. Jonara lost track of the time, but it wasn't long before the two reached Broadway Unitarian Church.

Evanita dropped from a jog to a walk with Jonara following the same moves. Evanita stood by the very bench where she had done so a few weeks earlier when she quit her Coming-Of-Age ceremony. A few birds chirped in nearby trees. Several cars were parked in the church lot, but not Eva's.

"Good, Mama isn't here," Evanita said. "How would I explain this to her?"

"The same way you always would," a familiar voice said. "That you just felt like running."

Evanita turned around and saw Eva.

"Where did you come from?" Evanita asked.

"I came here with a friend," Eva said. "Look, here she is now."

An older woman walked up to Eva and Evanita. Jonara did not recognize her.

"You remember Ms. Zyla?" Eva said.

"You're one of the mentors," Evanita said. "I had Mr. Robinson."

"Good afternoon, Evanita," Ms. Zyla said.

"Hi," Evanita replied.

"Ms. Zyla has offered to be your mentor for Coming-Of-Age," Eva said.

"Oh Mama, please! We've been through this!" Evanita said. "Do I have to go for another run?"

"Evanita, wait, please," Ms. Zyla urged. "I just want to have a little chat with you. What harm can there be in that?"

"You'll try to indoctrinate me—like the others," Evanita complained.

"Evanita, please, give Ms. Zyla a chance," Eva said.

"I gave this church a chance, and it didn't work. I gave Sheila a chance, and she's got Davino. Now I have to give church another chance?" Evanita asked, but she didn't expect an answer.

"I won't preach to you, Evanita. We can just talk," Ms. Zyla said.

"I'm done talking. I'm going home," said Evanita.

Evanita started running in place to loosen her legs which had tightened a little from stopping.

"We'll give you a ride home," said Ms. Zyla. "We were just on our way out now."

"See you at home, Mama," Evanita called.

Evanita jogged west across Broadway Bridge to Lovejoy Street, continued west to 23rd Avenue, north to Thurman, and west to the end of Thurman where she entered her neighborhood. She cut through the woods to her house where she went inside, grabbed a quick drink from the fridge, took a shower, and settled down to a movie. Her cat joined her and curled at her feet, which were nestled comfortably on the couch. She was just getting into the movie when the front door opened.

"Evanita, are you here?" said Claire's voice.

"Yeah, I'm in the living room. C'mon in," Evanita called.

"I have someone with me. And she has something to say," Claire said.

Claire entered the living room followed by another female.

"I'm sorry, Nee-nee," Sheila said. "I'm really, really, sorry."

"Yeah, whatever," Evanita said.

Evanita had worked out her frustration with the multi-mile run and was feeling rather good.

"May I sit down?" Sheila asked.

"Sure. You too, Claire. There are drinks in the fridge. Have some popcorn," Evanita offered.

Evanita had been snacking on a large bowl of popcorn and passed it over to Sheila.

"I'll get some drinks," said Claire.

Claire returned from the kitchen with drinks for Sheila and herself (Evanita already had a beverage) and was happy to find Sheila and Evanita laughing together with the movie.

"Did you want to see Davino's church?" Sheila asked. "It's at the corner of Hawthorne Bridge and Naito Parkway. There's no rush. We can see it anytime."

"Yeah, anytime. Let's finish the movie," Evanita said.

And they did.

CHAPTER 10

Arkham Atheist

2006 Oct 14, Sat Morn.

Jonara's backpack was lost for good. She had left it at the Portland International Raceway's parking lot, and the last she remembered while jogging with her mother was a car running over the backpack and dragging it along the rear bumper as it headed for Interstate 5.

"I'm sure it's disintegrated," Jonara said in a dark, misty room.

Jonara could not see, hear, or feel anything around her except a smooth floor. The mist smelled like a fresh spring night after winter had ended but before summer heat and bugs had added uric odor to the air.

Without warning, the floor slipped away from Jonara. At first she felt like falling, but there was no wind and no way to judge velocity. Blood and fluids pooled in her upper lungs and skull. Her nasal passages swelled, and her eyes felt pressure from behind the sockets, though not as much if she were standing on her head with Earth's full gravity pulling.

Jonara was alone. No backpack to swing around her, no relatives or friends to visit. Nothing. Had she gone blind and deaf? She gave a shout, but her ears heard nothing from the air. Only the resonance of her vocal cords against her skull registered in her ears. She sounded to herself as if under water, yet she breathed in and out without issue.

In the distance—was it in the distance or close to her? Jonara wasn't sure. It was a small pinprick of light, faint at first, but growing brighter. She waved her hands in front of her eyes. No, the light wasn't close—it was quite far away.

Jonara fell into water. It was quite obvious the liquid was water—first her feet, then her legs, her torso, arms, and face. The water was cool but urging—urging her to swim to the light. Waves pushed her toward the light, and she swam with one arm over the other in freestyle. She looked up at the light, and she realized—though still far off—the light was not a solid white color. There was a faint flickering. Not rhythmic, not predictable, but definitely a flicker. She continued swimming what seemed an eternity, and for most of the eternity, the light appeared no larger than a pinprick.

But Jonara did reach a point—what Jonara called the realization point—where the light was no longer an unrecognizable small flicker and instead was large enough to recognize. It was at this point the water shallowed and her feet touched something solid. At first, the feet touched sand, then stones, blocks, and steps. She climbed the steps over a small hill and to her surprise found an open-air cinema with people seated and focused on the light. The light was actually a screen—a movie screen—and a movie was in progress. The audience remained focused on the screen and was completely unaware of Jonara's arrival.

Or were they? At the back corners of the seating area, two people looked behind. No people sat behind them, and so they had no pressure to continue looking forward at the screen. They noticed Jonara and realized she was a newcomer and not yet absorbed into a seat and the movie. The one closest to Jonara (on her right) lassoed a rope in her direction to trap her. The first attempt missed. Jonara backed away from the lassoer on her right, but in doing so she didn't realize that backing away from the lassoer sent her in a more or less lateral path parallel to the back seats. In this way, she unknowingly backed toward the other lassoer. A lasso plopped over her head and caught her in the torso with her arms trapped at the elbows. Jonara struggled to get away, but she couldn't.

The lassoer who caught her pulled her to the front row and shoved her into a chair—forcing her to watch the movie. The full stares of those behind prevented her from rotating her head to either left or right direction. The lassoer in turn was free and left the cinema. Jonara did not know where—she was forced to look at the movie and could not turn away.

Jonara remained in the front row for quite some time. But gradually, other newcomers also sat in the front row. This process displaced people in a ripple effect where newcomers sent existing front rowers to the second row, second rowers were bumped to the third row, etc., until those in the last row were displaced and freed. As Jonara made the gradual transition from front row to back, she was able to turn her head more and more from left to right to left again. She was able to break her eyes from the screen bit by bit, but the light from the screen blinded her terribly, and if there were by some strange chance other lights from other movie screens, Jonara would not have been able to see them.

Jonara's time had come. She was in the last row and had to make a decision. Those in the last row who were ready to leave had to lasso a newcomer—there was no free escape. This changed things a bit—it meant Jonara would have to be willing to sacrifice an innocent newcomer's freedom in exchange for her own, and she'd have to compete with other back-rowers for this "privilege" of deceit.

Amazingly, each seat in the back row had a rope with lasso available. Jonara too had a lasso and watched intently for the next victim. She kept her eyes focused away from the movie screen and in so doing allowed her eyes to accustom themselves to the darkness.

"Come here, newcomer. Don't be afraid," Jonara beckoned.

Jonara thought she could tolerate such deceit, but a bitter taste traveled up her esophagus from her churning stomach. She thought back to Sharon's rifle as it shot out the tire of the neo-Nazi van. She tried imagining herself with a similar mission.

"The newcomer is a bad person, doesn't deserve freedom, isn't a real person, and is a nobody," she repeated.

Jonara initially felt guilty for saying such words—they weren't very considerate—and certainly not in keeping with how her mother (Evanita) had brought her up in the Unitarian church. Yes, Unitarian—but how did her mother get back to the Unitarian church when she was going from one church to another and avoiding her Coming-Of-Age ceremony?

Jonara didn't know, nor did she have much time to think. A newcomer, unaware of how the movie-ripple-effect worked, approached the back row from the distance. Jonara used her ears to judge the distance of the person, and without knowing what sort of person it was or even the gender, Jonara roped the young girl with the lasso.

The girl cried and cried. Jonara knew the system, or at least what the system had conditioned her to do—lead the girl to the front row and force her there. Jonara pulled the girl in close and began leading her up front. The girl cried. Not hard or screaming like a spoiled brat, but a soft whimper as if the young girl had been saddened before and knew all too well the consequences. The whimper simmered down, and the little girl's face pointed down in sullen dejection. Would the little girl's deprived freedom deprave Jonara of her moral sense? Could Jonara sell her soul to achieve a perceived short-term freedom without accounting for the long-term need of a soul?

Jonara hesitated, and this was recognized by those staring at the movie. Their eyes darted between the movie and Jonara's situation with the little girl as if to say:

"You'd better push her down in the front seat. We've been waiting a long time to receive our own freedom."

Jonara remained frozen in place—halfway between the front and back rows.

"Jail her," the people murmured. "Jail her."

The people continued this low chant in tempo with the movie. When the movie sped up, the audience spoke, "Jail her," more rapidly, and when the movie slowed, the people dragged out the words "Jail" and "her."

Yet there were no physical threats to Jonara and the little girl. The audience's attention was clearly fixed on the movie. They could not leave their chairs and gang up against the two—to do so would exhibit defiance of the movie and gain them their own freedom. No, they repeated, "Jail her," in full expectation their words would be headed. It was unthinkable to permit an alternative event.

Jonara attempted to remove the lasso from around the little girl's torso, but between the audience's chant and the blinding movie, Jonara could not.

It was the little girl who freed Jonara. She wiggled her arms free enough to enlarge the lasso. Instead of removing the lasso and succumbing to the trap of the movie and people, she beckoned Jonara to kneel a little. Jonara was able to do this, and the little girl placed part of the lasso around Jonara such that the two were both trapped in the lasso.

Jonara understood. She pulled the lasso tight. By being trapped in this smaller "world," she achieved enough freedom of will to move away from the front and exit the cinema at the back. But she could not do this alone. She had to work with the little girl, no, coordinate her movements with the girl such that for each backward step the little girl took (the two were facing each other), Jonara took a forward step. For every forward action Jonara took, the little girl took an equal and opposite backward action.

"It sounds familiar, like a law of Newton," Jonara mused.

The two didn't have to coordinate for very long. They left the cinema and found a dry spot well outside any back-rowers who would want to recapture them. The little girl removed the lasso from Jonara and herself. Jonara hugged the little girl, but they were interrupted. In the opposite direction of the movie screen, another flicker of light appeared. Jonara had not noticed it before, but she had never looked behind her when she first swam toward the first light. Nor could she have seen it while waiting to rope the little girl—the light of the movie screen had enough effect to obscure the faint light.

"Perhaps that light is better," Jonara said.

"No," said the little girl. "That light is just as bad. I escaped from there and thought your movie screen was safe."

"We'll be safe as long as we don't swim over there," Jonara said.

"No, it's coming closer. It's a ship like the one we just escaped. We have to leave this ship's waters before the other one collides with it," the little girl said.

"Then we must swim," Jonara said.

"Yes, we must. We must swim perpendicular to the ships to get away. And we must swim away from each other. They are drawn to us and would be pulled in our direction if we swim together. But if we swim away from each other, our draws will cancel each other out. It is the only way."

"That doesn't feel right. Loneliness cannot be the answer," Jonara said.

"For each answer, there is an equal and opposite re-answer," the little girl said, and she dove into the water and swam away.

Jonara dove in shortly after, and after hesitating again about whether to swim after her or not, she realized she had to swim away from the little girl to escape the two fast-approaching ships with their mesmerizing movie screens and obsessed audiences.

Eva's House.

Eva, Evanita, and Ms. Zyla sat around the dining table playing cards. There was light conversation about the weather and falling leaves but no mention of Ms. Zyla's desire to mentor Evanita. Jonara sat at the table between Evanita and Eva and wished she could play cards with them.

"Rummy on the board!" Evanita called.

"My eyes aren't what they used to be," Ms. Zyla said. "How did you miss that, Eva?"

"My daughter is too quick for me," Eva explained.

The telephone rang.

"I've got it!" Evanita blurted as she rushed to the telephone and picked it up. "Hello?"

Evanita returned to the table with the cordless phone in hand.

"Oh hi, Claire!"

At the mention of Claire's name, Eva and Ms. Zyla rolled their eyes. They didn't want Evanita spending time with Claire if they could help it.

"You are?" Evanita said.

"She's a confirmed atheist," said Ms. Zyla.

"Oh Zellie, what about tolerance?" Eva said to Ms. Zyla.

"They don't tolerate us—that's the problem," Ms. Zyla said.

"I'd love to go," Evanita chimed over the phone.

"Uh oh," Ms. Zyla said. "Doesn't sound good."

"I'll be ready in five minutes. I'm just finishing a card game," Evanita said.

"Finishing? We just started," Ms. Zyla said.

"Now Zellie, Claire is a good person. If she wants to do things with Evanita, what's the harm?"

"It's not what they do, it's what they say," said Ms. Zyla.

"Okay, Claire, I'll see you very soon! Bye!" Evanita finished.

"What was that about?" Eva asked.

"Claire and the Arkham Group are going on a garden spree!" Evanita exclaimed. "And I can go along!"

"I haven't seen you this happy in a long time," Eva said to Evanita. "So you're going to tour the different botanical gardens in the area, I take it."

"Of course," Evanita said. "That's what I said."

"You said something else too," Ms. Zyla said. "The Arkham Group."

"Yes, Zellie-Nellie, the Arkham Group. Claire is part of it, and I like 'em," Evanita said proudly.

"They have another name—the Arkham Atheist Group. Is that who you want to associate with?" Ms. Zyla said nicely.

"Zellie, I think we should—" Eva said.

"What's this 'we' stuff, Mama?" Evanita asked. "And I know what the 'other' name is—so what? Can't I enjoy the gardens around here? In Portland? The rose capital of the world? I'm going," Evanita finished with a smirk.

"No. Now you listen here, Evanita," Ms. Zyla started.

Evanita tuned her out. She hummed something in her mind and bobbed her head left and right.

"Those atheists—they don't think like we do," Ms. Zyla continued.

"No one thinks like anyone else," Evanita said with a monotone to suggest how bored she was getting.

"They want to mechanize the universe. They'd reduce the origins of life to a single mathematical equation if they could," Ms. Zyla said.

"Hah!" Evanita blurted, not knowing what she was hah-ing to, only that it was a good place in Ms. Zyla's oratory.

"And another thing—they don't want you to talk about God at all—not even once. They cringe in pain like you said Lucifer or Beelzebub. We're not stupid, Evanita. We know about them. They get too narrow-minded about things. Their world has to be their way. And they attack the Bible for every little perceived mistake they can find. But you don't hear them attacking every newspaper's typos or magazine's rant with the same passion. If only they'd loosen up," Ms. Zyla continued.

Claire knocked at the door. Evanita ran to the door with her things, let out a quick, "Bye," to Eva and Ms. Zyla, and out the door she leapt.

"Oh, youth these days," Ms. Zyla said.

Eva laughed.

"Claire!" Evanita said as she sat next to Claire in the middle seat of a full-sized van.

"What!" Claire said back.

The van was filled with music, joking, and laughter.

"What's Sheila up to?" Evanita asked.

"Oh you know," Claire replied. "She's memorizing books on Zoroastrianism—trying to convince Davino she is Zoroastrian."

"But she isn't," Evanita said. "That's why they wouldn't let Sheila and me into Hothrane Church last Sunday."

"Yes, but she got Davino to lie for her. Whatever. Hey, don't worry about her. Let's enjoy the gardens. First stop—our very own Portland Rose Garden!"

"Saving the best for first," said Evanita.

"Of course! No telling how much time we'll have," Claire said.

The van headed south from Evanita's house to the Portland Rose Gardens. It was late in the year, and Evanita didn't expect much, yet to her surprise there were roses and other flowers in the garden. The van unloaded quickly. Evanita was shocked—each person (other than Claire and herself) had some sort of electronic device. Most had cameras and shot off frame after frame—often capturing Claire and herself in candid poses. Some had other equipment—spectrometers, infrared scopes, and ultraviolet goggles.

"I feel like I'm on another planet," Evanita said. "Don't you get embarrassed?"

"Why would I? Look, isn't this a wonderful specimen of *Rosa chinensis*?" Claire asked.

"Huh?"

"That's a China rose," Claire said. "Or this one—*Rosa persica*. This one doesn't look like a rose, but it is—*Rosa pimpinellifolia*. That's a Scotch rose, Evanita."

"I guess I'm not as smart as you. I don't recognize any of those Latin names," Evanita said.

"Yes, Latin names," Claire said.

"Seems late in the year for flowers—how do they do it?" Evanita asked.

"You mean how do the groundskeepers keep the flowers blooming beyond their natural state? Science," Claire answered.

The two walked about the gardens as Claire explained. Jonara followed behind but had a sneaking suspicion a vine would thrust itself from the bushes and wrap itself around her legs.

"Taxonomy—I remember from biology class. But I could never memorize all the names," Evanita said.

"You're right. All life is organized by taxonomy—a hierarchical structure from the top levels of basic life structure to the lower detailed levels of fully-formed life. Used to be the Kingdom was the top level, but they've added a couple more for the moment—Domain and Dominion," Claire said.

"And when does it end? This naming and adding levels?" Evanita asked.

"Oh the naming will never end. Between genetic research and new life-forms being discovered, the naming will continue. But adding more levels above Dominion might not happen anytime soon—there's little left at the basic levels for differentiating life."

"Smile!" said one of Claire's friends.

The two girls smiled.

"So you're still a Bible thumper, aren't you?" Claire asked.

"Maybe," Evanita said.

"I heard about your Coming-Of-Age. Sheila told me," Claire said.

"Yeah?"

"Sheila's a follower. You know that. Something new comes along, and she jumps on the bandwagon," Claire said.

"She doesn't seem to realize it either," Evanita said.

"I think she does—later—when she's between fads," Claire said.

"Yeah, and the next fad comes along," Evanita said.

"And the next, and the next, *ad nauseum.* But not you—you're different. You challenge things," Claire said.

"I don't like to. Things just get under my skin. And I have to go on a run to get bad feelings out of me," Evanita said.

"You're feeling dissonance," Claire said. "Like hearing a musical instrument slightly out of tune. Others aren't as perceptive as you."

"I've never heard it explained like that," Evanita said.

"There's another part of dissonance that's very annoying. When two frequencies are close together, they seem to beat," Claire explained.

"Like this," said one of Claire's friends.

The friend pulled out two little devices and turned them on. Immediately, Evanita and Claire threw their hands over their ears.

"Turn it off, turn it off!" Claire ordered.

"I thought I'd help," he said.

"You 'helped' more than enough," Claire said.

"I've heard that before—on old science fiction shows from the 1960s—like some sort of overloaded ray gun or something," Evanita said.

"It was a novelty then. But as you can see, it's annoying. Dissonance does that—and when you see things in the world that are just a little bit off, it's subtle enough where you'll miss it on an analytical level, but intuitively it drives you crazy," Claire said.

"I know what you're going to say—if I see things as being a little off, but the world thinks it's fine, then I must be off. I must be crazy, I must be medicated. Isn't that the scientific explanation?" Evanita asked.

"Smart chick," said the guy who pumped out the beating frequencies. "And science would be happy to offer all sorts of prescription drugs to treat you."

"This is Adrian. Adrian, this is Evanita," Claire said.

"Have we met?" Adrian asked. "You look familiar somehow."

"No, I've never seen you before," Evanita said.

"Science doesn't always get things right," Claire said.

"Which is what engineering is for—to patch up the loose ends that science only gets partly right," Adrian said.

"Adrian is talking about those moments when a science theory is implemented in the real world—it's called percent efficiency, isn't it Adrian? Adrian?" Claire called.

Adrian was smiling ear to ear, but not because of anything Claire said. He was walking around the two young women and checking out their profiles.

"Adrian, what are you doing?" Evanita asked.

"Nothing," he said.

Adrian continued walking around the two.

"Dissonance?" Evanita asked, referring to what Adrian said versus what he was doing.

"Maybe," Claire agreed.

When Adrian walked behind Evanita, she turned her body to the right quickly and hooked her fist into Adrian's jaw.

"Oh, what are you doing there?" Evanita grinned.

"Okay, okay, I get the hint. I'll be over there if you need me," Adrian said.

Adrian walked over to some other friends and chatted with them, pointed at Evanita, they chuckled, and he stormed off to something else.

"Jerk," Evanita said.

"He's not like that normally," Claire said. "Must be the way you're wearing your clothes."

"There's nothing wrong with my clothes," Evanita said. "Other people have no problem with what I wear. But he has something wrong with him—inside."

"You're connecting with him on an emotional level," Claire observed.

"No. I don't like him. I'm not connecting."

"Hate is a form of connection, a sort of unpleasant bonding," Claire said.

"For a moment you sounded like Sheila. Let's not get philosophical, okay?" Evanita said.

"Why not? You sense things aren't right in the world. Don't you think you need to understand why, to resolve conflicting beliefs inside of you?" Claire asked.

"This almost sounds like indoctrination," Evanita said. "And I'm starting to resent it."

"Okay, I'll hold off on the deep talk for now—you need time to absorb these things. I remember how it was when I was your age," Claire said.

"Now you're trying to patronize me to get on my good side—but you're just making things worse!" Evanita said. "You may remember how you felt about things when you were my age, but you never knew what I felt at my age. Why is everyone trying to push their beliefs on me?"

"Science isn't a belief. It's science," Claire said.

"Isn't it a belief?" Evanita asked.

"It's subject to change—based on evidence and processed data. It's repeatable and falsifiable," Claire said.

"But how do you decide what data to gather, where to go?" Evanita asked.

"You gather data where the data is—where the object is you're studying," Claire said. "You're making this harder than it really is. The right data is always closest to the source."

"Is that science too?" Evanita asked.

"It's common sense. If I want to study the sun, I point the telescope at the sun—with a proper filter of course, or send a probe close to the sun. That's where the data is. It's common sense," Claire said.

"It's a belief. And it blinds you to other places where you might have data," Evanita said.

"Oh come now, you can't prove what you're saying, because to prove it you have to have data, and the data is at the sun— nowhere else," Claire said. "This is getting tiring, Evanita. I wish you'd learn to speak in more scientific terms."

"No, because that locks me in the scientific world, and that becomes a trap," Evanita said.

"You're talking philosophy?" Claire asked.

"A lack of evidence doesn't mean there isn't any," said Evanita. "If a tree falls in the woods and no one hears it—"

"It makes a sound. Instruments can detect it. Video cameras will catch the air vibrations affecting nearby small objects. It makes a sound."

"The source of data should be the tree, but it isn't. These nearby objects—" Evanita said.

"Are inconsequential. The tree makes the sound, not the leaves or twigs nearby. The energy difference is enormous," Claire said.

"That's the first hidden variable you've admitted to. Now your selection of data is based on where the most energy is," Evanita said.

"Better data with better energy," said Claire.

"Now 'better' is defined based on quantity. More is better, right?" Evanita asked.

"Oh please."

"What about solar wind, how it interacts with the Van Allen belts of Earth, the heliosphere, the termination shock, interaction of the solar wind with interstellar space, hmmm? What do those interactions tell you? What other interactions are out there that are far away from the sun that generate data? We may not know what other data about our sun is way out there," Evanita said.

"Many questions. Good. Science can use many questions. But be careful. Science doesn't like to come up with random answers to prematurely fill in the gaps of knowledge. All too often religion takes this up—and all too often religion keeps holding onto these fake answers when the real ones are discovered—by science," Claire said. "What do you have to say to that?"

"That may be true about religion, but I didn't bring up religion—you did—twice now. My *beef* about science is this—all too often the focus seems too focused—it easily ignores other little things that might be overlooked. Sometimes it's because no one thinks to look in other places, other times these other places are somewhat known but tossed aside as exceptions," Evanita said.

"Science does the best it can with what it knows. No one can ask for more," Claire said. "But religion."

"There, you did it again. You brought up religion. I keep thinking that science hates religion. And you said hate is a connection, a bond. Is science bound to religion? How can that be science? It doesn't make sense to me."

"Okay, Evanita, you win. There. I said it, you win. Isn't that what you wanted?" Claire asked.

"No, it isn't. I really didn't want to 'win'. There's nothing to win. I just want to get rid of this feeling I get in my stomach—when the world seems obsessed with itself. The best I can do is start running. Some people say I'm running away from things, but that's not what I feel. I feel I'm connecting with the world in a special way, a direct way without being polluted by world opinion."

Claire smiled. The others in the group concluded their photography and other scientific measurements. They prodded Claire and Evanita back into the van where the group visited other gardens in the city—Portland Classical Chinese Garden, Berry Botanic Garden, and the Japanese Garden Society of Oregon. The two didn't speak much more of science, and Claire didn't bring up religion again, except to joke about Sheila studying like mad for the first time in her life just for the pretense of being a Zoroastrian.

2110 Dec 27, Sat Noon. 376 Grey Road, Hamilton, New Zealand.

"Oh my, the morning passed by quickly," said the one-hundred-year-old Jonara. "I've talked your ears off without letting you get in another question."

"That's quite all right," Kristi said. "The more information the better."

"It's time for lunch," Jonara said. "May I get you two something? I have some leftovers from last night."

"We brought sack lunches," Kristi said. "They're in the news van."

"You don't have to eat out there," Jonara said. "Please, bring in your lunches and spend the noon hour with me. After lunch, I'll give you a tour of the house—if I can find the other rooms."

The three laughed.

CHAPTER 11

Cerossi Café

2110 Dec 27, Sat 1 pm. 376 Grey Road, Hamilton, New Zealand.

"And this is the third guestroom, if I can get the door open," elder Jonara said.

"It's filled from floor to ceiling with books, magazines, papers, and shoe boxes," Kristi said.

"It is a little inconvenient, but I'll get around to cleaning it out. Oh, there's so much I want to do," Jonara said. "But here, let's go to the next room. It's the fourth guestroom. Look, see? There's room to walk around. At least there is in the center. Watch your elbows. I have everything placed very carefully."

The room held stacks from floor to ceiling of toilet paper, paper towels, paper napkins, alcohol wipes, cotton swabs, cotton balls, and cotton wipes.

"Did you find a sale?" Kristi asked, but Margaret nudged her shoulder.

"What? Oh, well, I like to keep stocked up. I'll always need paper products," Jonara said. "This is just temporary until I clean out the basement. Oh, the basement. I hardly ever get down there. The steps need work, and well, I am full up to my armpits with things on the upper levels. But once I clean out the basement, then yes, I can clear this room out."

Margaret and Kristi looked at each other as if to ask, "What could the basement be like?"

"Begging your pardon, Mamma Maffet, but may we resume the interview?" Kristi asked.

"Oh, the interview! I forgot all about that. For a moment, I thought you were my grandchildren. Yes, let's go back downstairs," Jonara said.

The three returned to the living room. Jonara resumed telling about her past, and Kristi narrated as follows:

2006 Oct 21, Sat.

Jonara stood at the top of a steep cliff. Where? She did not know. It was twilight—as one might see during dawn or dusk—and she heard water trickling far below. She strained her eyes to see across, and as her eyes adjusted to the low light, she thought she could make out a corresponding cliff across from her, facing her, with the little girl she had seen earlier from the strange movie cinema.

"Hello!" Jonara shouted to the little girl.

"Hello there," the little girl shouted back.

"How do I get across?" Jonara yelled.

"I was going to ask you the same thing," she replied.

"My name is Jonara. What's your name?"

"Geneva," the little girl said. "I live in Spain."

"Are you my great-grandmother?" Jonara asked.

"Yes, but not yet. I have to grow up first," young Geneva said.

"There must be some way we can meet," Jonara said. "Do you see any bridges?"

"Not at our level. But if you look down, you'll see bridges," young Geneva said.

"All in the same direction?" Jonara asked.

"Mostly. They are one after another. If you were to jump, you'd fall past them all. And they have names," young Geneva said.

"You don't sound like a little girl. How old are you?" Jonara asked.

"Much older than I look. I only look like a little girl because you want me to," young Geneva said.

"What are their names?" Jonara asked.

"Names?"

"The bridges down there—what are their names?" Jonara asked.

"Broadway, Steel, and Burnside. Morrison, Hawthorne, and Marquam. Ross Island Bridge. And the last, the bottom, the bridge at the very bottom—you do not want to know its name. No one wants to remember—everyone wants to forget. Don't look for it, don't go that way, don't jump down," young Geneva explained.

"Then what should I do? All bridges are down," lamented Jonara.

"Is that where the evidence lies?" young Geneva asked.

"Yes. All bridges are down," Jonara said.

"You forgot what I told you before," young Geneva said. "For every answer, there's an equal and opposite re-answer."

"That was you? With the movie and the ships?" Jonara asked in surprise. "But tell me—how do I look where there's no evidence?"

Jonara looked down and around but saw no other bridges. Young Geneva nodded her head, "No," and pointed up with her index finger. Jonara looked up, and out of the twilight she saw another bridge.

"Fremont," young Geneva said.

"The re-answer," Jonara said.

"For the moment," young Geneva said. "But if I had chosen it as the answer..."

"The bridges below would be the re-answer?" Jonara asked. "Then which is right or wrong?"

Young Geneva laughed and laughed until she rolled on the ground and choked on her own laughter.

"By calling one right and the other wrong—it doesn't matter which—you have just polarized yourself. And you excluded us," young Geneva said. "Which of us is right or wrong?"

"That doesn't make sense," Jonara said.

"Doesn't it though? Which way is sense—up or down? Which way is sense—up and down, or forward and backward?"

"I just want to cross over to your side—I don't need riddles!" Jonara said.

"That's how it starts—with one desire, one goal. But where does that leave me?"

"On the other side waiting for me," Jonara said.

"Are you sure? I want to cross over to your side," young Geneva said.

"But you don't have to," Jonara said.

"Neither do you. But I want to," young Geneva said.

"So do I. Where does that leave us?" Jonara asked.

"In a riddle. And we are not alone."

At Eva's House.

Jonara appeared in the woods behind Eva's house. Well, not exactly like that. She felt she had sprouted and grown out of the ground. She looked at her attire and expected to see lots of yellows and greens but was surprised to find herself adorned in crimsons, dark reds, pinks, and violets. She wore a cerise-colored hat and shoes.

"I came out of the ground, and I'm not dirty," she said. "Am I going to someone's wedding?"

Jonara walked from the woods and entered Eva's house. Evanita was preparing breakfast—pancakes for her mother, eggs and fruit for herself. Evanita had just come back from a morning jog and wanted to eat before showering. Eva strolled in with a night robe and joined her daughter. Jonara sat at the dining table with the two and wished she could snatch a pancake or too with loads of butter and heavy maple syrup.

"Ah, it's good to have a day off from the clinic on a nice Saturday morning," Eva said. "How are you feeling today, Evanita?"

"I feel fine," Evanita said.

"Do you have—" Eva started.

"It's okay; I know you're going to ask me if I have any plans for today. I usually don't like the question. But today is different," Evanita said.

"Oh?"

"Yes. I think it's time for a change. Each weekend I've been going off to one church or another. Last weekend was with the atheists. I want to do something for me," Evanita said.

"I thought you were doing that all along. I certainly never stop you when you run off from a situation," Eva said.

"That's not what I meant. Anyway, I think I'll just stay home today and do nothing," Evanita said.

"What? Who stole my daughter and left this impostor?" Eva asked.

"You don't believe me?"

"Not for a minute," Eva replied.

"Maybe I can help you in the garden," Evanita said.

"Too late for that—the season is over, and I plowed everything under last weekend while you were at the city gardens."

"Clean the house?" Evanita asked with a grin.

"Funny. You know we have a cleaning person once a week," Eva replied.

"Maybe I can start taking care of the cars—like those mechanics do for Davino's car," Evanita mused.

"Our mechanic does an excellent job maintaining our cars. Evanita—is there something bothering you? Wait—why am I asking? When something bothers you, you go out for a run. Is it possible that for the first time in years my daughter is actually happy and has nothing preying on her mind?"

"I just thought we could have some mother-daughter time today," Evanita said.

"I know what I'd like to do with you, but judging by your past reactions, I don't think I should even mention it."

"You mean go to church—Broadway Unitarian?" Evanita asked.

"Not quite. It doesn't have to be that way. I was hoping you and Ms. Zyla could become friends—even if the mentoring thing doesn't work out," Eva said.

"Zellie?" Evanita asked.

"Yes, Zellie. I'm very fond of her, and I've known her for many years. She helped me when you were little, when—" Eva said, but she stopped short.

"When what? Did she know my father?" Evanita asked.

"Finally!" Jonara said with no one to hear. "I'm going to find out who my grandpa is."

Eva paused before saying, "No."

"Mama—can't you tell me about my father? I'm old enough now. My friends at school—the ones with divorced parents— well, they all know who their real parents are. They're old enough. I am too," Evanita stated.

"I keep hoping I'll never have to tell you," Eva said. "Some things are best left that way."

"Who is my father?" Evanita asked.

"You don't have a father," Eva replied.

"That's a lie. Everyone has a father. DNA evidence can prove it. Somewhere I have or had a father," Evanita said, feeling confident in her science.

"You don't have a father," Eva said.

"Mama—you're a dentist," Evanita said.

"Yes, you're right."

"You graduated from med school," Evanita continued.

"Without question."

"And in med school, you learned that a spermatozoa from a male human and an ovum from a female human produce a baby human," Evanita said.

"I learned that before med school, but yes, that's the story," Eva said.

"It's fact."

"Of course. Probably. Science says so," Eva said.

"Therefore, I have a father," Evanita said.

"Therefore, you should have a father. But you don't. And that's all I can say about the matter—for now," Eva said.

"Is there a re-answer?" Jonara wondered.

It was a major leap of faith for such a young girl, but the thought persisted. She was surprised her mother didn't think of the answer herself.

"Mama," Evanita said. "You were the one who told me that searching for evidence close to the sun doesn't always get the information one wants. Well? You're my 'sun', but you won't give me the evidence. Do I have to look elsewhere?"

"You want to have a father, don't you?" Eva asked.

"No, that's not it," Evanita said.

"Isn't it? Then why do you keep asking?" Eva asked.

"I need to know. I have to know. And you of all people should know who he is," Evanita said.

"Be careful, Evanita. You're speaking as if there is a father, giving as reference the pronoun 'he'. It's a dangerous thing—to go around speaking of things as if they are true when you really don't know for sure. Others begin to believe you. And they speak to you as if there is a 'he'. You believe it even more because it comes from their mouths. How can anyone go through life like that?" Eva asked.

"How can anyone go through life hiding the truth from her daughter?" Evanita asked.

"Is that what it looks like, that I'm hiding?" Eva asked.

"Yes, it does. You're hiding behind a lie—a lie stating that I have no father when everything in our understanding of human life says people have biological parents—a father and mother. We know all people have a father and mother," Evanita said. "Why is it so difficult for you to admit this simple truth?"

"Because, my loving daughter Evanita, some day you'll realize that all the science and knowledge and references to the phrases 'our understanding' and 'we know' don't mean a damn when something special happens in the universe beyond the laws and rules that men—and I mean men as in male humans—have placed on the universe as if men created it themselves—which they didn't. And I won't let a single man or men's science or any other patriarchal institution slander my origins or yours. The greatest struggle women face today is in dealing with the chains and concrete walls of phallic propaganda and conditioning," Eva explained.

"Mama! Now you're speaking in riddles again," Evanita said.

"It's only a riddle before you know," Eva said.

"And I want to know," Evanita said. "I do. That's why I ask."

"You will know," Eva said. "You're growing up so fast. I still remember when you were my precious little girl. You still are, but the patriarchal world *will* have its claws on you soon and *will* place its brands and scars on your psyche. I'm a selfish mother, I am. You are my only child, and I've savored every minute of our time together. I keep fooling myself into thinking the day will never come, that I'll always have you forever, but I know the world is more powerful than I. It will rip you away from me. And it will change you."

Eva was nearly in tears.

"Oh Mama!" Evanita said.

Evanita hugged her mother who was now sobbing softly.

"Silly Mama. I'll always be your girl," Evanita said, but she only said it to make her mother feel better.

Jonara hugged her mother and grandmother. Amazingly, she felt some semblance of their body warmth and emotional attachment. It was a special moment for Jonara too—beyond the laws of men and science.

The door echoed a knock. Not one, but several. Eva, Evanita, and Jonara jumped with a start. Their somber moment switched to alertness. Eva recognized the knock and offered invitation.

"Come in, Zellie," Eva beckoned.

"Good morning!" Ms. Zyla said. "How is everyone?"

"We are all fine," Evanita said.

"Good, good! Oh goodness gracious me!" Ms. Zyla started, noticing the two Evas at breakfast with Eva in a night robe. "I came too early. I didn't mean to—"

"It's quite all right. Make yourself at home," Eva offered. "Evanita and I were just enjoying a long breakfast."

"Wonderful, wonderful. I'll just wait here then for you two to finish before we start out," Ms. Zyla said.

"Start out?" Evanita asked. "Mama? What's she talking about?"

"Oh yes, I meant to tell you. Zellie has invited us to go pumpkin shopping today," Eva explained.

"That's an understatement," said Ms. Zyla. "There's a farm out in Happy Valley—Eileen Acres. They have pumpkins as big as—well, you just can't imagine how big. And they have other things too—crafts, pony rides, feed the animals—so much stuff to do."

"Eileen Acres. That sounds familiar. Have we been there before?" Evanita asked.

"We used to go there every October when you were younger," Eva said. "Yes, you remember the pony rides, don't you? You always loved the ponies. And feeding the animals."

"And hay rides. I remember the hay rides," Evanita reminisced.

"Oh we'll have a wonderful time!" Ms. Zyla said. "I'll even drive. You two will be my guests."

"That's not necessary, Ms. Zyla. You've been kind enough to give up your Saturday for us. I should drive," Eva said.

"Nonsense. Besides, I have a special surprise for later," Ms. Zyla said.

"Oh? What's the surprise?" Evanita asked.

"It wouldn't be a surprise if I told you now," Ms. Zyla said. "But I do need to drive for the surprise to work."

"Oh very well," said Eva. "Give us a little bit of time, and we'll be ready shortly."

The Evas did not take long. After a brief moment, they (and Jonara) entered Ms. Zyla's van and traveled to Happy Valley—approximately ten miles southeast of Portland. It was a cool autumn day with puffy clouds rolling along a sunny sky. There was little excitement beyond Evanita's fond memory of childhood, watching the younger people ride ponies, the Evas and Ms. Zyla feeding the animals, the walk along the craft tables, and the judging contests for best jarred produce in the area (applesauce, pickles—even tomatoes). Raffles, hay rides, clowns selling balloons, cotton candy, fresh-cooked corn—the list went on. The women could not do everything, and soon they forgot the most important reason for going. In fact, the Evas and Ms. Zyla were heading back to her van when they passed a small pile of pumpkins.

"Pumpkins. I nearly forgot!" Ms. Zyla said.

"This looks like a good size," Evanita said, walking over to the small pile.

"Oh honey, those are the little ones. They're for display only. Come this way—I remember where the prize-winning pumpkins are kept."

Jonara ran ahead. She had noticed the pumpkins before but of course could not say anything to anyone as they would not hear. She rounded a wooden fence and found them—some on the ground, others in a large wooden cart, and still more on large wooden tables—tables hewn from oak and maple. Jonara stopped short and realized that now leaving the pumpkin area with a rather large pumpkin on his shoulder was Johnny Pindus.

"Daddy!" she yelled.

Jonara ran up to him and hugged him. She felt his presence, and he reacted. He bobbled the pumpkin and nearly dropped it—disastrous as the pumpkin most likely would have split in two and be ruined.

"Who said that?" he asked.

Johnny regained his balance, but Jonara hugged him again. Again he jumped with a start, and again he nearly dropped his load, but he regained his composure and placed the pumpkin on a nearby bench until he could understand what was happening.

"Daddy, it's me—Jonara. Your daughter," she said.

"I remember you, voice. I heard you at the dental office," Johnny said. "You're my daughter? But I don't have a daughter."

"You will. You're my father," Jonara said.

"I remember what happened in the clinic. My sugar level was low. I was imagining things," Johnny said. He sat down and started to shake. "My sugar is low. I must eat something."

"No, please, don't go. Wait here a moment," Jonara said.

"I have a sugar pill with me," he said. "I'll just take it now."

"Daddy! Mommy is walking over here with Grandma and Ms. Zyla. Please stay," Jonara begged.

"Little voice, I know you can't be real. I can't let people see me talking to the air—they'll think I'm crazy. And they'd be right!" Johnny said, and he popped the sugar pill in his mouth.

"Daddy, I love you!" Jonara said.

Jonara repeated it several times. Johnny's blood-sugar level increased to a normal level, and his future daughter's voice faded into the background noise of leaves rustling and birds chirping. Jonara may not have been able to communicate with Johnny very long, but she did manage to delay him enough such that he'd bump into the two Evas and Ms. Zyla.

"No, these on the cart are better," Evanita said as she moved ahead of Eva and Ms. Zyla. "Maybe these," she said moving on to the table. "This one—this is perfect."

"Wait, let me see," Eva said.

Eva walked over to the table. Ms. Zyla followed. Eva saw Johnny sitting on the bench. She opened her mouth to say something to him but stopped. Instead, she held a finger to her mouth to keep him quiet and motioned him over to Evanita with her eyes. Johnny walked over to the table where Evanita hunted through pumpkins.

"Could be rotten on the inside," said Eva.

"It doesn't look rotten," Evanita said.

"Knock on it," said Ms. Zyla.

Evanita knocked on the pumpkin. It echoed back a "thump". A hand not of Evanita's touched the pumpkin.

"It's rotten," said the owner of the hand.

It was Johnny, but he disguised his voice.

"What about this one?" she asked the owner of the hand, not realizing who it was.

"Knock on it," he said.

Evanita knocked on the pumpkin, and he felt the vibrations.

"This one is good," he said.

"How do you know?" she asked.

"I'm Johnny Pindus," he said, restoring his voice to normal.

"Johnny!" she jumped in surprise.

Evanita turned around immediately to see him. Forgetting where she was or whose company she was in, she hugged him and kissed him on the cheek. Johnny surprised himself by not recoiling in horror from intimate contact. Evanita let out a big smile, and he managed to give a smile back. Evanita held a gaze with him for what seemed a long time, but in fact it was a few seconds. She suddenly remembered her mother and Ms. Zyla in her presence, and she broke off her embrace suddenly.

"Oh hello, Johnny. What a surprise," Evanita said, trying to be calm and unaffected.

"Hello. I was just buying a pumpkin for Halloween," he said.

"So were we," said Eva. "Did you find a good one?"

"Yes ma'am," he replied. "I have it right over there on the bench. Hey, that's mine!"

Johnny stole away to the bench to retrieve his pumpkin another person was about to take.

"So this is the Johnny I've been hearing about," said Ms. Zyla.

"What have you been hearing?" Evanita asked Ms. Zyla.

"Oh, did I say hearing about? I meant—what did I mean—I meant something like—" Ms. Zyla stumbled.

"Mama!" Evanita accused Eva.

"What? Why do I get blamed?" Eva asked with a sheepish grin.

"This is my pumpkin," Johnny said.

"It looks heavy," Eva said to break the blame pinned on her from Evanita.

"It is, but I can manage it," he said.

Evanita stared at Johnny and didn't say another word. Johnny wanted to say something back, but his tongue tied up in knots. Ms. Zyla and Eva kept silent too, waiting for Evanita or Johnny to say something, but they didn't. The situation became a little uncomfortable. Eva and Ms. Zyla smiled—they knew what was going on. Johnny looked around but wasn't sure what to do. Should he say, "Bye," and move on? That would be rude. He wished the women would say they had to run or something like that, but they didn't. Evanita spoke.

"Well, it's been nice...how've you been...what are you doing later...that's a really nice pumpkin," Evanita babbled.

"Huh?" Johnny replied.

He stared at her, she stared back.

"Somebody do something!" Jonara yelled. "Daddy, ask Mommy out on a date. Daddy?!"

Johnny swatted around his ear. Jonara's words sounded like a high-pitched flying mosquito in his left ear.

"What's the matter? Something wrong?" Evanita asked.

"I keep thinking there's a mosquito by my ear," Johnny said. "I can hear it, but I don't feel it."

"I'm not a mosquito!" Jonara said defiantly. "I'm your daughter! Now ask Mommy out on a date!"

Jonara walked from Johnny's left side to his right.

"Ask Mommy out on a date!" she yelled.

Johnny switched from swatting around his left ear to swatting around his right.

"I don't see any bugs," said Evanita. "Are you sure there's something there, there by your hair, your ear, you hear something, what do your hair-hear ears say?" Evanita stumbled.

Eva and Ms. Zyla giggled. It was quiet at first, but it grew louder and louder. The scene was nothing but comical to the older women. A young girl who normally is defiant and outspoken suddenly can't connect her words, and a young man flailing his arms around his ears at imaginary flying insects.

"I am NOT—" Jonara said as she stomped her shoe on Johnny's right foot.

"Ow!" Johnny reacted to the impact.

Johnny hopped on his left foot.

"—a mosquito! You will ask—" Jonara continued and stomped her heal on Johnny's left foot.

"Ow again!" Johnny said, now hopping on his right foot.

"—Mommy out on a date!" Jonara finished.

Jonara slugged Johnny in the lower right side just around the back, close to where his kidney might be.

"Ike!" Johnny screeched.

Johnny bent over and held his hand to his lower right back.

"Johnny, what's the matter, what's wrong?" Evanita said.

Evanita held him and assisted his backward steps to a nearby bench where he sat down.

"I don't know," he said.

Evanita sat next to him and tried to comfort him.

"Cramps, Johnny?" Eva asked.

"No ma'am," he said. "The pain was sharp, but now it's dull and burning."

"Have you been to the doctor lately? Have you been tested for gout? Are you dehydrated?" Eva asked.

"I—wait a minute—I can't keep up. I don't know about gout," he replied. "But I am a little thirsty."

"Mama, we can't leave him here. It's not safe—he could die or something. We should call an ambulance," Evanita panicked.

"Wait a minute there, Evanita," Eva said. "I think Johnny needs a little rest and a drink—thanks Zellie. Here, Johnny, drink this bottled water."

"Ah," he said after a few slurps.

"Better?" Evanita asked.

"Much," he replied as he poured some over his head and face.

"What was that for?" Ms. Zyla asked.

"Hot. Need to cool off," he said.

Johnny tried waving a hand in front of his face to cool off quicker, but the motion looked awkward and uncoordinated.

"More bugs?" Eva asked.

"Mama, the ambulance!" Evanita stated.

"Honey dear," Eva replied. "Your man Johnny is not in any serious danger at the moment. He might have cramps, he might have gout, or he might be dehydrated. Whatever. He won't die. This isn't that big a crisis. Remember—I've known him for quite a number of years—more than you, Evanita."

"But you can't let him go home like this—he should be monitored, observed, watched," Evanita said.

"Johnny, did you drive here?" Eva asked.

"No ma'am. The social worker gave me a lift. I'm supposed to call a friend to get a ride home," he said.

"Call your friend and tell him you have another ride," Evanita ordered.

Eva and Ms. Zyla looked at each other in surprise.

"She's quite assertive," Ms. Zyla said under her breath to Eva.

"Go, Mommy, go!" Jonara cheered.

"My friend is a *she*," Johnny said.

"What?!" Evanita asked.

Evanita jumped up from the bench and distanced herself a little from Johnny.

"You, you," she stammered.

"Are you jealous?" Eva asked.

"Stay out of this, Mama," Evanita said.

"An interesting reaction considering how 'well' you know Johnny," she added.

"Shhh," Evanita said back to Eva. Evanita turned to Johnny and demanded, "What's her name?"

"Her name is Claire. Claire Stout. She said she was a friend of yours," Johnny said.

"Why that two-faced, dirty atheis-. Stealing my ma-. How could she?" Evanita asked.

"How could she what?" Johnny asked.

"Evanita, didn't you say Johnny needed emergency treatment? What happened to the ambulance?" Eva asked.

"I'm giving him the 'emergency treatment' right now," Evanita replied. "And as for calling an ambulance..."

Evanita trailed off. She pulled out her cell phone and dialed a number from the cell phone's address book.

"Claire! How are you?" Evanita said.

"I'm fine, Evanita. What have you been up to?" Claire said.

"I'm here at Eileen Acres. I want to know what—" Evanita started.

"What a coincidence! I'm going to pick up a friend of mine there," Claire said.

"Oh you are?" Evanita played along. "Who's your friend?"

"Someone I met," Claire said. "Say, you sound a little agitated. Is everything okay?"

"I want to know more about your friend, and how you met him," Evanita said.

"I never said it was a 'he' or 'she'. What's this about?" Claire asked.

"You tell me. I met your friend," Evanita said.

Claire sighed.

"I didn't want to say anything—to protect Johnny—but I guess you know," Claire said.

"So it's true. You and Pindus," Evanita said.

"Evanita, Valeria Pindus was my best friend—even though she was Baptist and I'm an atheist. You sound like you know all this anyway, so I won't go into detail. Johnny kept choking on food after her death. I must have made five emergency visits to his apartment in three days. You know I'm a paramedic, right? Well, that's the story. I've been assigned to watch him from time to time—sort of like preventive medicine," Claire explained. "Johnny is too embarrassed to admit anything like that. People always accuse him of not being a man. Well, this would add fuel to the fire."

"You...helped Johnny...were Valeria's friend?" Evanita asked.

"You sound surprised. Actually, Valeria and Johnny taught me how to identify plants in the various Portland gardens. They both had impressive memories. Well, Johnny still does. That didn't come out right. I mean no disrespect toward Valeria or Johnny," Claire explained.

"Okay, okay, I get the picture," Evanita said.

"He was supposed to call me twenty minutes ago. I was going to take him home with his pumpkin. I don't know what happened to him," Claire said.

"He, uh," Evanita backpedaled. "We sort of bumped into him by the pumpkins."

"Oh that's wonderful," Claire exclaimed. "Any social interaction Johnny can handle is helpful for his recovery from Valeria's death. Sorry, I don't mean to be so blunt."

"Yeah, I'm here with my mother and Ms. Zyla from church," Evanita said.

Evanita sounded more cheerful with Claire than she had at the beginning of the conversation.

"We should be getting something to eat soon," said Ms. Zyla. "And Johnny is invited."

"I heard that," said Claire. "Johnny really needs someone to watch him while he eats. I don't want to impose on you, but if you are taking him out to eat, do you think—" Claire started.

"We'll watch him," Evanita said with a grin of victory. "I'll call you later then. Bye."

"Bye then. Say, 'Hello,' to Johnny," Claire said.

"I will. Bye again," Evanita said, and she hung up.

"We're giving you a ride home," said Evanita. "Isn't that right, Mama?"

"Yes dear, of course!" Eva said.

"I know exactly where to eat," said Ms. Zyla. "It's part of the surprise I was telling you about. That is, if you want to go, Johnny."

"I dunno, I guess. Do they have beef or pork?" he asked.

"Yes, they do," Ms. Zyla said.

"I'm sorry, I didn't catch your name," Johnny said.

"But I know yours. You're Johnny Pindus. My name is Ms. Beverly Zyla. Most folks call me 'Ms. Zyla' or 'Zellie'. You can call me 'Zellie'."

"Nice to meet you, Miss Zellie," Johnny said.

"If we're done with the introductions," Evanita said with impatience. "I'm getting hungry. Let's eat!"

"All right already," Ms. Zyla said. "Let's pay for the pumpkins and go."

Johnny offered to pay for the pumpkins, but Eva refused. She didn't say it out loud, but she did not like taking gratuity from a man—even Johnny—the man she'd treated since he was a small boy. Eva paid for her pumpkin, and Johnny paid for his. The four plus Jonara made their way back to the van and sat inside.

"Before we go," said Ms. Zyla, "I must ask each of you to put these on."

Ms. Zyla produced two blindfolds.

"Wait," she said. "I only have two blindfolds. I wasn't expecting Johnny."

"Blindfolds? What are these for?" Eva asked.

"It's part of the surprise. I want you to magically open your eyes and find yourself in a new place filled with music, food, and mystery," Ms. Zyla explained. "If you see how we get there, you'll think we're going to some ordinary café. I want this to be special."

"Hmm," said Eva. "I don't normally like surprises."

"It sounds like fun. I'll put my hands over Johnny's eyes," Evanita offered.

Eva's eyes opened up in astonishment.

"I'm beginning to wonder if there are other surprises the blindfold will shield me from," Eva said. "I'll put mine on—but on one condition."

"Name it," said Ms. Zyla.

"That Evanita remembers she is sixteen and Johnny remembers that both he is twenty-four and Evanita is only sixteen," Eva said with a sharp look at Evanita. "Sixteen."

"Yes, Mama," Evanita said with a bit of spice in her voice.

Jonara had no blindfold over her eyes and was able to observe where Ms. Zyla was going. King Road west to Mount Scott Boulevard. West on Idleman Road. North on 92nd Avenue.

"Is that the same 92nd Avenue? Does it go up to the Stout house? Sharon and Sheila?" Jonara asked.

"Are you doing something funny?" Evanita asked Johnny.

"I'm shaking my ears. I thought I heard something about 92nd Avenue," he said.

"You're peeking," said Ms. Zyla.

"Honest ma'am, I'm not. Evanita is squeezing my eyelids into my eye sockets," Johnny said.

"Well, we don't want to ruin the surprise, do we?" Ms. Zyla said.

Ms. Zyla proceeded west on Johnson Creek Boulevard for quite a ways until it ran into Tacoma Street.

"Something feels very unusual about this road," Eva said. "Like I've been here before—a long time ago. Strange."

"What would be strange about Tacoma Street?" Jonara asked.

Johnny mouthed the words to "Tacoma Street" without anyone hearing. Jonara saw Johnny mouth the words and knew he could hear her.

"Tacoma," Jonara said again, and Johnny repeated his lip movements.

Ms. Zyla turned north on Milwaukie Avenue. She continued north and turned left just before reaching McLoughlin Boulevard. She crossed railroad tracks and parked. The group was now close to the Willamette River, just east of Hardtack Island.

"You may open your eyes," Ms. Zyla said.

Evanita removed her hands from Johnny's eyelids. He opened his eyes, but everything was black.

"I can't see!" Johnny said. "The world is black!"

"Evanita!" Eva said.

"I didn't do anything!" Evanita said.

"You applied too much pressure against Johnny's eyes," Eva said.

"Wait," Johnny said. "My vision is coming back."

"You just needed a few seconds for your optic nerves to return to normal," Eva said.

"I'm sorry, Johnny," Evanita said. "I'll be more careful in the future."

"Where are we?" Eva asked.

"The Cerossi Café," Ms. Zyla answered.

"Never heard of it," said Eva.

"We must be close to the Willamette River," Johnny said.

"Now how would you know that?" Ms. Zyla asked.

"Oh Johnny has a strong sense of water movement," Eva said. "But I must admit, Zellie, you did find an interesting out-of-the-way place. I have no idea where we are—other than being next to the river. And I pride myself on knowing Portland."

The women and Johnny looked around. The parking lot was completely surrounded by Crimson King Maple and purple-leaf plum trees. There was no visible grass, and no other green plants in eye's view. Next to the parking lot was a building with a subtle sign—Cerossi Café. Its building design resembled something between a bamboo hut and a log cabin, yet there were very few straight lines. The logs or canes used in the building swirled and danced without moving. Surrounding the building at its base were violet plants.

"There isn't a single green leaf around," Evanita said.

"And you won't find one, either," said Ms. Zyla.

"I'm not sure if we're looking at a wicker building, an Easter basket building, a bamboo building, or an upside-down bird's nest—what do you think, Evanita?" Eva asked, turning to Evanita.

Evanita had walked over to the building with Johnny, leaving Eva with Ms. Zyla. Evanita looked closely at the plants around the building.

"Claire said you know a lot about plants. What kind is this?" Evanita asked Johnny.

"Coral Bells. Heuchera Frosted Violet. It's just..." Johnny trailed.

"Just what? Is it poisonous? Deadly? It's such a beautiful plant. Don't you think so, Johnny?" Evanita asked.

"It's just—I don't remember the full taxonomic name. I think 'Heuchera' is part of it," Johnny lamented.

Evanita giggled and said, "It's okay. I never could understand those Latin names anyway. Heurchera Frosted Violet is a nice name. I'd like one for home."

"Let's go inside," Ms. Zyla said, catching up to Evanita and Johnny with Eva. "Food is waiting."

Johnny ran up to the door and held it open for the women. Ms. Zyla went in first followed by Evanita. Eva walked up but did not enter. Instead, she stood there—and as she did, Jonara snuck in behind Evanita.

"Go ahead, Johnny, I'll follow you," Eva said.

Eva did not wish to say it to Johnny, but she wouldn't allow any man to do things for her like holding doors open.

Johnny went inside, and Eva followed him in. The four and Jonara walked through a dimly lit, short corridor with a low ceiling. Eva was the tallest of the group and had to duck a little to keep from bumping her head. The walls and ceiling appeared to be assembled from blocks of wood like brickwork, but when

Eva touched the ceiling with her hand, what looked like wood was petrified.

"The walls and ceiling," Eva started.

"Yes," Ms. Zyla said. "They're petrified wood."

Johnny reached to touch the wall along his right side (Evanita was to his left), and he withdrew his hand immediately.

"It shocked me!" he said.

"Your finger—it's bleeding. Here, put this on it," Evanita said as she handed him a small tissue.

"Don't touch it," he warned, "It will—"

He was cut short by surprise. Ms. Zyla touched the wall without a problem.

"I also touched the ceiling—it didn't hurt me," Eva said.

Jonara touched the wall about the same time as her mother, Evanita, did. Neither one experienced shock nor blood loss.

"I don't understand. It only hurts me?" Johnny wondered.

"You are especially sensitive to certain things. Could there be more to the wall than we can see?" Eva asked.

"They are special, yes," Ms. Zyla said.

"How many today?" a waitress asked.

"Three. And one male," answered Ms. Zyla.

"This way, please," the waitress said.

The four and Jonara followed the waitress to an arc-shaped table where two sat on the outer side of the arc and the other two sat at each end of the arc. Jonara sat on the outer arc of the table to Evanita's left. To Evanita's right sat Johnny, and to his right at the table's end sat Eva. Ms. Zyla sat on the other end. In this way, the party was able to view the central part of the café.

Other tables in the café had an arc shape. These arcs formed broken, multi-circular paths around the center object of the café—a ring of dim blue/violet fire—invisible in strong daylight, but easy to see in the dimness of the café. Inside the ring of fire were two, three-footed pedestals holding a glass sphere each, with an obsidian shard inside each of the two spheres. The shards had foreign inscriptions on them, of which no one in the café appeared to know what they meant or from what culture they came.

Johnny realized immediately that the café's patrons were mostly women. He didn't say anything, but it did seem a bit odd to him.

"I've never seen a café like this. Or a restaurant. In fact, I haven't seen anything like this at all," Eva said.

"I didn't think so," Ms. Zyla replied.

"Why the circle of fire and the funny-shaped tables?" Evanita asked. "What are those glass spheres in the center?"

"So many questions," Ms. Zyla said.

"What would you ladies like to order?" the waitress said. "Oh I'm sorry; I'm so used to saying that. I didn't see—"

"Quite all right," said Ms. Zyla. "Evanita, why don't you go first?"

"I would like the honey teriyaki chicken with pineapple, Italian wedding soup, and a cola," Evanita said.

"Eva?" Ms. Zyla motioned.

"I'll have the same—but I'll have, hmmm, I'm not sure if I want a white or red wine," Eva said.

"May I recommend a rosé then? We have a nice collection from Alsace, Champagne, and Provence," the waitress said.

"Hmm. Anything from Bordeaux?" Eva asked.

"Yes, we have red and white wine from Bordeaux. Would you like to see a wine list?" the waitress asked. "Sometimes we have rosés from Bordeaux, but they don't last long. Guests order them quickly."

"If you have a rosé from Bordeaux, I'll take that. Otherwise, red wine from Bordeaux will do."

"Very good," the waitress said.

"Johnny?" Ms. Zyla motioned.

"I, uh, there's a little problem," the waitress said.

The waitress whispered something in Ms. Zyla's ears about men never ordering before women in the café.

"I'm sorry," Ms. Zyla apologized. "Johnny, if you could just be a little patient. I'll order next. I'd like the pink salmon with teriyaki sauce, a Caesar salad, and mineral water."

"And you?" the waitress asked Johnny.

"I would like a steak sandwich," he said. "With minestrone soup."

"Would you like something to drink?" the waitress asked.

"Milk."

The three (and Jonara) looked at Johnny. Wasn't he too old for milk?

"We don't serve milk here," the waitress said, a bit annoyed.

"I think Johnny would like a root beer, wouldn't you?" Eva suggested.

"Yes, root beer works well," he said.

"Thank you, I'll be back with your drinks," the waitress said.

The waitress had barely left when she returned with beverages for all. She found a bottle of Bordeaux rosé to Eva's joy. The waitress also provided a pitcher of water and poured from this pitcher into extra glasses. Jonara took a sip from one of the glasses without being noticed. The water held in her mouth without passing through as she expected. She swallowed the water. It was surprisingly clean and refreshing—like springwater from a new mountain—not at all like the lake water where Sheila nearly died.

"All that fuss over a wine, Mama. What does it matter where it comes from?" Evanita asked.

"Notice the places she mentioned—Alsace, Champagne, Provence, and Bordeaux—are in France," Eva instructed the group.

"Of course, where else for wine?" Ms. Zyla asked.

"California makes wine," Evanita said.

"Hmm, yes, the one falling into the ocean. Ocean grape juice," Eva said.

"Hopefully, we have no one here from California," Ms. Zyla said in a hushed voice. "But I agree with you on the French selection—the character, the aroma. But why Bordeaux? The others are just as good."

"I have a rule when it comes to French wine. Now I have nothing against the French—they are nice people and all. They can't help who they have for a neighbor on the east. But my rule is this—I prefer a wine produced as Frenchly west as possible," Eva said.

"Because its neighbor is the Atlantic Ocean? California has an ocean neighbor—the Pacific Ocean," Evanita said.

"Not that kind of neighbor," said Eva.

"Oh, I know," said Ms. Zyla. "And it fits you like a cat's pajama. You don't want to be contaminated by anything German. Really, Eva, I'm ashamed of you. Tolerance for other faiths and all—where is it? Do we need to put you through Unitarian Coming-Of-Age again?"

"And look what tolerance for these 'faiths' has done to the world. These 'faiths' are allowed to take whatever they want," Eva ranted.

"That was a long time ago. Before you were born. Why don't you let go? It happened over there in the 1930s and 40s, hmmm?" Ms. Zyla asked. "Besides, your family came from Franco's Spain. Doesn't that bother you too?"

"Don't bring that up. You sound like my mother on her soap box again," Eva said. "How I tire of hearing those stories."

"Then don't you think people tire of hang-ups over other old regimes?" Ms. Zyla said. "There must be healing at some point."

"No," said Eva. "There mustn't. Especially when the regime follows you day and night into the present."

Evanita was surprised to see her mother so defiant. Evanita ascribed herself as the rebellious one—a feature her mother (Eva) often relegated to growing pains.

"You're not talking about Germany anymore, are you?" Ms. Zyla said.

"I should stop now given the mixed company," Eva said.

Eva was afraid Johnny would take offense to her words, but he was instead busily watching the dancing flames.

"Look at the fire in the middle of the café," said Johnny. "Isn't it mesmerizing?"

"It appears to be moving, but it isn't," said Evanita.

"The flames are stationary, but the colors shift from bright pink to dark blue and everything in between," said Eva.

"The colors are moving around the circle," said Evanita. "The bright pink is on one end, and opposite is the dark blue. They chase each other around."

"Looking down, the colors would appear to move clockwise," said Johnny. "But there are fluctuations at points in the circle."

"Yes, Johnny, I see them too. It's as if something pierces the circle of flames every so often. A flame drops low and almost goes out, but just for a split second," Eva said.

"There are three such points," Johnny said.

"They vary, too, in placement and time," Eva said. "Often I can see two of them pierce the circle at about the same time and not far from each other."

"What do you think it means?" Evanita asked Ms. Zyla.

"Means? There's no special meaning—none that I know of," Ms. Zyla said.

"Is it like lightning?" Evanita asked.

"It has a pattern, a rhythm. Not like lightning," Johnny said.

"That's what makes it so hypnotic," said Ms. Zyla. "People come in here, see the flames, and often reach new insight."

"What kind of insight?" Evanita asked.

"All sorts of things. Usually the insight is a unique solution to a problem the person has, though the solution is not in any sort of conventional sense that one might have in the outside world," Ms. Zyla explained.

"What do you mean, 'outside world'? Aren't we always in the outside world? What's the inside world, other than our inner spirits, our souls?" Eva asked.

"We are in our inner souls," Ms. Zyla explained. "This café—it's more than that. It's a meditation center. That's the best I can say. Words don't fully explain it, any more than a subconscious feeling can be fully explained."

The waitress brought the soups.

"Wait, Miss," Evanita said to the waitress. "Please—what do you call that circle of flames?"

"That?" she said, pointing to the flames.

"Yes. Does it have a name?"

"Indeed it does. The flames are called, 'Inside Indecision'. The two obsidian shards have the names 'Insight' and 'Intuition'. The flames and shards and glass spheres around them—all of it together—that's the Cerossi, and that's why we call this place the Cerossi Café," the waitress replied. She left the table and attended another.

"What confusing names," said Evanita. "The shards are 'Insight, Intuition.' What did she call the flames?"

"Inside Indecision," said Ms. Zyla. "It sounds a lot like the shard names, doesn't it? Inside Indecision, Insight Intuition."

"It is confusing," agreed Eva. "I wonder why—why the vague names? Seems more like a play on words than anything. Johnny, you're good with word games. Does it mean anything to you?"

"Inside Indecision," Johnny started. "Yes, 'inside' implies a wall or barrier separating a space contained by the wall and a space not contained by the wall. The space contained is the inside. 'Indecision' as in unable to make a decision, stuck, or caught in a loop. Or it could mean without decision, without the divisive wedge that creates a dichotomy—no polarization of two sides."

"Interesting," said Eva.

"That doesn't make sense. The word 'inside' is on one end of a decision, but there's indecision—isn't that a paradox?" Ms. Zyla asked.

"Yes, it is," Eva answered. "Unless the indecision is the wall, and something—"

"Or someone," Ms. Zyla cut in.

"Or someone is inside the thinking of the indecision," Eva continued. "What about the other two words, Johnny—'Insight' and 'Intuition'?"

"Devoiced and choppy versions of 'Inside Indecision'," Johnny replied.

"Intriguing. I never thought of that," said Ms. Zyla.

"I'm lost. Johnny, what do you mean?" Evanita asked.

"About which part?" Johnny asked.

"All of it. Devoiced, choppy—what do you mean?" Evanita asked.

"Devoiced. A term used in linguistics. Some consonants are voiced and involve using the vocal cords. Others are devoiced. In other words, devoiced consonants do not use the vocal cords. Consonants can be paired in this manner—the physical motions of the mouth are the same except for the use of the vocal cords. Voiced/devoiced pairs are *b/p, v/f, z/s, d/t, g/k, sh/zh,* and more."

"We get the picture, Johnny," Eva interrupted.

"The *tees* in 'Insight Intuition' are devoiced versions of the *dees* in 'Inside Indecision'," Johnny continued. "'Intuition' does not contain the extra *ess* sound—a fricative—that 'Indecision' does. *Dee* and *tee* are plosives—they go fast, especially devoiced plosives, whereas fricatives always slow things down."

"What?!?" Evanita asked. "English, please."

"That was English—English linguistics, that is," Johnny said.

"Okay, Johnny. So the flames are voiced and long while the shards are unvoiced and short," Eva explained.

"Devoiced," Johnny corrected.

"I like 'unvoiced' better," Evanita said. "The flames seem to speak to us, the shards do not."

"What do the flames say to you, Evanita?" Ms. Zyla asked.

"They say it's time to eat!" Evanita replied.

Evanita was joking, of course. She saw the waitress approach with their food, and this knowledge combined with the others' momentary lack of knowledge made her statement seem like a prediction.

"Mmmm," Eva said. "Looks good."

The four started eating. Jonara sipped on the fresh water without being noticed. The flames dimmed and brightened as if being commanded by the café patrons' thoughts. Jonara stared at the convoluted undulations circling through the flames—color variations and flickering that brought thoughts of sitting around a campfire. She was not alone. Most patrons stared at the flames and also thought of being around a large campfire.

"Look!" Evanita said.

Several patrons stood up and walked close to the flames. They positioned marshmallow twigs over the flames.

"I want a seat close to the flames next time," said Evanita, "so I can toast marshmallows with just a flick of my wrist."

"I wonder if—" Johnny started.

"No, they don't roast hot dogs here," Ms. Zyla said.

"It sounds like torture anyway," said Evanita.

"Not the animal dog," said Ms. Zyla.

"I know, I was just joking," Evanita said. "Who would ever think of burning an animal alive, or a human?"

"They used to. Back in medieval times," Eva said.

"Burning in fire was a last resort. Other methods were the rack, the boot, and the thumbscrew," Johnny started. "A favorite of some was to tie the victim's hands behind the back, pull the person up with a rope, and attach weights to the legs."

"Johnny, please! Let's not think of such unpleasant things as *strappado*," Eva said.

"Evanita, did you ever go back to that Catholic Church— what was it called?" Ms. Zyla asked, distracting Johnny from listing more torture methods.

"Saint Stellan. No, I didn't," Evanita replied.

"I'm glad too," Eva said. "It's unfortunate what happened, but—"

For Jonara, Eva's voice faded into a distant echo. The flames dimmed and went out, the room went dark and silent, and Jonara felt bewildered. She stood up from her chair but was thrust into the ground. She smelled dirt—Cemeterius dirt.

Saint Stellan.

"Recite the Act of Contrition!" Christine commanded.

Christine's heel dug into the back of Jonara's neck sending needles of pain through her back. Jonara convulsed briefly and found herself detached from the choir woman's body now on the ground. Jonara looked on the scene—the choir woman who was at one time defiant now deferred to Christine's authority of the heel.

"Oh my Christine," the trapped choir woman recited, "I am heartily sorry for having—"

"Go on," Christine said. "You are sorry for having offended me."

"I am heartily sorry for having offended you. And I detest all my speech because I dread the loss of choir and the pains of your heel. I resolve with the help of your grace to speak out no more and avoid the near occasion to speak. Allmen."

"There. That wasn't so bad, was it?" Christine demanded.

Christine pulled out a Cat O' Nine tails—a special type of whip.

"This is for mortification," said Christine.

Jonara watched as Christine whipped the choir woman on the back and prayed.

"I am the Vice of Christ," Christine said. "I release the vice on your soul, the demon that has placed a noooo on your tongue and forked it. Leave this poor child alone, demon. Possess her no more and leave her to silent holiness. I proclaim this in the name of the Christine, Rome, and Father Rick. Allmen. Rise, my rabbit of Christine. Go in peace and speak no more."

Jonara stood in the Cemeterius alone. She walked behind the headstone of A. Graves and found carrots, which she picked up. Plenty of fresh carrots with healthy, green stalks. Her vision blurred, and she spun in place. The carrots fell from her hands but circled around her as if in orbit. The spinning stopped. Daylight quickly faded to evening, to morning, and into the following day. Jonara no longer found herself in the Cemeterius. She was on a small porch with a rabbit hutch. She pushed the carrots through the hutch's chicken-coop wiring, and the rabbit ate them greedily. Jonara was amazed. She suspected the rabbit hadn't had fresh greens in a long time.

"No, you cannot do this!" someone shouted from a neighboring room.

Jonara left the rabbit on the porch and entered a rectory. Inside, she discovered Christine arguing with Father Rick.

"We must do it for the good of the church," Father Rick said.

"Father Rick, who was there for you in the beginning? Who gave you moral and spiritual support during your trial when that ungracious young man accused you of violating him?" Christine started.

"You did, Christine," Father Rick lamented.

"Who relieved you of your temptations to look at other men and boys in unholy ways? Who removed those vices and converted you back to the faith of men and women coming together in the physical bonds of Christ?" Christine continued.

"You always have been and will be, my special Vice of Christ," he said. "But there must be changes in this church."

"Changes? I have planned all architectural changes at Saint Stellan," said Christine. "The organization of our church into the Faithful and Catechumens, the altar and its step, the choir balcony, the ascending pew for bringing gifts to the altar—all these things I designed and had constructed for our purpose so we may serve the needs of the people. If there are any changes to be made, restore my choir to its rightful place on the choir balcony, and let the boys' choir sing where we are now."

"That was not my idea, of course," said Father Rick. "The bishop—"

"You really need to confide in me before going to the bishop. I know his methods, and not all are for the good. Trust me like you always have. Trust your Vice of Christ," Christine said.

Christine held Father Rick close to her and held his hands tenderly.

"The decision is out of my hands," he said as he released his hands from hers. "The bishop has issued a Decree of Removal. Here, read it yourself!"

Christine read the letter.

"You are relieved as Pastor of Saint Stellan effective...today?" she asked.

"Yes. Those are the orders."

"But why? There's no reason for him to transfer you to another church," Christine said.

"Read the fine print. This isn't a transfer. I'm to be defrocked," he said.

"No! This is a misunderstanding. I'll clear it up with the bishop myself," Christine said.

"You can't," he said. "Not this time."

"Don't try to stop me. I made you!"

"He knows about us!" Father Rick yelled.

Christine held silent for a moment and regathered her thoughts. Then her face turned red, and she was determined to go on a witch hunt.

"Who? Who told him? How did anyone find out? I always made sure we were alone in the rectory when...when we consummated our union in Christ. Did the bishop say who told him?"

"He didn't have to," Father Rick said.

"What do you mean?!" Christine asked Father Rick.

Christine suspected Father Rick was holding back and violating her trust in him.

"I..." Father Rick's voice trailed.

"How could you?!" Christine reeled. "I put my faith and trust in you, my own Pastor Rick. I helped you in your lowest moments, and you toss me to the lions the first chance you get?! What horrible injustice is this? Father Rick, confess your mortal sin, this slander against our church. Confess it now!"

"I did confess...to the bishop. That's how he knows. I went to Confession before him and told him everything!" Father Rick said.

"Impossible!"

"It's true. I wanted Absolution, a clean soul," Father Rick continued.

"Insane! Only I can give the kind of Absolution you can absorb."

"You have become too powerful, Christine. You've taken over everything. What am I, a puppet?" Father Rick asked.

"Who would you rather bend over for, the bishop or me?" Christine asked. "But that has always been your problem—you give in to the men above you. I offered you a chance, a life, something more than you were. And you turned on me and went running back to the life you had before. But now it'll cost you. You won't be a priest anymore. You'll have to find real work—some factory job or whatever. And I won't be there to help you. I'll be here—preparing the next pastor for his role as Father of Saint Stellan."

"This is for you," Father Rick said.

He handed her an envelope addressed to Christine from the bishop. Christine opened the letter, and her eyes widened with anger.

"I'm sorry," he said. "I didn't think—"

"You didn't think at all!" Christine yelled.

"You're banned from Saint Stellan. But look at it this way— you haven't been excommunicated," he said.

"He can't ban me from Saint Stellan. This is my church! I am this church!" Christine said.

The rectory shook, and a low, loud sound like that of a semi-truck bellowed across the airwaves. Was there an earthquake? Christine went for the door, but Father Rick blocked her.

"That's heavy equipment!" Christine said. "And it sounds close to our church."

"No, you can't. They have to tear down the church. It's part of the third letter here. The bishop sold the property to cover lawsuits," Father Rick said.

"Get out of my way!" Christine shouted.

Christine shoved Father Rick aside and lunged out the door, across the porch, and into the rectory lawn toward the church.

Jonara ran after Christine but could not keep up. She tripped over a rabbit hole in the ground. The hole secured her foot and twisted her ankle. Her body twisted and fell. Regathering her posture, she saw Father Rick on the porch opening the hutch door and allowing the rabbit to escape. Jonara turned around and sat on a tree stump. She gazed at the backhoe positioning itself to knock down the south wall—the side of the faithful. Jonara watched intently as Christine ran up to block the equipment.

Unexpectedly, a halo hovered above the church. It was white at first and circled like an oversized thin doughnut, or perhaps a frisbee with a large open center. The hue shifted from white to violet, and it expanded in diameter. In this way, it expanded to surround the church, which it did by descending over and around. The church grew pale and blue. Jonara could not hear the diesel engine or Christine shouting. But she did hear a familiar voice grow from faint to audible.

"...ran right into the demolition equipment," Eva continued.

Jonara was seated at the arc-shaped table in Cerossi Café with Eva, Evanita, Ms. Zyla, and Johnny. The others had eaten some of their meal while listening to Eva's tale of Saint Stellan.

"Did she get hurt?" Evanita asked.

"Christine suffered a broken arm and lost three teeth," Eva explained. "Demolition had to stop until an ambulance could take her to the hospital for the arm. The paramedics brought her over to my office for the teeth. She kept babbling about something, but I had to keep her quiet so I could work on her teeth. I gave her nitrous oxide. That settled her down."

"How did you find out what happened if she couldn't talk?" Ms. Zyla asked.

"Father Rick was with her. He told me quite a bit while the nitrous took effect. I made sure to speak with him in private so he'd speak freely," Eva explained. "But it's true. The bishop closed down Saint Stellan Church to pay for lawsuits brought on by Father Rick and his activities. He went to jail shortly after I saw him at the office."

"What about Christine?" Ms. Zyla asked.

"She's in a psychiatric ward," Eva explained. "She kept calling herself the Vice of Christ all the way out of the dental office. She's quite delusional."

"I can't believe they'd tear down a church and all," Evanita said, "even though it was creepy on the inside."

"There were strange things inside, but did you know that Saint Stellan was once a small factory?" Eva asked Evanita. "The crane that lifted you and your grandmother was once used to lift heavy equipment. The falling gate was part of a secure storage area—a crib is what I think it was called. The altar once held a small Port-O-Office where a supervisor could keep an eye on the factory."

"That's why it felt weird," Evanita said.

"Christine claims she designed everything in that church, but it's obvious she didn't," Eva continued. "Much existed already from when it was a factory. Evanita, I'm glad you didn't get caught up with those choir women. From what I heard, that was a tight-knit group controlled by Christine. She was making a power grab for running the church. She used her choir women to do whatever she felt needed doing to maintain her power. She tried to walk a narrow line—power from Father Rick through manipulation and the purported offers of help, and power over her choir women through threat and coercion. Christine was marginalized—all because she worshiped men—in particular Father Rick—and believed women should lean on men for power. Let that be a lesson of what not to do."

Eva took a big swig from her wine glass and swallowed. She let out a low sigh of satisfaction from a well-aged wine.

"Johnny," Evanita asked. "How was your steak sandwich?"

"Delicious. More than that, I have a warm feeling in my tummy that makes me feel good all over," he said.

"I'm glad," Ms. Zyla said. "Cerossi Café has excellent food here, and while I'm not a lover a beef, they do prepare it quite well from what I've heard."

"It reminds me of church picnics at Barnseed Baptist Church a few summers ago before everything started to change," Johnny started. "Cookouts, games, and good fun. We had the best steak—mine was always dry, but others liked steak sauce or barbecue sauce. I'd make a steak sandwich with pickles, lettuce, and tomato. And I'd take a little nap—right in the middle of the picnic! I'd wake up when the kids would start the three-legged races or start up the softball game. Oh how I miss those days."

"What happened? Don't you still have the picnics?" Evanita asked.

"No. They ended. He ended them," Johnny said.

"Who, Johnny? Who ended the picnics?" Evanita asked.

Johnny paused for a moment.

"Perhaps we should not ask Johnny any more questions," Eva offered.

"No, it's okay," Johnny said. "I have to learn how to deal with the situation. If I can think for a moment...yes, things

changed. Pastor Ephram took up hunting with some of the pa-
rishioners, and the church changed into a hunting lodge. Patty
was furious, but he kept control of the church operations including the finances. Do you remember the room on the left—
what I call the hunting room? It had stuffed animals—the whole
hunting lodge bit."

"Yes," Eva said about the same time Evanita said, "Yeah."

"No," said Ms. Zyla.

"It was supposed to be a church-sponsored day care. It was
Patty's idea, and Pastor Ephram went along with it—at first.
But when he started hunting with the church men, those plans
ended. He had new plans for the playground at church—he
wanted to convert it to a shooting range."

Johnny fell silent again. The flames shifted colors from blue
and purple to crimson and red.

"I'm sorry about your sister," Eva said.

"Johnny, we're here for you," Evanita said.

"Barnseed is changing again," Johnny said. "After Valeria
died, I took over her church gardening duties. It was time to
pull out the dead flowers and till them under for the winter. I
did this, tired as I was from working at the factory. I tilled them
under and watered the soil down for good measure."

Johnny paused again and stared at the fire. The flames
shifted their colors to dark pink and red.

"It came over me—what some call 'the gift' but what is really
a curse. I touched the water from the garden hose and sensed
an argument between Patty and Pastor Ephram. Patty was
cleaning up dishes, and—" Johnny said.

Johnny's voice trailed in the distance. Jonara lost sight and
sound of Cerossi Café and found herself standing next to her
father, Johnny Pindus, in the Barnseed Baptist Church's flower
bed. Johnny was watering down the soil but was lost in thought
as the water from the garden hose flowed freely over his hand.
For the first time, she noticed a finely-woven metal chain
around his neck. She was so used to seeing her father wear a
shirt with a collar—even turtlenecks—that she never noticed
the chain before. But he was working in the garden, and the

tee-shirt he wore allowed her to see this chain that traveled around the back of his neck and held something—perhaps it was a medal or keepsake—inside his shirt next to his chest.

Jonara reached around Johnny's waist and hugged him. His waist held firm and allowed her to hug him without passing through. Johnny could not see Jonara, but he felt her presence. He attributed this feeling to his "gift" for sensing things.

"The water has strange powers," he said.

Johnny's and Jonara's view of the garden faded. They continued hearing the water flowing over Johnny's hand, but now they were inside a house with Pastor Ephram and Patty.

"I can't believe it. Can you believe it? It's unbelievable, and who would think to pin it on me as if I, Pastor Ephram, did something. They can't do this!" Pastor Ephram rattled to Patty.

"Jeremiah—" Patty started while he popped three diet pills into his mouth.

"I'm going to miss my trip to the Convention," Pastor Ephram said. "All because of an investigation. She was bulimic, that's what I'll tell them. It's what I told everyone at the funeral service. Help me with my lie—I mean—help me with my tie."

Patty helped Pastor Ephram dress with his tie and his collar. She found his shoes for him and used a sticky roller to remove lint from his suit.

"Detective Sharon Stout—that's who's investigating. And that's the whole problem. A male officer would understand—he'd know how to close up this case quietly. But these women officers gotta drag things out," Pastor Ephram ran on. "They gotta make waves."

Patty made several gestures in sign language, saying it was his fault.

"What did that mean?" Pastor Ephram said, referring to her sign language.

"I said, 'Good luck.'" Patty lied.

"I'm on to you, Patty," Ephram said. "I know you twisted my sermon at Valeria's funeral. You disobeyed the laws of Jesus and the sanctity of marriage. The Bible does not allow these things. Take note, Patty. Reread letters from Paul again and again. I gotta go—I'll deal with you when I get back."

Pastor Ephram ran from the church house to the car, lit up the engine, and sped down to the police station leaving Patty alone. She dialed a number on the telephone and placed the receiver to her ear.

"Jan Haughf, please. Yes, I'll hold," Patty said.

In the few minutes Patty was on hold, she was able to finish the dishes and put them away. The water stopped running inside her house, and Johnny lost his link with her. He returned outside to his actual gardening. The water from the hose had created a large puddle at his feet. He finished up quickly and put the gardening equipment (including the garden hose) in the shed. Jonara followed him along the way, and when the two exited the shed, Johnny saw Claire Stout drive up. She parked and got out of her car with a big hug for Patty. The two looked over and saw Johnny walk up to them.

"Johnny, how are you holding up?" Claire asked.

"As well as I can," he said.

"Johnny, Claire and I are going over to Jan Haughf's office," Patty explained. "She's a senior partner at Haughf Telly. There are some legal issues that need to be performed. I wonder if you would come along. It would mean a lot to me."

"Did I do something wrong?" he asked.

"Haughf and Telly," said Jonara. "Where have I heard those names before?"

"Of course not, Johnny," Claire reassured him. "This is about the church's well-being. We're hoping you can help because we know how much Barnseed Baptist Church meant to Valeria and how much it still means to you. Would you like us to save the church?"

"Save the church, save the church! We must save the church! Yes, I'll come along to help!" Johnny said.

"Yes, that's where," said Jonara. "At Mommy's Coming-Of-Age. They were two of the mentors."

The three (and Jonara) entered Claire's car. Claire drove to Haughf Telly Law Firm. It was a beautifully architected building with dark masonry and sweeping lines. Claire parked and led the group up the elevator to the main office where a receptionist welcomed them into Ms. Haughf's office.

"They must have planned everything ahead of time," Johnny said to Eva, Evanita, and Ms. Zyla back in Cerossi Café.

"How do you mean?" Eva asked.

The flames tickled with tinges of yellow, but only briefly.

"Ms. Haughf had all sorts of papers ready for Patty to sign. Lawsuit papers, suing for divorce, full church property owner-ship, wrongful death—I think those were the major ones," Johnny explained.

"Ah, Patty! She held strong. I wondered how she would fare after signing her own version of Ephram's sermon," Eva said.

"Pastor Ephram didn't find out—at first," Johnny continued. "But word got around quickly to the men, and they let him know. Patty got scared, but Claire convinced her to see Ms. Haughf for legal advice and protection."

"I don't understand," said Evanita. "Is this the same Ms. Haughf who—"

"Mentored at the Coming-Of-Age at our church, Evanita? Yes. And so is Ms. Telly. They're both Unitarians," said Ms. Zy-la.

"They're Unitarians. Patty is a Baptist. And Claire—" Evanita started.

"Is an atheist," Eva finished. "Strange little world we live in, isn't it? Who would have guessed that women would connect across religious boundaries?" Eva said sarcastically.

"Don't make fun of me, Mama! I just think it's odd," Evanita said.

"They're all good friends," said Johnny. "We went out for a celebration dinner after the papers were signed."

"And Ms. Stout—Claire's mother—did the investigation?"

"That was Claire's idea," Johnny said. "Sharon would keep him busy with the investigation."

"Of course," said Eva. "It kept him from getting help from his buddies."

"If you mean his hunting friends in the Convention—yes, that was part of it. Part of the legal papers Patty signed sues to prevent joining the Convention. Ms. Haughf also made new friends in the American Baptist Churches, and she helped Patty start the process for our church obtaining membership," Johnny explained.

"A divorce can take a long time," said Ms. Zyla. "Patty will have a tough road ahead."

"It didn't help that Ms. Stout—Sharon that is—got caught up in that accident in Washington State," Johnny said.

"You mean the one where Sheila almost died?" Eva asked.

"Yes. How do you know? Did Claire tell you?" Johnny asked.

Evanita rolled her eyes. The flames lost their yellow tinges and red hues. They shifted back to crimson and violet.

"I got the story out of Evanita," said Eva.

"Mama!" Evanita said.

"It's nothing to be ashamed of," Eva continued. "Evanita saved Sheila's life. Her mother, Sharon, was an emotional wreck for a few days and took time off from work. I'm not blind to the world, Evanita, I know more than I let on."

"It's just that..." Evanita trailed.

"...That Evanita and Sheila got into a fight the following weekend," Eva continued. "Over a boy—Davino Vagatti."

"What?" Ms. Zyla asked. "I didn't know Davino was your boyfriend."

"He was never my boyfriend!" Evanita stated. "He's Sheila's boyfriend. And there's more."

"I don't understand why you had a fight," Johnny said. "Why, Evanita?"

"Sheila is her best friend," said Eva. "Sometimes we fight the people we love most."

"Sheila changed after the accident," Evanita said.

"The doctors said she suffered no brain damage," said Eva.

"Well I say she suffered some kind of damage," Evanita continued. "Davino is married. Maybe that's why she went after him. Married men seem more secure. She said she needed to find a man to lean on, to protect her so she wouldn't have to worry about being attacked again. I'm not sure if I believe her. Does Patty still lean on Pastor Ephram?"

"No, but things have changed again," Johnny said.

"How so?" Eva asked.

"Pastor Ephram is dead," Johnny replied.

"Oh that's terrible," said Evanita. "Who killed him?"

"No one, exactly. He died of heart failure," Johnny said.

"An overdose of diet pills?" Eva asked.

"Yes, it was the overdose," Johnny said. "Patty had been staying with Claire. Pastor Ephram saw the lawsuit papers and took more diet pills for strength. It was too much."

"How do you know?" Evanita asked.

"Johnny, did you—" Eva asked.

"No, I did not sense it," Johnny said. "I still can't read men. Sharon found his slumped body over the papers. He was supposed to report to the police station for another interview, and he failed to show up. The pathologist found the diet pills in his stomach. Oh, another death! Patty was worn out, but she held the funeral service, and now she's the pastor."

"Bravo!" Eva clapped.

"Mama! No one claps for death!" Evanita said.

"Bravo that she's the pastor. She's moving on then," Eva said.

"I wish Sheila would move on—from that Davino Vagatti," Evanita said. "He's got her doing all sorts of things for him. Helping out at the racetrack—for free! And now she's studying to be a Zoroastrian. Who is she kidding?"

"Claire told me about that," Johnny said. "Claire said Sheila has anxiety attacks at night—that she wakes up thinking she's drowning."

"I'm not sure I like how much time you spend with Claire," said Evanita with a tone of jealousy.

"Uh oh, here it comes," said Ms. Zyla.

"I may have to order another bottle of wine," said Eva.

"Stay out of this, Mama," said Evanita. "Now Johnny, this thing between you and Claire—"

"Valeria and I taught her taxonomic plant names," Johnny said. "Claire and Valeria were best friends and liked to garden together. Valeria would take care of the church gardening for years. Claire used to work at the Rose Gardens while studying to be a paramedic. I'm surprised you didn't know with Sheila being her sister. Sheila's your best friend, right?"

"Mostly. I only heard that Claire moved out from her mother's place years ago," Evanita said. "Sheila never spoke much of her sister, Claire. I guess she thought Claire was too independent."

"They don't agree on things, if that's what you mean," said Johnny.

"But Claire has some strange friends," Evanita said.

The flames had been burning a deep purple but now shifted into a bright pink.

"You mean me?" Johnny said.

"I didn't mean it like that," Evanita said. "When we went to the rose garden, her friends had all sorts of scientific equipment. They were measuring things about the flowers!"

"How rude," said Eva.

Eva finished her last glass of wine and wondered if she should order another bottle.

"There was one guy who gave me the absolute creeps!" Evanita said. "Creepy like nothing I've ever seen. He had a device, and it made an obnoxious sound, like some sort of vibrating drill or something."

"What was his name?" Ms. Zyla asked.

"Adrian," Evanita replied.

Eva looked up from her wine glass and stared directly at Johnny. Johnny returned the stare.

"What's wrong?" Evanita asked.

"Eva?" Ms. Zyla asked. "Your expression, it's like—"

"What name did you say?" Eva asked without moving a muscle.

"Adrian," Evanita replied.

"What was his last name?" Eva asked sternly.

"It was...I don't know!" Evanita said nervously. "Stop staring at me like that. I didn't do anything wrong."

"What was his last name!?" Eva asked more intently.

Eva stood up and shook her daughter.

"Stop it, stop it!" Ms. Zyla said. "She doesn't know."

"Johnny?" Eva asked. "You can find out—now."

"Ms. Carreña—I—if she doesn't know," Johnny stumbled.

"But you do," Eva said. "And you can confirm it with a simple test."

"It's not so simple. And it makes me tired," he dragged.

The flames shifted back to dark pinks and reds. Eva's blood started to boil, but Ms. Zyla and Evanita weren't sure why. Jonara didn't understand either, but Johnny knew something.

"What's wrong, Mama?" Evanita asked with a shaky voice.

Eva continued staring down Johnny. Johnny grimaced and sunk his head into his shoulders.

"What do you know, Johnny, what do you know?" Evanita asked. "Tell me! What's wrong with my mother?"

"Eva," Ms. Zyla said. "Relax."

"Johnny, hold Evanita's hand, and tell me what you see at the Portland Rose Garden," Eva commanded.

Eva shook the table—not with large disturbing shakes, but with a rapid, low-displacement vibration that sent small fast-moving ripples upon themselves in the beverage-filled glasses.

"What is going on?!" Evanita asked.

"Johnny, tell me what you see!" Eva commanded.

"Arkham Atheist Group," he started. "Portland Rose Garden. Adrian—close-frequency demonstration—frequency dissonance and beating."

The flames in Cerossi grew in height and waved back and forth in the air like wheat in a field with eddies blowing back and forth.

"Too much, too much!" Johnny said.

Johnny's face grew wet from perspiration, and he drew away from Evanita.

"Place your hands on the table," Eva instructed Johnny.

Johnny complied reluctantly.

"Mama, this is—" Evanita started.

"Shhh. Evanita, place your right hand on Johnny's left," Eva commanded.

"Eva, be careful!" Ms. Zyla said. "The flames feed off your emotional re—"

"Quiet," Eva commanded.

Eva placed her left hand on Johnny's right. Ms. Zyla reached her right hand out to Evanita's left, and the two held hands for support. Jonara could not touch her mother's hands, but she sufficed by placing her own hands on the table. Eva used her right hand to resume vibrating the table.

"What do you sense, Johnny? Adrian and the Arkham Group?" Eva commanded.

"Arkham Atheist Group. Adrian—looking at Claire and Evanita. Sense of recognition, Adrian thinks he knows Evanita. She doesn't know him," Johnny said.

Johnny took a sip of root beer and continued.

"Evanita's trip, Evanita's journey. Running. No, pushing the earth beneath her. Evanita in one place, the earth moving under her. Which way to go? Run the earth underneath her feet. Running from Sheila at the raceway. Claire offering help."

"Claire Stout," Eva said.

"Arkham Atheist Group," Johnny continued. "Running backward. Claire Stout, her mother Sharon Stout, Claire's sister, Sheila Stout. Sheila and Davino. Sheila afraid of drowning, searching for safety, to breathe, Hothrane Zoroastrian Church."

"Sharon Stout," Eva said.

"My child, my child!" Johnny said as if speaking for Sharon. "Raise my child, protect my child, make her strong and ready for the world. The world of injustice. Let no one attack my faith. Cannot be Jewish on the outside, the world is cruel. Spare Sheila from the world. What happened to my faith? Morris Synagogue. Sheila almost died, death of a daughter. Claire would lose a sister. Sympathy for Johnny Pindus and Valeria."

"Valeria Pindus," Eva prompted.

"Cannot stop working. Must save the church. Go, go, go. No rest. Cannot sleep. Cannot think. Cannot serve this man any longer. Must join the American Baptist Churches. No time left, no time. Force of men too strong, like steel, a machine, caught in the gears. Crushed. Friend Patty. Signs from God, gestures, peace and beauty of movement. Sign language. Read the scripture, read for love not power, for hope not hatred, for relief not debt, for life not machine. Machine. Gears and cranes. Chains and gates. Grandma Geneva, Josefene."

Eva paused. She wanted to skip over this venture into Saint Stellan.

"Back to Adrian," Eva said.

"The machine, the gears, Adrian, transaxle, Father Rick, Saint Stellan—so confused," Johnny said.

Johnny felt torn between focusing on Adrian in the Arkham Atheist Group and the unique internal architecture of Saint Stellan Catholic Church. The flames had waved rhythmically but now formed the outline of a long oval with an indentation in the middle.

"Look at the flames!" Ms. Zyla exclaimed.

The restaurant fell to a hush as the other patrons were amazed at the flames' animation.

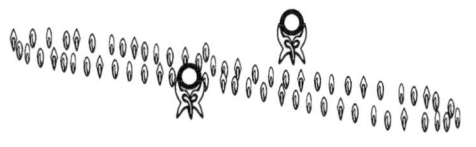

"It's an outline of something—a canoe, a sandal, a double-ended ice-cream spoon," said Evanita.

"It's holding steady," said Ms. Zyla. "Look how the flames form the outline without wavering."

"Flames and fire, fires of Gehenna," Johnny said.

"Genev...no, Josefene," Eva said.

"Working the faith, the dynamo, order and discipline, the voice of Christ, a voice is another's vice, turn off the brain, stop thinking, I must stop thinking. Latin, English, what is language? Catholic, universal, what is universal? Catechism, memorize, I must memorize, must recite things given to me, a handout, Coming-Of-Age, the handout, Sheila completed Coming-Of-Age, why couldn't I? Run and think, the earth turning

under my feet, run and think. Sheila, can you pronounce it?
Unitarian."

"Unitarian Universal-
ism," Eva said.

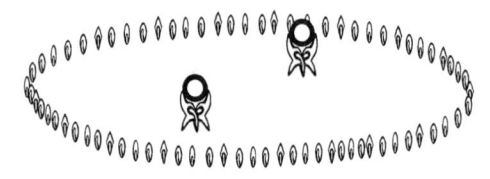

"Look!" Evanita said.
"The flames shifted. Now
the shape is more like a
circle."

"But not a perfect circle," Ms. Zyla said. "More like an inflat-
ed square. But the shape is wavering. It's changing back to the
canoe."

"No, it's the circle," Evanita said. "Now the canoe. It's shifting back and forth between the canoe and the circle. It's so fast
that it looks like both circle and canoe are being lit at the same
time."

"You're right, Evanita," said Ms. Zyla. "The flames shift back
and forth between
canoe and circle
like a pump, no a
heart, and it's
beating faster and
faster."

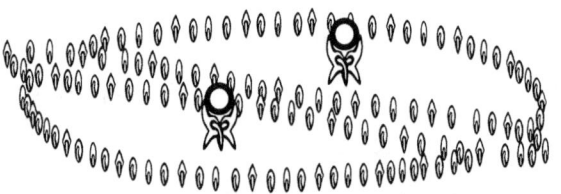

"Tolerance for all," Johnny continued. "Cannot tolerate everything. Must protect my daughter, must save Evanita. Must
save Sheila. The cat threatens, the rabbit hides. I am the shark,
I smell for the rabbit, the rabbit must not hide, must not die. I
am the shark but not for killing. Hunt to save the rabbit, not to
kill the rabbit. Sheila underwater. Eva underwater. Life from
death."

The flames roared back and forth between canoe and circular shapes. Sporadic yellow flames begat gray smoke. These yellow flames nearly reached the roof of the café's interior. The
waitresses stopped serving and looked around wildly for a way
to suppress the flames. One waitress guessed Eva's table
caused the up-flame and asked Eva to stop. Eva pushed the
waitress aside with her right hand. This interrupted Eva's vibrations on the table and broke Johnny's thoughts for a moment.

"Resume, Johnny," Eva said. "Adrian, who is Adrian?"

"The chain from present to past, from past to present. Unitarian, Catholic, Baptist, Jewish, Zoroastrian, Atheist, small tribe in a cave standing in a pool of strontium water. The place of the past and the present. Broadway Unitarian, Saint Stellan, Barnseed Baptist, Morris Synagogue, Hothrane Zoroastrian, Arkham Atheist, and Cerossi Café. These are the places—these are the chains, the threads, the bridges."

"What is Adrian's last name!?" Eva barked.

"Adrian has followed a bridge, Evanita the bridges, from there to here. Broadway, Steel, Burnside, Morrison, Hawthorn, Marquam, and Ross Island Bridge. Only one bridge left, one left. Sellwood Bridge—his name is Adrian Cracbern!"

The flames erupted into a fireball. The ceiling caught on fire, the electricity went out, and the patrons screamed as they evacuated the café. Eva stood up quickly and knocked the table over. She reached for Evanita's arm to pull her out, but as quickly as the ceiling caught fire, it went out. The flames from the circle ceased immediately. Poof! A faint smell of unburnt natural gas filled the air.

"Eva, Evanita, Johnny, Zellie," the voices called one another in the dark.

"Mommy, Daddy," Jonara called back.

The voices faded in the distance for Jonara. She found herself standing on the northern edge of Sellwood Bridge, halfway between banks, and staring at Ross Island. The current was swift in the Willamette River flowing beneath her. She peered across the haze and saw a van bobbing up and down the river. It forked to the east around Ross Island and disappeared around a bend into the island's lagoon. Jonara thought she smelled blood and salt—a strange sensation of blood lost while giving birth and blood lost while dying. The feeling was uncomforting and lonely for Jonara. She was tired of these bridges, tired of showing men how to build a pyramid, tired of addictive movie screens and being split into two people. Tired of power-hungry people. She wanted it to end. When would she wake up? When would the dream let go?

Chapter 12

Thoughtful Abandon

2023 Oct 4, Wed Early am. Jonara's Dream.
2006 Oct 30, Mon. Portland, Oregon.

Eva's House, the Living Room.

"It's final, do you hear? Final!" Eva said to Evanita.

"Mama!" Evanita said.

"No more going out to other churches, bridges, and friends I don't approve of in advance. You're grounded!" Eva said.

"Because of what, Mama? What?" Evanita asked.

"I should have moved us away from here years ago," Eva said.

"I like it here in Portland, and my friends like me!" Evanita said.

"You'll get along just fine wherever you go. Something will bug you as it always does, and you'll go for a run," Eva said. "Thank the stars you weren't injured by that fiasco in the lake."

"The doctors said I was fine, that the extra heavy bleeding and sloughing would go away. Just stress," Evanita said.

"Fortunately for us. I was all set to make an appointment for you—to have a D&C if necessary," Eva said.

"Mama! I'm not some old woman with sloppy innards!" Evanita said. "I take good care of myself."

"Still, one can't be too careful," said Eva. "The lakes and rivers around here are polluted with all sorts of chemicals and heavy metals."

"This is crazy talk! Why are you so possessive of me? Why can't I live my own life? I'm sixteen! In two years, I'll be a legal adult. Stop treating me like your helpless child," Evanita said. "I know what I need. I know what my body feels. And I know what to do about things."

"That's exactly the attitude that got me into trouble the first time," Eva blurted.

Eva turned away and darted into the kitchen.

"What trouble? What first time?" Evanita asked, following her mother into the kitchen.

Eva went silent except for one phrase, "You're grounded."

"Is this about my father?" Evanita asked. "Who is my father?"

"Never you mind!" Eva said.

"Does it have something to do with this Adrian Cracbern person? Is he related to me somehow?" Evanita asked.

Eva slapped Evanita across the face.

"Don't you ever mention that name in this house or anywhere else again. And don't make any wild claims of relation either. Got it?!" Eva ordered.

Evanita nodded her head in affirmation without saying a word. She left the kitchen, put on her jogging shoes, and opened the back door.

"Where are you going?" Eva asked.

"For a run," Evanita replied as she strapped on a utility bag to her waist.

"You're grounded!" Eva said.

"Am I grounded from running in the woods too? I'll see you in a couple of hours," Evanita said.

Evanita closed the back door behind her and jogged through the back yard into the woods from the edge of Holman Park to Forest Park. Eva threw her arms up in futility.

"What am I going to do with that girl?" Eva said to herself.

Jonara followed Eva to a room facing the south. It was well lit from the late-afternoon sun, and it had a view of Eva's bushes and flower garden. The birds were chirping, and two squirrels chased each other around the yard.

The room was Eva's exercise room. It was her spiritual haven, her place for regathering her inner strength and clarity of mind. One wall was little more than an oversized mirror with a handrail attached. The room also contained a complex muscle strengthening apparatus—more than simple weights but less than an oversized full-workout machine. The middle floor area was wood-tiled and varnished, giving a slick surface to anyone wearing socks.

Eva turned on a stereo. French ballet music filled the room. Eva warmed up with big stretches on the handrail in preparation for a few ballet moves. She had taken ballet as a young girl and loved it but gave it up for something she felt she could better support herself with—dentistry.

"One, two, three, four," Eva counted in each stretch position. "And one, and two, and three, and four," she continued with another set of muscles.

Eva completed her warm-up and walked over to a small desk. She pulled out a framed photograph from a drawer and placed it on the desk so she could see it during her workout. The photograph was a portrait of a young, carroty-red-haired woman. Jonara took a close look at the frame and noticed the name, "Roberta," written on the back. Eva laced up her pointy ballet shoes and stood on her toes. She bowed to the photograph and began dancing. She danced as if with a partner—extending her arms out at times and receiving another's arms at other times. She pirouetted, pliéd, extended, and circled her arms over her head. Eva performed other ballet maneuvers as well—many Jonara did not know the names of—but Eva finished her ballet with several grand jetés toward the photograph followed by an arabesque penchée, where Eva leaned forward with her face toward the photograph, her left leg remaining on the floor, and her right leg going nearly straight up into the air. Eva motioned her hands as if welcoming the photograph.

The doorbell rang and jolted Eva out of her pose. She rushed to the stereo and turned it off, unlaced her ballet shoes, and threw them in a corner. Eva toweled off her face as she prepared to exit the room. The doorbell rang again. She took a last glance in her exercise room and realized she'd left the photograph sitting out in full view. She ran over to the photograph and hid it in the desk, tossed the towel in the same corner as the ballet shoes, and rushed to the door only to answer it calmly as if nothing were afoot.

"Oh Zellie, it's you," Eva said. "Come in."

"You're perspiring," said Ms. Zyla as she walked in. "Busy workout?"

"I was just finishing, uh, doing some work," Eva started.

"With lace marks on your ankles?" Ms. Zyla asked. "How did the ballet session go?"

"Why do I bother hiding anything from you?" Eva confessed.

"Don't let me interrupt. Please, go back to your workout," Ms. Zyla said.

"Can I get you anything, coffee, tea?" Eva offered.

"Just bottled water is fine," Ms. Zyla replied.

While Eva went into the kitchen for the water, Ms. Zyla noticed the back door was a little ajar—in the familiar position Evanita would leave it when going out for a jog.

"Thank you," Ms. Zyla said as Eva handed her the water.

Ms. Zyla followed Eva into the workout room and turned on the stereo.

"French ballet music," Ms. Zyla said.

Eva placed her hand over Ms. Zyla's to turn the stereo back off.

"Must you be so nosy?" Eva asked.

"But of course. And now that I'm here and watching, you'll skip the rest of your ballet and proceed to weight lifting," Ms. Zyla said.

Eva shot Ms. Zyla a frown of having been caught sneaking a cookie from the jar. Eva did as predicted—she sat on the weight-lifting apparatus and exercised her arms' triceps.

"Push, push, push," said Eva.

"All alone in the house while Evanita is on a run, I see," Ms. Zyla said.

"She's grounded. And what am I going to do with you, Zellie, after that stunt you pulled taking us to that restaurant by Hardtack Island?" Eva said.

"It has a name—Cerossi Café," Ms. Zyla corrected.

"That black magic at Cerossi Café," Eva said.

"The flames are not to blame," said Ms. Zyla. "You and Evanita have much to work out."

"Evanita has nothing to work out. Life has not scarred her yet, and I want to keep it that way," Eva said, now working on her biceps. "And I'm working out my own stress. Lift, lift, lift."

"So is Evanita. She's out running, isn't she?" Ms. Zyla said.

"She's growing up. She needs exercise just for that," Eva said. "Besides, who's the mother here?"

"Eva, why don't you tell Evanita about her past? Hasn't she asked about—" Ms. Zyla started.

"Her father? She bugs me constantly about that. And I give her the same answer every time, that she doesn't have one," Eva replied. "Quads now. Umph, umph, umph."

"Tell her the truth. Tell her how she came into this world," Ms. Zyla said.

"She won't understand. I still don't myself. Sometimes it seems like yesterday, other times like centuries ago. My baby was the cutest little girl. Now she's a young woman. Where did the years go?" Eva said. "But the past is too painful to relive. I won't go through it or have Evanita go through it."

"Something scared you in the café, didn't it? You were obsessed with Johnny's insight. You wanted him to focus on that Adrian name," said Ms. Zyla.

"Like I was telling Evanita, I should have moved us away from here a long time ago. I never should have stuck around in Portland. Why did I think moving to the northwest corner of town would give us a safe haven? Just because it's next to Forest Park," Eva ranted.

"I think you know deep down, but you just don't want to admit it, not to me, not to Evanita, and not to yourself," Ms. Zyla said. "You want Evanita to know. You can't explain the situation to her on a rational level, but you're hoping that time will somehow create that magical moment when you'll be able to freely and candidly tell her, and all the past will be cleansed away. But that's not how life works."

"Who's to say how life works when a new kind of life comes along? Religion and science and engineering—what can they say about the unknown that's any more valid than what I feel?" Eva asked.

Eva stopped pumping the weights and sat up, not expecting Ms. Zyla to respond.

"You're not the first woman to raise a daughter without a man around," Ms. Zyla said. "In fact, I'm on my rounds today, and Sharon Stout is next on my list of single-mom families. Sheila's been quite a handful now that she's involved with this Davino."

"No, I'm not the first single-mom. But I am the first single-mom whose daughter never had a father," Eva said.

"Come come, Eva. Your situation is equivalent to all the other single moms in the world," Ms. Zyla said.

"Equivalent. Like a math equation? No set of teeth are the same, and my daughter is the only one of her kind!"

"I have to go over to Sharon's now, Eva," Ms. Zyla said. "But keep in mind one thing. You have me to talk to. Who does Evanita have? Sheila is Evanita's best friend, and right now there is a rift between them. You've grounded Evanita, and she's off running by herself. Who knows where she'll go or what she'll seek? And there's nothing more dangerous for a confused teenager than to seek answers in questionable places."

Eva waited for Ms. Zyla to leave before opening the refrigerator door and guzzling down a half bottle of the driest red wine she could find. She walked over to the back door and peered out the window, wondering where Evanita had jogged off to.

The world started to spin around Jonara. Her view of Eva faded, and Jonara expected to appear with Evanita and find out what she was doing. But the world cleared, and Jonara was with Eva again. Eva sat on the couch and read a magazine. The world spun and blurred again, but Jonara returned right back with Eva reading the magazine.

"Something is wrong," said Jonara. "I'm supposed to magically jump from here to there."

But Jonara didn't magically jump. It was as if something had run out of energy in her dream. Something she took for granted—something that always happened naturally in dreams was not working for her. She tried again. The world spun and blurred more quickly and with less effect. She was stuck in Eva's home.

"I can't be stuck," she said.

Jonara passed through the back door and ran into the woods after her mother.

"At least I didn't have to open the back door," she said. "But how long will that last? I could get stuck in this world if I'm not careful."

There was only one path into the woods, but after running for several yards, the path forked.

"Which way?" Jonara said.

From habit, Jonara reached back for the backpack, but it was gone. She checked her pocket for a map—no map.

"How will I track my mother?" Jonara asked. "Track, that's it. I must look for footprints."

Jonara searched the ground. Yes, there were shoe prints. Her mother veered to the right.

"Then right we must go," Jonara said.

Jonara ran along the trail and did not get tired, but she suspected that if her special transportation powers were bad, she would soon tire from running.

"Don't think about getting tired, too much thinking will make you tired," Jonara said.

The trees and underbrush ignored Jonara. Not that they were conscious as animals might be, but this was Jonara's first time running through these woods, and she was a little scared as to what might be waiting for her inside.

"Don't get scared, it will tire you out," Jonara said.

Jonara ran for what seemed like an hour or more. She was running northwest, and to her right she could hear a busy highway. Without warning, she came to an opening and faced the highway. It was Saint Helens Road, though Jonara didn't know it at the time. The ground changed from loose, woodsy soil to a sand and gravel mixture where only weeds and tall grass grew. Jonara looked beyond this light, weedy growth and saw a line of demarcation where no plants grew—perpendicular to her path from the woods. At that point was her mother, Evanita. Evanita stood by a large sign and regathered her breath while she gazed at a factory building. Jonara walked briskly up to Evanita and stood next to her. Jonara read the sign aloud:

EPA
United States Environmental Protection Agency
Region 10
DO NOT ENTER
HAZARDOUS CHEMICALS
Unauthorized Entry Prohibited

In smaller print at the bottom she read:

EPA Superfund
River Wood and Battery Site

Spray-painted on the back of the sign was graffiti which had the word "make" followed by pictograms of a heart, a rope with a knot, and a skull.

"Make love not death," Jonara read.

"This must be it, the old abandoned River Wood and Battery factory," Evanita said.

Jonara looked at her mother in surprise. Why would Evanita want to go here? It was an old and deteriorating building, with concrete and steel jutting out unpleasantly in several places.

"Mommy, don't go in there," said Jonara.

"If it's really so hazardous, how come people worked there to begin with? Just another sign to ignore," Evanita said.

Evanita sat down on a fallen tree trunk. She unstrapped the bag from her waist and placed it next to her leg on the log. Jonara stood behind her mother and wondered if Evanita would open the bag and find something like a Daily Missal, a Bible, or another book that Jonara had found in her now-lost backpack.

Evanita did have something like a small book inside. She retrieved the "book" and opened it.

"It's blank!" Jonara said.

Evanita held an unruled spiral notebook, about five inches by eight in size. In her left hand, she held two pens—one with a thin point, the other thick. Her right hand reached for the thick pen and drew outlines of the building and the surrounding landscape. Jonara watched over her mother's shoulder.

"I didn't know you could draw, Mommy," Jonara said.

Evanita completed the thick outlines and swapped pens.

"Details always take longer than outlines," Evanita said, not realizing she had Jonara in attendance.

Evanita did not finish the details. She tired of drawing details of such a decrepit building and decided instead to go inside. She placed the spiral notebook and pens in her bag and jogged to the building. She didn't bother strapping the bag around her waist but instead carried it in her left hand.

Jonara jogged with her. Their shoes crunched along in the sterile gravel, and when Evanita crossed the crumbled-up parking lot, she stopped at the door marked, "Employee Entrance Only."

"I'm grounded, which means I'm supposed to stay on the ground. If I enter this abandoned building, I'll be leaving the ground. I'll be going against Mama," Evanita said.

"Mommy," Jonara said to Evanita.

"I'm going to do it anyway. She can't ground me forever," Evanita said, and with that she went through the employee entrance and into the building.

"You are a rebel!" Jonara exclaimed.

Jonara followed her mother inside. The short hallway teed off—to the left was the factory, to the right a door leading to the front office. Evanita opened the door to the front office and walked inside. A middle section once contained cubicles, but all that remained of their presence were carpet impressions where the cubicle walls rested. A few banged-up metal filing cabinets rested on the floor next to a wall. On the floor by the filing cabinets, papers of old memos for picnics, lunches, and mission statements were mixed with company coffee mugs, mouse pads, and used pens.

Evanita nearly slipped on some papers as she walked from the center office area to one of the permanent offices—an office room with a window view. The sun shone through and lit up the room. The walls had undiscolored places where picture frames once rested, the carpeting was sun-bleached in places, and an old bookcase made of particle board rested against the wall with broken shelves and old books—supply catalogs, machining handbooks, hazardous waste manuals, lumber reference guides, and an old telephone book.

The office room had an old scratched-up wooden desk. Evanita opened one of the drawers, revealing an assortment of pens and paper clips. Reaching back into the drawer, she pulled out labels and pushpins. One of the pushpins punctured her index fingertip on her right hand, but she did not notice as the adrenalin from the run reduced her awareness of pain.

Evanita opened the other drawers—most were empty—but one had several pill bottles—aspirin, antacids, and decongestants. Reaching farther back, she touched an assortment of loose pills along with jelly beans and sunflower seeds.

"The junk these people kept," Evanita said.

Evanita left the office and explored the others but found nothing else of interest. One was full of cobwebs, and she swatted them away. She swiped her hand across her face to clear away cobwebs and in doing so unknowingly touched a drop of blood from her push-pinned finger onto the center of her forehead. Evanita cleaned the rest of the cobwebs from her hair. She bumped up against a tall bookcase and jolted dust loose from its top. The dust got in her hair.

"Yuck! This place is going to get me all dirty. Mama will know I've been somewhere. Better cover up my hair from the dirt," Evanita said.

Evanita had been holding the bag in her left hand. She placed the bag on a short filing cabinet and used both hands to tie her hair up in a bun. From the bag, Evanita produced a white dish towel she normally used for wiping off perspiration, and she fashioned it over her head such that the ends were tied together around the back of her neck. She looked something between a factory worker, a field hand, and a nurse's assistant of two hundred years prior.

"I had better strap this back on," Evanita said, referring to the bag. "No telling what else I'll encounter."

Evanita was referring to her bag. She strapped it around her waist and continued around the office. She found the reception lobby with a view of the Willamette River. She sat in the receptionist's chair, took her spiral notebook out, and drew a picture of the lobby, though she changed the picture into one with ornate plants, a magazine-laden coffee table, and nicely-framed hanging pictures. She pulled out a small pack of colored pens and gave life to the drawing—from a line drawing to a watercolor look. But Evanita felt strange. She sneezed several times. Was it the dust? She wasn't sure. Perhaps there was something in the office she was inhaling, something not good for her. Jonara felt no ill effects herself, but she urged her mother to go outside and get some fresh air.

"I just need to get moving," said Evanita. "I shouldn't sit for such a long time."

Evanita stood up and returned to the main office area when BOOM! She was startled by the clap of thunder, though the sky was clear outside. The ground shook, and dust shook from the ceiling onto her headscarf. Several ceiling tiles broke free and fell around her. One bounced off her shoulder. Her immediate reaction was to get out of the building, but instead of thinking her way out, her legs carried her out of the office from where she came, past the employee entrance, and into the main factory floor area. She felt lightheaded, the air didn't feel right, and it didn't look right.

"Boom!"

Another clap of thunder jolted her, but she realized the sound wasn't from outside but inside the factory. The thunder had multiple components—there was a low rumbling like a semi-truck approaching, a deep-encompassing thud, a loud pop, and the ringing of metal.

"Someone else is in here," she said to herself.

"Mommy, go outside," Jonara beckoned. "Here, this way."

Evanita could not hear Jonara. Evanita would have been better off leaving the factory and returning home, but something took hold of her mind. She suspected some bad drug remnant entered her punctured finger in that desk drawer. She looked around the factory, and it apparently came to life. Steel beams and cranes waved through the air like water lilies underwater. The ground vibrated with each boom and flowed with ripples like a pond receiving plunging debris. The daylight—shining through the skylights in the roof—took on a bluish tinge before fragmenting into hues of yellow and orange. Painted steel and concrete walls took on more lively colors from their normally dingy drab. Evanita passed her hand in front of her face, and her flesh glowed.

"Mommy, get out of here!" Jonara urged.

Jonara could not help. She reached to grab Evanita, but her hands passed through her mother. She yelled again, but it was no use.

"Maybe I can find Daddy. He'll know what to do," Jonara said.

But that was the problem—where was Johnny Pindus in this moment of need, and how would Jonara reach him? She closed her eyes and imagined spinning around with the backpack and landing near Johnny Pindus. She opened her eyes to find she was still with Evanita, who was now seated on a bench and drawing the factory structures surrounding her.

"Boom!"

The factory echoed with the thunder-pop again. Jonara wasn't sure what her mother was feeling, but by looking at Evanita's drawings, Jonara could guess. Evanita's solid and steady drawing strokes from earlier in the office had become more ballooned, more cartoonish. Her depiction of the factory was a mixture of I-beams and trees, cross-beams and branches, signs and leaves, painted floors, and grassy paths. She went through several pages of drawings. In each one, the steel and concrete looked more like trees, shrubs, and earth.

"Boom!"

One more drawing—that was what Evanita told herself, only one more, and she'd leave. But each time she completed a drawing, she felt compelled to turn the page and begin another one.

"I'll only draw a little," she told herself. "Just a line or two."

Evanita could not stop. Her trees and shrubs took on a less rounded look and acquired sharp angles—angles and motivation as if the trees were active machines coordinating with other machianic trees. What were the machianics doing? They were using their sickle-like branches to chop down more natural trees and feed them through a central, double-open-ended box. The tree entered from the left, endured a chattering screech, and exited from the right as a machinated tree.

"Boom!" rang the factory.

Evanita flipped the page and started a new drawing—one of dancing little people firing into the open-ended box. The bullets passed through the box from right to left and exited as apples. One of the little people with dark skin and Hindu background walked up to Evanita and held out his hand.

"Parvati—goddess of love, goddess of spirituality. Welcome to your palace! I am your servant, Vinay. As your servant, I will do the needful thing—I must show you your throne. Come this way. I will show you the way!"

Evanita stood up. The little people danced around the factory without noticing her. Vinay was real, however. Jonara followed her mother and this young Hindu man along an otherwise deserted factory.

"Boom!" rang the factory again.

"Parvati," Vinay said as he stared intently at Evanita's bloodstained forehead and scarfed head. "You are all the beauty of her goddessness."

Vinay was mistaking Evanita for the Hindu goddess Parvati. Yet he had a glaze in his eye and a sincerity that convinced Evanita in her altered state.

"Mommy, please! Do not go that way! Snap out of your trance!" Jonara begged.

Vinay placed a small tube to his nose and inhaled. His eyes fluttered for a moment before resuming his obsessive gaze upon Evanita. Evanita followed Vinay into the factory—past abandoned saws, scattered lead-acid battery parts, green sawdust, and cans of chemicals.

"Boom!" echoed the factory.

"Do not let the celebration frighten you, your great highness," Vinay said.

"Hey dudes!" called another voice. "It's Mother Bunny!"

Vinay led Evanita to a group of older teenage boys.

"This is Parvati!" Vinay said to the boys. "Not your mother! Make way for the goddess!"

"Oooo!" another voice mocked, known as Fat One. "Vinny got himself a girl!"

The boys sat on grated stands around an open pit. They threw green-colored wood into the pit. Evanita approached the pit but backed off as a flaming roar shot up toward her face.

"My royal goddess Parvati—be careful of the sacred flames!" Vinay urged.

Vinay rushed to her and pulled her away from the pit.

"Sacred flames, hear that dudes? We got a sacred flame going," said one of the boys (Skins), a tall skinny boy who smoked a cigarette.

"Let's get that sacred flame going really good!" said another (Doofus), who threw several more green-colored planks into the fire.

"Sit, my royalness," Vinay said to Evanita. "Sit and enjoy the celebration."

Evanita sat on the grated stand next to Vinay and the boys. She removed her spiral notebook and two pens from her bag and began drawing.

"Boom!" rang the factory.

"That sound," Evanita said. "What is that sound?"

"Your goddessness, it is the royal cannon!" Vinay said.

The boys laughed.

"It's Josh setting off a few rounds on the press. Look over there," said Doofus.

Evanita and Jonara looked to their right in the darkness but could not see anything.

"Doofus!" said Fat One. "Mother Bunny can't see anything in the dark! Here!"

Fat One passed his flashlight to "Doofus". Doofus shined the long black flashlight to the right. It gleamed and glared off a small press and a guy—Josh. Josh positioned a bullet cartridge on the press with the cartridge supported on three sides by the small metal lips of an old abandoned die set, aimed the bullet across the factory toward some barrels, took a step away from the press, and pressed his hands on two large buttons—the buttons being attached to an operator's stand. A spinning flywheel at the top of the press engaged the ram, and the ram descended into the cartridge. The cartridge ignited, the bullet shot across the factory, and it punctured a barrel. Fluid poured out of the barrel and onto the floor.

"Cool, dude! Can you catch venison that way?" asked Doofus.

"Shut up!" said another, a stocky weight lifter known as Beef. "You gotta be deep in the woods to hunt animal."

"No! My uncle killed a deer in his back yard, and that's no lie!" said a fat boy, known as Fat One.

"That's bullcrap!" said Beef.

"Gents! The goddess Parvati graces our presence! Show respect!" said Vinay.

"It's Devil's Night Out," said Skins. "That's all the respect we need!"

"Boom!" sounded a cartridge.

"How did he get that press running?" Doofus asked.

"He wound up a big rubber band and let it go," said Fat One.

"More bullcrap from Fat One," said Beef.

"Look at that machine on four wheels," said Doofus as he moved the flashlight around to highlight the machine on wheels. "It's a diesel generator."

"Now where did he get that from?" asked Fat One.

"I saw him, I saw him!" said Doofus.

"Where did you see him?" Fat One asked with a sigh.

"I saw him go into a locked storage room and pull the generator out," said Doofus.

"If it was locked, how did he get it open?" Skins asked.

"I broke it open for him, sir," Beef said to Skins. "Captain Beef, aka Break-Bones-and-Locks at your service."

"Boom!" sounded the press.

"Let's hear it for Devil's Night Out!" Skins applauded.

The other boys gave a general cheer in agreement. Evanita drew more pictures, but she was edgy and uncomfortable. She felt as if little bits of metal were filling her lungs. Her delusions continued, and she saw millions of little ash flies swarming through the air and flying into her lungs. She exhaled, and the bugs appeared to fly out. She dropped her spiral notebook onto the grated stand and swatted these ash bugs vigorously around her face, ears, and neck.

"They're getting me, they're getting me! They're eating me alive!" Evanita yelled.

"My goddessness, please, I will calm you. Rest here and enjoy the celebration!" Vinay said.

"Look dudes," said Fat One. "Mother Bunny is tripping out!"

"Boom!" echoed another bullet cartridge.

"Yeah, what's she on?" asked Beef.

"Did you give her some of our *acid*, Vinny?" Fat One asked.

"I don't believe in those demons," said Vinay.

"She stole our *acid*," said Doofus.

"Naw, I hid it real good in one of those desk drawers," said Beef.

"Here, my good Parvati, put away your notebook and bless us with your presence," said Vinay. "Say a prayer for the celebration."

"What are you celebrating?" Evanita asked in a monotone voice.

"Devil's Night Out!" said Skins. "Haven't you been listening? Stupid broad."

"Do not insult the goddess!" Vinay said.

"Boom!" sounded a cartridge.

"It's Mother Bunny!" said Beef.

"Hey Mother Bunny! Show us how to dance!" said Fat One.

"Dance Mother Bunny, dance Mother Bunny!" the boys chanted.

Evanita yielded to the power of suggestion. She hallucinated that she was an oversized rabbit with long ears and a furry coat. With her powerful running legs, she bent her knees and jumped several feet into the air and across the floor. The boys cheered and jeered. Evanita held her arms next to her ears and used her arms to imitate long rabbit ears. She hopped on alternating feet and rotated her hands as if listening in different directions.

"Stop, Parvati! Do not humiliate yourself!" Vinay said.

"Ah, shut up," said Beef to Vinay.

"Boom!" rang another cartridge.

"Mother Bunny, show us how to dance on all four legs," Skins said.

"No!" said Vinay.

"All fours," repeated Skins.

Skins stood up and pushed Evanita to the ground.

"Leave her alone," said Vinay, and he stood between Skins and Evanita.

Skins flicked his cigarette away and shoved Vinay aside. Evanita hopped as best she could on all fours and sniffed the floor like a rabbit looking for food. The boys laughed again, but their cheers and taunts turned more sinister and evil, like hoodlums at a stripper party.

"Mother Bunny is sniffing for food," said Fat One.

"Boom!" jarred a cartridge.

"What do bunnies eat?" asked Doofus.

"Carrots," said Fat One.

"Do we have any carrots?" Beef asked, setting up Skins for his line.

"Hey Mother Bunny, would you like to eat a carrot?" asked Skins.

Vinay's eyes filled with rage. He grabbed Evanita and placed her on some metal-grated steps leading to a catwalk for protection. Picking up a five-foot length of two-by-two wood, he turned around and struck Skins. Skins fell backward.

"Get the Indie," said Beef.

"Stand back! I know Silambam. The martial art of the cane!" Vinay yelled.

"Boom!" echoed Josh's cartridge antics.

Most of the boys jumped up and encircled Vinay. Fat One crawled after Evanita with lust in his eye. Evanita's head swirled with the commotion—her legs instinctively kicking away Fat One. Her spell of dancing for the boys ended, but she still felt like a rabbit. She moved up the steps and across the cat-walk—a narrow walkway that rose above the floor about eight feet and ran close to the pit—the very same pit with the roaring fire of pressure-treated wood. Fat One approached Evanita, and she kicked him back successfully, but it was only enough to hold him off temporarily. Evanita was confused and had her attention split between kicking off the intruder and witnessing Vinay fighting off the circle of boys.

Josh noticed the excitement and set two- and three-bullet cartridges on the press at one time. He cycled the press faster and faster, setting off more "booms" through the factory and spraying down several barrels at the same time. Barrels that were unaffected by earlier rounds were now being hit and drain-ing liquids onto the floor.

Jonara stood by her mother and urged her down the other end of the catwalk, but Evanita did not hear her. Evanita's eyes saw a "leaf devil" on the floor, with Vinay defending the vortex, and the boys swirling around him like leaves—attacking close and withdrawing away from Vinay's wielding stick. The leaf dev-il widened, as did much of the factory floor. Everything grew flat and wide. Evanita held her hand in front of her face and moved it away—her arm extended out several yards.

"Boom, boom!" echoed a two-shot from Josh's press.

"Give me an Easter present, Mother Bunny," said Fat One in a guttural voice.

"No," said Evanita, but her voice weakened. "No."

"Wait for me Parvati, I'll save you!" Vinay said while jabbing the boys with the stick.

The catwalk, which had railing for most of its span, had an opening next to the pit. Evanita regained some sense and start-ed kicking Fat One toward the opening. Inflamed, he reached for Evanita and attempted to throw her off instead.

"Don't fight me, Mother Bunny," Fat One said, who now had Evanita in his grasp. "Give me some Easter sugar."

"Eat this for Easter!" Evanita said.

Evanita kneed Fat One in the groin. He doubled over. Evanita kicked him again, and he fell off the catwalk. He reached for the walk as he went over and grabbed onto the edge with his hands. He dangled freely below the catwalk and yelled for help. Before Evanita had time to think, Josh activated the press and discharged three bullets. One of the bullets struck a barrel partially filled with inflammable fluid. It exploded. The shock wave loosened Fat One's grip from the catwalk, and he fell into the pit below. He screamed in pain. The shockwave sent Evanita off the catwalk where she too dangled from it. Her hands held the catwalk much in the same way and place as Fat One, and she struggled to pull herself up but could not.

"She got Fat One," said one of the boys.

"Get out!" yelled Josh, now running away from the press and toward the boys.

"I must save Parvati!" Vinay said.

While Evanita's predicament froze Vinay in shock, Josh and the boys rushed Vinay and dragged him out.

"Leave her!" said Josh.

"No!" Vinay said, but the boys grabbed the stick and used it against Vinay to force him away from Evanita and instead toward the exit.

"Help!" Evanita yelled.

A raging fire in the factory encroached on her position and that of the boys. Another partially full barrel caught fire and exploded. The shock wave loosened Evanita's grip from the catwalk and sent her plunging into the open pit of burning pressure-treated wood.

"She's gone!" said Josh. "Just like Fat One!"

"We can't leave them here!" yelled Vinay as the boys dragged him out.

"Fat One and Mother Bunny were sacrifices to one of your gods, Vinny," said Doofus.

"We don't believe in human sacrifice!" Vinay said.

"Those were the Aztecs, Doofus," said Beef.

Distant sirens struggled to pierce through the raging inferno's air.

"Police. Everyone scatter!" said Josh.

The boys ran out of the building and into multiple directions. Police and firefighters circled the factory. Most boys escaped, but the police caught Doofus and took him to the nearest police station for questioning. Firefighters realized the blaze was on a chemical site and took extra precautions to ensure their own safety while attacking the flames. These precautions meant delays for any attempt at finding Fat One and Evanita. Jonara remained in the factory building and looked for her mother, but she could not jump into the pit and find her. The flames formed some sort of barrier and prevented Jonara from crossing them. As the building continued to burn, the flames and smoke forced Jonara outside. She could not find her mother and realized she could be dead.

"But how can she be dead?" Jonara asked herself. "She must survive—she does survive!"

It was the last thing Jonara would say on the River Wood and Battery site. The flames and chemicals affected her presence. The world blurred into a fireball and remained engulfed in flame for quite some time. Jonara lost all orientation and felt miserably alone.

CHAPTER 13

Daddy, Daddy

2023 Oct 4, Wed Early am. Jonara's Dream.
2006 Oct 31, Tue. Portland, Oregon.

"*La madre de conejo,*" Evanita said. "*La madre de conejo.*"

Evanita was speaking Spanish in her hospital bed. She didn't know Spanish fluently, but Grandma Geneva had taught her some words and phrases. Roughly translated, Evanita was saying:

"Mother rabbit."

Evanita was semi-conscious and unable to think clearly. An Hispanic nurse spoke some soothing words to her in Spanish while she checked Evanita's chart. She told Evanita it was time for her pill and oxygen treatment.

"*La madre de conejo,*" said Evanita.

"Shhh," the nurse said.

The nurse handed Evanita a pill and glass of water and told Evanita in Spanish to take the pill. Evanita looked at the pill, placed it in her mouth, and swallowed it with water.

"*Bueno,*" said the nurse as she took the glass from Evanita.

The nurse told Evanita to place the tube over her nose for oxygen treatment and to breathe normally, relax, that's it—all in Spanish. Evanita breathed the oxygen and fell into a light sleep. A male doctor walked in and spoke with the nurse.

"She's taken her DMSA (dimercaptosuccinic acid) pill, and she's on oxygen treatment, Doctor Harris," said the nurse.

"Very good, nurse," said Doctor Harris. "How are the wounds on her legs where we removed the metal spikes?"

"Clean. No sign of infection on either leg. The stitches are holding well," the nurse replied.

"Excellent," he said. "I am amazed at this one."

"Why are you amazed?" the nurse asked Doctor Harris.

"It's a wonder she isn't dead," he continued. "She has an arsenic level that would be fatal to three grown men. We'll keep her on a sedative for three days as the arsenic is removed from her system by the DMSA."

"Any idea who she is?" the nurse asked.

"The police found no identification on her. They believe she's an illegal immigrant who couldn't read the English warning signs around the old River Wood and Battery factory. INS should be here soon to arrange for her deportation."

"She can stay with me," pleaded the nurse. "She's only a girl."

"She's old enough to have a baby on American soil and use that as an excuse to stay. No, she's not a girl. She can be deported," said Doctor Harris, and he left.

The nurse adjusted Evanita's sheets and pillows and was ready to leave when a group of children stopped by.

"Trick or Treat!" the children said.

"Oh how cute!" the nurse said.

The children were patients from the children's ward. Most were being treated for cancer.

"I'm an old man," said one boy.

The boy's hair had fallen out from the chemotherapy. He wore a false beard, overalls with a stuffed belly, and a cane.

"How adorable," said the nurse.

"I'm a robot," said a girl.

The girl's hair was also missing. She was dressed in a silver and black outfit and made stiff, robotic moves.

"And a very good robot, too," said the nurse.

"Oh, what happened to the lady?" asked another girl, referring to Evanita.

"She's just asleep," said the nurse.

"Is she going to miss out on Halloween?" the girl asked.

"Of course not," the nurse explained. "Today is Halloween."

"Yay!" the kids hollered and celebrated.

The kids jumped up, down, and around before running down the hall yelling, "Happy Halloween," to everyone.

"Halloween?" Evanita asked, awaking from the kids' yelling.

"Halloween," the nurse replied.

"Where is father?" Evanita asked in English.

"You spoke English," said the nurse. "Do you understand me?"

"Father—where is father?" Evanita asked again.

"That's a standard trick," said an officer who was standing by the doorway. "They try to make you think they're American by saying some English words."

"But the way she says it—she has no Spanish accent!" said the nurse.

"They're getting better at deception all the time. The Mexican girls are much better at it, too," said the officer.

The nurse shot a hostile stare at the officer, but he grinned.

"You disagree?" he said.

"She's not some deceitful little girl," said the nurse.

"You're right—she's not a little girl. But she's a deceitful girl," said the officer.

"How can you tell?" the nurse asked.

"I can tell just by looking at her. They all look the same," he said.

The nurse shot an even angrier look at him.

"Watch it there, nurse," he said. "Or I'll report *you* to Immigration."

"I'm needed somewhere," the nurse said, and she left.

The officer chuckled at the nurse's exit. He took a look at Evanita, chuckled, and waved her off as if getting rid of her. He returned to his post outside the room to ensure she didn't escape and others didn't smuggle her out.

Jonara stood by her mother and cried. Evanita appeared to be in bad shape. She had an oxygen tube like an old person, she had stitches on both legs, and her once-long hair was now singed to perhaps half an inch in length. Evanita's skin was black and blue from multiple bruises. Jonara tried to count the bruises on her mother but realized there were no single bruises—they all ran into each other and overlapped.

"Mommy, get better!" Jonara said.

But Jonara couldn't understand how her mother escaped the burning factory. Did firefighters reach her? Did she get out on her own? Jonara wondered these things and thought:

"Could I go back and find out?"

Jonara closed her eyes and remembered the fire, the hoodlums, the booming press, and bullet cartridges. Sounds of the hospital room faded, and Jonara felt herself spinning briefly, but when she opened her eyes, she was not at the factory.

"It's been over twenty-four hours," Eva said on the telephone from her home. "I told you she was missing, and she is! She never came home last night. Now what are you going to do about it?"

"Ma'am," said the police officer, "we'll do everything in our power to find her. Now what did you say her name was?"

"I've told you, her name is Evanita Carreña," Eva said. "She went out jogging yesterday morning. I called yesterday evening, and you people wouldn't do anything until twenty-four hours passed since her disappearance. It's over twenty-four hours, now find my daughter!"

"Just calm down," the officer said.

"Calm down?! I am calm! If I weren't calm, I'd be at the police station right now—kicking you in the shins until you get your lazy butt off your easy chair and start looking for my daughter!"

"Ma'am, I'm going to ask you to refrain from that tone. We can't help you unless you're perfectly calm. Now what did you say your daughter's name was?"

"She's not a *was*, she's an *is*! She *is* Evanita Carreña! And you're wasting time! Good day!" Eva yelled, and she hung up the phone.

The telephone rang.

"WHAT?!" Eva yelled into the receiver.

"Whoa!" Ms. Zyla said on the other end. "What's the matter?"

"Oh, it's you Zellie. I'm sorry," Eva replied. "I'm just worried and frustrated."

"I didn't hear from you this morning. I wondered what happened," Ms. Zyla said.

"It's Evanita," said Eva. "She's been missing since yesterday. I didn't think anything of it at first. She's done this before where she runs off and comes home in time for supper. But she never came home. Her bed was never slept in. And the police are giving me a smoke screen."

"I'm sorry to hear that," said Ms. Zyla. "I could call Sharon and let her know. I'm sure she'd love to help."

"She's on vacation," Eva explained. "I checked with Claire last night. Sharon took Sheila on a trip to California for some mother-daughter bonding. Sharon has her problems raising Sheila, and I have mine with Evanita. Sigh. When does it end?"

"Then I'll come over and help you search the woods. Maybe she hurt herself and can't walk," said Ms. Zyla.

"She could be anywhere," said Eva. "And there's no guarantee she's still in the woods. No, I have a better idea, but I'll need help from someone."

"Who?" Ms. Zyla asked.

"Someone I know. He—" said Eva.

Ms. Zyla gasped over the phone.

"I know, I know," said Eva. "I'm seeking help from a man."

"You always tell women to never accept help from a man. And now you suggest doing that very thing," Ms. Zyla said.

"I do," Eva agreed.

"That accepting help from a man weakens a woman," Ms. Zyla continued.

"It does," Eva agreed.

"And it feeds men's egos," Ms. Zyla added.

"I said that, yes."

"And women become too dependent on men and can't think for themselves, becoming dumb and subservient," Ms. Zyla finished.

"Yes, those are all true, and I said all those things," said Eva.

"But now there's an exception. How does the exception fit in with 'never accept help'?" Ms. Zyla asked.

Eva went silent.

"I'll come over, and we'll search the woods. It's settled then?" Ms. Zyla asked.

Eva kept silent then replied slowly, "Yes."

"Good. I'll be right over. Goodbye," Ms. Zyla said.

"Bye, Zellie," Eva replied.

Eva turned on her stereo and played an audio CD of singer Anacani. The song *Bésame mucho* aired through the speakers. Eva sat on the couch for a moment, stood up, paced back and forth, went into the kitchen, opened the refrigerator and looked inside, closed the refrigerator without taking anything, walked upstairs, downstairs, outside, around the flower garden, back into the house, into Evanita's room, into Evanita's closet, back into the hallway, the kitchen, and back to the living room. Eva picked up the telephone and called someone, but Jonara could not hear the conversation over the music. It was a short telephone call. Eva nodded her head in affirmation and hung up the telephone. Eva paced a few more times before going to her workout room and exercising her legs and arms.

The doorbell rang. Eva jumped up from her exercise machine and allowed the person in, ushering the person to a side room. Jonara didn't move as quickly as Eva and did not see who this person was. Jonara moved toward the room where the person went. Jonara expected to find Ms. Zyla in the room, but the doorbell rang again and diverted Jonara's attention. Eva answered the door and let Ms. Zyla in.

"Zellie," Eva said.

"Eva, you look exhausted," Ms. Zyla said.

"I am. Couldn't sleep all night," Eva said.

The two sat down on the couch in the living room.

"One moment," Eva said, and she turned off the stereo. "There, that's better."

"The first thing I want you to do is sit down and go over everything that happened," Ms. Zyla said.

Eva paced back and forth in the living room.

"Eva? Please, sit down," Ms. Zyla repeated.

From the other room, the sound of something falling grabbed Ms. Zyla's attention.

"What was that?" Ms. Zyla said.

"Nothing. Chipmunks," Eva lied.

"It came from the bathroom," said Ms. Zyla. "Are you telling me you have chipmunks in your bathroom?"

"Yes, no, they're in the walls," Eva fibbed.

"You're hiding something, Eva, and I'm going to find out what," Ms. Zyla said.

Ms. Zyla got up from the couch and walked to the hallway. Eva jumped over and blocked her path.

"Wouldn't you like some coffee or tea?" Eva asked.

"I think you're hiding something, Eva. I think you're hiding a man, and you won't admit to anyone that men have a useful purpose in this world."

"A purpose, yes. But their own purpose, and useful for themselves. However, there are times—" Eva started with a lowered voice.

Ms. Zyla's eyes opened wide in curiosity.

"Yes?" Ms. Zyla asked. "There are times they are useful, is that it? You're hiding a new love interest, aren't you?"

"How dare you!" Eva said.

"It's natural. You're a woman, and men are—" Ms. Zyla continued.

"You know me better than that. I only have one love—that's my daughter, Evanita. Now please! Back to the living room!" Eva said.

"What's that sound?" Ms. Zyla asked.

A vibrating tool sounded from the bathroom.

"I don't hear anything," lied Eva.

"That sounded like an electric razor. A big one too! How big of a man are you hiding?" Ms. Zyla smirked.

"That's a power tool," said Eva. "I'm having some sanding done."

"That's a power tool, all right. Move aside, Eva."

Ms. Zyla moved to push Eva aside, but it was a feint. Instead, she ducked under Eva's arm and snuck into the bathroom.

"Ah-hah!" Ms. Zyla exclaimed, but her grin turned to puzzlement.

"Oh hello, Ms. Zyla," said Johnny Pindus.

Johnny was standing by the bathroom sink. He had one hand under the running water, and a triangle-head cordless sander against his forehead.

"Johnny, why are you sanding your forehead?" Ms. Zyla asked.

"He isn't," Eva said.

Ms. Zyla grabbed the cordless sander from Johnny and inspected the triangle-shaped head.

"Strange, there's no sandpaper," she said.

"Johnny is conducting an experiment, Zellie. Now please!" Eva urged.

"I can't do it," said Johnny. "I can't focus."

"What can't he do, and what are you doing with Evanita's boyfriend, Eva?" Ms. Zyla asked.

Eva hushed Ms. Zyla down the hallway away from Johnny.

"Don't say that in front of Johnny. He doesn't know about Evanita's feelings, I don't think. And Evanita hasn't made her feelings known to him, although we see it," Eva said.

"Then what is he doing here? We should all go out and look for Evanita," Ms. Zyla said.

"We will, but Johnny must find her first," Eva said.

"Find? How?" Ms. Zyla asked.

"Remember when we were in Cerossi Café?" Eva asked.

"Yes, too well. It nearly burned down," Ms. Zyla said.

"Before that, when I was asking Johnny about that person, the person with the name beginning with the letter A," Eva said.

"You mean Adrian?" Ms. Zyla asked.

"Yes, and please don't speak that name in my house," said Eva.

"Why not?" Ms. Zyla asked.

"You should know why. It's his last name, and I don't need to hear it spoken," Eva said.

"I'm sure he wasn't old enough to remember the other one," said Ms. Zyla.

"Nevertheless, don't speak it here. Now do you remember how Johnny went into a trance?" Eva asked.

"That happens a lot in Cerossi Café. People receive all sorts of insight from the flames," Ms. Zyla explained.

"Johnny's insight, as you call it, is something else. He can sense things—physically—through vibration. His mind calculates shapes and positions. It's like an ultrasound," Eva explained.

"Is that why you were shaking the table?" Ms. Zyla asked.

"Yes, that's why I shook it. The vibrations shake his skull and allow him to feel other vibrations in the world," Eva said.

"That explains the cordless sander," Ms. Zyla said. "And a good thing it's cordless too—I hate to think he'd use a plug-in model with the way he had one hand on the sander and the other in water. He could electrocute himself. Speaking of water, why is his hand in water?"

"He uses the water to connect to other water bodies. It's his way of looking around the world quickly," Eva said.

"I can't focus," Johnny said down the hallway. "Too much interference. Too many other things going on."

"All right, Johnny, I'll help you," Eva said.

Eva walked into Evanita's bedroom and retrieved a school notebook. She took the notebook to Johnny.

"Hold the sander to the back of my neck," Johnny said.

Eva did as he asked. Johnny held his left hand under running water and Evanita's notebook in his right.

"Algebra. Ehks squared plus two ehks minus three is equal to—"

"No, Johnny, not school," Eva said.

"The absolute value of four wye times—"

"Concentrate on Evanita," said Eva.

"End of class. Lunch break. Eating with friends, watch my weight," Johnny said.

"Where did Evanita go?" Eva asked. "She ran into the woods yesterday and did not come back. Where is she?"

"This book shows me Evanita in school," said Johnny. "I cannot see where she went yesterday."

"Maybe something more personal. Her hairbrush," Eva said.

Eva rushed off to Evanita's bedroom and retrieved her hairbrush. She returned to the bathroom and handed it to Johnny.

"This all seems so occult," said Ms. Zyla. "Do you really think—"

"Shh," said Eva to Ms. Zyla.

"Hold the sander to my neck," Johnny said again.

Eva stood behind Johnny and held the sander to his neck.

"What do you see, Johnny?" Eva asked.

"Evanita. Brushing her hair. Mad about being grounded. Long shower yesterday morning. Need to go for a run," Johnny said.

"The woods, the woods," Eva said.

"Running through the woods, yes. Someone else running behind her," Johnny explained.

"That was me!" Jonara yelled.

"That was me, 'me' is here," said Johnny.

"Yes, you are here," said Ms. Zyla. "And with bad grammar, too."

"Don't interrupt, Zellie," Eva said.

"Who is here, Johnny?" Eva asked.

"The voice from Page Clinic, the voice who said—"

"Concentrate on the woods, Johnny," Eva said. "Where is Evanita?"

"Jogging in the woods. Leaving the woods. Warning sign. Can't read it—paint is too thin. Nothing grows past the sign, nothing to focus on," Johnny said.

"Focus, Johnny," Eva said. "Where did she go?"

"I can't see anything, can't see. Move the sander to my forehead," Johnny said.

Eva moved closer behind Johnny. She was practically hugging him while she held the sander to his forehead.

"Ballet," Johnny said. "Drilling teeth. Page Clinic."

"Don't focus on me," Eva said. "Focus on Evanita."

"Where is Evanita? Must find her. My only daughter. Love of my life," Johnny continued.

"No, not me!" Eva said.

Eva removed the sander from Johnny's forehead and withdrew.

"I'm sorry, but she went into an area I cannot read—a place where nothing can grow. A dead zone. Must be a toxic chemical site," Johnny said.

"Where is this toxic site?" Eva asked.

"On Saint Helens Road northwest from here," replied Johnny.

"There was something in the news about that last night," said Ms. Zyla. "The old River Wood and Battery factory caught fire. If she was in that building, she is —"

"No, I refuse to believe it. Evanita's too smart to go into a restricted site like that. Johnny, when did she leave that dead zone?"

"Leave? I didn't see anything about her leaving," he said.

"She must have left," Eva said.

"If she did, she would have come back here," said Ms. Zyla.

"No, not if she sustained an injury. Johnny, you must focus on the dead zone again," Eva said.

"I need something more than her hairbrush. Something more personal," he said.

"Nothing is more personal than her mother," offered Ms. Zyla.

"That won't work. Johnny started focusing on me instead of Evanita," Eva said. "Wait, there is something else. I'll be right back."

Eva ran to her workout room and returned shortly.

"Is that a lock of hair?" Ms. Zyla said.

"No time for questions," said Eva. "Evanita's life is at stake."

"That's not Evanita's hair. I know, because Evanita has black and dark-red hair. But you're holding a locket of bright red hair. Is that—"

"Shhh, not another word," Eva replied, and she turned to Johnny and said, "Keep holding the hairbrush, Johnny."

Johnny held Evanita's hairbrush in his right hand and kept his left hand under the running water. Eva "hugged" Johnny from behind. She held the sander against his forehead and the locket of hair against his chin.

"Johnny," Eva said softly in his ear. "I want you to think back many years to when you were a boy. Don't say what you see, yet. Wait until I ask you to speak. Now go back. I saw you in my office. Then you went to the other office—the one with the red hair touching you now. Nod if you remember."

Johnny nodded.

"The dentist with the red hair treated you by giving you a root canal. You remember that, right? Think about the two of us—the red-haired dentist and me. Focus on us," Eva said.

Johnny nodded yes to Eva's suggestions.

"Johnny, think about when we bumped in the hallway at the dental office. Do you remember? It was before my argument with the red-haired dentist. I was pregnant. You sensed my un-born baby completely. Do you remember my baby?"

Johnny nodded yes.

"Johnny—that was Evanita. Think back to Evanita when she was inside me."

"She wanted to run, even before she was born."

"Yes. I left the clinic for several years. I returned," Eva said.

"The red hair no longer fits," Johnny said.

"I know, but merge its feeling against my own and focus on Evanita as a baby inside me. She was in amniotic fluid—mostly water. Remember the water? Touch the water on your hands and reach out to Evanita," Eva said.

Eva placed the locket of red hair on the sink's counter top. She removed the hairbrush from Johnny's right hand. Eva re-positioned herself so she stood close to him on his right side. She moved the sander to the back of his neck. Eva took his right hand and placed it on her abdomen over the place where he once felt Evanita kicking inside her. Jonara walked up to Johnny's back left side and hugged him. Johnny felt her pres-ence and received enough strength from Jonara to continue.

"Remember how she moved inside me?" Eva asked. "In the amniotic fluid?"

"Yes, I remember," he said.

"Reach out through the running water and find her again. Where is she?"

"She went into the building. She acted strangely. Boys making a fire in a pit. Gunshots, a press cycling. Evanita on a catwalk, kicking a fat boy off. Fat boy falling into burning pit. Evanita falling into burning pit."

Ms. Zyla put her hand over her eyes and looked down. Eva bit her lip.

"Continue, Johnny," Eva said.

"Burning flesh, burning flesh," Johnny explained. "Evanita crawling through a scrap tunnel. Fire and smoke everywhere. Evanita in pain. Can't breathe. Legs ripped open. Metal in flesh. Bleeding everywhere. Crawling, crawling, so painful. Crawling. Dead end. Can't crawl. Plywood on the wall. Breaking plywood. Splinters in hands. Air and daylight, air and daylight. Crawl through the opening. Flashing lights. Fire trucks, police cars. Flashing lights. Ambulance. Riding in the ambulance. Darkness. Darkness. Ambulance to the hospital, the hospital, where is the hospital?"

"Yes, Johnny, where is the hospital?" Eva asked.

"Barnes Road, Lois Lane, the hospital is Vansen—"

The doorbell rang and startled everyone. Ms. Zyla went for the door, but whoever rang the doorbell now beat on the door loudly. Eva dropped the sander. She took the locket of red hair and rushed it back to her workout room. Johnny turned off the water and left the bathroom. He sat in the living room on the couch and fell into exhaustion. Eva returned from the workout room and gave Johnny bottled water. Ms. Zyla opened the door.

"Eva Carreña?" a burly police officer said at the door.

"No, but I'll get her," Ms. Zyla said.

"I'm Eva. Sorry, this will have to wait," Eva said.

"You're the one with the missing daughter?" the officer asked.

"Yes, I am," Eva said.

Eva gathered her purse up and motioned Ms. Zyla and Johnny to join her.

"Where are you going, Miss Carreña?" the officer asked.

"I'm going to find my daughter," said Eva. "Not that the police want to look for her. I've already wasted enough time trying to get your help."

"I'm here now. I want to help," the officer said. "Now let's start at the beginning. First, who answered the door? Second, where and when did you last see your daughter—her name is?"

"My daughter is Evanita Carreña. I last saw her yesterday. She took a run in the woods behind the house. Now please, I must go find her!" Eva said.

"Just a moment. You didn't tell me who answered the door. You said she went out in the woods?" the officer asked.

"Yes, yes, yes! Now we must be going," Eva said.

"But you're going out the front door, not the back. Are you going to drive through the woods?" the officer said.

"She's at Vansen Hospital," said Eva. "Now out of our way!"

"What leads you to believe she is there? Did the hospital call you?" the officer asked.

Ms. Zyla and Eva spoke at the same time. Eva said, "No," while Ms. Zyla said, "Yes."

"Which is it? All right, I'm taking you both down to the station. Something fishy is going on, and I'm going to find out what," said the officer. "Who's he?"

The officer pointed toward Johnny Pindus. Johnny was extremely tired and couldn't get up from the couch.

"He's sick," said Eva.

"That's not what I asked. Who is he?" the officer asked.

"I...am...Johnny Pindus," Johnny said.

"Oh, not you again. Crackpot psychic man. What are you three really up to?" the officer asked.

"We aren't up to anything," said Eva. "Now please, we must go to the hospital."

"Miss Carreña, do you have proof of this so-called daughter?" the officer asked.

"I do, but I won't show you now. If you like, you can drive with us," Eva said.

"Not so fast," the officer said as he grabbed Eva's arm and twisted it.

"Let me go, you grubby-handed man!" she said.

Eva twisted free of his grasp, ran for her car, and drove away. She left the house's front door open. Ms. Zyla and Johnny Pindus were surprised by her sudden departure.

"You two—stay here!" the officer ordered Ms. Zyla and Johnny. "Or you'll both be under arrest."

The officer jumped into his car and drove off after Eva.

"Come," said Ms. Zyla. "We'll go to the hospital in my car."

"But the officer said—" Johnny said.

"I know what he said. We'll try not to be spotted," Ms. Zyla said.

Jonara hopped in the back seat of Ms. Zyla's car while Johnny sat in the front passenger seat. Ms. Zyla finished locking up Eva's house and drove away, but she did not follow the same route Eva would have. In taking an alternate route, Ms. Zyla was able to avoid any possible interaction with the officer who was chasing Eva.

Jonara wondered what had become of Grandma Eva. Did she make it to the hospital? Jonara would soon find out. Ms. Zyla took slow, side roads and arrived at Vansen Hospital.

"This is the hospital," Johnny said.

"Are you sure?" Ms. Zyla said.

"Yes. It's the one I envisioned back at Miss Carreña's house," he replied.

Ms. Zyla parked the car by the emergency entrance. The three exited the car and walked up to the emergency receptionist.

"I'm looking for Evanita Carreña," said Ms. Zyla.

"Carreña, Carreña—sorry, there's no one here by that name," said the receptionist.

"She must be here," said Johnny.

"If she came through here, there'd be a record. I have no record. You can try General Admitting," the receptionist said.

"She must have come through here," said Ms. Zyla. "She was in the River Wood and Battery fire yesterday. About sixteen, black and dark-red hair, slim build?"

The receptionist gave Ms. Zyla and Johnny a quizzical look.

"Are you family?" the receptionist asked Ms. Zyla.

"No, I'm a friend," said Ms. Zyla.

"I'm sorry, I can only let family visit her," the receptionist said.

Ms. Zyla took Johnny aside and whispered something in his ear. Johnny looked at Ms. Zyla in surprise and shrugged his shoulders. The two walked back to the receptionist.

"This is Johnny. He is Evanita's brother," Ms. Zyla said.

"Oh, you're her brother," the receptionist said in a doubting voice. "She's in room 114."

"Thank you," said Ms. Zyla.

The receptionist kept a close eye on Ms. Zyla and Johnny, and when they left earshot range, she picked up the telephone and dialed a number.

"ER Reception. Yeah, another brother to visit the girl in 114. Calls himself Johnny. Yes, that's what he looks like. I did, they're on their way now. Understood. Bye."

The officer outside Evanita's door allowed Ms. Zyla and Johnny Pindus to enter.

"Evanita?" Ms. Zyla said.

Ms. Zyla and Johnny were surprised to see Evanita in her injured condition. Her hair was short, her face swollen and bruised, tubes ran to her nose for oxygen and her arm for intravenous feeding, and she was covered in a hospital gown and blankets. Ms. Zyla expressed her anxiety with a grim face while Johnny shook like a leaf.

"Father?" Evanita asked in a dazed state.

Evanita couldn't see around herself very well but was aware enough to realize a woman and man had entered her room. Her IV drip contained morphine to alleviate her pain, but it gave a dreamy sound to her voice.

"It's Evanita. I recognize her voice," said Johnny.

"Father, is that you?" Evanita asked.

The officer outside the doorway edged into the room a bit—enough to hear what was being said without being noticed.

"I'm Johnny Pindus, remember me?" Johnny asked.

"Johnny? Johnny! You're here!" Evanita said as she held out her arms in hopes of hugging him.

"I'm here, Evanita," he said.

Johnny gave Evanita a hug as best as he could. Evanita wrapped her arms around Johnny and hugged back. Johnny lifted her a little and in doing so was able to wrap his arms around her. She kissed him several times on his cheek and cried softly.

The officer heard the conversation yet maintained silence. He held a small, black, plastic device discreetly by his side. Jonara didn't like this officer and felt he was a threat to her mother and father.

"I don't know what happened," Evanita started. "I just went for a run, and now I'm here."

"I know," he said.

In hugging Evanita, Johnny was able to sense everything that had happened to her in the past forty-eight hours—in livid and vivid detail. Johnny's face scrunched up in pain as he endured the memory of what Evanita went through—the anger that sent her running to begin with, the altered state of consciousness and loss of control, the taunting by the boys, the attack from Fat One, the fire, witnessing Fat One's death and smelling his burning corpse, falling atop his corpse and bouncing off, impaling her legs into steel spikes, limping through the scrap tunnel, fighting her way out of the building to be frustrated by plywood, and breaking through the plywood only to be arrested by police—police who shuttled her off to the hospital without a friend or family member to hold her hand through the surgery.

"I...I..." Evanita tried to explain.

"You've been through hell. No, you've been in Hell. I know about jogging through Forest Park. I know about the River Wood and Battery factory and the pictures you drew. And I know about the fire pit, the press, the bullets firing, and how the factory caught fire. I know you nearly died and how you escaped. I know, Evanita, I know," Johnny said.

"Johnny. I want to give up," Evanita sobbed. "I can't live like this. Look at me—I'm a mess."

"You must live," Johnny said. "There is a spirit in you that won't die."

"I can't, Johnny. Not after what happened in the factory. I think someone died because of me," Evanita said.

"No, you didn't kill him," Johnny said. "It was an accident. Everything was an accident."

"I'm ugly. Look at me, Johnny. I'm ugly on the outside and the inside. I can't live with this guilt. Johnny, do you know what I'm feeling?"

"Yes, I do," he said. "I know."

"It won't go away. It's getting worse. There's no way out," said Evanita.

"Hold on to life, Evanita, hold on!" Ms. Zyla said, running up to Evanita and holding her hand. "You are not to blame!"

"It's getting dark in here," Evanita said.

Evanita's grip weakened, and her voice faded.

"Evanita?" Johnny called.

"Father?" she said in a faint voice. "Father?"

Evanita's grip around Johnny failed. She slipped into unconsciousness. Johnny lowered her back in bed and removed his arms from around her. Ms. Zyla released her too.

"Poor thing is exhausted," Ms. Zyla said. "Johnny—we should let her sleep."

"She isn't sleeping," said Johnny.

"Don't say things like that. Her heart is beating. She's breathing. Of course she's sleeping," said Ms. Zyla.

"No. She's slipping into a coma!" he said.

Johnny stood and looked around wildly, not sure of what to do.

"Nurse, nurse!" Ms. Zyla called out in the hall.

A passerby nurse reacted to Ms. Zyla's call for help and darted into Evanita's room. She took a quick glance at the machine indicating Evanita's vital signs. Alarmed, the nurse pressed an alert button. Other hospital personnel—doctors and nurses—rushed in, worked on Evanita, talked over each other, and forced Ms. Zyla and Johnny outside Evanita's room.

"Evanita," Ms. Zyla and Johnny both shouted from outside her room.

"Okay, you two. Step over here out of the way," said the officer to Ms. Zyla and Johnny.

"We only want to—" Ms. Zyla started.

"I know, I know. You're the mother and want to take her home. And you're her brother," the officer said.

"I never said I was her mother," said Ms. Zyla. "And as for Johnny—"

"May I have your name please?" the officer asked Ms. Zyla.

"Beverly Zyla," Ms. Zyla said.

"And where do you live, Ms. Zyla?"

"Is this an interrogation? I want representation," Ms. Zyla said.

"Just your address, please," the officer said.

"2525 Raleigh Street," she said.

"2525? That's Wallace Park! Your real address please!" the officer said.

"2626 Raleigh Street?" she said, but the officer shook his head in disbelief. "2727?"

"You—the 'brother'—what's your name?" the officer asked.

"Johnny Pindus. 3535 West Burnside Road. The Barnseed Apartments," he said.

"Oh I see, you want to play number games too," the officer said.

"It's the truth. It's a church-sponsored apartment complex. Barnseed Baptist Church," Ms. Zyla said.

"Oh the truth, is it? The same truth that says this is the patient's brother?"

"Well, not exactly," Ms. Zyla said.

"Well what exactly is the truth? Let me tell you—there were five other women posing as the girl's mother. Each one wanted to sneak the girl out of the hospital. And there were four boys claiming to be her brother," the officer explained. "Do you care to revise your stories?"

"We're just friends who wanted to see Evanita," said Ms. Zyla.

"Oh, now we're just friends. And the girl has a name, too. But you wouldn't happen to be the same friends who were at that factory, were you?"

"No, we weren't there," said Johnny.

"I suppose not. And that would explain how you knew details that only police know. Unless you were actually there," the officer said.

"What are you talking about?" Ms. Zyla said.

"I have everything here," he said, holding a tape recorder.

"You mean just now? That was just talk," Ms. Zyla said.

"You're under arrest," the officer said to Johnny. "You have the right to remain silent. Anything you say can and will be used against you."

The officer finished reading Johnny his rights. He radioed to a buddy who took over watch at Evanita's door. Ms. Zyla attempted to stay behind at Evanita's door, but the officer arresting Johnny turned to her and spoke.

"What do you think you're doing?" he asked her.

"I'm going to stay here and watch Evanita until—" Ms. Zyla started.

"Oh no you don't. You're coming to the station with 'Brother' Johnny," he said. "Now you can cooperate and we can go peaceably, or if you give me trouble—I'll handcuff you too!"

Jonara accompanied Ms. Zyla, Johnny, and the officer to the local police station. When they arrived, the officer spoke to a front-desk person.

"I have another 'mother' and 'brother' for the River Wood case."

"Right over there," the front desk pointed.

The officer took Ms. Zyla and Johnny to a waiting area where three women sat on a bench and four young men sat on another, waiting to be questioned. Ms. Zyla immediately recognized one of the women on the "mother" bench.

"Eva!" Ms. Zyla exclaimed.

"Miss Carreña!" Johnny added.

"Grandma!" Jonara said without an audience.

Ms. Zyla turned to the officer and spoke.

"Officer, this is the real mother—Eva Carreña."

"I'm the mother," yelled another woman on the bench, followed by another and another.

"Quiet," the officer yelled. "That's enough out of all of you. This ain't a *Spartacus* movie."

"Miss Carreña, we saw Evanita," Johnny said, running over to Eva.

"Hey you!" the officer said to Johnny. "Over here with the 'brothers'."

"No, I need to—" Johnny started.

"You need to do as you're told. Over here now before I drag you over," the officer threatened.

"I'll see you soon," Johnny said to Eva.

"Eva—this way, please," called an officer (Buke) to Eva.

Eva stood up and followed Officer Buke into a questioning room.

Johnny sat down next to four young boys—Doofus, Beef, Josh, and Vinay.

"Skins is in there," whispered Josh to Beef.

"He'll turn us in, I know he will," Doofus whispered to Beef and Josh.

"Shut up!" Beef whispered back. "Just play it cool and don't say anything. No one is turning no one in."

Doofus kicked his legs under the table in nervousness. Beef bit his fingernails, and Josh clasped his hands together. Johnny attempted to read them through the vibrations in the bench, but he could not. While he could sense agitation and anxiety among them, he was unable to read their direct thoughts. His gift of reading thoughts only worked with females. He never understood why there was a difference in gender, and he often made the attempt to read other male thoughts. Like before, he could not read these boys' thoughts.

Jonara hugged her father. Johnny didn't seem to notice, but he did calm down a bit. For the first time, Jonara felt something through him—worry about Evanita, Eva, and Ms. Zyla, shared suffering from Evanita's personal ordeal in escaping the factory, and Johnny's frustration in being unable to read the boys' thoughts. Yet Jonara knew what the boys had done and how Fat One had forced Evanita across the catwalk. The humiliation Evanita suffered acting as a rabbit, her badly injured body, her lovely hair—the thoughts boiled Jonara's blood. She released her grip from Johnny and marched into a questioning room where Skins was being interrogated.

"I told you, I was nowhere near that factory," Skins said.

"Let's take it from the top," the interrogator said, his name being Captain Agar.

"Oh, not again," Skins said.

"Why were you at the hospital?"

"To visit my sister," Skins replied.

"Your sister?!"

"Yeah, my sister," Skins replied.

"How did you know she was there?"

"The hospital called me," Skins replied.

"The hospital didn't call anyone about the girl," said Agar.

"Someone from the hospital called," Skins replied.

"What is your name?"

"Askin Roberts," Skins said.

"What is the girl's name?"

"My sister? Her name is Ashley Roberts," Skins said.

"How do you explain the fact that you two look nothing alike? She has black and dark-red hair, you have blond."

"We have different fathers. She's my half sister," Skins said.

"What about your gang out there? What were they doing at the factory?"

"Gang? What gang?" Skins asked.

"Those boys waiting out on the bench."

"Never seen 'em," Skins said.

"Not even the psychic?"

"What psychic?"

"Calls himself a brother of the girl. Johnny Pindus."

"Never heard of him," said Skins.

"We caught one of your gang running around the factory grounds," said Agar. "Donald Fessel. Says he goes by 'Doofus'. We had an interesting chat with him. What do you say to that?"

"Never heard of him," said Skins.

"I'm giving you a chance to come clean. Tell me what you know. That isn't your sister, is it? Those boys out there are part of your gang. Doofus is a rat. He confessed. But I think you can rise above them. Look at this document," Agar said.

Agar passed Skins a document with a pen.

"This document guarantees you a reduced sentence if you are willing to testify against your buddies out there—especially the psychic one. All you have to do is sign here," Agar said.

"I want to see my sister," Skins said. "In the hospital. She's all I care about. No one else matters."

Skins was obviously lying. He gave all answers in a monotone voice with a spice of belligerence. But he did not admit to any involvement with the factory fire.

"We're going to hold you for a little while, Askin. Or should I say, 'Skins'? Take him away," Agar said to an officer.

The officer took Skins away and brought in Beef.

"What is your name?" Agar asked.

"Buford Hamm," Beef said.

Captain Agar paused with silence. He took some notes, reviewed some papers, and filled out some forms.

"Aren't you going to ask me any questions?" Beef asked.

"No," Agar said.

"Good, then you'll let me go," Beef said.

"No."

"Then ask me some questions, man!"

Agar continued filling out a form.

"Okay, okay, you want me to crack. I won't crack. I can take the silent treatment. I got nothing to say, nothing to say. Aren't you going to ask me why I was at the hospital? Do you want to know why I was there?" Beef asked.

"No."

"Why, you think you're better than me, don't you? Who do you think you are, pulling me in here and asking me questions? I was visiting my sister, that's all, that's all."

"Your sister," Agar repeated as if bored.

Agar looked up briefly at Beef and back at his paperwork.

"Hey, you wanna pick a fight with me, don't you?" Beef said.

"I have no beef with you," Agar said.

"What did you call me? That ain't my name. My name ain't Beef. It's Buford Hamm. Buford Hamm. That's what my friends call me. Buford Hamm."

"Friends," Agar repeated as he checked off several notes and drew lines connecting one section to another.

"Hey, I don't know those guys out there on the bench. Not even the freaky psycho boy. And they don't know me."

"Excuse me," Agar said as he reached down and pulled a candy mint from a duffel bag. "Would you like a mint? Don't worry, it's clean. I keep it in my dooful-us bag."

"I'm not your Doofus or your Doofus bag," Beef said, getting agitated by Agar's use of 'dooful-us bag' instead of 'duffel bag'.

"It's a good mint," said Agar.

"So what? What's so great about a mint?"

"It's fresh, like the country air by a fire with freshly cut green wood crackling," said Agar.

Captain Agar pulled a stick and marshmallow from his duffel bag and handed them to Beef.

"Would you like to toast a marshmallow?" Agar asked.

"What!? You're crazy!" said Beef, who refused the marshmallow and stick.

"That's all right. I'm just Joshing you."

Beef held silent for a moment. His skin crawled. Agar knew something, but Beef didn't know what.

"What do you want from me, huh? A confession? I got nothing to confess. Not about her, not about you, not about anything," Beef said.

"I want nothing from you, Buford. Nothing at all," said Agar.

Agar removed some hand lotion from his duffle bag.

"What's that? A truth drug? You ain't gettin' nothin' out of me," said Beef.

Beef was very agitated. His eyes teared a bit, and he was ready to fight his way out of the interrogation room.

"This?" Agar asked. "Why this is lotion. It's a reward for good behavior. A reward for cooperation. A reward for my new friend, my Skins."

Captain Agar rubbed the lotion on his hands and arms, clasped his hands together in glee, and clapped twice. Beef stared at him in horror. He ran for the door and thrust it open, but an officer caught him.

"Aren't you going to offer me a deal? I'll talk if you give me immunity. I'll talk!"

"Too late," said Agar, who motioned for the officer to take Beef back to the bench.

"I don't understand," said Jonara. "Captain Agar didn't ask Beef a single thing. But Beef thinks Captain Agar knows everything."

Beef stumbled onto the bench with Vinay, Josh, and Doofus watching in bewilderment. Beef tried to whisper but couldn't keep his composure.

"He knows everything, he knows everything. Who told him?" Beef asked.

"Not I," said Vinay.

"Mum," said Josh.

"Don't look at me—I've been out here," said Doofus.

"You were caught at the factory. You're the rat, you're the rat!" Beef said.

"No, I didn't say anything!" Doofus insisted. "I only pretended to be her brother. I said everything was an accident—that she didn't mean to kill Fat One. It was Skins. Skins ratted on us."

"No way, man!" said Josh. "Not Skins."

"Someone did," said Beef. "They know everything."

"But how? What did he ask you?" Vinay asked.

"He didn't ask me anything," said Beef.

"What did he tell you?" Doofus asked.

"He didn't tell me anything," said Beef.

"Then why do you think they know everything?" Josh asked.

"It was what he did, the way he said things. I know he knows. I know it. And someone had to blab."

"Skins," said Doofus.

"It had to be. One by one they will put us away. Skins did the needful thing for himself," said Vinay. "It was Skins."

"Skins," said Doofus.

"Skins?" Josh asked.

"Skins," Beef grumbled. "I knew it. He got immunity before we did. They made a deal with him. Skins betrayed us."

"Not Skins!" said Josh.

"Skins," said Doofus.

"Skins," said Vinay.

"Skins!" Beef grimaced.

An officer took Josh to the questioning room.

"My name is Captain Agar. What is your name?"

"Josh Ephram."

"You're the brains of the operation?" Agar asked.

Josh laughed.

"You know, Beef is a character isn't he? I mean, he's wrapped up in everything around him," Agar said.

Josh laughed again.

"Nothing really bothers you, does it Josh? You're the only one of the gang who goes by his real name. Now that's confidence."

Josh kept a smirk on his face and folded his arms with a smugness suggesting he had nothing to worry about.

"You're also the girl's brother, aren't you?"

"Naw, man," said Josh. "I just made that up."

"That's what I thought. Your father is Bill Ephram. Runs a game and sporting goods store. I know him very well. My condolences on the loss of your uncle. Barnseed Baptist Church won't be the same without him."

"Yeah, he got a bad deal with Aunt Patty. The family doesn't speak to her anymore," Josh said.

"You're an 'A' student, Josh. What happened? Why the new friends? They're no good for you. Your father says you gave up hunting with him."

"It's not the same without Uncle Jerry," Josh said.

"Your father needs you most right now, and you need him. Don't look for a substitute father in these naïve kids," Agar said.

"What does he know?" Josh asked, but he didn't expect an answer.

"I've known Bill for many years. We were in the military together. He's seen a lot and knows more than you may realize. Things that one would rather forget. But there's a problem here, Josh. You're linked to the River Wood and Battery fire, and we have a possible homicide. We ID'd the body to one Greg Applefoot. If we don't clear your name immediately, there could be real trouble. The Applefoot family is wealthy and swings a big bat. Not to mention the Feds coming in with their own charges, starting with the EPA. Do I need to go on?"

"No. So what did Skins tell you, did he try to pin the blame on the rest of us?" Josh asked.

"I can't disclose that until the trial," said Agar.

"Trial!?"

"Yes, the trial! You'll be tried as an adult, along with those other boys and the psychic. And the girl, though it's unlikely she'll be able to attend. She's in a coma, and the Applefoot family wants to resolve this quickly. They won't wait for her to regain consciousness."

"I didn't know it was this bad," said Josh.

"It's very serious. Now, if you tell me everything you know, I'll work to lessen your charge," Agar said.

"I want a lawyer," Josh said.

"You have that right. But be aware, Josh, if you get a lawyer now, it will look very bad, like you're guilty and trying to prove your innocence," Agar said.

"But you...Skins could have blamed us...aren't you calling me guilty already?" Josh asked.

"No. This is just a preliminary chat. You're not formally being charged. But if we work together—and we can work with your father too if you want—we'll get to the bottom of this mess and find the daylight for you. But we need to do it now before things get out of hand with every man getting his own lawyer and throwing mud at each other in court. Now let's hear it."

"Okay, okay! I went to the factory with—" Josh started.

"Clarify please—which factory?"

"River Wood and Battery factory with Skins and his group," Josh said.

"Could you tell me the names and nicknames of each person?"

"You know I don't have a nickname—they call me Josh. Askin Roberts is Skins. He's the leader. Buford Hamm is Beef. He's the bodybuilder. Donald Fessel is Doofus. Not too bright. Vinny is—"

"Wait a moment as I write something down," Agar said. "All right, go ahead."

"Vinny's from India," Josh explained.

"And the others?"

"Just Greg Applefoot. Fat One," Josh replied.

"What about the psychic?"

"You mentioned him before. I don't know any psychic," said Josh.

"The man on the bench out there. He was sitting next to Doofus."

"Never seen him before. He wasn't there," Josh said.

"He had to be. He knows about the fire," Agar said.

"I'm telling you I've never seen him before. He wasn't part of the gang," said Josh.

"Is he now?"

"No. No, no, NO, NO!"

"What about the girl? She wasn't part of the gang either?"

"That's right; she wasn't part of the gang. I was busy getting rid of old bullets in a press when—" Josh started.

"Wait. Were these used bullets or new cartridges?"

"New bullets. Cartridges. I would put one or two in the press and push the buttons. The press would come down and destroy the cartridge," Josh said.

"Did it go off? Did the bullet travel?"

"Oh maybe a little," lied Josh. "It would plop off the side of the press."

"That's a lie!" Jonara yelled, but of course no one heard her. "You started the explosion with those bullets!"

"Josh, I should let you know—Forensics found bullets fired into the wall and into barrels from the press. Don't embellish now. They'll trace those bullets to you. You need to be truthful with me so we can work around Forensics. They're going on a hunch that leftover fuel in those drums drained and ignited. They'll pin the homicide charge on you unless we change that. So you must be positively truthful with me. Now, let's start with the cartridges."

"They did fire across the factory, and they did land into barrels and the wall. I just wanted to get rid of that ammo 'cause I don't want to hunt anymore," Josh said.

"What were the others doing? Skins, Beef, Doofus, and Vinny—what were they doing? And the girl, how did she get there?" Agar asked.

"Vinny found the girl. He called her Parvati. I guess that's a Hindu goddess. The other guys called her Mother Bunny. They were hanging out next to an open pit with a fire going. I wasn't with them—I was at the press firing rounds."

"Who started the fire?"

"Beef. Skins ordered him to start it. There wasn't anything to burn except that green wood," Josh explained.

"That green wood was pressure-treated wood," said Agar. "It was full of arsenic. Anyone inhaling the burning ashes would get arsenic in their system. How close were you to the fire?"

"Not close enough to breathe the fumes," said Josh.

"Good. You'll have to have a blood test, but if we're lucky, we'll be able to prove you had nothing to do with the initial fire. The ballistics, however, will be harder. Okay, so Vinny found the girl. She didn't set the fire? Hmmm. What happened next? Did you catch the girl's name?"

"No I didn't. She never told us. Like I said, the guys called her 'Mother Bunny' and made her pretend she was a rabbit. She hopped around and stuff. Then Vinny went nuts. He grabbed a two-by-two and started swinging it around like some kung fu master. I was still setting off rounds against the wall and barrels. The chick went up on the catwalk and Fat One went after her. It wasn't safe on that catwalk; she could have fallen off and killed herself. But Fat One risked his life for hers."

"Another lie!" Jonara shouted. "He attacked her."

"She killed him," said Josh.

"How?"

"He reached for her, but she kicked him in the groin. Then she kicked him off the platform. He hung onto the railing, but before anyone could get to her, she stepped on his fingers, and he fell into the burning pit. He yelled for a few seconds, but that was the end. We could smell his flesh burning. There was no way to put out the fire. We ran out of the building. Doofus stayed behind to watch the girl, but she escaped. That's all I know. I saw the news about the fire and was surprised to see that she was alive, so I went to visit her at the hospital."

"That's not how it happened!" said Jonara.

"Is this the truth?" Agar asked.

"No!" Jonara yelled.

"I swear, that's how it happened," replied Josh.

"All right. What I'm going to do for you, Josh, is prepare a transcript of our chat. I'll omit the part about firing the cartridges. We need to work around that for now," said Agar.

"So, like, is this a confession?" Josh asked.

"No, we won't use those words. You're supplying evidence as a witness—that's our angle. In exchange, I can get your sentence down to six months probation."

"Is that good?" Josh asked.

"It's excellent. It means as long as you stay out of trouble—which I know you will—there's no punishment to endure. No jail time, no community service, no nothing. How does that deal sound to you?" Agar asked.

"Cool, man!" Josh said.

"There are a couple of things you need to keep in mind. First, you can't tell anyone we had this discussion until it's revealed in trial. We don't want any unnecessary complications. Second—the trial needs to be unified."

"Huh?" Josh said.

"We don't want to have multiple trials, but if we're not careful, there could be. One for homicide, one for arson, one for trespassing—a trial for each person—it's too much. We have to streamline this trial—keep the costs down—and produce results. Results everyone will be happy with."

"Who is 'everyone'?" Josh asked.

"You, me, the police department, the media, and especially the Applefoot family. We're going to push for one trial—homicide—and funnel in the other crimes as component elements of the homicide."

"You're gonna pin everything on the girl?" Josh asked.

"Of course! She killed Greg, didn't she?"

"Well, yeah, but what if she testifies?"

"As I told you, she's in a coma. She'll stay in a coma until the trial is complete. Look, she's under eighteen. They won't give her hard time. And once her time is served, she'll be deported. Or she may be deported immediately. The point is, she's an easy means for dumping these charges so everyone else can move on," Agar said.

"I dunno," said Josh.

"Don't waffle now. If Defense clouds the homicide issue—makes it into an accident or pins the root cause on the pit fire or bullets—it would all fall back on you. And the prison time could grow quickly. So what's the best solution for all—a few months in juvenile detention for the girl who's on her way to Mexico anyway, or years of prison time for you? Don't answer. Think of this—by the time she comes out of her coma—"

"If she comes out," interrupted Josh.

"Yes, well, we don't need to worry about that. Anyway, if she comes out of the coma, it will be time served, she'll be deported, and everyone will be happy. It's a win-win situation!"

"Except for her," Josh said.

"Don't worry about her. She'll thank us all later when she's grown up and marries a man who can set her straight."

Captain Agar was quite pleased with his presentation to Josh. Josh agreed to the logic and promised to sign the document once Captain Agar had it typed up.

Jonara couldn't believe the conversation she'd just heard. Was it true? Did things like this really happen in a police station? She couldn't believe it. Something in her dream must have gone wrong. Perhaps Great-Grandma Geneva's diary was in error. Jonara trusted police stations—everything they did had to be honest everywhere in the world—especially in the United States. But there it was—Captain Agar the interrogator and Josh working out a deal. Jonara was disgusted. Decisions were being made about Jonara's mother, Evanita, without Evanita's knowledge.

Captain Agar led Josh to a side room away from Skins and the other boys. Jonara's attention shifted, and she wanted to know what was going on with her grandma. Jonara slipped through the doors and entered another interrogation room where Eva was being held.

"You have no right to hold me here," said Eva.

"We've been over this again and again, Eva," said Officer Buke. "You ran from a police officer and resisted arrest. You also claim to be the mother of the girl in the hospital who is clearly an illegal immigrant from Mexico. I got five other women claiming to be her mother. It's no secret. They know just as you do that the girl is going to be deported to Mexico."

"You can't deport an American national, and certainly not my daughter," said Eva.

"Again, you're not listening to reason. But here's the kicker—you're the only fake mother who ran from the police. This ain't Mexico."

"I'm an American like you. And my ancestry is Spanish," said Eva.

"Like I said, Mexican."

"Spanish. As in Spain. Europe. The same continent as your ancestors," Eva replied.

"How can you or anyone else prove you're that girl's mother?"

"That girl has a name—it's Evanita—and I have a photo. Here!"

"Every other purported mother has shown me a photo. Yours is no better. This doesn't look anything like the girl. Have you even seen the girl in the hospital?"

"No," replied Eva.

"And you expect me to believe this girl in the photo is the same? They look nothing alike."

"Because Mommy is all bruised, swollen, and her hair is burned off!" Jonara screamed, but no one heard.

"If I hadn't been dragged into this station by a male officer who obviously had no clue about a mother's concern for her daughter, I would have been able to see Evanita in the hospital, and there would be none of this," Eva said.

"None of this? You think this is some sort of circus just for your benefit? That girl is a murder suspect. You're only here because of your interference in this case. Face it, you're a nobody. You'll be charged with fleeing an officer and resisting arrest. You won't have to spend any time in jail, but you'll have to pay a fine."

Eva socked the interrogator in the jaw and caught his nose.

"Now we're talking jail time!" he said.

Buke's nose started bleeding, and he was forced to leave the room.

"Grandma!" Jonara screamed. "Don't give in to that bully!"

Eva sat down and buried her face in her hands. She sniffed twice, took a tissue from her purse, and dried the tears from her face. A female officer entered the room and sat across from Eva.

"My name is Officer Entz. Well then, you've put on quite a show, haven't you?" she asked.

"Do you have children?" Eva asked.

"Three daughters, and a boy who can't keep himself clean," Entz said, and she pulled out a photo of her four children.

"They're all cute," said Eva. "This is my daughter."

"She's lovely," said the officer. "She looks a lot like you."

"I know. She's all I have," said Eva.

"Miss Carreña," started Entz.

"Please—call me Eva."

"All right, Eva. I know you're stressed out and tired," she started.

"I just want—" Eva said.

"One moment please. Thank you. We know your daughter is missing—hold that thought—is reported missing for over twenty-four hours. Rules are a pain, aren't they? We do the best we can. We sent an officer to your house to help you find your daughter—Evanita—is that right?"

"Yes," said Eva.

"Things work well when everyone is calm. When people aren't calm, well, things get dangerous. And officers need to think quickly or people die. Now earlier today when—"

"I have something for you," interrupted Eva.

"Please, I'm almost finished."

"I just remembered I had it. It's in my purse—do you mind? I keep it in a special pocket," explained Eva.

"More photos won't do any good," said the officer.

"It isn't that kind of photo," said Eva, and she pulled an exposed X-ray film from her purse. "Look for yourself."

"They look like teeth. You're a dentist. I don't see the relevance," said Entz.

"This is a panorex of Evanita's teeth from about a year ago. Mothers keep all sorts of unusual lovesakes of their children. This is mine," Eva said.

"You could have pulled that out at random from anyone in your files."

"No," said Eva. "Not this panorex. It was taken at Vansen Hospital—the same hospital she is in now."

"The hospital you believe she is in," said the officer.

"Yes, whatever, the hospital I believe she is in. This is a copy of the original. Take it and have the hospital look up the name 'Evanita Carreña'. They'll find the original and verify what I'm saying. If it doesn't match then fine—I'll give up my 'belief' as you call it. I won't trouble you anymore. I'll pay whatever fine and do whatever jail time this department asks of me. But if I'm right, you'll release me and let me see my daughter."

"I can't drop any charges," said the officer.

"Take the panorex," said Eva.

The female officer paused. Eva held the panorex out to Entz. The light glistened and glared off the X-ray film of Evanita's teeth. The officer stared at the film of teeth and saw a person, a human being, a daughter.

"All right, I'll run a check. No guarantees."

Officer Entz took the film and placed it in a protective envelope. She left Eva in the interrogation room and faxed the film
to Vansen Hospital. Ten minutes later, the hospital confirmed a
match with the name, "Evanita Carreña." Entz went to a meeting room with the two other interrogators—Agar and Buke.

"Gentlemen, it appears we have an identity for the hospital
girl," said Entz. "Her name is Evanita Carreña. And her mother
is here at the station."

"What's the mother's name?" Agar asked.

"Eva Carreña," Entz replied. "Eva was right all along—the
girl is her daughter."

"We deport both of them, then?" Buke asked.

"No," replied Agar. "Eva is an American by birth. A promi-
nent dentist, too. Wait, now I remember. The secret trial back in
1990. Do either of you remember that?"

"No," said Buke. "I was in elementary school."

"I was living on the East Coast," said Entz.

"It was a crazy trial—paternity rights and the legal status of
this girl, Evanita," said Agar. "I can't believe we got the mother
and daughter in court again after sixteen years! The trial was
like something out of a movie. A weird movie."

"Well that's all in the past," said Buke. "You can't refer to
past cases in this trial."

"No, but there might be—" Agar started but he caught himself—he didn't want to let his thoughts out to Entz.

"Might be what?" Entz asked.

"I, uh, hmmm. I lost my train of thought," said Agar.

In fact, he had not. Jonara didn't like the look of Captain
Agar and was afraid of what he was planning to do.

"You can dismiss the other women," Agar said to Entz.
"They're cleared of any involvement. In fact, you can let Eva and
Johnny Pindus go as well."

Officer Entz left Agar and Buke in the meeting room and
dismissed the women including Ms. Zyla and Eva. She also released Johnny Pindus.

"You can't release the psychic!" said Buke. "We have a tape
of his conversation with Evanita. He admits to knowing about

the fire and how it started. He must have been there. We have to interrogate him further."

"What have you learned so far?" said Agar. "You interrogated him—what did he say?"

"He says he wasn't there," said Buke. "But he must be lying."

"I don't think so," said Agar. "And I suspect a blood test will be negative for arsenic. Those boys burned pressure-treated wood full of arsenic. If he had been there, his blood would be full of the toxin. No, we must let him go."

"But sir!" Buke protested.

"Trust me on this, Buke. We must let Eva and Johnny go— for now. If we hold them for much longer, they'll drag in lawyers and all sorts of legal headaches. Let them cool off a bit before we start the next round. I want everything ready when we launch the surprise attack."

"Yes sir," Buke said.

"One more thing," said Agar. "Call the fathers of these boys and have them meet me here at the station. We have a lot of work to do."

CHAPTER 14:

Evanita's Trial

2023 Oct 4, Wed Early am. Jonara's Dream.
2006 Nov 10, Fri. Multnomah County Courthouse. Portland, Oregon.

"All rise. Judge Gregory presiding," said the Court Clerk.

"What's going on?" Jonara asked.

Jonara was sitting with a twelve-person all-male jury in an old courtroom. The judge's bench was off to her far right, and the rest of the courtroom—plaintiff, defendant, and others in attendance—were off to her far left. Ornate wood and oversized paintings of past judges decorated the tall walls except for a section of the wall directly across from her—that position had windows to an outside of trees and people—trees with autumn leaves and people walking their dogs.

Voices echoed through the courtroom like a cave. The court reporter periodically urged people to speak up so she could hear them. Besides the judge and the Jury, Jonara recognized the boys at the factory—they sat in a row behind the plaintiff—a row shared with a British family, the Applefoot family. The plaintiff sat in the court to Jonara's closer left (and the judge's far left) while the defendant sat farther away on a slight left (and the judge's far right).

The defendant appeared to be Eva. She was accompanied by Jan Haughf of Haughf Telly Law Firm. In the row behind sat Claire, Sharon, Patty, Ms. Zyla, and Johnny Pindus. Sheila did not sit with her mother, Sharon, but instead sat behind Davino several rows behind the plaintiff. Davino's wife sat next to Davino.

"Your Honor," started the prosecuting attorney. "I motion we end the trial and find the defendant guilty of all charges for failing to show up."

"Motion denied, Mr. Manis," said Judge Gregory, also known as The Court.

"Sir, may I approach the bench?" Manis asked.

"No," said The Court.

"Sir," he said, "we're wasting valuable tax dollars with these formalities. Let's move on and find Evanita guilty of all charges."

"That's an outrage, Your Honor," said Ms. Haughf. "Prosecution is trying to shift blame for all crimes onto a comatose girl."

"Your Honor," said Manis. "The defendant has not shown up. The defendant cannot enter a plea. Is this not an automatic guilty verdict?"

"Mr. Manis. We have spent time assembling the court and selecting the Jury. The trial will continue," said The Court.

"I object," said Manis.

"To what?" asked The Court.

"This charade. We have a trial but no defendant. Are we to play solitary tennis against a brick wall?" Manis asked.

"I object. Prosecution is equating Defense to a brick wall," Ms. Haughf said.

"Prosecution denied. Defense sustained. Mr. Manis, I urge you to avoid these *ad hominem* attacks."

"I object again," said Ms. Haughf. "Unconscious people on trial are permitted legal counsel and representation in court."

"Unconscious people are permitted counsel, but not indirect representation in court," interrupted Mr. Manis. "Defense intends to prop the defendant's mother up as the defendant."

"Sustained, sustained. Unconscious people are permitted legal counsel. But the defendant's mother should sit in the row behind Defense. The mother is not on trial."

"Bullcrap I'm not," blurted Eva.

Judge Gregory slammed his gavel into a block.

"Order, order. Defense will restrain comments from the defendant's mother."

"Your Honor," said Ms. Haughf. "Defense is allowed to have anyone sit at the Defense table. The defendant's mother is merely sitting in for the defendant."

"Ms. Haughf—The Court cannot permit substitution. This is not a football game. And in light of the fact the Jury may confuse the defendant with the defendant's mother, I strongly urge Ms. Eva to sit in the row behind Defense," said The Court.

"Your Honor, this courtroom is not prepared to receive the defendant," said Ms. Haughf.

"For the love of God, I've now heard the ultimate fantasy," said Manis, "Defense is now claiming the courtroom is not good enough for the defendant."

"Do you object, Mr. Manis?" the judge asked.

"Most certainly I object. I object to Defense's *ad hominem* attack on this courtroom while I have been accused of the same toward Defense. I object to Defense stalling for time. I object to anything else preventing this court from a speedy verdict against the defendant."

"I object. Prosecution is babbling," said Ms. Haughf.

"I object!" Manis said.

"Overruled, overruled, overruled! Mr. Manis, Ms. Haughf—stop this petty bickering or I'll hold the both of you in contempt. Defense—move the defendant's mother to the row behind," said The Court.

"Conditionally," said Ms. Haughf.

"Not again!" said Manis.

"What condition?" asked The Court.

"That the defendant be allowed to attend," said Ms. Haughf.

"Granted," said The Court.

"Ridiculous!" said Manis. "Of all the—"

Manis stopped himself. Eva and Ms. Haughf picked up their table and moved it to the window.

"Your Honor, Defense is redecorating!" said Manis.

"Yes, Defense is!" said Eva.

Ms. Haughf moved a few chairs aside while Eva ran to the back of the courtroom. The audience murmured and whispered speculations. The room's double doors opened, and two hospital technicians rolled in a hospital bed with IV bags hanging and tubes running into a girl's arm. The girl was Evanita. Court-sanctioned photographers snapped photos of the wild scene. The courtroom launched into an uproar at the sight of a comatose Evanita being rolled in.

"Order, order!" The Court yelled while he slammed his gavel into a wooden block. "Order in this court!"

The technicians rolled the bed up the aisleway and stopped at the place where Ms. Haughf's and Eva's table once stood.

"Your Honor!" said Manis. "This is not a hospital."

"No, it isn't," said Ms. Haughf. "But The Court does not discriminate based on creed, race, gender, or natural origin. The defendant's origin is from the world of sleep."

"I object," said Manis. "Defense is speaking for The Court. Defense is stretching the Civil Rights umbrella. And that's 'national origin', not 'natural origin'!"

"Ms. Haughf. You do not speak for The Court. That is my job. Ms. Haughf—the defendant belongs in a hospital, not a courtroom. This is very unusual," said The Court.

"Yes, Your Honor. But I cannot allow my client to be kicked around like she's a nobody. She's a somebody. Now The Court, the Jury, and everyone else in the courtroom can see for themselves who this 'nobody' is—a young, sweet, innocent little girl who is lifeless, helpless, and in need of a fair hand."

"She may be young and sweet, but the Jury will decide the innocence or guilt of the defendant," said The Court.

Manis smiled to the judge's comment.

"But I know of nothing in the rules that says a defendant can be excluded from his or her own trial. The defendant may stay," said The Court.

Manis's smile turned sour.

"Your Honor, may I approach the bench?" Manis asked.

"No," said The Court.

Manis's face turned red. He clasped his hands together and knocked them against his forehead. He stared at Evanita, at his lengthy list of witnesses sitting in rows behind the Prosecution bench, and at the all-male jury.

Ms. Haughf sat next to Evanita's bed (by her feet) and close to the aisleway. Evanita's bed was positioned such that its length was parallel to the rows behind Ms. Haughf. The bed lifted Evanita's torso and head up to a thirty degree angle. Her head was close to the window. Eva sat next to Evanita's right side. She placed her hand on Evanita's right hand. To Eva's left stood a device to monitor Evanita's vitals—heart rate, respiration rate, brain activity, blood pressure, and temperature. The device chirped and sang tunes at different pitches for each vital sign.

"Your Honor, I object to this racket. Defense is holding a cage of cackling birds," said Manis.

"Ms. Haughf," said The Court.

"Your Honor," said Ms. Haughf. "My client requires this monitoring device to let us know her health. If she crashes, she'll need assistance."

"Ms. Haughf," The Court said again.

"Without the device, we would not know her medical state," Ms. Haughf continued.

"Ms. Haughf," The Court tried once more.

"And we do want to know the defendant's vital signs," Ms. Haughf continued.

"Ms. Haughf!" The Court said with a few gavel knocks. "The Court cannot continue with that racket. Certainly the audio can be turned off?!"

"Of course! All you had to do was ask," Ms. Haughf said.

Eva muted the audio.

"Thank you, Ms. Eva," said The Court. "Now if there are no more objections?"

Judge Gregory paused—expecting either Mr. Manis or Ms. Haughf to object to something.

"No objections? Good, we're ready for the charges. Would the Court Clerk read the charges?"

"The State of Oregon charges the defendant, Evanita Carreña, with the following," started the clerk. "First Degree murder of Greg Applefoot. Second Degree murder of Greg Applefoot.

First degree manslaughter of Greg Applefoot. Second degree manslaughter of Greg Applefoot. Possession of LSD. Use of LSD. Trespassing on restricted hazmat federal property River Wood and Battery Superfund Site. Arson on federal property of River Wood and Battery Superfund Site. Burning arsenic- and lead-bearing materials in the form of pressure-treated wood. Discharging ammunition without a permit. Discharging ammunition on a federally restricted property. Discharging a firearm without a permit. Discharging a firearm in a public thoroughfare. Discharging a firearm with intent to kill."

"You can add fleeing an officer, resisting arrest, and assaulting an officer," said Manis, referring to Eva.

"I object. Prosecution is attempting to alter the charges," said Ms. Haughf.

"Sustained. The Jury will disregard Mr. Manis's remarks," said The Court. Turning to Ms. Haughf he asked, "How does the defendant plead?"

"The defendant pleads 'Not Guilty' to all charges, including those from Mr. Manis," said Ms. Haughf.

Ms. Haughf shot Mr. Manis a snide look.

"A plea of 'Not Guilty' has been entered," said The Court. "Mr. Manis, you may call your first witness to the stand."

"I would like to call Vinay Vagatti to the stand," said Manis.

"Place your left hand on the Bible and raise your right hand," said the Court Clerk.

"I am not a Christian," Vinay said with his Hindi accent.

"Throw him out!" jeered someone in the courtroom.

Others booed and chanted, "Atheist, anti-Christ, atheist!"

"Order," The Court gaveled.

"I am Zoroastrian," Vinay said.

The Court Clerk removed the Bible and said, "Raise your right hand. Do you swear to tell the truth, the whole truth, and nothing but the truth?"

"I do," said Vinay with his right hand raised.

"Please be seated," said the Court Clerk.

Vinay sat in the witness stand.

"State your name and spell it for the record," said the Court Clerk.

"Vinay Vagatti. V-I-N-A-Y V-A-G-A-T-T-I," Vinay said.

"You may direct, Mr. Manis," said The Court.

"Mr. Vagatti," said Manis. "Where were you in the late afternoon of October 30th?"

"I was at the factory, the one that burned," said Vinay.

"Can you tell us the name of that factory?" Manis asked.

"It was River Wood and something," Vinay said.

"Would that be the River Wood and Battery Superfund Site?" Manis asked.

"Definitely," Vinay replied.

"Were you alone?" Manis asked.

"No, I was with a few other people," Vinay said.

"Who were those other people?"

"Skins, Beef, Fat One, Doofus, and Josh," said Vinay.

"Are those their real names?" Manis asked.

"I don't know. Those are the only names I know," Vinay said.

"Do you see those people in the courtroom today?" Manis asked.

"Yes, I do—except for Fat One."

"Can you please identify them?" Manis asked.

Vinay pointed out each boy. As he did so, he called them out by nickname, and each boy stood in response to his name being called.

"Let the record show the witness has identified Askin Roberts as Skins, Buford Hamm as Beef, Donald Fessel as Doofus, and Joshua Ephram as Josh," Manis said. He turned to the boys and said, "You may be seated." Manis turned back to Vinay and asked, "What were you doing at the factory?"

Vinay shook in anxiety. He looked into the courtroom at his brother Davino. Davino nodded in affirmation. Vinay settled down and began to speak.

"We were investigating," said Vinay.

"What were you investigating?" Manis asked.

"We saw a girl run into the factory with a spiral notebook. We followed her in," Vinay said.

"You were concerned about her safety and wanted to rescue her from trouble?" Manis asked.

"Objection," said Ms. Haughf. "Prosecution is leading the witness."

"Sustained," said The Court.

"Is the girl in the courtroom today?" Manis asked.

"Yes."

"Can you identify her, please?" Manis asked.

"There. In the hospital bed," Vinay pointed.

"Let the record show the witness has identified the defendant, Evanita Carreña," Manis said. He turned to Vinay and asked, "What happened after you followed her in?"

"We found her dancing by a fire," Vinay said.

"Did you start the fire?" Manis asked.

"No, it was already lit by the time I arrived there," said Vinay.

"How did she kill...what did she do next?" Manis asked.

"Objection," said Ms. Haughf. "Prosecution is pretending to make a slip of the tongue while leading the witness."

"Sustained. Mr. Manis, I'm warning you about your courtroom conduct," said The Court.

"What happened next?" Manis asked Vinay.

"She ran onto a catwalk. She was about to jump into the burning pit. I held up a pole to stop her. Fat One ran up the catwalk to help her. She kicked him and pushed him over the edge. He fell into the fire and screamed. He stopped screaming. He burned. The odor was unquestionable. It made me sick."

Johnny shook his head in disapproval. He knew Vinay was distorting the events. Eva was grim, but Ms. Haughf had a sense of determination.

"What happened next?" Manis asked.

"Something exploded in the factory. The girl in the bed fell into the pit. We all ran out. I don't know what happened next," said Vinay.

"No more questions," said Manis.

Mr. Manis walked away from the witness stand. Vinay stood up as if to leave, but Ms. Haughf stepped over.

"Wait a moment, Mr. Vagatti," said The Court. "Defense—do you wish to cross?"

"Yes, Your Honor," said Ms. Haughf.

"Remain seated for cross-examination, Mr. Vagatti," said The Court.

"Mr. Vagatti," said Ms. Haughf. "Are you a Christian?"

"Objection—relevance," said Manis.

"Ms. Haughf, I cannot—" The Court started.

"Your Honor, I intend to illustrate a facet of the witness that should illuminate the courtroom as to the validity of his story," said Ms. Haughf.

"I'll allow the question. But do not stray, Defense," The Court said.

"Thank you, Your Honor," said Ms. Haughf.

"Mr. Vagatti, you may answer the question," said The Court.

"As I said before, I am not a Christian. I am Zoroastrian," Vinay said.

"Your first name is Vinay?" Ms. Haughf asked.

"Yes."

"Does that have a meaning?" she asked.

"It's a Hindu name. It means 'good behavior'," Vinay said.

"Mr. Vagatti—may I call you Vinay?" Ms. Haughf asked.

"Yes."

"Vinay, who is Parvati?" Ms. Haughf asked.

Vinay shook again. He looked at Davino. Davino made no movements. He looked at Josh. Josh quickly winked an eye.

"Parvati is the Hindu goddess of fertility and power," Vinay said.

"Objection. We're now discussing mythology!" said Manis.

"Hinduism is not mythology!" yelled Vinay.

"Order, order!" The Court gaveled. "The witness will not speak out of turn. Ms. Haughf—your line of questioning—"

"Is very relevant. I am establishing credibility of the witness," said Ms. Haughf.

"Your Honor, if Defense wishes a *voir dire*, she should have done so during deposition. The Court says—"

"Objection. Hearsay," said Ms. Haughf.

"You two are irritating me," said The Court.

"Your Honor, *voir dire* applies to an expert witness. Defense is permitted to determine validity of any conventional witness without prior *voir dire* and in the presence of a Jury," said Ms. Haughf.

"Mr. Manis—overruled. Ms. Haughf—sustained. Proceed with cross," said The Court.

"Mr. Vagatti, do you have family here in court?" Ms. Haughf asked.

"Yes. My brother, Davino, and my father, Sam," said Vinay.

"Are their names Hindu?" Ms. Haughf asked.

"No," said Vinay. "My father and brother chose Christian names when we immigrated to this country."

"Atheist! Anti-Christ!" the audience chanted.

"Order!" The Court gaveled.

"What do you mean by 'Christian names'?" Ms. Haughf asked. "Are your brother and father Christians?"

"Objection," said Manis. "Hearsay."

"Your Honor. Certainly Mr. Vagatti knows the religious orientation of his father and brother without it being hearsay," said Ms. Haughf.

"The witness cannot speak for someone else. Objection is sustained. Rephrase your question, Ms. Haughf," said The Court.

"Mr. Vagatti. Do you believe that your father and brother are Christians?" Ms. Haughf asked.

"Objection, Your Honor. The same hearsay," said Manis.

"Ms. Haughf—The Court has warned you about this line of questioning. Objection sustained," said The Court.

"Your Honor. I am exploring the witness's belief, not the religious orientation of the witness's father and brother," said Ms. Haughf.

"Limit your question to his belief," said The Court.

"Do you have a belief about your father's and brother's religious orientation?" Ms. Haughf asked Vinay.

"Yes," Vinay replied.

"What is your belief?" Ms. Haughf asked.

"I believe they are Zoroastrians," Vinay replied.

"Mr. Vagatti. You testified that your father and brother chose Christian names, is this true?" Ms. Haughf asked.

"Objection. Question already asked," said Manis.

"Sustained."

"Why did your father and brother change their names?" Ms. Haughf asked.

"Objection. Hearsay," said Manis.

"Sustained."

"Hypothetically, Mr. Vagatti, why might a person change a Hindu name to a Christian name?" Ms. Haughf said.

"For Americans, Christian names are easier to pronounce than Hindu names," said Vinay.

"Did you change your name?" Ms. Haughf asked.

"No, I didn't," he said. "But sometimes people call me 'Vinny'. 'Better Vinny than Skinny' is what people tell me."

"Objection," said Manis.

"What are you objecting to?" The Court asked.

"The witness is engaging in hearsay," said Manis.

"Your Honor, I've been very patient with Mr. Manis's objections to hearsay. But if he keeps objecting to hearsay, we'll be here until Easter," said Ms. Haughf.

"Overruled. I'm going to give Ms. Haughf and the witness some latitude here," said The Court.

"Then I object for another reason, Your Honor. Defense has pursued this banal line of questioning. What have we learned about the defendant?" Manis asked.

"Defense—can you demonstrate relevance with this line of questioning?" asked The Court.

"Yes, Your Honor," Ms. Haughf said. "I submit that the witness is Hindu and not Zoroastrian, that he kept his name because of his belief, that his brother and father changed their names to blend in with Americans, that Vinay kept his name to retain his Hindu identity, that Parvati—a goddess of Hindu belief—is a name he called Evanita in the factory, that he is a master of Silambam—a martial arts technique with the stick from southern India—far from the Zoroastrian people of western

India and eastern Iran. That Vinay was raised in southern India by his uncle, explaining his different religious upbringing. I submit that Vinay has not been truthful and should be treated as a hostile witness."

The courtroom erupted in a roar of mixed discussion.

"Your Honor!" Manis tried to object, but the courtroom overpowered his voice. Manis tried to say, "She's fabricating," but again his voice could not be heard.

"Order, order," said The Court, but the courtroom continued to react. "ORDER!" The Court shouted with a loud gavel knock.

The courtroom settled down.

"I object, Your Honor. Defense is fabricating," said Manis.

"Ms. Haughf. Unless you have evidence to support—" The Court started.

Vinay shook again and mumbled something.

"Here is my evidence," said Ms. Haughf. "The witness is showing signs of anxiety—anxiety brought on by supplying conflicting information."

"Parvati," Vinay mumbled.

"Mr. Vagatti," Ms. Haughf said to Vinay. "Does your testimony in the courtroom today live up to your name? 'Vinay' is Hindu for 'good behavior'. I ask you, are you Vinay today?"

Vinay hesitated. He looked up and stared directly at Ms. Haughf. With sweat glossing his face, he turned toward Mr. Manis, the prosecution side of the courtroom, and looked back at Ms. Haughf.

"Today, I am not Vinay," he said.

"Order!" The Court gaveled in response to "Oohs" and "Aaahs" in the courtroom.

"But maybe I am Vinny," he tried with a weak effort for recovery, but his voice was drowned by random crowd noise.

"Your Honor, I request the right to recall this witness later," said Ms. Haughf, and she turned to Vinay and said, "No more questions."

"Granted," said The Court. "You may step down, Mr. Vagatti."

Vinay exited the witness stand and sat in the courtroom. He gave a dejected look to Mr. Manis. Manis ignored the look as if he had nothing to do with Vinay's testimony.

"Your Honor. I request a short recess," said Manis.

"Denied."

"May I approach—"

"Denied."

"I—"

"Denied."

"I wish to call my next witness!" Manis forced upon the courtroom.

Manis paused for a moment, expecting the judge to say, "Denied," but the judge did not impede Manis.

"I call Joshua Ephram to the stand," Manis said.

Josh left the audience area and stood in the witness stand. The Court Clerk placed a Bible before Josh.

"Please place your left hand on the Bible and raise your right," said the Court Clerk.

Josh did as instructed. The audience breathed a sigh of relief. Some whispered, "That's a good Christian," while others said, "He's Saved for sure."

"Do you swear to tell the truth, the whole truth, and nothing but the truth?" the Court Clerk asked.

"I do, so help me God," Josh replied.

The scattered clapping approved of Josh's words.

"Please be seated. State your name and spell it for the record," said the Court Clerk.

"Joshua Ephram. J-O-S-H-U-A E-P-H-R-A-M," Josh said.

Mr. Manis approached the witness.

"Mr. Ephram," started Manis. "Were you at the River Wood and Battery factory on October the 30th?"

"Yes I was," Josh said. "And I'm sorry I was."

The crowd murmured in naïve sympathy for Josh.

"Why are you sorry?" Manis asked.

"Because of what I did. Because of what happened," Josh said.

"What did you do at the factory?" Manis asked.

"I took a case of .22 caliber cartridges to the factory to get rid of them," Josh said. "I never wanted to see them again. I knew the factory was abandoned, and I knew it was breaking the law to trespass, but I thought I could get rid of them there without anyone finding them. I was wrong. And I confess this now to the court."

"What an actor," muttered Eva to Ms. Haughf.

The audience nodded and cleared their throats in approval of Josh's confession.

"What happened when you took the cartridges into the factory?" Manis asked.

"I wanted to get rid of them. I looked around for a hole to dump 'em. I saw a pit and threw the case in it," said Josh.

"Liar," muttered Eva, but no one heard (except Jonara).

"Were you with anyone?" Manis asked.

"No, not at first. But as I threw the case of cartridges into the pit, a girl ran into the building and saw me," Josh said.

"Is she in the courtroom today?" Manis asked.

"Yes," Josh replied.

"Identify her, please," Manis said.

"She's the girl in the hospital bed," said Josh.

"Let the record show Mr. Ephram has identified the defendant as the girl in the factory," Manis said. "What happened next, Mr. Ephram?"

"The girl walked up to me and said she was the Modern Eve. She asked what I was doing. I didn't want her to know about the ammo, so I lied and told her I was doing nothing. I think she must have seen me throw the ammo in the pit because of what happened next."

"Objection, Your Honor. Hearsay," said Ms. Haughf.

"Hearsay?!" Manis asked. "Of all the—"

"The witness is claiming to speak for the defendant," said Ms. Haughf.

"I did open the door for you with Mr. Vagatti," said The Court.

"Only a little bit," said Ms. Haughf.

"Overruled."

"What happened next?" Manis asked Josh.

"She asked me to take something from her, that she was the Modern Eve and wanted me to eat the apple from the tree of knowledge. I thought she was crazy or on drugs. There was no tree in the factory, and she had no apple. But when she told me to eat the apple, she handed me a tampon soaked in oil."

The audience broke into laughter.

"Order," gaveled the judge. "Mr. Ephram—remember you are under oath. Now is not the time to be a comedian."

"I swear as I have on the Holy Bible, the Word of God—I tell no lie. The girl said this to me. I told her there was no way I was eating a dirty tampon. She said it was for memento, wait, for-metto, for-meta? No, it was a meta-phor. That to eat a tampon was to light it on fire. I don't know what a metaphor is, but she didn't make any sense until she lit that tampon and tried to throw it in the pit where I dumped the ammo. Then I understood. I blocked her but the tampon burned some of my hair. That's why my hair is so short now—I had to get most of it cut off."

"My daughter would have never done that!" Eva blurted.

"Order. Silence from Defense!" Judge Gregory ordered.

"Objection, hearsay," said Ms. Haughf.

"You're a little late playing the 'hearsay' card, Ms. Haughf," said The Court. "The defendant cannot speak as to what she said. Testimony as to her conversation will receive the same legal treatment as that of a person's last dying words. I'll give Mr. Manis latitude. Overruled."

"What happened to the tampon?" Manis asked.

"I lost track of it at first—my eyes got watery from the flames, and I freaked out when my hair caught fire. But after I stopped myself from going totally bonfire-like, I saw her throw the burning tampon in the pit but away from the ammo. And it caught fire real good," said Josh.

"Did anything else happen?" Manis asked.

"Yeah. I saw other boys running in after her. They tried to get her under control, but she kept dancing by the fire and throwing green wood in it. I knew it was bad to burn that green wood, and I backed away so I wouldn't breathe the fumes. But I didn't know what to do. I know I should have helped the guys try to restrain the girl from hurting herself, but I was afraid."

More murmurs of naïve sympathy from the audience. One guy yelled, "Chicken," and another, "Wuss," but there was no other taunting. The Court gaveled again, but he was tired and didn't bother to say, "Order."

"Did you stay in the factory?" Manis asked.

"Not for very long. She had a piece of burning wood in her hand. Then she went up the catwalk. Fat One tried to stop her, but she threw the burning wood in the exact spot where I had stashed the ammo. It didn't blow up, and I felt good—I thought everything was safe. She kicked Fat One where she shouldn't have," Josh said as many groaned in the audience, "and shoved him over the edge. He fell into the burning pit that she started. But then everything went bad. That burning wood that she threw at the ammo must have set it off. There was a big explosion. I saw her fall into the same pit as Fat One, but I wasn't sure. The explosion blew me back. I barely got out alive. I dunno what happened to the guys, but I'm glad to see 'em alive in court."

"Can you identify the boys?" asked Manis.

"Yeah," Josh said, pointing to each boy as he spoke. "There's Skins, Doofus, Beef, and Vinny."

Each boy stood as Josh identified them.

"Let the record show the witness has identified Askin Roberts as Skins, Donald Fessel as Doofus, Buford Hamm as Beef, and Vinay Vagatti as Vinny," Manis said.

"You may be seated," said The Court.

"No further questions," said Manis.

Like Vinay, Josh stood as if ready to leave. Judge Gregory said nothing, but Ms. Haughf stepped quickly toward the witness stand and cautioned Josh.

"Have a seat if you please, Mr. Ephram," said Ms. Haughf. "I would like to cross-examine you."

"Will it leave me cross-eyed?" Josh asked.

No one recognized Josh's attempt at humor, and the courtroom fell painfully silent. Manis rolled his eyes. Ms. Haughf firmed her facial expression. Judge Gregory turned toward Josh and waved his finger as if to say, "Nah, ah, ah."

"Mr. Ephram, your last name—where have I heard that before?" Ms. Haughf asked.

"My uncle, Jerry Ephram, was the pastor of Barnseed Baptist Church," Josh said.

"Yes, that's right. Tell us about your relationship with your uncle," Ms. Haughf said.

"Objection. Relevance," said Manis.

"Your Honor, I intend to establish the witness's character as it relates to his events at the factory," Ms. Haughf said.

"Overruled. Mr. Ephram, please answer the question," said Judge Gregory.

"He taught me everything about the Bible and about being a good Baptist," Josh said.

Several claps from the audience.

"And we went hunting with my father—the three of us," Josh continued. "Uncle Jerry taught me how to hunt. And we didn't pretend to go hunting like some guys who sit around and drink beer. We were good, honest hunters. Every one of our kills was legal."

"You loved your uncle?" Ms. Haughf said.

"Yeah," Josh said. "But that all changed when Aunt Patty killed him. I never forgave her. But I couldn't go on hunting. I got rid of the cartridges we used in the hunting rifles."

"Mr. Ephram. The coroner pronounced Pastor Jeremiah Ephram dead due to heart failure from an overdose of diet pills. How do you figure Patty killed him?" Ms. Haughf asked.

"She sued him for everything. But that's what women do to nice husbands," Josh said.

Several men cheered. The women groaned. One said, "Ah, shut up!" Jonara thought Sharon shouted that comment, but she wasn't sure. Judge Gregory pounded his gavel into the block as usual, and Jonara wondered if that gavel was ready to split as much as the splitting headache she was getting from hearing Vinay and Josh lie about what happened at the factory.

"Mr. Ephram, did you enter the factory with the other boys you identified?" Ms. Haughf asked.

"No."

"Did you leave with them?"

"No, no," Josh repeated.

"Do you hang out with them?" Ms. Haughf asked.

"Not really," Josh said.

"What do you mean by 'not really'? You either do or you don't. We have Mr. Vagatti's testimony that he, the other identified boys—the same boys you also identified—entered the factory together. And now we have your testimony, that you entered the factory independently of the identified boys, that you left the factory independently of the other identified boys, and that you 'not really' hang out with them. Mr. Ephram, do you wish to restate your story about the factory?"

"Objection, Your Honor," said Manis. "The witness has already taken an oath to tell the truth, so help him God."

"He'll need God's help," Eva said over her shoulder to Sharon.

Sharon grinned.

"Sustained. Mr. Ephram, you do not have to answer the question," said Judge Gregory.

"Mr. Ephram, what is a cartridge?"

"It's a bullet before it's been fired. Some guys call it a bullet, but it ain't. It's a round of ammo, a metal case with a bullet, gunpowder, and primer inside. You can stick it in a rifle and fire a bullet out. Then the cartridge is empty. You gotta get rid of the empty cartridge before firing another cartridge."

"Mr. Ephram, in your testimony you state you threw your case of cartridges into a pit, and the defendant threw a burning piece of wood into the same pit, causing the cartridges to explode," Ms. Haughf said.

"Yeah, that's about right," Josh said.

"Is it also about right that bullets from that case of cartridges were found in a wall along a line running from a stamping press where cartridges had been placed?"

"I don't know about that," said Josh.

"You don't know about that. Forensics knows about that. Would you like to see the report?" Ms. Haughf asked.

"Objection. Evidence from Forensics does not report anything about bullets in walls," said Manis.

"Your Honor, an independent forensic lab with no liaisons to Prosecution has provided a report of bullets in the factory wall and evidence that these bullets were fired by a stamping press. Furthermore, fingerprints on the buttons of the press's operating stand match those of the witness," said Ms. Haughf.

"Objection again. Defense cannot surprise The Court with supposed evidence. Prosecution has the right to review all claimed evidence before trial begins," said Manis.

"Objection, Your Honor," said Ms. Haughf. "Request a *voir dire* on Mr. Manis to establish his credentials as a competent lawyer. Defense has the right to all Prosecution documents, not vice versa."

"Approach the bench, both of you," The Court said as he motioned Manis and Ms. Haughf forward. "And bring your forensic report, Defense."

Manis and Ms. Haughf approached the bench. Ms. Haughf handed the forensic report to Judge Gregory.

"Mr. Manis," started The Court.

"Your Honor, she can't surprise me like this," said Manis.

"Shut up, Mr. Manis," said The Court.

"Yes sir. I am only doing what I—"

"Mr. Manis," said The Court.

"Yes sir?" replied Manis.

"Shut up."

Judge Gregory reviewed Ms. Haughf's forensic report.

"This is a well-established institution," Judge Gregory said to Ms. Haughf, "but this document is not entered as court evidence."

"Your Honor, I just received this report moments ago. Had Prosecution's forensics department performed the same thorough investigation as my independent forensic company, we wouldn't be whispering to each other now," Ms. Haughf explained.

"I want a copy of this report. I want a recess," said Manis.

"You do not have the right to request this report," said The Court.

"Your Honor, in the interest of a speedy trial, I would like to enter the report as a court document. And I'll even allow Mr. Manis to read it before continuing trial. Because I'm a nice person," said Ms. Haughf.

Manis's eyes lit up in surprise when he heard, "I'm a nice person." The judge paused for a moment and spoke aloud to the courtroom.

"We will adjourn for twenty minutes. Will the Court Clerk enter Ms. Haughf's document as evidence and provide a copy to Mr. Manis."

With two knocks of Judge Gregory's gavel, the trial fell into recess.

CHAPTER 15

Sheila Testifies

2023 Oct 4, Wed Early am. Jonara's Dream.
2006 Nov 10, Fri. Portland, Oregon.

Jonara followed Mr. Manis from the courtroom into a small side office. In the office stood Captain Agar.

"How the hell did Haughf get a forensic team into that factory? Your boys were supposed to put an iron ring around it and keep everyone out!" fumed Manis.

"We did, boss. No one got through without us knowing," said Captain Agar.

"A copy of the report, sir," an aide said as he walked into the office and handed Manis a document photocopy.

Manis skimmed through the document and saw everything Prosecution was trying to hide from the case.

"This is it. The ballgame is over. Haughf's got details of what really happened," said Manis.

"But how?" Agar asked rhetorically. "No one but firefighters and EPA were in that factory."

"I'll tell you how—your boys dropped the ball!" Manis said.

"We didn't drop anything!" Captain Agar said in a raised voice.

"I need to think quickly," said Manis. "Even if one of the kids talked—"

"Which they didn't. I had their fathers coach them on exactly what to say," said Agar. "Vinay and Josh—"

"That's another thing. You didn't coach everyone together. You had Vinay say everyone went in as a group, but Josh said he went in alone and the others came in later," said Manis.

"I'm working on that," said Agar.

"It's too late to work on that," Manis said. "We can't use the kids anymore. Haughf is gonna recall Vinay, and she'll probably start going after the other kids. She'll expose them as liars and debase our case. She'll push us into defending the kids. No, we're Prosecution, we're the offense. We've used up these kids. We have to dump 'em somehow and distance our case from them. It is mandatory we attack the defendants directly."

"I'll have 'em roughed up. Scare 'em into silence," said Captain Agar.

"No. I don't trust Haughf," said Manis. "She must have spies. Look at how she got forensic data out of the factory. No, we must use a wedge and drive these women apart and against each other. It's an old technique, Agar."

"Very old, but handy," said Agar.

"One minute remaining," an aide yelled into the room.

"We'll be there," Manis yelled back. He turned to Captain Agar and said, "Be prepared to issue arrest warrants. I'll send a message as to who and when."

The court reconvened. Jonara returned to the courtroom but stood at the head of her mother's bed instead of with the Jury.

"All rise. Judge Gregory presiding," said the Court Clerk.

Judge Gregory entered the courtroom and sat down.

"Defense, would you like to continue cross-examining Mr. Ephram?" The Court asked.

"No further questions," said Ms. Haughf.

"Mr. Manis, call your next witness," said The Court.

"I call Sharon Stout to the stand," said Mr. Manis.

"Objection. Ms. Stout is one of my witnesses," said Ms. Haughf.

"Mr. Manis?" The Court asked.

"Your Honor, given how Defense plans to recall one of my witnesses, I see no harm in calling one of hers," said Manis. "And yes, I do intend to demonstrate relevance."

"Objection overruled. However, Defense may call the witness at a later time," said The Court.

"Naturally, Your Honor," said Manis.

Sharon Stout took the witness stand.

"Place your left hand on the Bible and raise your right," said the Court Clerk.

Sharon almost placed her hand on the Bible but recoiled.

"Is there a problem, Ms. Stout?"

"I would like to know what kind of Bible I am swearing on," Sharon said.

Groans in the audience.

"The only Bible, the Holy Bible," said the Court Clerk.

"I won't swear on a Christian Bible," said Sharon. "But I will swear on a Jewish Bible."

The audience broke out into random reaction. Some yelled, "Atheist," but others yelled, "Get out, Jew." One yelled, "Jesus killer."

The Court Clerk looked around and realized there was no Jewish Bible available. He set the Christian Bible aside and simply asked Sharon to raise her right hand.

"Do you swear to tell the truth, the whole truth, and nothing but the truth, so help you God?" the Court Clerk asked.

"I do," said Sharon.

"Please be seated. State your name for the record and spell it," said the Court Clerk.

"Sharon Stout. S-H-A-R-O-N S-T-O-U-T."

"Ms. Stout," said Manis. "What is your profession?"

"I'm a police officer for PPD," Sharon said.

"I'm sorry, what is 'PPD'?" Manis asked.

"Portland Police Department," Sharon said.

"Ms. Stout. What were you doing on September the 29th of this year?" Manis asked.

"I'm not sure what you mean. That was over a month ago," said Sharon.

"Let me refresh your memory. I have a police report filed by you, that on the 29th of September you pursued a van from Morris Synagogue to the State of Washington. The van crashed into a small lake off Interstate 5. Do you remember that day?" Manis asked.

"Yes, now I remember," Sharon replied. "I did pursue a van from Morris Synagogue to Washington State."

"How did the van end up in the lake?" Manis asked.

"The van drove along Interstate 5, left the interstate, and plunged into the lake," said Sharon.

"Yes, of course. How did you force it off the road?" Manis asked.

"Objection. Naked assertion," said Ms. Haughf.

"Sustained," said The Court.

"Ms. Stout. Your police report states you disabled the vehicle by shooting out a tire. Is this correct?" Manis asked.

"Yes," said Sharon.

"Then Your Honor, it is not a naked assertion to ask the witness how she forced the van off the road. Clearly she forced it off by shooting the tire out," said Manis.

"Objection. Speculation," said Ms. Haughf.

"Sustained. Direct-examine the witness, not yourself, Mr. Manis," said The Court.

"Ms. Stout. What happened after you shot out the van's tire?"

"The tire deflated, the van lost control, and it veered off the road and into the lake," said Sharon.

"Would you say then that this action of shooting out the tire forced it off the road?" Manis asked.

"Yes," said Sharon.

"And would you say, in short, that you forced the van off the road?" Manis asked.

"Yes, I did," said Sharon.

"Ms. Stout, have the van's fugitives been identified?" Manis asked.

"Yes, they have," Ms. Stout said.

"How many fugitives were in the van?"

"Two."

"Are they in the courtroom today?" Manis asked.

"Only the driver. The other is not present," said Sharon.

"Would you identify the driver, please?" Manis asked.

"He is Askin Roberts," said Sharon. "Also known as Skins."

"Thank you, Ms. Stout. Please wait a moment. Your Honor, if it pleases The Court, I would direct attention to Exhibit 102—a forensic analysis of bullet holes in the fugitive's van."

Mr. Manis pulled out a large chart and placed it on an easel.

"Objection, Your Honor. Relevance," Ms. Haughf said.

"Your Honor. This chart was entered as evidence during deposition," Mr. Manis said.

"Mr. Manis," The Court said. "Unless you can demonstrate relevance..."

"That's what I'm trying to do," Mr. Manis said, "if Defense wouldn't object so much."

"Overruled," The Court said.

"Are you familiar with this exhibit?" Manis asked Sharon.

"Yes, I am," said Sharon.

"Then could you explain why there are two different hole sizes?" Manis asked.

"I don't understand what you mean. The exhibit shows bullet holes in the van. One is near the right tire. The other is near the driver's door," said Sharon.

"That is exactly what I mean. Forensics recovered the bullets and determined two different types of bullets caused the holes you identified. Also, the type of bullet that caused the hole near the left rear tire also penetrated the tire itself and left an identifying mark on the rim. Ms. Stout—how many shots did you take at the van?" Manis asked.

"Two."

"What weapon did you use to fire the bullets?" Manis asked.

"An FN Special Police Rifle," said Sharon.

"And what size bullets does it use?" asked Manis.

"It does not use bullets, it uses cartridges—.300 caliber cartridges," Sharon explained.

"Forensics identified the hole by the left tire was created by a .300 caliber bullet, and the deflation of the tire was caused by a .300 caliber bullet," said Manis. "The scratch pattern in the hole matches your rifle."

"That would make sense," said Sharon.

"Yet the bullet hole by the driver's window is much larger. It was not caused by a .300 caliber bullet. It was caused by a .400 caliber bullet. What do you think caused that hole?" Manis asked.

"Objection. Prosecution is asking for subjective speculation, not hard evidence," said Ms. Haughf.

"Sustained."

"Ms. Stout, did you have your service revolver on the 29th of September when you gave chase to the van?" Manis asked.

"Yes. A Smith and Wesson M&P .400," said Sharon.

"Your Honor, I draw the courtroom's attention to Exhibit 400, Officer Sharon Stout's Smith and Wesson M&P .400 service revolver," said Manis.

The Court Clerk produced the weapon enclosed in a clear plastic bag.

"Is this your revolver?" Manis asked, handing the bag to Sharon.

"Yes it is. I thought it was lost," Sharon said.

"Would you explain why you thought it was lost?" Manis asked.

"It fell out of my car during the chase," said Sharon.

"It didn't just 'fall out', did it? Evanita dropped it while firing at the van," said Manis.

"Objection!" Ms. Haughf yelled.

The courtroom gasped and grew disruptive at the news of Evanita firing Sharon's revolver at the van. Random voices spoke the following: "What kind of girl does that?" "She's no innocent little girl." "She's a killer."

Mr. Manis took a few steps toward Ms. Haughf and said, "Relevance."

"Order, I say!" said The Court with another gavel strike against the block.

"Your Honor, Prosecution is leading the witness," said Ms. Haughf.

"Objection is sustained. Mr. Manis—we cannot afford these disruptions. Direct your questions to the witness," said The Court.

"Your Honor, I present Exhibit 402—fingerprint analysis of Officer Stout's Smith and Wesson revolver," Manis said.

Mr. Manis placed a split-view chart on an easel for the courtroom.

"As you can see, the left frame shows fingerprints taken from the trigger of Officer Stout's revolver. On the right are fingerprints of the defendant upon admission to Vansen Hospital. Analysis shows a match. Ms. Stout—as an officer of the law and trained in reading fingerprints, would you say these prints are a match?" Manis asked.

"Yes," said Sharon.

"Did Evanita Carreña fire your Smith and Wesson M&P .400 caliber service revolver while on Interstate 5 at the fleeing van on September 29, 2006?" Manis asked.

"She was just trying to—" Sharon started.

"It's a 'yes' or 'no' question, officer," said Manis.

"I told her to—" Sharon started again.

"Officer Stout—you are a trained policewoman. You know what a yes/no question is. I ask you again—yes or no—did Evanita fire your revolver?"

Sharon paused for a moment. She gave a brief look to Eva and shook her head as if to say, "I'm sorry."

"Yes," Sharon replied to Manis.

The courtroom echoed her words, "Yes, yes, yes, yes," but quieted down by itself.

"No further questions," said Manis.

"Your witness, Ms. Haughf," said The Court.

"Ms. Stout, would you explain the circumstances where the defendant fired your Smith and Wesson revolver?" Ms. Haughf asked.

"I'd be happy to," Sharon said. "I was pursuing a van that had kidnapped my daughter. The van would not pull over. Backup arrived but was caught up in traffic. It was up to me to stop the van. It shot at me and hit my left hand. I couldn't disable the van with my revolver. I asked Evanita to shoot out the rear tire. Understand—the van had my daughter inside as hostage. Evanita missed, and the revolver fell out the window. I was able to disable the van with my rifle, thanks to Evanita's help. She steadied the rifle while I fired. Evanita helped me disable the van. I take full responsibility for asking her to fire my weapon."

"Ms. Stout, do you normally pursue vehicles with civilians in your own vehicle?" Ms. Haughf asked.

"No. It's against the rules. I admit—I broke the rules. But there was no time. A young male kidnapped my own daughter, and police rules or not, I wasn't going to let anyone cause harm to her," Sharon explained. "Evanita was not out to kill anyone. She didn't want to hold the revolver at all. But she saw the pain I was in and how difficult it would be for me to shoot, so at my request, she fired the revolver. I know it breaks all rules of the book, but again—I take full responsibility—Evanita had nothing to do with the pursuit."

"No more questions, Your Honor," said Ms. Haughf.

"You may step down, Officer Stout," said The Court.

Sharon left the witness stand and rejoined her daughter, Claire, in the row behind Ms. Haughf and Eva.

"I call Askin Roberts to the stand," said Manis.

"Place your left hand on the Bible and raise your right," said the Court Clerk.

Skins complied with the Court Clerk.

"Do you swear to tell the truth, the whole truth, and nothing but the truth, so help you God?" the Court Clerk asked.

"I do," Skins replied.

"Please be seated. Recite your name and spell it," said the Court Clerk.

"Askin Roberts. A-S-K-I-N R-O-B-E-R-T-S."

"Mr. Roberts," asked Manis. "Were you driving a van on September the 29th?"

"Yeah," Skins said.

"Were you pursued by another vehicle?" Manis asked.

"Yeah," Skins replied.

"Did you know the vehicle pursuing you was a police officer?"

"Nope."

"Did you have any passengers in the van while being pursued?" Manis asked.

"Yup."

"Could you identify them, please?" Manis asked.

"George Gango, and Sheila Stout," Skins answered.

"Are they in the courtroom today?" Manis asked.

"Only Sheila," said Skins.

"Would Sheila Stout please stand?" Manis asked.

Sheila stood from her position behind Davino.

"Was she one of your passengers?" Manis asked.

"Yup," Skins said.

"You may be seated, thank you," Manis said to Sheila. Manis turned to Skins and asked, "What was Sheila's reason for hitchhiking with you?"

"Triple objection," said Ms. Haughf.

"A simple 'Objection' will do, Ms. Haughf," said The Court. "Now what is your objection?"

"I have multiple objections. Prosecution is leading the witness. Prosecution is asking the witness to engage in hearsay. Prosecution is making a naked assertion that Sheila was hitchhiking," said Ms. Haughf.

"Sustained, sustained, sustained," said The Court.

"Mr. Skins...er...Mr. Roberts," Manis asked. "Why were you fleeing a police officer?"

"I object," said Skins.

"You cannot object," said The Court. "Only counsel may object. Answer the question."

"I didn't know I was running from the cops. I thought it was some crazy woman following me. And she shot at me. Wouldn't you run?" Skins testified.

"You could have slowed down and pulled over. Why didn't you?" Manis asked.

"Sheila kept telling me to drive faster," said Skins.

"Objection. Hearsay," said Ms. Haughf.

"Sustained," said The Court.

"No more questions," said Mr. Manis.

"You may cross," said The Court to Ms. Haughf.

"Mr. Roberts, were you at the River Wood and Battery factory on October the 30th?" Ms. Haughf asked.

"Aren't you going to ask me about Sheila hitchhiking in the van?" Skins asked.

"Your Honor," Ms. Haughf said. "Permission to treat the witness as hostile."

"Granted," said The Court.

"Your friends know you as Skins. You led them into the River Wood and Battery factory, didn't you Skins?" Ms. Haughf asked.

"I—" Skins started to say.

"You're trying to divert attention from this by asking if I'll cross-examine you about the van chase," Ms. Haughf continued.

"That isn't—" Skins continued.

"You were already in the factory when Evanita arrived. Your gang didn't follow her in. You had already led your gang there. You ordered Beef to start the fire with pressure-treated wood, didn't you?"

"Wait, I just want to say—" Skins tried to say.

"Josh *did* want to get rid of his ammunition, but by using a stamping press. You allowed it. What did you care? Isn't that right?"

"But it could be that—" Skins stuttered.

"Your gang used the factory as a meeting place. It was Devil's Night Out. Why wouldn't you have a fire and do drugs? You had LSD stored in the factory—several places—but one place was in the front office," said Ms. Haughf.

"What the Devil! How can you—" Skins said.

During this exchange, Manis sent a text message on his cell phone to Captain Agar. Agar rushed into the courtroom.

"Askin Roberts is under arrest," Agar said.

"Outrageous!" said Ms. Haughf. "Your Honor, I object!"

"Captain Agar, I take it you have a good reason for disturbing my courtroom?" The Court said.

"I am taking Mr. Roberts into custody," Captain Agar said.

Captain Agar walked up to the witness stand and pulled Skins aside.

"You have the right to remain silent," said Agar as he read Skins his Miranda rights. "Anything you say can and will be used against you in a court of law."

"He's already in a court of law. And his words were being used against him," said Eva.

"Objection," said Manis. "The arrestee has a right to hear his Miranda rights without interruption."

"Sustained. Ms. Carreña—you will refrain from outbursts while Mr. Roberts is being arrested."

Captain Agar completed reading Skins his Miranda rights and marched him out of the courtroom.

"Your Honor," said Ms. Haughf. "Certainly the judicial branch of this country—The Court—will permit witness cross-examination without intrusion by the Executive Branch—a police arrest."

"Counsel would be wise not to dictate what The Court will and will not permit," said The Court.

"I wish to re-examine Mr. Roberts at a later time," said Ms. Haughf.

"At the convenience of The Court," said The Court.

"Your Honor, this is an illegal arrest!" Ms. Haughf said.

"Ms. Haughf. You are currently defending Miss Evanita Carreña. I suggest you limit your scope to your client," said The Court.

"Your Honor, I call Sheila Stout to the stand," said Manis.

Sheila left her place and walked to the witness stand.

"Place your left hand on the Bible and raise your right," said the Court Clerk. "Do you swear to tell the truth, the whole truth, and nothing but the truth, so help you God?"

"I do," said Sheila.

"Please be seated. State your name and spell it for the record," said the Court Clerk.

"Sheila Stout. S-H-E-I-L-A S-T-O-U-T," said Sheila.

"Ms. Stout, do you know the defendant?" Manis asked.

"You mean Evanita? Yeah, I know her. She was my best friend," Sheila said.

"Is she your best friend now?" Manis asked.

"No. Not after what she did," said Sheila.

"What did she do?" Manis asked.

"Lots of things. But the worst was when she stormed out when I was timing Davino's laps," said Sheila.

"Could you clarify what you mean—Davino's full name, if he's in court, what are 'Davino's laps' and what do you mean by 'she stormed out'?" Manis asked.

"Huh?" Sheila asked.

"You're forgetting the age of the witness," said The Court.

"Yes, she is young. Apparently not as sophisticated or devilish as Evanita," said Manis.

"Objection. Biased subjective statement," said Ms. Haughf.

"Sustained," said The Court. "Mr. Manis—you are to direct-examine the witness, not babble your opinions to the courtroom."

"Ms. Stout. Is Davino in the courtroom today?" Manis asked.

"Yeah. He's over there," Sheila said.

"Let the record show Ms. Stout has identified Davino Vagatti," Manis said. "Ms. Stout, tell us what happened when the defendant 'stormed out' as you say."

"Me and Nee-nee were—" Sheila started.

"I'm sorry," said The Court. "Who is Nee-nee?"

"Nee-nee. Eva-nee-ta. Don't you get it?" Sheila said to Judge Gregory.

Judge Gregory rolled his eyes and turned his attention back to Prosecution.

"Proceed, Mr. Manis," said The Court.

"What was the next question?" Sheila asked.

"What happened when the defendant 'stormed out'?" Manis asked.

"We were at Portland International Raceway. Davino was doing laps in his race car. I was timing him with a stopwatch. Nee-nee, I mean Evanita, was supposed to help. But instead she was rude," said Sheila.

"How was she rude?" Manis asked.

"She said—" Sheila started.

"Objection. Hearsay," said Ms. Haughf.

"Your Honor, I am attempting to establish the defendant's character through direct examination of a witness," said Mr. Manis.

"Your Honor, attempting to put the defendant on the stand through the words of another person is hearsay," said Ms. Haughf.

"Your Honor," Manis countered, "The Court did allow latitude during Mr. Ephram's testimony regarding the defendant in the factory. If the Court Reporter would reread The Court's response...where was that...after Defense objected to Mr. Ephram's testimony about the Modern Eve."

"I won't have the Court Reporter digging through old dialog when she's already busy taking dialog to begin with," said The Court.

"But Your Honor," Manis pleaded.

"Your Honor, you only allowed latitude with Prosecution's direct of Mr. Ephram after you allowed latitude with Defense's cross of Mr. Vagatti," said Ms. Haughf.

"The Court remembers what The Court said," said The Court.

"Mr. Manis—can you establish the hearsay as having relevance to the crimes for which the defendant is charged?" The Court asked.

"I'm establishing character," said Manis, "that the defendant is—"

"I want relevance to the crimes, not character. This courtroom has more character than it needs!" said The Court. "Objection is sustained."

Mr. Manis took several paces away from Sheila, looked at the floor, took several deep breaths, and walked back to Sheila.

"Ms. Stout, how do you feel about boys?" Manis asked.

"Boys are...well...they're boys!" Sheila said.

The courtroom laughed.

"Yes, of course," said Manis. "Do you like boys?"

"Some," said Sheila.

"Which ones?" Manis asked.

"Davino. Before him there was George Gango," Sheila said.

Some of the audience gasped. Davino's wife elbowed Davino in the jaw. Others were confused. Who was George Gango, they whispered.

"And before Mr. Gango?" Manis asked.

"I guess I had a crush here and there," said Sheila.

"How was your friendship with Evanita before Mr. Gango?" Manis asked.

"Huh? Before Gango?" Sheila asked.

"Before you took that joy ride with Mr. Gango," said Manis.

"Objection!" Ms. Haughf tried to say, but the other half of the courtroom who'd forgotten Gango now remembered and related him to kidnapping Sheila.

"Or did he kidnap her?" the whispers echoed.

"Mr. Manis, you're doing it again. Objection is sustained," said The Court.

"Ms. Stout, on September the 29th, did Mr. Gango kidnap you and hold you against your will?" Manis asked.

"Not really," said Sheila.

"It should be a 'yes' or 'no'," said Manis. "Please explain what you mean by 'Not really'."

"I only pretended to be kidnapped. At least at first. Then Mom flipped out. I got scared. George went berserk. And Skins drove faster. Everything got out of control. Evanita shot at us—she could have killed any of us. We almost died anyway when our van went off the freeway," Sheila said.

"Sheila, stop that nonsense!" yelled Sharon.

"I don't have to do what you say, Mother!" said Sheila.

"Order, order!" The Court gaveled.

"So Evanita spoiled my thing with George Gango. I had a little crush on Skins before I moved on to Davino," said Sheila.

"You're too young for these boys," said Sharon.

"Like Evanita is too young for Johnny Pindus?" Sheila retorted.

The courtroom murmured gossips about Evanita and Johnny Pindus.

"Order," said The Court. "I'll have no cat fights in my courtroom."

"Ms. Stout," Manis asked Sheila. "How would you characterize your relationship with Evanita before your interest in George, Askin, and Davino—and during your interests in the three?"

"Uh, characterize. That's a big word," said Sheila.

The courtroom laughed.

"What I mean is this—before George, were you and Evanita good friends or bad friends?" Manis asked.

"Good friends. Best friends," said Sheila.

"And while you were with George?" Manis asked.

"Bad friends," replied Sheila.

"And after that?" Manis asked.

"After that was Davino. We were bad friends again. And now after what she's done at the factory to Skins and his friends, we're still bad friends. When I'm hanging out with a serious boyfriend, we're bad friends," said Sheila.

"Thank you, Ms. Stout," said Manis.

"Do you wish to cross, Defense?" The Court asked Ms. Haughf.

"Yes, thank you," said Ms. Haughf.

Ms. Haughf, as she had done throughout the trial, stood from her chair next to Evanita's bed and walked up near the witness.

"Ms. Stout. You have taken an oath to tell the truth, isn't that right?" Ms. Haughf asked.

"Yeah," Sheila replied.

"And Ms. Stout, the courtroom is not the place for vague opinion. We're here to discover facts—facts of truth. Guessing doesn't count as the truth. So when I ask you the following questions, I want you to be sure you're telling us the facts—the truth. Will you do this for me?" Ms. Haughf asked.

Sheila looked nervous, though not as frightened as Vinay had earlier.

"Yeah," Sheila replied, shrugging her shoulders.

"I want you to take a good long look at Evanita in her hospital bed over there," Ms. Haughf said, waving her hand toward Evanita. "I want you to take a look at what she's been through and what she's going through and tell me—would you ever do anything to hurt her—on purpose?"

"No," said Sheila.

"Do you think she would ever do anything to hurt you?" Ms. Haughf asked.

"Nah, not really. I mean, she gets mad sometimes, but she just runs away. She never attacks me," said Sheila.

Sheila felt a little sad and almost said, "I'm sorry," to Evanita.

"Do you think Evanita could ever hurt anybody?" Ms. Haughf asked.

"Objection," said Manis. "Defense is asking the witness to speculate what the defendant thinks."

"Your Honor, I'm asking the witness what she thinks, not what the witness thinks the defendant thinks," said Ms. Haughf.

"That's exactly what you're asking the witness to do," said Manis. "You've gushied-up the witness with this good-feelingism and worked her up in an emotional state where she's answering subjectively—all this in the guise of her giving facts as the truth."

"The witness appears to be sincere," said The Court to Manis.

"Your Honor, appearances are deceiving. An emotion is rarely a truth," said Manis.

The courtroom broke out in split uproar—the Prosecution side roared in approval, while the Defense side moaned in disappointment.

"Mr. Manis," said The Court. "Are you dealing in absolute facts?"

"Yes, Your Honor," said Manis.

"Then perhaps you care to explain what 'Rarely a truth' is?" The Court asked.

"It's about the same as being rarely a man," said Eva.

The courtroom behind Defense roared in laughter while the Prosecution side fell into distasteful silence.

"I object. An outrage, Your Honor," said Manis.

"Oh dear, look at the time," said The Court. "It's noon. We must wrap up examination of this witness so we can break for lunch. Any objections, Prosecution?"

"No, Your Honor," said Manis, "except you never ruled on my objection."

"Sustained," said The Court. "Any objections from Defense in wrapping up cross-examination?"

"None here, Your Honor," said Ms. Haughf.

"Very good," said The Court. "Please proceed, Ms. Haughf, and after you finish we'll break for lunch."

"Ms. Stout. Were you at the River Wood and Battery factory on October the 30th?" Ms. Haughf asked.

"No, I wasn't," said Sheila.

"Then it's fair to say that since you weren't there, you don't know for a fact what happened," said Ms. Haughf.

"Objection. Defense is drawing a conclusion and leading the witness," said Manis.

"Hmmm, I'll give Defense some latitude provided the witness answers. It's not a far-fetched conclusion, Mr. Manis," said The Court, and Judge Gregory turned to Sheila and said, "You may answer Ms. Haughf as to whether her conclusion is true or not."

"Yeah, it's true. I don't know for a fact what happened to Nee-nee at the factory," said Sheila.

"And since we're not speculating and not asking you to guess what Evanita was thinking when she fired your mother's revolver at the van, can you say—in all factuality—why Evanita fired at the van on September the 29th—the van you were riding?" Ms. Haughf asked.

"In all factuality, no, I don't know why. I wasn't in the car with her. I heard things afterward—" Sheila started.

"But to recite them in court would be hearsay, as Mr. Manis would say, isn't that right Mr. Manis?" Ms. Haughf asked as she turned her head toward Prosecution.

Mr. Manis shot back a scowl.

"No more questions, Your Honor," said Ms. Haughf.

"Wonderful! We'll adjourn for lunch and reconvene at—" started The Court.

"I wish to redirect," said Manis.

"What?" asked The Court. "Now of all times? We're all very hungry, Mr. Manis."

"I'm hungry too. And I wish to clarify my witness's testimony," said Manis.

"You have the right," said The Court. "You may redirect the witness."

"Ms. Stout—take a look at the defendant in the hospital bed. You testified you would never hurt her, isn't that right?" Manis asked.

"Yeah, I'd never hurt her," said Sheila.

"Would she ever hurt you?" Manis asked.

"Objection," said Ms. Haughf. "Prosecution is asking the same question he objected to."

"You're objecting because he objected to the question when you wanted an answer yourself?" The Court asked. "Overruled."

"No, she'd never hurt me," Sheila answered.

"Now based on your conversation with Evanita at the Portland International Raceway, would she ever hurt a boy, or a man?" Manis asked.

"Objection. Prosecution is asking the witness to draw a conclusion for the defendant," said Ms. Haughf.

"You opened the Pandora's box when you asked the witness what the defendant would or wouldn't do," said The Court to Ms. Haughf. "I'm going to give Prosecution a little more latitude—and hopefully we can tidy up examination for lunch. Overruled."

"I think if the boy or man made her feel inferior. She blamed me for being a slave to Davino when I was timing his laps. But I'm not a slave—I'm a good helper. Nee-nee is good about helping me, but not good about helping me help my guy friends," said Sheila.

"Ms. Stout—have you ever had a lesbian relationship with the defendant?" Manis asked.

"Objection! The court is no place for discussing one's sexual orientation!" Ms. Haughf said.

"Your Honor, it's very relevant. Ms. Stout's testimony indicates the defendant would never hurt her, but that the defendant would hurt a male who makes the defendant feel inferior. I'm getting to a point," said Manis.

"Then get to it quickly," said The Court. "My stomach is grumbling. Overruled."

"I won't answer that," said Sheila.

"You must," said The Court, "or you'll be committing perjury."

"What's 'perjury'?" Sheila asked.

"It means I get to treat you as a hostile witness among other things," said Manis. "Request permission from The Court."

"Yes, anything to get this wrapped up for lunch," said The Court.

"You were intimate with Evanita. You called her, 'Nee-nee'. You may or may not have had a lesbian relationship with her—that doesn't matter. Ms. Stout, was Evanita a lesbian?"

"I don't know," said Sheila. "And we never had a lezzy relationship."

"But she became emotionally detached from you when you shifted your emotional bonds to a guy friend. She distanced herself from you at the raceway when she stormed out. She fired at the van when you were inside with Gango and Roberts. And she pushed Greg Applefoot into the factory fire. Why? I'll tell you why. Because the defendant doesn't want men to have an upper hand over women. Greg happened to be on the catwalk when she was. She couldn't handle that. To demonstrate her deluded superiority, she pushed him over the catwalk into the fire. And where does she get that from?" Manis asked rhetorically.

Manis paused to develop tension in the courtroom, but to his surprise, Sheila answered.

"Her mother," said Sheila.

"Hang her!" yelled a guy in the audience on the Prosecution side, referring to Evanita. "No, burn her at the stake," said another. "Wait for her to wake up, and burn her at the stake," said a third.

The courtroom erupted in chaos. People stood and shouted at each other. Everyone was tired, hungry, and irritated by the constant objections and the back and forth rhetoric. Eva misplaced her hand on the diagnostic equipment and accidentally turned on the audio indicators. The equipment cheeped and chirped at Evanita's heart rate and breath rate—and the chirps sounded out more frequently as if Evanita were also agitated by the commotion.

Evanita opened her eyes for a moment and said, "Mama?"

Eva turned around and hugged her daughter. She kissed her on the cheek and said:

"Yes, baby. Mama is here."

Evanita replied that she was cold. Evanita slipped back into her coma just as Judge Gregory got the mayhem under control with repeated gaveling and shouting of, "Order, order!"

"Order in this courtroom!" The Court shouted one final time. "Mr. Manis, are you quite done with your redirect!?"

"Yes, Your Honor. No more questions," said Manis.

"You may step—" started The Court.

"I wish to re-cross," said Ms. Haughf.

"My poor stomach, my poor stomach," said The Court. "Go ahead, Defense. But please be aware of the time. The lunch hour will be over soon!"

"Thank you, Your Honor," said Ms. Haughf. "Ms. Stout, would you say Evanita was like a sister to you?"

"Yes, she is like a sister," said Sheila.

"Then would you say you feel sisterly love for the defendant?" Ms. Haughf asked.

"Yes. We love each other like sisters. We fight like sisters. We make up like sisters," said Sheila.

"Do you have any feelings beyond that—the ones Prosecution asked about being a lesbian?" Ms. Haughf asked.

"No. Never," said Sheila.

"Objection, Your Honor. One female loving another is lesbianism. The witness is confused. I wish to re-redirect after the re-cross," said Manis.

"Your Honor, I understand why Prosecution cannot differentiate between sisterly love and lesbian love. He is, after all, male," said Ms. Haughf.

"Overruled, Mr. Manis," said The Court. "Does anyone have saltines?"

"I have a teething biscuit in my purse," said a woman sitting on the Defense side of the courtroom.

The courtroom laughed.

"I'll take it," said The Court.

The Court Clerk took the biscuit from the woman and passed it to Judge Gregory while Ms. Haughf continued questioning Sheila.

"Your Honor, I object. The Court must remain impartial," said Manis.

"I am impartial, Mr. Manis, but my stomach is not. Now dry up—at least until lunch!" said The Court.

"You were not at the factory, were you Ms. Stout?" Ms. Haughf asked.

"No, I wasn't," said Sheila.

"So Mr. Manis's claims about the defendant while questioning you are really not meant for you to answer, are they?" Ms. Haughf asked.

"No, I shouldn't have said Nee-nee got her attitude about men from her mother," said Sheila.

"How does Evanita feel about boys? Does she have boyfriends?" Ms. Haughf asked.

"Object—" Manis started.

"Shhhhhh!" The Court said to Manis.

"She's careful. Like I said, she doesn't like boys ordering girls around. But if she finds a boy she likes, she's loyal to him," Sheila said.

"Like she's loyal to you?" Ms. Haughf said.

"Yeah. I know she likes Mr. Johnny Pindus. He's special to her," said Sheila.

"Is he in the courtroom today? Could you identify him?" Ms. Haughf asked.

"He's there," said Sheila, pointing to the row behind Evanita's bed.

Johnny Pindus stood up and sat down.

"For the record, the witness has identified Johnny Pindus,
who is male. No further questions."

"We'll adjourn for an hour!" The Court said followed by two
gavel knocks.

CHAPTER 16:

Evanita's Defense

2023 Oct 4, Wed Early am. Jonara's Dream.
2006 Nov 10, Fri Afnoon. Multnomah County Courthouse. Port-
land, Oregon.

Jonara returned to the head of her mother's bed after lunch break.

"All rise. Judge Gregory presiding," said the Court Clerk.

Judge Gregory entered the courtroom and sat down.

"Mr. Manis, your next witness, please," The Court suggested.

"I call Doctor Harris to the stand," said Manis.

Doctor Harris—the same doctor who had promised Evanita would be deported to Mexico—took the witness stand. The Court Clerk placed a Bible before the doctor.

"Please place your left hand on the Bible and raise your right," said the Court Clerk.

Dr. Harris complied.

"Do you swear to tell the truth, the whole truth, and nothing but the truth, so help you God?" the Court Clerk asked.

"I do," said the doctor.

"Please be seated. State your name and spell it for the record," said the Court Clerk.

"Arton Harris, MD. A-R-T-O-N H-A-R-R-I-S. The 'MD' is for Doctor of Medicine," Doctor Harris said.

"You may direct," said The Court.

"Doctor Harris, you're currently an ER surgeon at Vansen Hospital, isn't this so?" Manis asked.

"Yes," said the doctor.

"And you treated the defendant when she arrived in the hospital," Manis continued.

"Yes," Doctor Harris said. "I treated her for first-, second-, and third-degree burns, arsenic poisoning, and lead poisoning. I removed metal spikes from her legs. She had sepsis and was in shock. Yes, I treated her."

"Did you perform any blood tests on the defendant?" Manis asked.

"Yes, I had several blood tests performed," said Doctor Harris.

"What foreign substances did the blood tests reveal?" Manis asked.

"Arsenic, lead, lysergic acid diethylamide, and a high level of the Streptococcus bacterium," said Doctor Harris.

"Did you investigate how the defendant acquired the arsenic and lead?" Manis asked.

"Yes. I took sputum from her lungs. The lab reported a very high level of arsenic and lead. In my professional opinion, Evanita was poisoned by breathing arsenic- and lead-based fumes," the doctor explained.

"Then she inhaled the burning pressure-treated wood at the River Wood and Battery factory," Manis suggested.

"Objection. Prosecution is leading the witness to draw a conclusion," said Ms. Haughf.

"Sustained. Rephrase your question, Mr. Manis," said The Court.

"Could the defendant have been poisoned by inhaling burning pressure-treated wood?" Manis asked the doctor.

"It's possible. It would have to be the older wood before the toxic components were minimized," said Doctor Harris.

"You mentioned something else in her blood—lysergic something or other," said Manis.

"Lysergic acid diethylamide," the doctor clarified. "It's more popularly known as 'LSD'."

"Was there enough LSD in the defendant's system to send her on a *trip*?" Manis asked.

"If you mean to experience the hallucinatory effects of LSD, the answer is 'yes'," the doctor replied.

"Was there LSD in her sputum?" Manis asked.

"No. She did not inhale LSD," said the doctor.

"No more questions," said Manis.

"You may cross," said The Court to Ms. Haughf.

"Doctor Harris," said Ms. Haughf. "When you received the defendant as a patient, how was she?"

"In very bad shape. As I testified, she had multiple-degree burns. Her extremities were edematous, and her legs were badly damaged from impaling metal spikes. Blood pressure low. Delirious. Very serious shape."

"And her clothing—was it also in bad shape?" Ms. Haughf asked.

"Objection. Relevance," said Mr. Manis.

"Your Honor, I'm attempting to determine the defendant's condition as she left the factory, even to the detail of any torn or dirtied clothing," said Ms. Haughf.

"Overruled. But Ms. Haughf, please keep your questions on focus," said The Court.

"Thank you, Your Honor," said Ms. Haughf.

"Her clothes were torn and burned. What's left of them was dirty with factory grease and filth. She had nothing else on her," the doctor explained.

"In the course of treating the defendant, did you make a search of her body and clothes? Did she carry anything else?" Ms. Haughf asked.

"I did search, but there was little to search. Most of her skin layers throughout her body were burned to some extent. This necessitated discarding her contaminated clothes, treating and cleaning her skin, and dressing her in a hospital gown," said the doctor.

"You mentioned the clothing was contaminated, doctor. Did you dispose of it?" Ms. Haughf asked.

"No, I sent it to the lab for testing to determine what surface chemicals entered through her skin," said the doctor.

"Did the lab find any chemicals, and if so—what chemicals did you find?" Ms. Haughf asked.

"Arsenic, lead, industrial oil lubricant, gear grease, benzene, and sulfuric acid," said Doctor Harris.

"Did the lab find LSD on the clothing?" Ms. Haughf asked.

"No, not a trace," the doctor replied.

"Doctor Harris. In what way or ways can LSD be taken?" Ms. Haughf asked.

"LSD is usually ingested by consuming a candy laced with the drug. LSD is very powerful for its size—ingestion can occur by simply licking the candy," the doctor replied.

"Can a person become under the influence of LSD without actually consuming the drug?" Ms. Haughf asked.

"I don't understand. A person would have to take LSD to become under its influence," said the doctor.

"You just said 'take' and not 'ingest'. Are there other ways to acquire LSD without ingestion?" Ms. Haughf asked.

"Injection," said Doctor Harris.

"Are you familiar with Swiss chemist, Albert Hoffman?" Ms. Haughf asked.

"Of course. He's the father of LSD," said Doctor Harris.

"And how did he first 'ingest' LSD?" Ms. Haughf asked.

"He did not 'ingest' it. By accident, he absorbed some through his skin," replied Doctor Harris.

"Then isn't it possible the defendant also absorbed LSD through her skin?" Ms. Haughf asked.

"It's possible," replied the doctor.

"Did you pump the defendant's stomach and test its contents?" Ms. Haughf asked.

"No—neither were performed," said the doctor.

"What part of Hoffman's skin absorbed the LSD?" Ms. Haughf asked.

"His fingertips," replied the doctor.

"Did you examine the defendant's finger tips?" Ms. Haughf asked.

"Yes. They were burned. But her right index finger had a puncture wound—most likely from a needle or pin. I gave Evanita multiple tetanus shots for the multiple puncture wounds she received in her feet, legs, and her index finger," said the doctor.

Ms. Haughf walked over to Evanita's bed and held up the unconscious girl's right index finger.

"Is this the finger you treated?" Ms. Haughf asked. "Step down from the witness stand and take a closer look."

Doctor Harris walked to Evanita's bed and examined her right index finger. He removed a bandage from the finger, looked at the wound, and reattached the bandage. After inspection, he returned to the witness stand.

"Yes. That's the finger. A puncture wound from a needle or pin," said the doctor.

"You testified that Albert Hoffman absorbed LSD through his fingertips. Could Evanita have absorbed LSD through a puncture wound?" Ms. Haughf asked.

"Yes, very easily," said the doctor.

"No further questions," said Ms. Haughf.

"You may call your next witness, Mr. Manis," said The Court.

"No further witnesses at this time. I would like, however, to reserve the right to call additional witnesses after Defense presents its case," said Manis.

"Only a small number of witnesses," said The Court. "Prosecution should present its case upfront and should not employ a 'wait and see' approach."

"I understand, Your Honor. I only intend to call an additional witness or two should any new information come to light during Defense's examination," said Manis.

"Very well. I grant that right. We'll move on to Defense's witnesses. Are you ready, Ms. Haughf?"

"Ready, Your Honor," said Ms. Haughf.

"You may call your first witness, then," The Court said to Ms. Haughf.

"I call Officer Entz to the stand," said Ms. Haughf.

Officer Entz approached from the back of the courtroom where she had been guarding the door. She stood in the witness stand.

"Place your left hand on the Bible and—" started the Court Clerk.

"I'm Jewish," said Entz.

"Oh, another one of you," the Court Clerk said, and he set the Bible aside. "Raise your right hand. Do you swear to tell the truth, the whole truth, and nothing but the truth so help you— Yahweh is it?"

"I do," Entz said. "You can say 'God' instead of 'Yahweh' if you like. 'God' isn't a dirty word."

Loud cheers and applause from the audience. Judge Gregory initially lifted his gavel to strike it against the block, but he paused and allowed the crowd to continue cheering. He waved a hand, and the applause subsided.

"Please be seated. State your name and spell it for the record," the Court Clerk said.

"Officer Ezra Entz. E-Z-R-A E-N-T-Z," said Entz.

"Ms. Entz," started Ms. Haughf. "According to police records, you were the first officer to take the defendant into custody."

"That's correct," said Entz.

"What steps did you take to arrest her?" Ms. Haughf asked.

"Before I arrested her, I noticed the defendant was in shock. I placed her head at the same level as her heart and elevated her legs until the ambulance arrived. I read the defendant her Miranda rights. The defendant did not seem to be aware and kept saying something in Spanish," said Entz.

"Did it sound like, '*La madre de conejo*'?" Ms. Haughf asked.

"Yes, that was part of it," said Entz.

"On what charge or charges did you arrest the defendant?"

"Only one—trespassing on restricted federal property," said Entz.

"Did you search the defendant?" Ms. Haughf asked.

"Yes. I searched the defendant thoroughly—not only to check for illegal items, but also to determine what sort of injuries she sustained. I'm also a trained paramedic."

"I see," said Ms. Haughf. "Did you find any illegal items?"

"Negative."

"No LSD?" Ms. Haughf asked.

"No LSD, no illegal drugs, no weapons, no paraphernalia— nothing."

"Tell us what happened next," said Ms. Haughf. "Did you accompany the defendant to the hospital?"

"The ambulance arrived. The paramedics loaded the defendant onto a gurney and into the ambulance. I followed the ambulance in my cruiser to Vansen Hospital. I watched over the defendant while she was in surgery. Relief arrived, and I returned to the station to follow-up on paperwork," said Entz.

"By 'relief arrived' do you mean another police officer took over watch of the defendant in your place?" Ms. Haughf asked.

"Yes," said Entz.

"When you filled out your paperwork, what charge or charges did you file against the defendant?" Ms. Haughf asked.

"The one I already mentioned—trespassing on restricted federal property," Entz said.

"Did you add other charges later?" Ms. Haughf asked.

"No. Other charges were added later as the investigation proceeded," said Entz.

"And what was your role in the investigation?" Ms. Haughf asked.

"My role was to determine the identity of the defendant. Initial speculation suggested she was a Mexican national. Numerous Latin women showed up purporting to be her mother. Others showed up anyway and offered a home for her until she could heal," Entz said.

"How did you determine the identity of the defendant?" Ms. Haughf asked.

"Through interrogation of Eva Carreña. She produced a panorex of the defendant," said Entz.

"Could you explain to the courtroom what a 'panorex' is?" Ms. Haughf asked.

"It's a panoramic X-ray taken of a patient's teeth. It shows all teeth and the jaw. It's used primarily in dentistry, but we also use it as a forensic tool for identification—particularly when other means are impossible. In Evanita's case, she carried no identification cards, and her face was and still is badly bruised and swollen beyond recognition," said Entz.

"Officer Entz. How were the other charges added to the defendant?" Ms. Haughf asked.

"As I said, they were added as part of the investigation," said Entz.

"And this investigation revealed these charges in what way?" Ms. Haughf asked.

"I'm sorry, I don't understand the—" Entz said.

"There must have been evidence linking the defendant to each of the charges. What was the evidence?" Ms. Haughf asked.

"Objection, Your Honor. Defense is attempting to conduct the entire trial through one witness," said Manis. "Defense has access to all Prosecution evidence linking each charge to the defendant."

"Sustained," said The Court. "Please phrase your questions carefully, Ms. Haughf."

"Officer Entz—did you participate in gathering evidence against the defendant?" Ms. Haughf asked.

"Other than establishing identity of the defendant, no," said Entz.

"You must have worked with other officers in gathering evidence against the defendant, no?" Ms. Haughf asked.

"Yes, I worked with other officers," said Entz.

"How did they come up with their evidence?" Ms. Haughf asked.

"Objection. Could be leading to hearsay," said Manis.

"Your Honor, I am attempting to establish credibility of the evidence against my client," said Ms. Haughf.

"Which proves my earlier objection. Defense is attempting to conduct the entire trial through the witness, and now she's about to engage the witness in hearsay," said Manis.

"Sustained. Ms. Haughf—you cannot pursue this line of questioning with the defendant," said The Court.

"Yes, Your Honor. No more questions," said Ms. Haughf.

"You may cross," The Court said to Manis.

"No questions," said Manis.

"You may step down, Officer Entz," said The Court.

"I call Doctor Zavuski to the stand," said Ms. Haughf.

A well-dressed woman with short hair took the stand.

"Please place your left hand on the Bible and raise your right," said the Court Clerk.

"I don't believe in Bible," said Zavuski with a Russian accent.

The audience gasped. Yells of, "Get rid of the Commy," and "Atheist Ruskie," filtered through the courtroom before Judge Gregory gaveled the courtroom back into order.

"Raise your right hand then. Do you swear to tell the truth, the whole truth, and nothing but the truth, so help you G...so help you?" the Court Clerk asked.

"I affirm," replied Zavuski.

"Please be seated. State your name and spell it for the record," said the Court Clerk.

"Antonina Zavuski, Ph.D. A-N-T-O-N-I-N-A Z-A-V-U-S-K-I. The 'Ph.D.' is Doctorate of Philosophy in Chemistry," said Zavuski.

"Doctor Zavuski, what is your relation to this case?" Ms. Haughf asked.

"I am president of Zavuski Forensic, Incorporated. My company provided independent forensic testing of River Wood and Battery factory after October 30th fire," Zavuski replied.

"Objection. Request *voir dire* on the witness," said Manis.

"You had your chance for *voir dire* during the hearing and declined," said The Court. "I want no unnecessary delays. This is Friday, and I have yet to prepare for my appearance in tomorrow's Veteran's Day parade."

"Your Honor. May I point out that banks and federal buildings are celebrating Veteran's Day today. I move we adjourn for the afternoon and resume on Monday," said Manis.

"I realize the inconvenience of being the only courtroom—probably in the nation—that is convened on a national holiday. I wouldn't have made the special request except I realize the importance of a speedy resolution to this matter. We'll hear the Defense's case this afternoon," said The Court. "Proceed with direct, Ms. Haughf."

"In your analysis of the River Wood and Battery fire, what was the cause of death for Mr. Greg Applefoot?" Ms. Haughf asked.

"Mr. Applefoot burned to death in pit fire of pressure-treated wood," replied Zavuski.

"Can you determine how the fire was started?" Ms. Haughf asked.

"Analysis is unclear as to how fire first started. Metal gasoline can was found in pit with greasy fingerprints belonging to Buford Hamm. Old book of matches was discarded in area near pit with fingerprints matching Mr. Hamm," said Ms. Zavuski.

"Can you identify who placed the pressure-treated wood in the pit?" Ms. Haughf asked.

"*Da.* By gathering fingerprints from partly burned wood, we identified three people who tossed wood into fire—Buford Hamm, Donald Fessel, and Greg Applefoot."

"Did any wood contain fingerprints of the defendant?" Ms. Haughf asked.

"*Nyet.*"

"Did you find the defendant's fingerprints anywhere?" Ms. Haughf asked.

"*Da.* We found them on door handle leading in through old employee entrance. Her fingerprints were on unburnt office furniture and desk drawers. Desk drawers contained push pins and LSD-laced jelly beans. She sat in receptionist lobby area. She also left finger- and kneeprints on floor next to open fire pit," said Zavuski.

"Those prints on the floor—did they leave a trail? Did they have a direction?" Ms. Haughf asked.

"Finger- and kneeprints led to catwalk. Defendant appeared to walk backward along catwalk. Her handprints were on railing up to and leading to point where catwalk opens on one side to pit. Her prints jumped to bottom of catwalk along edge near pit. From there she left prints in pit and along tunnel to outside of building," explained Zavuski.

"Doctor Zavuski—you also took fingerprints of the deceased. First, explain to the courtroom how you were able to identify those prints as belonging to the deceased," said Ms. Haughf.

"Greg's left hand was in good enough condition to take finger- and handprint sample. Rest of his body was too badly burned to be usable, but by using his left hand as reference, we were able to identify his progress through factory floor," said Zavuski.

"And what was that progress?" Ms. Haughf asked.

"Mr. Applefoot left handprints on railing suggesting he walked forward. The prints' positioning and spacing suggest he matched defendant's speed and stride. His prints were also on catwalk edge just over pit, but parts of his prints were covered with particulate residue suggesting explosion forced him to lose grip of catwalk and fall into pit," said Zavuski.

"Did the defendant have the same particulate covering on her prints—the ones where she too was hanging from the catwalk's edge?" Ms. Haughf asked.

"*Nyet.* Her prints were on top of residue. From this we deduce that explosion threw Mr. Applefoot into pit and the defendant onto edge of catwalk," said Zavuski.

"Were there any footprints or other marks suggesting the defendant stepped on or forced Mr. Applefoot's fingers to release their grip on the catwalk while he was swinging over the edge?" Ms. Haughf asked.

"*Nyet,*" Zavuski replied.

"In your opinion, what led to Mr. Greg Applefoot's death?" Ms. Haughf asked.

"Accidental fall from catwalk into burning pit," said Zavuski.

"No further questions," said Ms. Haughf.

"Doctor Zavuski," started Manis. "Take a look at this—Exhibit T100."

Mr. Manis handed Dr. Zavuski a sealed, clear plastic bag with what appeared to be a partially burned oil-soaked tampon.

"And this, Exhibit T101," Manis said, and he handed Zavuski a forensic report.

"Unusual," said Zavuski, looking at the supposed tampon and the forensic report.

"Forensics found this partially burned tampon in the open pit. The chemical analysis shows traces of asbestos, carboxy-methyl cellulose, dioxin, rayon, and cotton soaked in vegetable oil. The same chemicals were found in the pit. You are aware of the ingredients of a tampon, are you not?" Manis asked.

"*Da,*" replied Zavuski.

"And this report agrees with you—this is the flaming tampon that started the fire," said Manis.

The audience behind Prosecution erupted with outrage. The audience behind Defense sat silent with many rolling their eyes.

"*Nyet,*" said Zavuski. "I not agree with report."

"You just said—" started Manis.

"I know ingredients of tampon. Most chemicals listed not belong in modern tampon. Some did at one time, others never," said Zavuski.

"Your Honor, this is why I wanted a *voir dire,*" said Manis.

"Are you objecting to your own question, Mr. Manis?" The Court asked.

"I object to the claim that this is an expert witness," said Manis.

"Overruled. Continue, Mr. Manis."

Manis paced back and forth a few steps—frustrated with Doctor Zavuski's testimony. He'd meant to ask more questions, but they escaped him at the moment. Judge Gregory tapped his fingers on his wooden desk in anticipation of Mr. Manis's cross-examination. Manis walked over to the witness and retrieved the sealed bag and document from her.

"No more questions," said Manis.

"I wish to redirect," said Ms. Haughf.

"Proceed," said The Court.

"Doctor Zavuski, please explain to the courtroom why the chemicals listed by Prosecution could not be from a modern tampon," said Ms. Haughf.

"Carboxy-methyl cellulose was once used in 1980s but was determined to cause toxic shock syndrome. It was withdrawn from market in early 1990s. Dioxin is supposedly by-product of bleaching process used in tampon material, but studies show U.S. manufacturers have no dioxin in their tampons. Rayon—yes—that is component. Cotton also. Asbestos is not and never was component," said Zavuski.

"What does this tell you about the exhibits Prosecution just showed you?" Ms. Haughf asked.

"Not tampon, or tampon contaminated with additional chemicals, or forensic report error," said Zavuski.

"Doctor Zavuski—in your opinion, could Exhibit T100—the supposed tampon soaked in oil—have caused a fire on pressure-treated wood?" Ms. Haughf asked.

"Not in way fire actually started," said Zavuski.

"I don't understand. Could you explain?" Ms. Haughf asked.

"*Da.* First, lighting tampon soaked in oil burn up entire tampon. But exhibit only partly burned. Second, oil burns for little time on isolated piece of wood, but not enough heat energy to start up entire pile of pressure-treated wood. Finally, if initial fire on tampon not completely burn it through, resulting pit fire of pressure-treated lumber burn tampon completely," Zavuski explained.

"No more questions," said Ms. Haughf.

"Do you wish to re-cross, Mr. Manis?" The Court asked.

"No," said Manis.

"You may step down," The Court said to Doctor Zavuski.

"*Spasiba* (Thank you)," said Zavuski to Judge Gregory.

"I call Johnny Pindus to the stand," said Ms. Haughf.

Johnny Pindus took the stand.

"Are you willing to swear on the Holy Bible?" the Court Clerk asked, who was tired of wondering why everyone wouldn't just swear on the Bible and be done with it.

"Yes," Johnny replied.

"Place your left hand on the Bible and raise your right. Do you swear to tell the truth, the whole truth, and nothing but the truth, so help you God?" the Court Clerk asked.

"I do," replied Johnny.

"Please be seated. State your name and spell it for the record," said the Court Clerk.

"Johnny Pindus. J-O-H-N-N-Y P-I-N-D-U-S," he replied.

"Is that your legal name?" The Court asked.

"No. It's what everyone calls me," said Johnny.

"Please state your legal name and spell it for the record," clarified the Court Clerk.

"Johanidan Pindus. J-O-H-A-N-I-D-A-N P-I-N-D-U-S," said Johnny.

"Johnny, you have an amazing ability to see into a person's mind and body and understand what that person is going through, isn't that true?" Ms. Haughf asked.

"I do have a gift like that, yes," said Johnny.

"Is it true you used your gift to understand what happened with Evanita at the River Wood and Battery factory on October the 30th?" Ms. Haughf asked.

"Yes. With my sense of touch, I learned exactly what happened with Evanita that day," said Johnny.

"Objection, Your Honor. Are we going to allow psychic testimony in a court of law?" Manis asked.

"Your Honor," said Ms. Haughf. "Mr. Pindus does indeed have this gift."

"Does he? Prove it. Wait, what am I saying?" said The Court.

"It's not like that. He can't sense what men are doing," said Ms. Haughf.

The audience on the Prosecution side erupted in laughter, including Judge Gregory.

"Oh how convenient," said Manis sarcastically as the laughter died down. "So you rehearse things he should say, is that it? I might have known you'd stoop to such a level. Your Honor, the witness should be charged with perjury."

"The witness hasn't testified anything," said The Court, "so he can't have perjured himself—yet. But Ms. Haughf, I wonder—how do you intend to establish credibility of the witness. Are you placing Mr. Pindus at the level of expert witness?"

"Yes, he's an expert at clairsentience—the ability to sense others through the vibrations of touch," said Ms. Haughf.

"Request *voir dire*," said Manis.

"Granted," said The Court. "But I think I'll keep the jurors here. I don't want to slow things down with leaving, entering, and getting settled all over again."

"Thank you, Your Honor," said Manis.

Mr. Manis turned to Johnny Pindus and asked his first question.

"What is your occupation?" asked Manis.

"I'm between jobs. I was a forklift driver at Willamette Copper and Brass. Next week I'm starting a job as a custodian at Portland Junior Rehab," said Johnny.

"Why did you leave your job at Willamette Copper and Brass?" Manis asked.

"I didn't voluntarily leave. I was let go. I was told my job has been eliminated," said Johnny.

"Was it a personality conflict? Didn't the people like you there?" Manis asked.

"I thought they did. I was only let go when news got out about the trial," said Johnny.

"How did your job as forklift driver or your new job as custodian qualify you as a—what was that name—yes, a clairsentient?" Manis asked.

"It doesn't. It's not something one works to—" Johnny started.

"In your academic career, what research have you performed, what papers have you written in defense of your expertise?" Manis asked.

"I don't have much of an academic career. I was a B student in high school. I graduated with my class. I didn't attend college. And I haven't written academic papers except term papers in high school," said Johnny.

"That would answer my next question—do you have any university degrees?" Manis asked.

"No."

"Do you have a permit in this state—or any state—licensing you to practice clairsentience?" Manis asked.

"No."

"That would mean you have served no time as a certified clairsentient specialist, is that right?" Manis asked.

"I've been a clairsentient most of my life," said Johnny.

"A certified clairsentient. Certified. How long have you been certified by a licensing agency?" Manis asked.

"Not at all. None," said Johnny.

"Have you taught or lectured in your field? Have you conducted tests of clairsentience in an academic setting for peer review?" Manis asked.

"No. No," said Johnny. "But I do tests for people all the time."

"In an academic setting for peer review?" Manis reiterated.

"No. Not in an academic setting. But I have many peers," said Johnny.

"Unbiased academic peers—not friends," said Manis.

"No."

"Are you a member of any clairsentience professional society? Do you have any academic or professional awards or honors in your field?" Manis asked.

"Not a member anywhere. But I get thanks from the people I help," said Johnny.

"Again—academic or professional awards or honors in your field by unbiased peers—not private friends," said Manis.

"No, not unbiased peers," said Johnny.

"Have you acted as a professional consultant to any government agency including law enforcement? As a professional consultant, you would have to be licensed and paid for your services," Manis said.

"No."

"Have you given testimony as an expert clairsentient witness in any court of law prior to today?" Manis asked.

"Yes," said Johnny.

"As an expert clairsentient witness. An expert," said Manis. "That means passing a *voir dire* test. Have you passed a *voir dire* test for an expert clairsentient witness in a court of law? Remember, you are under oath, and any disingenuous answer will be considered an act of perjury."

"Yes, I said yes," said Johnny.

"When? What court? What state?" Manis demanded.

"In the State of Oregon. It was here—in this courtroom. And it was July of 1990," said Johnny.

"What case was that?!" Manis asked. "What case?!"

"Eva Carreña vs. Marcus Cracbern," said Johnny.

"Order, order!" The Court gaveled, but the courtroom was absolutely silent. "*Voir dire* is over."

"Your Honor, Mr. Pindus has answered 'no' to almost all *voir dire* questions. By every measurement standard, he is not an expert," said Manis.

"Except by one standard—precedence," said The Court.

"Your Honor," Ms. Haughf said. "Pursuant to precedence set by Mr. Pindus's testimony as an expert witness in the 1990 court case of Carreña vs. Cracbern, I am tendering Johanidan Pindus as a qualified expert witness in the field of clairsentience."

"Johanidan Pindus is hereby qualified as an expert witness in clairsentience," said The Court. "Ms. Haughf—you may direct."

"Thank you, Your Honor," said Ms. Haughf.

"Of all the outrageous things, Your Honor!" Manis yelled.

"Mr. Manis—if you do not control your temper, I'll have you gagged for the duration of Defense's direct examination of the witness. Do I make myself clear?" The Court asked.

"Yes, Your Honor," said Manis.

"Your Honor," Ms. Haughf said. "Before I start, I would like to perform a demonstration for The Court to verify Mr. Pindus's ability. While it's true Mr. Pindus cannot read the thoughts and physics of a man, he can of women and other life-forms. For this demonstration, I would like The Court to select a female volunteer in this courtroom."

"Very well," said The Court. "Hmmm. It seems the women are all sitting on the Defense side."

"Which I would object to," said Manis. "It would lead to a biased demonstration."

"The Court chooses the Court Reporter. But the demonstration must not interfere with her duties," said The Court.

"Not a problem," said Ms. Haughf. "I will need Mr. Pindus to leave the witness stand temporarily so that he may touch the Court Reporter."

"May I remind the witness that he is still under oath," said The Court.

"Yes sir," said Johnny.

Johnny Pindus left the witness stand and stood next to the Court Reporter. She glanced briefly at him but continued working. Ms. Haughf passed a battery-powered electric toothbrush to Johnny.

"Mr. Pindus will now turn on the electric toothbrush, hold it to the back of his neck with one hand, and touch the Court Reporter on the shoulder with the other," explained Ms. Haughf.

Johnny did as Ms. Haughf explained—he turned on the electric toothbrush and held it to his neck with his left hand while placing his right hand on the Court Reporter's shoulder.

"I would ask the Court Reporter to think of something said between her and The Court that no one else knows—a conversation or something. Johnny will attempt to read those thoughts from the Court Reporter," said Ms. Haughf. "Johnny, what do you sense?"

"Chording letters for words," said Johnny. "Punching keys. Chording, chord-ing."

"Focus, Johnny," said Ms. Haughf. "Go beyond the stenography machine."

"Lunch. Chicken salad with ranch dressing and iced tea. The dressing was bland. Oh well, it was fat-free," Johnny said.

The Court Reporter smiled.

"Your Honor," said Manis. "Anyone could have seen what the Court Reporter had for lunch."

"Mr. Manis—shush," said The Court.

"These high-heeled shoes are killing me. I just bought them last week. I have blisters on my feet," continued Johnny. "Crap, I have a run in my nylons."

The Court Reporter smacked Johnny in the chest.

"Focus, Johnny. What did the Court Reporter hear? What did she hear today—outside of the courtroom?" Ms. Haughf asked.

"I need better earrings," Johnny said, speaking for the Court Reporter's thoughts. "These nickel-plated things are irritating my skin. Need gold, need gold," said Johnny. "Money. The judge promises I'll receive overtime and holiday pay for today. What was he complaining about? Yeah, the security at the door made him throw away his fingernail clippers before entering the building this morning—could be used as a weapon. I told him he shouldn't clip his nails at work—it's rude. He said only his wife is allowed to speak to him like that, that she says the same thing to him. I said she's right, and he should clip his nails at home. He says he doesn't have time with the yard work he's always doing. What, she has you doing her flower garden again? The season is over. Yes, the squirrels dug up everything. You should have used that red pepper like she said—don't you listen to your wife?"

"Order," said The Court. "That will be quite enough."

The Court Reporter blushed. Judge Gregory seemed annoyed as if no one should know what goes on between himself and his wife.

"Your Honor—is it true about the yard work?" Manis asked.

"The Court knows what was said outside the courtroom. The demonstration is over. Please move on with direct, Ms. Haughf," said The Court.

"Johnny, did you exercise your clairsentient gift with Evanita at Vansen Hospital?" Ms. Haughf asked.

"Yes," he replied.

"Did you learn what happened at the River Wood and Battery factory?" Ms. Haughf asked.

"Yes, I learned everything she did," he replied.

"Let's go through the charges one by one, beginning with the van chase of September the 29th. Did Evanita discharge a firearm without a permit?" Ms. Haughf asked.

"Yes. In Officer Sharon Stout's car, Evanita fired Sharon's Smith and Wesson revolver," said Johnny.

"Did she discharge the weapon in a public thoroughfare?"

"Yes. She was on Interstate 5 at the time."

"Did she fire the weapon with intent to kill?" Ms. Haughf asked.

"No. She was aiming at the left rear tire and missed. The revolver kicked up, bounced off the top of the window frame, and fell onto the interstate," Johnny replied.

"Let's move on to the River Wood and Battery fire of October 30th," Ms. Haughf said. "Did Evanita burn arsenic- and lead-filled pressure-treated wood?"

"No. When she entered the factory, the wood was already burning in the pit. She did not add any wood to the fire," said Johnny.

"That would answer the next charge—did she start the fire?"

"No."

"Did she possess LSD?" Ms. Haughf asked.

"No. She didn't use it either—not on purpose. She was rummaging through a desk drawer in the old office area. Her finger got pricked with a pushpin. Without knowing, she touched a jelly bean with LSD on it. She started feeling the effects when she left the office and entered the main factory area," Johnny explained.

"Did Evanita plan and kill Greg Applefoot?" Ms. Haughf asked.

"No. Her senses were distorted. The boys called her 'Mother Bunny' and convinced her to hop around the floor like a rabbit. They pretended to feed her carrots. Vinay got mad and swung a stick around at the boys—Skins, Beef, Doofus, and Fat One. Evanita tried escaping across the catwalk. Skins, Beef, and Doofus kept Vinay busy. Fat One followed Evanita. Josh kept setting off cartridges in the press. It was like thunder. Fat One attacked her. She defended herself by kicking him. He fell over the side but held onto the edge. Josh fired more cartridges, and there was an explosion. It threw Fat One into the burning pit. It threw Evanita over the edge, and she was hanging. Skins, Beef, Doofus, Vinay, and Josh ran away without helping Evanita or Fat One. Another explosion sent Evanita into the burning pit. Evanita bounced off Fat One—his blubber cushioned her fall and saved her life. His body created a temporary thermal insulator that reduced how much she burned. She crawled through a scrap tunnel from the burning pit. The scrap tunnel ran under the stamping presses and was filled with metal scraps and dirty oil. The scrap tunnel led to a bin outside the building. The bin had built-in rungs on the side. Evanita climbed down those and crawled away until she was far enough from the fire. Officer Entz found her. She remembered nothing more until she woke up in the hospital. I was there. So was Ms. Zyla. She felt cold, almost dead. She slipped into a coma. That's all of it."

"Thank you Johnny. No more questions. You may step down," said Ms. Haughf.

"Objection," said Mr. Manis.

"Yes, now what is your objection?" said The Court.

"Defense is presuming to be The Court. She has given the witness permission to step down," said Manis.

"Sustained. Mr. Manis, do you wish to cross?" asked The Court.

"Most assuredly," said Manis. "First, I wish to add some new-found evidence to the trial."

"Objection," said Ms. Haughf. "Prosecution cannot introduce evidence without first sharing it with Defense."

"What is the nature of this evidence?" The Court asked.

"I have an audiotaped confession of the murder—by the defendant herself," said Manis.

The audience groaned, murmured, and carried on. "This is the final nail in her coffin," said one. "She'll get the death penalty for this," said another.

"Order," said The Court.

"I object again, Your Honor. Use of audiotapes of anyone without their knowledge is against the law," said Ms. Haughf. "I submit his audiotape is illegal and should be seized. The person making the tape should be prosecuted."

"Hmmm, it is a bit of a quandary," said The Court. "And it's 3:30 pm already."

"Your Honor. Prosecution tolerated the parapsychological testimony of Mr. Johanidan Pindus, which could be considered a form of hearsay. I request Prosecution be given the latitude to submit factual audio using proven science of the tape recorder," said Manis.

"I'll give you that latitude," said The Court. "Objections from Defense overruled. The evidence will be entered at this time as Exhibit A10."

"Thank you, Your Honor. And now I would like to play the tape for the courtroom," said Manis.

"Proceed, Mr. Manis," said The Court.

Mr. Manis rewound the tape and selected the "Play" button. The recorder's speaker carried the voices of Ms. Zyla, Johnny, and Evanita throughout the courtroom:

Zyla:	"Evanita?"
Evanita:	"Father?"
Johnny:	"It's Evanita. I recognize her voice."
Evanita:	"Father, is that you?"
Johnny:	"I'm Johnny Pindus, remember me?"
Evanita:	"Johnny? Johnny! You're here!"
Johnny:	"I'm here, Evanita."
Evanita:	"I don't know what happened. I just went for a run, and now I'm here."
Johnny:	"I know."
Evanita:	"I...I..."
Johnny:	"You've been through hell. No, you've been in Hell. I know about jogging through Forest Park. I know about the River Wood and Battery factory and the pictures you drew. And I know about the fire pit, the press, the bullets firing, and how the factory caught fire. I know you nearly died and how you escaped. I know, Evanita, I know."
Evanita:	"Johnny. I want to give up. I can't live like this. Look at me—I'm a mess."
Johnny:	"You must live. There is a spirit in you that won't die."
Evanita:	"I can't, Johnny. Not after what happened in the factory. I think someone died because of me."
Johnny:	"No, you didn't kill him. It was an accident. Everything was an accident."
Evanita:	"I'm ugly. Look at me, Johnny. I'm ugly on the outside and the inside. I can't live with this guilt. Johnny, do you know what I'm feeling?"

Johnny: "Yes, I do. I know."

Evanita: "It won't go away. It's getting worse. There's no
way out."

Zyla: "Hold on to life, Evanita, hold on! You are not to
blame!"

Evanita: "It's getting dark in here."

Johnny: "Evanita?"

Evanita: "Father? Father?"

Mr. Manis turned off the tape recorder. The courtroom fell
silent. Most of the jurors who listened to the tape had stared at
Evanita's comatose body and imagined a sweet, innocent girl
speaking to the courtroom. It left a stain of sadness in the air,
that a young girl was reaching the end of things, and this was
her goodbye message. Ms. Haughf forced herself to hold a grim
expression, but the women sitting behind were sniffling and
crying as quietly as they could. Eva bit her hand and tried to
remain calm, but her limbs shook, and she could not contain
herself. She stood up, hugged Evanita, and cried:

"Don't leave me, my baby! Don't let go of life! You can't leave
your mother on this earth all alone. Don't go, baby child! Don't
go!"

Eva carried on and wailed like this. The Court Clerk and a
bailiff took Eva by the shoulders and escorted her out of the
courtroom. Eva had finally snapped.

"Mr. Manis, I take it you have a good reason for presenting
this audiotape?" The Court asked.

"Yes, Your Honor. I intend to cross-examine the witness
based on this audio confession," said Manis.

"Objection. There's no confession on the tape," said Ms.
Haughf.

"Oh but there is. If you'll permit me to continue," said Manis.

"Overruled. Continue, Mr. Manis, but please be brief. The
weekend is nearly here, and the Veteran's Day parade is tomorrow," said The Court.

"Mr. Pindus. Mr. Pindus!" Manis yelled to Johnny.

Johnny had sunk his head into his palms and quivered. Manis took hold of one arm and shook him.

"You are still under oath. Pay attention and answer the question—unless you wish to be considered a hostile witness," said Manis.

"No, I'm not hostile," said Johnny.

"Good. What did Evanita mean by the statement, 'I think someone died because of me'?" Manis asked.

"She was referring to Fat One," said Johnny. "She blamed herself for his death."

"By 'Fat One' you mean 'Greg Applefoot'—is that correct?" Manis asked.

"Yes. But she was not thinking straight," said Johnny.

"That's not what I asked. You testified that she kicked him over the edge, isn't that so?" Manis asked.

"Not quite. She—" Johnny started.

"Isn't it true that she blames herself for his death because of that action—because she kicked him over the edge?" Manis asked.

Manis looked over toward Ms. Haughf and expected her to object, but she didn't. Johnny paused a moment before answering.

"Yes, that's why she blames herself. She believes she kicked him over the edge. But he hadn't completely fallen yet," Johnny tried to point out. "She didn't really kick him over the edge."

"Your Honor, it's clear from the audiotape and the witness's testimony that the defendant killed Greg Applefoot. I submit you end the trial now and pronounce sentence," said Manis.

"Objection. The Court will decide—" Ms. Haughf started.

"Sustained. Yes, The Court will decide on the proceedings of The Court. Mr. Manis, are you finished with cross-examination? It sounds to me like you're jumping into your closing statement," said The Court.

"No more questions, Your Honor."

"Ms. Haughf. Do you have any additional witnesses?" The Court asked.

"No," said Ms. Haughf.

"You did reserve the right to recall some witnesses. Do you wish to recall them now?" The Court asked.

"No, Your Honor. The Defense rests."

"Mr. Manis—did you wish to recall any witnesses?" The Court asked.

"Not at this time. Prosecution rests."

"Very good. We'll hear closing arguments," said The Court.

Jonara walked around the courtroom and stared at the various people while Mr. Manis gave his closing argument. He focused on the 'Modern Eve' and how Evanita had lured the boys into the factory, tempted them with fire, and lured Greg Applefoot to his death. Manis blamed Evanita for planting LSD, suggesting she had been to the factory before and used it to manipulate the boys. He labeled her an unstable, emotional juvenile, who ran off when irritated, fired guns at boys, and all-in-all hated men for being men.

Jonara walked back to her mother's bedside and tried holding her hand, but her own hand passed through her mother's. Ms. Haughf gave her closing argument by showing how Prosecution's evidence was flawed and how Defense's evidence was coherent. She listed and structured the evidence in a way that showed how Evanita was adventurous at times, did not do drugs to escape but instead did healthy exercise in the form of jogging, how she was helpful to law enforcement personnel by attempting to disable the fleeing van, and how she acted in self defense when Greg forced himself on her.

"At this time, I wish to thank everyone in the courtroom for their patience and good-faith efforts to bring this trial to a speedy conclusion," said The Court. "I won't keep you much longer. And on that matter, I won't keep the Jury here today. The Jury is to report here Monday morning to deliberate on the charges brought against the defendant. On Tuesday we will all reconvene here for the verdict and sentencing. I want to wish everyone a happy Veteran's Day, and I hope to see you at the parade tomorrow. Court adjourned."

CHAPTER 17

Veteran's Day

2023 Oct 4, Wed Early am. Jonara's Dream.
2006 Nov 11, Sat. Veteran's Day Celebrated. Portland, Oregon.

Eva's House.

Just after daybreak on Saturday the 11th of November, Eva jogged from her house into the woods along the same path her own daughter had taken on October the 30th. Eva reached the same EPA warning sign her own daughter had ignored, but unlike her daughter, Eva did not trespass. She stared at the charred factory building from a distance and wondered how things had gone so terribly wrong. She grounded her daughter, yes, but apparently that wasn't enough.

"A mother should lock her teenage daughter in a room until she's old enough to make good decisions," Eva blurted while staring at the EPA sign, but she realized it was a crazy thing to say. "All she had to do was turn around and return home, like this."

With that, Eva put the sign and factory to her back and returned along the trail until she reached home. She would have welcomed the outdoor air and natural environment—trees, birds, and long early-morning shadows tickling the ground. But her jog was for a different reason—it was a form of compulsion—a rehashing of recent events in an active way. Too long had Eva sat alone at home in the evening while her daughter remained comatose in the hospital. Eva had initially spent every evening with her daughter at the hospital—talking to her and holding her hand in hopes of pulling her back to consciousness and the land of the living. But it was futile. Sure, a mother doesn't give up on her daughter, but Eva was exhausted. It wasn't the time or effort she spent in just sitting next to her daughter—it was the emotional and analytical gears that kept churning at lightning speed—a crisis mode that Eva knew had to be resolved quickly.

Yet Eva could not resolve it quickly, and it frustrated her. She could not stop her brooding, her searching and thinking of what should have been done, what could be done, and everything in between. A mother doesn't stop going over the facts and emotions of the past, present, and hopeful future until her daughter is safe and well. It was a power that Eva hadn't anticipated, but the power held her hostage. She loved her daughter, yes, but why did she have to deal with the painful side of love too?

It was with some relief that Johnny Pindus visited Evanita in the evenings, though Eva had some hesitations. She knew Johnny since he first sought treatment from her in 1989—back when she first moved to Portland from Corpus Christi, Texas. But now he was a man, and Eva had strong suspicions of men no matter what their personalities. It was an analytical problem Eva knew too well and wished she didn't rehash in her brain as often as she did—given a certain set of environmental parameters, a man will violate a woman. Could Eva set aside the analysis—could she deceive her own brain or at least distract it long enough to "trust" Johnny that he could be a friend to her daughter without hurting her? Eva wished life were that fair, that honest, and she hated how honesty made her see ugly realities of life.

"I need a shower," said Eva.

Eva took her shower—a long hot one, and she alternated between holding her face and the back of her neck under the shower head. There was something therapeutic about a shower with hot water massaging her tense facial muscles. She was thankful she didn't have to rely on the hot shower as some did with migraine headaches. Still, she understood the power of the shower, and she embraced its soothing strands of water while she contemplated what to do with herself for the day. The week had been long in preparation with her daughter's trial, and she didn't know how she'd recover quickly enough over the weekend to face the verdict on Tuesday.

"I'm not as young as I used to be. How I wish I had the energy of Evanita with the experience of my own years," Eva said.

There was never a worry about running out of hot water in the shower. When Evanita started taking long, hot showers (resulting in a sudden change from a hot to cold shower as the hot water ran out), Eva had her hot water heater replaced with a tankless water heater. The new heater never ran out of hot water. It was a certain freedom Eva wished she could enjoy in other parts of her life.

But reality set in, and Eva knew she had to drag herself out of her comfortable shower. She turned off the water, toweled off, and threw on some clothes. She knew it was time to eat something but couldn't decide what to do for breakfast. Should she eat yogurt? No, she'd been having yogurt every morning all week. What about going out for breakfast—some eggs and bacon? No, too heavy with the grease.

"I'll make something," she said.

Eva retrieved some vegetables and fruits from the refrigerator—celery, tomatoes, carrots, an apple, and a pickle. She also selected a banana from the countertop and proceeded to make some sort of breakfast salad. Eva placed the celery on a chopping board and diced it easily with a large knife. She tossed the celery in a bowl and moved on to a tomato. Here she could not so quickly chop the tomato as she did with the celery. The tomato required her to hold it steady with one hand while slicing it with the other. Her hands held steady at first, but as she drew the blade against the tomato's skin, her hands shook. They trembled—for the first time in Eva's life, her hands trembled when she was about to apply a steel instrument against the skin of a life-form. It was unheard of—she had gone through med school, dental school, and serviced countless teeth with the smoothest of touch—as smooth as her ballet dancing. But now in this strange moment of dread—a weekend that felt more like the eye of a hurricane than anything else—she could not hold her hands steady.

Frustrated, she set the knife aside, took a frying pan, and beat the tomato to its pulp. The pulp splattered ninety degrees from the motion of the frying pan—sending it laterally across the countertop in all directions, including onto Eva's shirt.

"What a mess I'm making!" said Eva.

The doorbell rang. Eva rolled her eyes and said, "The doorbell never rings at a good time."

Eva answered the door.

"Zellie," said Eva.

"Oh, did I catch you at a bad time?" Ms. Zyla asked on seeing Eva's stained shirt.

"Come on in. I was trying to make breakfast, but I ended up making a mess. Can I get you anything?" Eva asked as Ms. Zyla entered Eva's house.

"Is it safe?" Ms. Zyla joked. "Sorry, I was being funny."

"Well don't. I don't know how much more of this I can take," Eva said.

Eva returned to the kitchen where she cleaned up the tomato mess. Ms. Zyla followed. Instead of returning the vegetables to the refrigerator, Eva simply threw them all into the garbage can.

"Did the vegetables do something wrong? Are they spoiled?" Ms. Zyla said.

"Yes. No. Something is spoiled. It's not the vegetables," said Eva.

"Then why throw away good food?" Ms. Zyla asked.

"I need to throw something away. I need to get rid of this tension that's been eating at me this past week, a tension that will rear itself on me Tuesday morning when the verdict is read," said Eva.

"Oh that," said Ms. Zyla as if it weren't much.

"Oh that! Yes. Is there anything else? What else could there be? Things can't get much worse. A daughter on the edge of death, a trial of men who don't give a crap. An all-male jury. I don't have to guess what they'll decide—it's pretty obvious," said Eva.

"Come come now, Eva. You're beating yourself up too much," said Ms. Zyla.

"Others beat me up. What can I do?" Eva asked, though she didn't expect an answer.

"I'm glad you asked," said Ms. Zyla.

"I didn't really ask you, I was just—" Eva started.

"Of course you were," said Ms. Zyla. "And I have the answer. I'm a mentor, remember? Anyway—you're hungry for breakfast, right? So am I. That's why I'm here—to invite you out to breakfast. What do you say?"

"Hmmm. I was hoping just to get something here and rest a bit," said Eva.

"You mean brood. Anyway, we can see what luck you're having with homemade breakfast. Take a load off your shoulders and let someone else make breakfast for you," said Ms. Zyla.

"Someone else. Yeah," Eva said sarcastically.

"Let a man make breakfast for you," said Ms. Zyla.

Eva's eyes opened with brief excitement at the thought of seeing a man being subservient to her, but she suppressed her excitement.

"Who's to say he won't make it badly and give me indigestion?" asked Eva.

"Who's to say you won't enjoy yourself at the sight of a man working to please you? People need to enjoy themselves once in a while," said Ms. Zyla.

"Not me. Not until my baby is safe," said Eva.

"Eva. I've known you a long time—since you came up here to Portland from Corpus Christi early in your career. You get into these destructive ruts by obsessing too much about things you cannot change for the moment. So I'm here to change the moment. Let's get something to eat. I know the perfect place," said Ms. Zyla.

"Uh oh, not again. I remember the last place you took us to—Cerossi Café," said Eva.

"What was wrong with Cerossi?" Ms. Zyla asked. "Didn't you like it? Oh maybe it was a little strong for your first visit, but given enough time, you'd learn to enjoy it. But forget Cerossi for the moment. The place I propose is a little Japanese restaurant in Hollywood—you know, off of I-84 just a little east from here."

"Hollywood?" Eva asked.

"Not the one in California," said Ms. Zyla.

"Hollywood. The Veteran's Day parade. You're trying to sneak me into that," said Eva.

"I can't get anything past you now-a-days, can I? No, I'm not trying to 'sneak' you into the parade. Just close enough to watch it," said Ms. Zyla.

"And watch Judge Gregory and all his male courtroom pals bask in the glory of old men marching who can't fit in their juvenile war uniforms anymore. Tanks and guns and flags—"

"And high school bands, baton twirlers, clowns, the Girl Scouts, and something you can appreciate—bagpipes," said Ms. Zyla.

"I don't play the bagpipes," said Eva, trying to distance herself.

"But you once knew someone who did. Someone very special," said Ms. Zyla.

"Don't bring her up. I won't have anyone tarnish her name," said Eva.

"I mean no disrespect," said Ms. Zyla.

"But others might. It's best I keep her in my private memory," said Eva.

"You have to tell Evanita about her sometime," said Ms. Zyla.

"Now it's too late, isn't it? My daughter is in a coma and may never come out. I'll never get to tell her about Roberta," said Eva.

Eva slapped a hand over her mouth when she realized she'd let Roberta's name slip out into the open air. The name was very sacred to Eva—as if uttering "Jesus Christ" or "God the Almighty". Eva's hand shook over her mouth. Ms. Zyla removed Eva's hand, placed a finger over Eva's lips, removed the finger and placed the same finger over her own lips as if to say:

"My lips are hushed just as yours wish to be."

"I will always be your confidant, Eva Carreña," said Ms. Zyla. "Let's talk more. The restaurant is waiting. I've already phoned ahead. We have a special reservation at an umbrella table outside next to the sidewalk. We can have breakfast and enjoy the day. And if you want to sit with your back to the parade, that's fine too. I hear Mr. Enoki has an excellent wine list—rice wine, plum wine, and a special import based on the Muscat Bailey A grape."

"Some say the Muscat Bailey A grape can make red wine as full as wine from Bordeaux. I wonder if it's true," said Eva.

"You'll have to find out. Let's go," said Ms. Zyla.

Ms. Zyla drove east from Eva's house to the Japanese restaurant. She could not take Sandy Boulevard as it was closed off for the parade. Ms. Zyla meandered around side streets until she arrived at 4802 Sandy Boulevard—Enokidake Restaurant. An elderly Japanese man pointed and gave instructions to a younger Japanese man who was dressed in a restaurant uniform—apparently an employee. Ms. Zyla parked, and the two exited her car and walked toward the restaurant.

"The parking—do not let other people park. Only customers park here," said the elderly man.

"Mr. Enoki," Ms. Zyla said to the elderly man.

"Ah, Miss Beverly," said Mr. Enoki. "And who is this lovely young girl?"

Eva blushed at being called a "young girl".

"This is Eva Carreña. Eva, this is Mr. Hiri Enoki," said Ms. Zyla.

"A pleasure to meet you," said Eva.

"The honor is mine, Miss Eva. Please come this way. I have your table ready," said Mr. Enoki.

Mr. Enoki led Eva and Ms. Zyla to a round table alongside and outside of the building. The table had a large beach umbrella sprouting from the middle, which gave Ms. Zyla and Eva shade from the sun, though in November there was no concern about getting too hot.

"It's warmer that I expected today," said Eva. "And the wind is calm."

"An excellent day to be outside," said Ms. Zyla.

A waiter placed two paper mats on the table—one for Eva and one for Ms. Zyla—along with napkins, sets of fork-knife-spoon, and chopsticks.

"I am Harry Enoki," said the young Japanese man of maybe twenty-something years. "I will be your waiter today. Would you like some green tea?"

"Yes please," said Ms. Zyla.

"I'll have some too," said Eva. "Are you related to—"

"Great-Grandfather Hiri owns the restaurant, yes," Harry said.

Harry poured green tea for both Ms. Zyla and Eva.

"Our miso soup is excellent. Our noodles, rice, and mushrooms are also excellent," Harry Enoki said.

"I expect you would have mushrooms—the restaurant is named after a mushroom, isn't it?" asked Eva.

"Yes. 'Enokidake' is a mushroom. Great-Grandpa thought it was clever, I guess—mixing the family name with a mushroom. But the food is good—I eat here all the time with my girlfriend," said Harry Enoki.

"I imagine you would," said Ms. Zyla. "I'll have some miso soup, some noodles, and—oh dear, I'm losing my memory, what is it called? A fruit and vegetable bowl."

"I know what you mean, Ms. Zyla," said Harry. "And you?" Harry asked Eva.

"I'll have the same. Also, I would like a glass of wine. What do you have for a wine list?" Eva asked.

"We have *saké*—that's a rice wine. We also have a wine made from plums, and a special wine Great-Grandpa makes himself at the micro-vineyard—it's—" Harry started.

"The Muscat Bailey A wine?" Eva asked. "I'll take that."

"—based on a grape—yes—how did you know? It's very good," said Harry Enoki. "I'll have your food out in a bit. In the meantime, here are some pencils if you care to solve the cryptograms on the place mats."

"Thank you," said Ms. Zyla, taking the pencils.

"This is an odd place for a restaurant," said Eva. "It's a block away from two gas stations, a fast-food chicken place, and a funeral home."

"And across the street from a Chinese Restaurant," said Ms. Zyla. "Not that unusual."

The women took sips of green tea from their glasses. Both returned expressions of satisfaction.

"It's good green tea," said Eva.

"The parade is starting," said Ms. Zyla. "They'll be marching down this way soon. Look at the people lined up on both sides of Sandy Boulevard. I remember my mother telling me about the parades they watched in the late 1930s. They would hold an arm up in the air to salute the people in the parade. What did they call it? A 'something' salute."

"A Bellamy salute," said Eva. "But the Nazis turned it into a pejorative gesture. And you're going to say that's why no one salutes like that in the U.S. anymore."

"Yes, I was going to say that. How did you know?" Ms. Zyla asked.

"Geneva—my mother," Eva said. "She spent my childhood lecturing me about all the different dictatorships. Well, what could I do? She was so obsessed with telling me about the Franco regime that I'd do anything to get her talking about something else. Guess one dictatorship wasn't enough—she went on about the Nazis, about Latin America—you name it, she knew about it. And yes, she knew about the Japanese Empire, at least before it crumpled in the 40s. Anyway, let's not talk about that."

"Here you are—miso soup, noodles, and vegetable bowls. And here is your wine," Harry said. He placed the food on the table and asked, "Is there anything else I can get for you?"

Both women indicated, "No."

"Most towns start the holiday at 11 am," said Ms. Zyla. "We like to start here at 9:45, but it takes a little while for them to reach the end of the parade route, which is where we are. See? It's 10 o'clock, and they're already arriving."

The parade led with a color guard—men in blue uniforms carrying the American flag—followed by the first wave of veterans.

"Old men in old uniforms recapturing the good old days," said Eva sarcastically.

"You don't really mean that," said Ms. Zyla. "There aren't many of them left—the World War II vets, at least. There are other ones from Korea and Vietnam, and of course the newer ones from the Gulf, Afghan, and Iraqi wars."

Eva ate her noodles and sipped her miso soup. Young white teenage boys ran around throwing water balloons at one another. One threw a balloon at the Enokidake Restaurant and yelled:

"Go home, nine-iron."

Hiri Enoki ran out the front door and chased the youth down.

Eva was amazed at how quickly the eighty-plus man could travel on foot. He didn't seem to need the cane—instead, he carried it like a weapon. Hiri caught the youth and put him in a hold, wrapping the cane behind the youth's back and upper arms to restrain him. The other teenage boys laughed at the subdued youth and teased him to no end—that he was weaker than an old Japanese man.

"Go on, get lost!" he said at last, releasing the youth from the cane.

The boy ran off without looking back. The other teenage boys stood for a moment making fake Japanese sounds as if they were challenging Mr. Enoki to a fight, but he stepped up to one youth, tapped the cane sharply on the boy's body in key spots, and caused immediate pain in multiple places. Outwitted, the boys ran off.

Mr. Enoki hobbled back on his cane, re-becoming the tired old man the years had prescribed on him. He sat on a bench close to Ms. Zyla and Eva and watched over the exterior of his restaurant like an old guard dog.

"That was impressive," said Ms. Zyla.

"Oh, I'm not as fast as I used to be," said Mr. Enoki. "But youth today are so immature—they don't learn survival skills as they should."

Two high school bands followed along the parade route and played patriotic military songs. Mr. Enoki waved at the group.

"I watch them every year," said Mr. Enoki, referring to the parade. "And I enjoy them just as much as the first time."

"What first time?" Eva asked.

"When I came over to this country, a long time ago. Back in '47, I think. Yes, 1947," Mr. Enoki said.

A high school's JROTC group followed next, attired in their dress uniforms.

"I remember when I was their age too," Enoki said. "A good soldier. The best. And loyal to my country during the War."

"Mr. Enoki," said Eva.

"Please, Miss Eva, call me Hiri," Enoki said.

"All right, Hiri. When you say, 'the War', do you mean World War II?"

"Yes. Everyone calls it the War. Everyone used to," said Enoki.

"Just what side did you fight on, if you didn't come over here until 1947?" Eva asked.

"The Japanese. I was a Zero pilot," he said with an expression of shame on his face.

"That was long ago," said Ms. Zyla. "People are different today."

"No, they still remember," he said, pointing to more veterans walking along the parade route. "They are thinking about their comrades who died in the war. So do I. But I do not hate Americans—that's why I came here—to make up for my part in the war."

"And you've done very well. Your food is excellent," said Ms. Zyla.

Eva rearranged her dishes to begin eating from her vegetable bowl. In doing so, she noticed enciphered words.

"These are unusual placemats," said Eva. "There's a cryptogram here—CFKUT NMLMJIF'A ADV. What does it mean?"

"Happy Veteran's Day," said Enoki. "At the bottom is the method for deciphering the code. That one is called the 'Shawnee' Cipher, after a boy who sent it to me about fifteen years ago. His name was Shawnee Pindus."

"You mean Johnny Pindus?" Eva asked.

"Yes, Shawnee Pindus," Enoki agreed.

"Small world. I didn't know you knew him," said Eva.

"He used to play around here years ago," Mr. Enoki said. "Look at the bottom—you will see the method he used. It is a shift cipher, like Caesar used. But Shawnee changed it—he used the length of the word to determine how many characters of the alphabet to shift. A three-letter word would mean to shift each character of the word three positions in the alphabet. And he added a twist. Each word has its letters marked as odd or even depending on its position counting from the left. An odd-positioned letter would have a subtraction shift, but an even-positioned letter would have an addition shift."

"Sounds like something Johnny would do," said Eva. "He always likes puzzles. Did he use these circles and letters to help him encipher it?"

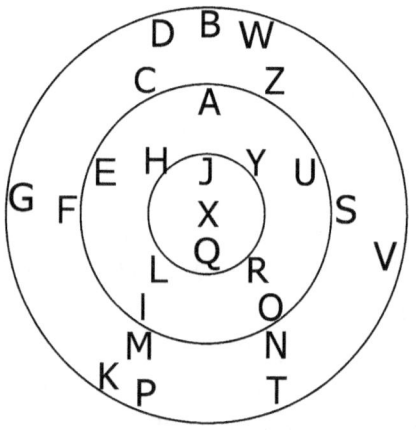

"No," said Mr. Enoki. "That is a cipher circle by Valiwa. His sister made that."

"You mean Valeria Pindus?" Eva asked. "I didn't know she made cryptograms."

"Oh she was very clever," said Enoki. "Very clever. Look at her cipher for 'Happy Veteran's Day'—it looks a little like a real language."

"Laddh Vuturoz'c Por," said Eva. "It's almost pronounce-able."

"Those two would send me ciphers and ask me to solve them. I always knew Shawnee was sending me a cipher message. But when Valiwa sent me this cipher, I thought it was a European language, and I didn't know which one. Then she felt sorry for me and showed me the diagram."

"How does the Valeria Circle work?" Eva asked.

"She uses a shift cipher, like Shawnee. Also like Shawnee, she uses the word length to determine how many letters to shift. But Shawnee used the same alphabet list for doing all shifts. Valiwa would look at the letter in the word, match it to one of the circles, and count along the circle counterclockwise by the number of letters in the word. There are six groups of letters, so there are six circles, but only three circle lines are shown. The center circle is 'X' and does not change. The next circle is 'J' and 'Q'. The next is 'H', 'Y', 'R', and 'L'. So for example, in the word 'Happy', the word length is five. To encipher the first letter 'H', she would count five times counterclockwise around the circle—'L', 'R', 'Y', 'H', and 'L'."

"Later, she invented a better cipher with a key, but I never printed it. The key would be the word lengths of all words in the sentence. For 'Happy Veteran's Day' the key length would be three—583—and she would shift letters based on the key—'H' in 'Happy' would shift 5 places, 'a' would shift 8 places, and 'p' would shift 3 places, then the key would repeat—the next 'p' would shift 5 places, and the 'y' would shift 8. Using this key, 'Happy Veteran's Day' would be 'Lowdy Detuyoc'n Doh'."

"It sounds complicated," said Eva.

"Oh but it was fun. Those were the days before every kid had a cell phone and did text messaging," said Enoki.

Bagpipe players, clowns, and baton twirlers passed by while Mr. Enoki explained the ciphers. A fire truck sounded his siren playfully, and the men onboard threw candy out to the children along the side of Sandy Boulevard.

"It's good to see that children still enjoy the parade," said Ms. Zyla. "Sometimes I wonder if the day will come when we forget what fun is."

A military flyover thundered through the air. Mr. Enoki shuddered, looked down, and placed a hand over his face.

"Are you all right, Hiri?" Eva asked.

"Just a thought of old times," he said, "when I was flying over Midway. The Americans had broken our code. We didn't know it at the time, but Midway showed us the sleeping giant could fight back. They knew our plans, and they were ready. I was an ace pilot, and our planes were superior to the American planes. But they tricked us somehow. I didn't know how, but every time I closed in behind an American plane and went in for the kill, it veered away, and another American plane came at me and fired. I had to break off for a little bit, but when I pursued the American plane again, it veered away again and another American plane came right at me—head on. How did they know? There was no radio contact between them, not even in code. I could not shoot down the American's inferior plane, and that's when I knew we were beaten."

"Did you ever find out how they did it? The trick, where they veered off and caught you head on?" Eva asked.

"It was an aerial maneuver invented by the Americans—called the Thach Weave," Enoki said. "Two planes fly together. They watch each others' positions. One airplane turns in toward the middle, a point of intersection, but they never plan to collide. The other sees this and also turns toward the middle. The first plane clears the middle first; the second plane reaches the middle around the time the tailing enemy plane reaches it—and tat-tat-tat-tat-tat with machine guns. If there is a miss, the planes keep weaving until the second plane shoots down the enemy."

"Everyone knows about it now," continued Enoki, "but back then, it was a complete surprise to Japanese pilots. One of the vets at a parade not too many years ago told me a story about two Americans who were low on fuel and were being chased by a Zero. They couldn't make it back to the carrier at full throttle—they had to reduce throttle without being shot down by the tailing Zero. They slowed to half power and used the Thach Weave all the way home. The Zero never got a clean shot—he kept breaking off each time they wove."

"What a story!" said Ms. Zyla. "I think I read about that story somewhere in a history book, but I didn't remember the maneuver name. And breaking the code—I read that somewhere too."

"The Americans made a duplicate of our Navy's enciphering machine. The Americans called our machine 'Purple'. We had deluded ourselves into thinking 'Purple' could never be broken, but it was. During the war, we were informed by the Germans it had been broken, but we did not believe them—not until after the war. The Americans were always full of surprises. We didn't believe they had a superbomb either, until they dropped it on two Japanese cities. After my first wife died in Hiroshima, I learned to be wary of the American military."

"I'm sorry for your loss," said Ms. Zyla. "War is an ugly business."

"Yes," said Mr. Enoki. "It is. So I am glad for parades—the clowns and baton twirlers and marching bands. It helps to forget the unpleasant memories."

Someone yelled at Mr. Enoki, and he waved back. Another group of folk marched down the parade field—a group protesting the war in Iraq. It demanded peace.

"There aren't as many peace groups these days as there were in the 60s," said Ms. Zyla. "And I hear a peace group was banned from marching in the Veteran's Day parade in one of the other Portlands—the one in Maine. Ironic, isn't it?"

"What's ironic?" Eva asked.

"When a group starts marching for peace, conflict and fighting results," Ms. Zyla replied.

Shortly after Ms. Zyla spoke, several youthful spectators alongside Sandy Boulevard threw ice cubes at the peace demonstrators. The demonstrators continued marching along, doing their best to ignore the ice cubes, but the cubes were knocking off hats, glasses, and causing harm. Mr. Enoki ran down the sidewalk with his cane and whacked a few of the spectators over their heads, and he took their ice. He returned to the restaurant and went inside with the ice.

"The parade goes on," said Ms. Zyla. "But we don't have to stay for the end. Judge Gregory will be walking by soon, and he's going to give a speech at the flagpole. Then there will be a ceremony inside the funeral home with refreshments and—"

"Mr. Enoki's wine is excellent," said Eva.

"Good!" said Ms. Zyla.

"But I think I've heard enough war stories for one day. I'm sure the veterans will spend the rest of the day exchanging stories, but that's not for me," said Eva.

"Are you sure? A fiery person like you?" asked Ms. Zyla.

"Oh please," said Eva.

"Oh please! You sound like Evanita," said Ms. Zyla.

"I should go see her," said Eva. "I haven't seen her—"

"Since yesterday at the trial," Ms. Zyla said. "She's doing fine. And you can do better."

Eva and Ms. Zyla finished their late breakfast and sipped beverages. The plates were cleared, and Eva stared at an enciphered poem:

Endruth Cipher	Translation
O tushsh sal yai,	A kiss for you,
A rudrk as ny boy.	O light of my day.
O shkol sal ne,	A star for me,
Ka sung ny ahm hoy.	To find my own way.
U raze o ruse,	I love a life,
As loum slan che shty.	Of rain from the sky.
Noy fahel ogaze,	May power above,
Duze hushban o kly.	Give wisdom a try.
Ma laan sal che woke,	No room for the hate,
Am rong as ail Eolch.	On land of our Earth.
Cane zhaum huch ne mah,	Come join with me now,
Um ruse as meh gulch.	In life of new birth.

"It's a strange cipher—where 'love' is 'raze', and 'hate' is 'woke'," said Eva.

"It's not just any old shift cipher, is it?" said Ms. Zyla. "It shifts the language. A person looks at words differently—in skewed fashion."

"Oh really? I think it's just a cipher, Zellie. You're overanalyzing it."

"Am I?" asked Ms. Zyla. "Look at the Valeria Circle. It's interesting the letters are not spaced evenly."

"So?" Eva said.

"So? Don't you think the circle resembles a stick person stepping on something?" Ms. Zyla asked. "I think Valeria was trying to say something—something she did not approve of."

"That is the problem with overanalyzing. People read more into situations than what is really there. All the superstitions and myths in the world come from wild interpretations," said Eva.

"Wild interpretations. And how does one know what is wild and what isn't?" Ms. Zyla asked.

"Mr. Enoki," Eva called. "Mr. Enoki."

Mr. Enoki tended to Eva and Ms. Zyla.

"Yes?" Mr. Enoki said.

"Is there a special meaning to this poem?" Eva asked. "Are the words twisted on purpose?"

"Twisted?" Mr. Enoki replied. "I not know about twisted. It is Endruth cipher. Valiwa's last cipher. *Gh* to *dr, ph* to *st, wh* to *shl, ng* to *nd, nd* to *ng, nk* to *nt, nt* to *nk, qu* to *tw, j* to *zh, x* to *ts, a* to *o, o* to *a, i* to *u, u* to *i, g* to *d, d* to *b, b* to *g, p* to *f, f* to *s, s* to *sh, sh* to *th, th* to *ch, ch* to *p, k* to *t, t* to *k, h* to *w, w* to *h, l* to *r, r* to *l, m* to *n, n* to *m, v* to *z,* and *z* to *v. C, e,* and *y* not change."

"That was a mouthful," Ms. Zyla said.

"But the poem," Eva said. "Does the poem have a twisted meaning?"

"No, no twisted meaning," Mr. Enoki said.

"There, you see?" Eva said to Ms. Zyla.

"What about the name of the cipher?" Ms. Zyla asked. "What does *Endruth* mean?"

"*Endruth* is Endruth for *English*," Mr. Enoki said. "Excuse me."

Mr. Enoki tended to another customer. Eva and Ms. Zyla's attention was diverted by a thumping sound. On a podium next to the flagpole at Thompson and Sandy stood Judge Gregory. He tapped on the microphone several times and spoke. Eva and Ms. Zyla paused to hear the speech. Eva noticed the judge—he had his wife and two children standing next to him. His wife kept the children well-behaved while he prepared to speak. Next to the judge stood two other men—Mr. Manis with his wife, and Captain Agar with his wife. The wives looked out of place, like they would have rather been somewhere else doing something more interesting instead of pretending to support their husbands. Eva picked up on this trait immediately.

"Subservient wives," blurted Eva.

Jonara looked around and realized no one heard her grandmother.

"Men and women of our armed forces, welcome!" started Judge Gregory. "And for those who have come out to support our veterans, thank you very much. It was at this hour—eleven o'clock—on this day—November 11th—in 1918 when our troops signed the Armistice bringing to a close the war to end all wars. And in 1954, President Eisenhower changed it to Veteran's Day. Let's hear it for all veterans!"

Large round of applause. Some yelled, "Amen, amen!"

"Some people confuse Veteran's Day with Memorial Day— thinking we are celebrating the military twice a year. Some would even say twice too many times," said Judge Gregory.

"Boo to them," shouted one. "They're crazy," said another. "Insane left-wingers," shouted a third.

"Memorial Day goes back to the end of the Civil War, when we honored those who'd fallen. But we've learned as a people that we cannot go through life remembering only those who have paid the ultimate price for freedom—we must support those who also fought both in war, and in the terror that follows afterward—terror of being back in battle, watching their comrades die, and feeling guilt that they survived at the expense of these fallen heroes. Let no veteran carry his burden alone—find another man and share your story. For today is Veteran's Day— and we thank you for your service!"

Another round of applause. Many veterans chanted in approval and did not wish to stop. Husbands hugged their wives, wives hugged their children, and children waved flags. Jonara watched Eva turn livid as she (Eva) stared at the crowd's expression of approval.

"Eva—if it weren't for your olive skin, I'd say you're turning green," said Ms. Zyla. "Judge Gregory is touching the people with his words. Have you no feeling of compassion for our vet-erans?"

"Our veterans. Veter-mens," said Eva.

"The judge said 'women and men'," said Ms. Zyla.

"He said 'men and women'—in that order. That was just a cover. 'Let no veteran carry his burden alone—find another man'," said Eva. "Vetermen."

"It's just a limit of the English language. There is no neuter pronoun for *he/she*," Ms. Zyla said.

"The judge should have rephrased. I did so now—I could have said, 'He should have rephrased'," Eva said. "He's a male sympathizer."

"Another irony—that's two," said Ms. Zyla.

"What are you talking about now?" Eva asked.

"In the first irony, peace marchers incite violence. Now the very person who accused me of overanalyzing something is her-self overanalyzing the judge's speech," said Ms. Zyla.

"Call it what you like. I'm not shmoozed over by a slick-talking male who has his own wild interpretations. Yes, here's an example of a wild interpretation," said Eva.

"Oh come now, the people didn't find his words that wild. But if he bothers you that much, just tune him out. Enjoy the rest of the parade. Like Mr. Enoki says, a parade helps to forget unpleasant memories," Ms. Zyla said.

"I see what the rest of the parade represents. Did you see the progression of power, the pecking order? Men started it—they hugged their wives," said Eva.

"I'd rather have a hug than a bruise," said Ms. Zyla.

"Ha, ha," Eva replied sarcastically. "It was followed by the wives hugging their children."

"A mother's love," said Ms. Zyla. "You can't deny that—you above anyone would admit to that."

"And the children waving the flag," said Eva.

"Patriotism at its best. So what are you complaining about? It's the perfect family," said Ms. Zyla with a laugh.

"I know you're 'pulling my chain', Zellie," said Eva, who wasn't laughing. "But you see the same thing I do. As isolated events, the hugging and flag-waving seem natural. But a trained eye—like you and I have—sees the real picture, that the symbol of patriotism is a man defending his country so he can initiate love to a family."

"I believe Judge Gregory was getting to that," said Ms. Zyla.

"How dare you!" Eva said.

"I saw his speech ahead of time. It's printed in the paper for all to read," said Ms. Zyla.

"Then he manipulated the press to his advantage," said Eva. "How conceited."

"Who was talking about wild interpretations from overanalyzing?" Ms. Zyla asked. "Who, Eva, who?"

"You're turning the tables on me," said Eva.

"You bet I am," Ms. Zyla said with a grin.

"Men don't initiate everything. And they haven't," said Eva.

"You'd be hard pressed to convince everyone here," said Ms. Zyla, "that what you're saying is anything short of patriotic heresy."

"But I know it to be true," said Eva. She paused before continuing and said, "You know it too—the burden I've carried. And I don't just mean raising Evanita as a single parent, though that has had its challenging moments."

"We each have our battles to fight," said Ms. Zyla. "In a way, we are all veterans. But I agree with you, Eva. You have faced quite an uphill battle. Yes, you have your own war with a few allies. Many do not accept you after the incident with Roberta. I do not mean it as an offense, but her name must be spoken. She doesn't deserve to be hidden in your private thoughts any more than those who've fallen in war should be buried in a nightly anxiety attack known as the flashback."

"The world isn't ready for what Roberta stood for. Look at our world, Zellie," said Eva, pointing to the folks attending the parade. "How many ice cubes would they throw my way if I didn't keep Roberta safe from ridicule?"

"Eva, listen to me," said Ms. Zyla. "War is like that—there are those who oppose us because they do not accept us, and somehow we pose a perceived threat to their way of life, their thoughts, and their very language."

Eva's expression turned from irritation to sadness and exhaustion.

"I'm tired, Zellie. Tired of fighting the battle alone, with only a photograph to give me strength. Where is feminism today? Ask most of the girls Evanita's age—the Sheilas of the world—do they even know what it means to fight for rights? They think suffrage is what happens when people get old and suffer in pain."

"Don't be so down," said Ms. Zellie.

"Things are just good enough for them. They settle for a man. And if he's half kind to them, that'll do for the moment," said Eva. "And if he's half mean to them, they'll put up with it until he grovels back later."

"Eva, you're tearing yourself apart. Try not to think about it for the moment. You need rest—for your daughter's sake," said Ms. Zyla.

"I can't stop. When I see other women who have given in, it makes me all the more irate. And all the more determined to trudge on," said Eva.

"And you don't sleep because of that. What good can you do then, hmmm?" Ms. Zyla asked. "You can't carry the world on your shoulders."

"I don't need to carry the entire world—just the female half," said Eva.

"I have just one last thing to say, and then I think we should go," said Ms. Zyla.

"Yes, we should go. I don't want to hang around the parade anymore. It's skewed," said Eva.

"That's what I want to warn you about. It's all too easy to apply a shift cipher to any particular event and skew the results into something that appears like legitimate knowledge but in fact is not."

"You think so. I think we have to unskew the damage done—damage that has largely been unchecked since the male model was invented," Eva finished.

Ms. Zyla paid the bill and took Eva toward home. Halfway from the Sandy Boulevard flagpole to Eva's house, Eva yelled.

"Stop the car!"

Ms. Zyla slammed on the brakes, took a sharp turn, and careened into a parking lot. The car lurched to a stop. Ms. Zyla slapped the transmission selector into Park and rolled down the windows.

"What's the matter, what's the matter!" Ms. Zyla asked.

"Don't take me home," said Eva.

"Are you sick? What's the matter?" Ms. Zyla repeated, her hands now shaking out of fear that Eva was in dire straits.

"Take me to the hospital. Take me to Vansen Hospital. Hurry, Zellie, Hurry!" Eva said.

Ms. Zyla slapped the tranny selector into Reverse, whipped backward into a Y-turn, slapped the tranny into Drive, and stomped the accelerator to the floor—sending the two out the parking lot and down the road, swerving around cars and racing through every yellow light on their way to Vansen Hospital.

CHAPTER 18

Dirt Prairie

2023 Oct 4, Wed Early am. Jonara's Dream.
2006 Nov 11, Late Sat Afnoon. Portland, Oregon.

Ms. Zyla whipped into the hospital driveway and pulled up to the emergency entrance.

"Why are you driving here? Park in the lot," said Eva.

"What?!" Ms. Zyla asked. "I thought you were on your deathbed!"

"No, no, no," said Eva quickly. "Not me. I need to see Evanita. A mother should hug her daughter every day."

"What in all madness is going on?" Ms. Zyla asked.

Ms. Zyla rolled her eyes and shook her left fist out of view from Eva, or so she thought.

"I see you shaking your fist," said Eva. "I didn't mean to alarm you. But there's something I've got to try."

Ms. Zyla parked. The two entered the building and walked briskly to Evanita's room. By her bedside, Johnny Pindus held his vigil.

"Ms. Zyla, Ms. Carreña—hello," said Johnny. "Evanita hasn't awakened yet. I've been reading to her. I thought if she heard a voice, she'd wake up."

"Yes, Johnny. Come, I have a favor to ask you," said Eva.

"What are you up to?" Ms. Zyla asked.

"You'll see. Something I learned from our friend, Mr. Enoki," said Eva.

"Mr. Enoki. Did you see him today? I used to write ciphers to him when I was a kid," said Johnny.

"Yes, Johnny. Later. Listen—I want to tell you something," Eva said.

Eva pulled Johnny aside and whispered into his ear.

"What are you saying?" Ms. Zyla asked, but Eva continued whispering.

Johnny nodded his head several times but froze at the next whisperings.

"I've never done that before," Johnny said. "How should I—" he started, and Eva whispered something else after his pause.

"But that would mean..." Johnny continued. "Are you sure ...it might be too much...who will hold the...I won't have a free hand...okay...do you think she will...shouldn't we tell the doctor...it could be dangerous if there's no doctor around...okay, I'll stop at the first sign of trouble...yeah...yeah...I'm ready...Are you ready...Are you sure you want to do this?"

"Yes, Johnny," Eva said aloud. "We must. Zellie—we're ready to begin."

"Begin what?" Ms. Zyla asked. "I couldn't hear a word you said to Johnny."

Jonara nodded in agreement.

"Take this," Eva said while handing Ms. Zyla an electric toothbrush, "and be prepared to use it when I tell you to."

"I still don't understand," Ms. Zyla said. "What am I supposed to—"

"Okay," said Eva to Johnny, "let's move her over."

Eva and Johnny carefully lifted Evanita and shifted her to Evanita's left side of the bed.

"Zellie—help us move the bed away from the wall," said Eva. "No, not that way. The head of the bed needs to be away from the wall. Yes, that's it. Good. Thank you, Zellie. Johnny—you now have a place to stand."

Eva reclined onto the bed next to Evanita's right side. There was barely enough room for the two without one of them rolling off. Eva was determined to make 'it' work. Make what work? That was the question in both Ms. Zyla's and Jonara's minds.

"Eva...should you be...what if someone sees?" Ms. Zyla asked.

"Zellie," said Eva. "I'll explain later. For now, I need you to stand next to Johnny and hold the electric toothbrush next to the back of his neck."

"This is crazy," Ms. Zyla said. "You don't really believe I will just—"

"There's no time for lengthy discussion," Eva said. "Here—you might as well hold onto my purse too, just in case."

"In case of what?" Ms. Zyla asked. "You're acting very strangely, Eva."

"I'll explain later. Now turn on the toothbrush. Good. Hold it against his neck—not the brushes—use the back side. Don't worry about toothpaste. Good," said Eva.

"How can you tell I'm doing it right?" Ms. Zyla asked.

"By the sound. Johnny, is the—" Eva started.

"I'm not sure how this will work," said Johnny.

"Yes, you said that already," said Eva. "You'll be fine. Just do the best you can. Now begin."

Eva placed her right arm across her abdomen and placed her right hand onto Evanita's right hand. Johnny stretched out his arms and placed each hand atop the Evas' foreheads—his left hand on Evanita's, and his right on Eva's. His hands trembled—causing the Evas' skulls to shake slightly yet gently.

"I don't feel anything," said Eva. "Do you sense anything, Johnny?"

"I must concentrate," he said. "I can sense worry in you, Ms. Carreña. But I get nothing from Evanita—just cold darkness."

"Remember what I said," continued Eva. "Imagine you are riding a horse. Evanita and I are also riding horses. You're following us, but you're alternating between following her and me. Focus on that, Johnny."

Jonara wished desperately to sense what Johnny sensed. Could she see into his, her mother's, and her grandmother's thoughts? Jonara stood on the other side of Johnny where Ms. Zyla was not, put her arms around his waist, and hugged him.

"It's working," Johnny said. "I'm seeing something."

Jonara no longer stood in her mother's hospital room but was instead in a place where her immediate surrounding was lit but the distance was dark—as if she were on stage and a spotlight shone in her immediate area. Yet she knew she wasn't on a stage or inside a building. She was possibly outside, as there was dirt below her feet with scattered prairie grass. There were no other plants. Voices did not echo. Eva and Johnny were with her, and there were three horses with Western-style saddles.

"Where's Evanita?" Eva asked Johnny in the locally lit area. "Aren't you linking in with her?"

"She's very distant," he said, and without warning, two closely spaced flashes zipped past the three.

"What was that?" Eva asked.

"I'm not sure," said Johnny. "But something just flew past us."

"Something, or some things? There were two flashes," said Eva. "Could the flashes be Evanita?"

"I don't know," said Johnny, "but I'm getting tired."

"We just got here. How tired are you?" Eva asked.

"Very tired. I wasn't expecting the heavy drain," Johnny said.

"Let's leave then," Eva said.

Johnny physically released his grip from Eva and Evanita. He held a hand up to Ms. Zyla so she'd know to stop with the toothbrush. He was back in the hospital room, and so was Eva. Jonara released her grip from her father, and her grandmother stood up from the bed and spoke to Johnny.

"Why can't you reach her?" Eva asked as she stood up.

Johnny paused for a moment and caught his breath. He stretched his arms and wiggled his fingers to restore circulation.

"She's running in her mind, running away from something at incredible speed. I don't know how to reach her, and I don't know why you chose horses," Johnny said.

"Could someone please tell me what's going on?" Ms. Zyla asked.

"I'm trying to bring my daughter out of her coma," said Eva.

"How?" Ms. Zyla asked. "And why were you napping next to Evanita?"

"I wasn't napping. I was trying out an idea," said Eva, "that if Johnny and I appeared in her subconscious mind, we could help her resolve whatever sent her into the coma to begin with."

"Is this a medical procedure?" Ms. Zyla asked. "Eva—you're a professional dentist. You graduated from med school. I'm surprised to hear you talk like a mystic."

"This is why I didn't want to explain it to you—I don't have time to argue the scientific merit of the procedure. I'm more interested in getting my daughter back—and if that means getting the Easter Bunny herself to appear, so be it," Eva explained.

"Ms. Zellie might be right," said Johnny. "I've never tried to appear in someone's mind, and I've never tried to link people's minds together. I've only—and with great difficulty—been able to read people's minds within a special set of circumstances. I don't know if this will work, Ms. Carreña."

"Why don't we get a Ouija board in here and hold a séance?" joked Ms. Zyla. "And we can call on friendly spirits to help us. Of course there's the danger of contacting evil spirits pretending to be helpful."

"Don't patronize me, Zellie," said Eva. "Wait—Johnny, can you sense people who have passed on?"

"Whoa! My gift...what I do...it's just another sense like seeing or hearing. My mind takes the external information and converts it into concepts. That's in the here and now," said Johnny.

"Well, it's the here and now," said Eva. "And I'll try anything now to get Evanita back here."

Johnny paused for a moment and thought.

"What was that all about—with the horses?" Ms. Zyla asked.

"That was the second part of my idea—which I got from Mr. Enoki."

"He's never had a horse," said Ms. Zyla.

"No, but he was part of the Thach Weave," said Eva, "and I thought that if we could reach Evanita's subconscious and convince her she's riding a horse, I could ride parallel with her on another horse, and we could turn our horses toward one another so I could pick off whatever is chasing her."

"That's fantasy," said Ms. Zyla. "Besides, he was talking about airplanes, not horses."

"Horses are more friendly and proper," said Eva.

"Proper? How?" Ms. Zyla asked.

"A Spanish woman should never be without her legs. And a horse's legs are an extension of her own, a connection to the earth, a fulfillment of—"

"Oh, you have visitors, Evanita," said a nurse walking in.

The nurse's appearance startled everyone in the room except Evanita, who was still comatose.

"Let me check your vitals. Everything looks fine. Hmmm, you moved over to the side. Did she roll over or become violent?" the nurse asked anyone who was willing to listen.

"No," answered Ms. Zyla.

Everyone stood still as if being interrupted from something they did not wish the nurse to see.

"Something strange is going on here. Is everything okay?" the nurse asked.

"Well, that's a question I asked—" Ms. Zyla started before Eva cut her off.

"Everything is just fine. Evanita is doing fine. We're just visiting, that's all," said Eva.

"Oh. Well, visit all you like. I'll be down the hallway if you need me. Or you can press the button on the wall, and I'll come, or someone will come if I can't," the nurse said.

"We'll do that," said Eva.

The nurse left.

"Don't touch that button no matter what," said Eva. "Zellie, hand me the toothbrush. Good. Now watch the door."

"I can't believe I'm doing this—and at my age," said Ms. Zyla.

"Shush," said Eva to Ms. Zyla. "Johnny—you'll have to manage the toothbrush without Zellie."

"The toothbrush won't be powerful enough," said Johnny. "I was just receiving information before. Now I must send information. 'I must shift from being the catcher to the pitcher.' I heard someone say that to me sixteen years ago."

"Yes, I did say that," said Eva. "But what will you do for an energy source? I don't understand your condition well enough to recommend a source."

"There is one possibility," said Johnny. "By mistake, I learned of it when the doctors were trying to revive my sister. I was electrocuted. Now what I propose—"

"You can't just stick your finger in an electric outlet," said Ms. Zyla.

"I agree with Zellie. Johnny—you'd electrocute yourself," said Eva.

"No—the defibrillator," said Johnny.

"You want to shock your heart?" Eva asked.

"No, my brain," said Johnny. "The doctors were arguing, and in the confusion, I was pushed into the path of the defibrillator. That's how I was shocked."

"Oh my," said Eva. "That's bad. I didn't realize you were injured like that. But you can't electrocute yourself again."

"It wasn't bad the first time—not really," Johnny explained. "I mean, everything turned white for a split second, then I saw my sister somewhere else—on a waterfall—but she was walking up the waterfall while the water was going down. And the sun was shining over the edge of the waterfall, so when she reached the top, her face and hair glowed golden, and a wind blew her hair back. That's when I knew her spirit had moved onto something better."

"He's delusional," said Ms. Zyla.

"Perhaps," said Eva.

"What?!" Ms. Zyla asked in surprise. "Did I hear a 'perhaps'?"

"I know about AEDs (automated external defibrillators). You probably took a large charge, Johnny," said Eva. "However—"

"However?! You sound like you actually approve—" Ms. Zyla started.

"You just watch the door, Zellie!" Eva said. "Johnny, look—there's an AED next to you. But a word of warning—the semi-automatics have little leeway for altering the output energy level. Furthermore—"

"Semi-automatic! Are we working with Tommy guns?" Ms. Zyla asked.

"I told you to watch that door!" Eva said with a little playfulness in her tone.

"I'm watching, I'm watching," said Ms. Zyla.

"Furthermore," Eva continued to Johnny, "they have automatic detection so they won't work outside their intended use. You definitely will be going outside their intended use."

"A nurse!" said Ms. Zyla. "No wait, she's going in another room. I thought she was—"

"Please be more accurate, Zellie!" said Eva. "Johnny, let's take a look at this AED unit here. Hmmm yes, I recognize this model. It has a manual mode. Good, that's what you'll need. And the energy levels are set with these up and down buttons. It ranges from 2 Joules to 360. You must start with the lowest setting to be safe—that's 2 Joules. Do you understand?"

"Yeah," said Johnny.

"Now this model will recharge in 20 seconds—8 if you don't mind running out the battery. You can't receive a constant shock—this won't be like the electric toothbrush where you'll be receiving a constant vibration," Eva explained.

"I know. I'm ready. Tape the paddles to my forehead and the back of my neck," said Johnny.

Eva took some bandaging tape and strapped it around his skull several times over the electrode paddles—affixing the paddles as he suggested to his forehead and back of his neck.

"There's no automatic mode for sending a shock at regular intervals. I'm guessing you'll need regular intervals to maintain the link," Eva said.

"I'll need to control how often the shocks are sent anyway," said Johnny. "Somehow, I'll have to press it as needed, but I won't have a free hand."

"I'll switch hands with Evanita—I'll hold her right with my left and press the AED with my right hand—but you'll have to tell me when," Eva said.

"I won't have to tell you," Johnny said. "When the link begins to fade, press it."

"How will I know?"

"The light will shrink to a small point around you—from your view it will be like being in a blizzard—you'll only be able to see a foot or two in front of you. Everything else will look dark.

You'll only have a second or two before everything goes black and the link is lost," Johnny said.

"Okay, okay. Let's do it," Eva said.

Eva reclined on Evanita's bed again but with her left hand on Evanita's right hand. Eva tried placing the AED on the bed under her relaxed right hand, but the paddle wires would not reach that far.

"You're pulling me," said Johnny. "It won't reach."

"Okay, I'll hold it next to my head...no, that's awkward... above my head...that might work," said Eva.

"That might work. I can still reach around and touch your forehead," said Johnny.

Johnny placed his hands on the Evas' foreheads as before. Jonara walked around and hugged Johnny again.

"Press the button, Ms. Carreña," Johnny requested.

Eva pressed the button. Flash! Eva, Johnny, and Jonara were back in the dirt prairie with three horses. Johnny and Eva could not see Jonara, but otherwise the three shared the same visual experience. The initial flash into the world was blindingly white. The world lit up—both near and far. Jonara realized she was on a vast plain—perhaps somewhere in the middle of the United States. The plain stretched for miles in all directions, but in the extreme distance along the horizon was a long chain of mountains. In fact, the chain was circular and completely engulfed the plain.

The flash of light lit the distant mountains only briefly—like a lightning burst. The mountains quickly returned to darkness, and darkness carried across the plains closer to the six such that after twenty seconds, the light shrank to a small circle just barely large enough to illuminate the three people and three horses. The speed at which the darkness engulfed the six did not appear linear. It started slow—keeping the mid-distant plains lit for perhaps a good sixteen seconds. But after the sixteen seconds, the shadow closed in on the six quickly such that the last second seemed to be a sort of a half-flash—the half where light goes into darkness.

The enshrinking light diminished to a few feet around Eva. Eva was so dazzled by the environment that she neglected to press the AED button and had to be urged.

"Press the button, Ms. Carreña," said Johnny.

Eva pressed the button. Flash! The light was blindingly white and repeated as before as it illuminated the mountains briefly and shrank with the advancing darkness in twenty-seconds.

"Again," said Johnny when the light shrank to a point on Eva.

Eva pressed the AED button once more and established a conditioned reflex such that she would press the button just before the light shrank into nothingness.

"Do you see her?" Eva asked Johnny.

"No," Johnny said.

"We must get moving," said Eva. "We must ride the horses and find her."

Johnny climbed up on a medium- to smaller-sized gray-spotted white horse with a long, matted mane, dusty coat, and a heavy Western saddle. Eva climbed onto a tall, black horse with a white-splotched forehead and white fur above its hooves. The horse's mane was short and uniform, its coat glistened in the light, and its solid black hooves gleamed like highly-polished stones. A third horse—the one Eva hoped Evanita would find her way to—was not quite as tall as hers but taller than Johnny's. It was like a chestnut—trims of black mixed with dark to light browns—as if a painter had taken his pallet of colors and gradually worked the browns into the blacks. It too had a white splotch on its forehead though not as large as Eva's horse. Its hooves, however, were unusually light—like polished ivory.

"Evanita's horse must ride with us," said Eva.

The light continued its cycle of full-flash and shrinking light. Eva and Johnny didn't even discuss it as Eva was now pressing the button out of habit.

"I'm not much good at riding horses," said Johnny. "Maybe we can use our horses to push the brown horse along."

"For the first time since I've known you, Johnny, you spoke like a male," said Eva. "You can't push a horse any more than you can push a woman. But a horse who is happy with its company will follow along. We won't be pushing the horse, and I don't think we need to have it trail behind on a rope attached to one of our horses. If we travel along in unison and in friendly stride, the horse will follow. So what are the horses' names?"

"Names?" Johnny asked. "I...it's all I can do with the link...the shocks...the lighting...you want names?"

"All horses have names," Eva explained. "Don't worry—I've already decided on a name for my horse—I'll call her Obsidiana—after black volcanic rock. Evanita's horse is quite obviously Chestnut. Have you thought of a name for your horse?"

"Yeah," Johnny said with a sneeze. "His name is Sinus."

"That's not a horse's name," said Eva.

"It is now," Johnny said with another sneeze. "And I think I'm allergic to him."

"Dear me! Do you want to switch horses?" Eva offered.

"No, it won't matter. I created the environment anyway, so I'll be allergic to any horse," said Johnny.

"Can't you just unallergic yourself?" Eva asked.

"It doesn't work that way. What I believe is what I get," said Johnny. "It's much harder to unbelieve something than to never have believed. I've always thought I'd be allergic to horses."

Jonara climbed Johnny's horse and sat behind him, holding her arms around his waist.

"We must ride on," said Eva.

Eva nudged her heals into Obsidiana and made two clicking sounds with her tongue and teeth. The horse did not move.

"Come on, Obsidiana, let's go," Eva urged, but again Obsidiana did not move. "Johnny—why isn't my horse responding?"

"Mine isn't either. But I thought that's because I don't know how to ride a horse," he said.

"You should be able to press your heels into the horse on both sides like this," said Eva as she pushed her heels into Obsidiana. "You shouldn't have to kick the horse unless you want her to go into an immediate run. But Obsidiana won't even walk."

"Not enough energy," said Johnny. "I need to increase the power on the AED...two Joules is not enough...this will be awkward...if I keep asking you to make adjustments...that will be too slow...wait a moment...here...I'll take the AED."

Without leaving their world on the plains, Johnny half-returned to the hospital room and lowered his body so he could extend his arms. In this way, he could (and did) place his right forearm on Eva's forehead while keeping his left hand on Evanita's forehead. With his barely free hand, he pivoted his forearm (to retain contact with Eva) and attempted to reposition the AED between Evanita and Eva. It wasn't working. He released his link with Eva for a second. Eva returned to the hospital room but kept her eyes closed.

"I'm on Obsidiana, I'm on Obsidiana," Eva repeated in an effort to return to the dirt prairie.

"One moment," said Johnny.

Johnny completed positioning the AED between the two Evas and placed his forearm on Eva's forehead. He increased the energy level to five Joules and pressed the "shock" button. Flash! Eva and Johnny returned to the dirt prairie.

"There, that's better," said Eva. "Be careful you don't increase the power too much. You might go into convulsions."

Obsidiana responded to Eva's nudging, and the horse started walking. Chestnut followed Obsidiana. Johnny nudged Sinus a little too hard. The horse launched into a trot and in doing so kept hopping Johnny and Jonara up and down until both lost balance and fell off. Yet Eva only saw Johnny fall off.

"Oh dear, Johnny, you don't know about posting in a trot," Eva said.

"My back aches, and not just from falling off the horse," said Johnny. "I have to lean over to reach you, the AED, and Evanita. Ms. Zyla—can you bring a chair over so I can sit down?"

Ms. Zyla heard Johnny and brought the chair over. Jonara saw herself in both worlds simultaneously. It reminded her a bit of when she was both Modern and Victorian, but in this situation, she was the same person in different places instead of two different people in the same place. Currently, Jonara wasn't doing much more than holding onto Johnny—quite different from her more active roles earlier. Was she deferring to her environment? One thing was certain—she was exhausted.

"There," said Eva while the flash was still strong. "Shadows passed over us—high in the air."

"I don't understand why they were flashes the first time and shadows this time," said Johnny.

"It doesn't matter," Eva said. "You need to get back in the saddle, Johnny."

Johnny did just that, and Jonara sat behind him as before.

"Let's go," Eva said. "Now start with a walk, Johnny. Gently press your heels into the horse. There, Sinus is walking. Now I'll walk with you. Look, Chestnut is following us."

Johnny turned around to look at Chestnut and in doing so let go of the reins. He instinctively held onto the saddle's horn as if that would steer the horse. Sinus wandered, slowed, lowered his head, and nibbled on prairie grass.

"What are you doing?" Eva asked. "I said 'Let's go,' not 'Let go'. This isn't the time to let your horse graze."

"I—the reins, I must hold onto the reins," said Johnny.

"Yes! Here—don't dismount. I'll get the reins for you," said Eva.

She slipped off Obsidiana as gracefully as when she danced in front of Roberta's photo. She handed the reins to Johnny.

"Now don't let go of these," said Eva.

"Yes ma'am," said Johnny.

"And pay attention to where you're going," said Eva.

"Yes ma'am."

"And don't let Sinus stop to eat grass," added Eva.

"Yes ma'am."

"And don't call me ma'am," said Eva. "Makes me feel like I'm mothering you."

"Yes ma...I mean...thank you, Ms. Carreña," said Johnny.

Eva returned to her horse and lifted herself to the saddle.

"Walk," said Eva.

Obsidiana started walking.

"Walk," said Johnny.

Sinus did not move. Obsidiana sensed this and stopped.

"*Caminas,*" said Eva in Spanish (walk).

Obsidiana walked and lifted her front legs high with each step—the Spanish walk. Johnny was amazed that Obsidiana responded to English and Spanish. He thought of saying something to Sinus to get him walking, but what? He thought about what might work with the little stone around his neck—the secret of his gift. He saw two concentric circles floating above Eva, and at first he thought of the cipher wheel, but then an oblong, canoe-shaped object crossed the paths of the circles—much like the shape he saw in the fire at Cerossi Café. He focused on the outer circle, and a word came to his mind.

"*Zhoipo,*" Johnny said.

Sinus went into a fast walk and caught up to Obsidiana.

"That's it, Johnny. Stay focused. Do what you have to do to keep up. Keep the reins firm but not too tight or loose. Guide Sinus, don't force him. Excellent."

"Ms. Carreña," said Johnny. "A strange thing has entered this world. I'm seeing a cipher circle floating above you, but I don't understand why."

"The Valeria Circle?" Eva asked.

"Not quite. Some other cipher circle," Johnny said. "How did you know about my sister's cipher circle? Have you been thinking about ciphers?"

"I saw it at the Enokidake Restaurant," said Eva. "Your sister was talented."

"Yes she was. She taught me ciphers," said Johnny.

"Johnny, I'd love to chat about ciphers, but we have to get going and find my daughter," Eva said.

"I understand," he said.

Eva waved her hand up in the air, and the cipher circle dissipated.

"Now we're ready," Eva said. She turned to Obsidiana and shouted a Spanish command to run, "*Corres.*"

Obsidiana broke into a solid gallop. Johnny reacted by commanding Sinus.

"*Laomo*," Johnny called to Sinus—a command which means, "Run."

All three horses thundered along the prairie. Obsidiana led, Chestnut followed half a horse's length back on the left, and Sinus followed half a horse's length back on the right.

"Go, Daddy, go!" Jonara said, hanging onto Johnny for dear life. "Now how does this work? I'm dreaming, but I'm...like...in Daddy's dream or something? And he's riding a horse. I've never seen Daddy ride a horse!"

In commanding the horses to run, the cycle of white flashes were engulfed more quickly by the darkness, as if Johnny's energy for the light was being drained by the horses' motion.

"Just hang on, you're doing fine," said Eva. "There, did you see it? Did you see the shadow pass over? It went by more slowly. I think I saw Evanita flying on something."

"I'm seeing all kinds of things—the AED keeps me busy with the flashing, your horse's hooves are kicking up dirt at me, and Sinus's mane is flapping in my face," said Johnny.

"Don't say, 'Your horse.' Say her name, Obsidiana," said Eva. "Again, there. Do you see the shadow flying overhead?"

"Yeah, I see it now. We're matching its speed," said Johnny.

"We must go faster," said Eva. "*Corres, corres. Persegues!*" In other words, "Run, run. Pursue!"

"Ms. Carreña, wait!" Johnny yelled. He gave a command to Sinus, "*Vauriko idu daupu zhubaina!*" which means, "Follow at top speed!"

As Johnny completed the command, he adjusted the AED to pump 10 Joules through his cranium. The cycle of flashing and engulfing darkness reduced in frequency and lengthened in period. This was the desired effect to maintain the connection with Eva and Evanita.

"She's not just a shadow," yelled Eva over the thundering horses. "Look—she's riding a large blue bird."

"I see her. And she's being followed by something on a large black bird," said Johnny. "We're nearly as quick as they are."

"If only we could reach them. How do we attract their attention?" Eva asked. "Evanita! Do you hear me? Evanita! Down here!"

Evanita did not respond. Johnny increased the AED to 15 Joules. He pressed the "shock" button as before. Flash! With the shock to his skull, Johnny sneezed. The sneeze carried into the dirt prairie world as thunder and a gust of wind. Each time he pressed the "shock" button, the sneeze followed, as if the shock were causing him to sneeze.

"It's getting stormy," said Eva. "We have to reach Evanita."

Johnny had increased the AED to give him some sort of energy to reach Evanita. He envisioned a lasso rope. Eva found the lasso attached to Obsidiana, wielded it in her hand, and threw it to latch onto Evanita. Miss. The lasso could not travel high enough or far enough to reach Evanita.

Johnny increased the AED to 20 Joules. The horses morphed into giraffes—tall, graceful animals but with the same fur pattern as their horses.

"What happened?" Eva shouted with the giraffes running as quickly as the horses were. "Where are the horses?"

"I thought we could reach them this way," said Johnny. "I'm climbing onto my giraffe's neck."

With Jonara remaining in the saddle, Johnny climbed his giraffe's (Sinus's) neck and sat on his head. With the motion of running and the extra mass atop his long neck, Sinus's head swayed back and forth like an upside-down pendulum. Johnny swung along with Sinus's head. He felt like he had climbed a tree too high and was about to fall off.

"It isn't working," said Eva. "You can't reach Evanita from there. She's still too fast and just a little too high. Johnny, you're going to fall off! Go back down to the saddle!"

Sinus as the giraffe ran through a small dip in the prairie and jumped over a fallen tree log. The motion sent Johnny airborne. Sinus tried using his head to catch Johnny but could not quite align with Johnny. Johnny missed the landing on Sinus's head but was able to throw out an arm and catch a bit of mane on the back of Sinus's neck. Johnny swung underneath Sinus's neck such that his other hand grabbed onto the mane from the other side. This positioned Johnny on the front side of Sinus's neck. Johnny slid down the neck and bumped against the front chest of Sinus. He dangled freely, with Sinus running at full speed. Johnny was in great danger of being trampled by his own steed. Jonara saw this and reached for her father as he attempted to swing his legs around and over to the saddle. On his own, Johnny would not have succeeded, but with unknown help from Jonara, Johnny was able to swing onto the side of the saddle and climb back up.

Johnny was exhausted. The giraffes slowed to a canter, and the flashing decreased in period length—a sign Johnny was running out of energy for the dirt prairie world. The giraffes reverted to horses.

"Whoa," said Eva.

Obsidiana and Chestnut slowed to a walk. Sinus along with Johnny ran past Obsidiana and Chestnut. Eva shouted for him to slow up, and at length Johnny yelled, "*Sheriasho,*" which means, "Slow."

Sinus slowed to a walk, and Johnny directed him back to Obsidiana and Chestnut.

"I got a good look at Evanita," said Eva once Johnny pulled alongside her. "She was riding an oversized blue jay. And there was a grotesque creature following on an oversized grackle. It looked like a dogfight. Evanita kept turning, diving, and climbing, but for each move she made, the creature followed. Johnny, we can't reach her with horses, giraffes, or any other earthbound animal. We must take to the skies."

"How? Throw wings on our horses? The mass is too great. We'll never catch up with—" Johnny started.

"Wings, yes. We must fly," said Eva.

"A griffin—you're saying we need to be riding griffins? Out of mythology?" Johnny asked.

"No, I'm not asking to ride a griffin. That isn't a proper horse anyway. How about a Pegasus horse or three?" asked Eva.

"Or three? The mass, Ms. Carreña, the mass. Mass needs energy," said Johnny. "How about a friendly eagle, or even a sparrow? And maybe just one of us should go flying. How about you go up alone?"

"And I catch up to Evanita," started Eva.

"And you go into the Thach Weave to take out that black thing," continued Johnny.

"On a sparrow no less," Eva added. "And Evanita falls straight out of the sky and onto the ground shattering every fiber of her being."

"Or her blue jay makes a soft landing," said Johnny.

"Or her blue jay flies away with no chase to keep it occupied and in the area," said Eva. "And with the blue jay goes my daughter. A blue jay cannot run on the ground."

"It can walk," said Johnny.

"It can hop," said Eva. "A Spanish woman must have her legs and must be riding an animal that has legs meant for walking and running on this earth."

"If I give you a Pegasus, will you go up alone?" Johnny asked.

"I have a feeling it won't work, because you don't believe enough for all three horses to be Pegasi," said Eva. "And if you don't believe enough for all three, you won't have enough belief for one to work. We still have the problem of getting Evanita onto a horse. I don't think she could make the transition to mine very easily."

Johnny opened his mouth to say something but stopped himself short.

"Look, Johnny, we've been at this for a while, now. I'm worried that you're enduring too much for try-and-fail, try-and-fail, and more try-and-fail. You can't last much longer without sustaining injury if we keep at it like this. We must get a quick resolution. Give wings to Obsidiana, Chestnut, and Sinus. Let's go get my daughter. Are you with me?"

"Yeah," Johnny said.

Johnny reached for the AED and prepared to turn up the energy.

"One more thing—don't run the AED at full power," said Eva. "Do I have your promise?"

Johnny hesitated. He set the AED to 50 Joules and pressed the "shock" button. The sky flashed white with little sparkly balls shooting around—like the shooting stars one sees after hitting one's head. The usual shrinking circle of light was less regular and had a more spiral-like spin to its character. This spiral pattern illuminated the prairie and spun slowly—slower than a disco globe. It was as if Eva, Johnny, and the three Pegasi were traveling on the image of a galaxy. Yes, Pegasi. Johnny added wings to Obsidiana, Chestnut, and Sinus.

"Yeah sure," Johnny said half-honestly, responding to Eva's request to avoid full AED power.

"Excellent," said Eva. "I imagine we need to simply run, and the horses will take flight."

Eva made two clicking sounds, tapped her heels, and Obsidiana broke into a gallop. Her wings extended, flapped, and Obsidiana took flight—carrying Eva with her. Chestnut followed, and the two flew together.

"Giddy-yup," said Johnny, but Sinus didn't seem to know what to do with his wings. "They're wings, silly. You flap them like a bird."

Sinus extended his ragged wings, and fleas jumped out. Johnny reeled from the cloud of insects and batted them with his hands.

"Who ever heard of wings with fleas? Who ever heard of a horse with wings? Fly, Sinus, fly," Johnny commanded, but Sinus kept tripping over his wings. *"Fuifo, fuifo,"* Johnny commanded.

Sinus went into a trot and held his wings up without tripping over them.

"Fuifo boshu loreifu zhubaina mahilu!" Johnny commanded, translated as, "Fly with all speed, now!"

Sinus bucked back and forth like a bronco.

"This isn't a rodeo!" Johnny yelled, but before Sinus could buck Johnny and Jonara off, Sinus jumped into the air and took flight.

"Hurry up, Johnny," said Eva flying ahead.

The Pegasi lined up as follows—Eva on Obsidiana, Chestnut following Eva, and Johnny with Jonara on Sinus. To the left of the Pegasi flew Evanita on the oversized blue jay, and the creature followed her on the oversized grackle. Eva waved at Evanita to get her attention.

"Johnny, she doesn't hear me," said Eva. "We must reach her and tell her to veer in toward me so we can perform the Thach Weave."

"She doesn't hear any of us," said Johnny, "and I have the AED cranked up to 75 Joules."

"Johnny!" Eva explained. "That's too much!"

"It had to be done. I couldn't get Sinus up in the air without the extra power. I'm afraid to increase the power any further," Johnny said.

"Then don't. We'll have to fight off the creature ourselves," said Eva. "I'll go first."

Eva took a position to the right of and slightly higher than the creature. She drove Obsidiana down at the creature's bird to block pursuit of Evanita. The creature veered slightly to the left but directed its bird to peck at Obsidiana as she passed. The beak caught Eva on her left leg. Eva reacted in pain and directed Obsidiana to break off the blocking position and fly to the left of the creature.

"That creature got me on the leg!" shouted Eva. "Johnny— Evanita did not respond to my weave. We have to go after the creature ourselves, and we have to do it rapidly—in a one-two-three punch. If we can braid a block, we just might do it."

"A braid? How?" Johnny shouted.

"All three of us—one at a time—will have to go in for brief blocks," Eva explained. "Our paths will form an English braid. You know, like braiding hair."

"I'm confused. I've never braided hair."

"Just follow my lead. We'll alternate sides," said Eva.

"How do we get Chestnut to braid at the proper time?" Johnny asked. "No one is riding Chestnut."

This was Jonara's cue. Still holding onto Johnny around the waist, she pulled at his reins, directed Sinus above Chestnut, had Sinus perform a roll into an inverted position, and Jonara let go of Johnny. Jonara fell, managed to rotate her body in the air, and landed in Chestnut's saddle.

"I'm riding Chestnut now," Jonara yelled.

Johnny recovered from the roll and pulled in behind Chestnut to regain his composure.

"What happened?" Eva asked.

"The girl's voice—the one at your clinic and at the pumpkin farm—she's riding Chestnut," Johnny said.

"An English braid, eh?" Jonara said. "Like this?"

Jonara directed Chestnut up and slightly to the right of the creature. She descended into a dive and pulled up in time to land Chestnut's hooves onto the creature. Before either could react, Jonara directed Chestnut to the left, where she descended slightly and pulled up to clear the area quickly. Clear the area for what? For Eva to continue the braid.

"Now it's my turn," said Eva.

Eva took a position slightly to the left and above the creature. She descended much like Jonara had, but from left to right instead of right to left. Obsidiana landed her hooves solidly into the creature, followed by a quick descent to the right to avoid retaliation. Before the creature could pursue Obsidiana, Johnny directed Sinus to a position up and to the right of the creature. Johnny descended onto the creature and hoofed him but good. He descended to the left, and Jonara was already waiting her turn—up and to the left of the creature.

Jonara descended from left to right, Eva from right to left, Johnny from left to right, Jonara from right to left, Eva from left to right, and so on. The attacks on the creature were unceasing. The left-right beatings kept him off stride, but on the whole it forced him down, down, down, until the creature's grackle scuffed the dirt. Hooves upon hooves beat the creature. A final hoof to the creature's head (from Obsidiana) knocked it unconscious, and the grackle flipped over and buried the creature into the prairie dirt. There the grackle remained, upside down, with the creature under the grackle's back.

"She's saying something," Johnny said. "Evanita is saying something."

"Blue Jane, Blue Jane," said Evanita.

"Johnny—the blue jay she's riding—she calls it Blue Jane," said Eva. "I understand something I didn't before. Johnny—

quick—there's no time to explain—change Blue Jane into a Pegasus."

"Mass is energy," said Johnny.

"We can't transfer her to Chestnut," said Eva. "Chestnut is not for Evanita—Blue Jane is. Hurry, Johnny."

Johnny cranked the AED up to 200 Joules. He pressed the "shock" button. Flash! Blue Jane the blue jay became Blue Jane the Pegasus. The light did not hold up long—it shrank in a matter of ten seconds. Flash! Johnny pressed the "shock" button again. The four Pegasi took formation—Obsidiana lead, Blue Jane followed, and Chestnut followed Blue Jane. Sinuo took a position to the right of Blue Jane.

Flash! The Pegasi landed. Flash! The horses lost their wings and slowed to a trot. Flash! The horses slowed to a walk. Johnny sneezed, gagged, and fell off his horse. The horses disappeared, the Evas and Jonara fell to their feet onto the prairie, and Johnny reached one last time to press the AED.

"No!" Eva yelled.

Jonara ran to her mother to hug her as Eva ran to Johnny. As Evanita and Jonara embraced, Eva grabbed Johnny's hands and contained them—preventing him from pressing the AED. They shook—whether from raw nerves or from the beginnings of a convulsion—Eva wasn't sure.

"End it now, Johnny. Break off the link!" Eva shouted.

Eva, Johnny, and Jonara returned to the hospital room. Eva ripped Johnny's hand from the AED, and with the sudden loss of electricity from the device, he felt lightheaded, lost his balance, and fell off the chair. Eva jumped from the bed, and Ms. Zyla rushed over to help. While Eva removed the tape and paddles from Johnny's head, Ms. Zyla returned the chair and AED to their original positions. Smoke rose from Johnny's head—smoke that smelled like burning flesh.

"Can you stand?" Eva asked. "Try to stand and act normal."

Johnny stood, but he shot Eva a glare.

"Normal? After that?" he asked.

The nurse returned to the room.

"I heard a crash. Is everything all right?" she asked.

"We're fine," said Eva. "Just fine."

"There's a dirt mark on your forehead, sir," said the nurse to Johnny.

"There's a what?" Johnny asked.

"Oh you know these men—they can never clean themselves," Eva lied.

"Well this is a hospital, and we like to keep things clean. There's a sink and soap in the lav right there," the nurse said. "If you need anything else, let me know."

"We will, we will," said Eva.

The nurse left.

"Quick—wash that off," said Ms. Zyla, not realizing what the dark mark was.

"It won't wash off," said Eva. "It's a burn mark from the electrode."

"Will it ever come off?" Johnny asked.

"It might grow out," Eva started to explain, but Evanita said something.

"Where's my horse? Where's Blue Jane?" Evanita asked groggily.

"Oh Evanita, Evanita! Wake up, honey. Your mama is here with you," said Eva.

Eva massaged Evanita's legs to get circulation in them. Johnny wobbled on his feet, and Ms. Zyla walked him over to a side chair and had him sit down.

"Wake up," said Eva.

"I am awake," said Evanita. "What was I saying? Something about Blue Jane?"

"Yes, Blue Jane," said Eva. "That was the name of your horse, the horse you rode to return to the living. She brought you back, Roberta's mother, she brought you back."

"Mama, are you feeling all right?" Evanita asked. "I'm hungry. What's for dinner?"

"Oh sweetie!" Eva said as she hugged Evanita. "You may have whatever you want for dinner! See if you can stand up."

"These tubes in my arm—they hurt," said Evanita.

"We'll have them removed soon enough," said Eva. "Here—I'll move the IV drip stand with you. Now place your feet on the floor. Easy, your muscles haven't been used in days."

Evanita placed both feet on the floor. She attempted to stand up, but she fell back on the bed in a sitting position.

"My legs hurt," said Evanita.

Evanita's eyes grew tired, and she made a motion to return to sleep.

"No, not now, not yet!" said Eva. "You don't want to slip in a coma again, do you? Here, let's try again."

Eva rubbed Evanita's legs again to loosen them up. She propped Evanita on her shoulder and lifted Evanita onto the floor in a standing position. Eva allowed Evanita to place some weight on the floor, but not too much. The Evas took a step, then another, and another.

"Zellie, the stand, can you help me?" Eva asked.

Ms. Zyla hurried over to the IV drip stand and carried it such that it did not get tripped up with the Evas.

"I'm...walking," said Evanita. "I'm walking again."

"You're doing it, my baby sweet. You've got your legs back," said Eva.

"Will I be able to run again?" Evanita asked.

"Yes," Eva replied, now with tears of joy.

Eva hugged Evanita as hard as she could without adding to Evanita's injuries, and said:

"You'll run again. I promise."

CHAPTER 19

The Verdict

2023 Oct 4, Wed Early am. Jonara's Dream.
2006 Nov 14, Tue. Portland, Oregon.

"All rise for Judge Gregory," said the Court Clerk.

Jonara found herself back in court with Mr. Manis, Mr. Applefoot, the Skins gang, Davino, and Sheila on the Prosecution side, and Ms. Haughf, Eva, Evanita (with crutches), Ms. Zyla, Sharon, and Claire on the Defense side. Judge Gregory entered the courtroom.

"Be seated," said the Court Clerk as Judge Gregory sat down. "Welcome back, Ms. Evanita. You're looking very well today."

"Thank you, Your Honor," said Evanita.

"Are you ready to accept the verdict and sentencing this Court is about to pronounce?" The Court asked.

"We are ready," said Ms. Haughf.

"Would the Court Clerk please escort the Jury into the courtroom?" The Court requested.

Twelve men entered the courtroom and sat in their assigned jury seats.

"Has the Jury reached a unanimous decision?" The Court asked.

"Yes, Your Honor," replied the Jury foreman. "We have."

"Please read the charges and the verdict," said The Court.

"For the charge of discharging a firearm without a permit—Guilty. For the charge of discharging a firearm in a public thoroughfare—Guilty. For the charge of discharging a firearm with intent to kill—Not Guilty."

For each verdict of "Guilty," the Prosecution side expressed approval rumblings. When the verdict was "Not Guilty," the Defense side expressed approval. The foreman continued.

"For the charge of discharging ammunition on federally restricted property—Not Guilty. For the charge of possessing LSD—Not Guilty. For the charge of using LSD—Guilty. For the charge of trespassing on federally restricted property—Guilty. For the charge of burning arsenic bearing pressure-treated wood—Not Guilty."

The foreman paused for a moment before continuing.

"For the charge of murder—Not Guilty, for the charge of first degree manslaughter—Not Guilty, for the charge of second degree manslaughter—Guilty."

The courtroom reacted most strongly to the "Guilty" verdict for second degree manslaughter. The men applauded while the women yelled, "Outrage," "Sexist," "Appeal it."

The Court Clerk passed the verdict document from the foreman to Judge Gregory.

"This is the verdict of the Jury—let no one come between the accused and the justice of the State of Oregon and the United States. Evanita Carreña, you are hereby sentenced to eight years in prison of which three will be served in juvenile detention followed by five in adult prison," proclaimed The Court. "In addition to prison, there is a $2000 fine."

"Your Honor, may I approach?" Ms. Haughf asked.

"Objection, Your Honor. The Court does not entertain deals," said Mr. Manis.

"Mr. Manis—you can no longer object," said The Court. "Prosecution rested last week. And as for what The Court does or does not entertain, that is up to The Court. Now restrain yourself."

"Your Honor, I am merely—" Manis started.

"Enough!" The Court said with a gavel blow to the block. "Ms. Haughf, are you trying to entertain a deal?"

"No, Your Honor. Defense requests options on sentencing— probation, community service, fine for time. This is a sweet little girl we are condemning," said Ms. Haughf.

"According to the Jury, she's not so innocent," said Manis. "And she should get twenty-five years for murder, not eight for manslaughter."

"Manis—I warn you," said The Court. "Ms. Haughf—each year of the adult prison sentence can be commuted by a fine of $50,000 plus probation and community service. The first year of juvenile detention has no option—it is mandatory. The second and third years can be commuted by a fine of $50,000 for each year plus probation and community service."

"Your Honor, if I understand the options correctly, my client can serve her sentence with one year of juvenile detention, seven years probation, seven years of community service, and a $352,000 fine," stated Ms. Haughf.

"That's correct, Ms. Haughf," said The Court.

"Your Honor, this is a travesty against our legal system," said Mr. Manis. "The rich can buy their way out of prison."

"Your Honor, Miss Carreña is hardly rich," said Ms. Haughf.

"Her mother's a dentist. That means rich," said Manis.

"Her mother serves the impoverished community," said Ms. Haughf.

"Nevertheless, she—" Manis started.

"Order!" gaveled The Court. "Ms. Haughf—have you reached a decision on sentencing options?"

Ms. Haughf quickly whispered with Eva, and the two nodded their heads.

"Yes, Your Honor—the $352,000 fine option," said Ms. Haughf.

"Very well," The Court said. "The Court hereby revises sentencing of the defendant, Miss Evanita Carreña, to one year juvenile detention, seven years probation, seven years community service, and $352,000 in fines. Case closed."

With two knocks of the gavel, Evanita's trial ended. The courtroom was mixed with emotion—Prosecution felt the sentence was too light, Defense felt Evanita had been unfairly judged and grossly fined.

"We'll appeal," said Ms. Haughf. "I'm sorry, but I have to rush off to help Patty Ephram with some wrangling over church business. If you'll excuse me."

With that, Ms. Haughf left. She pointed to Sharon, and Sharon followed her along with Claire. Eva, Evanita, Ms. Zyla, and Johnny Pindus exited the courtroom and went out for coffee and brunch. Soon afterward, the four sat at a comfortable round table in a local restaurant where they ordered brunch and engaged in conversation.

"Don't worry, Eva. If anyone can appeal the verdict, Ms. Haughf can," said Ms. Zyla.

"What's the point?" asked Eva. "The town has made up its mind."

"Don't give up now. There's always hope with an appeal," said Ms. Zyla.

"My lifesavings and my house are paying the fine. We'll have to start over," Eva said. "And Evanita was convicted of crimes she did not commit."

"Mama, I'm sorry I'm such a burden to you," said Evanita.

"You're not a burden, sweetie," said Eva. "You're not to blame. We'll get through this somehow."

"You shouldn't give up your house for me," Evanita said.

"I should have said, 'Our house'," said Eva. "It's as much yours as mine. What good is it if you're not around to enjoy it? No, I made the right decision."

"Selling your house may not be necessary," Ms. Zyla said. "Jan works wonders with appeals and creative financing."

"I hope you're right," Eva said.

"Will you visit me at the detention center?" Evanita asked.

"Of course, sweetie!" Eva said with a big hug for Evanita.

"I'll visit you too," Johnny said.

"Thank you, Johnny," Evanita said, giving Johnny a hug. "You're a peach."

"Evanita, you're taking this very well," said Ms. Zyla, "Better than your mother, I think."

"I blame myself—for everything," said Eva. "I have to."

"Like I said before, there's no sense in beating yourself up," said Ms. Zyla.

"What will happen to the others?" Evanita asked.

"Others?" Ms. Zyla repeated.

"Ms. Ephram. Sheila's mother—Ms. Stout," said Evanita.

"Patty is in the final stages of taking over Barnseed Baptist Church," Ms. Zyla explained. "There's some opposition in the congregation—"

"Male opposition?" Eva interrupted.

"Of course!" replied Ms. Zyla, and she continued. "But I think Patty will do fine with Ms. Haughf helping her. And Patty is not alone. She has a new person helping her co-minister the church."

"I didn't hear about that," said Eva.

"Who, Ms. Zyla, who?" Evanita asked.

"I know," said Johnny. "Patty told me already."

"Who is it, Johnny?" Evanita asked.

"Miss Sharon Stout," he replied.

"Really?" Evanita asked in excitement.

"Good for her," said Eva.

"After Sharon was permanently suspended from the police force—" Ms. Zyla started.

"Because of me?" Evanita interrupted.

"No. She takes full responsibility for the way she handled the chase on Interstate 5," said Ms. Zyla.

"But I was there. I fired the gun that got her in trouble. I helped her," lamented Evanita.

"Helping your friendly woman is never in the wrong," said Eva. "The courts may say one thing, but deep down Sharon knows you and she did the right thing."

"Yes, Sharon believed she did the right thing," said Ms. Zyla. "Unfortunately, those in power do not agree. She paid by losing her job. She applied to other districts but was turned down—and very quickly too. They made it quite clear she wouldn't be a police officer again. Patty extended an open arm of Baptist ministry to Sharon, and...well...Sharon accepted. She'll need all of our support, especially with Sheila behaving the way she is."

"What about Sheila?" Evanita asked. "What happened to her? I know she was hanging out with Davino."

"I'm afraid that's another sad story," said Ms. Zyla. "You missed most of your trial, Evanita."

"Evanita was there," said Eva with a grin.

"I was?" Evanita asked.

"Yes, you were," Ms. Zyla continued, "but you weren't aware of the proceedings or of what was said. In short, Davino is the brother of Vinay, and Vinay is part of the Skins gang—the hoodlum of boys who got you into this trouble to begin with."

"That's the problem with men," added Eva. "They begin as boys and don't grow up."

"Some do," said Ms. Zyla winking at Johnny.

Johnny blushed. Evanita took Johnny's arm and gave him a side hug.

"My apologies, Johnny. You are, of course, not the typical male," said Eva.

"He saved my life," said Evanita. "He pulled me out of a coma."

"The doctors call it a miracle," said Ms. Zyla. "They've never seen someone who went from sinking deeper into a coma to regaining immediate consciousness. They were beginning to give up on you, Evanita."

"Do they know yet? Do they know how Johnny pulled me out?" Evanita asked.

Eva looked down in despair.

"I didn't say anything, I promise," said Johnny.

"I know," said Eva. "It's not your fault. I should have checked the room first."

"They know? How?" Evanita asked.

"There was a security camera in the room—in case someone tried to sneak you out of your room, or kill you," said Ms. Zyla.

"No one would have killed her," said Johnny. "I would have made sure of that!"

"Don't be too sure," said Eva. "The men in that courtroom all but killed my baby girl. I wouldn't put it past them, given how badly their side of the trial went."

"They should have lost—completely," said Ms. Zyla.

"But they didn't. I was kidding myself in believing that an all-male jury would be impartial," said Eva.

"There will be an appeal. You know Ms. Haughf will fight for you to the end," said Ms. Zyla.

"That's what I'm afraid of, that this is the end. I can't afford to pay for any new legal fees now that I have that fine," said Eva. She looked at Evanita, read her expression, and said, "You'd do the same for your own daughter. You may not understand now, but I hope someday you will. The 'understand' part, not the part about paying a male-penalty of $352,000."

"I hope I never have to pay a male penalty," said Evanita.

Eva and Ms. Zyla applauded Evanita's words. Johnny smiled, admired Evanita's style, and thought:

"If only she were a little older."

Johnny had developed true affection and caring for her during her coma, but being in her presence while she was awake was all the more captivating.

"Johnny," said Ms. Zyla. "Don't you think Evanita speaks the truth?"

"Yes, she does," Johnny replied. "She always does."

"So there's the Sheila thing," said Evanita. "She sat on the Prosecution side! I can't believe my old friend deserted me completely."

"Like I said," Ms. Zyla reiterated, "she's indirectly involved with the Skins gang through Davino. I can't tell you how much it upset Sharon to see her own daughter sit on that side and follow in their footsteps of deceit."

"It's the ultimate assault on women—to coerce them into the male world of following whatever they think and getting women to parrot whatever they say," said Eva. "Too easily the young woman falls into the male trap."

"I'm afraid that's what happened to your friend, Sheila," said Ms. Zyla. "She's completely given herself to Davino and his friends."

Was this the same Davino who was so nice to Jonara? It was a question Jonara had asked before. She couldn't understand how the nice man pretending to be her uncle and having a wonderful daughter in Cerafina could be part of some male-oriented cover-up.

"I was right to leave her at the raceway," said Evanita. "And I'm sorry she's not my friend, but I couldn't hang around her—the way she was acting."

"It's tough—when a friend changes," said Eva.

"And I can't see myself ever dealing with her again," said Evanita. "I never want to."

"Be careful, honey," said Eva. "She may have fallen into a trap, and she's obviously blind to it, but she might suddenly see the failure of her ways. And when that day comes, she'll be in desperate need of help. Don't throw her away forever—she may yet come to her senses, though I fear it won't be for many years."

"Mama," said Evanita.

"Yes, my sweet," replied Eva.

"What about the camera in the hospital? Is anyone in trouble?" Evanita asked.

Eva paused and tried to think of an answer.

"I should be to blame," said Johnny. "I used the AED. Ms. Carreña, you shouldn't have—"

"It's done," said Eva. "Sometimes we make sacrifices, and I made another one. But I have your word, Johnny Pindus."

"Yes, my word. I will never forget the promise I made," said Johnny.

"What promise? Mama, what's happened? What's going to happen?" Evanita asked.

"Evanita," Ms. Zyla said, "Unfortunately as the expression goes, 'When it rains, it pours.' Well, it's raining very hard. The camera caught everything, and Johnny was going to be thrown in jail. But your mother—"

"Your stupid mother said it was all her idea," said Eva, "and claimed she forced Johnny to perform the procedure. There, I did it. I sold my soul to the patriarchal devil."

"No, Eva, no you haven't. Deep down you know you did the right thing," said Ms. Zyla.

"Because you took the full blame. Because you shielded Johnny," speculated Evanita.

"Yes, yes. And as much as I'm almost fond of Johnny, it rips me apart knowing he belongs to the male race. Why couldn't you have been female, Johnny? I would have done anything for you without hesitation," said Eva.

"I...can't help what I am," said Johnny. "But I know why you shielded me. It was for Evanita, wasn't it? I read your thoughts when we bumped into each other in the hospital hallway—when you were trembling."

"One of these days we need to end that thought-reading process of yours," said Eva.

"I wish I could stop reading people's thoughts," said Johnny. "It's like a trap, and I can never hear my own."

"You...spared Johnny...for me?" Evanita asked.

"Yes, yes! Must we repeat it?" Eva said.

"Because you know...you know...that I love Johnny. And you have a soft spot for love," said Evanita.

Eva tried to appear strong and upstanding, but she was practically in tears. She wanted to hug Johnny and Evanita together, but the anti-male vibes prevented her. She started to stand as if reaching over to hug Johnny, but she sat down. Twice she performed this awkward maneuver. Seeing the conundrum she was in, she stood fully.

"I need a drink, fast," said Eva.

Eva walked over to the bar, sat on a stool, and requested a Piña Colada from the female bartender. The bartender complied, and she drank her beverage.

"Like taking medication for an allergy—a male allergy," Eva joked with the bartender, who nodded and winked in agreement.

"Your mother is very proud," said Ms. Zyla, now that Eva was outside earshot, "but she doesn't wish to appear weak in front of men. Johnny, don't take offense to Eva—she never means to direct any of her anti-male hostilities your way."

"I understand," said Johnny. "I've known her since I was a little boy, and I never felt she meant any of it toward me."

"Good," said Ms. Zyla.

"What will happen to my mother?" Evanita asked.

"She could lose her dentistry license," said Ms. Zyla.

"That's not fair!" Evanita said.

"It's yet another price your mother is paying for love," said Ms. Zyla. "A price she has been paying since you were born."

"Because of my father?" Evanita asked. "Is it his entire fault? Why does she protect him?"

"Oh Evanita! Your mother must explain that to you someday, though she'd better hurry up," said Ms. Zyla.

"But *you* know, Ms. Zyla. *You* know what happened when I was born. *You* knew my father, didn't you?" Evanita asked.

"I did not know anyone claiming to be your father," said Ms. Zyla.

"He didn't even admit to being my father? No wonder Mama hates men," said Evanita.

"No, no, no. Evanita try to understand—"

"I understand. I understand my father abandoned me and wants nothing to do with me. My mother feels guilty—I know— she drinks when she's upset," said Evanita. "I lost the house, and I'm going to jail for a year."

"It's not like that," said Ms. Zyla.

"You're trying to make me feel better," Evanita continued.

Evanita took several bites from her salad. She swallowed with difficulty and clutched her abdomen. She grimaced in pain.

"What's wrong?" Johnny asked.

"This salad—something's wrong with the salad. Is it spoiled?" Evanita asked.

Ms. Zyla drove her fork into and consumed the salad. She tasted, she chewed, and she swallowed.

"It's excellent," said Ms. Zyla.

"Are you sure?" Evanita asked.

"Honey—you're talking to the queen of geriatric intestinal problems. If there were something wrong with the salad, I'd know it immediately," said Ms. Zyla.

"Something's wrong," said Evanita. "I'm going to be sick."

Evanita stood from the table and rushed to the restroom. Jonara followed close enough to hear her mother throw up.

Jonara returned to the table with Ms. Zyla and Johnny, unsure of what to do or where to go.

"Do you see what is happening here?" Ms. Zyla asked Johnny.

"Things aren't going well," said Johnny.

"More than that. The Evas are apart—Geneva, Eva, and Evanita—at the time when they should be together," Ms. Zyla said. "Geneva is in Texas because Eva wants to raise Evanita without so-called interference, Eva is at the bar soothing her nerves with drinks, and Evanita is most likely throwing up her brunch due to nerves."

"I don't understand," said Johnny. "Valeria and I always helped each other. I wish she were here—she'd know what I can do to help."

"Johnny—Eva and Evanita are in danger," said Ms. Zyla.

"Danger of what? Is someone going to kill them?" he asked.

"No, they are in danger of growing swiftly apart. We must not let that happen," Ms. Zyla explained. "Each blames herself for the other's problems and believes the best solution is isolation. Oh sure, they love each other and do things to help each other, but there's something deep that says isolation is also a part of love."

"I don't understand. How can isolation be a part of love?" Johnny said. "I loved my sister, and Valeria loved me. We never spoke of separating from each other—never. And now I'm isolated from her—and it hurts."

"Isolation does hurt," Ms. Zyla said, "but sometimes people feel it is for the best, out of love. Eva and Evanita are a lot alike, and their silent rule of isolation could rip them apart. We can't let that happen."

"How? How can we prevent it? Both are so—"

"Stubborn?" Ms. Zyla asked.

"I was trying to think of something more polite," he said.

"They're stubborn," Ms. Zyla emphasized. "But I think I know what we can do. I'll work with Eva, and you work with Evanita. Keep an honest dialog open with Evanita—don't let her clam up. If she gets sick or doesn't want to talk, find some way to help her."

"I still don't understand," said Johnny.

"You will. You'll sense her disposition and figure out a way to keep her in tune with the world. Help her spirit recover into full strength. She must not fall into the trap of believing she is to blame for her and her mother's situation."

"I think I understand. I'll do my best," Johnny replied.

"Meanwhile, keep in touch, but don't let Eva or Evanita know about this conversation. They might think we're plotting against them," Ms. Zyla said.

"Aren't we?" Johnny grinned.

"No, we're plotting with them," Ms. Zyla replied. "Okay, hush now. Here comes Eva."

"What happened to Evanita?" Eva asked, returning from the bar with another drink.

"She felt sick and went into the bathroom," said Ms. Zyla. "Look, here she comes now."

"I feel a little better," said Evanita, returning from the bathroom. "I don't know what was in that salad, but it didn't stay down. I guess I'm nervous."

"We're all a little anxious," said Ms. Zyla. "But the important thing is to stick together and have a high level of tolerance."

"Tolerance," said Evanita. "That's like the Unitarian faith, isn't it? I guess I should have just filled out that form and read it for my Coming-Of-Age. Running around to other churches didn't do any good. Now it's too late."

"It isn't too late," said Ms. Zyla. "God does not set deadlines, and neither does our church. If you like, we can work with you during your detention, to study and prepare for a real Coming-Of-Age."

"Will you do it? I'm sorry I didn't ask earlier. I know Mama wanted me to have you as my new mentor. I'm sorry I didn't listen to you, Mama," Evanita said.

Eva smiled and squeezed Evanita's hand.

"Yes, I'll be your new mentor," replied Ms. Zyla. "Our church has established a program in the detention center. Make sure you sign up for it—it's called Y-O-U. It stands for Youth Outreach Unitarian. Mentoring is only a small part of YOU—there are other things too—but it's important you sign up early. You'll be accorded certain privileges the other detainees won't have. It will also look good on your record, and it will help with the appeal and parole process. Look for me each Sunday afternoon!"

"I will. Oh thank you, Ms. Zyla! Thank you!" Evanita cried.

Evanita stood up to hug Ms. Zyla but knocked over a glass of water.

"Oh dear me!" said Eva. "I'll take care of that. Hug Zellie all you like, sweetie!"

"It's almost time," said Johnny.

"Must you be so technical, Johnny? Sorry," said Ms. Zyla.

"Our police escort is getting restless," said Johnny. "One of the officers is coming inside the restaurant."

"Yeah, we have to go," said Eva.

Eva paid the bill. The women and Johnny exited the restaurant where the officer intercepted them.

"We'll follow you down to the detention center," he said.

Eva returned a weak smile or a grimace of acknowledgment—Jonara wasn't sure which. But Jonara was sure that the moment was sad. Ms. Zyla drove, Johnny sat in the front seat, and the Evas sat close together in the backseat crying and holding each other. Jonara had a small place she could sit on the free side of her mother, and she did the best she could to place her arms around her mother even though her arms kept passing through her mother.

"I wish I could hug you, Mommy," said Jonara.

Only Johnny was able to hear her words, and just barely.

"I wish I could hug you and Grandma," Jonara added.

Jonara cried along with her mother and grandmother. Johnny bit his hands to keep from being consumed by the overflowing sadness emanating from the Evas and Jonara. Ms. Zyla held a stern check on her emotions just to get through the day, but later she would collapse in grief once her job in transporting the Evas was complete.

The moment arrived. Ms. Zyla parked her car in front of the juvenile detention center. Johnny carried a suitcase for Evanita and handed it over to one of the matrons. Evanita hobbled to the check-in station on her crutches and sat. While Eva completed some paperwork and signed her name, a matron opened Evanita's suitcase and inspected every item—clothing including undergarments, toiletries, photos, and a sketchbook. Evanita's few sacred items were now on display to the world. It was the last form of humiliation, or so she thought. Evanita signed the paperwork, and she was asked to reassemble her suitcase. Evanita repacked everything, and another matron took the suitcase away.

Evanita hugged Ms. Zyla, hugged Johnny, and hugged her mother. Eva kissed Evanita on the cheek and asked her daughter to be good. Evanita turned around on her crutches and hobbled away as directed by the matron.

"She's gone," said Eva.

It was too much for Eva. She buried her face in her hands and returned to Ms. Zyla's car. Johnny offered her the front seat, but she declined, preferring to hide her anguish in the back seat.

"I can't believe," said Jonara, "that all the zany adventures with Saint Stellan, Barnseed Baptist, and all the other churches have come down to this—a bunch of stupid boys, a fixed trial, and my mother going to juvenile detention. And she never told me about it. Grandma never told me. No one told me! Mommy, wait for me!"

But Jonara could not follow Evanita. The main prison gate closed, boom! Jonara turned around in time to see Ms. Zyla speed away with Eva and Johnny. And there Jonara stood by the main gate, alone, and at the center of a divergence—her mother going to prison, and her grandmother returning to what little remained of her questionable dental practice and loss of home. Jonara stared down the length of the fence line—the fence line preventing people from going in and out of the detention center. The day was late, and Jonara stood there and watched as the sun turned orange, flattened like a pumpkin, and disappeared below the horizon, leaving its last orange flickers of light on the treetops and the edges of cumulus clouds.

The sky faded from orange to black, the stars twinkled in the cool night, and Jonara felt a shivering cold. She grasped the fence and shook it. The fence did not yield. She stared at the stars and watched them travel across the sky—stars that had been around much longer than Jonara or any person who had ever lived. Stars that were there in the beginning of life were now twinkling for her. She made out star patterns and realized they were constellations but did not know their names. She only remembered something she'd read where the ancient Egyptians chose their pyramid locations to mirror star positions.

Jonara could not forget the misery she'd seen on her grandmother's face. She looked up to the stars in hopes of seeing some pattern that would guide her in what to do and what to think so she could endure this moment. Jonara walked around the fence line perimeter but only found tall grass. Tall grass. She ducked down in the grass, and the night turned to dawn. She was no longer in Portland but in some ancient land along an ancient river. She heard a splash and walked to the river where the grass changed to reeds. A grieving mother placed her son in a basket and placed the basket on the river in hopes of sparing him a deadly fate. She covered the basket and pushed it along the river, sending it into the tide where the basket left her hands and entered God's. The woman whispered goodbye to Moses and returned home.

The dawn had not faded. Jonara ducked in the reeds but heard horses. She stood again and found herself close to a hut—a hut she entered. A mother was feeding her baby some mushed up grain. The baby cooed and happily took spoonful after spoonful. The baby drooled with mushed grain, and the mother took the spoon and scooped the mush back into the baby's mouth. The baby lifted his head and happily swallowed the grain.

The horses grew closer—horses sent from a king in another ancient time—a king jealous of his reign being disrupted by the prophesy of a newborn, a newborn who would change the world and end his. The horses entered the village and bore men of ill will. It was still dawn, and the men dismounted and charged from hut to hut slaying every baby in the village. Jonara watched the young mother hide from the slayers. She heard the screams and wails of the other mothers—a sound as instinctive as a rabbit hearing the death shriek of another rabbit. The soldiers found the mother and ripped the child from her, ending its life physically and her life spiritually.

Dawn. An ancient Greek woman had given birth to a baby girl. Her husband was displeased—she had not given him a boy. Tradition afforded him the right, and he exercised it. By his will and against her own, she took her baby girl, ascended a slope, and abandoned her daughter among the rocks for the Gods to decide its fate.

It was still dawn. Jonara was now on eastern shores in the west Pacific. A group of ancient people refused to bind their baby girls' feet according to the ancient tradition. While men argued over whether the group should be executed or sold into slavery, the group stole away before the day started. They erected a square sail on a ship and prepared to sail east into what many thought was the edge of the earth. Crimes of thought, crimes of freedom—these were the accusations. The group was desperate for some fair judgment, and their God was their last hope in the vastness of the Pacific. The group took to their ship in full fear that their end had come. They sailed into the sunrise, a sunrise that remained a sunrise until the group's ship arrived on the eastern edge of the Pacific, the western shores of a new land with a mountain chain stretching like the human spinal column. It was the lamina—the barrier plates of mountain and might that would either kill them off or provide passage and protection to a new life of unknown fears and challenges, but a life nonetheless.

It was dawn when Jonara stood by the bedroom window. She didn't know how long she'd been watching stars ascend above the horizon in her great-grandmother's house. The arrival in Corpus Christi and the visit to her pregnant mother in the hospital with Davino and Cerafina seemed years ago. She was tired, horribly tired, but she was afraid to sleep.

A hand touched her on the shoulder. She knew it was her father and did not jump. He stared out the window as the breaking dawn obscured the last of the prior night's stars.

"It's morning," said Johnny Pindus.

"Yeah," Jonara replied.

"You're up early," he said.

"I know," she replied.

"Would you like some breakfast?" he asked.

"All right," she replied. "Daddy?"

"Yes?"

"Do you ever look at the stars and feel they are speaking to you?"

"All the time," he said.

"They seem to have their own stories," she said.

"They do."

"Daddy?"

"Yes, Jonara?"

"Do you think the stars know about us?"

"They may."

"Daddy?"

"Yes, dear?"

"I love you."

2110 Dec 27, Sat 6 pm. 376 Grey Road, Hamilton, New Zealand.

"There is more," the elder Jonara said, "but I am too tired to remember."

"Do you mind if we come back tomorrow?" Kristi asked.

"I insist. There's so much more to tell. I feel I have hardly started, and yet an entire day has gone by. But please, stay for dinner," Jonara said.

"I'm afraid we must be going," Margaret said. "We have some unrelated editing to finish up at the news station in Hamilton."

"Goodness, I forgot all about the editing!" Kristi said. "That's another two hours!"

"Then you best get going," Jonara said.

"Mamma Maffet, will you be all right tonight?" Kristi asked.

Jonara laughed.

"I have always lived alone in this house since I immigrated to New Zealand in 2050," Jonara said. "I have plenty of experience. Sure, I'll be fine. You two finish up your work at the news station and rest tonight. I imagine I'll talk your ears off tomorrow."

"We look forward to it," Kristi said. "Goodnight Mamma Maffet."

"Goodnight," Margaret said.

"Goodnight, and have a safe journey," Jonara replied.

The story continues in book two, Lamina.

Characters

Kristi Fernandez
Television journalist for Channel-A news interviewing Dr. Jonara Carreña Pindus in 2110 at Jonara's home. Kristi is nearly nine months pregnant with her wife's child. She is married to Margaret McAleese.

Margaret McAleese
Television camerawoman capturing video and audio of Kristi's interview with Dr. Jonara Carreña. She is married to Kristi Fernandez and is the other biological mother of Kristi's unborn baby.

Carreña Family

Geneva Carreña
Geneva is born on February 4, 1939 in Girona, Spain, to a Spanish woman and a French man. She grows up in Spain during the Franco regime and migrates to the United States in 1964. She marries Colonel Gracer in June 1964. She gives birth to her only child, Eva, in July of 1964, raises her initially in San Antonio, Texas, and later in Corpus Christi, Texas. She lives the remainder of her life in Corpus Christi.

Geneva is the matriarch of the modern Carreña family. She has strong Catholic values and cares very deeply for her daughter and descendants. Even though her daughter, Eva, is against Geneva's religion, Geneva still loves Eva and pursues any opportunity to bring Eva into the faith. Geneva strikes up a strong relationship with her granddaughter, Evanita. This relationship leaves Evanita heartbroken when Geneva passes away on October 3, 2023 at 84 years of age.

Geneva has several artifacts—primarily a special diary Geneva's Great-Granddaughter Jonara uses to witness family events of the past. Another artifact is a *viol de gamba* that allows Jonara to see into the future.

Geneva is around five feet, six inches tall, has short, black hair, brown eyes, olive skin, and is a bit on the heavy side. She becomes a nurse in the United States and works for a local clinic in Corpus Christi.

Eva Kelicacha Carreña

Eva is born on July 2, 1964 to Geneva Carreña and Colonel Gracer in San Antonio, Texas. She barely remembers her father and later grows up in Corpus Christi, Texas. Eva's intelligence drives her to pursue a career in dentistry. She graduates with a medical degree from the University of Texas Houston. She moves to Oregon and receives a pediatric dental degree from the Oregon Health and Science University. She practices dentistry at the Page Street Clinic building and specializes in treating low-income families.

Eva never marries but gives birth to an only child, a daughter named Evanita in June of 1990. Eva keeps the knowledge of Evanita's biological parentage a secret from Evanita for most of Evanita's childhood.

Eva believes in equal rights for women, and that men are the root cause for almost all problems women have.

Eva has straight, shoulder-length black hair, brown eyes, and an olive complexion that could suggest her place of origin as southern Spain, Armenia, or the Middle East. She is somewhat tall—at least five feet, eight inches in height. She enjoys a variety of French wines and is an accomplished ballerina.

Evanita Soledad Carreña Pindus

Evanita is born in June 14, 1990 to Eva Carreña. The identity of her other parent is kept secret from Evanita for many years, though she questions her mother repeatedly about it. Evanita grows up in Portland, Oregon. Her life is the primary focus in book one of the *Carreña* series.

Evanita is raised in the Unitarian Universalism faith. She struggles with the Coming-Of-Age ceremony as she thinks it is some sort of joke or pretense. She looks at other faiths but realizes they are not for her. Evanita, like her mother, feels a need for pursuing freedom, but for Evanita this is expressed in jogging. Ultimately, this leads her to the River Wood and Battery factory where her life changes for the worse.

Evanita has curly, long, mostly black hair with some streaks of dark red. She questions where this red hair comes from, but this is never revealed in the first *Carreña* book. Evanita begins a romantic relationship with Johnny Pindus and eventually marries him to produce two children—Jonara and Robert.

Evanita has a strong relationship with her Grandma Geneva and witnesses Geneva's death, which sends Evanita into shock and into the hospital. Evanita's health problems are compounded by the permanent metal poisoning she receives at the River Wood and Battery factory.

Evanita's nicknames: Nita, Nee-nee, Parvati, Mother Bunny, Ashley Roberts.

Jonara Carreña Pindus

Jonara Pindus is born September 29, 2010 to Evanita Carreña and Johnny Pindus in Portland, Oregon. Her birth date coincides with the first full moon after the first day of autumn. She is the eldest of two children, her younger brother being Robert. Her mother is the last to carry the Carreña family name—a name passed down for hundreds of years from a family living in Carreña, Spain. Jonara is named after her father, Johnny.

Jonara is very intelligent—like her mother, grandmother, and great-grandmother. She aspires to be a doctor—unlike her Oregon friend, Almarita, who believes success for a woman comes through luring and hooking a powerful man.

Jonara quickly becomes friends with Cerafina Vagatti, a girl just a little older than Jonara who lives in Corpus Christi close to Geneva's house. Cerafina shares in some of Jonara's adventures, and the two become good friends.

Nicknames for Jonara: Joni, Jo, Victorian, and Modern Jonara. Christine (from Saint Stellan Church) refers to Jonara as Ishtar, Bastet, Al Kardai, Hekate, Lilith, Prosperine, Lamia, Mara, and Tunrida.

Jonara has golden blond hair with a very light orange-red hue to it.

Robert Pindus

Robert is born October 14, 2023 to Evanita and Johnny Pindus in Corpus Christi, Texas. He is the younger brother of Jonara Pindus and is named after Roberta, an acquaintance of Eva Carreña.

Very little is known about Robert in book one. At some point in his youth, he uses Geneva's diary to travel back in time much like Jonara does. Jonara and Robert meet in Barnseed Baptist Church in the past by accident.

Robert is an albino and has white hair.

Martin Sixpence

Geneva's British grandfather on her mother's side.

Pindus Family

Valeria Pindus (Valiwa)

Valeria is born February 1, 1971. At age 18 years, she moves into her own apartment and shortly afterward brings her younger brother Johnny to live with her.

Valeria finishes raising Johnny—providing food, clothing, and transportation to school and church. The two grow up as Baptists, and Valeria often reads Johnny Bible stories. Valeria is a very strong Baptist and credits her faith for giving her day-to-day strength.

In Valeria's final years, she champions the rights of women pastors, and she pushes for the conversion of Barnseed Baptist Church from the Convention to the American Baptist Churches

USA. Her skin develops vitiligo patches, and Valeria sees a doctor too late to treat the root cause. She dies of Addison's disease on September 21, 2006 at 35 years of age.

Nickname: Valiwa by Hiri Enoki.

Johanidan Reginald Pindus (Johnny, Shawnee)

Johnny Pindus is born in 1981 to Aromani Pindus and Deladi Sweets. At age eight, he moves in with his sister, Valeria, until he is eighteen years old, at which time he moves into his own apartment.

Johnny is a near albino in that his hair is a light gray but not white. He is tall and thin, considered geeky, and has difficulty with fluid movement and speech. He is very intelligent and has an excellent memory. Johnny is a strong supporter of Barnseed Baptist Church and often performs sign-language duty for the deaf.

Johnny finds an unusual stone when he is eight years old. The stone is activated by vibrations, and Johnny learns to use the stone to internally visualize objects in three-dimensions—much like a sonogram. Through the stone, Johnny learns to use water pipes and other water bodies to extend his extra-sensory skills. This enables him to find people and learn of their condition.

Johnny is a lifelong dental patient of Eva Carreña at the Page Clinic. He meets and marries Eva's daughter—Evanita Carreña. The two have two children, Jonara (his namesake), and Robert.

Using the stone for years gives Johnny the shakes and makes him miserable. Yet he puts his own suffering aside for the sake of his family and church.

Vagatti Family

Sam Vagatti

Sam is a petrochemical engineer from Gujarat, India, and lives in Portland, Oregon circa 2006. He is the father of Davino and Vinay Vagatti. Sam's religion is Zoroastrian.

Vinay Vagatti

Vinay is the son of Sam Vagatti and the younger brother of Davino. He is raised by his uncle in southern India before migrating to the United States with his father, Sam, and his brother, Davino.

Vinay is a member of the Skins gang—a group of teenage boys led by Askin "Skins" Roberts who hang out at abandoned buildings. Vinay has a short crush on Evanita at the River Wood and Battery factory in 2006.

Vinay is Hindu. He mistakens Evanita for the goddess Parvati.

Davino Vagatti (Uncle Fostero)

Davino is the elder son of Sam Vagatti. As a youth, he races cars at Portland International Raceway and—despite being married—has an affair with Sheila Stout. Davino is divorced over the affair and moves to Corpus Christi where he works as a petrochemical engineer. He meets and marries Marina Ancona and converts to her faith, Catholicism. The two have a girl, Cerafina Vagatti.

In book one, Davino poses (briefly) as "Uncle Fostero"—a pretend uncle of Jonara so that she can visit her mother, Evanita, in the hospital.

Davino has black hair and a heavy-set build.

Marina Ancona Vagatti

Marina is the daughter of Elina Ancona. Marina runs a shrimping business and meets Davino when he is drowning at sea. Marina marries Davino in the Catholic Church and has Cerafina. Marina is Roman Catholic and believes strongly in her Italian heritage. She has short, black, and curly hair.

Leo Vagatti

Leo is born in 2005 to Davino Vagatti and his wife (not Marina, and not Sheila). He is half-brother to Cerafina. Leo has short, brown, curly hair with squinty polar-bear eyes. Leo has a heavy-set build like Davino.

Cerafina Ancona Vagatti

Cerafina is born on April 3, 2009 to Marina Ancona and Davino Vagatti. She has long, thick, curly hair with the Mediterranean complexion of olive skin and large, round eyes. She lives in Corpus Christi, Texas and becomes good friends with Jonara Pindus.

Stout Family

Sharon Stout

Sharon is a Portland police officer circa 2006. She is tall, strong, has defined facial features, and dark brown hair with drifting large curls. She has two daughters in order of age: Claire, and Sheila.

Sharon was raised in the Jewish religion but switched to Unitarian when she was older. Her Jewish church was Morris Synagogue.

Claire Stout Foster

Claire is the eldest daughter of Sharon and the elder sister of Sheila. Claire is a paramedic. In 2006, she provides rescue help to Portland International Raceway. In 2023, she has Jonara over for a weekend visit with her (Claire's) daughter, Almarita.

Almarita Ellen Foster

Almarita is the only child of Claire and Mr. Foster. She goes by the nickname, *Allie*. Almarita is good friends with Jonara circa 2023.

Almarita believes that equality for women is dead, and that a woman should resort to her feminine charm to hook a power-ful man. These thoughts contrast with Jonara's, who believes women should be just as opportunistic as men.

Sheila Stout

Sheila is the younger daughter of Sharon Stout. She has brown hair. Sheila is good friends with Evanita circa 2006, but the two have a falling out. Sheila has an affair with Davino Vagatti who is married at the time. Sheila later breaks off her relationship with Davino.

Corpus Christi People

Anna
Geneva Carreña's housekeeper circa 2023. Anna is Mexican by birth and an American citizen through naturalization. She speaks fluent Spanish and English.

Dr. Reegen
Attending physician to Evanita during childbirth of Robert circa 2023.

Portland Religious People

Unitarian Coming-Of-Age Volunteer Mentors Circa 2006
Ms. Blackmoore, Ms. Haughf, Mr. Miller, Mr. Robinson, Ms. Telly, Mr. Tombaugh, Mr. Tulson, and Ms. Zyla.

Beverly Zyla (Ms. Zyla)
Goes by *Ms. Zyla* for most people. Eva calls her *Zellie*. Ms. Zyla is a mentor at the Broadway Unitarian Church. She is good friends with Eva.

Mr. Robinson
Evanita's initial Coming-Of-Age mentor circa 2006.

Todd, Glen
Church teens in Sheila's and Evanita's Coming-Of-Age class circa 2006.

Josefene
Evanita's Catholic friend during the visit to Saint Stellan Catholic Church circa 2006.

Father Rick
Pastor at Saint Stellan Catholic Church circa 2006.

Christine
Lead choir woman at Saint Stellan Catholic Church. Former nun. Nickname: *The Vice of Christ.*

Jeremiah Ephram
Pastor at Barnseed Baptist Church circa 2006. Jeremiah is mentally abusive to his wife and believes strongly in male power over women. He is against women assuming roles of power in his church. He dies after taking too many diet pills.

Patty Bugle Ephram
Patty is the wife of Jeremiah Ephram. She performs sign-language service for the deaf section at Barnseed Baptist Church. Patty is often at odds with Jeremiah's male-chauvinistic ways. After Jeremiah's death, she completes Valeria's work and switches the church's affiliation from the Convention to the American Baptist Churches USA. Patty and Jeremiah have one child, a daughter named Denise.

Denise Ephram
Daughter of Jeremiah and Patty Ephram. Young girl at Carreña Dental when Evanita first meets Johnny. Johnny's church friend.

Bill Ephram
Jeremiah's brother.

Joshua Ephram
Bill Ephram's son. Jeremiah's nephew. Josh is a member of the Skins gang.

Portland Court People

Jan Haughf

Mentor at Broadway Unitarian Church and lawyer at Haughf Telly Law Firm. Ms. Haughf acts as defense attorney at Evanita's trial.

Askin Roberts

Known as *Skins*. Leader of the Skins gang. Skins is a tall, skinny boy. He smokes cigarettes and has blond hair. Skins drives the getaway van that Sharon chases when George Gango kidnaps Sheila.

George Gango

Sheila's first boyfriend. Kidnaps Sheila at the Morris Synagogue resulting in a chase from Sheila's mother, Sharon. George is a member of the Skins gang.

Greg Applefoot

Nickname: *Fat One*. Member of the Skins gang. Dies at the River Wood and Battery factory. Evanita is blamed for his death. Greg is from a British family.

Donald Fessel

Nickname: *Doofus*. Member of the Skins gang.

Buford Hamm

Nicknames: Beef, Captain Beef, Break-Bones-and-Locksbody. Member of the Skins gang.

Dr. Arton Harris

Emergency Room doctor at Vansen Hospital circa 2006. Attending physician for Evanita after River Wood and Battery fire.

Officer Buke

Portland police officer. Interrogates Eva regarding the factory fire.

Captain Agar
Portland police officer. Interrogates members of the Skins gang.

Officer Ezra Entz
Female Portland police officer. Finishes interrogation with Eva.

Judge Gregory
Presides at Evanita's trial.

Court Clerk
Assists at Evanita's trial.

Zeldweeb Manis (Mr. Manis)
Prosecuting attorney at Evanita's trial.

Dr. Antonina Zavuski, PhD
Doctorate of Philosophy of Chemistry. Russian atheist. President of Zavuski Forensic, Inc. Testifies at Evanita's trial. Granddaughter of Alina Zavuski. Emigrated from Asia to Alaska and later moved to Portland, Oregon.

Marcus Cracbern
Defendant in lawsuit against Eva Carreña in July 1990.

Portland Other People

Hiri Enoki
Japanese restaurant owner, former WWII Zero pilot. Played cryptography games with Johnny and Valeria.

Harry Enoki
Waiter, great-grandson of Hiri.

Marinda, Shirl
Workers at Carreña Dental. Marinda is an office clerk while Shirl is a dental assistant.

Adrian Cracbern
Son of Marcus Cracbern. Member of the Arkham Atheist group. Has an interest in Evanita. Evanita is warned against Adrian.

Animals

Obsidiana
Eva's horse in Evanita's 2006 coma.

Chestnut
Jonara's horse in Evanita's 2006 coma.

Sinus
Johnny's horse in Evanita's 2006 coma.

Blue Jane
Evanita's blue jay bird/horse in her 2006 coma.

Timeline

2006 Sep 10 Sun
Evanita's first Coming-Of-Age event at the Broadway Unitarian Church in Portland, Oregon.

2006 Sep 16 Sat
Evanita visits Saint Stellan Catholic Church.

2006 Sep 21 Thu
Eva makes plans with Evanita for Evanita to visit Carreña Dental the following day. Valeria Pindus dies.

2006 Sep 22 Fri
Evanita assists her mother at Carreña Dental and meets Johnny Pindus for the first time.

2006 Sep 23 Sat
Valeria's funeral at Barnseed Baptist Church. Contrasting sermons presented by Pastor Jeremiah Ephram and Patty Ephram. Jonara deals with split personalities of Modern and Victorian Jonara.

2006 Sep 29 Fri
Sheila is kidnapped from Sharon Stout at Morris Synagogue.

2006 Oct 7 Sat Afnoon
Evanita and Sheila have an argument at Portland International Raceway about Sheila's boyfriend, Davino Vagatti.

2006 Oct 14 Sat
Evanita visits the Portland Rose Gardens with the Arkham Atheist group.

2006 Oct 21 Sat
Evanita, Eva, Johnny, and Ms. Zyla eat at Cerossi Café.

2006 Oct 30 Mon
Evanita visits the River Wood and Battery factory, interacts with teenage boys, and is involved in an accident where a boy dies and she is seriously injured.

2006 Oct 31 Tue
Evanita is in Vansen Hospital for injuries from the River Wood and Battery fire. Johnny uses his gift to find her. Questioning at the police station begins.

2006 Nov 10 Fri
Evanita's trial begins.

2006 Nov 11 Sat
Eva and Ms. Zyla watch the Veteran's Day parade. Eva and Johnny revive Evanita from her coma.

2006 Nov 14 Tue
Evanita's trial concludes. Evanita is transferred to detention.

2023 Sep 29 Fri Eve
Jonara's thirteenth birthday celebration. Evanita leaves with Eva for Texas after learning of Geneva's worsening condition.

2023 Sep 30 Sat Early
Eva and Evanita arrived at Geneva's house in Corpus Christi, Texas.

2023 Oct 2 Mon
Geneva's condition deteriorates further.

2023 Oct 3 Tue

Geneva dies. Evanita falls ill and is admitted to Corpus Christi Hospital. Johnny and Jonara fly down from Portland, Oregon to Corpus Christi, Texas. Jonara makes a secret visit to Corpus Christi Hospital with new friends Davino and Cerafina Vagatti. Jonara finds her Nanna Geneva's diary and begins adventures in the past.

2023 Oct 4 Wed

Jonara continues dreaming she is in the past, and she witnesses her mother as a teenager.

2110 Dec 27 Sat

Kristi Fernandez and Margaret McAleese begin interviewing Dr. Jonara Carreña Pindus at her home in New Zealand.